Wrath Rising

UnderVerse Book 10

By
Jez Cajiao

Jez Cajiao

CONTENTS

<u>THANKS</u>

Hi everyone! Well, me again, yet another book, and yet another thanks!
First of all lets start with **<u>you</u>**.
You've made it to book 10 of the UnderVerse, which is no mean feat, this represents about 2.5m words so far, and that's just the ones that you see, it's closer to five when you consider rewrites, polishing, edits, all that good shit.
You've stuck with me, you've read on, listened, and occasionally swore at me, I know, and it's been fun, but I wanted to thank you, because it's meant a lot to me to be able to share these stories with you.
I know I mentioned it before, that we were holding back the releases for eBooks and physical in order to be able to get the audio to tie up better, but that means I'm now speaking to you from even further in the past than before!
Yes! I'm deep, deep in the past, all the way back in November '25 currently, and as I write this, I've actually completed book 11, and I'm working on 12.
Now, I'll always have these to write, because as much as writing the book is a solitary affair in many ways, it's really not in others.
I spend at least eight hours a day on Discord, now you might not see me, but that's because I spend most of it in a private authors section, sprinting with like-minded.
What that means is that I sprint with others, we write a bunch of words, take a break, talk some shit, and then write again.
Its a little strange at first, but after a while it becomes almost like you're in a shared office, and it makes things a lot more fun, if I'm honest.
It also really helps when you're searching for that elusive word that you just know begins with a… no, wait, isn't it a… you know, the one that means…
Regardless, this time around I want to thank the team, mainly Lars, Chrissy, Chatfield, Adam, Kev, Dimi, Ben, KT, Dasha, Eric, Nathan, Darla… there are a lot of us, and that's just the regulars.
The point is though, you make the hours fly through, and you make what can be a slog at times, much more fun.
Thank you all.

-Jez
05/11/25

Jez Cajiao

<u>BOOK 9 SYNOPSIS</u>

After defeating the spider goddess Illoth in single combat, Jax and his companions arrived at the nomadic tent city of Sonra, which housed endangered species and races persecuted throughout the continent. Learning of the extensive slave trade operating around Sonra, Jax demonstrated his imperial power by freeing over twelve thousand slaves through a massive magical working. Many of these freed individuals swore the imperial oath, becoming citizens of Jax's reborn empire.

Wilhelm, of House Granth arrived with representatives from noble houses that fled Earth centuries ago, seeking to negotiate territorial boundaries. Jax refused to recognize their authority, demanding they swear allegiance to him instead. The goblin Cleq revealed that Jax's next objective should be the Tower of Gaij—an ancient imperial outpost now controlled by succubai with strategic importance.

At Gaij, Jax discovered the city was caught in a power struggle between multiple factions: the local nobility led by the Council of Gaij, the Dark Legion serving Nimon, warriors from Earth's House Malakai, and the succubai who had nominal control of the tower. Through his succubus ally Sehran, Jax learns the succubai weren't the tower's masters but its prisoners—they had been sustaining the damaged structure with their essence for centuries, unable to leave without causing its collapse.

After forming an alliance with the succubai, Jax devised a plan to simultaneously claim both tower and city. He invited all factions to the tower's roof, where he revealed he had already claimed the tower with the succubai's support. Unleashing a massive spell, he disrupted all other magic in the city while channeling enormous amounts of mana through himself and Sehran, and into the tower. This power surge began to repair the structure dramatically. Simultaneously, Jax activated his imperial power to free all slaves in the city, causing control devices to detonate and killing many slave owners.

Jax successfully claimed Gaij and the surrounding territory of Carrmor, earning the title "Arcane Administrator." He established new power structures, appointed the succubus Seraphina as steward of the tower, and set up defenses, as intelligence revealed armies massing to attack the city.

Two threats approached Gaij: an army from Kronk with approximately 12,000 soldiers and a Dark Legion force of about 5,000 elite troops sent by Nimon. The gods revealed these armies had made a deal orchestrated by the gods Nimon and Baphomet, who had broken divine rules of non-interference.

When the battle began, Baphomet physically manifested to interfere, breaking ancient divine law. In response, Darakin, God of Battle, appeared and challenged Baphomet to divine combat. After a spectacular duel that reshaped the battlefield, Darakin defeated Baphomet, claiming a tenth of his divine essence as prize.

The next day, the armies attacked the walls of Gaij. Through cunning strategy and effective use of magic, Jax and Primus Daralen orchestrated a devastating defense. They concealed their true numbers, letting the enemy believe they faced only a token force before revealing their full strength. The legion's disciplined use of magic, combined with cavalry attacks, resulted in the total destruction of both enemy armies, with minimal losses on Jax's side.

During the victory celebration, the goddess Lagoush appeared to Jax with urgent news: wisps at the Cradle of Feshcan'un were under attack and dying. She asked Jax to destroy certain artifacts in the Vault of Stone beneath the tower to give her enough power to temporarily assist the wisps. Though the artifacts provided significant benefits to children born in their vicinity, Jax ultimately agreed to destroy them to help Oracle's people and potentially save their unborn child.

Jax, Oracle, Sehran, and a small group set off in a gnomish airship for the Cradle. After several days of travel across increasingly blighted landscape, they arrived at the Cradle—a lush valley surrounded by wasteland. Oracle realized the Cradle was draining life from the surrounding land, concentrating it unnaturally.

When they landed, Jax met strange pale creatures who warned that the temple was a place of pain. Inside the temple, they found wisps who were dying and corrupted. The wisps offered to help stabilize Oracle and the baby, who were reacting badly to the concentrated mana of the place.

While Jax left to defend their position from an attack, Oracle was taken through a portal by mer creatures controlled by Xenefier—the malevolent entity Jax encountered previously. Xenefier revealed it wanted their unborn child as a vessel, as the baby represented a bridge between worlds that would allow Xenefier to use mana and merge all realms into one.

Despite Jax's desperate battle against corrupted creatures, he failed to reach Oracle before Xenefier took her through the portal. The temple collapsed around them as Jax's rage manifested in uncontrolled power. Baphomet briefly appeared, mocking Jax and revealing he had prevented the other gods from sensing what was happening.

In his grief and fury, Jax underwent a transformation—the compassionate prince was set aside, and only "Amon's Heir" remained, intent on teaching the realm "…some motherfucking respect."

<u>PROLOGUE</u>

"What do yer mean she's gone?" Lydia whispered, staring at the perfectly dressed figure that had appeared in her cabin, standing at parade rest with her back held straight and her hands clasped firmly behind her, her tails swishing nervously.

"Just that," Tenandra said quietly. She paused, then sighed and shook her head, forcing herself to relax slightly. "Lydia, I can feel Oracle due to our nature, and I know that she still lives. But the distance between us? She's no longer even on this *continent*. She was, until very recently."

"But Jax *is* still 'ere?" Lydia asked, clearly worried that she and the others had endured months aboard the ship, traveling from Dravith to Carrmor, only to have their friend and leader take a portal back without them.

"He is, and that's the worst part," Tenandra assured her, before taking a seat.

Lydia had been relaxing, laid back in bed, just drifting off to sleep, when Tenandra had appeared in the small, private cabin she enjoyed as the optio of her squad, and had warned that something had gone very, very wrong.

Now Tenandra sat in the chair—after carefully setting the piled clothes aside—and looked at the feared Valkyrie.

"I don't know much more than that," she admitted, concern clear in the way that she kept her voice down. "We can all feel Jax, the direction and a rough distance... that's easy. But for me, with our species being as close as they are, and being bonded to Jax, and Oracle being part of that bond already; as I said, I can sense her as well. It's not as clearly as we can all sense him.

"Lastly, as you well know, I'm also bonded, though more distantly, to Sehran. I sense little beyond that she is in pain, and still with Jax."

"Okay, but Oracle's gone? Gone where?" Lydia muttered, brushing her hair back out of her eyes and frowning. "Ah mean, she's got t'be due inna few months, right? Why would she leave Jax behind? Has 'e sent her home ahead?"

"I don't think it was by choice," Tenandra admitted, wringing her hands as she'd seen humans do when they were nervous. "I sensed pain, fear, and then a significant distance. Something has hurt her, and now I feel uncontrolled rage from Jax. Terrible, terrible anger, and..."

"And?" Lydia prompted when Tenandra stayed silent.

"And something else." She shook her head, as if having difficulty explaining it. "He's in pain, and he's bathing himself in it, deliberately hurting himself, I think, and using that pain to make himself harder."

"Ah shit." Lydia closed her eyes, understanding what Jax was doing at an instinctual level.

Her own years spent in slavery had been filled with that. When her husband Berin had sold her—sold his wife, like a cow or a pig, when she failed to give him the sons he'd wanted—she'd spent the first entire year being taken advantage of. The sweet, kind, and fearful woman who had entered slavery had died in its ungentle embrace over that time.

The woman who had been freed? She was different, harder, and far less concerned with the minor niceties of life. She'd hurt others, deliberately; she'd backstabbed and she'd seen people die, starving, while she forced food down, refusing to share.

She'd abandoned others during escape attempts, desperate to save her own skin, and she'd still be recaptured, then forced to spend weeks and months alongside those she'd left behind.

All of this, though, had come after it'd been done to her, over and over and worse. For every failure of her soul, of her morals and of her conscience, she'd done it only after it'd been done to her, again and again.

During the long nights in the slave pens, she'd replayed the things that others had done to her, the way they'd stabbed her in the back, the way they'd cheated, they'd tattled to guards and ruined her chances of escape, all because she couldn't take them with her—that was what Jax was seeing, she knew, somehow.

He was bathing his soul in the failures, in the pain that others had inflicted on him, and in return, he was growing even greater calluses on his soul.

She'd been capable of almost anything when he'd rescued her. She'd barely been brought back from the edge by the ministrations of Cai and the others, already expecting to die, at any time, and that all hope was lost; she'd been ready to just quietly lie down and let it all go.

Then he'd come for her. He'd freed her, fought off the slavers, taught her, trusted her and healed her. He protected her, and once again gave her life meaning, before finally taking her back to where it'd all began, giving her closure.

She was the first living Valkyrie in around six hundred years, self-taught. But no Valkyrie could survive without a master or mistress. They existed to protect, to serve and to save, and that was what her soul had learned and called out to do after all that Jax had done for her.

He'd freed her, healed her, and raised her up. And his past? It was the same as hers. Not the same in that he was kept a slave for years, but that he'd been forced to do things, abused, hurt, and had his life filled with pain.

Despite all of that, he'd still turned out as he had, choosing to become the master of the great tower, the scion of the empire, and the prince who was freeing them all.

That was in part to Oracle—that wonderful, crazed goddamn wisp, who spent half her time trying to calm him, to pour water on the flames of his soul and make him consider his actions, and the other half trying to choke herself on his damn dick.

She was as insane as he, but they were the perfect counter to each other.

That she was pregnant—something that not even the gods understood the mechanics of—had been greeted with rapturous joy. Not just for their friends, not just for their family, but for the empire.

The succession was secure. A belief was spreading across the sworn territories that tomorrow might actually be better than today, and there was hope.

Genuine hope.

But when Oracle had been taken from him before—only for a few days, but still—the other side of Jax had come out. That hard, brutal side that had kept him alive so long.

The man who would beat a SporeMother to death with his bare hands.

The man who casually hung nobles and commoners alike because it was a punishment that was deserved, with absolutely no concern as to the possible repercussions.

The man who had literally gone oh so quiet and gentle-sounding, as he questioned the drow, the only survivors of Oracle's first captivity.

Then he'd tortured that drow, and he'd done it with less fear or concern about the morality of it than Lydia would have shown squashing a mosquito.

He'd shown he was capable of things that had terrified them all in that brief pause, made even worse by his incredible and almost instinctual mastery of magic.

Lastly, worst of all, he'd had the mad emperor Amon in his ear.

He'd seen and learned things that the empire had done in its deep, dark past that brought absolute compliance and obedience from rebelling nations.

He'd seen island chains destroyed, continents reduced to archipelagos, and entire species enslaved, tortured, and maimed, because it needed to be done for the greater good.

Jax had hated what his empire and his grandfather had done back then. But when he was pushed, when Oracle had been taken from him, he'd shown that blood will out.

He'd forced himself to take the gentler path when he could, but Lydia knew what most of the squad—save Bane—probably didn't.

Jax *wasn't* a good man.

He wasn't a born guardian of the light and instinctual taker of the moral high ground.

No, he had to *work* at it. Every day, he got up and he *chose* to try to help people, to give them a chance, and to then show mercy when it was warranted.

Oracle was that moral compass for him. He tried to be good without her, sure, but when he'd found her, that one person who was meant for him in every way?

He'd fallen in love, and he worshipped her.

That she'd been taken from him? That he was searing his soul to enable him to do whatever he was planning?

That *terrified* Lydia.

"We need t'get t'him," she said abruptly. "We can't leave 'im be. 'E needs us."

"He does," Tenandra agreed. "But we're already straining my engines past limits that should have never been broken. I can't push harder, not without the very real risk of catastrophic failure or detonation."

"'Ow long?" Lydia watched as Tenandra stood, smoothing the royal-blue jacket that she wore over the white shirt and smart pants.

"Four days," she said. "That storm we were forced to loop around cost us too much time."

"I told yer we shoulda gone through it!" Lydia muttered unthinkingly.

"No, you agreed that we couldn't, actually. And even had the entire crew demanded that we push through, I would have still refused. The damage done through skirting the outer edges made it clear enough that we'd not have survived a direct pass. But regardless, you need to decide on the next course of action."

"What?" Lydia blinked. "Why me?"

"You are the optio and leader here. In place of Jax, all look to you, and you have to decide if we should share this knowledge with the others to prepare them or keep it to ourselves. There is, after all, nothing that we or they can do to affect things until we arrive."

"Dammit, I wish yer'd not told me!" Lydia growled, and Tenandra smiled understandingly.

"Would you truly have preferred I not tell you?"

"Well, no, but…"

"Exactly." The wisp smoothed her uniform unnecessarily again, then spoke. "Lydia, your sponsor, the goddess Vanei, may be able to push us a little faster, or grant us additional aid, but… I doubt she would respond to me?" She looked at Lydia imploringly.

"I'll ask 'er now." Lydia nodded. "Then spread t'word—squad meetin' in t'galley in half an hour."

"Just your squad?" she asked, the inference being that there was a second legion squad aboard, and that they'd been training with regularly.

"Dammit, no, both o' them," Lydia spat. "Ah hate this. T'damn fool shoulda put someone else in charge."

"Such is the burden of command." Tenandra smiled. "I'll wake Jian now."

With that, the wisp vanished, her seemingly solid form disintegrating into mana that sank back into the structure of the hull in a flare of light and color.

"Damn wisp," Lydia muttered, though there was little heat in the curse. "Buggerin' off t'wake 'er boyfriend while I've gotta figure all this shit out."

"It is a pressure that all leaders face, my Chosen."

The goddess's words in her ear made Lydia bolt upright, before staggering, then sinking to one knee.

"Ah'm sorry, ma lady!" Lydia hurriedly said. "Ah'd not realized…ah mean…" Shit, how the hell did you apologize for not noticing a goddess, Lydia wondered.

"Be calm, my child. There is much to tell you, and we may only speak quickly, due to our opposition having broken so many rules already in their actions. Are you ready?"

"Uhhh…"

"Then I suggest you dress, and I'll explain, even as I offer what aid I can to your vessel. What has happened to Jax and Oracle is…"

CHAPTER ONE

She was *gone.*

That was the one thought that kept running through my mind.

Oracle was gone, taken from me, and it was because of my failure—my *weakness*—that she, the love of my life and our unborn child, had been abducted.

The thing that we'd identified as Xenefier—that the system had identified as Xenefier, anyway; it'd never claimed a name as far as I could remember—had chosen our child to be its ultimate host.

Something about what it was, a sentient fucking slime monster from the depths of the realm, had meant that it could never touch or interact with mana.

I had no clue why, but from what I understood, between the conversations with it and Malthus—its offshoot—and the little details that the gods had shared, plus when I'd briefly been forced into its hive mentality and had limited access to its memories, I'd seen that it was unbearably old.

I didn't mean it was a thousand years old and had a fucking bad back and crystals forming in its joints, or was going senile.

I meant it was a creature that remembered the rise of multiple generations of gods—and that was a fucking surprise. The fact that the gods I knew were just the latest uppity bastards to claim the title and were much weaker than those of antiquity was quite the bombshell.

This thing was there when the gods first came about. It remembered that what we all thought of as this terrible cataclysm—when the moon fell and ninety percent of all life perished, when the empire was laid low and the gods were banished—was only the most recent in a long string of horrific cataclysms.

It had fought the gods in the deep dark past, and due to its nature, as a fucking slime thing, it'd survived each and every attempt to eradicate it, losing only mass.

Xenefier had survived in the depths of the realm, miles underground in caverns and holes that would never see the light of the sun.

It'd survived the pressure, the lack of food or oxygen, and it'd never cared.

It had no need of them. In ways that I just didn't understand, it existed: a sentient gloop that could pour itself into the bodies of the flesh things around it and puppet them. It could sink its tendrils into their minds and recover memories; it could be anyone and anything, limited only by its utter alienness.

It didn't understand us, because it didn't care to.

For it, a creature that had fought the gods, that had existed since before time began, the lifespan of even the longest-lived flesh creature was the blink of an eye.

It saw nothing about us that was of interest, beyond as puppets to play with; to check and see whether the hated gods still waited, watching for it.

It'd been lurking, plotting and trying to come up with a way to escape the depths, but something about mana and it just weren't compatible.

Mana was the one thing that had stumped it every time it'd tried to break free.

It was massive and ancient, but it was also patient, and had been slinking through the depths, watching, anticipating. Who knew what it'd done for millennia, until that dumbass motherfucker in the prax had opened a portal to one of its locations.

They'd found a hidden, long-buried city.

A place that was filled with the long dead, and those dead had in turn been filled with Xenefier, who had lifted them up, walking them around, to capture others, others who could be questioned and tempted to cross the portal to come and play.

I'd had the feeling that the creature hadn't been concerned that it'd been found, not by us, and it had some way to hide from the gods…the "weak and ineffectual" ones that I knew, anyway.

But when it'd found Oracle, a magical creature transformed and given a physical form, made flesh, and pregnant?

Something about our child had driven it wild.

Through our child, it believed that it could finally manipulate mana; that it'd be able to gain access and control over it, and that in turn it'd be then able to kill the gods.

It'd be able to supplant them, to rule over everything and become "the one who is all," as its mouthpiece had said, while they took my love from me.

It didn't understand the issue, or it claimed not to, saying that it'd take our child, but as long as I didn't chase after Oracle and the baby, then it'd return the "brood mare" once the baby was born.

It claimed that there was still a lot of growth involved, but that it was beneficial, not required, so if I fucked with it? It'd just kill Oracle and possess the baby now.

It fully fucking intended to kill my love, I knew, and there was no fucking way on God's green earth or off the fucker that it was getting my child.

I would free them.

I would rescue them.

I would burn the fucking realm to ash if I had to.

My problem was that I'd been *weak*.

We'd come here to help the wisps, the creatures of the Cradle of Feshcan'un, because the gods had said that they sensed wisps here and abundant life mana, so much so that this was the best place for us to go. The best place for Oracle to give birth. And we'd need those fucking wisps to help her through it.

We'd been attacked, and Oracle had sent me from her. She'd trusted the wisps; she'd believed in them, despite their obvious wrongness—the black lines of what I now realized was infection, the weakness, the weirdness, all of it—and then, when I'd been gone, they'd turned on her.

They'd captured her; they'd almost killed Sehran, and a handful of the bodies that Xenefier had been using had gone through a portal that the wisps had somehow powered it.

Mana was deadly to the fucker; it couldn't interact with it, I'd thought, but clearly it could force others to use it.

Once on the other side with its prize secured, everything on this side had been released, and the gloop that made up Xenefier had poured itself into the cracks and deep places of the Cradle, leaving the rest of the bodies.

Now I was alone here, with my heart ripped out and torn to shreds, filled with nothing but anger and shame and fear and pain.

I'd failed them all.

I'd failed my love, I'd failed my unborn child, and I'd failed my friends.

I'd failed my empire—their next ruler was gone. And I'd failed the realm, because if Xenefier did what it intended, then it'd kill or infect everything.

It had no intention of fucking off and leaving us to it, just shaking hands and strolling into the sunset with its new body.

Oh no.

It was planning to kill the gods, and that was just for *starters*.

I'd failed *everyone*, and even now, those around me were trying to help me, not understanding what a monumental fuckup I was.

I didn't deserve to be the prince of the empire.

What kind of a man couldn't protect those they loved? What kind of a man let anyone take their child?

I sat there; the hours rolled past, one blurring into the next, with only the sound of the dripping water, falling from the roof overhead as my company.

The others came and they went; only Sehran remained by my side. She'd sent them all away, somehow knowing that the last thing I needed right now was the judgment of those I should have better served.

She'd also been careful to keep the others away as well.

The survivors of the infection.

Survivors of Xenefier's touch, now abandoned when they served no more purpose.

Dozens of wisps, the very creatures that had opened the fucking portal for her to be taken from me—*dozens* of them—had survived, and they'd tried to speak to me.

I'd been so filled with rage when they'd come near that it was only Sehran's quick intervention that had kept me from slaughtering them all.

Others were there as well: Minotaurs, the hairless creatures that had made up most of the attackers. A pod of mer—the Tia'Almer-atic, creatures of the same species as my friends Bane and Flux, Cheena and Ame and the others.

All of them had tried to come to me, and Sehran had driven them away before my rage could ignite into a devouring flame.

Instead, I was left.

As the hours rolled past, as the sun set and rose again, still I sat there, staring at the perfect gleam of my gauntlets.

My body beneath my armor had long since been healed of the wounds I'd taken; and the massive surges of mana, uncontrolled in my rage, had repaired my armor.

So now I sat, covered in dried blood, the inside of my armor stuck to me. I stared at my fingers, and beyond them at the water that shimmered and rippled gently.

I couldn't have said how long I sat there like that, beyond that I was desperately in need of following nature's demands, and still I couldn't rouse the interest, when the first of them arrived.

It was the overpowering sense of presence that always hit me first, and right now, that was the initial thing that made it through.

Unfortunately, as Darakin appeared, smashing my rising naginata aside, the arrival of the gods had also triggered the absolute rage I felt at their betrayal.

"Jax, please listen!" Jenae shouted as I surged to my feet, weapon leveled; water streamed from my armor from where Darakin had shoulder checked me and thrown me back.

"You did this!" I roared. My voice echoed off the walls and sent the water shivering backward with the pressure. "You sent us here!"

"Please my champion, listen!" Jenae begged.

Instead, I lunged forward, intending to bull through the arriving gods. My hate-filled eyes locked on Lagoush's regret-filled face.

Darakin was there again, this time his sword crashing into my naginata and flipping the blade aside as he tried to disarm me. His own massive weapon slid down the haft of mine, giving me the option of releasing it or losing fingers.

I reached inward and *pulled.*

Scales flared in response to my call, folding out of my flesh, rippling across the armor as something about the ancient praetorian plate accepted them, and guided them.

Darakin's eyes widened as he realized I wasn't going to let this go so easily. As he turned his blade, twisting it and gripping it in his other hand, ramming the flat of it against my chest and shoving me backward, the scales continued their flow.

They poured up and over my chest, sealing my throat and gorget, running like liquid quicksilver across the gleaming red metal of my armor, to encompass me in silvery scales.

Shustic's gift, the scales of the Maiden of the North, reinforced by the blessing of her mate, Tuthic'Amon, sealed across me, and my latent draconic bloodline, carried through all the way from Amon, rose in me.

The one creature that even the gods were warily polite to was the greater dragon, and the blessing of two of them, through bone and blood, through magic and meaning, rose in me, and I. Felt. *Rage.*

I dug my feet in, stopping the slide, then spun my weapon, locking Darakin's arms at the same time as I hooked my leg behind his, and shoved.

Even the God of Battle, when in physical form, was limited by the physical. He staggered backward and then crashed to the water, rolling to come to his feet, only to feel it as I discarded my weapon, grabbed him by the back of the neck and the base of his cuirass and hefted him, twisting to rob him of any grip or brace points.

Then I spun, throwing him aside to crash into the water.

He was up in a second, back in a blur, even before I'd fully recovered my weapon. As I was straightening, his blade tapped down on my own.

"Jax, my friend, don't make me do this," he said softly. *"We have come to talk…"*

"Then stand aside," I growled. "*She* did this. She sent us here. She put us here, for Oracle to be taken! She lied to us about the wisps. She hid other places we could have gone, to make us come here! She did this!" I roared that last at her, and the gods, now all of them, stood around me, staring, with Lagoush at the back of the group, half hidden behind the rest.

"Jax, please, let me explain…" she tried.

I snarled, lunging forward again, only for both Darakin and Sint to move. Cruit, Lord of the Earth, was a few seconds behind them; as I roared and fought, trying to get free of the pair, he lumbered into the fray and grappled me, driving me back.

Where Sint and Darakin were warrior gods, Cruit was the God of the Earth. Literally, he was massive; solid in a way that suggested mountains were weak and the pillars that held up caverns were meaningless.

He wrapped his arms around me, pinning me as Darakin and Sint got my weapon free. I glared into his eyes and sucked in a deep breath, feeling the core of the earth's heat as I prepared to unleash dragon fire into the fucker's face…

Only to have Tuthic reach out and twist. I felt the knotting of my powers, the support that he'd given me, as he yanked back, frantically trying to stop me from breathing literal dragon fire into the face of an allied god.

My scales shivered; pain radiated outward. My armor buckled as he deliberately weakened me, and I hauled back, then headbutted Cruit.

He blinked in confusion, his grip lessening slightly. I planted my left foot on his right knee, then shoved as hard as I could. He tilted, staggered, and I roared, ripping my left arm loose and bracing it as I tried to do the same for my right.

I felt the pain as they tried to stop me.

I heard their voices; I heard the pleas and the anger, and still I fought.

Cruit shook off the blow and glared at me. Tightening his grip around my waist, he dove and threw himself forward, crashing into the ground. The impact was enough that part of the roof gave way; massive blocks fell free, along with a surge of water that roared like a waterfall into the formerly hidden grotto.

I cried out in pain, my breath crushed from me under his immense weight. I struggled to get free, as Sint and Darakin each dropped down onto either side of me to grab my arms and pin me, as Tyosh, a god I'd barely spoken to, moved in.

He knelt; his long orange robes growing filthy with the stagnant water. He gripped my helm and pulled it free, before tossing it aside. Then he laid his hands on my temples, staring down into my eyes.

I shouted and bucked, determined to break free, even as the scales fell as Tuthic continued to fight me.

They held me there, pinning me, forcing me into immobility, as my body suffocated; as the mana that I needed, the air, the very beating of my heart was forced to slow by that calm, purple-eyed gaze.

The God of Time and Reflection held me there, staring, stopping the world, and giving me the time to cool off, even as three others worked to hold me in place.

I blinked, and was…somewhere else.

A place that I instinctively knew was His. The place that Tyosh called His own, a part of the realm of the gods and yet not, aside from all the others.

I saw it. I felt it, and I…stared at Him, feeling empty.

All emotion drained away.

All my cares, the fear, anger and loss.

Instead, I stood there, in a new cavern, one that was also circular and filled with water. But where the one I'd been taken from was old, made of worked stone and filled with the forgotten glories of past ages, this was seemingly all natural.

Grey basalt and onyx made up the walls, with a gentle flow of waters across them here and there.

Moss covered shelves and ledges, glistening in the silence, and overhead, a small space let in the gentle light of the sun.

I stood atop a ring of slightly raised and drier land, with an inner ring of water ahead, water that rippled gently as tiny fish flicked this way and that across the gravel that made up the bottom.

Sea grass, or seaweed—I'd never known the difference—but green and lush, flowed with the ripples covering most of the shallow pool's bottom, and the fish slid in and out, their silvery scales reflecting the light.

In the center, in the very heart of the chamber, sat Tyosh in a lotus position, waiting atop a slab of marble.

He watched me, His eyes glowing gently. His clean-shaven face and head made Him look almost boyish, with the lack of any wrinkles. The robes of yellow and orange that made Him almost monkish in demeanor were drawn across His body, leaving one shoulder and His sinewy arms exposed.

His chest showed He was well muscled, though He was hairless. His feet were tucked from sight beneath His folded robes.

And still He watched me.

Those eyes radiating strength. Calm. Control.

"Will you speak with me, my guest?" He asked politely.

I swallowed hard, sucking down a breath, and tried my best to hold onto some of the rage that had filled me…the horror and the loss.

"What have you done to me?" I whispered.

"I have brought you here," He said. *"Nothing more, nothing less. All that you feel, or do not, is down to yourself. We sit on the cusp of the realms, at the point of nexus in the veil, between life and death, between the realms of light and dark, and here I contemplate all. You are one of only three guests to see this place, but I judge you worthy of its grace and calm."*

"I…" I swallowed hard. "I…"

"Be not afeared, Champion," He said. *"Here, all is one. No other may enter, nor leave, and you cannot offend me. You are worthy, Jax Amon, else you could not be here. Anything you say or do in this place will not change the outside realm. None shall know what we discuss, nor can they."*

"I don't know what to do," I whispered, in a small voice. "I didn't mean to fail them…"

"I know," He assured me. *"But you must understand: you did not fail them."*

"I lost her. I lost them both."

"They were taken, not idly discarded. You did not fail them, nor we you. What was, is. What yet may be, none save the Arbiter can see. Do you accept this? None, not even we gods, can see the future truly, else how would we have been banished in the first place? Baphomet had shrouded this place for truth, and we could not see inside until he was driven back."

"Okay," I accepted, the coldness and peace that rolled through me forcing me to see that simple truth.

"When Lagoush asked you to attend the Cradle, yes, She hid things. She dissembled, and She played to Her own gains. She wished for Her temple to be recovered, for the wisps that lived here, and all the other creatures that once revered Her, to be Her new priests and worshippers.

"There was greed, in that She sought to grow faster than all others, that She thought to gain—and to share, yes—but to gain before the rest. She guided you to where She believed you would find the things She needed, but She did so out of a desire not for power, simply for power's sake.

"She did this to make a better world. She believed that in your coming here, you would free Her long-lost children. The Cradle would offer up its power and help, and—She has admitted—that She believed Her home here could have become the heart of the empire.

"She hoped you would see this location, held safe from the enemies around by the great Plain of Bones, with abundant mana and resources, and you may wish to make it the heart of your new empire, affording Her much in the way of additional power.

"Although foolish, and in no small part selfish, it was not, as it may have appeared to you, malicious. A combination of two competing situations has led to our current crisis, and it is, regretfully, one that requires an old secret be shared. First of all, in this place, emotions are limited, allowing greater meditation, for those who are new to its gifts. Do you wish to discuss this with me here, or return to the outside realm?"

"We can talk here," I forced out. A combination of the loss I felt, and the confusion and disbelief that through those events, I'd just attacked my allies, all mixed to make me both deeply saddened, even distantly, and concerned that I'd just damaged my empire, and through it, the chances for Oracle's recovery.

"Thank you," Tyosh said. *"Very well. The greater secret is one that may only be shared, both because of the path that you walk, and this location. Here certain rules are, by their very nature, relaxed.*

"First, I ask that you accept that there are things that even the gods, seemingly so powerful from your position in the grand scheme of things, are either unaware of, or have forgotten.

"Some secrets are left for good reason. Others are simply lost, while a rare few are bound behind doors of our own creation.

"The truth about the creature known as Xenefier is one such secret. Our information is limited; much is hearsay, and still more are details pieced together from our past incarnations, ancient legends and more. But what we know beyond doubt is that it is our ancient enemy.

"The information we have is... poor. Please understand that we, the pantheon that you know, arose at differing times. We took up the reins of this realm, when others had fallen, and the information we have on the deep past is spotty at best. Horrors that were passed on in faded memories, cryptic warnings, and more...these are the places that we have gathered information from, though it is known that there are other, more detailed sites that can be explored. What we know is this:

"Xenefier was believed destroyed at least thrice before, so perhaps it is not that surprising that it has risen again. But where the first two probable incidences of its existence were in the deep past, the last was troublingly recent.

"Every time Xenefier rises, the realm is thrown into turmoil. The limited memories we have of our previous incarnations—much as you were gifted many from your grandsire Amon—are spotty and clouded, but we believe that the first two incidents were around fifty thousand or so of your years apart; the third, a little under that, at around forty thousand and change.

"This gives us hope, although such records are unclear, that each time Xenefier has appeared, it has reduced the realm—above and below ground—to a barren wasteland. The gods have been fought to a standstill, many perishing in the attempts to stop its rise, before it was eventually defeated.

"That this last sighting was a 'mere' fifteen thousand years ago is thus a hopeful occurrence. It suggests that the creature is not yet ready for a full rise. That although it survived, again—unfortunately—before, it has taken many thousands of years for it to believe it was ready to face the realms of light and life. That this time it is doing so without that time to prepare, and instead out of desperation, may be our only hope."

"I don't care," I intoned. "I can't… I'm sorry, Tyosh, truly I am, but all I care about is her—*them.* I have to rescue them."

"I know, Jax, and this is nothing to be ashamed of. You still care for the rest of the realm, I sense this, but it is right that those you love are held more closely in your regard. To move ahead, though, there are things we must discuss, and little time to do it in.

"That Xenefier is real, is something that we all hoped would never be proved, but regardless, it is. The identity of the creature was itself lost. All that we knew was that there was a creature of darkness and hatred that had attempted again and again to erase all life. Much as Nimon Himself has attempted. And as such, we are guilty of mixing legends of the past and our own hated brother into one. Creating a fictional, but beatable boogeyman, if you will."

"What?"

"Nimon…we have assigned Him much of the same hatred and disgust that the legends warned us were Xenefier's hallmarks, and as such, perhaps we pushed our brother away, helping to create the situation that endures today. Regardless, however, the truth is simple.

"Xenefier exists, and it has worked to rise and destroy all life. More troubling than that is that another, namely Baphomet, has conspired to hide Xenefier's existence from us.

"It was He, make no mistake, and we suspect Illoth, who provided this most cunning of traps, enabling Xenefier to spread here, while shielding it from our gaze. As such, once the subtle hints and trap was laid, Xenefier, most likely unaware of the aid it was receiving, hoped to entice you here with others of Oracle's kind.

"The trap worked, regardless of which hand baited it, and now it has all that it needs to rise in power over all, to swallow the realm in darkness absolute, and to ensure that those you love are forever lost." He paused then, clearly contemplating his words, before going on.

"Oracle is—we believe—as safe as she can currently be. The creature will not risk her, as the best time for a joining between it and the child will be at the

19

moment of birth. You remember how it struggled to take Oracle? Where she was defenseless, and yet still, it struggled?

"We believe your child was indeed granted much by the wild mana of the Cradle, and far from being defenseless, it was the reason that Oracle was taken, instead of slain and disposed of.

"It fights, even now, but in the moment of its birth, it will be vulnerable, and then is when we believe Xenefier is most likely to strike.

"For the child to be already aware speaks to its power, though it is likely to fight to remain within the world it knows, comforted by the slumbering Oracle. We believe—and again, we know little more than you—but given all that we have seen, we believe that it is capable of survival now, outside the womb. But, as the creature itself has claimed, for the child to grow, to become all that it could be, it still requires more time."

"I remember it." A dim memory flared. "Shit, I remember it…when the thing attacked me, when it'd gotten its mess into my brain, it was looking at my memories, and I could see into its memories as well. Into its mind."

"Go on."

"It was splitting off sections of itself, preparing. It needed things. When it thought it had me and Sehran under control, and Oracle already captured, it was searching for things…" I tried to remember.

Tyosh nodded slowly. *"May I?"* He tilted His head to one side in question.

"May you what?" I asked.

"May I enter your mind?" He clarified. *"We are here, in the nexus, and you are partly in my mind, hence our contact, but I would be loath to dig deeper without your permission, mine ally."*

"What would you be doing?" I asked uncertainly.

"I would sink deeper into your mind. It will not be pleasant for you, but in doing so, I may glean much, including likely locations that she is being held, or one that is being prepared to host her yet."

"You can find her?" My eyes widened.

"I do not know for sure," He said firmly. *"Jax, understand this: I cannot guarantee anything, but if it was thinking of specific places of power or artifacts it needed, we may be able to delay the birth by removing or recovering those artifacts before it can reach them, and then facing it at the location it seeks."*

"Do it," I said, resolute.

Tyosh didn't wait, didn't offer a chance to back out. Instead, He struck. The calm waters of the pool, the shimmering reflections vanished; the water turned steel-grey as it lunged upward, forming into a tight spear of solid grey. It stabbed into my skull, piercing me like a lance driven through flesh.

I stiffened. The pain…

Then it was gone, and instead I stood beside myself in my memories. I was back in the forgotten city, deep under the earth. My body was climbing to its feet, jerkily; the eyes rolled back in their sockets, black as pitch, and the thing rolled around, burrowing deeper.

I saw bulges under my skin as the fucker sank into my flesh and traced organs. I felt it as the thing rooted around, but as it did, I felt the same being done in return by my divine companion.

Tyosh was beside me, the fractured memories that I had tasted from Xenefier were being pulled free, examined from every angle, and then set aside.

I sensed locations that Tyosh identified, places that were impossibly far away, that would take centuries to travel to on foot, never mind as a slime thing creeping through the tight gaps in the earth. There was a solution, though, and I saw what it'd decided to do. I saw more now than I'd been capable of absorbing at the time: a simple plan, inelegant, but all that was needed.

It couldn't touch mana, it couldn't bear it, but those it infected could, even though the very act of their channeling helped to free them from its control, while simultaneously killing them.

It'd forced the wisps to bend space and time, and seeing this, how it remembered its puppets dying in the attempt, made it clear the price they'd paid for it using them that way. Dozens, probably on top of dozens of others that I'd not seen, had died in the attempt, but that was what it would do again.

Portals were inimical to its kind—usually, at least. The portals that the empire had used—huge, carefully designed creations that had been fixed in place—were unintentionally lethal to them.

With the act of stepping across the threshold terminal, the gloop that made up its form would collapse. But one of its creatures could power a portal, march up and throw things across. It couldn't travel itself, which meant long weeks and even months for the thing to puppet its playthings around the realms to collect what it needed. But once there?

The artifacts could be returned quickly, provided the location already had a portal, or there were hundreds of wisps and other mages who it could force to kill themselves creating a portal it could use.

Tyosh quickly identified three places that could be the heart of the mass, and in each, yeah, a portal existed.

They were there, waiting, but even as my heart surged, the possibilities springing to mind, I felt it as Tyosh released me. The meditation place, the nexus, appeared before my eyes again as the steel-grey mass retreated, becoming water again.

"We cannot go," Tyosh said. *"Not yet."*

"But…" I started, shaking my head in disagreement. "Oracle *has* to be at one of them! I can feel her, there, in the distance, in that direction…" I pointed, my heart following my finger to the distant sense of her. "I could…"

"My ally, the portals are most definitely closed and already protected. And even where they are not, you would be jumping into the heart of the creature's domain. Once there, you would face a creature that has endured for so long as time has had meaning, and beyond.

"You would have to fight something that has killed and consumed gods— not fought them to an honorable defeat and claimed a portion of their power, but that has literally consumed them.

"Gods rise and fall by the focus of their faithful, their power waxing and waning, but regardless, if this thing could fight the ancient gods in their prime, then even now, it is likely beyond you."

"But you could help," I pointed out, not liking how desperate I sounded, how whiny. But this was for Oracle and my kid, dammit!

"We cannot, though now that I see this, I believe there are other things that we may yet do. Jax, as I explained, there are secrets, long lost and forgotten by ourselves, but hints remain. Those three sites are one such, as is, more to the point, the fourth site that lies in the heart of the other three.

"They form a triangle, and in the center of that triangle lies a single point, one that was deemed incredibly important in all the memories of our past, even long before the empire rose and claimed it, reinforcing it as Amon named it Dai'Amaranth.

"We cannot enter those three places—not 'will not,' not 'don't wish to'…we **cannot.** *We have long been blocked from certain areas, and the greatest of them is beneath Dai'Amaranth, where our legends claim that death awaits.*

"I must speak with my brethren about this, but please, Jax, understand that although we will search for an answer now, the location cannot be a coincidence. We know only that we cannot enter this location. In the deep past, many of our kind have tried and have never been seen again.

"That Xenefier is likely there tallies with what we know, and explains much. There is something there, something put in place by our ancestors to prevent us accessing it, and presumably, to trap some part of the creature's power as well.

"That we cannot go there directly ourselves, however, does not mean that we cannot find a solution, nor that we cannot aid you. But for now, you must give us the chance to examine it.

"We will aid you, we will, but there are legends of terminal counters in place against us, that were put in place by other gods to prevent something. That it is there, that it has turned what may be a stronghold of our past against us, makes terrible sense—else how would such a creature have survived so long? No, Jax, as we are, I fear that attempting a rescue now would lead only to the loss of your Oracle.

"But, that is not to say that the situation is hopeless." He said it quickly, holding a hand up as I opened my mouth to argue. *"Please, listen. This is why we came to you, not simply to apologize for our part in the deception and loss. We were well intending and similarly duped, but even so, we came to offer apologies, and, we believe a solution, though it be a drastic one."*

"What solution?"

"It will not be easy, Jax, and it will be filled with risk…"

"If it has a better chance for me to rescue them, then I want to hear it, now," I said firmly.

"Hence the reason for this discussion."

"Then fucking tell me, Tyosh. Stop beating around the bush and say it," I snapped. Even here, in this place of perfect contemplation, my anger rose again.

"Is it not clear?" He cocked his head to the side. *"You must ascend to true godhood, and once again raise the banner of the empire."*

CHAPTER TWO

"Hold the fucking front door, what?!" I blinked, staring at the clearly deranged god. "I'm already trying to goddamn do that!"

"You have been," He agreed. *"However, you have been attempting to ascend as but one of many projects. You have been attempting to rebuild the empire, searching out ancient relics, raising armies and more. You have been helping your partner and protecting your child, as well as attempting to resolve wider economic issues for your people. Although that is laudable, it is not what must be done now, Jax.*

"If the creature known as Xenefier is back, if it has, as we suspect, been shocked into making a preemptive action when it is yet unprepared, then we have yet a chance. Conversely, should we not take immediate action, then we believe the results would be catastrophic."

"Yeah, for me and Oracle," I growled, but he went on as if I'd said nothing.

"All our limited advantages, our strengths that have served us so well in the past...all could be taken from us, Jax. If that creature gains true access to mana, that will be the end. I know, and I understand, your goal is that of freeing and protecting those you love. I approve most heartily of this, but ours, as the gods of this realm, must be the survival of all reality.

"From what we know, Xenefier is a living entity that is not constrained by size, nor composition; it is itself, be it a grain of sand or the size of the greatest of the oceans.

"In the past, our legends have named 'the great enemy' as being unable to stand the touch of mana, and limited to more mundane abilities to face us. Should it gain access to mana, however, imagine the power that a creature that filled entire oceans would be able to call upon.

"We are gods to you, but in facing something like that? It would be our nadir. Therefore, we must act, and act now.

"With that aim in mind, there are ways we can help you. Ways that will require us giving up power that we were gathering, secrets each of us were working to uncover. Where we are indeed prevented from accessing these areas, however, you, as a mortal—of sorts—are not. Not in the same ways. We propose to aid you, to enable you to grow in power at an exponential rate, in order to permit you to battle Xenefier as our champion and to rescue those you love."

"Let's do it," I said flatly. "Right now."

"No, Jax... just listen. There is more, and you must understand why, before you can understand how." He watched me, seeing the impatience, even battling past the emotional restrictions that this location placed on me, and He nodded.

"Understand this as well, Jax—much of what we can tell you is pieced together, knowledge that was passed in memory or conversation. There are, however, other sources, and the greatest of these is the lost Library of Souls.

"Its location is unknown, deliberately hidden until a time of great need. But, as ever, our forebears left a method to circumvent this. We will need your help, and I must speak to the others. We must discover all we can, pool our memories and knowledge, but it is my belief that the others will agree, and that the hunt for the Library will begin.

"I hope that should we find it, then we can discover the full story. First, though, and foremost for you, is the recovery and claiming of additional fragments themselves. You must also understand what they are, and why they are important," He said. *"To be clear, each form, each aspect in reality, formed ten fragments naturally, or so we believe.*

"The original gods, the first of our kind, rose to sentience through those fragments. They were the personification of those aspects: Order, Magic, Knowledge, Love, Hatred, Life, Death… there were hundreds, possibly thousands.

"What happened was that the originals warred between themselves. Why, we do not know, nor is it important—but war they did, and when some claimed fragments of another's power, they grew stronger.

"Smaller gods gathered to tear down larger; larger preyed on the smaller; and for long eons, this was the way of the world. Some claim that Xenefier is the true God of Evil and Hatred, bound away from mana's touch to prevent his rise to the peak. The truth is we don't know. But for whatever reason, this is how the original aspects were split across the realm and the first gods fell.

"In time, others rose in their places, and where once there were hundreds, or even thousands of gods, and their fragments numbered in the tens of thousands, much was lost. The original knowledge of reality and the secrets of magic were splintered; in their place rose imperfect imposters, claimants to the thrones that were based on power and not knowledge; not true devotion to their ideals.

"This is when Xenefier, came. Rising to battle to gods for command of the realm. Over and over gods were thrown down, hundreds dying before the greater being was destroyed, or so they believed. The fragments that made up the destroyed gods were captured where possible, both by it to deny us those fragments, and by other gods to fuel their growth. But mainly, they were lost. Their power leached into the realm you know, which developed and grew in power and beauty.

"The first mortal lives that roamed the realm had no concept of mana, nor any way to touch it, not until so much of the God of Magic's essence had been lost to the realm. As the races evolved, some lived in places that gained from that, learning to touch it, and thus increasing their range and breadth.

"As time went on, the realm evolved again, along with the life that it held, and the fragments were further disseminated. The issue, and the detail that you must understand, is that those fragments were not all lost. Some remain in the hands of minor gods, others, greater, and still more are in the hands of what were once mortals.

"You may be wondering why we permit this. Why the greater gods don't simply eliminate the lesser, and then from there grow to be the One Who is All." He paused and looked at me.

I nodded. Yeah, it'd crossed my mind a time or two why the hell Nimon permitted lesser gods to exist at all, and why the others didn't just band together and hunt down the enemy smaller gods.

"The reason is simple. We cannot."

"Oh, well, that was fucking helpful. Thanks so much for the comprehensive explanation," I snapped.

"I mean it literally, Jax. A god who takes a fragment of another, after that god has fully ascended, must dedicate a huge amount of their effort to absorbing it. Darakin took that fragment from Baphomet, and now both of their powers are less than it was before, not greater. For Darakin to fully absorb and gain the power of the fragment will take years—possibly decades or even centuries, should the fragment he claimed be less compatible with him. The reason for this is that his power is already fixed.

"As a god ascends, their power settles into specific forms, built around the way that particular god uses their powers. For Darakin, He uses most of it physically and through enhancements. As such, His power must be absorbed, guided, and redirected, lest the new fragment's power ruin long centuries of work with its undirected surges and mistakes.

"For Jenae, Her focus is fire and knowledge. Should She absorb something of death? She would have to break it into the relevant forms. She must focus that power into the death that comes from consumption through Her flames, and also, to maintain balance, work to breathe new life into Her other aspects to ensure balance.

"That power must come from somewhere, and the effect on Her, should She absorb something of death, would be to remove Her from the realm as an active participant for possibly the next several centuries. Knowing this, and we do, we are still largely incapable of passing up such an opportunity.

"These are consequences of the action, and yet do not touch upon the true issue, which is that hunger that we all feel. The greater the number of aspects that we are bound to, the greater the hunger. We are driven to complete our focus. For me? Reflection, meditation, time…all are constantly calling to me, desperate for more of who they, and I, once were.

"Should you come before me with a Fragment of Time, unbound, the hunger…the compulsion to take it, to assuage my hunger would be unbearable. As it is, you possess Darkness, holding it close to yourself, hidden within, and although I have no such aspects, I feel a ravenous desire to take it."

"So, what you're saying is that you can't just take the others? Like if you were to track down and trap that dickbag Baphomet, and you all fell on him and killed Him, you couldn't just take the fragments for yourself?"

"We could, and worse, we would be driven by our very nature to fight one another to capture more. As soon as one of us had all the fragments they could gather, they would flee, abandoning all else to absorb them before the others could claim them, risking that we could fall to internecine war."

"Fuck me, well, that's… Wait, how does this help? I mean, if you all do this and then you're out of the fight, that means that Nimon and their side, if they just sacrificed one of their number, you'd all be gone! He'd be able to do what he wanted and fuck us all!"

"Yes and no. First of all, that would require the others to serve one of their own up to us, and in doing so, they would be equally driven to take those fragments from their victim. They could no more do that than you could simply decide that you were now a water breather, and walk into the ocean.

"Yes, in theory they could do that, but they wouldn't, just as we could sacrifice one of our own to take the others out of this war. What Darakin did was both incredibly brave—as He lowered His own strength to do it—and foolish, but He would not be dissuaded from assisting you."

"He's a good one. I do fuckin' like the guy," I said. "Okay, so I owe Him my thanks, but how does this help us?"

"It helps us, because for now, until the fragments are bound and your divine form is complete, you gain only a relative small boost in your power from each fragment you claim. You are not yet formed, and you are therefore not yet limited.

"When the time of ascension comes, you could have gathered the ten fragments needed, or you could have gathered a hundred. In those first moments as your form takes shape, you are unlimited by such things. Should you bind dozens, then your power would grow to surpass us all."

"Okay, great theory, but how does this help us now, and how does this help me with Oracle!" I snapped, frustratedly; the calmness that this place brought warred with the rage that filled me still.

"It helps, Jax, because although Xenefier will have plans in place to block the gods, it is still vulnerable to our power, and as you have defeated a small concentration of it already, it believes it has your measure. It also cannot understand nor conceive of cooperation of others, as for it…it is alone.

"It has, in the past, been destroyed only when large numbers have faced it at once. And as it is a creature in isolation, it presumably will want to face us in such as well.

"The legends we have counsel against facing the 'deep dark' and 'that which walks between' alone. We believe this is why. So, we must face it as a concerted effort, or we will be destroyed in isolation.

"Groups, to its mind, are likely coincidence, happenstance, not coordinated. As such, we have an advantage. If you were—with our help—to gather more fragments, to specifically build yourself to be the reflection of the empire, and all that you are capable of becoming, then you would be able to face it."

"But you said it'd take years for me to ascend, right? That once I take my power from the fragments, that's it…I'm out of play for centuries."

"Again, yes and no. If you do this after you have ascended, claim ten and then try to bind more afterward? Yes. If you capture many, and hold them? Hold them in place, and then bind them as you cross the threshold into its sanctuary? Once inside, whatever shields that place from us would be circumvented.

"You would have a chance—only that, mind you—but a chance, and you could therefore rescue your love and your child. You could free them and potentially destroy the creature. Through evading the protections it has, and then ascending, you may defeat it. May I say, there is one last reason we believe

you capable of this, and not simply because you have held Illoth's fragment so long and still have not yet bound it."

"Go on."

"Jax, as the focus of the empire, you could become the god of imperial might. Or civilization. Of order against chaos. You could claim your place as the god of the empire, and even the citizens who worship us would tithe a portion of their mana to you each day, provided we were careful in our design."

"How? I mean, shit, I don't want to fuck you all over, but how?"

"Simply this: we create a symbol that is blessed by the gods that incorporates the empire and the god of their choice. As they pray to their god, we take our tithe, and the remainder as they continue, recovering their mana and moving on, is channeled to the imperial throne, to power those abilities.

"Once you have ascended, as the focal point of the empire, as the emperor, you will have access to all that power. With so much, with the power of millions behind you, you could destroy the creature."

"This doesn't make sense," I said after a few seconds. "I'm sorry, but fuck me, Tyosh, there's so much that can't be just 'it's that way, so it is.' You say the gods are blocked? Well, how the hell do you know that if you're blocked? How do you know that once I'm there, I won't just be killed instantly, or puppeted and it gets control of the power of the throne and my fragments! How do you know I can destroy it? Why the hell wasn't it destroyed in the past then, if you know we could do it now!"

"For two reasons, Jax. First, we know this because Xenefier was defeated at least twice in the past, and the way to face it again was left to be discovered. We know not exactly what happened, beyond mixed and incomplete memories, but many of them reference the Library of Souls. Although we know it is not here—not a one of us hasn't given over decades to searching for the Library in the past—many of those memories say that Lembiq is part of the secret.

"What it is, and why, we cannot say. But too many threads lead there. And so, we suggest you be exceedingly careful when you conquer it—or, even better, you assimilate it without damage. We have concluded that like the sites that Xenefier hides within, the Library is somehow hidden from us. Should you find it, then likely you will find out why, and how.

"Secondly, because in the past, the gods only fought together only grudgingly. Xenefier was more powerful, and they banded together to kill it, but as soon as their part was done, they retreated, or they fought, desperate to capture fragments from their fallen brethren. You have carried a fragment for weeks. They have little hold on you, and we cannot understand why. You put off leveling, the most simple and easy growth that can be imagined, and you put it off until later, when you 'have time for it,' and you spend your time mating for recreation instead. Jax, there is much that is unique about you and that mystifies us, but this we have seen you do already. And frankly, with the life of your love and your unborn child upon the line, there can be no greater drive."

There was a moment of silence as I nodded, flatly staring at Him, before He went on.

"Jax, we wished for you to grow, but we also wished for ourselves to do so. We coveted secrets of power. We saw those who claimed fragments and stayed hidden, and we have each planned to take from them, but because of the situation with Nimon, we have not. We have observed them, hidden them from one another, and we made plans.

"What we see now is that, most likely, as things stand, we will lose. Some if not all of us will die, and any survivors, tempted by the fragments and dissipating power, will be driven to claim them, allowing Xenefier its chance to flee again.

"As you ascend, though, as you fight for those you love, there will come a time that you have the power of the empire, the power of the gods, and your own pure heart still, before the hunger takes hold of you. In that time, you will be able to fight it, and devote all your power to the task.

"At least, that is our hope, and in exchange for aiding in the potential rise of the One That is All, we accept that the realm will change. We run less of a risk, now, and more later, because there is the risk that once fully ascended, you will—instead of fighting for us, instead of bringing order—you will choose to feed upon us all.

"That is the risk we run, that we could, in seeking to remove the threat of Xenefier, once and for all, to slay the boogeyman, we instead give rise to our own destroyer. In this, is the greatest risk for us, but we choose hope. We choose trust, and we do this in part in contrition. Had we helped you in the way that we could have before now, had we been focused as our memories demand, on preventing the rise of this creature, instead of blaming its worst aspects on Nimon and dismissing the threat, then perhaps this might have never come about."

He bowed His head, His last words carried on the breeze, barely above the sound of the rippling water.

"We will guide you, Jax. We will aid you, and in turn, we will give birth to our successor, enabling the thing that Nimon has most feared to come to pass...the rise of the Overgod."

CHAPTER THREE

There was a long silence, as I processed this, processed what I was being offered, and promised, and the history fucking lesson that had come with it.

The knowledge that if I did this, this would be the end and the beginning. That I would no longer be Jax, not even Prince Jax. I'd be a god, literally the one god above all the others. The god who could, in theory at least, smash Nimon into fucking paste, when I fully ascended.

If they couldn't really come to one another's aid when it was serious because of the hunger that would overcome them, if I considered the power that I gained from each fragment, and I instead bound only up to nine fragments of divinity and then held any more I gained, then I could…

I could fight the gods.

Not challenge them and then be forced to accept that when they had their full power, I was an ant. No, if I claimed nine fragments, and then just held the others, I'd be still gaining some power from each.

That would mean that I couldn't bind them—not then, at least—but with say, nine fragments bound and then another ten unbound, I'd be a beast. I'd be able to hunt down Baphomet. I'd be able to hunt Illoth.

And on top of challenging them, on top of ripping a single fragment free, I'd be able to use the ability that the first fragment granted me properly.

With Illoth, I could stop Her from fleeing, and keep Her close.

I could harvest Her of *all* Her fragments.

I could kill Her and Baphomet. I'd need to harvest a lot of other fragments, but once Nimon figured out what I was doing, once He realized I wasn't taking one, that I was taking them all? He'd step in; He'd have to.

If I could escape then, with the rest of their power, then chase down others? If I could change from what I was, into the assassin and predator of the gods?

Then there was no limit to what I could become.

With the other gods helping to pick out my targets, guiding me, I could do it.

The other cities of the empire could be recaptured as well. It'd not be easy, and I'd have to move—and move incredibly fast—but I *could* do it. With the help of the gods, literally, I could target the cities in ways that I hadn't before now.

Hell, with the way that I'd taken the cities so far, it'd been more or less the traditional way. I'd marched in armies, and I'd pulled sneaky underhanded shit. But I'd been doing it the "right" way. The normal way. If instead I was to claim some more fragments, bind them and then go for it?

In theory, at least, I could literally march the fuck in the front door, or better yet, fly over the wall, land and smash the top dicks who were in charge, make it messy and obvious as fuck that they posed me no threat, and then demand their surrender.

That of the survivors, anyway.

I'd need spies, information—I'd not want to take out someone who wasn't a dick. But if I was to fly into the cities, eliminate their leadership—personally, I mean—and then free the slaves, open the gates, have the legion march in and take control, then summon the secondary leaders to the palace or whatever, give them their new orders, put one of them in charge with a legion minder I could trust and an example of the mess when I got annoyed, then fuck off?

"I could do it," I whispered, seeing the potential. In a few days, I could take a city, literally. Take a few of them? Put people I trusted in place to rule them, then move on? Have them all swear the oaths, so that I knew the city wouldn't be fucked the second I turned my back, and then just…

It was possible.

I hated that it meant leaving Oracle in the hands…tentacles… claws…*whatever* of that fucking creature, Xenefier. But it meant that there was a better chance that I'd actually be able to free her.

If I went screaming in now and died? That'd achieve nothing. I'd leave the empire to flounder, for all the time it took for Xenefier to join with our child, and then all life would be over.

It'd be everything and everyone, as it said.

I hated it, I *hated* it with the fucking burning passion of a thousand French farmers facing a minor inconvenience, never mind the much weaker burning passion of the sun.

I hated it, but I also knew that I needed to do it.

It felt…wrong. It felt like I was some sneaky-sneaky fucking rogue planning to slip in and steal the city rather than fight like an honest man. But…this way would not only save Oracle and our child, save all of life if it worked, but in the short term? It'd probably save a buttload of lives as well.

No armies marching and facing one another, when I damn well needed these people surviving and joining the empire.

It could be done, and that meant that I needed to do it. I needed to face the gods, I needed to face my people, and I needed to get moving, because I'd be damned if Oracle was going to be in the hands of that fucking thing one second longer than was absolutely necessary.

I looked at Tyosh, who nodded in clear understanding, before closing His eyes, and the world around us vanished.

I blinked, and I was on my back again, looking up, seeing the gods: Tyosh as He straightened and stepped back, a gentle smile on His face as He spoke to the others; Cruit, who held me down on my chest; and both Sint and Darakin, on my left and right, respectively.

"It is over. He is clear of the madness now. You may release him." That was all He said, but the others moved hesitantly at first, as if expecting me to suddenly throw them off.

That oddity suddenly registered, as all my emotions roared back with horrific force.

It'd taken three gods to hold me down.

Three. Fucking. *Gods*.

How the hell had that worked? I knew they could only project a limited amount of their power here—otherwise, Nimon could simply manifest and step on me like the bug I was, ending our quarrel instantly, but still…

"Are you well, brother?" Darakin asked me gently, and I looked at Him, at the exhaustion and uncertainty in His eyes.

"No," I rasped, my voice full of unshed tears. "No, I'm fucking not… But I will be, brother."

"Then know that we mourn with you, and will aid you until she stands with you again."

It was a simple thing, something that could be easily put aside, or so it seemed. When a god said something like that, it had an effect.

I felt it. And more so when Sint spoke up as well.

"The road has been a hard one for you, mine ally and friend, but we shall stand with you and finish the journey yet. Until then, know that we believe in you, and are here."

"And there is much to say, and explain…" Jenae added, before pausing as Tyosh shook His head. *"Ah, I see."*

"Yeah, I know," I muttered, swallowing hard, feeling the rasp as my dented armor caught on my flesh. Once again, I wondered how the ever-living fuck I'd done that.

In part, I knew; it was because of the limitations of the gods, and also, my dragon form.

"Tuthic'Amon?" I called in the silence of my mind. I felt him, as he reached back to me—that immensity, that solidity, as one of the greatest creatures of the realm put his attention to me.

It wasn't like the gods, who weren't here, not really. They were always—at least, in part—in that realm far away. They were beings of power that existed in a thousand places at once, anthropomorphic manifestations of abstract concepts given life by will and luck and ascended living people.

Dragons were all in this realm, and they were terrifying. The dragon form I'd been granted was incredible, and I barely understood its most basic capabilities, and yet…

With it active, I'd held off three gods.

I felt Tuthic's regret that he'd had to choke off that power, and yet the pride that I'd lasted so long.

It wasn't entirely because of him; it was a gift of the bloodline, tied to Shustic, his mate, and Amon, my grandfather. But what one greater dragon could give, another who was also bonded to me had been able to choke off.

"I am sorry, little one…" he rumbled, before correcting himself. *"And twice over for the dishonor of the address. I shall do better. I am sorry, Amon's Heir, and one who made his passage complete. Jax, heir to our joined line, I am here. I sensed your rage, and your need, and regret that I had to step in. But I believe you understand why?"*

"Yeah," I said softly, internally, even as I struggled with a feeling of betrayal, despite knowing he was right to do it. *"I got it."*

"Then you understand why I had to act as I did. In a battle with a true enemy, not your shame-filled allies, I would not do so, but…"

"I got it," I repeated. *"Can you see what happened? Do you understand why I did it?"*

"I did and I do." He nodded his magnificent head. *"And as such, I add to your blessings, that I shall not do so again, unless you face an ally in such a way. Act with honor, and claim your birthright."*

"I will." I wanted to ask for more—hell, I wanted to *demand* more. That fucker had reached out and choked off my gift, and now I wasn't confident in using it again. I'd be worried in the middle of a fight that he might decide that he liked my opponent more than me, but I also knew the reality of this.

In the eyes of the greater dragons, the empire broke its oath. It failed to do what it promised and Shustic died. And then, compounding that failure—one that came about thanks to that fucking dickbag of a father of mine—it failed again when the legions were supposed to be sent to protect the newborn dragons.

That Tuthic had literally shown the restraint he had in not flying over with the others of his kind and burning what was left of the empire from the realm was an incredible act of generosity on his part, and one that, as the prince of the empire, I was really starting to understand.

He could have, probably should have even, and it was out of respect for Amon that he hadn't.

That was it.

A dragon's moral compass and that of lesser beings just weren't compatible, or at least not in the same way.

It was like me worrying about whether an ant I stepped on was owed recompense.

No, we understood each other, and although I could probably push for a single favor, it'd be a one-time thing, and that would be it. Asking for anything now? Not yet. When I knew where Oracle was and I was going for her?

Yeah. When I wanted the deep places of the realm burned to a cinder, that was when I'd ask for his help. The mental nod he gave me let me know that he understood, that he had sensed all those thoughts, and that when I called, he'd answer.

Once.

I bowed my mental head and sent him a sense of respectful thanks, and then he was gone.

I blinked. A second or less had elapsed in the real world, and I found the gods all facing me still, though in the middle was Lagoush, who went to one knee and bowed Her head.

"Jax, my ally and our savior, I am sorry." That was it: no explanations, no begging or denunciations over the action I'd taken on seeing Her, nothing beyond, "Hey, I fucked up, and I'm sorry."

Ironically, it was the only thing that She could have done that wouldn't raise my ire. I forced myself to push down the anger and nod that I understood.

She stood and backed away, as Jenae spoke again.

"You have been made aware of our offer?" She clearly meant the help that Tyosh had offered, and I nodded. *"Will you accept it?"*

"I will," I said flatly.

"Then I suggest you begin with the fragment that you took from Illoth. Will you trade it, as we discussed, to Tamat?"

"I will," I growled, before looking over at the Goddess of Dark Deeds. "The Fragment of Order."

"I agree." Tamat nodded. *"You will need to bind it in a place of order."*

"Or," Sint interrupted, *"perhaps a different choice would be wise?"*

"What?" I glanced at him.

"There is a Fragment of Chaos, held by Brakuus, the lord of Kronk," Sint said. *"If you were to take that, and then bind it…the city is a place of chaos already, so that would suffice, and then the resultant surge of order when chaos is removed would power the Fragment of Order as well."*

"Well, there's a fucking plan," I growled. "Two birds, one stone, and one fucking dark dwarf dickhead fucked up in the meantime."

"Be aware, Jax, that as he has this gift, a Fragment of Chaos, he will have a similar level of power to your own at this point," Jenae warned me.

"Maybe." I shrugged. "Know what he doesn't have?"

"What?" She asked curiously.

"An absolutely urgent need to fuck someone up." I cracked my shoulders, shifting and twisting my neck, feeling the ache and the pain of the last who knew how many hours of being stationary, then I nodded to Her. I still had a serious issue with rising rage around them, and I was relieved as they faded back, stepping from our world into the next.

"Use that anger, channel it; let it speed your strikes and aid you, but never permit it to control you." Darakin nodded to me.

In seconds, they were gone, save Sint.

"Jax, although I understand, and I sympathize, you must understand the risk that this path represents to us all. Please understand that although I believe in you, I shall also be watching. Should you fall under the spell of the Fragment of Chaos, should you lose yourself in it, then for the respect and admiration I bear you, I will step in and end your suffering."

And then he was gone.

I stared after Him. My blood boiled again as rage, anger, and self-recrimination roiled through me, on and on. He would kill me? If I lost control doing what they needed me to do, to fix their fuckup and to rescue my love, because of their actions?

He'd kill me?

No.

Not a *fuckin'* chance!

I'd do this, and I'd damn well make it look easy.

A Fragment of Chaos followed by a Fragment of Order?

That sounded like military service to me. An oxymoron, I'd heard it called, like "Army Intelligence" or "peaceful occupation" or "honest politician."

I shook it off, as I realized that there were two sensations fighting desperately for my attention.

One was pain, and the other? A burning, agonizing hunger. And both of them came from Sehran.

I turned, blinking and seeing her for the first time since I'd lost Oracle and retreated into myself.

She looked *terrible*.

She was starving, literally. As I looked at her, she straightened, wiping tears from her cheeks and sinking to her knees again, trying haltingly to explain her failure.

Her *failure*.

"Stop," I rasped out, before stepping forward and dragging her from her knees to stand. I enfolded her in my arms, crashing her to me, as I pushed out the bond to her again and shared my soul.

She'd been bonded to Oracle, and then Oracle to me. The duality of our natures meant that Oracle's lesser mana pool of six hundred was more than enough to sustain the succubus, and then Oracle could draw from mine, enabling us to be safe working in tandem.

Sehran, by her nature as a demon, needed to feed on either mana or life to remain in the realm. That she'd survived as long as she had?

I looked around, seeing the dead that lay near her, and feeling the pain that rolled through her, understanding that she'd been feeding on the dead, and that was a big no-no for her kind.

Hell, it damned well should be for any kind, obviously, but for a succubus, they needed life-bearing fluids.

One of the main reasons they were always portrayed as filthy fuckers wanting to suck on guys all the time was that they literally wanted that fluid. It was ambrosia for them, the liquid of life…though it was also because, you know, demons of lust and all that.

Now, I would not be offering *that* to Sehran—and the bodies around had their necks savaged, so I guessed it wasn't that she'd been snacking on. Although, for her kind, it'd be totally acceptable and the whole "cheating" thing wasn't really an issue for demons, I damn well knew that Oracle would be the first to make me do it, if we had to, to save her life. But no.

She could survive just fine on blood, or on mana, if she was bonded to someone.

Usually to stay here, she was bonded to Jian, and yeah, she also got her little treats from him, which was obviously a *massive* treat for him.

Since we'd been cast adrift here, though, so far from Jian, I'd bonded her, and then Oracle and I had shared the bond. With Oracle taken, that bond had broken, and she desperately accepted my offered link as I pushed it out.

My mana channels creaked as a fresh wedge was driven into them, one that siphoned off my mana to the succubus, who urgently drank, almost collapsing as she took it and her body recovered.

"Don't," I whispered, feeling it as she opened her mouth, still held against me. "You didn't fail her. *I* did." My heart broke all over again. "I failed them both."

"No, I did. You ordered me to protect them and—"

"And they almost killed you," I pointed out. "Xenefier, that fucking thing, set this trap up. It created all of this, just to get her, and that absolute shitehawk Baphomet helped."

There was a sensation of pressure as my invoking of the god drew His attention, and I raised my gaze to the ceiling.

"I know you can hear me," I said softly. "I *know* you can. So fine. Until now, this was something that I was doing for the empire. Had you stepped aside, had Nimon Himself chosen to accept neutrality, to put all of this behind us, despite the deaths and the shit? I'd have taken that."

There was a silence, as the sensation of other gods watching grew.

"No more," I growled. "Baphomet, you crossed the *fucking* line. You made this *personal*. You involved yourself with goddamn Xenefier—the fucking boogeyman of your worst legends. You helped to take the love of my life from me, to punish me, just because you mouthed off and got spanked by Darakin for it."

There was a feeling of anger, but there was also the same feeling as I'd had from Nimon and Illoth right after the fights: a feeling of injury, of weakness…and a hint of fear.

"You're wounded. Recovering. Hiding!" I called out, letting go of Sehran and stepping to the side; she sank to sit in the cool water. "You thought that *this* was the way to get even? You thought this was the way to pay me back for the mess you got yourself into?"

I was getting louder as my anger finally had a viable target.

"You thought you'd fucking do this and then walk away! NO!" I roared. "You thought this was between us, Nimon? Well, let me make this fucking crystal goddamn clear. Until now, *I didn't give two shits about this fight beyond keeping my people safe!*"

I felt the change in the air as the gods listened, as Nimon, I was willing to bet, actually started to consider it.

"Beyond that? I'd have written it all off! The war, the fucking murder of Amon, all of it—I'd have been sensible and for peace, if that was the price. I'd have listened, and I'd have damn well even apologized if I had to… BUT NO MORE!

"THAT FUCKING COCK-GOBBLING, FURRY-FACED FUCKUP JUST MADE THIS *PERSONAL*!" I roared. "YOU HEAR ME, BAPHOMET? Until now, you didn't rate highly enough for me to even give a shit about you! This was all me responding to Nimon, and you being too dumb to get out of the way. But now? I'M GONNA RIP YOUR HEAD OFF AND SHIT DOWN YOUR NECK!"

There was a long, frozen moment before a bellow like a raging bull echoed out.

"FOOL! Weakling! You think to goad me? To draw me forth to grace you with my presence! I shall crush you like a grape beneath my hoof! Enjoy your last days, for my armies shall hunt you down and decorate my altars with your entrails!"

"Fucking bring it, you dumb shit!" I yelled at the sky, before turning my back on Him and moving to Sehran. Even as thunder and lightning crashed overhead, the gods protected me as He hammered down blow after blow on a shield that the gods hastily erected, followed suddenly by a terrible shriek of pain.

"Intervention declared," came that same, cold, calculating and somehow alien voice that I'd heard when Baphomet and Darakin fought last time. ***"The little bull interferes with what must be yet again, attacking the one who rises directly, without honor or care for the compact. Intervention is called for and noted. The cost is zzzzzzzz…"***

There was a long instant of a buzzing, like a thousand bees driven wild, their hives destroyed and the roar of the queens as they demanded restitution; then it shattered, and the sounds of the world and that great voice slid back.

"And must be borne. Let all bear witness: intervention has been offered."

"Say you accept the intervention, quickly!" came a whisper from Sint into my ear.

I cleared my throat, before calling out, as he'd suggested.

"Very well. In recompense, the location is claimed and healed. The price is paid from the bull, and let all take note. Mortals or not, beware, lest ye be adjudged, as none are above the laws of the compact."

There was a long silence, before the ground shook, the walls blurring, as Baphomet's screams echoed again.

The carvings that covered the walls sharpened; the water that rose to my knees in here shivered and then retreated. Collapsed masonry lifted and rolled through the air, shattered edges reforming.

I turned slowly, seeing on all sides as the damaged temple was reborn. Shattered friezes, long lost to the constant onslaught of water, were again repaired, dragging themselves across the floor, snapping into completion and lifting, floating to the walls and then sealing themselves back in place.

Running water burbled and bounced as it was shifted, limited to set channels that were clearly designed long ago to enable the water to flow. Roots withered, breaking free and flaking into dust as blocks that should have taken a hundred men to move slid from the water; their edges reformed into pristine glory, as they slotted, one by one, into their original homes.

It took minutes to rebuild this section of the temple, that was all; but the entire time, Baphomet screamed and roared, his rage and pain clear to all, and I fucking loved it.

This was a fraction of what I'd do to that bastard. But something small in the back of my mind warned me against further antagonizing him, or reveling too openly in his punishment.

Whatever was doing this, whatever the gods had appealed to for intervention, was clearly holding them accountable for rules—rules that we were somehow blocked from hearing.

That left us in the shitty position of knowing that we might make a mistake that cost us everything, and more so, that if this thing, whatever it was, could do this so casually to a god?

I mentally marked it as something NOT to fuck with.

No, I'd gotten what I wanted, which was to make sure Baphomet knew I'd be coming, and that when the time came, he'd be stupid enough to accept my challenge.

Beyond that, I had shit to do.

The sounds of his pain gradually fell away, reducing to hoarse whimpers, before stopping entirely as the last sections of the temple were locked back into place. I offered my hand to Sehran, helping her upright, as the surviving legionnaires and their companions approached.

Dozens of others were behind them, more of the hairless apes, the wisps, and even a small contingent of mer. They stayed well back; the mer moved closer to a recessed pool by the far wall.

I felt it as they checked the pool, their Worldsense—a form of sonar that enabled them to "see" the world around them as they were normally blind—washed out over me. But the majority, I felt as it sank into the depths, vanished into the distance.

Looking around, I saw the temple had been restored, the pool clearly leading out into the lake for the mer and any other aquatic species to be able to come here to worship, and I even felt something below us.

My senses had gradually become, through constant fucking repetition, attuned to the divine. I could feel the altar that now graced the temple, and a second that waited somewhere below, presumably for those species that wouldn't—or couldn't—come to the surface.

And more than that, I felt it as Lagoush did something, and this place, this heart of Her worship, a fully restored temple that could have been the focus of Her sole worship, blurred, and was instead converted to the worship of the Pantheon of the Flame.

There was no way that the situation could have been clearer that contrition was the order of the day: Lagoush had given up Her place as the first in the temple; She was sharing the power, the mana that it brought in, and She'd stepped back as the primary deity here.

Admittedly, I still wanted to kick Her teeth in. And the thought of what She'd done, and the cost to Oracle and our child, filled me with rage, but…

Whoosah.

Calm.

I forced myself to be as calm as possible, as cold, reserved and just cool—not raging, nor tearing the building down around our ears. Instead, I checked that Sehran was okay. I saw the hurt, the pain and the shame on her face, and I resolved that we'd talk later; I sent a brief sensation to her through the bond of caring, of trust, and of reassurance.

I sent one to Oracle as well, though that one was filled with fear, shame, and a desperate love and hope. But I wasn't surprised when I felt nothing back.

She was too far away, and although our bond was strong—iron was weak in comparison, as was titanium—the distance meant that nothing reached back. That and I was fairly sure that Xenefier wouldn't be allowing her to wake up and nuke the place.

That meant that, for now, as much as I absolutely hated this, I had to accept that I wasn't going after Oracle right now. I had to instead sort out my shit—and then, and only then, could I let my rage burn.

CHAPTER FOUR

As the sensation of the gods' direct attention faded—though the air remained charged with them, as they reveled in the repaired temple—I turned to Sehran, casting both a Scour and a Complex Healing into her. As the last injuries faded, the covering of matted blood and filth fell free.

She was left exhausted, hollow-eyed, and deeply broken inside by our loss. I wrapped her in my arms again; I, as much as her, needed the comfort.

I didn't dare let myself weep, knowing instinctually that feeling that filled me—the cold, brittle calm—was all that kept me upright.

If I let go of my control, if I stopped, there was no telling how long I'd be broken for. I'd already been lost to the world for too long. In truth, I didn't even know how long it'd been since the fight.

Since she was taken from me.

I vaguely remembered the calls of night creatures, the hooting of owls, and a darkness that had swept across the room. But it'd seemed meaningless to me, as lost within my personal funk as I had been.

It couldn't have been a full day and a night, surely.

I knew that, intellectually, I'd been there for a while, but the reality?

No.

"How long?" I asked Sehran slowly. Haltingly. "How long was I…?"

"A full day and a night, and half the next day," she said.

"Fuck. No wonder I need a piss," I muttered, and she snorted, then choked off her laugh, shaking her head and starting to apologize. I painted a smile on my face and patted her on the shoulder. "It's all right," I assured her.

"She'll be okay," Sehran lied. "They both will. I know it."

"Of course," I lied in return. Both of us knew it, and saw it.

"What…what do we do now?" she asked. "Did the gods tell you? I saw them pin you, then everything changed. A second later, you were up and calmer again."

"A second?" I shook my head. "I was talking to Tyosh for about half an hour, it feels like. Doesn't matter, though…" I had a sudden feeling that I was being watched, and I changed what I was going to say, just in case that intervention was still ongoing. "He meditated with me, and just told me that they were with me, and shared in my loss."

"That's it?" She blinked, before she must have seen something in my eyes and played along. "Ooookay, so, did your meditation give you the chance to come up with a plan?"

"I'm working on it," I said, not wanting to make it too obvious. "But for now, we need to check on the survivors, then get ready. Tenandra, Lydia and our people are getting closer by the minute, but they're still a few days away, and we can't wait for them."

"So, you want to see the others?" She turned and gestured to the legionnaires to come closer.

I hated the look of fear and shame on their faces, but I understood it as well. They jogged over; the formerly knee-deep water that had covered the floor was entirely gone, as was the mulch and filth of centuries.

Instead, with every step, the metal of their boots and the jingle of cuirass, the clatter of steel and the grinding of material rang out. All of it dropped away as they went to one knee before me.

Of the seven I'd brought with me, Vislen was their optio, a grizzled, but frequently smiling veteran of hundreds of fights, with short, cropped light-brown, almost blond hair. His eyes were usually blue, bright and clear. But now they were red rimmed, and clearly he'd had a damned hard time of it the last few days since the fight that went so disastrously wrong.

His right hand had been Lembas, a half-elven legionnaire who had taken to magic like a duck to water, but he'd been killed, brutally so, his head crushed along with his helmet. As I glanced around, I saw that both of the scouts, Bern and Toci, were missing.

I vaguely remembered seeing them in the fight, when I'd been desperate to get to Oracle, but not since. And the creatures that we'd been facing?

I glanced toward them at the back of the room. They nervously shuffled their feet, clearly ready to run.

I turned back to my people. I'd deal with the others soon enough.

Kneeling next to Vislen was Kato, the succubus he'd bonded to; dark-haired and almost petite next to the massive legionnaire. She knelt on both knees, hands pressed to the ground before her, head bowed and wings tucked in.

Her horns were almost dainty, they were so small.

On the other side of Vislen knelt Orden, in the legion style: one knee and one fist to the ground, the other fist to his chest. Orden was taller, rangier, and had the "look of eagles," as I'd heard it said about those natural warriors in any army.

He was a focused, intensely driven legionnaire who rarely joked and had a very dark sense of humor when he did. But he was always the first to check on others as well. He was the one who got a coffee ready for the next on guard duty as soon as he handed over, and pushed himself hard.

His partner, the incubus Hador, knelt on the far side of him, both fists pressed to the ground, on both knees. In direct contrast to Vislen and Kato, he was actually bigger than Orden, wide-chested and heavily muscled.

He also wore a much more respectable outfit than the one that Kato wore— which, frankly, I was thankful for in all sorts of ways.

Kato was a succubus and had all the overwhelming sexuality and submissive sex-kitten persona that many associated with her kind. While Hador?

He was huge, and after seeing him wandering around on the airship on the way here in the buff, the last thing my ego needed in its current state was to have that thing on display.

I just hoped he'd been careful when he knelt.

That was it, though.

"I'm sorry." I meant it.

"My prince?!" Vislen whispered, looking shocked. "No—no, *we're* sorry. We failed—"

"No." I cut him off. "No, you didn't fail. I led you into an ambush, and then I lost…" I changed what I was about to say, forcing back the tears as my voice roughened. "No, what happened, happened."

"We should have—" Vislen tried, and I cut him off again.

"I told you to hold the entrance," I reminded him. "I ordered you all to keep them out, never realizing that they were already inside. I was the one who left Oracle in a position to be taken, and I was the one who left Sehran on her own to be brutalized by the monsters as they tried to take her.

"She fought to protect my love, and the future of the empire, and I hold her and you all blameless for their loss. We fought against a creature that killed the ancient gods, and that was helped to hide, to fucking ambush us, by Baphomet."

"Baph…" Orden growled, and I nodded.

"Oh, I'll be dealing with that one personally, don't worry," I assured him with a snarl. "For now, though, he crossed the lines and this…" I gestured at the surrounding temple. "This is the result. There are apparently rules when the gods war, and he broke one, so this happened. I don't know more than that, so please don't ask. Just accept it."

"Of course, my prince." Vislen nodded.

"And get the hell up, man. I just spent nearly a week trapped in a small room with you farting like a steam engine, so quit that shit."

"Ah, yes, sorry…" He blushed, and Sehran spoke up from behind me.

"He means the respectful attitude and not meeting his eyes, not that you have to stop farting," she assured him.

"Oh, thank God." He smiled.

"Are you sure?" Hador interjected. "Could I change your mind on an injunction of that order? We're from hell, and it literally smells better there half the time than around him."

"Regardless, what happened, happened, and as much as I want to pound someone into ground beef, now's not the time," I admitted, as Sehran again interjected as both Kato and Hador smiled.

"Not either of you," she said firmly. "He's not talking like that, and if he was, there's a line to take part…"

"Fucking hell." I sighed, rubbing at the bridge of my nose. "Fine, so, Vislen, give me an update please, and stand up, for fuck's sake. At ease."

He did, as did the others, and he nodded as he spoke. "The Xenefier creature—our notifications named the kills as Xenefier-infected—is that the enemy?"

"Yeah," I replied flatly.

"The creature released the locals as soon as it had what it came for," he explained. "Those who are still alive mainly fled. Small numbers of their groups have been arriving since, and the wisps are the most desperate.

"They were apparently captured, or as many as possible were, and then half were infected, while the remainder were pressed to the altar and were tortured to death in an attempt to draw the eye of Lagoush and the others.

"With a third party—Baphomet, I guess—holding a shield over the area and hiding it from the other gods, it meant that they had no clue what was happening here until we arrived and the shit hit.

"The creatures we met out in the jungle when we first landed are the original inhabitants of the area, mutated by centuries of living in proximity to the wildly surging mana here. They're not…well, they're mad, but I don't think it's their fault." He looked over at them.

"Whatever happened here, they don't have the words to describe it, just that it was done intending to help them, and instead it's been killing them ever since. Something magical was done, and over the following months, the lumps and bumps started showing up. They're strong and fast, but they're also very short-lived. Like, the leader is called 'old Jamus' and he's nearly *six*.

"Whatever happened here, it massively boosted their growth and strength. They all have a garbled history that they repeat to one another each night to make sure it's kept alive, but they only live between four and seven years. Their childhood, from birth, is six months.

"Pregnancies are about eight weeks, and about one in ten is viable. The others…" He looked at me and choked off what he was going to say, considering the situation, and just shook his head instead.

"Okay, so they were captured by Xenefier?" I asked once I'd gotten my emotions sharply reined in again, and he nodded quickly. "All of them? And are we sure it's gone?"

"They claim to have all been taken over, or those who are with them now were never captured. But we only have their word for it, and we have no way of verifying their claim," he admitted. "I considered pinning one down and cutting into them—we have healing spells, after all—but there was just no other way to be sure."

"And if you did that, all the creature has to do is move ahead of the knife and it'll look like you're just murdering someone," I finished for him, and he nodded.

"Exactly."

"Well, there's the cleansing fire spell, you know, Frostfire Circle of Cleansing," I muttered, rubbing at my chin and trying to focus, when everything in me screamed that I needed to be moving, to do…something!

"If they swear to me, then they can stand inside the circle and when we order them to tell the truth, they'll have to. It's about as clear as I can think a way to make sure, but…" I shook my head. "That fucker's powerful, but honestly, I don't think it's sneaky enough to pull tricks like that, not consistently.

"Sure, there's probably some of it still here watching us, but they're going to be tiny bugs or just the gloop itself, hidden in shadows or crevices. That's its body, by the way, so it only uses other bodies, physical humanoid bodies, for specific tasks. Why risk being caught for nothing?" I swallowed hard, shifting as I tried to keep myself on track, and not start screaming, raging, or break down into tears. Instead, I forced myself to listen as he went on.

"I think it's likely they're no longer infected, but they are also weak, mutated and abused, and terrified. They have spent the time since they were freed either running from us, or desperately trying to make contact, but at the same time, if a twig breaks, then they run for the hills.

"The wisps are the worst of the lot. They know their value, and they know that they were what convinced us to trust the trap. They fully expect that we're going to take at least some of them as slaves, and they are just hoping that if they give up a small number now, then we'll leave the rest alone."

"They're that bad?" I asked, and Vislen nodded.

"They're genuinely terrified, and yet they also see us as their only hope. Their groups are split, from what I've seen, with a few almost sacrificial victims being sent to us, willing to be taken if that protects what's left of their families."

"What about the mer?" I asked.

"No contact." He shook his head. "I mean, they're there…" He inclined his head in the direction of the small group on the far side of the room, and went on. "But if we go near them? They just dive in the pools and vanish. That water there? They check it constantly, I think to make sure there's not a gate or something that's closed and trapping them here. But if we approach them, that's it…they dive straight in and swim away. The only way we see them is if we give them a lot of space like this and wait. Then they gradually come out of the water and sit and wait."

"They came through over there before the temple was repaired?" I asked, and he nodded. "So, they knew the pool was there, but it may have been blocked in the past or been a place that they had issues with. Okay, I'll speak to them. Lastly, the scouts and the gnomes?"

"We lost Toci, killed in the fight, but Bern is alive and currently guarding the gnomes. The mad little bastards only saw one enemy since we landed, and they've built something that shoots a flaming liquid when they press a handle, so whatever else, the creature stayed clear of them. They're fine, but they say that the ship won't fly far. There's too little resources to fix it and too few stones."

"It can fly, though?"

"For a few days maybe, but that's it." He nodded. "And it's been rebuilt again. The wood they had…too much was broken in the crash, and it's down to half the size it was after their fixes. Even now, there'll barely be enough room for us all, and that's using green timber from fresh-felled trees."

"That's fine." I nodded, forcing a smile. "Thank you, Vislen. Thank you all." I got a crash of fists to chests for that, with both Hador and Kato mimicking their bonded partners' actions, with very different results; Kato bounced for a while afterward while Hador looked to be almost as solid as the legionnaires' plate armor was.

I turned to the mer on the far side of the chamber, keeping my distance, and spoke.

"I know your people, and I have friends who are mer back on Dravith, which is why I damn well know that you can hear me just fine from that distance and have been listening to the entire conversation.

"I also know that you'll have a few others of your pod scattered around, ready to fight if something goes wrong here, so let's cut the crap. You wouldn't be here if you didn't want to talk, but I can't hear you at this distance. I'm going to come over, alone, and you either talk to me, or you can fuck off, because I've not got the time to deal with your shit right now."

I said it flatly, then waited for thirty seconds, before telling the others—including Sehran—to stay here.

"Want me to speak to the wisps?" Sehran asked quietly. "They've been watching us while I waited with you, and they know that I'm yours already. They might listen to me more than the others."

"Go for it." I nodded. "If they won't listen, then Tenandra will be here soon, and they can listen to her. We need their support, though, because when I get Oracle back, we might need them for the birth still."

"I'll explain and get them to join us," she said, resolute.

I nodded, feeling proud of how dedicated and how far she'd come. Hell, we'd all come so far that the people we were before all of this wouldn't recognize us.

God knows the idiot who had gone to Lou's house that night would never have expected this shit, that's for sure.

I walked over to the pool and the waiting mer, all the while channeling mana into my armor, aiming it specifically at the neck and upper chest, feeling the tiny fixes it made as the mana sank into the ancient armor.

By the time I got halfway, the mer dove into the water, and I kept going, speaking again.

"Either you're coming here because you want to speak to me, or you're coming here because you want to have access to the gods. I'm the champion of Jenae, and my brother Thomas is the champion of Lagoush, this I swear." I injected mana into the words as I spoke them, and the air shimmered with the feeling of an oath sworn, and then kept marching.

One of the larger mer in the middle of the group jerked to a halt, seconds from diving in, and instead turned to stare at me.

"That's it, huh? You want to speak to the gods, but you're not able to for some reason yet. I can feel an altar below us…you could easily reach that underwater, so why show yourselves? Why come here?"

"Because the gods will not speak to us, unless we speak to you first," the mer called out, his voice harsh and clipped. "The gods refuse us for our crimes."

"For the shit you did when possessed by Xenefier?" I asked, continuing to close the distance.

"Yes, and more."

"What else?"

"None of your business!"

"Fine. What do you want then?" I snapped.

"To speak to the gods."

"Then fucking speak, you prick," I growled. "They're here—you should be able to feel them listening. If not? Then it's your problem, not mine. Lagoush and the others are allied to me and my empire. We're helping each other and spreading their worship. You saw what this temple was like before and what it's like now."

"Full of evil."

"It was, wasn't it?" I snapped. "Now that evil's gone and it's taken my wife and unborn fucking child with it!" Okay, wife was a bit of a stretch—I'd not asked yet, nor put a ring on it—but I damn well was going to…and before I ascended the steps as emperor as well.

I'd rather have done it before ascending to godhood too, but let's face it…I was already a god in the sack, so it wasn't like it was going to be much of a change for Oracle when I got her back.

"So, let's make it clear, you dick. One of yours took her, and I could choose to believe that this shit was because of you and blame you for it, or I can be a fucking adult and say no, that it's not your people's fault. But either way…"

"It is."

"We need to be able to—wait, what?"

"It *is* our fault."

"Fucking come again?" I asked slowly, calmly, as something gripped my stomach and twisted.

"Ret'cha, the one that you speak of." The mer's voice echoed slightly as I strode across the last ten meters toward him. "Ret'cha found a cavern deep below the lake, followed it to another, and still more.

"He was gone long months, and we all believed him dead, until suddenly he was back, weeks ago, and infected. We knew not what with before, but our runesmith was determined to heal him, and spent long turns of the daystar working.

"She sickened, as did others, but we believed she would find a cure, as always before. And so, when he started moving more, exploring the lake as if new to our ways, we viewed it as the sickness having hurt his head.

"We believed in him, and her, until it was too late. Had we realized and instead of driving the infected out, we'd killed them? This would have been different."

I came to a halt, standing, staring down at the mer as I processed that.

If this stupid fucker had…well, if he'd killed one of their pod who seemed confused and ill after a long absence, supposedly lost to the depths, then this might not have happened. Might.

In order to have that situation come about, the group would have to be willing to kill any of their own pod who acted confused or lost, so how the hell would they act toward outsiders?

I wanted to find fault.

Fuck me, did I.

I wanted to scream and rant and rage and damn well rip his head off his shoulders, but…fuck me, in order to do that, I'd have to expect them to be murderous xenophobic assholes. And if I thought that about them? Why the hell would I want to speak to them at all?

"It's not your fault," I ground out, even my own voice fighting me as I struggled to tell him it was okay. "You tried to help someone who was sick. That's all."

"We did, but it resulted in this," he spat, shaking his head. "We should have—"

"You did exactly what you should have. And this fucker, Xenefier, came to the surface for one reason only." I forced myself to go on. "He came here to hunt me. He came here, and he's probably been in a dozen other places doing exactly the same thing, in order to trap me…to get at Oracle, my love, and my unborn child. Fuck me, I hate having to repeat this, but this isn't your fault. And you know what? I'm done. It's not my fucking fault either.

"This is Xenefier's fault, nobody else's, and I'm going to fucking kill it for this shit. So, what do you want and what are you offering?"

"What?" He seemed startled, by the way his tendrils flared.

"I asked *what you want*," I growled. "Listen, this place? It's all kinds of messed up, but I'm pretty sure if this isn't the heart of the territory, it's going to count as it once I smash Kronk into paste. As such I need your support, and the empire—I'm the prince of the old empire, sorry, should have led with that, but fuck it—but the empire needs you to at least be neutral so that I can claim the territory and drive Illoth out."

"The…goddess Illoth?" he asked, clearly trying to keep up.

"Yeah, that spidery bitch." I grunted. "You've seen the notifications about me kicking Her arse and Nimon's?"

"That's you?!" he hissed, his voice going up into a higher register in surprise and fear.

"Yeah. Me." I snapped my fingers. "Focus, dammit. Do you want to be neutral, or better yet to join the empire?"

"I… We… No." He shook his head. "We are neutral at best. We wish no wars. We will not join you."

"Neutral I'll take, for now." I nodded. "Sorry, but I've not got time for this shit, so here it is. Think about what you want, the price it'll take for you to join my empire, and tell me, or tell one of the others. If I can do it, I will. If not, well, how many of you are there?"

"I will not tell!" he hissed.

"Well, let's be clear…that lake is small, I doubt it'd hold two hundred of you, and although it might go places underwater, they're not going to be far. If you fuck with me, then I'll boil that lake dry. Otherwise, you do you, boo, and we let each other be. But…if you want the support of the gods, and access to them, then you join us."

"You cannot withhold access to the divine…" he started, clearly trying to get a word in edgewise.

"I can and I fucking will. If you weren't what you are, this would be a different conversation. But with the desert outside the valley and your small numbers? No fucking way you're causing a problem for me beyond doing something stupid to the temple. Let's be clear, you do that shit? You'll wish I'd boiled you all to death.

"Now, you think I'm an asshole, and you're not far wrong, but here's the rub— I like you. Not you, personally—I don't swing that way—but your kind. One of my best goddamn friends is a mer, and I goddamn miss him like my arm's been cut off. He'll be here soon, and he can deal with you, see if there's a deal to be struck. But if there isn't? Fine.

"If there is? Name it! You want ten tons of gold? A frickin' shark with a laser beam on its head? Fine. I. DON'T. CARE. Just don't waste my fucking time and name it!" I broke off, suddenly aware I was panting and shouting, and I attempted to calm down.

"Look, I'm sorry. I'd say I'm not usually an asshole, but that'd be a lie. I do usually hide it better and I play the game more, but that slimy, good-for-nothing piece of shit took those I love more than life itself. I'm here, dealing with this crap instead of tearing the realm apart with my bare hands, so here's the offer.

"Join the empire, and get access to the gods, to whatever support you need, and most of your people all get to stay here. You'll get access to equipment, food, magic, and more. You've got sick? We'll teach you healing spells.

"You're in need of learning new runes for your runecrafter? Great, Ame—one of our people and another mer—is a runecrafter. She's also a healer. It'll probably take a few months, because we'll need to get portals sorted out, but I can ask her to come here and speak to your runecrafter. Set up an exchange or something."

The rapid-fire barrage had clearly flummoxed him, and I sighed.

"Look, just consider it. Remember to play nice with the other kids and don't do anything stupid, all right? Oh, and pay attention to the notifications you get over the next few months, because one way or another, you're going to be hearing about me."

With that, I turned and started to walk away, before spinning on my heel and staring at him.

"Dammit!" I cursed. "Knew I'd forgotten something…what's your name?"

"Vash."

"Fine, talk to your people, Vash. I'm Jax." And with that, I was marching again, this time toward the wisps and the hairless apes.

"You're getting good at diplomacy," Vislen muttered, falling in with me.

"No I'm not."

"No, you're not, but fucking hell, sir, that was hard-nosed."

"Why?" I asked.

"You basically tore him a new arsehole like a new recruit and then tossed the whole thing off and left him in bits. He doesn't know if it's bum or breakfast time."

"Has he gone?"

"Well, no, he's still watching us."

"Listening, too," I pointed out. "I mean it, Vash. We'd like to be friends but we've got no time to sugarcoat this." I spoke directly to the mer I knew was still listening, and after a few seconds, I heard a splash as he dove into the water.

"Sorry," Vislen muttered, and I shook my head.

"Doesn't matter. He'll pass the word to his people and that's all I needed. Right, how's Sehran doing?"

"Uh—"

"I'll check myself." I cut him off and reached out through the bond. *"How we doing?"*

"Very, very nervously," she replied. *"Absolutely the gentlest you can manage."*

I sent a feeling of agreement and then walked closer, before stopping a dozen meters away and speaking loudly. The two groups, the hairless apes to my right and the wisps to my left, both watched me—equally skittish.

"You're here because you want to know what to do. You want to know where to go from here, and you're worried that I'm going to blame you for what happened and hurt your people in some kind of reprisal," I said curtly.

"Let's get that out of the way right now. Yes, I feel that I want to blame you, and no, I don't hold you responsible. What happened was that we were all attacked by a thing older than sin and that's as evil as shit.

"You were captured, tortured, and used against your will to hurt me and my people, killing some of them, and then helping that fuckstick to take those I love away.

"I'm going to get them back, all that it's taken. I'm going to hunt it down and kill it. But before I make it clear how I'll do that, I need to know that I can trust you, and you need to know that you can trust me, so here's the deal.

"You want access to the gods and the temple; you want help, protection, healing and all that good stuff, right?" I looked around, seeing the hesitant and even scared looks on their faces as I continued. "You want a legion force attached to here and others sent out to protect your kind, to make damn sure they're safe and there's none of the atrocities of the past. But given that I'm literally going to be marrying a wisp, and she's the mother of the next prince or princess of the empire, you were probably feeling pretty hopeful.

"Right up until you were instrumental in her being taken from me, and now you're panicking that I'm going to blame you, or somehow enslave you."

Absolute silence now.

"Well, this is the deal. You are your own beings. I can't guarantee your safety, just like I couldn't fucking guarantee that of Oracle. What I can guarantee is that if anyone fucks with you, then they have to go through me.

"I WILL rescue Oracle. I WILL bring my child home. And if I have to shatter the realm to dig into the depths to find Xenefier and burn that fuckstick to death? You better believe I will!"

That last part was shouted loud enough that it echoed off the walls, and I visibly strained to calm myself.

"What's going to happen, and I mean in the next few hours or days, is that I'm going to surround the temple in a powerful spell, one that will burn anything that's not sworn to me out of existence. I'm going to do that again and again. I'm going to make it permanent, and this temple, mark my goddamn words, will become a place free of the scourge of Xenefier and anyone else who isn't an imperial citizen.

"For those of you who are? You'll be able to come here, whenever you want. Live within the boundaries of the spell and know that those around you are sworn by magical oath not to harm you. That anyone who tries to harm, hunt, or enslave you will have to cross the entire length of the temple, burning at every step to do it, and that the Imperial Legion will be here as well, tasked with protecting those of you who are citizens.

"Now, what better option do you have? How else are you going to survive the coming war of the gods and the battle with that fucking slimy bastard?

"You can run, sure, but considering the shit-storm that is coming, there's nowhere that's going to be safe to run to. Add in that unless you think you can survive the Plain of Bones outside, you will not last long enough to get captured by an enemy.

"You can hide, just like you've been doing for the last seven hundred years. Tell me, how's that worked out for you? Or, you can join me. You can learn, you can grow and be protected, and, for a very few of you who are strong enough, you can fight! We'll teach you to fight, to defend those you love, and next time, when anyone comes for you, they get mauled to shit for even thinking about it!

"For you wisps, there's another option as well. Some of the free wisps in my lands have bonded with artifacts, towers that are vast repositories of magic and might, airships that fly across oceans and that rain hellfire down on our enemies and more. You can choose to do this, or not. But if you want to see the world? How the hell else do you think you can do it while being powerful enough to fight a fucking dragon and eradicate armies on the ground that would threaten those you love?

"THEN, the Imperial Legion will be sent as well. You think Kronk is a threat to you here? Give me a fucking *week*. I'll level that shithole and salt the earth. I'll free the enslaved and, as the gods are my witness, I'll fucking slaughter those who think attacking me and mine was a good idea!"

I was ranting, raving almost. The anger was in full flow, but I could feel it as well...the nervousness changing to hope. I almost had them.

"I'll teach you to heal the others around you, to create a safe haven. In the empire, no citizen may harm another, and all have the right to call upon the legion, and ultimately me, *personally*, to defend them, or if they cannot be defended, to be avenged. You—the wisps, I mean—were shit upon from a great height in the past. You were enslaved, abused, and hunted to the point of extinction. Well, it's time the empire made that right.

"I will protect you. I will avenge you, and I will teach you. I'll raise you up and grant you a home that's as safe as any can make it. And if you're willing, and if you need the most possible and strongest protection I can give you, I'll make you a home in the heart of the empire's strength on this continent.

"At the top of the Tower of Gaij, with the legion around you, with the succubai and incubai between you and the rest of the realm, with golems and armies between you and any possible threat, I'll make you a home filled with balanced mana. A place that the gods visit and call their home.

"That's where I'll protect you, if you feel that this isn't safe enough. The choice is yours. But to prove to you all just why you want me protecting you, and why you want to be imperial citizens, with all that entails, I'll do what I've said I'll do. You're aware that Kronk is out there, that it has sent armies back and forth and caravans searching for you here, seeking to conquer you all…"

I was going on instinct here; I had no clue whether it was true or not, but it sounded plausible. I was gambling that they'd at least be aware of the place.

"So, I'll show you proof of who and what I am first. I will conquer Kronk, free those it has enslaved, and remove that threat once and for all for you as well. You worry that you can't trust me and my empire? You worry that you don't know what I'm capable of or even if I am strong enough to do this? Fine. I'll prove it! I'll conquer your enemies, I'll eliminate the threat of Kronk, and in return, you'll join me!"

I got a handful of nods, carried away with the emotions of the speech. But most weren't sure, until the divine presence of Lagoush spoke up.

"I stand witness to the claims of the Imperial Prince. If he should conquer Kronk, the city that has already dispatched an army to slaughter wisps and succubai and legionnaires, then I will give my blessing to those who swear. I, Lagoush, Goddess of Healing, of Calm Waters and Peaceful Shores, will grant you all my blessing, but turn my face from those who refuse my ally's aid."

That was clearly the clincher; I received a quest notification, and I skimmed it.

You have been offered a Divine repeatable Quest: My God is Better than your God (6)

Lagoush of the Pantheon of the Flame has offered you a Quest. Destroy the fortress city of Kronk, eliminate its leaders and shatter its armies, free those unjustly enslaved and prove your worth to the people of the Cradle of Feshcan'un.

Bonus: Repair the Temple of Quiet Waters and rededicate it to the worship of the Pantheon of the Flame 0/1

Kill Brakuus, Lord of Kronk: 0/1

Destroy enemy Elite forces 17/72

Capture the city of Kronk: 0/1

Destroy the city of Kronk: 0/1

Bonuses will be given for exceeding these numbers.

Reward: Territorial Claim increased, 5,000+ Citizens and loyal inhabitants of the Cradle of Feshcan'un, Access to Kronk treasury and loot, 6,000,000xp

Accept: Yes/No

Well, let's face it. I wasn't going to refuse it.

CHAPTER FIVE

The Cradle of Feshcan'un. I read the words again, stuck on that. The "cradle of shattered mother-fuckin' hopes" was more like it, I reflected inwardly. That was what this place was. I stared at the quest notification. I forced myself to stuff down the mingled desperate need to drop to my knees and sob my heart out, and the equally pressing need to drown the world in fire and blood until they were with me again.

No.

I needed to be better. For her. For them. A heavy sense of resolve settled on my shoulders as I swallowed my feelings and looked around.

I'd make this place a temple and fortress to keep those here safe, so that when the time came, we had their support, and in the meantime, I'd wipe Kronk off the fucking map.

Yeah, I had some serious issues I needed to work out, and Kronk? Well, with all the shit they'd pulled, and given that they were being led by someone I needed to gut anyway? It was a perfect target.

I accepted the quest without a thought and then turned to the expectant locals. They watched me for any sign that I was about to go on a murderous rampage, their bodies tense like deer ready to bolt.

"So. That's the deal," I announced, making them jump. "I'll show you who and what I am by eliminating the threat of Kronk once and for all. In return, I expect your support, and your pledge of allegiance to the empire."

Once, I tried to be gentler, I thought grimly. Once, I would have worried about their feelings more. But then, once I fucking had Oracle with me.

A small group of wisps drifted forward, glowing orbs of light, pulsing with different colors. One, a soft-blue light with tendrils of mist trailing behind it, approached closer than the others.

"Prince of the Empire." It spoke, its voice like the whisper of wind through reeds. "I am Erista, elder of what remains of our colony. We agree to your terms but ask one thing: protection for our young. Protect them, but leave them exempt from your wars. They are few, and all that remains for our race to continue."

Something twisted in my gut at the mention of young. *My child, my Oracle, my future, taken.* I pushed down the rage that threatened to consume me again.

"Your young will be under the protection of the empire," I managed. "As will all of you. But they still need to swear. This isn't me being a dick and trying to use them. If I trigger the spells I'm planning to use and they're not sworn to me, then they'll be viewed as an enemy. They could be killed, by the very magic I'm trying to protect you with. You understand?"

The little light bobbed and shifted, then moved closer. "What will you demand of us?" Erista asked. "For the protection of our children?"

I heard the fear in her voice, and I mentally damned all the assholes who had butchered her ancestors to every hell I could imagine.

"I'd ask, and I mean *ask*, that you help me teach my legionnaires magic, as well as possibly helping with the management of the Great Tower of Gaij. I'll be clear, by my oath and word—you will never be forced to bond against your will, nor enslaved to serve the towers nor anything of that nature that I can prevent. I will fucking protect you. Oracle…she was captured, burned out and forcibly bonded to the tower of Dravith nearly a thousand years ago. I met her there over the last year and when she found me injured, she bound herself to me to save my life.

"As such, I have her views on the whole thing, and I've offered freedom to all the wisps who were bound when I met them beyond her. They've chosen to stay as they are, but they also know that they can leave at any time. My plan for you is that you'll help the legionnaires to learn magic for several hours a day and the rest of the time is your own. Explore the cities, stay here if you want, but be ready to help. As the legionnaires meet you and understand what was done, expect them to try to protect you against *everything*.

"That's why they're legionnaires—their primary desire is to protect the weak and innocent, and there's fuck all I've met as deserving of protection as a wisp. For now, though, I need to understand this place better. This temple, the Cradle…I can feel that there's something wrong with the mana here."

"Wrong?" Erista's light flickered uncertainly. "It is abundant. It is why we survive."

"Well, yeah, but it's damn…uh…unbalanced?" I replied, glancing at Sehran, who had moved to stand beside me again, smiling. "It's killing everything outside this valley, draining the land like a parasite. That's not natural, and that's not how temples to Lagoush are supposed to work. I know that much."

The wisp's light dimmed slightly, a clear sign of discomfort. "There is a…place. Deep beneath the temple. It feels wrong, and we cannot enter."

That confirmed my suspicions. "Then that's where I need to go. Show me."

"I will guide you," Erista offered cautiously. "But please understand, I cannot enter. The mana there…it burns. It twists…those who enter never come back."

I turned to Vislen and the other legionnaires. "I want you to scout the temple. If you can, get the gnomes and whatever the hell they've done to the airship inside the temple somehow. Then no one in or out without my say-so. I'll deal with this, then…fuck's sake."

I hung my head, suddenly aware of just how scatterbrained I was right now.

I'd made a deal with them all that I'd smash Kronk to prove my power and that I could protect them, and then I'd also said that I'd make sure that the temple here was safe for them, that Xenefier and so on, none of them could enter and harm them.

I'd said it knowing that Oracle and I could alter the spell that we'd used in Narkolt to scour the citadel of rats—both the usual kind, and the kind that hid between the walls and listened or spied through keyholes.

Well, that was great and all, but I didn't have fucking Oracle to help me. And even if I did, I'd just agreed that I'd flatten Kronk before I did any of that!

I couldn't just wait a damn few more days while the others got here. I just couldn't. If I lay down to sleep without scouring the damn temple of that gloop, what was to stop it from sliding up between the flagstones by my ear when I was fast asleep and pouring into my brain?

Fuck all, that was what!

That meant… "Ah, fuck it." I shook my head. "Sehran, go to the wreck and get any manastones you can. In fact, search the temple as well and get any and all you can find. Do it now."

"Jax—" Sehran protested, not wanting to leave my side.

"No." I cut her off sharply. "I need you to do this, and while you do it, I'll sort this shit out. If something happens to me, you're the one who'll need to guide the others when they arrive. And when I've sorted it? You're the one who'll be with me for the next job."

What I didn't say was that I couldn't bear to risk her too. Not after Oracle. The bond between us was my only tether to sanity right now, and part of me was damn well terrified of what I'd do without her as well.

She nodded reluctantly, looking like she wanted to argue further but knowing better. The rage and pain I was barely controlling had to be clear as glass through the bond, after all.

"This way." Erista floated toward the far end of the temple, away from the pool where the mer had gathered.

I followed, and as I did, I looked at the unsubtle changes in the temple's structure since its restoration.

What had been a crumbling ruin was now a marvel of ancient architecture. Intricate carvings of water scenes decorated the walls: mer swimming beside dolphins, people bathing in healing springs, farmers standing beside irrigated fields. All of it was dedicated to Lagoush's domains: water, healing, and fucking calm.

Something I was desperately in need of, but yet was also in incredibly short supply of.

It was all made worse by my senses, honed by months of being bonded to Oracle, of personal growth and understanding. The mana here wasn't flowing naturally; it was being pulled, concentrated, forced into here. The more I paid attention to it, the more it made my skin crawl.

Erista led me to what looked like a solid wall at first glance. But as we approached, the tightness in the air of the mana, the subtle wrongness, grew.

I reached out, running my fingers over the wall, feeling the faint ridges of the hidden door that was blatantly here. The mana of the world was barely stopped by solid matter, after all; it sank through walls, floors, and more. But there was a slight resistance here, where mana was being compressed as it tried to flow through the wall and then beyond.

"Can you see anything?" I asked Erista, not really expecting an answer, and instead looking at the wall as I searched for a hidden trigger.

"The door?"

I paused, glaring at it, before speaking as calmly as I could.

"Of course the fucking door, Erista. I…" I paused, frowning. "Wait, why the hell do you have names? The other wisps I met didn't until they were given them?"

"We were named by those you ignored."

"What?"

"Those." The wisp shifted into a more or less spiky star shape, then grew one of the arms longer, pointing to the bald ape-like creatures.

"I didn't ignore them." I dismissed its comment. "I asked them to join us, the same as I asked you."

"But you had a plan for us, a need. You asked the mer to join you and serve, but for them, you just…told them to serve?"

"You mean I didn't have a specific plan for them?" I asked, distractedly, running my fingers over the wall.

"Exactly."

"I still don't," I admitted. "Fuck me, I don't even know what they are."

"They are those you ignored," the little fucker repeated. "Is that not enough? You see them, you spoke to them, and then you dismissed them. You have no interest in them, and yet you come here, an outsider, and you choose to change our lives. You decide that the mana that sustains us is wrong and that you must change it, but you've not asked for our opinions on it.

"Of all of us who survive here, they are perhaps the most physically punished by it, the most twisted and damaged. But did you ask them if they want you to change such a central point of their lives, or ours?"

"No," I growled, feeling suddenly shitty about it, but still struggling to make myself care enough to actually make the effort.

"Will you now then?"

I glared at it. "Why?" I snapped.

"Because you say you're different. Different from those who take without asking. Different from those who enslave and punish. But your actions…"

"Fuck me," I growled, before closing my eyes and resting my forehead against the wall. "Fuck's sake, fucking fuckity fuck, fuck, fuck!"

"Is this wrong?"

"What?" I glowered at the wisp.

"That you do not wish to speak to them? Have they offended you beyond attacking you when under compulsion?"

"Quit that." I forced myself to stand upright, then marched across to the small group of hairless ape-looking motherfuckers, seeing the way that they backed up, scared as I approached.

The legionnaires had broken off as ordered and with their partners were scouting the rest of the temple. Most of the others—the mer, the wisps, and the apes—had gone, but a small group stayed. I walked up to them, took a deep breath, and manned up.

"I'm sorry," I said to them. "I was rude. I'm exhausted, stressed, and worried for those I love, but I still should have been better. Is there one of you who speaks for the group?"

"I speak." One of them pushed forward, bracing himself on one knuckle, his arms longer than his legs, almost making them look four-legged rather than two, as he shifted and swayed from side to side uncertainly.

"Do you have a name?" I asked.

"Yesss."

"What is your name?" I asked through clenched teeth.

"Oto."

"Oto, I'm Jax…"

"Knows this, we do."

"I fucking know you know, all right?" I snapped. "I was trying to be polite!"

"This shout is polite?"

I glared at him, wondering whether he, like the wisp, was actually asking a question, or whether he was fucking testing me. I decided that no, he was asking a question, and responded as such.

"No, it isn't, but as I said, I'm tired and stressed."

"Shouting is wrong?"

"Depends on the situation," I muttered. "Sometimes it's warranted. Look, what are you?"

"The people."

"You're the people?" I cocked an eyebrow. "Okay, if you're the people, do you have a name for your people? And what do you call everyone else?"

"Not people."

"We're…the not people?" I tried.

"We people. You not people."

"Okay, all right, whatever. What do you want and what can you bring to the table?"

"What is table?"

"Do you as a people have skills?" I tried again.

"Yes."

"What skills?"

"We are the people."

"I…whoooo boy, okay, one more time," I muttered. "Look, I need to find out why the mana here is so messed up, and I'm going to stop it, slow it down to normal levels, okay? Is that a problem?"

"Mana same, not same." He shrugged, then stood on his bandy little legs and spread his massive arms to the sides as he gestured grandly. "Mana all go, all come. Change some."

"So… I'm going to stop it," I offered, then waited.

"All change!"

"Okay, good talk!" I forced a smile as he dropped back to bracing on his knuckles, then turned and walked away.

I marched back across the room to the strange section of wall, and all the way, my internal monologue was an ongoing litany of swear words and screaming abuse.

By the time I made it to the wall a second time, I was desperate for a little of the calm that Lagoush was famous for—though, right now, as much as the time in Tyosh's little meditation sanctuary could have massively helped as well, I was fifty-fifty whether I'd have rather had that or a fight with Darakin.

That was madness, actually—as distracted and angry as I was, Darakin would kick my fucking arse.

Though…it had taken the combined efforts of three of the gods to stop me before, and that…that wasn't a small thing.

Whatever had been different about that, beyond that I'd been incredibly furious and ready to burn the world down, I'd done something that should have been impossible.

I had a feeling it was partly to do with the dragonscale armoring. That blessing had kept me going at times when I should have been very, very dead, after all.

The other side, I was willing to bet, was because of the increase in my status—from a regular mortal to godhood, I mean—and that even though I'd not bound the fragment to myself yet, I was still getting some benefit from it.

From what I understood, the gods were limited in what they could do on "this side" of the divide between their realm and our own.

I wasn't a creature of that side—I was all this side, baby. And in the future, as my power was mainly going to be coming from the worship of the empire…I wasn't going to have the same side effects and diminishment of power that they had as well, I guessed.

Yeah, all right, every single flame was in a small way a prayer to Jenae, and so she gained a horrific amount of mana every second, in general terms, but her mana was also stolen away to help feed all flames, etc.

For me? I'd be gaining a small amount of mana and therefore power from every single imperial subject, every single day. That was always going to be less than every single flame, sure, but the imperial subjects were only going to be clawing back the mana that I was giving up by choice.

They didn't need this mana to live or they'd all die.

The only expectation on me with it was that I'd not go mad with power and that I'd protect my people.

That, I'd do all day long.

With bells on.

Also, I'd be able to spend a lot of every day when I was a god with, well, Oracle on, not just bells.

I'd have all that power coming in, and my responsibility would be to be the empire, nothing more. To do what I'd be doing with the power of the empire and my own personal power as well.

The difference was that my power would be hundreds if not thousands of times greater than I should have had as a ruler, and that for every single day that I ruled, I'd grow in strength.

This was how Amon had been able to smash island chains and so on.

He'd been a demigod without the limits that the other gods were constrained by, and I bet that he'd known some of it, too.

That was why and how he'd been what he was.

I paused as I reached the wall, my mind still racing over the details of his ascension and the potential that I had to surpass him. I thought for a few minutes about it, as Erista buzzed and flew around me.

If I could take the fragment from Kronk's ruler, then bind it to my soul along with the Fragment of Order? I'd jump significantly in power—and I mean "dick caught in the space shuttle's door on launch" power levels rising.

Then, with that? With that, I could challenge Baphomet. I could challenge all of them, knowing that they'd be limited by the challenge.

Yeah, all right, they'd be limited to an avatar of equal power to me, but my stats were only half the story, I had started to understand. Hell, maybe even less.

I frowned, still musing over that, until I noticed a slight redness on the wall. I squinted at it, and watched it. The glow grew brighter—a tiny difference in the wall, but one that once you noticed it, was almost impossible to ignore.

Squatting, I stared at it: a pair of faint lines, waves, that ran left to right in the general marking of the scene.

It was something to do with a lake, a general image, or so I'd thought. But looking at the carving, or fresco or whatever it was…the more I stared, the more I noticed.

These two little lines were out of place, which was why I'd spotted them, but overall? If I took the mental image of the temple out, and cut the jungles back from their inane overgrowth, that lake…

I pressed the symbol and felt a slight tugging in my finger, something that… *Mana.*

I pushed out life mana on instinct, just because there was so much around me at the moment that it was on my mind, but that did nothing. No, I needed water, I realized.

Pushing that out, feeling the mana flow, there was a momentary resistance, then a sense of recognition as the wards apparently accepted it. The door slid open silently, revealing a steep staircase that descended into darkness, thick slabs of stone on all sides boxing it in.

"Wait here," I ordered Erista. "If I'm not back in two hours, tell Vislen to secure the temple and wait for Tenandra."

The wisp bobbed in acknowledgment, though yeah, there was apparent reluctance and fear. "Be careful, Prince. The mana grows wilder below. I can go no farther."

"Figured as much." I nodded grimly and stepped through the doorway. The stairs were carved from the same stone as the temple, but they felt older somehow, alone and separate, untouched for millennia. As I stomped down the steps, the air grew heavier, charged with mana so dense I could almost taste it—metallic, thick, and wrong in so many ways.

As I went, I was struck with a sense of why it felt so weird.

Mana was ephemeral: unless you could use it, unless you did use it, it was just there. Like air. You only noticed it when there wasn't any, or when it was contaminated. Like a fart in an elevator.

Here, I could both "feel" the rush of mana pouring down the stairs and ahead of me, and at the same time, I only felt it through my senses that were attuned to mana.

I didn't feel the rush of air like I would have a breeze across my skin, or the pressure change in my ears like I could when I went high or low.

No, instead, I felt a feeling like an oil slick atop clean water.

The water was fine, it was pristine and beautiful even, but whatever was being done here was fouling the surface, making it impossible to touch the water without also touching the scummy mess that floated atop it.

The stairway eventually opened into a large circular chamber, lit by a flaring, pulsing light at its center.

The walls were lined with alcoves filled with strange crystalline formations that stunned me—massive manastones. The smallest were the size of my torso, and the largest? At least as tall as I was. They glowed with internal light, primarily blues and greens, the colors of water and life mana. They filled the alcoves, bulging out and angling inward, reaching toward whatever was in the center of the room.

A device there drew my attention. A metal, onyx, and stone creation, clearly imperial in design, rose from the floor to about waist height. It looked something like a lotus flower made of bronze and silver, its petals spread wide to reveal a swirling shallow bowl of life mana at its heart.

It was almost like the way that the wisp manawells condensed the mana that they were given to form their bodies, but here the mana that was being sucked in was being compressed, forced into a solid and then fed into other areas.

Tubes and channels ran from the device to the walls, ceiling, and floor, pumping mana throughout the temple and beyond. The drain on the natural order, the way that mana wasn't supposed to be formed into a solid, was then acting as a vacuum, and pulling more and more of the mana inward.

"Well, fuck me sideways," I muttered, approaching cautiously. "Someone built a mana collector."

Mana collectors weren't uncommon in imperial structures—towers, encampments…hell, even the prax all had them—but they were designed to gather ambient mana and distribute it evenly. This one had been modified, and heavily so.

Additional components had been grafted onto the original design, creating something that looked more like a parasite than a tool.

I slowly circled the device, examining its structure. The modifications were crude compared to the original elegant imperial column, but effective in their own way. They'd been designed to pull mana from a much wider area than intended, concentrating it here in the temple.

Just looking it over—and with the advantage of the new knowledge that I'd gained from the Constellation of Secrets—I could identify the mana conduits that ran here and there.

Looking at them, and seeing the patterns, I guessed they must extend out into the surrounding areas as well. The Plain of Bones beyond must have something in them, some kind of focus that pulled inward, and this…this was where it all collected.

Why, though? I mean, Lagoush and the others pointed out that this was a place that was overfilled with life mana before all of this, so what the hell had done this?

"Who the fuck thought this was a good idea?" I wondered aloud.

As if in response to my voice, the orb at the center pulsed brighter; my skin tingled at the corresponding wave of mana. My own mana responded, rising to meet it. I felt a sudden connection to the device—not through any deliberate action of mine, but through my imperial bloodline.

The collector was active, and had been forever, but as imbued with life as it was, it felt almost aware as well.

I could sense the wrongness clearly now. The collector had been modified to pull mana from miles around, concentrating it here. The effects were twofold: the area immediately surrounding the temple was supercharged with mana, augmenting the lush paradise of the Cradle, while everything beyond was drained to the point of death, becoming the Plain of Bones.

This wasn't what it'd been like in the past, I knew at an almost instinctual level as I looked around.

No. It was wildly unbalanced and getting worse. The device was pulling in more mana than it could properly distribute, storing the excess in the manastones lining the walls, and forcing them into desperate growth. Some were so saturated they developed cracks, threatening to release their energy all at once in a cataclysmic failure.

"Okay, so this isn't fucking good," I muttered to myself, moving closer to examine the central mechanism. "It looks like it's gonna blow at this rate."

I stared at it, then saw something concealed by the column. I stepped to the side and stared down, before cursing.

It was a body—or, more accurately, three bodies.

One was dressed in rough homespun clothing that had rotted slowly. The robes and nearby broken staff—it looked like it'd detonated at some point—made me mentally mark that one as "hedge wizard" or druid or some such.

The other two bodies wore silks, though clearly stained and travel-worn even before the owners were hit by whatever had killed them, and then they'd bled out in here.

I looked from the shattered staff to the bodies, and back again.

Was it that simple?

The device on the collector was unusual, but it wasn't anything that was incredible. If the wizard had done something in here and his staff had exploded, was it as simple as the survivors—injured and trapped down here—had been messing with the collector, probably trying to heal themselves?

I mean, I could understand the collector being here; the more I looked at it, the more I did. Natural excess of mana? Why leave that to go to waste, after all? Instead, set up a collector and grow some stones, then hand them over to the empire in tithe and everyone wins.

Maybe they sold them; maybe they just liked the shiny rocks. Regardless, my plan that Sehran find some manastones to get us to Kronk just kinda stopped mattering as much.

After all, why the hell waste the handful of tiny ones that we had, when I could stop the collector here, or at least deal with it, and then take some of these?

I stood before the collector, considering my options. I could try to restore it to its original state, but that would take time and knowledge I didn't have. I could destroy it, but that might trigger the very catastrophe I was trying to prevent. And that would also leave me a collector down, when this one was perfectly usable. Even if it was a bit weird, it was still pulling in mana, right?

Or I could modify it further, redirecting its flow and harvesting some of the stones.

I placed both hands on the device, channeling my own mana into it, along with sharing who I was.

Something about the stone responded to me; it'd recognized me and my imperial authority, I felt. I didn't know how—it was a bit like the way that some dogs automatically liked some people…no clue why, they just did. Take that mentality away—the upper levels of it at least, and the limited awareness—and you had what this felt like: a drowsing puppy, barely aware of the world around it, but trusting, and…and thankful.

Fuck me, more than the mer, the people—whatever the hell they were—and the wisps…this rock, the bloody least likely to be aware of them all, was the one most thankful for me being there.

I pushed further, feeling for its controls.

It didn't have a control mechanism, not really, not in the way that I was used to finding for the towers and the various imperial sites I'd claimed. But it did have…something.

I could feel paths, places where the commands were expected, and should flow.

Normally, Oracle would have been here doing this, and she'd have been great at it. Hell, I could probably have Erista help and…

And it and the others couldn't come down here, could they?

I suddenly remembered that. And more so, I realized that the sense of "wrongness"—the itching, creeping feeling that everything was off, that it was dangerous and that, weirdly, it was almost like I was gaining or losing genes in uncontrolled mutations—it'd all stopped.

I felt a warmth.

A sense of relief, of welcome and…and a sense that everything was going to be okay.

It took a second to click. Then I shook my head in disbelief, remembering that old "never attribute to malice, what can be explained by stupidity" quote.

The stone was aware, sort of.

It was a collector, and it'd spent hundreds of years being guided to drag all the life mana it could down here and through itself. It'd probably had the last seconds of the two wounded people in here—judging from the way they'd died in each other's arms—where they'd been desperately begging for healing, for *life*.

The stone had been created for a purpose: to pull life mana down here and share it. So, when they'd done that, they'd given it a powerful need to draw in all the life it could. And I mean *all* the life mana.

In doing so, when the stones couldn't keep up with the powerful desperate out-gassings of a system under strain, it'd then radiated it out, along with a warning that something was wrong.

It'd been trying to let out the mana it'd been ordered to draw in, and it'd been wanting help all this time, while releasing insane amounts of life mana that corrupted and mutated all those that lived nearby.

With that in mind, and no longer looking for some kind of hard control method, I instead searched for something else. A sort of "ghost in the machine": a need, a drive to consume, to pull the life in. It didn't take long to find it.

When I did, it was like…I don't know how I'd describe it. Actually, it was like a memory, triggered by a scent, when it suddenly rushed back to you, clear as crystal. I felt the horror, the pain and the sadness, the knowledge that the one who touched the strange tower was dying, and that everyone else already was.

There were monsters outside, and the old priest had brought them down here, to hide. There'd been a bang; the priest had collapsed and without his authority to open the doors, they were trapped down there.

A young girl and her father—though, by the clothes, I'd guessed mother, they were so lacy—had been hammered by the fragments of the staff.

The priest was dead instantly. Her father had died moments after, having barely managed to pull himself upright, holding her, and then had succumbed.

She'd lasted a little longer, but for most of it, thankfully, had been unconscious. As the last moments of their lives had passed, they'd both been thinking of life, of health and being together, and something in their thoughts had imprinted on the nascent awareness of the stone.

Now I reached along faint threads inside the stone, smoothing away the panic and the fear, as the memory faded, the scent gone. I could feel the flow of mana through the device, see how it had been diverted from the steady accumulation of excess mana, and instead forced into a desperate, panicked concentration.

Working carefully, I adjusted the flow, redirecting it to just collect what wasn't needed, to stop pulling from outside, to stop pulling at all, and instead to just absorb. But first?

I pulled on the stones.

It was delicate work, probably requiring precise control with an absolute buttload of things that should and could have gone wrong. Sweat beaded on my forehead as I manipulated the ancient rock without any kind of guidance.

Hours seemed to pass, though in reality it was probably only minutes.

Finally, I felt the shift as the collector settled into a new flow. The pull from outside the Cradle was reduced, dropped down to "normal" levels, like the ones I'd felt from the tower when it worked, but with one noticeable difference.

Instead, until it was changed, the excess life mana that had been fed into the manastones around me was being fed back along the conduits and into the dead land beyond.

The crystal's glow dimmed slightly as the dangerous pressure shifted. Although it was never going to be instantaneous, just that the mana wasn't being forced into them—second by second, hour by hour—clearly helped.

I moved methodically around the chamber. Some of the stones, most even, were fine, but some were so close to rupturing that I had to drain them almost completely, absorbing the energy myself. As soon as the "shit, it's gonna blow" feeling lessened, I broke more off the mass and slid them into my bag.

For each stone that I drained, I had a 'simple' solution to deal with it. Namely, I jogged up the stairs, put my hands on the altar, and pushed almost all my mana into it over the space of about a minute. Then I ran back down, drained more of another stone and then ran back up, refilling myself, then draining, over and over, until the stones calmed.

It took hours—again—but by the time I finished with the last stone, my body ached from the passage of excess mana and my armor gleamed. But the gods were getting the "good stuff" and it wasn't being wasted, which was a hell of an improvement.

I gathered a few dozen more of the remaining stable manastones—my bags had at least a hundred in there now—and made my way back up the stairs. My mind was clearer than it had been since I'd left the meditation nexus with Tyosh, and in myself, I felt better than I had since Oracle was taken.

I didn't feel good, not at all, but achieving something, no matter how small, was a start. And, more importantly, the manastones I'd recovered that were in the bag were more than enough to get me to Kronk.

They were enough that once I was there, I wasn't going to be worrying about mana at all in fact, and that opened the door to a fucking ass-whooping that nobody there was going to forget.

The stones I'd taken separately were literally a gift for the gods, to be fed into the altar and to boost them as well, in thanks for their help and understanding.

When I left the tunnel again, Erista was waiting where I'd left her. Her light flickered anxiously. She'd tried to talk to me several times already as I rushed past, and I'd been having none of it, too focused on my task.

"You survived." She almost sounded surprised.

"Found the problem." I held up one of the smaller manastones. "Someone modified a mana collector centuries ago. It's been pulling mana from miles around, feeding it into the Cradle and storing the excess in these."

The wisp drifted closer, examining the stone. "Oooh, pretty!" She sighed, staring at the stones with a hunger I could feel.

"They've been collecting and concentrating mana for, well, probably since the cataclysm. Centuries, at least," I explained. "I've stabilized them and adjusted the collector to reverse the drain on the surrounding land. It should help the Plain of Bones recover eventually."

"And these stones?" Erista asked. "Can I have them?"

"Most will go to the gnomes, to power their airship repairs. Some I'm keeping for myself." I shook my head. "If you have a need for them, then explain why and I'll consider it, but otherwise, no. I'll need the power they contain to deal with Kronk."

We emerged back into the main temple, where Vislen waited with Sehran. Beyond them, I could see the hairless apes—a different group of them from the ones who had been there earlier, guessing from the marking on their bodies—and other wisps watching cautiously.

"Vislen, anything to report?" I asked the legionnaire as I marched past him, both of them hurrying to join me.

Sehran and Vislen quickly moved to help me with my arms full of the stones.

"Temple secured, sir," he replied promptly. "No sign of any further infected or hostile forces. The gnomes are okay, and they're on about the fifteenth rebuild. The ship now looks more like a horse mounting the balloon, but they say they're ready to begin the major repairs as soon as they have materials."

"Good." I nodded. "Change of plan with that. Instead of collecting the manastones from them, I've now got part of what they need right here." I gestured to the altar and then down at the manastones. "These are for the gods, and there's more in my bag for the gnomes. They should provide enough power for what we need."

"So, the stones that I ran around searching for and collecting…" Sehran sighed.

"Totally not needed," I admitted. "Sorry, Sehran. They need to go back to the gnomes."

"You have no idea what those crazy little bastards offered me if I'd forget some of the stones and leave them with them," she pointed out to me, shooting over a black look.

"Then tell them you changed your mind and you'll take the payment," I suggested. "Everyone wins."

"I don't." She snorted. "Remember, Giint is a freak of gnomish nature. He's bigger than almost all the gnomes I've ever seen, and I mean in all ways."

"I've seen Giint naked, as much as I'd love mind bleach to get that image out forever. If he wasn't bigger than most of his race, I'd have been frankly terrified. The little bastard has an inbuilt stabilizer!" I grunted.

"Exactly. But if it's any consolation, it's the short legs that make him look so blessed."

"I don't believe we're having this conversation, and I don't want to have it anymore," I said firmly. "Tell the gnomes whatever you want. In fact…"

I handed several of the stones to Vislen. "Get these to the gnomes. Tell them to focus on getting the ship airworthy enough to get us back to Gaij. Nothing fancy, just enough to get you all there."

"Just us, sir?" Vislen frowned.

"Sehran and I are going to take a detour," I clarified. "I can't wait for Tenandra and the others. Kronk has something I need, and frankly, I'm out of fucking patience and I need to blow off some steam."

"With respect, sir," Vislen began carefully, "would it not be better to wait for reinforcements? You said your ship will arrive in just a few days, with your full squad aboard."

I knew he was right, but I couldn't shake the burning need to start. To do something. Every day Oracle was in Xenefier's grip was another day that she could be killed, that the baby could be taken forever. Every minute spent waiting was another minute of failure.

"We don't have a few days," I snapped, my voice harder than I intended. "The longer we wait, the more time Xenefier has with Oracle. The more time Baphomet has to recover. No. I need to start moving now."

Sehran reached out, putting her hand on my arm. "Jax, please. Vislen's right. We should wait for the others. For Lydia, my Jian and the rest of the squad. For Bane."

For a moment, I was tempted to lash out, to remind them that they weren't the ones who'd lost everything. That they couldn't possibly understand the urgency driving me. But I caught myself, taking a deep breath.

"I understand the worry." I made an effort to sound reasonable. "But this isn't just about Oracle. The people of the Cradle need proof that I can protect them. I can't secure this place until I've had them swear, and they won't swear, thanks to that stupid damn phrasing of mine, until Kronk isn't a threat anymore. Plus, it needs to be fucking stomped into the ground regardless. If I wait, more innocents will suffer."

I looked around at the gathered wisps, the ape things, and the few mer who had returned and were watching me. "I promised you all I'd show you what the empire can do. That means acting now."

Before anyone could argue further, a familiar divine presence filled the temple. The air shimmered with gold and crimson light as Jenae manifested, not in Her full divine glory, but enough to make Her presence unmistakable.

"My champion." Her voice resonated through the hall. *"You have done well to uncover and stabilize the collector."*

I bowed slightly, acknowledging Her presence. "Jenae, thank you," I said. "I'm going to prepare for the assault on Kronk now."

"So I hear," She replied. *"Jax, your eagerness to act is understandable, but perhaps unwise. Brakuus of Kronk possesses a Fragment of Chaos. He is dangerous, especially to one in your…emotional state."*

My jaw tightened. "I can handle him."

"Can you?" She challenged gently. *"Your rage burns bright, Jax. It gives you strength, but also blinds you. The Fragment of Chaos will have granted him significant power, much as the Fragment of Death has you. The difference is that you were human—more or less—when you began. He was a deep dwarf. He already had bones and flesh far stronger than any normal surface dweller. The Fragment of Chaos will have increased that significantly."*

"What would you have me do?" I demanded, struggling to keep my tone calm. "Wait? Hide? While Oracle suffers?"

"We would have you prepare properly," came another voice. Sint materialized beside Jenae, His form stern and unyielding. *"The fight yet to come will be significant, possibly one of the hardest you have yet faced. As such, rushing into it without rest, without time to plan or to prepare, is folly. Tell me, Jax, when were you planning on leaving to face Brakuus?"*

"Now," I admitted. "Well, as soon as I'd gotten whatever here needs done, sorted out."

"Exactly." He nodded. *"I understand your concern and your desire. All of us do, Jax, and we applaud your drive. But please, rest first; sleep and let your body recover. It might not feel like it, but you are still limited by physical flesh, and it has weaknesses."*

"I…" I started, ready to tell Him to go suck a barrel of dicks, when a third form blurred into ghostly appearance.

"Jax, brother. Would you take a dull weapon to war?" Darakin asked. *"Armor that had not been fitted properly?"*

"No," I admitted with a growl.

"Then why would you expect to take companions and a body that is exhausted into the fight?"

I hesitated, deliberately not looking at Sehran, even as I felt her through the bond—the pain she was in, the tiredness, the absolute bone-deep exhaustion…and that was for a demon.

For a human? If I was mortal, my body would be broken, I suddenly realized. And the legionnaires?

Glancing at them, I saw what I'd not allowed myself to see before, what I'd missed, because it didn't fit with my needs.

They were all broken…maybe not in terms of healing and injuries, as they'd all received that already, but definitely in terms of their mental and spiritual sides.

I'd barely given the legionnaires time to learn magic, something that they'd never had access to before, and then I'd had them drain their pools over and over again in fight after fight.

They'd lost friends, people they'd known days and people they might have known years…decades, even.

I'd put them in a position where they'd seen their principal, the one person above all that they HAD to protect, be taken away. Sure, they might think that was me, and on paper, on an org chart or whatever, it *should* be me, but I fucked gods up.

I faced down armies and I called the God of Death out on His shit and had His skull back home as a goblet.

Oracle, though, and the next prince or princess? They needed that protection, and these legionnaires had seen them taken.

They were full of failure, even though it wasn't their fault. Panic, exhaustion…they were basically hopped up on adrenaline and gung-ho "can-do" attitude.

That was great for a while, but the one thing that couldn't do, not for long, was keep them alive.

Oh, it could keep them fighting, forging forward, but sooner or later they'd make a mistake, one that they wouldn't do normally, and that would be it.

Most of all, I saw what they were saying, because as I let myself relax slightly, searching, I felt it as well.

I wasn't that far behind them.

Even gods rested.

I wanted to argue, to tell them to go fuck themselves and their caution. But the small part of me that wasn't consumed by rage recognized the wisdom in their words. I'd faced Illoth with discipline and strategy. Going after Brakuus in a blind rage might get me killed—and that wouldn't help Oracle.

"How?" I asked finally. "How do I prepare?"

Sint approached. His divine presence made the air around Him shimmer. ***"You let those who support you do their job.***

"There are others with you who can help. And here, in this place, where we are strongest, although we cannot take a direct hand, we may observe, and one of us will at all times. Rest today and tonight, Jax. In the morning, then you take action. Until then, meditate and prepare."

With that, the gods faded away, and I stared into the empty air after them for long seconds, before stifling a curse as a sudden whisper invaded my mind.

"When you meditate, use the stones…"

It was Jenae, I knew, but the sense of Her presence was gone in a second, leaving me stupefied. *The stones?*

What the hell was I going to do with the stones? I stared for a few more seconds then shrugged it off. I'd figure it out.

"Vislen, go to the gnomes. Tell them that they have to rest, and then bring them back here. Bring everyone in here. Six hours of rest is an order, as a minimum. Twelve, if you can. I know how fucking insane gnomes are, but still. Take the stones, show them one and tell them they'll get the rest after they've taken some rest."

Vislen saluted and departed with the manastones, while Sehran lingered, worry flowing through the bond as she reached out and hugged me.

"Jax," she said softly, "I know you feel you have to do this alone, but remember, you're not. We're all with you. Oracle is with you, in spirit if not in body."

I swallowed hard against the sudden tightness in my throat. "I know," I managed. "But I have to be strong enough to save her. To save our child. And to do that, I need power."

Sehran nodded, understanding in her eyes. "The fragments," she agreed, understanding and knowing what we'd discussed before.

"That, and more," I replied, thinking of the manastones I'd kept for myself. "We'll need every advantage we can get, but we'll fucking well do it."

She hugged me again. "Just don't lose yourself in the process. Oracle would never forgive me if I let that happen."

"I won't. I promise."

Sehran left me then. I didn't know where she was going, probably just giving me a little space to myself, to be honest. I found a quiet corner of the temple and sat cross-legged on the cool stone floor.

I took out a handful of the manastones I'd kept and arranged them in a circle around me. Their gentle glow shone through as I closed my eyes, focusing on my breathing and trying to find that balance Tyosh had shown me. The eye of my storm. The still point between rage and control, where there was nothing. I reached deep for the same place that I went when I fought Darakin, and slid into it.

The void.

It wasn't easy. Every time I started to find calm, images of Oracle in Xenefier's clutches would flash in my mind, sending fresh waves of fury through me.

But gradually, I managed to separate the emotion from the purpose. To hold my rage as a tool rather than being consumed by it.

As I meditated, I slowly started to sense the manastones responding to my presence. Their mana resonated with mine; a pulsing worked through me—a heartbeat that was inside and out—and I slowly immersed myself deeper and deeper.

Hours passed like that, the outside world fading as I worked. When I finally opened my eyes, the temple was bathed in the golden light of sunset, and the manastones around me glowed with a new intensity, pulses of light synchronizing with my heartbeat.

I gathered them up, feeling their weight—both physical and magical—as I stored them in my bag of holding, smiling to myself. I didn't know what the difference was, why they now felt so attuned to me or how that was going to help, but they did. And if I could pull from regular manastones just fine, I wondered what the difference would be with these.

Regardless, tomorrow, I would use their power to reach Kronk, to fight that piece of shit Brakuus, and claim his Fragment of Chaos, and to take one more step toward saving Oracle.

One step closer to becoming what I needed to be to destroy Xenefier once and for all.

When the sun set, knowing that the gods were literally watching over us and that the wisps, the ape things, and the mer were too, we slept. Despite everything, despite my sure knowledge that I was fine and I didn't need the sleep…

I slept like the dead.

CHAPTER SIX

"Well," I said sardonically to Sehran as the pair of us sat atop the small rise, staring down at the city of Kronk in the distance. "It's a real shithole, eh?"

"Absolutely," she growled.

We'd arrived a little under two hours ago. With the airship still needing a ton of repairs, what we'd ended up doing was—as I'd expected—leaving the others behind and flying ahead.

The flight hadn't been easy. It'd been a long time in the air in fact, for both of us, and because of the sheer distance involved, I'd sustained myself with dozens of manastones.

What had made it worse was that I could push harder and therefore go faster, using more mana, but Sehran was limited by the biological efforts and limits of her wings. I'd been forced to let her sit on my back and ride me.

The comments as we hurtled through the air with her whooping had been ridiculous. Fortunately, she'd limited herself, knowing that now really wasn't the time for the usual stuff she'd say; she'd instead treated me like a horse, rather than a sex toy.

Which I'd usually have low-key regretted, but given everything of late, I was instead thankful for.

We'd gotten here, and given that it was a little after midnight and the stars were hidden behind low scudding clouds, we'd made the decision that Sehran would scout the place out for us.

When I say "we," I mean that she'd badgered me incessantly on the way in, until I finally gave up and agreed, on the grounds that although normally I'd not want a woman on her own walking through the streets of a crime-ridden shithole of a city after dark—or any other time, for that matter—she *was* a demon, after all.

As much as she was hot as hell to look at, and generally a wonderful person who, if push came to shove, I loved and viewed as my little sister by now; she was also a psychotic murderous demon when the mood took her...so, you know, anyone who attacked her in the darkness, thinking she was a defenseless young woman, deserved anything they got.

What I'd not expected was that she'd have to stop feeding on those who tried to attack her, because she was too full.

Literally, she'd flown close enough under the cover of darkness to find that there were all of seven people she could spot "guarding" the walls. Avoiding them was easy, so she'd simply flown into the city and landed in an alleyway.

Then she'd been attacked as she walked to exit the alley, by a beggar she'd stopped to ask a question of. Then someone had seen her standing over the body, and had attacked her.

That one had been reasonably clean enough that she was willing to feed on him. And then, a few minutes later, as she walked down the street, two of the local "guards" had asked her business there. Then they'd dragged her into an alley to "discuss things."

Needless to say, the full-fledged demon form that she shifted into to deal with the scumbags wasn't what they'd expected.

The worst part was that the entire goddamn city was like that, as near as she could tell. Seventeen times she'd been attacked before she'd stopped walking around with her demonic features disguised, and had gone as a full succubus in public.

Six more attacks as she crossed the next four streets and, in the end, she just took off and flew out of the city.

"Honestly, I've never seen the like," she growled, glaring at the city. "The only children I could see any sign of in the entire city were the ones in chains, and I looked! I was going to try to get you to be careful, to show some mercy, and that a city that size has to have innocents in it…"

"And?" I prompted after she'd paused.

"And I think we need to free the slaves, then burn the city from one end to the other!" she declared. "No mercy, no chances. The things those people were doing…"

"Bad?"

"I've seen hell, and this is worse." She shook her head. "I mean it. I know dukes of hell who would tear through this city in abject fury over the vileness I saw. An hour I was there, and I saw that there was no way, no way at all, that anyone who wasn't at least as much of a murderous bastard as these people could ever walk those streets. Anyone who was an innocent would be dead, or enslaved and probably wishing they were dead."

She shook her head again, staring across the empty mile or so toward the city, then spat on the ground and shook her wings out. "I mean it, Jax. That place needs to be burned from one end to the other—the entire place. There's nothing there worth saving. Nothing I could find."

"Then that's convenient, because personally, I need to work off a little fucking steam," I growled, rolling my shoulders.

"One thing…"

"Yeah?"

"Well, two actually," she admitted. "First, I know Oracle is always complaining about you leaving your notifications until the last minute. Are they all dealt with?"

"Yeah." They were. I'd spent a lot of the hour reading over the bastards, and the way they were, well, I'd gotten angry all over again.

Congratulations!

You have been given a Quest by the Goddess Jenae: Bring balance to the Realm!

The Goddess Jenae has granted you a quest! The wisps, long believed to be the most innocent of all creatures in the UnderVerse, are on the edge of

extinction, driven into hiding, captured, tortured, and driven insane by the demands placed upon them. There are now less than a thousand wisps known to exist.

You have secured the Cradle of Feshcan'un, but although you have laid claim to it, you have yet to root out the watching evil that still lingers. Only once its borders are secure will you be able to complete this quest.

Discover, recruit, and protect a viable breeding population to assist Oracle in the birth of your child, and welcome a new species to the realm.

Discover, recover, and protect wisps: 57/50

Secure their home: 0/1

Reward: A chance at an easier birth for Oracle, Balance being restored, Unknown, Unknown, 5,000,000xp

So there was that: as soon as I could secure the Cradle, then I'd get five million experience, which I damn well wanted. Until then, though, that was pretty much the order of the day.

Congratulations!

You have been given a Quest by the Goddess Jenae: Protect Gaij!

The Goddess Jenae has granted you a quest! The city of Kronk has ever been a thorn in the side of the true and honest people of Gaij, and everyone else as well! The army of Kronk marched on your territory, as they've done many, many times in the past to all that they could reach.

This time the army was destroyed, leaving you with an opportunity! Conquer or destroy (preferably destroy) the city and eliminate the threat it poses.

Defeat the invading army: 1/1

Remove the threat posed by Kronk: 0/1

Reward: Secure borders, Safer trade routes, 5,000,000xp, loot, and a more experienced and stronger workforce! (Possible additional rewards based on performance.)

So that was nice, as clearly even the gods wanted that shithole cleansed, and so was the last quest to be updated.

You have received a Divine repeatable Quest: My God is Better than your God (6)

The dark power of Kronk grows like a tumor. No longer satisfied with raiding the caravan routes or smaller villages and settlements that surround it, the city of Kronk turned its gaze westward, to Gaij.

That proved to be a costly mistake, as the army met its end on the verdant plains of your territory, leaving the city partly unprotected, as hundreds of the enemy flee, broken, for any cover.

You have destroyed the army of Kronk; now deal with its homeland to secure a second territory on Carrmor!

<u>**Bonus:**</u> Claim the Cradle of Feshcan'un: 1/1

- **Kill the leader of the army of Kronk**: 1/1

- **Kill enemy officers**: 47/50

- **Capture the city of Kronk**: 0/1

- **Throw down the altars of the Dark Pantheon: 0/50**

Bonuses will be given for exceeding these numbers.

Reward: Territorial Claim increased, 40,000+ Citizens, Access to City treasuries and capabilities, 6,000,000xp

All told, that was sixteen million experience, which wasn't a small amount by anyone's standards. Admittedly, yeah, all right, I was conquering cities and ruling over territories, so the experience *should* be significant, but still.

It would have been enough for a nice couple of levels when I was lower down the totem pole. But now? I'd get one. Maybe, if I was very lucky, two—and that'd depend on how many of Kronk's citizenry I slaughtered. But that was fine.

I'd read over my other notifications as well, finding a few that had slipped through the net at some point, showing that my staffs skill had reached level twenty-nine—one more, and I should get a fresh specialization—and my heavy armor skill was at forty-seven.

I'd not even noticed that going up, but considering I literally lived in my armor these days, that was understandable.

I wanted to ask Restun about it, to understand whether my armor skills were reaching "acceptable" for a legionnaire yet, or whether I was still as he often made me feel: that I was only being allowed to play with the legionnaires because I was the boss.

I had a sneaking suspicion, though, that when the time came for us to have our next catch-up and training session, he was going to be a little surprised.

Mind you, I also planned to have ascended to godhood by then, or to be close enough that I could see the horizon on a good day, so I had to hope that would impress him.

I really didn't know what would, though, because even after seeing me ripping the God of Death a new asshole, he'd been all "meh," after all.

The fucker.

Regardless, I'd sorted my notifications, though the kill one was…difficult to read.

I'd closed it after reading the first line, and refused to read more.

That I'd killed wisps—infected, sure, but still wisps—had made me feel physically sick.

That they and the other defenders of the Cradle had almost all been alive and had been internally screaming for help as I did it only made it worse.

As such, having spent nearly an hour dealing with that trauma, and feeling the disgust from Sehran—even if at a mile plus, it'd been too far to speak clearly— it'd been exactly what I needed to get ready for this.

As I stood, Sehran joined me, and I absently asked the question as I stared at the rusting, distant iron walls.

"What was the second thing?"

"What?"

"The second thing—you asked if I'd done my notifications, and said that there were two things to check."

"Uhhh…oh! How do we get the slaves out?" She vaguely gestured toward the city, as it huddled, grim and leaking foul smoke, in the distance.

"What?"

"The slaves. You're going to free them all, right?"

"Of course." I waved that aside.

"In that case, I know that you do something that surrounds them with a shield and heals them, but in this city, we're going to need to do more than that."

"Go on…"

"In this city, as soon as the shield breaks and those people are free, anyone nearby is going to try to kill or recapture them. The people who aren't going to be affected by the control keys being destroyed aren't because they're innocent—it's because they can't afford a slave. That doesn't mean they won't attack an easy, and probably weak, target as soon as they see them, so what do we do?"

"Shit!"

"You didn't think about that?" she asked, clearly a little disappointed.

"I didn't," I admitted. "Fucksticks. I thought, I don't know, I figured we'd free them and whoever was nearby would run for it as they usually do when the slaves are free. We've always had…" I broke off and groaned.

"We've always had the legion or our other allies nearby to help and to create a safe zone," she agreed. "We don't have that here, though."

"I… Dammit!" I snarled, not wanting to send back to Gaij for our forces, and not really knowing what to do beyond that.

"Would you be against a suggestion?" she asked me carefully.

"I'd not be against fucking astrology right now," I grumbled. "What are you thinking?"

"Well, we've got two options, if we don't include run away and deal with it all another day," she pointed out. "First is that we could do a deal with some more from my home realm, but I think that might be a mistake, as the slaves, when they've just been freed, might accept me as your property—I know, I know, you don't think of me that way, but it's a reality, and it's one that I embrace wholeheartedly! Get Oracle back and forget those stuffy ways and we can all have a lot of fun after the baby is born."

She grinned then blanched as she saw that her joke hadn't hit home; instead, it'd been a sucker punch. She moved on, quickly.

"Or, the other option is that we start in the arena."

"The arena?" I gestured for her to go on, to get us past that awkward point. "Okay, tell me about that."

"There's an arena in the city. I saw it on boards and heard conversations about it. I'd intended to go and visit it on my scout, but never made it that far. I bet in a city full of people who act the way they have, they're not going to have an arena that uses volunteers only."

"And the people who are usually the top target for anyone who has an arena are legionnaires." I nodded. "Okay, that works. An arena is going to be a fairly solid structure as well, probably easily defensible too," I muttered, thinking of the ones I'd seen so far.

"We take the arena. It's late, so they're likely to be shutting down for the night. We break in, slaughter the guards, free the slaves and have them swear, then move slowly and methodically until the shit hits the fan. Once it all goes up, then you and the legion go freeing the slaves and we'll choose the nearest gate and you lead them out of it.

"I free everyone with an ability and do the whole fuck this city routine, tear the walls down, smash the top fighters to paste, and draw out their leader.

"Bish-bash-boom, I feed him his own face, claim the fragment, and then bind it. At that point, you're going to need to be out of the city…" I paused. "Or are you?"

"What are you thinking?"

"Well, when I bound the Fragment of Death, it removed all the death mana in the area. It literally reversed death for some. Add in that, as the gods said, a city in the middle of being razed is going to be the perfect place to bind a Fragment of Chaos…you know, that or any fucking airport…but when I bind it?

"What'll happen as all the chaos is absorbed and sucked out is that the order in the city, the literal mana of order, the discipline that the legion is built upon like a bedrock will rise, and…crap."

"The disorganized enemy will suddenly be able to organize very well." She nodded. "That's not going to help."

"No, it's not," I agreed, scratching my chin in thought. My beard, which was growing in well now, itched like mad. "Fuck, I mean, they wanted me to bind the Fragment of Order right after, but it's gonna be like seconds after, isn't it?"

"It must be," Tamat whispered, stepping out from behind the tiny damn tree on the hill and almost giving me a heart attack. *"And for you to do that, you must have the fragment now. That in turn means opening ourselves to both temptation and the risk of an attack, and doing it here, far from any aid."*

"Fuck's sake!" I snarled, before wiping the fury from my face and forcing myself to bow, acknowledging the fucker. "Sorry, Goddess, that was just a bit of a surprise, all right?"

"I know. That's why I did it." She smirked. *"Jax, we need to be quick about this. The less time anyone else has to react, the better for us all. Are you ready?"*

"I am." I took a deep breath and blew it out. "What do I do?"

"Simply take the fragment out and offer it to me," She purred into my ear. The sudden physical form of the goddess—clad as always in fucking tight leather and covered in knives—slipped from beside the tree and around me almost as fast as I could turn my head to look. ***"Reach out and offer it up, and I shall take it…"***

"I bet you will." I snorted. "And the Fragment of Order?"

"Once the Fragment of Darkness is safe, I'll split it off and—"

"Not going to happen," I said firmly. "We do it together, or I'm not giving it up."

"You're irritating me, boy," She hissed.

I heard as much as felt the tip of a dagger suddenly being pressed to my armor and drawn across the back of the cuirass.

The squeal and slight dragging, snagging feeling let me know She was literally carving a line in the metal, and the fucking gloss. I spun, coming face-to-face with Her glare.

"You think I like this?" I bit out. "I can bind that fragment right now—it's dark enough that I'll still gain from it. That Fragment of Order you're offering me is worthless until *after* I've bound the one of Chaos!

"I'm walking into a fight, weaker than I should be, to help you out, Tamat, and we both know the temptation that you're feeling right now. That's only gonna get worse. So tell me, which of us is more likely to be trustworthy here? The goddess who needs the fragment, or the guy who's held onto it for weeks, uncaring because I didn't need it yet?

"Who's going to try to stiff the other here? Knowing that if I do it, I fuck my allies over *and* I'll lose my chance at freeing the one I love?"

"You dare insinuate—"

"I fucking dare!" I roared, stepping closer. "Yeah, I damn well do! You know I shouldn't trust you. I can damn well see it in your eyes! That hunger, that *need*! Well, I need it as well. I need it to free her, so give me the fragment, Tamat, and by my word, I'll give you the one we agreed upon, or both it and your own back in compensation!"

I injected mana into my words, making an oath that shimmered in the air, the feeling of magic all that kept the goddess from shanking me as we stared at each other.

"Bargain struck, boy…" She stared into my eyes, a hint of madness clearly there, as well as the hunger that I knew was driving Her. ***"But if you try to fuck with me, know I'll gut you and make a pouch of your flesh!"*** She tapped the pouches that I saw dotted here and there about her body.

As I looked properly at them, yeah…that didn't look like normal leather.

Fucking psycho.

I had a momentary flashback to the lunatic I'd yeeted off the top of the tower back home…Toka? Yeah, that was its name. A person so fucked up, so tortured and enslaved, that they'd become a torturer and had gotten off on the pain they'd caused.

They'd been wearing outfits of human leather as well, and I'd gone all "Street Fighter" and Hadouken'd them off the tower.

Good times.

I blinked; the sudden flare of memory had distracted me for a second. When I looked back, it was to see Tamat staring at me, as She unzipped the front of Her leather outfit to the waist, slipping a hand inside and gasping in pain.

I wondered what the hell She was doing, when things resolved for me.

The darkness beneath the leather wasn't Her flesh; I could see that higher at the neck and a touch lower at the stomach, exposed. Instead of the pale skin that She revealed there, I saw a terrifying void, a hole into darkness, one that was filled with…

My mind shuddered away from the things I'd seen in a half-second's glimpse: teeth, eyes red and glowing, flashing blood and silvery blades, pain, shrieks of torment, murder most foul, and the screaming redness of desire, of hunger and pain.

I was left with a sensation like the kind of rough desire that made you both break all the furniture in getting the job done. The kind of situation where you were left panting and broken afterward, where the room was reduced to kindling and you hoped the neighbors didn't hear anything.

Where the pair of you were covered in bruises, bites, scratches and worse, and where you both looked at each other a little shocked and surprised at what you'd done. That special place where you didn't know whether you should apologize or thank them; you just knew that when you recovered, you'd want to do it all over again.

Just…not right now.

All that hit me in an instant, and then She was hissing in pain, panting and drawing a gleaming fragment free of that terrible void, clutched in shaking fingers.

"Now, now, you're not supposed to be looking at me like that…" She whispered, sweat beading on Her skin as She held it clutched there, Her breathing ragged. *"You're supposed to be offering me something up! Quickly, before it's too late…"*

I cursed, blinking away sensations that vanished like morning mist before the noonday sun. I focused, willing my own fragment, the one of Darkness, to fill my hand.

It did, bubbling up from my fingertips like oil, spreading out to form a jagged framework, then backfilling, creating a serrated shard that seemed to suck in the dim light of the night.

"Quickly!" She hissed, shoving Her own shard at me, and snatching the Darkness one free.

I reached out, grabbing at the one She offered; I felt it, for just a second, as She tried to hold on, clearly fighting with herself in Her desire to hold to it, to keep both. Then She snarled and twisted aside, releasing the shard and vanishing as space around Her folded.

She was gone in less than a second; the world seemed to buzz with the compressed power of the shards and whatever that opening into Her had been.

Then I swallowed hard, the feeling of desperately searching attention growing as I made the new fragment vanish into me. I didn't know how—I just felt it fold space and time, vanishing into my flesh and my soul, somehow inside me and yet…elsewhere.

The sense of eyes upon me lingered, and I looked up—no clue why; I knew the gods weren't in the sky, but it always felt like they were—and those who I sensed there?

It wasn't just the usual suspects.

The presence of two fragments of divinity, unbound, out in the open had drawn…others.

Hell, I felt the true attention of more than just gods in those seconds as well. I felt the veil, brought close by my Fragment of Death, always a gossamer thread away, and on the other side? I felt the Valspar.

The hungry, desperate need to consume…that boiling, festering hatred of all life…the need to destroy it all.

For the first time, as I sensed their presence, they weren't aware of me. Their gaze was drawn aside, searching, desperate for the power that they sensed on the other side of the barrier, and I stared into nothing, as I felt the connections forming.

They were evil…but, not?

They'd smash the universe given the chance. They'd feed on the last remnants of every living being's minds, tearing them apart and desperately consuming every sensation. But not because they were evil, I suddenly realized, as it clicked.

That was where Amon had gotten it wrong.

Where his researchers had failed and misled him.

The void they'd opened had been "between the stars," I remembered from his memories. They'd found the Valspar there, waiting, and they'd burst through the veil, attacking and growing, desperate to kill and destroy.

They were the antithesis of all life, a force that existed only to destroy, and that was occasionally sentient, but usually seemed simply mindless, driven by hunger.

That's because what they were…

They were *entropy*.

They were the cleaners of the universe, driven by an absolute need to strip everything apart, to free the souls within!

They weren't evil, not in the way that Barabarattas had been evil, or the vampyrs. They didn't revel in the punishments they inflicted.

I sensed the need, the desperate hunt for power, power that would enable them to cross over to this side, to consume everything.

They were a part of the natural order, there to strip all life away and to free the souls to return to…something.

When they attacked, it was with that in mind…that need to free us of the prisons of flesh and the foul touch of mana. The magic that was life.

I felt it, as I recognized that the creatures on the other side were searching, but they were also blank in ways that the ones that I'd encountered before hadn't been. They were blank in the mind. There was no evil need to cause as much pain as possible, no need to twist us…no.

In my experiences, all that was evil like that? I recognized in people.

That sealed it for me as the last connections were made. The Valspar weren't fucking evil. Not in that sense. The desire to hurt, to tear us apart and to rip our souls free wasn't evil; it was just like the urge to drink, or to eat. It was needed, it was instinctual, and that was all.

When they tore us apart, though, as more and more of the souls were filtered through them and passed through the veil, they were contaminating the pure force of entropy!

That was what I'd found before, what I'd filled myself with that had driven everything around me wild. The magic of both sides of the veil, the way that my own mana had interacted with the entropy was like fusion—like goddamn nuclear fusion!

For a split second, as fusion occurred, it was like a super-fuel. Or maybe that was wrong…my own scientific background was fucking lacking, which made this harder…but maybe it was more like matter and antimatter.

They both existed out there, in the galaxy as I understood it. They just didn't exist together, because when they did? MASSIVE KABOOM.

That was more like what had happened.

My mana—which at its heart, I was starting to understand, the power that *created* everything—and entropy—the power that *destroyed* everything—had combined…very, very imperfectly.

It'd supercharged my spells, but it'd also, if I had this right in my head, had to have massively failed as well.

If I'd been understanding this right, then when I'd cast my spells, I'd been guiding the mana and releasing the entropy. The entropy had just sort of…spread out and vanished, probably taken up ripping the air apart and dissolving that into its component parts or whatever.

A little was probably carried along the spell, just caught up and dragged with it, and when the spell went boom, so did it.

I was blundering along in the dark here, feeling for the elephant in the room, and touching its trunk—blindfolded—while hoping that it was the trunk, and I wasn't about to find a massive pair of bollocks next.

The notification that flashed up, though, let me know that I was on the right path.

Congratulations!

You have made progress in your Quest: The Deeper Secret

Where once you thought you sensed the truth, now you feel its reality in your heart, and may at last begin to unravel its power.

Entropy is the name you give to the seventh power, and it sings in your ears as all truth must. Congratulations, young wielder, you have grown, and you make progress in your travels along the road to your destiny.

Forms of Magic Discovered: 7/10

Reward: New forms of magic, 10,000,000xp, Unknown

I blew out a long breath as the searching presences faded slightly, though I could still feel the attention of the gods, and—or so I thought—their shadowy observer.

Either way, I was fairly sure that unless I did something stupid right now, the gods who might have decided now was the perfect time to play silly buggers and attack me, risking it all to claim my fragments, were less likely to than ever before.

That made me grin as I settled my helm into place and tightened the straps on my armor.

"So, feel like winging it and slaughtering a city?" I asked Sehran, feeling that desperate need for a little good old-fashioned violence rising in me.

"After my visit?" She grinned in the darkness, her pristine white teeth shining. "Oh, hells yes!"

CHAPTER SEVEN

The darkness was a wonderful helping hand as we closed on the walls of Kronk.

There was no moon tonight, and the clouds had gradually thickened, leaving only the occasional guttering torch along the wall to mark the plodding guard's presences.

Considering that carrying a damn torch in this situation just made sure you saw nothing beyond about three meters, I wasn't worried about being spotted by them. Perfect conditions for what we had planned, all things considered.

"Stay low," I sent to Sehran as we closed on the wall. The pair of us kept barely above the ground; her wings made almost no sound in the night as I flew on magic alone. *"Let's find a section without patrols."*

I didn't need to say it; as soon as the words were out of my mouth, I knew that, but, you know, I was both hopped up on adrenaline and an urgent need to let loose with some insane levels of violence. And at times like that, it was the equivalent of asking each other if you were ready before the big game.

She'd been in there already, seen the filth of the place up close, breathed its stinking air, and she just nodded, staying silent, as I sent a mental "sorry" feeling and the sensation of being wound tighter than a watch.

She grinned at me in the darkness again, and I snorted. The ground flashed past, less than a meter below me. It was broken, the occasional scrub brush and spotty grass all that survived out here. The earth was cracked, looking as if it'd not seen rain in a decade or more.

The black iron walls loomed ahead of us. Rust ran down them with what I hoped was just condensation, but considering the smell as we got closer…

Literally, the closer we got, the more the stench hit me: sewage, rot, unwashed bodies…and something else. Something rancid and metallic. Most of all, though?

Blood. Lots of it. Old and new.

As we got to within a hundred meters of the wall, I couldn't help but shake my head at the stupidity. Seven guards, spread thin, most of them barely moving, probably drunk or worse, and the wall was at least a few miles long as it looped around the city.

"There," Sehran sent as she pointed to a section where the rust had eaten through part of the *metal* wall, creating jagged holes; the parapet there looked to have collapsed. *"I flew over it earlier. The holes are big enough that I doubt the guards can cross it, so I think they just avoid it entirely, making an even bigger blind spot in the patrol routes."*

I nodded, and we flew on, reaching the wall without so much as a shout being raised, which was just pathetic. The metal was jagged, and my skin crawled at the thought of what a cut from that mess would do to someone. Sehran followed me, flashing over the wall and then dropping into a graceful landing beside me, in a cluttered alleyway.

Kronk was even worse than I'd thought.

The alleyway we landed in was a narrow channel of shit and abandoned filth. What might have once been cobblestones were now just broken rocks jutting from a mix of mud, rotting food, and gods knew what else. But the narrow space that I could stand in that wasn't clearly piles of shit or bodies was covered in a miasma that suggested that the rotting rubbish that was stacked here and there concealed even more bodies as well.

The buildings leaned inward like drunks about to collapse; the walls were stained with soot and worse. What few windows there were had been boarded up or covered with rags; occasional, faint yellow light leaked out from behind them.

"We should stay off the streets," Sehran sent, pointing upward. *"The roofs will be faster and cleaner."*

I nodded, and we leapt into the air again, landing on the nearest rooftop. It creaked under my weight but held. Having seen what passed for a street here, the concern that someone might see us on a roof was just not an issue.

From here, we could see more of the city as well. The arena had to be toward the center, where the larger buildings were—I mean, why the hell have it anywhere else? These kinds of places always kept their entertainment close enough that the important people didn't have to go far, and there was no way that anyone with a working nose was coming down here out of choice.

We moved from roof to roof, staying low and silent, usually walking but occasionally jumping and boosting ourselves with flight when someone heard us and screamed out vile threats.

Voices drifted up from below as we went: harsh laughter, screams, pleading that went unanswered until too late. We reached the scene of one such place just as a body fell. A single look was enough to know that no amount of healing was going to bring him back from that.

I almost intervened, until I noted the outfits they wore and that their "victim" wore were identical, or near enough: blacks and greys, browns, with a mask to cover their faces and a dagger on the hip.

We'd literally—looking at the bag that the winners were rummaging through and grinning over—chanced upon a burglar getting mugged and murdered.

Once, I made the mistake of looking down into an alley where three figures were hunched over something. When one of them moved, I saw what was left of a person, still bleeding as they divided up the spoils. I wasn't sure if it was a "professional" hit or just dinner being served, but fuck me, the more I saw, the more convinced I was that the best thing to do with this city was napalm it from one side to the other.

"Normal night in Kronk," Sehran sent to me, following my gaze. *"Trust me, that's tame compared to what I saw earlier. Considering who and what I am, and these people turn my stomach?"* She shook her head.

I clenched my jaw and moved on. We were here for a purpose. Everything else was just another reason for the fire I planned to start later.

We'd covered about half a mile when the first real obstacle presented itself: a gap between buildings that was too wide to jump, and a street below filled with actual torchlight.

Unlike the rest of the city, this area seemed to have less of a piss-poor attempt at order—armed figures patrolled in pairs, and the street was relatively clean.

"Think we're getting closer to something important?" I asked. *"I don't see any of these buildings being anything useful, do you?"*

Sehran shook her head. *"Guild territory, I'm betting. There're big signs out in front of the buildings, and I think—not sure—but I think that's the sign for the Caravaneer's Guild, isn't it?"*

I looked at what she'd indicated. It could be, sure, but the combination of the angle, the drunken swaying of the sign—it had a corner loose and the wind was picking up—and the darkness meant it could have been anything, really.

"I'm guessing a place like this is going to have assassins as well, so maybe we should keep our eyes open. I mean, can you see the thieving bastards we've passed so far just staying away from here without a good reason?" She nodded to our left. *"I think we're better off going around."*

As we changed course, a door below us slammed open, and a man was shoved out into the street. His hands were bound behind him, and blood streamed from his face. Behind him came three figures in dark leather, one of them holding a thin blade that gleamed wetly in the torchlight.

"Please." The man was sobbing as he was turned around to face away from the three and out into the darkness. "I'll get the money. I just need more time!"

"Time's the one thing you don't have," said one of his captors, a woman with a grating voice like broken glass, from what looked like an old neck wound she showed off proudly. "Guild policy's clear. You don't pay, we make an example."

Before I could even think to move, her companions already had. One of them grabbed the debtor's head, yanking it back to expose his throat. The other drove his blade into the man's gut, then yanked it across with a rough, sawing motion. The victim's scream turned into a gurgle as the first did the same with his throat and his guts spilled onto the street.

Blood violently sprayed out, and the man collapsed. Then the one holding him yanked his head back, angling him to stare upward at the night sky, half sprawled on the ground.

But they weren't done. The woman produced a small metal tool from her belt, something like a corkscrew but with blades on the edges instead. She stepped in, stood over the dying man, and jammed it into his eye socket with a twist.

"His eyes are forfeit to the guild," she called out to the night, as what I guessed were her apprentices grinned and stared out, clearly seeing the few passersby who angled wide around them, before lowering her voice and presumably speaking to the pair with her. "Always take the eyes. They fetch a good price from the right buyers."

I reached for my weapon, but Sehran's hand on my arm stopped me.

"Not now." She shook her head. *"We have a mission. We can't save everyone, and anyone doing business or borrowing money from those like this aren't going to be innocents either."*

She was right, of course. But fuck me, no wonder she'd wanted to burn this place down.

We skirted the guild territory, taking a longer route that brought us closer to what had to be something like the local equivalent of the commercial district.

Here, the buildings were taller, and light spilled from more windows. But it wasn't the warm light of homes or honest businesses. It was the garish red glow of brothels, gambling dens, and drug houses. Even from the rooftops, I could hear the sounds: forced laughter, arguments, the occasional sob quickly muffled.

We passed a smithy, or an armory maybe. Peering down into the wide square behind the building, I growled involuntarily.

Four slaves were held there: two on the bellows, keeping a massive forge glowing; a third digging out coal from a pile and staggering under the weight of a shovelful. And the fourth?

Laid on their back, staring upward, clearly dead.

That the other three—all wore chains that encircled their neck, and were clearly unmagical, meaning we might have problems freeing them with my usual abilities—simply stepped over or around the body, and that they were apparently uncaring, just made this worse.

Kronk was a place that hopes and dreams went to die.

I hesitated, then shook myself and turned back, seeing how Sehran watched me.

"We'll come back for them," she promised.

I nodded, hating that I was leaving them there, but I had to be sensible about this. If I secured a place for them to retreat to, then they had a much better chance of survival.

No, we hurried on, passing houses that were pitch black, and others that had light shining from every window, as men and women of multiple species danced and laughed, wearing what looked like elaborate ball gowns and fucking masks.

That house, rising above most of the others on the edge of what I guessed was a deep dwarf zone—there were a collection of buildings that looked very different, angled backward as if collapsing, but wider and lower than any others, built with an eye to strength that was missing elsewhere—was one that I *really* wanted to see burn down.

And then, rising above it all as we passed the sounds of the party, we saw our target. The arena.

It was the tallest structure in Kronk by far, a massive circular building of dark stone and iron. Unlike the rest of the city, it showed signs of actual maintenance. Its walls were straight and its roof looked intact. Torches blazed all around its perimeter, and even at this hour, crowds were still filtering in and out through its many entrances.

"Fuck me sideways," I muttered to Sehran. "It's in full swing."

"We should have thought about that," she responded grimly. "A place like this, they probably run blood sports around the clock."

"Yeah, well, I didn't think about that," I admitted, having been thinking more about Mal's one back in Himnel, with its clear opening and closing hours.

We paused on a nearby rooftop, watching the flow of people on the plaza below. The crowd was a mix of Kronk's 'citizens'—or scumbags, depending on your point of view.

Some were clearly rich, dressed in gaudy, shiny shit that might have passed for finery anywhere else, accompanied by guards or slaves or both.

Others were more normally dressed but moved with the casual cruelty of people who were used to having power over their fellow men.

Lastly, scattered among them were the desperate ones, hollow-eyed and twitchy, betting their last coins on the night's entertainment.

What struck me most was how many of them were armed. Not just the obvious guards who stood on either side of the entrances, sneering at the poor and bowing when the rich tossed them a coin, but nearly everyone.

Knives, clubs, crude swords…here and there, obvious magical weapons. This was a population ready for violence, and expecting it at any moment.

"Well, that changes things," I growled, before looking around at the other buildings in the area. "We can't wait for the place to empty."

Sehran nodded. "I was afraid you'd say that. How do you want to do it? The guards might not look like much, but I bet they'll remember us. I don't see the public areas leading down to the slave pits. I think we'll need a special entrance."

"There has to be one inside. Go through and then find it—" I broke off, sighing. "And anyone inside who sees us opening locked doors is going to spread the word. Even if they don't care, they're going to see it as a distraction so they can play silly buggers elsewhere, aren't they?"

"Now you're thinking like a criminal." She smiled. "But, seriously, you're right. We need to either find a way to get uniforms and pass ourselves off as guards, which is going to be hard, or find another, less obvious way in."

I scanned the arena's exterior, looking for weaknesses. The main entrances were well-guarded, but there were smaller doors spaced around the circumference, probably service entrances. And below, almost hidden in the shadows between the arena and the surrounding buildings, I could see grates and drains. The sewers had to connect to the arena somehow.

"Fuck it. We split up," I decided. "You take the air, circle the arena, find a way in from above. If you can, start picking off any guards you get the chance to, as long as it's quiet. I'll go in through the sewers and see if I can find the slave pens from below. We meet in the middle."

"Are you sure?" Sehran frowned. "I don't know, sounds like a bit of a stupid plan to me. No offense, Jax, but once you're inside? You're not gonna be able to pass yourself off as anyone who's not been through the sewers, right? Reeking and covered in shit?"

"I will." I grinned. "Believe me, I don't like the idea, but Scour will clean me up nicely again."

"Still, seems a little…"

"Think it'll be worse than the sewers under Narkolt?" I asked flatly.

"Well, no." She shuddered at the thought of all the filth we marched through there, literally through shit that was deeper than we were tall. "But then we'll need to find each other as well."

"We can do that easily." I tapped the side of my head. "The bond, remember? Just reach out and sense me. Fuck knows you usually know when I'm doing anything fun!"

"Well, yeah, but that's a feeling I want to feel. You wading through shit? Not so much."

"Okay, plan B…*you* want to go through the sewers and *I'll* go through the roof?" I asked.

"I've got a great idea!" she said quickly. "Why don't you go through the sewers?"

"Yeah, that's what I thought." I snorted.

She didn't look convinced, but she nodded. "Fine. But be careful down there. If what I saw in the streets is any indication, the sewers are going to be horrific."

I gave her a grim smile. "Again, Narkolt's sewers…after that, I don't think these are going to be on the same level. Go, and I'll see you inside."

She squeezed my arm once, then launched herself into the night sky, a darker shadow against the clouds. She arced away, clearly looking to pass from another angle.

I watched her go, then made my way down to street level, moving to the edge of a nearby alley and jumping, boosting myself "up" a little with my Soaring Majesty ability just before I crashed into the filth, then released it, barely making more noise in landing than I did in walking.

"S…shpare a coin…" a drunken beggar I'd missed under a pile of rubbish asked.

I glanced at him; then, hearing a soft noise behind me, I kicked out on instinct.

The unseen mugger doubled up. The air whooshed out of him as he folded around my armored boot, and his dagger—barely a piece of sharpened metal and a cloth grip—clattered to the ground.

I straightened, grabbed him by the back of the head, then threw him at his accomplice, who'd just gotten to his feet, scowling and pulling another knife—a better made one this time—free.

I stepped into the short gap between us, punching twice, then turned away. My limited good mood from the banter with Sehran was gone as I scowled at the stench that hit me full force as soon as I took a real breath down here.

Up on the rooftops, the night air had diluted it somewhat, but down here, it was a physical assault. I gagged, forcing myself to breathe through my mouth as I slipped between buildings, making my way toward one of the drainage grates I'd spotted.

I had to duck into a doorway twice to avoid patrols. Not the organized guild patrols we'd seen earlier, but roving gangs of armed men who moved like predators, eyes constantly scanning for targets.

The second group had a prisoner with them—a young woman, barely more than a girl, stumbling along with a chain around her neck. Her eyes were vacant, her body marked with fresh bruises. I had to physically restrain myself from intercepting them. *Soon,* I promised myself. *Soon they'll all pay.*

The grate was old and rusted, but still solid. I examined it carefully, looking for a way to remove it without making too much noise. Finding none, I drew my dagger and began working at the mortar around the edges, chipping away bit by bit until I felt the grate loosen.

It took nearly a full minute of careful work before I could pull the grate free without filling the air with a squeal of tortured metal.

The opening it revealed was dark and reeked like exactly what it was, but it was big enough for me to slip through. I lowered myself down, feeling for a foothold, shaking my head in disbelief when the stench enveloped me.

Gods, what was that? Not just shit—no, it was something else. Something *worse*, as hard as that was to believe.

My feet touched a narrow ledge, slick with substances I didn't want to identify. I closed the grate above me, leaving it slightly ajar for a quick exit if needed, then relaxed as my eyes adjusted to the darkness. Darkvision kicked in.

The sewer was a broad channel, the "water" level thankfully low, though what flowed through it was more sludge than liquid. The ledge I stood on ran along the side, just wide enough for single-file passage. Ahead and behind, the tunnel curved away into darkness.

I oriented myself toward where I thought the arena should be and started to walk, one hand on the slimy wall for balance. The sound of flowing sludge masked my footsteps, but it also made it harder to hear whether anyone—or anything— was approaching.

I hadn't gone far when I heard it—a splashing sound, different from the steady flow of the sewer…something moving through the foul mess. I froze, pressing myself against the wall, and waited, my naginata pulled free of my bag and leveled, ready.

The splashing grew louder, accompanied now by a wet, snuffling sound, like an animal scenting the air. I held my breath as a shape emerged from the darkness ahead.

It might have been human once. It walked upright, more or less, but its proportions were all wrong: limbs too long, back hunched, head oversized and misshapen. It moved through the sludge with practiced ease, stopping occasionally to plunge its hands into the filth and bring something to its gaping mouth.

A tunnel scavenger of some kind, I guessed. Some kind of wretch that lived in the sewers, surviving on whatever they could find, slowly changed by disease and the toxic mess. Its skin was a patchwork of weeping sores and growths, its eyes milky white and, I was willing to bet, completely blind.

It stopped suddenly, head swiveling in my direction. It sniffed the air aggressively, then let out a low, gurgling growl.

I didn't have time for this, I decided. I stepped forward, thinking I'd stab and kill the creature quickly and quietly. As soon as I moved though, it hissed, spun to face me fully, and lunged toward me with a howl that echoed through the tunnel.

I barely had to brace myself; it might be fugly, but it wasn't big. Clearly, living on what floated around in a sewer wasn't great for personal growth, considering that it weighed about the same as a geriatric patient. The creature stiffened as the blade punched through its chest, then went limp, sliding down into the sludge without another sound as I shucked it off the blade.

I hit my weapon with a Scour and moved on, faster now as I guessed the scavenger's cry might have drawn some attention. I needed to find my way to the arena before anyone came looking.

The tunnel branched several times, and I had to make some wild-ass guesses about which way to go. Twice, I had to turn around and go back to choose the other passage when they got too narrow or collapsed entirely.

The whole time, the weight of the city pressed down on me, thousands of sick fucking bastards doing who knew what to their prisoners and then merrily going about their business above while I slogged through their literal toilets.

It was also obvious, as I got turned around again, that it was only the areas like this that had sewers at all. There weren't any passages that led into the rest of the city, just these few dozen tunnels that all seemed to lead to the same place, a massive cistern that I found mid-search.

It was full of movement, rats, bloated flies and other insects, twisted shapes like the scavenger I'd killed earlier, all feeding on the bodies of what I guessed were the arena's slaves.

When they were killed, they were clearly tossed down here, which meant that there had to be a way in and out. I just needed to find it.

After what felt like hours but was probably only twenty minutes, I noticed a change in the tunnel ahead. The ceiling rose higher, and the passage widened into something more deliberate—a maintained section of sewer, with actual brickwork that was clear enough that I could see it, instead of almost totally buried below "high tide" deposits.

Sure enough, the passage soon ended in a grated section, and beyond that it opened into a second, larger chamber where several tunnels converged. In the center was a circular pool of relatively clean water—compared to the sludge where I was, anyway; it only had a few turds floating in it that I could spot at this distance—and I was willing to bet it was some kind of filtration system.

Then, on the far side, set into the wall, was a heavy iron door.

I checked the grate that was between me and the new area. Then, once I was sure there were no traps or guards, I fed mana into the naginata until it shone white-hot and I used it to casually cut through the bars where they joined to the wall on one side.

That done, I shifted and braced, and pushed the grate back. A slight squeal still sounded out, but was easily lost in the roars of the crowd that now filtered down distantly from overhead.

Once on the far side, I bent the grate back, figuring it'd pass a casual glance, and hit myself with a Scour, then another, then a Heal for good measure, shaking my head at how much stinking mulch cascaded free of me.

Regardless, once I was here, I was more or less clean again. This chamber was deserted. The door on the far side was locked, of course, but it looked simple to bypass.

I literally powered the blade with mana again, slid the tip down into the gap between the locking mechanism and the hole in the wall it sank into, and sawed slightly.

I had it open in seconds, revealing a narrow staircase leading upward.

The smell changed as I climbed: less raw sewage and death, more sweat, blood, and fear. The air grew warmer too, with the sounds of distant cheering getting louder by the second. I was under the arena now—I had to be.

The stairs ended at another door, this one seemingly barred from the other side. I tugged my helmet off and pressed my ear to the metal, listening.

Movement was clear on the other side: heavy feet, the clink of metal, low voices and general arguing. Guards, I was willing to bet.

I needed a distraction. Looking around, I spotted a chunk of loose mortar on the staircase. I picked it up, then pounded on the door with my fist.

"Hey! Someone locked me in down here! Help!"

The voices stopped, then one called out, muffled through the metal. "Who's there? How'd you get down there?"

"I'm with…maintenance?" I bullshitted. "Checking the drains, yeah. Someone closed the door behind me, and I got turned around and now I'm stuck. Can you let me out?"

A pause, then: "Wait there!"

"You can't really be that dumb, can you?" I whispered under my breath to myself in disbelief.

Footsteps receded, leaving at least one guard still by the door, judging by the occasional shuffle I could hear.

I waited, tense, ready to go. After a minute, I heard returning footsteps, then the metallic sound of a key in a lock, then the sound of at least two people heaving with something heavy.

Guessing it was a bar or something, I shrugged and then kicked the door open with all my strength. It slammed into a pair of guards on the other side, sending them both staggering backward to crash to the ground under a massive ironwood bar.

Clearly, they were used to having to keep the door sealed for a reason, which made me think that this wasn't the usual method of disposing of bodies.

I was through the doorway in a blur, grinning beneath my helm as I struck out, my naginata in my right hand and the chunk of mortar I'd scooped up in the other. I hurled the mortar at another guard, catching him in the face as he reached for his weapon, then closed the distance to the pair on the ground and swung the blade from left to right, angled low, relieving them of their heads—more or less—before they could recover.

The guard I'd just stunned shook his head and blinked blearily; his nose gushed with blood, his eyes watering. He opened his mouth to shout.

I silenced him with a fast stab to the throat, the minute grating sensation as the glowing-hot weapon carved through the bottom of his skull and into his brain almost being lost in the hiss as his blood evaporated where it touched the weapon.

Then I turned, staring around and expecting more guards, only to find that was it, all done. I shook my head at the stupidity of the fuckers.

Then I grunted as I remembered that a stupid guard stayed a guard, until he died. A smart guard either moved up the chain, or got out as soon as they could.

I dragged them back through the door and tossed them down the stairs, out of sight of anyone who might pass by. Then I took a moment to look around.

The room I was in was a guard post, clearly: five bunks around the wall, each with a small cot on the bottom and the top, a chest at the foot of each, and then a collection of chairs scattered about.

The table in the middle of the room had a few coppers on it and some cards, as well as small mugs that stank of shitty ale.

Beyond that—and the traditional stench of farts, sweat, and poor dietary choices that always came with a bunkhouse—there was nothing worth noticing.

I plucked the coins free, adding them to my pouch, before considering that I'd tossed the bodies without a thought. I'd not even bothered to loot them. Hell, when did I ever these days?

Coin was generally something I ignored; I just tended to accumulate it. The food I was likely to get off a body—despite the common tropes of all the skeletons in forgotten ruins in games having fresh bread on them—would never be something I wanted to put in my mouth.

That left you generally with valuables—no guard was likely to have any—or weapons and armor. Considering the armor I had and my gear? Fuck no. Not worth my time.

As I opened the door to the corridor, a second detail popped up, and I sighed, shaking my head as I thought it through.

Sure, they were useless to me, but to the slaves I was about to free?

Fucking priceless.

I growled and stepped out; the corridor beyond was empty. Figuring confidence was better than stealth, as I was piss-poor at it anyway, I marched forward. Despite everything that should have happened, it took me another five minutes to find any sign of life down here.

When I did, it was in a long and low-ceilinged passage, lit by widely spaced torches. The walls were stained with old blood here and there…and worse. Unlike below, the floor here was what looked like sawdust and old reeds, strewn about and still damp in places.

From somewhere not far away came the now much louder sounds of the arena, the roar of crowds, the screech of metal on metal, and worse, the screams of the mutilated and dying.

And beneath that, closer and desperate: Voices. Whimpers. The rattle of chains. Frantic arguing, begging and prayers.

I moved down the corridor, following the sounds, checking each door I passed. Most were locked storerooms, some filled with weapons, armor, or supplies, most with damaged gear and even occasional props like what looked to be poorly made-up forgeries of Imperial Legion gear.

That had gotten my attention. Although I'd grabbed weapons and armor intermittently, piling it all in my bags, I moved straight for this—torn between fury they had it, and hope that I would find more of my people.

Then I snarled as I saw the truth.

It was imitation shit. Barely thick enough to hold together when they put it on. Anyone wearing this would do better to fight naked. I hurled it down and stomped out, my anger—never far away these days, admittedly—rising sharply.

But as I went deeper, the doors changed—heavy wood reinforced with iron, with small, barred windows at eye level. Cells.

Cells filled with people.

CHAPTER EIGHT

I peered into the first one and saw three men huddled together on a pile of straw for warmth. Their bodies were covered in scars old and new, one still smeared with recent blood, and the room smelled of sickness. One of them looked up as my shadow fell across the window, then he turned away, shaking and biting down on his hand, clearly terrified.

"Please no…" he whimpered, and I shook my head.

"Soon," I hissed. "Be ready." Then I hit each of them with a healing spell, and moved on to the next cell and the next. Between the mana reserves I had, the stones, and the potions, I could afford to cast when I had the chance, and damn, those people needed it.

Not a one of them had been chained up. Clearly the arena wasn't going to "waste" magical restraints on them, not when they could just leave them in rags, half-starved, and surround them with guards who could kill them easily.

There were dozens of cells now, small rooms on either side of the corridor that varied from packed in like sardines to empty, with the empty rooms on the outer ring, and the deeper I went the more people.

The corridor branched, and I followed the sound of the most voices, peering around the corner from the closest I could manage to stealth. I'd found a larger space—a central chamber where a dozen guards sat or stood around a trio of rough tables, drinking and playing dice and cards.

Beyond them, seven more corridors, lined with more cells, were laid out like the spokes of a wheel, all leading into this area in the middle.

I'd found, I guessed, the main holding area for the arena slaves.

I counted quickly. Twelve guards, all armed, some in partial armor. Too many to take quietly, and a fight would alert the entire arena. I needed Sehran if I was to take them all quietly.

I mean, I could always do this messily, and a little voice inside cried out that was *definitely* the way to go here, but no. I wanted these people ready before anything ruined the surprise.

So, instead I retreated to a shadowed side corridor a little farther back, then focused on our bond, sending a pulse of awareness outward, searching for her presence. I felt her almost instantly; she was inside the arena already, moving through the upper levels, trying to find a way down.

"I've found the slave pens—they're underground. Twelve guards or so. You close enough that I should wait, or…?" I pushed the thoughts through our connection, visualizing the layout as best I could.

I felt her understanding, a sense of "just give me a goddamn minute," before a sense of movement as she changed direction, heading downward. Now I just had to wait and avoid detection until she reached me.

It didn't take long. Within minutes, I heard a commotion from the direction I'd come—shouts, the clash of metal, a scream cut short. The guards in the chamber looked up, alert now, reaching for weapons.

"What was that?" one asked.

"Go check," ordered another, clearly the leader. "You three, with me. The rest, stay here and watch the slaves."

Four of them headed toward the noise, which had intensified. I distantly heard Sehran's voice now, raised in a song, and smiled grimly.

Well, it wasn't the distraction I'd wanted, considering the whole "let's be stealthy" plan but fuck it—at least this time it wasn't me who fucked up.

Made for a change, actually.

Regardless, she created exactly the distraction I needed.

I waited until the four were out of sight, then moved. The remaining eight were focused on the sounds of fighting, their backs to me. I silently closed the distance, triggering Mana Overdrive and Hyper Cognition, and readying my naginata. Then I struck.

The first two guards died without a sound; my blade passed through the gaps between their helmets and chest armor, literally popping their heads free. The third had just turned when I stabbed it into him, ramming it through the center of his chest and impaling him for the sheer fucking look of it.

The others reacted then, screaming in panic as he shrieked and gurgled. They drew their weapons, but they were scattered, surprised, and oh so slow.

I caught the fourth with a kick to the knee that sent him sprawling, then parried a sword thrust from the fifth, with my left forearm, releasing my naginata as I decided that a little "hand-to-hand" was in order here. Stepping inside his guard, I headbutted him hard enough to crack his skull and carve a divot in his forehead with the attached head blade on my crest.

The sixth and seventh came at me together, but they got in each other's way. I stepped aside as the first tried to stab me, grabbed his wrist and yanked him forward to use as a shield against the other's attack. Then I grabbed them both by their faces and slammed their skulls together with a sickening crunch.

The eighth landed a blow on my shoulder. But his sword bounced off my armor with barely a clang, the cheap iron that made it doing practically nothing but scuffing the gloss.

I caught his wrist, snapped it with a twist, then yanked him into a headbutt that crushed the front of his skull in.

There was a ninth who I'd missed until now, but he was backing away, eyes wide with fear, when five Magic Missiles slammed into the back of his neck from behind, burning through his flesh and crashing him to the floor.

Sehran stood in the doorway, her wings fluttering as she turned, looking for any more targets…then sighed, in disappointment. Behind her lay the bodies of the other four guards, broken and bloody, along with one in much better armor that I guessed she'd charmed to do the actual work as she hurried to help.

"Sorry about that." She stepped over the corpses. "It was going so well, until I took the stairwell that opened out into the main guardroom. I had to kill them all. Well, all but their commander, and he seriously didn't deserve the armor he was wearing."

"Amateur?" I asked casually, stepping over to my naginata and yanking it free, before wiping the weapon on a dead guard's cloak, then hitting myself with a Heal, restoring my burned-through health from the Mana Overdrive.

"Urgh, it's so annoying. I mean, gear like that, you assume he's going to at least know how to use it, right?" She rolled her eyes, gesturing to the body. "He was barely a good meat-shield."

"Disgraceful, really." I sighed, then grinned at her, pulling my helm off and peering back the way she'd come as I scratched my hair.

"Getting long again," she pointed out, and I nodded.

"Fuck everything on this continent, I need a portal home so that Isabella can trim it again for me." I sighed. "Any chance someone's going to wander along and find the bodies behind you?"

"Probably," she admitted. "No time to get them hidden, and honestly, nowhere to do it either. I had to make it fast, and it was a bit…messy."

"Never mind." I shrugged. "We're inside now, and we've found some of the slaves at least…can't be helped. I always preferred heavy stealth anyway."

"Nobody can say anything, if everyone's dead." She grinned. "Feels almost like Grizz is with us, doesn't it? Oops, found the keys!" She lifted one hand and jingled them, smiling.

With that, we moved quickly now. Sehran took one corridor, me the other, unlocking cells and freeing prisoners. Most were men, fighters in their prime or slightly past it, their bodies bearing the marks of countless battles. But there were women too, and even a few children—the next generation of gladiators, being broken in early, as foul as that sounded.

The worst was the cells farthest away, where dozens were crammed into spaces that would barely hold them, starved, weak and mainly naked, presumably there as the local equivalent of cannon fodder.

Regardless, for each group, I gave the same quick message: "We're freeing everyone. Arms are in the storerooms back that way. When you hear the signal— and trust me, you'll know it—that's when you move. Kill your former masters, free the others, and get ready. Hold the arena. We'll be sending more slaves here to get ready and to be safe."

They listened in stunned silence at first, then with growing joy and a determination to seize the chance as the reality sank in. By the time Sehran and I had opened all the cells, nearly four hundred slaves had gathered in the central chamber, arming themselves with weapons from the storerooms that we'd found.

I'd not even needed the weapons I'd grabbed on the go, there'd been plenty, and as we got ready, we knew there'd be even more soon because the cheers were winding down from above.

"Will you lead us?" asked an older man with a network of scars across his face and chest as he cinched a leather chest piece closed with a practiced movement.

"No, we have to secure the rest of the arena first." I shook my head. "We'll start moving up, killing the guards and sending any more slaves we free down to you. Wait here until the signal, then move out and seal up the entrances and exits. Be ready to open them when we free more people. There are thousands more slaves in the city yet, and we need a safe place to protect you all."

"What signal?"

"Like I said, you'll fucking know it." I shrugged.

"Why take control of the arena?" he asked me suspiciously. "You a gambler?"

"I am." I snorted. "But not like that. We need a safe place to send the slaves as we free them. The Imperial Legion doesn't abandon its people."

"The legion?"

"We're not just here for them, we came for all of you, but yeah."

The man nodded, staring at me in stunned amazement, as he realized the sheer fucking audacity of the plan. "You're going to free all of Kronk."

"That's the plan, yeah," I admitted distractedly as I looked around at the gathered faces, seeing a little hope replacing the despair. Most of the faces showed only a grim readiness to fight, but fuck it, that was better than the terror I'd seen in the first cell. "What's your name?"

"Varec," he whispered, as if he'd almost forgotten he had a name. "I've been fighting in this pit for fifteen damn years."

"Well, Varec, consider tonight your retirement. Once this is over, you'll be free citizens of the empire—provided you choose to serve, anyway."

"The empire?" someone else asked. "What empire?"

"Mine," I said simply, and left it at that. Fuck it, if this went badly, it wasn't going to matter, after all.

Sehran and I headed back the way she had come, climbing stairs that led up into the arena proper, thinking to meet the guards as they escorted the wounded and surviving slaves back down to their cells.

Unfortunately, just as we reached the stairs to what she assured me was the ground level, we heard the distant sounds of fighting breaking out, *behind us*.

Shouts, the clash of metal, screams.

"Fuck," I hissed. "They just couldn't wait, could they?" I spun around, looking back down the stairs.

The sounds of fighting grew louder, spreading through the lower levels. From somewhere a few rooms over, a clanging rang out as a bell was rung in iron warning, and suddenly more shouting broke out on this level as well.

The slaves hadn't waited for our signal. They were already moving, attacking guards.

"The arena." Sehran groaned. "There must have been another passage down. The guards must have…"

"Fuck it then; change of plans," I said grimly. "We need to make sure they don't all get slaughtered. We need to get back down there. They'll need help dealing with the professional gladiators."

We moved in the direction of the shouts and followed the sounds of battle. The corridors were chaos now, filled with fighting men and women. Former slaves were fighting guards and arena staff as they came boiling down out of multiple stairways and passages; the confined space made it a brutal, close-quarters melee.

I waded in, daggers in both hands, no room for my naginata in the mayhem, and cut a path through the guards who tried to restore order. Sehran bounded off, her demonic form fully fledged now—wings spread wide, claws extended— ripping through armor and flesh with equal ease. She stunned and confused with her songs, forcing the occasional one who looked worth the effort to switch sides and fight their friends.

We fought our way through corridor after corridor, freeing more slaves as we went and taking them with us until we found ourselves at a heavy portcullis. It was one of the gates that led onto the arena floor. Through the iron bars, I could see the sands lit by torchlight, a battle already raging there.

The slaves who had escaped first had made it to the arena proper and were engaged with the gladiators: free men who fought for sport and profit, better armed and armored than the slaves, and trained in the art of public killing.

The crowd in the stands was in an uproar. Some fled; others cheered on this unexpected bonus, throwing coins and placing bets on who was gonna win.

Well, fuck that. Time for me to go play, too, I decided, kinda annoyed it'd taken us that long to find it.

I shoved people back, sheathing my daggers and drawing my naginata. Feeding fire mana into it sure as hell made people back up as it gleamed the bright white of superheated steel.

I slashed three times, then kicked out. The central mass of bars creaked outward to crash into the blood-soaked sands of Kronk's arena.

It was like something out of a nightmare.

Slaves and gladiators fought desperately on all sides, bodies already littering the ground. The stands above were a riot of screaming spectators, some now throwing not just coins but weapons, food, anything at hand. And in a high box overlooking it all, a group of richly dressed figures watched with expressions ranging from anger to amusement.

"The arena masters," Sehran said, following my gaze. "And probably some of the city's elite, I'd imagine. Should we go for them?"

Before I could answer, a roar went up from the slaves as they spotted us, both those out on the sands and those who streamed around us, heading to fight with their brethren.

Some of the gladiators turned too, glaring at us and clearly pissed off.

One of them, a mountain of a man in some damn nice articulated plate armor, stepped forward, pointing a massive war hammer in our direction.

"Who dares interrupt the games?" he bellowed, his voice carrying over the chaos of the crowd. "This is sacred ground, and you have defiled it!"

I couldn't help but laugh, the sound harsh and cold even to my own ears. "Sacred? There's fuck all sacred in this shithole of a city. But I'm about to make it a holy place—holy with the blood of every slaver, every torturer, every piece of shit that calls Kronk home."

The gladiator spat. "Bold words from a dead man. Do you know who I am? I am Gorgas! Champion of the arena, undefeated in three hundred matches!"

"Well, ain't that nice? I guess this'll be a change for one of us then, considering I've not lost an arena bout either!" I replied, readying my naginata. "Better pucker up, fuckface, it's time to kiss your arse bye-bye!"

He charged, faster than I was expecting for his size, hammer swinging around in an arc that would have killed me had it landed.

I wasn't in the mood to play fair, though, not with the way that everything had been, not with the fucking few days I'd had.

Instead, I slammed my naginata into the ground and powered both my usual suspects, Hyper Cognition and Mana Overdrive. The difference was I doubled, then doubled it again, plowing so much mana into myself that the world seemed to slow to the point he was barely moving.

I strode forward, stepped inside his reach, plucked the weapon from his hands with my right, and grabbed him by the throat with my left. I let inertia take the weapon around and I simply guided it, as the poor fool who had been used to slaughtering half-starved, poorly trained slaves came to a jarring halt.

For him, it must have looked like I just blurred across the sand, ripping his hammer free and snatching him up. Certainly, that must have been what the fans in the arena stands saw, as a sudden shocked hush replaced the baying for blood.

Then I spun the hammer around and drove the head of it into his face, even as I pulled forward, holding him by the neck.

The result was that his head snapped back, shattering around the metal of the hammer, and his neck broke. The raised lip of the armor where it ran around the back of the neck didn't do him any favors either, as his flesh was markedly softer than either, and so, of all the options to give up, it was that, and his head was ripped free in a welter of bloody chunks.

There was a second, even more stunned silence, and that was when I swung the hammer around twice to build up a little momentum, and then I hurled it at the arena masters' box, smashing through a shield that they'd clearly expected to be more than they needed, and turning a particularly unlucky celebrant into paste.

Then I turned and walked back to my naginata, plucking it from the sand again and calling out unconcernedly, "Well, that was a disappointment. Anyone else want to try their luck?"

For a moment, there was silence in the arena. Then a sound I hadn't expected: cheers.

Not from the stands, but from the slaves. They raised their makeshift weapons in salute, their faces bright with fuckin' glee to see their masters' favorite fall.

The other gladiators looked, well, a bit less amused. They formed a loose circle around us, wary now, realizing we weren't ordinary intruders. In the stands, the mood had shifted too. The excitement of unexpected blood sport was giving way to fear as more and more slaves continued to pour out onto the arena sands from the tunnels below.

In the high box, the arena masters were shouting orders, pointing, clearly trying to organize some kind of response. One of them, a corpulent man in gaudy robes, was screaming at an equally fat man in a gold embossed suit of armor.

"I think it's time for the fun to really begin." Sehran sidled up next to me. "The original plan's done now anyway."

She was right. The plan was never a great one, being more or less "let's see what happens and make it up as we went along," but now it'd become a full-blown slave revolt, and there was no calming that down. Better to embrace the chaos and turn it to our advantage.

"Actually, if we view it as we were always going to make it up as we went along, I think we're still on track," I mused. "In fact, this is probably the longest one of our plans has lasted without going wrong."

We both looked down at the body of the previous arena champion, and I went on. "Well, you know, *wrong for us*, is what I mean," I hastily added.

"Yeah, I think his day ended poorly." Sehran grinned.

I winked at her, then raised my voice to address the slaves who had gathered around us. "Slaves of Kronk! You're now free, but others, your brothers and sisters, aren't. They're out there, locked up, chained to serve shitbag masters and beasts, so how about we change that?"

A cheer went up, ragged but heartfelt.

I kept going. "This is just the start! Through this city, others are trapped but not for much longer! We're going to free them all. But before we do it? We need a safe place for them to go. A safe place for the slaves...no, for our *free people* to be!

"We need somewhere with strong walls, food, weapons and space, and look! How convenient—it looks like we've got just that right here!" I gestured around us at the walls and seats of the arena. "All we have to do is kill the fucking rats that infest it first!"

The slaves roared their approval, a sound of primal rage that echoed off the walls. The gladiators who were surrounding us in a thin line, sensing which way the wind was blowing, began to back away. Some even dropped their weapons in surrender as the slaves closed on them.

I turned to Sehran, a grim smile on my face. "Ready to go crash a party?"

She flexed her wings and grinned at me. "I thought you'd never ask!"

I crouched and then launched myself up into the air. Sehran rose with me, her wings beating hard, as we closed on the masters' box and the screams started again below us.

CHAPTER NINE

The arena masters' box hung over the sands like a vulture's perch, all gaudy gold and silver decorations and battered, faded opulence.

As we closed on the box, I caught a clear view of the panic unfurling inside thanks to the thick glass floor.

Of the seven figures, three were fat men in robes with so much gold thread that they had to be Olympic-class athletes under the flab to even move.

Clearly I was wrong, though, because they all struggled to move quickly; one had to roll out of his chair and onto all fours on the ground to get up. Their clothing was stretched taut over their bulging, flabby bodies, and one of them grabbed at two women dressed in finery that couldn't hide their hard, cruel faces to drag him upright.

The final two men were in armor that might have been impressive…if they weren't so clearly for show rather than function.

One of them, I assumed, was the head of the city guard or the army maybe. He barked orders at a servant, his face purple with rage as he frantically gestured at the carnage below. The others were already struggling back toward the exit, looking for escape.

"Too late!" I growled as I landed on the edge of the box.

The shocked silence as I dropped in was broken by a scream from one of the women, high and piercing—almost a fuckin' sonic attack, it went on that long.

The armored men grabbed for weapons—a sword for one, a mace for the other. The first charged, his sword raised high overhead…a textbook example of how *not* to attack, as it caught on the glittering chandelier and was nearly ripped from his hand.

I sidestepped, then clotheslined him with my arm. As he dropped to the floor, gasping, I reached down, grabbed him by the back of his fanciful armor, and tossed him out behind me over the railing.

His scream was cut short by the wet *crunch* as he hit the sands below. The slaves closed on him, and I turned away from what followed.

The second armored man hesitated, his mace wavering.

"So nearly the smart choice!" I congratulated him.

His moment of distraction cost him his life, though, as Sehran landed behind him. Her claws ripped through the exposed back of his neck.

"You know, if not for her," I finished.

"The door!" one of the fat men shouted, and they all surged toward it in a panicked rush. It burst open before they reached it. Instead of escape, they found themselves face-to-face with a group of six guards rushing in. The collision sent two of the would-be escapees sprawling.

"Perfect timing," Sehran snarled. Her wings expanded to their full span as she launched herself into the cramped space, claws extended.

I followed, naginata whirling, and together we turned the masters' box into a slaughterhouse. The guards were professionals, at least, but they were boxed in, fighting in a space too cramped for anything like the room they needed, and they were caught between us and their desperate masters trying to shove past them.

"Please," one of the fat men squealed as I cut down the guard in front of him. "I have gold! Lots of gold!"

"Not interested," I told him flatly, and rammed my blade through his chest.

"Their stash," Sehran called as she snapped the neck of one of the women. "Might as well take the gold for your coffers, and we'll need it for the slaves."

"I suppose. Fuck it," I grunted as I grabbed the next nearest of them, a short, balding man with a jeweled collar so tight it was cutting into the folds of his neck. "Where's the vault? I know you fuckers will have one!"

"B-Behind the painting," he stammered, pointing to a garish landscape on the far wall. "The key is…the key…" He fumbled at his belt pouch, and I reached down, ripping it free.

"Too slow," I growled, and threw him over the railing to join his friend. His scream was short and cut off sharply with a wet smack.

"Uh, Jax?" Sehran called as I moved to the painting, tore it down, and found a small iron door set into the wall.

"Yeah?" I looked at the lock, shaking my head in disgust. They'd clearly relied on the fact that they had a shitload of guards, rather than hiring someone good at making locks.

"Might want to look before you throw next time. You nearly killed someone with that last one."

I snorted, seeing the grin on her face, and then drew back and slammed a single mana-enhanced blow into it with my fist. The door buckled; two more blows, and I pulled the buckled door open. Inside was a small fortune in gold and platinum, gems, and what looked like betting receipts, but little else.

"Bit pathetic…" I frowned, looking it over.

"Another for the crowd?" Sehran held the last arena master—one of the women this time—by her throat. The woman's feet kicked frantically as she dangled over the edge, her face turning purple as she tried to beg.

"Your choice," I told her, uncaringly.

Sehran pretended to consider, then smiled wickedly at her captive as yells rose from below. "I think the people have spoken." She released her grip, and the woman plummeted from sight with a shriek.

A massive cheer went up from the sands below as the slaves saw another of their tormentors fall. The box was ours now, and from here we could see the full scope of the arena from above. It was bigger than I'd realized—a sprawling complex with multiple rings, practice yards, and what looked like a small section off to the side for private showings.

"Let's move." I emptied the vault and the small pile of valuables and pouches that we'd taken from the group into my own bag of holding. "We've got a lot more work to do."

We left the box, stepping over the bodies of the guards and the arena masters, and moved back out into the main building. The corridor outside was empty now, but I could hear fighting elsewhere echoing up, the sound of metal on metal and screams.

We followed the sounds, moving through a maze of corridors decorated with trophies of past "champions": bloodstained weapons, scraps of armor, even what looked disturbingly like preserved body parts. Each room we passed showed us just how far a group that saw themselves as having the right to do whatever it wanted and no moral compass could do.

From the rooms where new slaves were presumably "broken in," to lavish viewing chambers where the wealthy could enjoy private death matches, this was an absolute shithole. The farther we went, the more I wanted to hurt people.

Each time we freed the slaves held in the rooms—of all ages, and many having been locked into torture devices and worse—we killed their captors and abusers.

Guards appeared periodically—sometimes alone, sometimes in groups, sometimes escorting wealthy patrons trying to flee. We didn't care; we just killed them all. I lost count of how many fell to my blade, how many Sehran tore apart with her claws, her whip, daggers, or even enthralled into fighting their own comrades.

We used magic sparingly; we could use it, but there just wasn't a need here.

"Does this place have no end?" Sehran muttered as we cleared yet another corridor.

"It's fucking ridiculous." I had a weird sense of déjà vu, remembering a day out at a local flat-pack furniture company when I was seeing an ex.

She'd loved the place; I'd seen a maze that was designed to make sure you went round and round and were only let out when you were flat broke.

This place reminded me of that, having to go through room after room after room. I groaned, realizing that we might have been too hasty in slaughtering the masters, as there was no way they'd have been marching on and on to get somewhere.

I just knew this place was going to have some secret fucking doors somewhere. And as for that vault? It was tiny, and I was willing to bet it was just for show. It all clicked in my mind.

I considered going back and searching, but we just didn't have the time, so fuck it. Instead, we kept going, passing what had to be the entrances to the poor people's stands, and finding the detritus left behind after hundreds of people had run for it.

We didn't bother going looking inside the arena anymore, instead following the trampled rubbish. At last, we found the main entrance hall.

It was a vast chamber with marble floors—cracked and stained with shit—and high ceilings.

Here, a pitched battle was just getting going between a group of slaves who had somehow beat us here, fighting against a last stand of guards who were pushing in through the main doors.

Behind the guards, I could see wealthy assholes trying to flee, pushing and shoving one another in their desperation to escape.

"Fuck it, time to let off a little steam," I muttered, and launched myself into it.

The battle was short and brutal. The guards fought desperately, but they were caught between us and the exit, and they fell one by one. The crowds screamed and ran, but a lot didn't make it. The slaves showed no mercy. Honestly, I couldn't blame them. There were no kids, or I'd have insisted on it, but the people who'd been baying for their blood only an hour before? Fuck them, and the horse they rode in on.

When it was over, we stood in a blood-soaked hall, surrounded by freed slaves with makeshift weapons. They looked at us, presumably waiting for some orders.

"Secure the building," I ordered them. "Seal the entrances. Post guards at every gate and get ready. More of your brothers and sisters are gonna be coming, and they'll need help."

Varec, the scarred gladiator I'd met earlier, stepped forward. "What about the guards, or anyone who tries to take it back?"

"Kill them," I said. "This place is yours now. Anyone who tries to take it back is your enemy."

A grim smile spread across his face. "I like that."

I turned to the gathered slaves. "Are there healers among you? No? Okay, anyone with medical knowledge?"

A few hands went up hesitantly for the latter, where none had for the former.

"Good. Set up areas for the wounded. We'll need food, water, and weapons handed out. Organize watches. Make sure no one gets in who shouldn't. And, be ready…because when I do this, there's gonna be a LOT of attention right after, and I want you all to be able to seal it up and ride it out."

They nodded, already moving to carry out the orders. There was a different feeling in the air now, a sense of purpose that hadn't been there before.

"Come on," I said to Sehran. "We've got a goddamn city to burn. And then, at some point, one of the fuckers is going to go running for Brakuus and we can really start to play."

We left them to their work and made our way out of the main doors and then flew up to the roof. The night air was thick with smoke now. In the distance, fires broke out across Kronk. The chaos was spreading even without us taking part, and I couldn't help but grin at that.

The street outside, where there'd been various people wandering about and waiting guards when we first arrived, was now deserted. But in the streets to either side, I could see more people gathering, and the glint of armor and weapons being made ready.

I sat down heavily on the edge of the roof, my body suddenly reminding me of the toll this was taking. My mana reserves were slowly sinking, and I could feel Sehran's need through the bond.

She needed my mana like I needed air, and although she'd been good about it—the practice of the weeks since we came here and she was bound to Oracle, and Oracle to me having helped her to be more selective—but still, she needed mana, and so did I.

She'd managed to feed multiple times if I knew her, which was why she wasn't draining me overly, but still.

That meant that while I was recovering a little, it was a lot less than I was burning through.

With Oracle, she'd been able to take all her mana pool, as I understood it, and Oracle had in turn used my own. That'd acted like a dam in the river, stopping Sehran from drinking it all. Now, without Oracle's to draw on and limit her, she was having to be careful and focus all the time, lest she take too much.

"Hold on." I pulled out two mana potions from my bag. I downed one, then hesitated, and looked to her. "Question—can you drink these?" I handed the other to her. The familiar sensation washed through me as my reserves refilled, not completely, but enough for what came next.

"I can, but as I don't regenerate mana here, it's not the same." She sighed, before handing it back, and I nodded and downed it as well.

Sehran stood, stretching her wings. "I'm going to take a little tour of the neighborhood," she said with a wicked grin. "I see some very important-looking people trying to organize down there, and you know, I think a few of them would really appreciate a little attention."

"From a spell or two?" I asked, smiling one-sided.

"Well, I don't think we've got the time for me to take a personal hand with them all, and I think taking out the leaders will help. Plus, isn't it better if they focus on me for this bit?"

I waved her off. "Have fun. Just stay in sight and keep them away from me."

As she flew off to rain havoc on the scrambling city leadership, I got up, moved back from the edge and where I could be seen, then sat on the rooftop and closed my eyes, beginning to prepare.

What I was about to do was something that Oracle did regularly, but I'd never attempted myself, beyond that one fuckup with the tower when I nearly sucked it dry and blew myself up.

I was used to doing my bit—the manifestation of imperial power, using it to shatter bonds, break chains, and kill the enslaving bastards while I freed their victims—but to do it in a way that gave them all at least a bit of guidance was going to need a bit more concentration and control than I usually managed.

I focused, drawing on the power that flowed through me, the need, the desire, and the goddamn motherfucking right that I had to do this.

I ruthlessly squashed the little voice that the necromancer bastard had put in the back of my mind with his talk about me not having the right to enforce an imperial claim on these lands, and I damn well did it anyway.

Visualizing the city spread out below and all around me, I could sense the thousands of enslaved souls trapped within its walls. I knew they were there, those I'd already freed and those yet to be free.

I couldn't tell where they were, not like I could those who swore to me. The bonds that tied us all together told me so much. I felt their emotional state, to some degree; I felt their location and a rough sense of who and what they were. If they were human or mer, gnome or goblin, whatever they were doing and if they were safe, scared or injured.

I felt an overwhelming amount from them, but only when I concentrated. Otherwise, I'd be reduced to insensate by the overwhelming input.

No, this wasn't the magical bonds that held them.

Instead, I reached out into the ether, feeling the mana, and the world around us through its interactions with mana.

I felt the fluctuations, but little more. Pushing harder, and searching for the death mana that I knew was there, I found a horrific amount, literally everywhere.

The arena was a massive source of it, of course it was, but reaching out into the city beyond?

I felt it everywhere, so much, rolling out of the limited few sewers, out of the warehouses, buildings here and there, vats… I couldn't tell anymore.

The rising death mana that I'd expected to find wasn't just part of the spectrum here, with life being sucked away by the twisted mess that had been made of the Cradle, which had left death to rise unopposed here in massive quantities.

I couldn't find the people, not like Oracle could. There…there was just too much, so fuck it.

I reached into my bag and pulled out ten of the manastones, setting them around me, and downed another mana potion, before focusing on what I could feel.

The focus for me, as ever, was rage.

Rage at what had been done, rage at how low these fuckers would go. At the bodies I'd seen, both young and old, laid cooling in the sands of the arena, floating through the sewers and that lay huddled in the cells.

The people who were chained up, naked and clearly terrified, probably abused already in all sorts of ways, kept in stocks, cells, or chained to the walls in public fucking places.

The fact that these people, fucking *people* had their lives written off, their worth reduced to a handful of copper—or, if they were lucky, silver and gold— and then they were traded.

Anything that their new masters wanted to do to them was their master's choice. It didn't matter whether they were willing or not, whether they wanted to do whatever, be it household chores, or provide other, darker services.

No, all that mattered was that one had power and the other didn't, and the citizens of Kronk had reveled in it. In the ability to inflict every indignity, every forceful degradation they could on these people. And then, when they'd grown bored of them, they'd sold them to the arenas, so that even their deaths could be an amusement.

Well, no more.

As always, the anger over this, the feeling of wrongness, of something that must be set right, rose in me, and along with it rose the power. The imperial ability that I'd first manifested and that was still the only one that I really understood to any degree.

I understood its power now as well, that it was fed from a constant wellspring of devotion to the empire. That every legionnaire and citizen, as they thought of the empire and all it could be, was basically offering up the equivalent of a tiny prayer each time.

The legionnaires were the most powerful fount of that mana, of course. They wore armor that tied them to the empire, wielded its weapons, marked themselves with tattoos and more. Each of these things served as a focal point, but I felt more than that as well.

As I once again expanded the empire; as I brought people to its safety, they worshipped it, and though I'd never expected or wanted it, they worshipped me.

It'd felt wrong, disgusting at first, that I was basically swapping one form of slavery for another, but no more.

They wanted safety. They wanted security, and they wanted a future that was at least a little better, day by day, from what they had until now. That was the deal that was struck.

I gave them that and more. I gave them a home, and I gave them my blood, sweat, and tears. And in return?

Every single drop of mana that was fed into the empire was slowly becoming part of me as well.

I couldn't use it without the guide rails Amon had unknowingly created for me. Had he not been a part of me before, I could never have tapped into it in the first place. But I had, and now, day by day, I was coming closer to full access.

I was growing to be more of a god than my single bound fragment could justify, and that was only the first step.

Now, as the rage over what had been done to these people reached its peak, I gathered it up.

"HEAR ME, KRONK," I whispered, though my voice rolled across the city from wall to wall and beyond. "I am Jax. Some call me Prince of the Empire, or Maurice, and some call me the gangster of love. Others call me Scion. Lord, duke, or Godslayer… "

I didn't know why I'd added it, just like yelling 'Hadoken' at that fucker back at the tower, it was ingrained into my very bones, not that any of them had gotten the reference, but fuck it. I mentally cursed and soldiered on.

"I am the one who killed Nimon's avatar. I am the one who killed Illoth and banished the drow and her servants from all my territories. I am the ruler of Dravith, overlord, and demigod ascending.

"I am the one who has come to your city, having slaughtered your armies, to free your slaves. I will raise them up, and set them free. I will kill those who trespass against the laws of the empire, and I will rain hellfire down upon those who think to walk past the weak as they are abused.

"My legions were sundered. My people were enslaved. Those I love were taken. No. More. I am here, now, to make this right. You have a single chance. Release your slaves, surrender, and face judgment. If you do not do this, right now, then you forfeit any chance at mercy from me. You deserve all that is to come.

"To the slaves, to those who are weak or strong, those who were forced into servitude, those who even now weep in the darkness, I say this: *come*.

"Come to the arena. I am here. I will smite your enemies and I will erase their forces. I will burn this city from one side to the other. Not one brick will be left standing atop another when I'm done.

"If you have small children, if you believe you are innocent, or you are responsible for those who are—take them from the city. Now. You will not be offered another chance. I have walked your streets and I have seen nothing—bar the slaves—that deserves so much as a second's grace, but I give you this one chance.

"You're hearing my voice already. You'll be given the chance to swear the oath, and to become an imperial citizen in a minute, but first, for all who doubt me? FEEL. MY. POWER."

The power rose to a crescendo and then burst forth in a wave, hurtling outward. The air filled with crackling lightning and pressure waves that were unstoppable, sweeping through the streets and buildings of Kronk. Wherever it touched a slave's bonds, those bonds shattered. And thanks to the mana of the stones around me being fed in as well as the imperial ability, I supercharged it enough that even the physical chains, not just those that were magical, all shattered.

The effect was immediate and catastrophic. All across the city, control collars exploded, shackles crumbled to ash, and enchanted brands, runes, or sigils burned themselves out in magical backlash.

Hundreds, perhaps *thousands* of slave owners or mages, died screaming as their own control devices detonated in their hands or the backlash as the broken enchantments exploded, the feedback burning through them.

I heard the screams, the panic and the howls of disbelieving joy, and hope. Thousands were suddenly freed; their confusion and fear and hope rang out over the city, as bells rang in warning.

I didn't have long, I knew, exposing myself like this. Shouting out to all where I was meant that there were those who couldn't do anything but come for me. Those I'd freed needed advice. They needed their desperate urge to run to be tempered, or they'd just be caught and killed. I reached out again, this time pushing a much more direct message:

"You are free. The empire claims you as its own. Come to the arena for protection. Swear the oath, and never be enslaved again."

I felt it as the message took hold, resonating through the newly liberated minds as one by one, ten by ten, and finally hundreds at a time spoke the words that I shared with them.

"I swear upon pain of death, to faithfully execute all that the Emperor decrees, and that Prince Jax Amon speaks for the empire until his ascension. I swear upon my soul that I shall stand for the Empire when it calls. I shall be strong when the weak need me, generous when the poor are at hand, and merciless when my fellow citizens are threatened. I shall worship the Gods of my fathers, respect my elders, and raise up my children to stand tall.

"I am an Imperial Citizen. I claim the right to call upon the Legion in my hour of need, to hold those that wrong me to justice, and to be avenged if I cannot be saved."

"I swear to obey Prince Jax and those he places over me; I will serve to the best of my ability, speak no lie to him when commanded otherwise, and treat all other citizens as family.

"I will work for the greater good, being a shield to those who need it, a sword to those who deserve it, and a warden to the night."

"I will stand with my family, helping one another to reach the light, until the hour of my death or my lord releases me from my Oath.

"Lastly, I will not be a dick!"

It wasn't a compulsion—I wouldn't replace one form of control with another—but an *invitation*, a beacon in the darkness.

The response was overwhelming. I sensed thousands swearing both outside and below me; hundreds turned toward the arena, beginning to move through the streets.

But I also sensed resistance and fear, pain and terror as guards, soldiers, and Kronk's citizens rallied to stop them, to recapture what they saw as their property.

I opened my eyes, panting slightly from the effort. I pulled two more potions out as I saw my mana bar was flatlined and the stones around me reduced to dust. The headache made it hard to see, and my health bar was down to half.

I downed them, then hit myself with a Complex Healing. Sighing, I clambered to my feet and moved toward the edge again, staring down at the city from at least five levels up.

The city was flaring into full chaos now. Fires flickered to life, burning in a dozen places. The streets were filled with people. Some fled, be that toward the arena or away. Others fought. And there had to be plenty just lost in the confusion.

Sehran landed beside me, her face flushed with excitement. "That got some attention, all right." She smiled. "I saw collars and controllers exploding all over the place. But, I think we need to get Oracle back in the future. You look like shit."

"Thanks, but yeah," I muttered, taking a moment to steady myself. "That took more out of me than I thought, and…"

A crossbow bolt cut the air an inch to the left of my head, swiftly followed by three more, and both Sehran and I started to cast.

She returned fire ten seconds or so later with an Explosive Compression. The spell smashed into the barrier the small group were hiding behind, and reduced it—and them—to a ball of weeping flesh and metal.

For me, I cast a shield around us, realizing just how obvious a target we were, and cursed myself.

"Was it worth it?" Sehran asked, as the spell took hold, and we stared out, picking out more potential targets.

It didn't help that a lot of the streets had only a torch here and there, and the damn clouds were still blocking the stars and moons.

Although I had Darkvision, it wasn't unlimited. When I stared at something directly on the other side of a torch—as the streets were—it was hard to make anything out as it would be with normal eyes.

"Look." I pointed to one of the wider streets below, where small groups of former slaves were already joining up and fighting their way toward the arena, overwhelming the scattered attempts to stop them.

"They're coming," Sehran said with satisfaction. "But so are others." She pointed to where armed groups were forming, moving purposefully through the chaos.

"The city guard?" I asked.

"That, or what's left of the army," she confirmed. "Plus whoever they could round up. They know they're in trouble now."

I stretched, as my strength returned. "Let's give them something else to worry about," I suggested, popping another mana potion and getting ready.

We launched ourselves from the roof, flying over the chaos below. The city was transforming before our eyes, no longer an organized hellhole, but a battlefield where everyone seemed to be out to fight.

There were at least as many people using the confusion to rob each other or settle old scores, as there were who were interested in the slaves.

I saw people standing back to let slaves out of a building, then racing in behind them, already looting.

We couldn't be everywhere, so instead we struck where we were needed most, breaking up formations of guards trying to corral fleeing slaves with a spell or a strike from behind, landing and carving our way through them, eliminating squad leaders attempting to organize resistance, and clearing paths for groups of the newly freed to reach the arena.

Dozens of the former arena slaves joined us, pouring out from the building to help their new companions. Many of them, unlike the guards, had been forced to fight for their lives daily, meaning that when they actually had to fight? They tended to slaughter the less experienced locals.

Here and there were groups that moved with purpose and discipline, using their hard-won fighting skills to protect the weaker, unarmed slaves fleeing toward safety. One of them cried out as I flashed past, landing in the middle of a concentration of soldiers and gutting three of them, before I launched myself back into the air, leaving the survivors reeling and shell-shocked.

"LEGION!"

I spun and stared down. A group of seven sprinted at the guards; they wore shitty armor and were scarred, several of them bleeding, but I felt each and every one of them through the bond.

"Legionnaires!" I bellowed, lifting my naginata high, before casting a circle of frostfire into the middle of the enemy. "Into the circle, trust in the empire!" I roared, before turning as my shield flared, a staccato of arrows slamming into it.

I snarled. Others ran to join the first few archers, and a dozen formed up right behind a group of spearmen. The enemy were finally overcoming their shock and getting organized.

Shame, that.

I still stayed right where they could see me, though, as they peppered me with arrows, my shield flaring all the way to failure.

My favorite trick of making a shield blind the one inside from the world beyond might as well work in reverse. I subvocalized, my fingers writhing, practically ready to snap as I dual cast, dropping my naginata into my bag to free both hands.

As the shield finally popped, and a cheer went up from the archers, thinking they were winning, I was revealed. Unfortunately for them, so was a ball of Pyroclastic Blast hovering above both palms.

Four hundred mana a pop, and fuck me, that was increased to nine hundred in total with the dual cast. I hurled the pair of spells into the right and left of the formation, deliberately letting their fields of effect overlap...

The result was what basically looked like a pair of fireballs unleashed detonations that should be restricted to the heart of volcanoes.

Of the forty or so who had gathered, ready to defend their right to fuck people over and steal their shit, perhaps two survived.

If they'd lived longer, they'd probably have had serious PTSD when it came to minor things like fire, heat, air, life…you know, that kinda shit.

As it was, with almost all their companions reduced to charcoal briquettes and their armor glowing with a cheery, cherry redness, the two almost-survivors were left rolling and screaming with severe burns.

Right up until a group of slaves they'd caught and had been planning to do unspeakable things to, chose that time to pick up a few available weapons and put them out of their misery, despite the waves of heat rolling off them.

I pulled my weapon free again, recast my shield, and then saluted the ragged band, who cheered and raced toward the arena. I turned and flew toward the next fight—drinking a bloody mana potion *again*—and hating the taste.

As the fight went on, I sensed the oaths taking hold. Each freed slave who swore became another citizen of the empire, another soul under my protection. With each oath, where once I'd felt only a binding cord, tying them to me, now I felt a tiny spark of power flow into me, a reminder of the responsibility I was taking on, and a reward, as they individually, silently or overtly, worshipped me.

"Jax!" Sehran called, pointing toward the eastern quarter of the city. "Look!"

Through the smoke and chaos, I saw movement, and this time it was organized…*deliberate*. A column of heavily armored figures marched through the streets, their formation tight and their weapons gleaming in the firelight. They were shorter than humans but broader, their armor dark and heavy, probably heavier than most other races could even lift.

"Deep dwarves," I growled, recognizing them from descriptions and the briefings I'd been given.

The elite of Kronk, the true rulers of this cesspit, finally came out of their enclave to deal with the threat.

"That's him, isn't it?" Sehran asked, her eyes narrowed. "The one with the fragment."

At the head of the column marched a figure whose armor seemed to shimmer with wrongness, the metal itself flowing like liquid in places before snapping back to solid form. His beard was braided with what looked like small bones, and the massive axe he carried radiated with glowing runes that made my eyes hurt to look at it directly.

"Brakuus," I breathed, feeling the pull of the Fragment of Chaos he carried. It called to the Fragment of Order I now held, two opposing forces seeking to neutralize each other.

The deep dwarves marched relentlessly toward the arena, cutting down anyone in their path: slave, guard, citizen—it made no difference to them.

Their discipline was good, their weapons and armor clearly better than anything we'd seen in the city so far.

"What's the plan?" Sehran asked, as the pair of us landed on a rooftop, watching them in the distance.

I watched as Brakuus split his forces with hand signals and barked orders, sending teams to secure key intersections, setting up a perimeter. These weren't mindless thugs; they were trained soldiers following a planned response to the uprising, and they were culling anyone and everyone they saw.

"We let them come," I decided. "Let them commit their forces, spread out. Then we take Brakuus."

"Just like that?"

"Just like that," I confirmed, my eyes never leaving the deep dwarf leader. "He wants the fragment I'm carrying. I can feel it calling to him the same way his calls to me, a sort of…well, a weirdness. He won't be able to resist a direct confrontation."

"And then?"

"And then I take his fragment, drive everyone out of the city, and bind both of them. Then we burn what's left of this city to the ground."

The deep dwarves continued their advance, stomping forward like a tide of iron. Citizens fled before them, and even the newly freed slaves realized it was pointless, turned and ran.

The guards had given up, though here and there, on the rooftops to the sides, I spotted movement—movement that vanished as soon as I looked at it, telling me that this wasn't the same grade of opportunistic scumbag we'd seen so far.

"They're going to reach the arena soon," Sehran observed. "Should we warn Varec and the others?"

"They already know." I pointed to where the arena slaves formed up at the main entrances, weapons ready. "They've been fighting all their lives. They'll hold as long as they need to."

Then, on instinct, I cast a Frostfire Circle of Cleansing, dropping it onto the roof under our feet, and waited. I drank a potion, then another, getting my mana up to full.

"Be ready to feed as much as you need to with this one," I said to Sehran in a low voice. "I'm probably going to need my mana."

"Understood." She nodded. "Um…just as a side note, I've never…"

"You can have one of the deep dwarves." I nodded. "Just not him. He's mine."

"Usually, considering I'm going to be sucking on my dinner, it sounds all sorts of wrong when you say it like that," she quipped. Despite everything, the reminder that she knew just how childish and crude my humor was, to get me with a joke like that, made me laugh.

That got his attention, of course. I mean, hell, I stood on a building a hundred meters ahead, with a succubus by my side and with a fragment of divinity in my possession that had to be screaming at him to come for me, so it wasn't like I wasn't going to be noticed.

Still, I doubted that genuine amusement and seeing me shake my head as I laughed was what he'd expected as he deployed his elites.

Brakuus stopped in the center of the main avenue leading to the arena, his troops forming a semicircle around him. He planted his axe in the ground, the stone cracking beneath its weight, and raised his voice in a challenge that carried even over the chaos of the city.

"Face me, fool!" he screamed, his voice surprisingly deep for his stature. "Face me, or watch my slaves die by the hundreds!"

I rolled my shoulders. An icy rage flared in me as I looked down at the fuckstick that had sent an army to my gates. "Alrighty then; time to end this."

"Be careful," Sehran warned. "That fragment gives him power we can't predict, don't forget."

"Oh, I know," I assured her, readying my naginata. "But he doesn't know what I carry either."

I leapt from the rooftop, using my Soaring Majesty ability to fly, and landed twenty feet from Brakuus in the center of the avenue. Around us, the fighting seemed to pause as all eyes turned to the fight that was coming.

On instinct, I wanted it back behind us, in the open plaza that ringed part of the arena, but that would mean we were closer to the slaves, and that was the last thing that I wanted.

Up close, Brakuus was even more unsettling. His armor didn't just shimmer: parts of it constantly restructured themselves; plates shifted and reformed in ways that defied physics. Either he'd had the fragment and that armor long enough for it to wreak changes in it, or…or it was enchanted all on its own.

His eyes were pools of swirling energy. And when he smiled, his teeth seemed to rearrange themselves in his mouth.

"So," his voice distorted slightly, as if multiple people spoke almost in unison, "you're the one who dares challenge Kronk."

"Kronk," I spat. "A shithole of a city that deserves to burn."

"Chaos is the natural state of all things," Brakuus replied, pulling his axe from the ground with negligent ease. "The strong dominate the weak. Order is a lie, a temporary state that cannot last. All turns to chaos in the end."

"Well, fuck me, you're just full of cheerful thoughts, aren't you?" I asked, circling slowly. "You really believe that, or is that just what you tell yourself to justify the shit you're pulling?"

His eyes narrowed. "You've brought me another fragment." It wasn't a question. "One to bring balance, to end the madness, to make it sing!"

"I've taken my fragments from gods," I told him. "I'll give you one chance. Kneel, give up your fragment, and I'll make this quick. You're nothing special."

He laughed, the sound fracturing into multiple tones. "Then come, Godslayer. Face us. Face the Lords of Chaos. Let us see what you're made of."

Behind him, the deep dwarves raised their weapons, ready to charge. Above, I sensed Sehran circling, waiting for her moment. And all around us, the city of Kronk burned, set alight by those fleeing and looting.

A fitting pyre for the confrontation to come.

Brakuus raised his axe, and the fragment's power flared around him like a dark halo. "Your empire ends, and mine begins! All will worship! All will serve!"

I readied my naginata, feeling the Fragment of Order resonating within me, unbound. It was weaker than his, though still responding to the challenge. "Uh, no," I growled. "I'm gonna fuck you up, you short-arse little turd."

CHAPTER TEN

Brakuus moved like nothing I'd ever seen, the Fragment of Chaos warping reality around him. One moment, he was twenty feet away; the next, he was on me. His axe descended in a blow that would have split me in half if I hadn't already been running both my Mana Overdrive and Hyper Cognition.

This time, though, I didn't limit it to that.

I knew that the fight was going to be hard. However long he'd had the fragment, he'd developed powers from it. Just in case, I activated the first ability that I'd gained from the first of the fragments—well, the only "real" ability so far, though I could feel things from the Fragment of Death already, hints and powers that were growing.

No, I triggered the tether.

The Soul Anchor.

It lashed out, even as I leapt backward. A flaring tether of multi-hued light embedded into the mad dwarf's chest, sinking into his fragment and locking the pair of us together, even as a shield flared to life around us in a dome.

"What is this!" he screeched, hacking at the tether, and achieving slightly less than he would have done, had it been actually made of smoke.

Instead, he staggered about, swaying and shrieking, looking like a fucking stupid drunk, before spinning and eyeing me, just as I'd been considering whether I could stab him in the back while he was distracted.

"You."

"Me?" I wondered who the fuck else he'd been thinking could have done it.

"You want this."

"I…dude, that sounds so wrong."

"My soul."

"Your fragment," I corrected. "The Fragment of Chaos. Give it to me, Brakuus."

"NEVERS!" he shrieked, blurring toward me.

I backed up, cursing as his axe seemed to be everywhere at once. "Fuck this shit!" I snarled, triggering a third ability.

Temporal Fluidity made the world seem to stutter as it activated. Everything slowed down, but my Hyper Cognition helped to make the world flow right. Mana Overdrive doubled and then redoubled as I powered myself to the limit. And then I pulled hard on my dragon armor as well.

I twisted away; the axe cleaved the air where I'd been standing, and I countered with a thrust of my naginata. The blade pierced his armor, but the metal flowed around it like quicksilver, sealing the wound before it could penetrate deeply.

"Fuck," I muttered, dancing back as he pressed the attack, somehow blurring, vanishing from point to point; he appeared to the left, to the right, behind me and above…there for a fraction of a second before swinging his axe in a maddening blur.

I slapped it aside. Using my temporal flow, I simultaneously kicked him in the face, stabbed his left knee, carved a line across his right bicep, and kicked the back of his axe, driving it aside at the last minute. And yet still the little fucker pushed me back. My armor flowed out, my skin allowing it release, and poured across my actual armor, fusing them both into one.

All around us, the battle raged. Deep dwarves clashed with arena slaves and newly freed citizens. Sehran was a blur of motion overhead, diving to tear out throats and blind eyes before soaring back into the safety of the air.

Brakuus laughed, the sound distorting into a chorus of mocking voices. "You understand nothing of the power we wield," he sneered. "Chaos cannot be defeated. We must rule!"

I circled him, watching how the fragment's power manifested. It wasn't just his armor that flowed and shifted; the very ground beneath his feet seemed uncertain of its state—sometimes solid, sometimes seeming to ripple like water.

"Go fuck yourself, little man!" I threw back at him, and launched another attack, this time aiming for his head.

He brought up his axe to block, but at the last moment, I shifted my aim. The naginata's blade slipped past his guard to score a line across his cheek. Blood welled, black and then green, and then seemed to freeze in place before dripping upward, defying gravity.

"More of your blood spilled." I grinned. "How's that chaos helping?"

His eyes narrowed, and the power around him intensified. The air crackled with energy, and reality strained at the seams. "You want chaos?" he shrieked. "I'll show you chaos!"

He slammed his axe into the ground, and the world fractured. The stone beneath us cracked—not in the normal pattern of fractured rock, but in impossible geometries that hurt the eye to follow. From these cracks poured not dust or earth but…*wrongness*. I glimpsed fragments of what might have been, what could be, and worst of all, what should *never* be.

I leapt back, barely avoiding a tendril of something that reached for my leg. Where it touched the ground, the stone transformed: in one spot becoming glass, in another turning to writhing maggots, in a third dissolving into pure light.

"Nice party trick," I called, trying to sound more confident than I felt. Brakuus had either had it long enough that his control was incredible, much better than my own, or…or he had no control over it and was just riding the wave.

He grinned, his teeth rearranging again. "This is but a taste," he hissed. "When I take your fragment and add it to mine, I'll reshape this whole miserable world."

I needed to end this quickly. The longer I ducked and dove, the fucking harder this was going to be, because half the space around me was now…well, it wasn't somewhere I could fight, put it that way.

The longer we fought, the more damage his chaotic power would do to the area, making it impossible for me to avoid the holes in the ground and the fucking glowing maggots and shit.

The deep dwarves were solid and skilled soldiers, but they were outnumbered. And the freed slaves fought with the desperation of those who knew defeat meant death, so there was nothing to lose.

Sehran had organized a group of the more capable fighters into a unit that was methodically picking off the dwarves from the flanks.

But it was all unimportant compared to the confrontation between Brakuus and me. This would end when one of us fell, and not before.

I circled him again, this time feeding power into my naginata, making the blade glow with heat. "You know what chaos fears, Brakuus?" I called, trying to distract him. "It's not order. It's purpose."

"Funny words. Silly words." He snorted, advancing steadily. "Words won't save you."

"I have what you'll never have, you know that? I have purpose." I thought of Oracle, of our child, of everything that had been taken from me. "And that makes me infinitely more dangerous than you." My building rage channeled into action.

I charged, pouring mana into my movement, becoming a blur of speed. Brakuus raised his axe to block, but I wasn't aiming for him, not directly. Instead, I plunged my superheated naginata into one of the cracks he'd created in the ground, driving it deep into the heart of whatever the chaotic shit was, and I pushed the weirdness that I felt surrounding the Fragment of Order out, through the naginata.

The result was instantaneous. Reality shrieked in protest as order met chaos at its source. The cracks flared with blinding light, then sealed themselves, order reasserting itself over the chaotic intrusion.

Brakuus howled in rage and pain, staggering back as his connection to the chaotic energies was severed. For a moment, just a moment, his armor solidified, losing its fluid, shifting quality.

I didn't waste the opportunity. I abandoned my embedded naginata and charged, drawing my daggers in a fluid motion. Before he could recover, I was inside his guard, driving both blades into the gaps of his now-rigid armor: one at the armpit, one at the neck.

Blood—normal, red blood this time—spurted from the wounds. Brakuus gurgled, his eyes wide with shock and fury.

I opened my mouth, drawing deep on my powers and feeling the heat building, the dragon fire...but the fragment's power wasn't finished. Even as he fell to his knees, chaos energy exploded outward from him in a desperate, uncontrolled burst.

I was thrown arse over tit, skidding across the ground. All around us, reality warped. Buildings twisted into impossible shapes. The air itself seemed to solidify in places, becoming crystalline, while elsewhere it thinned to nothing, creating pockets of vacuum. I grabbed at the ground, growling in fury as I stopped myself, feeling a pull from behind me as gravity flipped and tried to tell me that back was down.

Deep dwarves and ex-slaves caught in the effect suffered horrific transformations, even outside of the bubble: limbs elongated, flesh melted into stone, eyes multiplied across their bodies. Those closest to the blast contorted in ways that would haunt my nightmares as they screamed and wailed.

Instead, I triggered my flight ability and rocketed back toward the heart of the chaos, aiming straight for Brakuus. The chaos energies buffeted me, trying to transform me as they had the others. My skin rippled, my bones attempted to rearrange themselves, and my blood turned to fire in my veins.

Instead of concentrating on that, I activated a final ability.

Essence Sight sent the world exploding in all directions as its underlying magical structure was revealed. My mana dropped like a drunken blonde on spring break, but I could see!

I could see everything, and that meant that I could see the path through.

I saw how chaos contaminated and twisted everything, but it was also everywhere and nowhere.

It was a featherlight touch here that had a terrible effect, and it was swamping a cobblestone there with a horrific amount of power, to absolutely no effect.

I didn't need a huge amount of power from my own Fragment of Order.

Not at all. As chaos was literally everywhere, it was weak everywhere. While order? I sheathed myself in it, and I passed through the flickering twisting holes in reality, unharmed.

I crashed into Brakuus with all the force of my abilities, driving us both into the fractured ground. He was barely recognizable now, his body a writhing mass of constantly shifting parts. Only his eyes remained to show the dwarf he had once been.

I pinned him to the floor as he writhed, and grabbing the hilts of the weapons I'd left embedded in him—his skin was like iron and it was only because I'd put so much force into the blows that they'd made it through, never mind the armor—I braced myself.

The pressure in my throat, the need, the pure heat and rage and hatred and love that was creation's greatest weapon, dragon fire, roared out of my mouth and slammed into the little fucker. And where it touched…he simply ceased to be.

It wasn't a case of his own abilities nullifying mine. No, it was that dragon fire was literally just that goddamn hot, and there was fuck all that was walking away from it.

I tracked it down from his face to his chest, then aside, leaving the middle of his chest uninjured as I sensed a change happening there.

Sucking down a deep breath as the last of the fire faded, I slapped my palm against his chest, and felt the Fragment of Chaos as it flowed up from him.

I grabbed it; its power surging through me like acid in my veins. It fought me, trying to corrupt my flesh, my mind, my very soul. The Fragment of Order within me responded, rising to the surface, and turning my body into a war zone as the two opposing forces clashed.

I knew what I had to do. There would never be an opportunity that was more chaotic than the middle of a battle, and especially when the opposing force had just lost its leader.

I formed the Fragment of Chaos in my palm, then rammed it into my heart, into my soul.

I *screamed*, the sound lost in the cacophony of reality tearing itself apart around us. Through the haze of agony, I saw Brakuus's body collapse in on itself. The chaotic energies that had sustained him vanished with the fragment as instead it compressed in around me, and then flared wildly.

Buildings warped. The sky thundered and twisted. Cobbles by my feet, once driven deep into the ground, got up, sprouting legs and running away.

The chaos spread faster now, the area of effect growing with each passing second. I could sense the terror of those caught in its path, feel the fabric of reality straining at the seams as it flared… and then just as quickly, suddenly it was fading, the chaos on all sides ripped from reality and sucked into me, drilling deeper and deeper into my soul, searing into me at every level.

I could feel it, the pain as it twisted and tore at me, as the world shuddered and shivered. As my mind turned inward upon itself, I saw something else as well.

My Essence Sight was still active, and I saw the flooding of all reality around me, as the long-suppressed mana of order, of the right and proper march of the seasons, of all things in order and balance, suddenly flared brighter and higher.

Without the compressing power of chaos, order rose, flaring to levels it'd not reached in millennia. And as soon as I saw that?

I knew it was time.

With the last of my strength, I reached deep within myself, to that place where the Fragment of Order resided. I ripped it free and rammed it to my soul as well, binding it all over again.

The process was instant and excruciating, like having my essence rewritten at the most fundamental level. The fragment's power became truly mine, flowing through me like molten metal being poured into a mold.

Then, with Order and Chaos fully a part of me, I turned them on each other, giving them both a space in my soul and forcing them to seal the other down to a manageable level.

I imposed structure, pattern, meaning onto that which rejected all three. It was like trying to cage a hurricane or give shape to a nightmare, even as I gave freedom to Order, spreading it loose and letting what could be, be.

For one terrible moment, I thought I had failed. The chaos energies redoubled their assault, tearing at my newly ordered essence, seeking to unravel everything I had just become.

Then, suddenly, it yielded. Not gradually, but all at once, as if some critical threshold had been crossed. The Fragment of Chaos stilled in my soul; its jagged edges smoothed, its erratic energies calming under my control.

I have no memory of what happened next. Sehran told me later that the chaotic effects simply…stopped. One moment, reality was unraveling, buildings warping, people transforming; the next, everything snapped back to normal, or as normal as it could, given the damage already done.

She said I rose from the crater wrapped in a corona of light so bright it was visible across the entire city, and that the sight of that much power, combined with the clear death of the former demi-god of Kronk, was all that was needed to finish most of the resistance off.

I had flashes of memory, hours later when I could think again, of walking through the streets of Kronk, feeling the city respond to my presence. To my will.

To my absolute hatred of it.

I remembered the former slaves kneeling as I passed, not in subjugation but in awe. I remembered the remaining deep dwarves throwing down their weapons and fleeing back to their enclave.

Behind us, bare meters from the last in line, the city just.. unraveled. Cobbled stones rolled. Bricks shuddered and mortar shattered, caves fractured and streets tumbled into them.

The pressure of the deeps, where the dwarves fled to, roiled. Increasing hugely to shatter the structures around, and then crumbling like poorly fired clay.

I remembered leading the slaves and the tiny number of innocents who joined me out of the city, onto the hill that Sehran and I had looked down from, raising my hands, and declaring in a voice that carried to every corner of Kronk:

"This land is now imperial territory. Its people are under my protection. Its slaves are freed. Its crimes now face my justice."

Through it all, it was like I hovered behind myself, removed from the situation as I processed it all, and instead my body worked on auto-pilot, leading the people to safety and free of the devastation, as Kronk just... failed.

When I fully regained awareness, I was sitting on the hill, looking down at a fucking crater.

Sehran stood beside me, watching as the sun rose over a scene of utter devastation. Fires still burned in places, and the scars of battle were everywhere. But mostly? It was disturbed earth, shattered stone, and smoke.

"Welcome back," Sehran said softly, apparently seeing and feeling that I was aware again. "How do you feel?"

I took a moment to assess myself. The two fragments within me had settled into an uneasy balance. Order and Chaos coexisted in a state that wasn't quite harmony but wasn't open warfare either, with Death sealing them both in place.

Their power flowed through me, more substantial than before, more integrated with me at a level that I could barely understand.

"Different," I admitted finally. "Stronger. But...stretched thin, somehow."

She nodded, as if this made perfect sense. "You bound two divine fragments in a matter of seconds. I don't know if I'm impressed or scared. But the gods have kept quiet the entire time, and nobody from the other team came to try to fight you, which I think says a lot."

I looked down at my hands. They appeared normal, but I could sense the change in them, in all of me. "What happened after I...after the binding?"

"You happened," she said with a small smile. "You walked through the city like some avenging god, and everything just...changed around you. The fighting stopped. The deep dwarves ran. And most of the city? They just thought it was over, I think. They stayed back and let us leave—well, apart from a single assassin who was terminally stupid. Do you remember that?"

"No?"

"They jumped at you, and before anyone could react, everything in that direction, from the assassin to the buildings and the roads, was gone...just smoking ruin. That got some attention, I can tell you."

I frowned, trying to piece together the fragments of memory. "The people?"

"Safe, most of them. There's a little camp behind us that's full to bursting with former slaves. Varec and the others have done an incredible job organizing them. The citizens who fled the city but haven't joined us are being rounded up for questioning. As for the rest? Well."

She shrugged. "I don't think there's anything left of those who attacked us. It's like the time you grew that forest and brought the dead back outside of Himnel, so much power bursting free that it just...did it."

I nodded, then winced as a wave of exhaustion hit me. Despite the immense power now flowing through me, my physical body was still mostly human, still subject to mortal limitations.

"Maybe get some sleep?" Sehran suggested, seeing the state of me. "The people are okay. They're not going anywhere."

"Oracle is," I reminded her weakly. "Every moment we delay…"

"You won't help her by collapsing," Sehran countered. "A few hours of rest, that's all I'm asking. Then we can figure out our next move."

She was right, of course. I could feel the world rolling as I slumped onto my side, my eyes closing without my say-so. "Fine," I mumbled. "A few hours. But then we move on."

As the world slipped away, the last thing I saw was a familiar shape on the horizon, flying high, but closing on us, her engines driving her toward us at full power.

"Tenandra…" I whispered. A vast wave of relief poured through me at the sight.

"And Jian and all the others," Sehran agreed with a smile on her lips and relief I could feel. "Sleep, boss. We're safe. I promise."

And I fucking did.

CHAPTER ELEVEN

I woke slowly, oh so fucking slowly, as the world dialed in again.

The first thing was sounds, as always. A mumbling as the volume crept up, building from inaudible incredibly slowly as I lay there. Other senses came online as I listened, distantly.

Softness.

Warmth.

Comfort.

There was the feeling of…of sheets. A blanket and a soft bed.

The voices continued to rise, gradually settling at a low buzz of conversation in hushed tones.

The warmth of the bed and the blanket was a wonderful change, especially after so many times waking on the ground in some shithole, still wearing my armor or laid in shitty, scratchy sheets.

No, these were familiar.

Comfortable, in a way that suggested cool water, or maybe…silk.

The drow's gloom silk spider sheets.

As soon as that twigged for me, so did other details.

I was laid in a bed, feeling those familiar sheets on my skin, and that meant that I wasn't in my armor. I'd been stripped, laid into a bed, and one that had familiar sheets. Oracle?

No.

She was *gone*.

That last recollection burned the fog from my mind, and I went from drifting, half aware and half in slumber, into fully active, sitting up quickly as the entire room came into focus, and the conversations were sharply cut off.

I blinked, staring around at a familiar cabin, one walled with teak and oak, the melding of two radically different ships into one Frankenstein's monster.

I felt them all, even as I saw them—the rest of the team.

I was surrounded in seconds as everyone crowded in, not even caring about the fact that I was in bed, and presumably naked apart from a sheet. No, they were there. They were hugging me and there were so many tears, rough voices, and so much swearing that it was insane.

The first few minutes were a blur, as everyone from Lydia to Grizz to Tang to Giint to Yen and Arrin, and even that goddamn bard Ronin hugged me.

They were all there. Even those who weren't in the room, I could feel were approaching.

I felt Tenandra all around me, and the door burst open just as things calmed slightly to let her—in her physical form—as well as Jian and Sehran in.

That just started it all up all over. Just the feeling of them all being there, the knowledge that they were back, was incredible.

Then it was Bane's turn. The big fucker stepped in and hugged me tight for a few seconds.

"You all right?" His voice was a low thrum that was almost too low for anyone else to hear.

"No," I admitted. "But I will be."

"We're here for you, my brother," he said softly, before breaking free and shoving me backward.

The edge of the bed caught the back of my legs and sent me tumbling into it. The entire bed creaked under the sudden impact before the sheet was tossed over me unceremoniously.

"Now put that away—nobody needs to be reminded how pathetic a specimen of manhood you are," he finished, the hum of amusement in his voice as I glared up at the big mer.

Others approaching—others who were bound to me, I could feel—but for a few seconds, I just looked at him.

He cocked his head to one side, clearly waiting.

"He really is broken," he said eventually. "What, no abuse?"

"Honestly, at this point, responding to a joke about my manhood in comparison to your sex life would be like kicking a puppy." I sighed and laid back, dragging the blanket across myself to give the illusion, at least, of modesty, as others paused at the still open door, and were then waved in.

It was Flux, Ame, Lio, and Cheena, which was a surprise, though a welcome one—mostly, Ame was still a fucking nightmare at times with her vicious temper and lack of anything like a filter—but behind them were a handful of legionnaires. And at the front of them? Their optio, Hennen.

It was fucking old friends' week, all right. Seeing any of them was wonderful, but honestly, where yesterday, to see one of them—any one of them—would have been incredible—it was having my team there, it was knowing that I wasn't alone anymore that made me shake with relief.

Sehran had been with me all that time, and it was a bit shitty to say that I was alone in being with her, and honestly, I could probably throw a rock in a deserted forest at midnight and still hit someone who would give their back teeth for some quality time "alone" with her.

Instead, it was that of all the squad, I was probably the *least* close to her and Yen. That wasn't because they were women, as I knew some dickbag would think.

I was pretty close with Lydia; it was just that we thought completely differently so much of the time. With Yen, it was a hundred percent duty and she was so serious; with Sehran, she constantly teased me.

Now, don't get me wrong, I loved being teased usually. The problem was that I damn well knew that if I said something like "God, I really need a blowjob," then even though she was with Jian, and was committed to that actual relationship, there was still a good fifty-fifty chance that she'd just decide it'd make me happy and drop to her knees to do it.

I loved her as a friend, but I felt like I always needed to watch what I said, and I was actually relieved in more ways than one that the others were back with me now, because as least she'd be getting her "fix" from Jian again.

I realized that there'd be a notification from her in the mix waiting as well, and I blinked as dozens of notifications instantly popped up.

The first to pop up was the kill one, and *shiiiiiit*, it just kept going!

I dismissed it, promising myself I'd look at it later, then found the one that I knew was going to be there.

Your bonded slave Sehran requests her freedom to bind to another…do you wish to release her?

Yes/No

I hit the Yes option, and she grinned, spinning to Jian, who'd clearly been waiting. I saw the way they both sighed, relaxing slightly and then kissed. I relaxed as well, knowing that I had my full manapool back.

"What 'ell 'appened, Jax!" Lydia growled. "Fuck's sake, you know 'ow long it took t'get 'ere?"

"Yeah." I snorted, shaking my head. I waved both Flux and his people in, and Hennen, before nodding my thanks as the big optio closed the door in the faces of the rest of the legionnaires.

I got that they wanted to hear it from me, I did, but right now, I just couldn't face even more randoms.

"Did Sehran fill you in?" I asked the room at large.

"More or less, yes," Bane grated out. "You've been doing some very stupid things, though we're not exactly surprised."

"Yeah, well, sue me," I muttered. "You're all okay though? Nothing went too badly wrong after…"

The door opened again, and this time it was to admit a legionnaire carrying…Bob!

"Bob?" I gasped, staring at the massive skull that the legionnaire, grinning, carried. "Holy shit, dude. What the hell?"

"We couldn't repair 'im," Lydia explained as he was set down on a table nearby. "Without yer, 'e's bin like this since t'prax, an' t'bones that made up t'rest of 'im, they just crumbled."

"Ah, shit, I'm sorry, buddy." I shook my head. "I bet that's been shit."

"*It…was.*" His voice appeared in my mind like the leaden sound of fallen slabs. "*Rebuild me.*"

"I will," I assured him. "Do we have the rest of his body?" I looked around.

"Nope." Grizz sighed, as he gestured vaguely toward the back wall and down. "We brought a load of bones, but they're all just random ones. His own just collapsed into dust, boss."

"Fuck's sake." I sighed. "Okay, uh, Legionnaire?" I directed it to the man who'd carried Bob in.

"Yes, my prince?" He stiffened and crashed his fist to his chest in salute.

"Bring the bones we have to the deck, and I'll try and build him a new body after this, please."

"Now," Hennen growled to him as he hesitated.

The legionnaire, clearly hoping to listen in and be included, colored, braced and then raced out of the door.

"Okay, what do you know?" I asked the room at large.

"You got yourself lost, and we were all forced to come to find you, boy," Ame replied before anyone else could. "Even from here, I can sense the damage done to you, and little of it is physical."

"Well, you're not wrong." I nodded. "I'm very fucked up, but that's only half the story. I know Sehran probably told you, but that thing that we found underground, Malthus, is a spin-off colony of a very old, very fucked-up creature called Xenefier. You got that, right?" I looked around the room to a variety of nods.

"Great, that'll simplify things then. That's the fucker that took Oracle. It's old, powerful, and a fucking nightmare to kill. It's killed and eaten gods, as far as we know, and although I don't think it can use the fragments it must have gained access to, because it's something like the antithesis to mana… Shit."

"What?" Grizz asked, when I fell silent, my mind racing.

"Fragments." I groaned, rubbing at my face and sucking down a deep breath before starting that conversation, as my mind worked to link up the connections I'd just made. "All right, look, I'm ascending—that's part of the plan here, that I ascend to godhood. Basically, when I killed Nimon, I stole a fraction of His power, and in binding it, I started myself on the path to ascension. I told you all that before, right?"

"Dammit," Bane growled. "We leave him alone for five minutes and he's trying to become a god."

"Heh, well, if it's any consolation, this started when you were there, not since, remember?"

"Yeah, but I hoped you'd gain some sense."

"Well, it wasn't exactly a big focus for me. The empire was. But once I ended up here…" I deliberately left out *saving your fucking asses.* "I needed all the power I could get. I fought Illoth, and claimed ten percent of Her power as well."

"So, you're twenty percent to a god now?" Grizz frowned at me.

"Yes and no," I replied. "I'm more powerful than I was, but the way that it works, don't ask me why, is that I need ten fragments first and then I'll completely ascend and most of my power will unlock at that point. As it is, I have three fragments—Death, Chaos, and Order. Once I bind seven more, I'll ascend. Depending on the mix of fragments and how powerful they are, I'll reach— hopefully—the same level as a minor god like that dickhead Baphomet, or Illoth."

"You mean Lolly the Turd Spider?" Tang asked, and I grinned.

"YES!" I pointed at him and nodded firmly. "Yes, fuck's sake, thank you. Let's keep that as her name—I keep accidentally reverting."

"So, yer stole a fragment from Lolly an' one from t'God of Death, but yer said three. T'chaos one is from t'city that's no here anymore?" Lydia asked.

"Yeah." I nodded. "Shit, about that…we're still here, I mean, by the city?"

"I've landed next to the hill and stayed there," Tenandra said calmly, though still smiling. "We were unsure as to plans with regard to the refugees and freshly sworn."

"Shit, the people." I groaned. "Okay, we need to deal with them, but long story short, the gods keep trying to kill Xenefier, and like I said, Xenefier is the shitbag that stole Oracle and our baby. It seems to think when the baby is born, it can then take over and possess it, and through its link to magic and the empire, it'll be able to then use magic itself and destroy basically everything.

"Wherever it is, there's something that prevents the gods from going there, and so the plan, at this point anyway, is that I get more fragments of divinity, go to wherever the fucker is to free Oracle, and bind the last fragment when it tries to stop me.

"The hope is that wherever it is, there'll have to be a place that it can take Oracle to and that the baby can survive, so it's not going to be the center of the realm or ten miles down in a lava flow. Wherever it is, it'll be there, ready to possess them, and when I get there, the gods will help me kill it. What just occurred to me is that there are other fragments out there. Our plan relies on me gathering up enough that I can ascend, but what I'd not considered is that if he can possess my child and get access to mana, what it can do then is bind any fragments of divinity it has.

"If it killed the ancient gods, dozens of them before it was driven off, it might have taken captured fragments with it. In which case, as soon as the baby is possessed, it'll then be feeding itself those fragments. That could send it leapfrogging in power through the ranks that any of the current gods can reach and really make it the overgod."

"So, what I'm hearing is, that as usual, boy, you've just discovered that you have no time to achieve the things you must, and yet none but you are capable of it, is this so?" Ame asked, and I winced.

"Yeah, more or less."

"And you must save all of reality?"

"Yeah."

"And you must become a god, a literal one?"

"Yeah."

"Then it is time you grew up."

"Ye— What?" I blinked.

"You heard me. A leader does not lay in bed, telling stories. He dresses, he leads, he deals with his problems or he delegates them. He cannot simply push it aside to deal with later. Understand?"

"Yeah, I do," I growled. "Fuck's sake, Ame, I've literally been doing this. I've got a territory here that's now been cleansed of the drow, and…wait."

I pulled the notifications up again, searching and quickly finding that there still wasn't one for claiming the area, which meant that the group around the temple either hadn't heard that I'd won yet, or they'd not kept their word.

I was betting it was just that they'd not heard, but still. That meant that I couldn't purge the area of the drow, and that I couldn't expand my territory. Fuck's sake.

"Right, we need to get to the Cradle," I rumbled. "Once we're there, we can claim this territory—I think—and then when those people swear to me, we're covered for a lot. We burn any trace of Xenefier out, we load up the ship here with manastones, and we show the gnomes what a real airship looks like.

"Then we take them and everyone here back to Gaij, and the team there can work on integrating them and the territory, while we get out there and start slaughtering the enemy, claiming more fragments and I try to figure out some godly powers."

"He makes it all sound so easy." Grizz grinned at me. "Damn, it's good to have you back, boss."

I looked at him, then around at the rest of the group, and frowned. "All right, why do you all look like shit?" It was true. "I mean it—you all look like you've done nothing but hit the training field and eat really healthy. I don't think there's a single one of you who's not lost fat and gained muscle, but you look exhausted. What the hell were you doing on the way here?"

"Training," Flux said.

"To make sure we could kick your ass again no matter what crazy shit you'd pulled," Lio added, and I pointed at her without looking.

"I can sense you there, so I guess that means I've got an advantage at last then!"

"Keep telling yourself that." She snorted, and I went on, looking around the rest of the group.

"All right, so you're telling me that you all spent what, two months doing nothing but eating healthy and training, all day, every day?"

"Essentially," Flux confirmed. "Though many of us attempted to balance our time with study as well, and—"

"Fucking hell." I cut him off, rubbing at my face. "Tenandra, is that right? All they did was work out, train, and study?"

"They also spent a highly unhealthy amount of time in self-recrimination and arguing over who bore responsibility for your situation," she replied helpfully.

"Well, fuck me." I groaned.

"I tried—you kept saying no," Sehran pointed out, and I glared at her.

"Jian, this is an order…you ready?"

"Yes, boss." He straightened.

"When we're done here, you and Tenandra are to take Sehran aside and the pair of you do your absolute best to wear that fucker out. She's made my life hell with teasing, and I want her punished in the best possible way."

"Yes, boss!" He grinned so widely that the top of his head was in danger of coming off.

"Right, now that's out of the way, let's make this clear. Who's in charge here?" I growled, looking around.

"You," Flux said. The others echoed it, though it looked like that admission cost Ame something.

"Excellent. And do any of you get to give me orders?" I asked. "Think about it carefully."

"On t'training field, a bit, ah guess, but not really," Lydia admitted.

"Great. Last question. Did any of you deliberately get captured or help the enemy capture others onboard the prax?"

"No!" That response came from everyone, and was clear.

"Then it was none of your fucking faults, then, was it," I growled. "Fuck's sake, *I* led the mission, *I* gave the orders, and you all suffered for it. We could have lost people, but we were damn lucky in that we only lost one, and that was *my fault.*

"Unlike all of you, I knew what Earth weapons were like and I led you into that meat grinder." I glared around. "What happened here was I didn't defend my love hard enough, or she'd be here still. I need to live with that. But my real failing wasn't a lack of effort; it was that I didn't fucking *evolve*. I didn't grow or change, while even the sentient gloop monster from the land that time fuckin' forgot managed that. It assessed how I fought, how I reacted and moved, and it fucking learned to combat me.

"It threw enough bodies at me it held me back because I couldn't use any of my more powerful weapons and abilities without hurting her. It controlled the battlefield, it controlled the engagement, and it goddamn won. Well, no more! I have to evolve, and that means so do all of you."

I paused, looking around, and then sighed. "Look, I get it…genuinely, I do. I'm not blaming myself for Oracle being taken. I'm blaming myself for not evolving, because if I'd done that, if I'd learned and grown, I wouldn't have been who that shit fought last time. It holds the blame for taking her, and it holds the blame for all the deaths, not me.

"The blame I hold is for the one thing that was under my control. I didn't change. I didn't improve enough. Now, I'm working on that—I am, and so will all of you. But, the truth is, right here and now, that none of you were responsible for me ending up here. I made the decision I did, and we're where we are now. What we need to do now is deal with it, so this is what's happening;"

I looked around at the slightly embarrassed and ashamed looks on most of their faces, as well as the blatant "get the fuck on with it, dude; I've got better things to do" one on Jian's face.

"We're going to make a plan for these people. We're going to go to the Cradle and sort that place out. And then we—and that means me and all of you fucking lunatics—are going to conquer the shit out of this entire, goddamn continent."

I glared at Ame as she opened her mouth to speak, and I went on as if she'd not tried to interrupt.

"On top of that, I'm going to find each and every goddamn other demigod I can, and I'm either going to recruit them or I'm going to kill them. When I finally find Oracle, I'm going to do what the gods fucking failed to do over millennia— I'm going to kill Xenefier. I'm going to ascend to godhood. And then I'm gonna rule the fucking empire as a living god.

"One that'll damn well have Oracle as my wife, and my fucking conscience because, right now, I have neither her nor anything to stop me from burning this goddamn continent to ash! I literally destroyed a shithole of a city yesterday. Not trashed it. Not took it over.

"I reduced it to a handful of fucking bricks, and I killed thousands. *Tens* of thousands. And you know what I'll do tomorrow if I find another city like that? I'll do the exact goddamn same thing again.

"I thought Dravith was bad, but fuck me with an electric boogaloo, this place is worse. If I have to hold the entire goddamn land under the sea until it learns to behave itself or the infection is purged…I WILL!"

I realized I was back on the ragged edge, and probably wasn't making much sense.

"You don't know what I've had to do, and you don't know what I'll do again, so please, I'm fucking begging you, help me. Help me cure this place of the fucking infection of Xenefier, of the disease that is the nobility, and let's see what can grow in its place. Let's make the land a home for these people again. You all need to rest, and…and so do I," I finished.

"Boy, you're as broken as I've ever seen you," Ame said. "But the one thing that I've never had a doubt about is that you love your people. So, answer me this: if we help you, will you save more than you kill? Will tomorrow be better than today?"

"It will," I said quietly. "That's why I'm doing this. Hell, it *has* to be in comparison to what's coming. Xenefier will kill everything, everyone, and the gods themselves can barely sense it exists. Whatever it truly is, it's taken tens of thousands of years after each battle with the gods to grow powerful enough to challenge them again. This time, it'd barely had a chance to blink since the last time it was defeated.

"That's why we have a chance. That's why we have the chance to end this. The gods who are here now are weaker than the ones of the past, but give them time to grow powerful again and they'll reach just as high. The problem is that over that time, their enemy grows as well.

"Where we stand now, either Xenefier is going to find a solution that enables it to leapfrog thousands of years of both sides growing in strength, by killing my baby and possessing its body, or we kill it.

"We kill it when it's weak enough that we genuinely can face it. We fight it, and we stand a chance not only to win the war, forever, but in doing so we rescue Oracle and the baby. That's what I need from you all. To understand that we need to do this, that the next few weeks and maybe months are going to be hard and possibly horrific.

"We're going to fly like we never have before, we're going to be fighting enemies who have spent centuries growing like cancers, and we're going to be dropping into cities that have never seen an airship before. We're going to cheat, and sneak, and conquer the shit out of this continent in short order. We're going to teach these people that honor and sacrifice isn't something that other people should die for. That it's not a loophole to manipulate so that they get what they want.

"No, we're going to teach these fucks that actions have consequences. And while I'm at it? I'm gonna fuck that useless, tiny-testiculed, mince for brains bull Baphomet up."

The rumble of thunder that came from me saying that was immediate.

"You heard me, fuckface! I'm gonna fuck you right up! You took a side! You did this, and when I'm finished with you, you're gonna wish that Darakin had ended it all for you, because I'mma make what he did seem like fucking *foreplay*!" I was on my feet again, this time at the window and it was thrown wide as I screamed up at the darkening sky.

Thunder rolled, but absolutely nothing else was done. The idiot apparently decided that now wasn't the time to start something, be that because there was an intervention in place—still didn't understand that, but hey—or because he was sufficiently wounded still after Darakin defeated him.

Either way, though, it was done: I was clear on where I stood, and the others were there, with a chance to tell me to go fuck myself or not.

Unfortunately…I was also standing at the window, a massive bay window with those floor-to-ceiling glass walls that were all the rage back in the age of sail.

Think the captain's quarters in a galleon, where they could be thrown wide to let the breeze in—the real captain's quarters were above and were Jian's, Sehran's, and Tenandra's, but still—that was the look of the place, and it would have been great except for one thing.

The windows came from my knees to the ceiling, and I was standing in the middle, with them thrown wide, yelling at the sky, while naked.

And there were a LOT of people camping around the landed ship.

Fuck's sake.

CHAPTER TWELVE

"You know, just once, I'd like to be somewhere that the entire population doesn't think he's a sexual degenerate," I heard Bane casually say from behind me, and, not sure what else I could do, I forced a smile, waved at the nice people, and then closed the windows again.

"They don't think that in Gaij." I glowered at him, before snatching the blanket back up and covering myself.

"In a city ruled by the succubai?" He snorted disbelievingly.

"Well, yeah, all right, but they've not all seen me naked," I snapped.

"Actually…" Sehran opened her mouth, and I glared at her, then looked to Jian.

"Fuck's sake, little help here, dude? Go! Get her out of here so she doesn't spread any more wildly accurate tales about me!"

"Yes, boss!" He grabbed his girlfriend and spun her around, hurrying her toward the door while she laughed, and Tenandra grinned after the pair.

"Very well. It's good to have you back, Jax. Now, if you'll excuse me? I think they need a little help…" She nodded in the direction of the retreating pair, and I waved her off.

"Go—go on, get. Most of you can bugger off, go rest up and relax a bit, but before you go, thank you. You all came here to help, and I love you for it. All of you. I owe you."

"You owe us. Giint want to be a god too." The mad little bastard spoke up.

"Fuck to the no," I replied flatly. "Though I'll offer you a compromise."

"Giint listening."

"I'll not beat you to death and I'll arrange for some other gnomes and goblins for you to play with. They're trying to build an airship."

"Okay, sounds fun." The mad little bastard shrugged. "Giint can teach."

"Gods, that scares me so much," I muttered. "Please tell me he hasn't managed to find a girlfriend while I've been away."

"Nope, we're keeping him away from the ladies." Grizz grinned. "Last thing the realm needs is little Giints."

"Good man!" I let out a relieved sigh. "Right, you buggers all go, sort yourselves out and get some rest. I need…" I looked around, then shrugged. "Lydia, Yen, Flux, Ame, and Hennen here. The rest of you can go cause trouble somewhere else."

"Oh, thank God," Tang muttered in a voice that carried. "Bane, it's your turn— I'm getting out of here before he starts swinging his cock around again."

"Dammit," Bane growled. "Hey, Lio, Cheena…any chance…?"

"Nope." Cheena was heading to the door already.

"Fuck no," agreed Lio. "I've seen enough that I'm gonna have nightmares as it is."

"Go on, get out." I grinned around, then sighed and gestured to a chest of drawers attached to the wall next to Lydia. "Please tell me I have some clothes in there?"

"Yer do," she said after checking. "Gloom silk pants and…"

"Oh, thank fuck—gimmie." I gestured, and she grinned, pulling some underclothes out and tossing them over, before a pair of trousers followed.

I dressed quickly, even as I spoke.

"Okay, seriously, thank you all for coming, and sorry for being naked, *again*."

Normally I'd not have apologized—they were in my room, after all, and I'd obviously not been intending to flash them—but Ame was here, and she wasn't one of the usual group in that way.

"So, what do you need from us before you sleep again, boy?" She settled into a small chair and watched me as, now decent, I stood and stretched, feeling muscles creaking and popping.

"We need to make a plan for the next few days," I said. "First and foremost, we need to deal with the refugees. They swore to the empire and that makes them my problem, but my plan overall…" I trailed off, and Ame nodded firmly.

"You planned to save them and to kill their lord but nothing beyond, is that correct?"

"Yeah, basically. Sounds stupid when you say it like that, though."

"That's because it *was* stupid," she growled. "Very well. There are, according to Tenandra and the leaders of the refugees, some nine thousand, seven hundred or so of them. Around a quarter are former arena slaves, nearly two hundred are legionnaires, and the rest are either captured skilled workers and artisans, household or pleasure slaves.

"Of those who had the chance, roughly half grabbed anything they could, presumably having long had plans and desires to escape. That means that we have enough food, or so it's believed, for around five days for everyone, if we are willing to enforce a reasonable control over their meals, which, given the current situation, shouldn't be hard to do."

She looked at me, waiting, and I nodded.

"That sounds good. Does it include any food aboard ship?" I asked, and she nodded.

"Beyond a two-week supply of food reserved for the entire ship's company, the rest has been added in and that is helping to stretch the food to this point. I suggest foraging parties as well. But given the local land, I doubt there is much to be gained from that.

"As such, the decision to destroy first and then plan second was an incredibly stupid one on your behalf, though from Sehran's information, I understand it. Now we are left to feed and protect thousands, and to do that properly, we need you to make it clear what the end goal is. Are these people to settle here and rebuild the city? To migrate? To travel with us or to be directed to a location and then checked in upon later?"

She looked at me in question, and I made myself think about it carefully.

"I think we need to be realistic," I said after a brief pause. "First of all, the best place for them is probably the city of Gaij. But if we march the largest concentration of people out of the territory, and considering we don't even know for sure if this is the main population center for the territory, we're likely to lose it.

"What we need to do first of all is get to the Cradle, the location we were at before we came here, which is a few days' flight to the northeast, less probably for Tenandra.

"Once we're there, I need to have the locals there swear to me. Hopefully they all will, but the mer didn't seem that interested and—"

"You found a pod of mer?" Ame interrupted.

"And yeah, we found mer." I smiled suddenly as two problems canceled each other out. "And for interrupting me, you get to be ambassador to them. They have a runecrafter of their own, so you'll be able to speak to them on a level they'll understand—and I don't swim that well." I shrugged.

"So, we go there, hopefully the wisps and the…whatever they are…the *locals* all either swear to me or remain neutral, and then we're in a position to claim the territory. Once that's done, we need to figure out a plan for the area, get a decent up-to-date map in place, and we can figure this shit out."

"You haven't found a map yet?" Yen frowned. "I've heard of technologies being forgotten in places, but…"

"Nah, they've got maps," I admitted. "I've seen them. The problem is that the old imperial territories and the current cities aren't the same. We're not sure how much it'll effect it moving forward, but the Cradle was a major landmark in the past, and this area of the old empire was fairly well spread with population.

"That means that with me now having wiped out the biggest concentration of enemies in the area, and then we claim the Cradle, that should be enough to claim the territory…I *hope*.

"If it is, then we give the people a choice. They can stay in the Cradle, it's certainly big enough, and hopefully the locals there will be welcoming. And if not, we leave a small number and march the rest back to Gaij.

"While we do that, we need to be checking out the other possible centers of power in the territory. Once it's declared for us, we can trace the lines and we'll know of any cities or settlements we need to hit, but it's pretty sparse and grim here," I finished.

"Sehran explained what 'appened t'land. Yer think it'll recover?" Lydia asked.

"Definitely." I nodded. "Without the raiders of Kronk and their general shitty attitude around, and the semi-sentient fucking mana collector that was draining the place to death all dealt with there's nothing here, so if we get the sections of Sonra that still want to migrate—did she tell you about them?" I looked around, getting nods.

"Great. Well, with them under our control as well, we just move the migration pattern across. It'll be a chore to feed them all, but it's doable. And with the environmental mages marching behind them, and the land no longer being drained of life, it'll recover in short order." I paused, thinking, then nodded.

"All right, Tenandra, sorry to interrupt what I'm sure is a lot more fun than this conversation, but I need some advice. You there?" I asked, looking to the ceiling.

"Always," the wisp assured me, stepping back into the room through the wall, as if it were a door, as she reformed her body entirely from mana for the conversation.

"Okay, thank you. So, how much of the food these people need would you be able to carry, and how long would it take you to make a trip from here to Gaij?" I asked.

She moved over to stand next to me and created a map on the small table in my room, gesturing to it as she spoke. "Can you confirm Gaij's location, please? We distantly flew past a city but my data may be inaccurate."

"Here." I checked the location on my map and tapped the great tower she had marked. "It's still there."

"Excellent. From here or from the Cradle, please?"

"Uh, from the Cradle." I sighed. "And then to return to it as well."

"About half a day from here to the Cradle at full speed, and then two days from the Cradle to Gaij, with approximately two and a half to three to return. There are constant high winds from the east that will slow me slightly."

"So roughly six days for the round trip." I grumbled, "Shit, I need these people fed before then."

"I would suggest that we take the weakest and eldest of the group with us, travel to the Cradle and they take up residence there, as well as calling here on the return trip with any food that we are permitted to harvest," she said. "Beyond that, there is one other option that may offer a lifeline."

"Go," I encouraged.

"Sehran stated that the crops of the area—the limited amount that they were able to raise locally to Kronk—represented only a fraction of what must have been required to keep the city fed. Perhaps there is a regular shipment of food that one of the refugees would be aware of?"

I grinned. "Yes!" I nodded, before looking around the room. "Yen, can you take care of that? You and I also need to speak soon about the laws and so on, but that's a conversation that can wait—the food can't. Oh, and pass the word for—" I broke off. "How many can we fit aboard?" I asked Tenandra.

"Approximately two hundred and fifty of the weakest, should we make the most of every space."

"Then we need them all made aware and moving." I nodded.

"I'll take care of it, boss. Good to have you back." She saluted, then left the room.

I grinned, glad to have my team back and to know that when she said it would be done, that meant it was as good as done already.

"Right, now that's taken care of, what you'll do as well, Tenandra, is not just take the food you need and come back—I want you to take Sehran and Jian with you. Yes, it's partly a reward for her helping me and having my back, but mainly it's because she'll be able to speak directly to the Mistress of Gaij.

"I want her to arrange for a caravan to be put together, enough food for several months for the refugees, plus tents, clothing, all that kind of stuff, and seeds to set up a large enough farm to feed at least ten thousand. It'll also need a significant escort, and whatever they'll need.

"They can set off as quickly as possible and head straight for the Cradle. Then, once they've made it there, whoever doesn't want to stay at the Cradle from here, we can use the caravans to move back to Gaij, until we come up with a plan for the territory anyway."

"Aye, sounds doable." Lydia grunted. "Flux, any issues yer seein'?"

"Several," he said calmly. "Do we have a secure place at the Cradle that we can hold?"

"Yes and no." I shrugged. "We have a fully rebuilt temple to the gods there, a massive one, and that's going to be the center of whatever the Cradle becomes. The gods are literally watching over the place, but I need to find a way to kill anything that sets foot, claw, or tentacle inside it that's not sworn to us.

"The problem isn't having somewhere defensible to hold…it's more that the current locals are fifty-fifty about serving the empire. They're gonna have some serious issues around the temple—it's their home. Most were tortured and puppeted around it by Xenefier.

"I just rocked up, and we were attacked by them—which is part of the reason they're feeling a bit more guilty about shit right now and are more likely to listen to us—and they're scared of me personally. They offered to sacrifice a portion of their population to serve us, in the hope we'd fuck off. Instead, we rebuilt the temple, and now the gods are there.

"They want access to the gods and they want our protection, but the gods have done us a solid and said that basically they'll only deal with them if they join us. I carried them along with an offer to sign up to join the empire only if I smashed Kronk, and then we did that pretty much overnight. They're going to be in shock. I need to consolidate things, and get them sworn in before they have the chance to change their minds.

"Showing up with ten thousand refugees and eating all the food they have isn't going to endear us to them. We need to be careful, and make it clear this is a short-term thing, but still move a significant portion into the area to help anchor the territory.

"Lastly, the ground is almost certainly going to have some traces of Xenefier in it. I don't see the fucker just leaving as it pretended, so I need to set off a kind of general area of effect spell that's going to heal our people when they cross the lines, but keep that fucker out," I explained.

"There may be a way to do this, using my runes, but it will require a power source, one not easily exhausted, and significant time," Ame replied.

"We can do that." I nodded. "There's a collector there and a shitload of manastones. If you can tap into them, you can power anything you need."

"Child's play," she assured me.

I nodded. "Great. Then, in that case, that's your job once you've dealt with the local mer. As much as I'd like to stay with the people here while we march across, that's not going to happen. I need to be at the Cradle, and frankly, I can't afford the time. So, Hennen?" I turned to him, and he saluted.

"I can take my squad and lead them, boss." He smiled. "If you're going to be at the Cradle anyway, I can feel the bond to you, so…"

"I'll ask Jenae to issue you a q—"

"Got it." He held a hand up as it apparently appeared for him. "And it even comes with a marker to head to—ain't that convenient?"

"Thank you." I sighed, casting a glance upward, before going on. "Right, if that's the refugees sorted, more or less, then we're going to set off for the Cradle as soon as everything here is sorted out.

"I'll need to offer the oath again, as there's going to be a load of people who never swore, I have no doubt, but then we'll use a few of the manastones I have to power a circle of cleansing." I looked around at the waiting faces.

"It's the best way we found to weed out anyone who hasn't sworn the oath. We have everyone march through the circle—it heals them, which is nice, but it also burns anyone who's not sworn, so they can be booted out, and we don't have people who we're feeding and protecting who aren't ours."

"Brutal, but effective," Flux said simply. "As spymaster, I approve. But personally, I wish there was a better way."

"I know," I said softly. "Honestly, I hate that we need to do this shit, but with all the spies, assassins, and more we kept coming across, it's what we have to do.

"Also, side note, there was a guild that Sehran and I guessed was a guild of assassins in the city. We saw a few examples of them being brutal fucks, but nothing else. Now, it might be that they just haven't got a contract on me yet, and so they're staying small and quiet until they do, or they were still in the city and are already all dead or just aren't interested. But personally, I doubt that'll last long, considering I just smashed their city to dust."

"Then I'll view it as you're at precisely the same risk that I always do, and we'll keep you under constant watch." Flux let a thrum of amusement filter through his words, and I shook my head in disgust.

"Dammit, why did I miss you guys again?" I muttered.

"Because you know you need to be kept under constant supervision or you tend to destroy cities," Ame said flatly. "That is something we need to discuss, boy, because the mana required to do what you did here is incredible. How? How did you do such a thing?"

"I bound two fragments of divine power," I admitted. "A Fragment of Chaos…" I saw the way she stiffened at that. "And a Fragment of Order. Opposing powers that cancel each other out in some ways, and yet give me their gifts still. Don't ask me how—they just do."

"And that you bound such specific fragments, was this blind luck?" she continued; I looked at her and shook my head slightly. She hesitated, then inclined her head in recognition that this wasn't a detail to press, and instead moved on.

"Very well. I presume you intend to bind more fragments soon from what you said, so a simple question—are you to hunt those who hold such fragments or is there another method? Are they something that will be left in ruins, lost to the ages, or secured in vaults?"

"No." I winced as the thought of all the vaults and so on that I destroyed in Kronk suddenly came to mind. "Dammit, I never looted that place properly."

"You know this how?"

I sighed, knowing what she was referring to. "Because they're fragments of the power of the gods." I shrugged. "The current gods aren't going to leave fragments of the predecessors' power just lying around."

"And yet they leave those who have claimed such prizes to wander and claim more?"

"Yes and no. There are reasons." I gave her another look. I left unsaid it was because the gods would be essentially broken and weakened after claiming them for a while. If the observer knew that I knew that, they might wonder why, and I wasn't sure whether I was supposed to know.

"Very well. So, with the refugees taken care of—loosely—and a plan in place for the next few days, what else must be dealt with right now?" she asked when I left it at that.

I paused, then shrugged. "Nothing I can think of."

"Then I suggest Tenandra assists you to offer an oath to the people, we assure them that there is a plan by speaking to the leaders of their groups, and then you rest, boy. Divine you might be, but you're still exhausted, and what I sense feels like you need a week's rest in peaceful waters."

"I'd take it as well, if I didn't have a thousand things to do," I admitted. "Truthfully, just the time we're losing by arranging food for the refugees is going to be a horrific loss, considering that we need to be picking out the next target and moving already."

"But the other option is we allow them to starve," Ame said. "And that you will not do, understand me, boy? They have chosen to follow you at your invitation after you destroyed the life they knew. That makes you responsible for them."

"I know," I said. "All right, I need my armor—where the hell is it, by the way?" I glanced around.

"There's a trio of armorers working on it." Tenandra spoke up, still seeming a little distracted and distant. "It's two rooms over, and one floor down, with a legionnaire on the door. But one of the armorers is a legionnaire as well, and as such, I viewed it safe."

"What are they doing?" I asked curiously.

"Attempting to repair it to pristine condition, though they are commenting that the gloss appears resistant to their efforts."

"Shit, no—I can fix it. It's magic. They probably can't damage it, but they're just wasting their time. Ask them to bring it here please." I sighed. "Is my under armor…?"

"Cleaned and repaired. Do you wish that brought as well?"

"Gods yes, you have no idea how bad it'd be to wear that fucker without the padding." I snorted. "Okay, once I'm dressed, we can go sort things out. But for now? I think I need to look at my notifications."

"Why don't we give you a few minutes?" Flux suggested diplomatically, and the others agreed, all save Lydia.

"Yer all go," she said. "Ah need a word."

The others left quickly, and I didn't even get the chance to say anything, before Bane stood and filed out as well.

"What's up?" I asked her.

She waited until the others were gone, before speaking.

"Yer all right?" She dropped the hard-bitten act as soon as the others were out of the room and it was just the two of us. "Ah mean it—are yer okay?"

"Honestly?" I sighed. "No. No, I'm fucking not, Lydia. I can feel it, like an itch, you know? In the back of my mind, constantly pointing at the clock and counting down how many hours and minutes we have until the baby is born and Xenefier can destroy them both.

"It's made worse because I don't fucking know if that's going to be half an hour from now or six years away. We just don't fucking know, which means I have to move as fast as I can. I could see a notification at any second that my baby and Oracle are dead, and it's fucking game over for basically all of life."

I stared out the windows for a few seconds, mastering my breathing, fighting down the sudden surge of terror and heartache, the fear that I could lose them all. My eyes filled with tears.

"Fuck's sake," I muttered roughly, dashing the back of my hand across my eyes and sucking down a deep, ragged breath. "No, I'm not okay, but I will be."

"Come 'ere, yer big idiot," Lydia growled, stepping in close.

I turned around and she grabbed me, dragging me into a hug that threatened to break me, to send me sobbing brokenheartedly on her shoulder, as my friend, my protector, held me tight.

<u>CHAPTER THIRTEEN</u>

It was nearly an hour later when I was finally dressed again—not because I'd been stripping for shits and giggles, but because I needed time to get into my armor and get control of myself again.

That meant that by the time I was outside, the ship was already a hive of activity as legionnaires were moving around, food was being arranged, and the weapons were being organized.

The people were being drawn up in groups around the ship. The legionnaires and the dozens of ex-professional soldiers we'd found in the slaves' ranks were doing wonders as they essentially formed people up into cohorts, each of a thousand, and organized them to make it easier for management.

The legionnaires who had been rescued were overjoyed to meet their distant cousins from Dravith, and Hennen, already by dint of being a centurion and having spent some time as interim tribune of the Narkolt Legion, took charge of them effortlessly.

I wondered at one point, why a man who was so well trained and experienced was on my ship in a mere optio's slot, when realistically, he massively outranked everyone by experience alone, never mind his official roles, and then it clicked.

Lydia was still growing into her role; she was doing well, but she was still learning the ropes, as it were. So, having a more experienced soldier along, but who was the same rank? Perfect for her. Thinking about it, I had no doubt that the hands of Romanus and Restun had been involved.

A legionnaire who could do whatever role he was needed for, probably up to and including that of primus, was a hell of a loss to the legion back home. But here? Just when I and Lydia were likely to need him?

Looking out over the well-regimented ranks and hearing the easy and confident way he directed the majority into place, I was just damn thankful.

I was also more thankful than I could ever say that my squad was back with me. That was also why I could never say it, because that wasn't how these things were done. Instead, I coughed, then sighed.

"Dammit, I'd gotten so used to breathing clean air that I wasn't ready for the chemical warfare division to return," I said in a low voice that carried to my people. "You're standing behind me to my left, aren't you Grizz, with Giint by your side?"

"We're here, boss," the big legionnaire assured me.

"What him say?" Giint asked.

"He said you smell." Yen snorted.

"Me not smell." The little gnome was apparently backsliding in his phrasing again, and I glanced at Lydia in question.

She was by my side—she'd pretty much maintained being less than five meters from me since I'd woken up—and the pair of us now stood atop the ship's main deck, staring out over the thousands of people forming up.

The sheer number of people who stared, pointed, and talked constantly was getting intimidating. That's why I'd started with a little joke, but I also knew it wasn't entirely for me.

Her armor was impressive, but the most obvious thing that people were pointing out had to be her wings.

The first Valkyrie in six hundred or so years was an imposing sight. Her gleaming white wings reflected the sunlight and her white-blonde hair only added to it. She was incredible, and although the people watching had no idea of the nerves that being before so many people raised in her, the fact was, she was the stuff of legends. That was even before the people considered that she was the personal guard of the imperial prince.

"'E spent most o' t'trip when ah couldn't find 'im and make 'im work out, off 'is tits on drugs," Lydia growled under her breath. "'E somehow smuggled two crates o' 'is little treats aboard, an' that's just what ah could find. How 'ell 'e's still breathin' is beyond me."

"And the rest of the time?" I asked. "When you could find him, I mean?"

"Trainin' and work on t'ship. Tenandra said 'e was useful," she admitted. "Mean's we didn't see much o' 'im, an' when we did, like I said, 'e was mostly off 'is tits."

"So, he's barely spoken to anyone and just hid in the dark places of the ship, off his face on drugs and working." I sighed. "Ah well, at least he's alive, I guess, and so are all of you."

She'd brought me up to date on a lot of little details while I was getting ready and dealing with my own emotional baggage, one of which was that Grizz had blamed himself for me being captured, and for whatever reason, Thomas had publicly done so as well.

That'd sent the big legionnaire into a spiral of depression, one that he'd been self-medicating with booze, and Yen had needed to step in. Even though, as a knight of the legion, he had to outrank her, he'd had enough subsurface guilt and awareness that what he was doing was wrong, that when she'd ordered him around, his oaths had still triggered.

I guessed that was why—and the fact that he loved and respected her—he'd been reduced to being utterly driven into training for the entire trip, creating a wedge between the couple, as neither knew how to deal with the situation.

Now, with me ordering them all to accept that it was my fault—which they didn't really believe but had to accept to some degree as I was in authority over them—they were free to try to patch things up.

Bob was marching around, trying to get used to his new body. But he wasn't happy with it, and I knew I'd need to completely rebuild him as soon as we could get some decent bones again, because what the team had brought with them was basically a load of "regular" bones, and Bob was so far beyond them that it was insane.

Bane was nearby—I could sense them all through the bond—and at the front of the people below me, were the leaders of the various groups that Yen had already gathered.

Tang was off to the side and below, stealthed by the gangplank leading up to where I stood. The rest of the group were spread out, with only Tenandra, Sehran, and Jian missing.

As I had that thought, the door to the control center and captain's cabin opened, and Jian and his partners walked out. Sehran and Jian held hands, beaming, and Tenandra marched along calmly, despite the small, satisfied smile she wore as well.

"Mission accomplished," Sehran whispered, as she practically limped up to me, deliberately bumping me with her elbow.

"Glad to hear it." I snorted, before shooting Jian a wink, knowing that if he'd done the deed so right that a succubus was walking like John Wayne, then he'd indeed done well.

"I'm ready to assist, if I may?" Tenandra asked me formally, and I nodded, holding a hand out. She reached out, taking my hand and focused, as I approved a request to permit her access to my mana.

As soon as that was done, she smiled, then nodded to me that she was ready, released my hand, and stepped back, as did the others.

"Citizens of the empire!" I called out, my voice carrying. I waited as the conversations wound down and people turned, attention building.

"All hail Prince Jax!" A roar suddenly rose from the legionnaires. Ten of them at the foot of the ramp up to me crashed their swords against shields as one, and silenced the few who thought it was fine to keep talking.

"Well, yes, thank you, Legionnaires." I smiled, before hopping up to stand on the railing that ran around the outside of the ship's deck, making it easier for everyone to see me.

"Citizens of the empire, welcome to the beginning of the rest of your lives! Today, you all make a choice. That includes those who have sworn to me already, and those who have chosen not to.

"First, if you have not chosen to follow me, understand that I wish you no ill will, but you must leave, and do so now. When I finish speaking, preparations will begin for the long march. As part of that, I will do my best to heal you all. Most have been fully healed already by the same magic that I used to free you, but those who have not, or who had injuries sustained after that point, I will heal again.

"The spell that we use for this is one you may have seen already, but it requires courage to face. The circle that I cast will heal all those it recognizes as a friend. The definition is simple: if you are my ally, or sworn to me, then it will heal you. If not, the flames will attack.

"This sounds brutal, I know, but the simple truth is that I am a warrior, and my spells are designed to aid in battle. When I use this in a fight, it heals my allies and burns my enemies. What could be better than that?

"As such, it means that if you cross the border of the spell without swearing to me, then you will be seen, not as someone who means me no harm and is simply passing through, but as an enemy. The magic is simple, and cannot be made to choose.

"The reason we ask that all of you pass through it is also simple. Our enemies count among their number creatures that can infect and take over our allies. This spell will burn them out, freeing those who may have been infected without their knowing.

"Lastly, you all know of the drow. Those sneaky fuckers are thrown out of my territories by divine magic, but nothing stops others with similar skills and desires from sneaking into our ranks. Nothing but this spell, and we are currently outside those safe lands.

"As such, it will be cast over and over as you travel, when you sleep, and when you are injured. You will be healed, you will be protected, and you will be fed. But again, understand this: I cannot—and will not—make the spells choose. Instead, should you not swear to me, and then still attempt to follow along, then you will be harmed. Understand that this is not my choice to make—it is yours, and you must accept that risk.

"So, I ask again, if you have not sworn, leave, or, if you instead wish to swear, then I ask that you take the oath with your brothers and sisters now…" As I said the words, I felt the draw on my mana, as Tenandra siphoned mana from me, mixed in mana she drew from the ship's reserves and then pushed out the oath, as a servant of the empire.

Well over a thousand more people, who presumably hadn't taken the oath before out of fear or uncertainty, now took it up.

"For those who have simply mouthed the words, hoping that it will be enough, please understand that to leave here with us, you will walk through the circle. Last chance."

There was a brief silence, and then hesitantly, a good two hundred more on top of those who'd already joined started to recite the oath again.

I waited until it was all done. I'd also taken note of the feelings of the bond, before I took a deep breath and went on.

"Now that that is done…" I paused, giving anyone that last chance to leave. The feelings I was getting weren't changing, so I pointed to the ground before me, as the legion—who'd been prewarned—split.

They moved into formation. Two stood at the right-hand side of the first large group, at the front, and the others spread out so that two stood at the corners of the first group of a thousand.

They were formed into squares, and as I cast the first circle on the ground before the group, the leaders of the refugees—including Varec, the former arena slave—lead the way into the circle.

He'd seen and been healed by it before, and was confident—outwardly, at least—as he marched across the line.

The circle was a large one, twenty meters across, and he and the others strode through, stepping over the glowing runes that ringed the outer edge. Flames leapt to them, landing on feet and legs, flowing up across their bodies, tasting them, verifying them, and with one of the group, healing a minor sprain, before flowing free.

The first two lines of the refugees were next, striding through, led by the legionnaires, as a handful, then hundreds to marched through the spell.

It didn't take long for the first of the gathered people, being led toward the circle, to break and run.

They were gathered up by arena fighters and former soldiers who were ready and waiting, and were escorted to the side. More and more joined them as the minutes passed. Soon it changed from one or two people, to entire families; then, all at once, the exodus started.

Dozens of people turned and pushed free of the second battalion in line, and more were dispatched to deal with them. We'd discussed this when I'd first come out on deck with the local leaders, making the point that we couldn't feed those unwilling to contribute, and we couldn't give warning after warning to people. When asked if we could just accept these people, I'd refused, pointing out that in order to flush out spies, thieves, and murderers, we were going to be using the spell repeatedly.

That meant that now was the final chance for many people, and we'd be checking the groups of runners to find out whether they were just scared of the circles—it looked pretty terrifying, after all—or whether we'd just caught spies.

Ninety percent would be scared people who had simply been after a free meal, I was sure, but still, that other ten percent was the target.

Regardless, over the next hour, I went through a dozen more potions and ten small manastones, and Tenandra drained another quarter of her reserves as well, before it was done.

We'd not have caught all of them—I wasn't stupid; after all, all they had to do was stealth and stay out of sight to escape a lot of these kind of tests, which was why Tang was where he was. He stayed close to the bottom of the gangplank, so that if anyone tried to get past him, he'd sense them.

Bane was close to me, as was Ame. Cheena and Flux roamed the camp, along with Lio.

By the time it was done, I'd come up with a dozen different possible flavors to add to the goddamn mix for the mana potions, and I was gloomily certain that they'd all cause issues with the recipe. But I was still determined to try it.

Fuck the constant flavor of mint that I was subjected to. How the hell had I once liked that horrible taste?

Still, it was done, and the important thing was that now, with the nearly three hundred people who'd been carved out of the mass, we were ready to get to work.

"Okay, everyone, for those who needed healing, I hope you're feeling better now. As you all saw, many people weren't willing or able to swear the oaths. For some, there will be a valid reason, but considering the situation and the intention behind the oath—that you are all safe from one another—I'm sure you're all feeling a little relieved that those people have been caught and removed.

"For anyone who found a way around it, be aware—the spells will be cast on a regular basis along the march and around cooking pots and so on, so you better be ready to go hungry!"

I let that one hang there for a long minute before I went on.

"So, again, thank you all for your trust, and now it's time to get to work! Obviously, this area…well, let's be clear. It's a shithole! Nobody wants to live here. It might have been fine for the deep dwarves—for the rest of us, it's anything but.

"What will be happening now is that the weakest and most in need of aid will be brought aboard my ship, and we will be setting off for our next destination. I'm afraid I can't share it at the moment—there might be some little birds mixed into the group, after all—but you'll find out where soon.

"What's important at this point is that there is food already being arranged, as well as somewhere to rest and recuperate. But it's a long walk, I'm afraid. On foot, it will take days. Again, I can't be more specific yet, but you will be protected en route, and once you get there, there's plenty of food and water waiting for you.

"You'll make camp, and as we protect you there, my airship will be flying to another of the cities that has sworn to me, gathering up all that you'll need, and will head to meet us. Some will then put down roots and start building a life—a new one, under the gaze of the gods, as well as their protection.

"Others will instead return with the caravan and be granted a home in the city, ready to restart their lives. The choice will be yours. But between now and then, please take the time and think about what you're looking for from the empire. We'd rather you be happy doing a job that interests you, than stuck hating your lives, and that's a genuine thing, because when you hate what you do all day, you tend to give minimum effort. When you love it? It shows.

"You'll be offered training, opportunities, and respect. But please, remember, those you meet will be citizens as well. What they have, they've earned—and regardless of their species, you WILL treat them with respect, understand?" I glared out and saw the looks of confusion on many a face, but fuck it. I wasn't having them be dicks to people like Greg and Cleq.

"Lastly, I'm sorry to say that for the next week or two until the caravan reaches us, we're all going to be on short rations—two meals a day, I believe, morning and night—but as soon as we have more food for you, you'll get it. Thank you all." With that, I turned and strode away, a ragged cheer rising here and there from the group.

"Well, look on the bright side, boss…" Grizz smiled widely.

"Go on," I growled, knowing what was coming.

"No matter how far you rise, no matter how incredibly powerful you become, there's always something new to learn. One day, if you really, really try, you might be merely crap at rousing speeches."

"I hate you."

"We love you too, boss." He grinned unrepentantly at me.

"Lydia, does that fucker owe me any push-ups?" I asked hopefully.

"Nope."

"Pity."

"Sucks to be you!" He chortled.

"Fortunately, 'e owes me some." The Valkyrie glanced over at the big legionnaire.

"What? No, I don't!" Grizz retorted desperately.

"Oh, ah'm sure you do." She smiled. "Fifty, ah think it was? Or am ah forgetting somethin'?" she mused. "Was it fifty push-ups, or was it that leaf that ah lost this morning on t'far side of camp? You know, the one that if yer bring me a leaf that *isn't* t'one that ah lost, yer get fifty push-ups anyway?"

"You've been spending time with Restun," I approved, as Grizz stared at her, mouth opened in horror.

"Which was it, Grizz?" She quirked an eyebrow in question at him.

"Fifty push-ups." He sighed mournfully, but I could see from the faint twitch pulling at the edges of his lips that it was all a game.

There was no way that Lydia would actually genuinely abuse her position, and to a man like Grizz, fifty push-ups was barely a warm-up. It was all just fucking with each other, and the group were past masters at that by now.

"So, when do we leave?" Tenandra stepped up to my side as I led the way into the control room, pausing and looking around at the massive upgrades that had come about since she first took over the ship.

"As soon as the people are aboard and the food is off," I replied. "Any minute that can be shaved off is a minute we need, I'm sorry to say."

"Then let's get moving."

I sat and looked around the cabin, before sighing. "As much as I'd love to relax for a bit, we damn well need potions—there's never enough, so, I know where I'll be for the next few hours."

CHAPTER FOURTEEN

The alchemy lab that Tenandra had set aside for me was already feeling like home, even if it was, well, a little fuckin' cramped, considering how many people were in it when I got to it.

I stared at the, oh, seven or eight people, mainly in their sixties, who'd been bunking in the room, before turning to Tang, who leaned against the wall nearby, watching me.

"You've got two options," I said to him. "Take these people to my quarters and make sure they don't damage anything, especially of Oracle's, or you can join me and learn some alchemy."

"Well, sounds like you all get a cabin upgrade!" he called into the room, grinning widely. "Come on, grandfathers and grandmothers, time to move to a little roomier spot. Believe me, the last thing you want is to be around the smells that are going to be coming out of this room."

I counted down, and on three out of five, he went on as predicted.

"I mean it! And the smells will only get worse if he starts doing alchemy, so come on, let's move it or lose it, people!" He beamed around, and I gave him the finger.

Within a handful of minutes, they were all gone. Lydia and the others—apart from Bane—were firmly told to go somewhere else and let me work. I finally closed the door, knowing that although Bane was definitely there—crouching in the corner—he was also a reassuring addition, not a distraction.

The familiar scents of herbs and reagents filled the cramped space as I worked. My hands moved through the practiced motions of grinding, measuring, and mixing, determined to replenish my damn potion stash. Frankly, as much as I wanted to rest and just, well, catch up with everyone, I also knew that I wasn't ready for it.

I'd almost broken down when Lydia started talking to me about it, and I damn well knew the others would do the same. They'd want to discuss it, to show they supported me and they were there for me. That was the last fucking thing I could handle right now.

So instead, I was here.

Mixing more fucking potions.

"I won't ask if you're all right. I know you're not. But I'm here," Bane said quietly. "We don't need to talk, but know this—I'm not letting you get more than ten meters from me from now on."

"I'm… I'll be fine," I corrected.

"Maybe," he grunted disbelievingly. "How about we find some people to hurt badly and then see how you feel after?"

"Gods, yes," I muttered, closing my eyes and sighing in relief that Bane understood me so well.

That was all that was said, and it really damn well helped me.

I'd been at it for about an hour when a knock at the door interrupted my concentration. I looked up from the mortar and pestle, blinking away the focus that came with the work.

"Come in," I called, setting down my tools.

The door opened to reveal Yen, and behind her stood a woman I didn't recognize. She was maybe in her forties, with the kind of weathered hands that spoke of years of hard work. Her hair was pulled back in a practical bun, and despite the clean clothes she'd been given, she still had that slightly hunched posture of someone who'd spent too long being careful not to draw attention.

"My prince, this is Marta." Yen showed a little more formality than was normal. "I've just found out she's an alchemist when we were organizing the refugees, and thought you might want to meet her."

I straightened, blinking as a genuine distraction, and one that could really help, appeared. "An alchemist? Yes, damn good job, Yen. Thank you. Uh, Marta? Come in, please."

Marta stepped into the little shipboard lab hesitantly, but I saw the way her eyes immediately jumped from one thing to another: the kit that I had set up, the ingredients laid out, the half-finished mana potion cooling on the end, waiting for the final straining and distillation process.

Professional curiosity looked to be overriding whatever nervousness she felt for the first few seconds, then she ducked her head and stood silently, clearly waiting for an order.

"You know your way around a lab," I said quietly.

"Fifteen years, my lord," she replied in a low voice. "Though not...not by choice."

"The slavers had you making potions?"

"Yes, my prince."

"Okay, well, what kind of potions? Please, Marta, relax. I'm not going to hurt you. I'm curious...I want to know what you know."

She nodded, swallowing hard. "Buffing potions, mostly. Strength, Agility, Stamina. Mostly just things to make their gladiators fight longer and harder. And then other things, things to drug the ones they didn't want to win the fight." She looked ashamed, and bitter. "Never really made any healing potions or mana, though. The ingredients cost too much to waste on slaves."

I gestured to the stool across from me. "Well, you're not a slave anymore. You're a citizen of the empire, and if you want to keep practicing alchemy, we could use the help. But it's your choice now. I mean it."

I looked at her for a few seconds before going on when she hesitated. "Look, for me? I'm a journeyman, but pretty much all I do these days is healing and poisons, or much more often, fucking mana potions." I sighed.

"Seriously, I hate the taste of the damn things, I use them that frequently. And yet, if I try to substitute other ingredients? It fucks with it. It's always that goddamn mint!"

She sat slowly, as if stunned that I understood enough to know that adding something to change the flavor of the end product would also—minor detail—change the fucking effect. "I...I'd like that, my lord. It's the only skill I have besides..." She trailed off, and I didn't push.

"That's a hell of a relief. And it's just Jax, or boss if you really need a title when we're working together like this. 'My lord' makes me feel like I should be wearing a powdered wig or something. Outside? Yeah, fine, it needs to happen…the titles, not the wig, I mean…"

I forced myself to stop rambling and took a deep breath.

That got a small smile from her. "Yes, my… Jax."

"So, buffing potions." I pulled out a fresh notebook. "I've been focused mainly on mana and health potions, with some poison work on the side, like I said. Never really had time to branch into buffs. What can you teach me?"

Her eyes lit up, the first actual sign of interest from her. "Oh, there's so much. Basic strength enhancement is simple enough…bull's blood, powdered iron, and essence of giant's toe fungus—that's a mushroom, despite the name—but the real art is in the proportions and the brewing temperature…"

The next several hours flew by. Marta was a natural teacher once she got over her initial nervousness, and I frantically took notes as she walked me through recipe after recipe. We started with the basics—a simple strength potion that would give a temporary boost to physical power, though it took a little experimenting because did we have bull's blood? Of course we damn well didn't. What kind of a lunatic keeps bulls for their blood?

"The key," she explained as we worked, side by side, "is the crystallization process. See how the mixture turns cloudy? That's the iron bonding with the essence of Garn that we extracted from the monk's leaf plant. Now we add the fungus…just a pinch, too much and it becomes a poison. Have you seen the…"

I observed as she demonstrated, then tried it myself. My first attempt produced something that looked more like mud than a potion, but Marta just smiled.

"Better than my first try. I accidentally made a poison that made them shit themselves until they passed out instead. The guards were really unhappy with that one."

"Seriously? I did the same thing! One of my poisons does that…well, and a few other things. But the look on the target's face when it kicked in?"

We both laughed at that, and I realized it was probably the first time she'd been able to laugh about any part of her slavery. Admittedly, I left out the whole "I poisoned a goddess with it" bit because that shit sounds a bit ridiculous, but that's not the point.

"Excellent!" I grinned, holding up the successfully completed potion on the third try, making a note of the details. "What's next?"

Strength Buff		Further Description *Yes/No*	
Details:		This is a basic strength enhancement potion, granting a 2 point increase for 73 seconds.	
Rarity:	Magical:	Durability:	Potency:
Common	Yes	100/100	2/10

"Speed enhancement," Marta said, already pulling out new ingredients. "This one's trickier. You need quicksilver essence—just a drop, but I saw you had that in the list—along with feverfew and wind-touched sage."

"Quicksilver? Isn't that poisonous?"

"Everything's poisonous in the wrong dose," she said with the confidence of someone who knew their craft. "The art is knowing exactly how much won't kill whoever you give it to."

We worked through speed potions, perception enhancers, and even a basic berserker draught that Marta warned me about extensively.

"Never, ever let anyone drink more than one dose in a day," she said seriously. "I saw what happened when they forced gladiators to double-dose. The rage doesn't stop, and eventually their hearts just…" She shuddered.

I made notes about all the warnings, remembering my own experiences with pushing too hard. The notification about poison mastery from my experiments made me want to share the methods I'd found, but also, right now I was learning shit that I'd totally missed, and I really needed that.

Instead, I let myself just…learn. Losing myself in the process as the hours went past. Honestly, I enjoyed it as much as I could.

"These are incredible," I said as we took a brief break, both of us sipping water and stretching out the kinks from hunching over the workbench. "I can see how the squad can use them, and I sometimes forget that mana and health potions aren't everything."

"Your squad?" Marta asked curiously.

"My personal team. We tend to get into…interesting situations. Every advantage helps."

"You mean you get us in the shit as easily as you breathe," Bane corrected.

She almost shit herself, having no clue he was in the room with us.

"Don't worry." I sighed. "He's not a pervert—well, not totally—just a bodyguard who doesn't understand boundaries," I quipped.

"I understand them, but what kind of a bodyguard would I be if I left you in here with a strange woman?"

"See?" I asked her. "Boundaries."

"Uh…" She looked at me uncertainly, and I sighed, then had to explain that it really was the alchemy that I was interested in, and that it was just a joke between friends.

She nodded nervously. "I could teach you combination potions too. Things that enhance multiple attributes but for shorter durations. The guards used to call them 'oh shit' potions, for when everything went wrong at once."

"Now that's sounding fun." I grinned. "Show me."

We were deep into the intricacies of multi-effect brewing, including shit that had never occurred to me about "complementary mixtures," when Tenandra's voice echoed through the makeshift lab, making the poor woman shit herself all over again, though thankfully not physically as far as I knew.

"Jax, I'm sorry for interrupting, but we're approaching the Cradle. Do you have any specific directions?"

I glanced at Marta, who was already cleaning up. "We'll continue this later?"

"Of course, my lord. Whenever you need me," she said, and I could tell she meant it, which made me sigh.

"Seriously, Marta, I want you to think about what you know and what you'd like to do. In the empire, you're valued for your contribution. We need potions, desperately, but if you want to close the door on this side of your life, and become, I don't know, a farmer? That's fine. I'd ask that you help to train up a replacement who can help make potions, but you can walk away from this if it's not what you want to do."

"I…I will think on it," she answered. "But I think I'd rather continue, just, with a little payment for the work, if that's not too much to ask?"

"You'll be paid," I assured her. "For now, I'll need to get things in place, but all of that will come. Right now, out here, there's not much I can do, because there's no economy and so on, but here." I gave her two gold coins and a handful of silver and copper I plucked from my bag. "Take this so you've had something as payment, and we'll sort it out later, all right?"

I left her blinking in shock and made my way up to the deck, squinting at the afternoon sunlight after hours in the relatively dim lab. The first thing I noticed was the crowd gathered at the rail. Refugees and crew alike stared ahead and around us with various degrees of awe and apparently naked terror as some of them hadn't realized that we were going to be flying and were now clinging to the railing for dear life.

How the hell else a literal ship had ended up outside their recently destroyed city and what they thought was going to happen, well, I chose not to ask.

The Cradle of Feshcan'un was spread out before us, a valley of impossible green surrounded by the bleached bones of the deadlands. Even from here, I could see the restored temple gleaming in the sunlight, its waters cascading in carefully designed channels that sparkled like silver threads through the greenery.

"It's beautiful," someone whispered nearby.

"Why is it so green?" another asked. "Everything else is dead."

I didn't answer, not wanting to get into the complicated history of mana collectors and centuries of fucking up. Instead, I strolled straight past them, let them just enjoy the sight of something beautiful after the hell they'd been through.

I made it to the control room and checked in, glancing around quickly to make sure the trio of usual suspects were clothed and not engaging in horizontal refreshment.

Seeing Tenandra and Jian were standing and sitting at the pilot's desk, respectively, I went in.

"How's it looking?" I asked.

"Highly enjoyable," Tenandra declared seriously. "Do you wish us to land next to the temple?"

"Yeah, sounds good and… Wait." I frowned. "Why are you looking like that?" I asked Jian, who looked both terrified and distracted.

"No reason!" He whimpered.

"You look like…" I closed my eyes and covered my face with one hand. "Sehran's under the desk, isn't she?"

"I…"

"Fuck's sake!" I groaned. "Tenandra, just…make sure we don't crash!" I ordered over my shoulder, as I slammed the door shut behind me on my way out.

Making my way to the foredeck, I found Grizz and Yen leaning on the railing, enjoying the breeze. I stepped up alongside them, nodding and smiling at Ronin, who'd been surprisingly quiet so far.

Usually, he was constantly pestering me to tell him what I'd been doing or tales of my past on Earth. But clearly, he'd gotten that this wasn't a good time, which I was thankful for. Instead, he was merrily strumming a tune that was both soothing and uplifting.

I didn't know how the hell he did it, but that bloody music was truly magical.

That thought, of course, made me think of the harp, and I quickly banished that thought, before focusing on the forest ahead and below.

As we descended, I could see figures gathering, mostly the gnomes I'd left working on their blimp-like attempt at an airship, which now looked even more ramshackle next to Tenandra. They were jumping and pointing, clearly excited. I also spotted movement near the temple and the lake, locals coming to see what was approaching.

"There." Lydia pointed. "Ah guess that's t'legionnaires yer left."

Sure enough, the small group of legionnaires sprinted over from the temple toward our obvious landing spot, armed and ready to fight, if need be.

Tenandra settled to the ground with barely a bump, her landing legs perfectly absorbing the impact. Almost immediately, organized chaos broke out as a handful of refugees tried to run off the ship, while others tried to run belowdecks and still more milled about uncertainly, with my people moving to help maintain order.

I made my way down the gangplank to find absolute mayhem waiting. The gnomes had surrounded their distant kin who'd been aboard the ship both as crew, and those who had been freshly freed from Kronk—a pair of ancient gnomes who looked like they might drop off at any second—and they all chattered at a mad speed, while none of them bothered to listen to the other's responses.

I caught Giint in the middle of it all. From the reverential looks the local gnomes gave him, word had already spread about his divine connection. Or was it just that the mad bastard was half again the size of them and had already punched someone?

"Wrong!" one of the local gnomes was saying. "No wood has enough coefficient to—"

"Giint show you coefficient of shut up." Giint produced a wrench from somewhere and waved it threateningly. "Ship flies. Ship carries many people. Math work whether tiny brain understand or not."

"Wood principles—"

"Principles?" Giint laughed, a sound like grinding gears. "Giint blessed by Svetu! God of Craft and Making! You think him not know better than you?"

That shut them up real quick, though I could see them muttering among themselves, probably trying to figure out how to argue with divine mandate when enforced and claimed by a mad bastard.

"Giint," I called out. "Play nice. We need their help."

"Giint being nice!" he protested. "Only threaten with small wrench! For now… Giint have bigger wrench when needed."

I shook my head and moved on, spotting Vislen approaching with the other legionnaires I'd left behind. On seeing me, he relaxed a little, helped along, I was willing to bet, the moment they saw their distant kin from Dravith.

There was a moment of formality as Tang appeared before them, dressed in legion gear and clearly a fucking badass; then Grizz was there, backing him up, and Yen, before a shouted "they're all right; I know them" was yelled out at me—and a circle of frostfire just to be sure; I wasn't an idiot, after all—and then it was like they'd known one another forever.

The circle not burning them proved for everyone that they were all sworn to me, and that was enough.

"Prince," Vislen said after the initial reunion, snapping back to attention. "The area's been secure. The locals have been…nervous but cooperative."

"Good. Are their representatives here?"

"Approaching now, sir."

Indeed, I could see Erista's familiar blue glow leading a group of wisps, while Vash emerged from the lake with several other mer. The ape things—I really needed to find out what they actually called themselves beyond "the people"—hung back near the tree line, watching warily.

"Prince Jax." Erista's light pulsed nervously. "The notifications shared that you were successful. That Kronk is…"

"Dust and rubble," I confirmed dryly. "As I promised. The threat of Kronk is over, and you now know that I keep my word and I'll destroy any threat to you."

I left it unsaid that if they fucked with me and went back on the sort of agreement that we'd managed before…well, maybe I'd not be so happy with them.

There was a long moment of silence, then whispers broke out among all three groups. I let them talk, knowing they needed to process this.

Some random guy shows up, claims he'll destroy what they've been told is an ancestral enemy, and then actually does it in a single night? That had to be a lot to take in.

Finally, Erista floated forward. "Then…we will honor our agreement. The wisps of the Cradle will swear to your empire."

Vash emerged farther from the water, his tentacles writhing in what I'd learned was agitation. "The Tia'Almer-atic have discussed. We…we will consider…" Clearly, he saw the way I frowned, and he went on quickly. "We do not refuse. We simply ask that we are given time to speak to your companions, to learn more about you. Others here are willing, but we cannot chain our young to you without considering their future."

"That's fair." I sighed. "Look, Vash, back home, I have a rule that nobody who's not of the age of majority for their species can swear the oaths. Here, I can't offer that, mainly because if you need protection and you come to the temple—where we plan to make the place as safe as possible through magic—if anyone not sworn to me, such as your children in this situation, tried coming here, the spells would treat them as enemies."

"It is true." Flux spoke up, stepping forward. "We have only been allied with the empire for a matter of months, but since that time, we have received gifts that surpass any we had known before. I am granted a place of high honor by Jax's side, and when others have claimed rights based on species, it has been shown that this is not the way of the empire. All have an equal chance to rise, to earn greatness."

"Then perhaps you will speak to the pod, and we will decide soon," Vash invited.

Flux nodded, checking with me that it was okay, before diving into the water with Ame. The pair of them vanished, with the majority of the mer.

That left the ape things. Oto knuckled forward, the others of his kind following. "People think. People talk. People say…yes. You strong. You protect. People follow strong-protect."

Not the most eloquent acceptance speech, but I'd take it.

"Thank you," I said simply, hoping that this would be enough, as I took a deep breath and started to sort the oath out.

Tenandra appeared at my side, reaching out and touching my skin. I accepted her request and let her access me and my mana.

Ten seconds later, the groups around me—the wisps and the apes—were speaking. Their oaths kicked in as they read through and accepted the offers, making me relax infinitesimally, second by second.

The magic built with each word, that familiar pressure that came with multiple oaths. I could feel the bonds forming, over a hundred new threads connecting to the great web of the empire.

I waited as they all spoke, knowing that I probably should have waited for the mer, but considering the offer of "soon" might be an hour or a month, fuck it.

"I hear your oath," I responded formally as the last voices fell silent. "Be welcome, citizens. The empire stands with you."

As I said it, I pulled the notifications up, and…fucking yes!

Congratulations!

You have taken command of the Cradle of Feshcan'un and have the prerequisite authority and abilities to claim this location and the surrounding land (2,048 square miles), adding it to your territory as a claimed location.

Warning: The Cradle does not contain a control facility of suitable size and power; the territorial control point has been destroyed and must be rebuilt.

That was pretty clear-cut: either I or someone else had fucked up the control facility—probably me by smashing Kronk, but bugger it. I moved on, reading the next few lines.

You have secured enough of the local population and have the prerequisite authority and abilities to claim this structure and the surrounding land, adding it to your territory as a claimed location. As this territory holds less than ten (10) percent of sentients that are actively hostile to your rule, it can be claimed.

Do you wish to annex this territory now?

Yes/No

I mean, obviously I chose Yes. A heartbeat later, another notification flashed, jumping to the top of the list of the little buggers waiting for me.

Congratulations!

You have annexed new lands onto your own, providing the following benefits if the land is worked:

Blessed Location: This land has long been considered blessed by all that beheld it. Although there have been issues recently, that does not detract from the value of a location blessed by a god.

Gain 0.5 modifier to all life production facilities inside the territory known as "the Cradle of Feshcan'un."

Primary Cathedral: The temple of Feshcan'un has been rebuilt and increased upon, and now qualifies as a primary cathedral for the faith of the Pantheon of the Flame! Gain 2.5x mana investiture for all divine actions in this area.

Beware: Should the cathedral fall into enemy hands, a minus modifier will be imposed upon the Pantheon of the Flame!

"Motherfuckers," I growled to myself, knowing damn well that I just gained another location to damn well protect. Still, that's life. I pulled up the next notification in line.

Attention, Citizens of the Territory of Carrmor!

The Cradle of Feshcan'un has been claimed by a worthy aspirant of ancient bloodlines!

All Titles, Deeds, and Laws in the claimed territories of Carrmor are held for review, and can be revoked, altered, annulled, or approved.

All Hail Prince Jax of Dravith and Carrmor! Scion of the Empire and master of the Cradle of Feshcan'un!

*

Congratulations!

You have completed your Quest: Bring balance to the Realm!

The Goddess Jenae has seen that you have completed her quest. The wisps, long believed to be the most innocent of all creatures in the UnderVerse, teeter on the brink of extinction, driven into hiding, captured, tortured, and driven insane by the demands placed upon them. There are now fifty-seven more free of their species to aid in the land's recovery.

You have secured the Cradle of Feshcan'un, the wisps and askanari have accepted your lordship over their home, and the territory surrounding the Cradle has been absorbed into the empire, banishing those who are among the worst of the wisps' unnatural predators.

Discover, recover, and protect wisps: 57/50

Secure their home: 1/1

Reward: ~~A chance at an easier birth for Oracle~~, Balance being restored, Manastone mine, ~~Unknown,~~ 5,000,000xp

Seeing that Oracle's hope for an easier birth and one of the unknown rewards had been removed kinda pissed me off. That was an understatement, but still. I went on, seeing that I'd now found that species name at least for Oto and his kind: askanari.

Congratulations!

You have completed a Quest granted by the Goddess Jenae: Protect Gaij!

The Goddess Jenae has accepted your completion of Her quest! The city of Kronk was long considered a thorn in the side of the true and honest people of Gaij. The army of Kronk marched on your territory, as they've done many, many times in the past, attacking all that they could reach.

This time, as several times before, the army has been destroyed, but you have made the most of that opportunity, by deciding to destroy the city and eliminate the threat it posed once and for all.

Defeat the invading army: 1/1

Remove the threat posed by Kronk: 1/1

Reward: Secure borders, Safer trade routes, 5,000,000xp, 9,766 new citizens

*

You have been offered a Divine repeatable Quest: My God is Better than your God (6)

Lagoush of the Pantheon of the Flame has offered you a Quest: Destroy the fortress city of Kronk, eliminate its leaders and shatter its armies, free those unjustly enslaved and prove your worth to the people of the Cradle of Feshcan'un.

Bonus: Repair the temple of Quiet Waters and rededicate it to the worship of the Pantheon of the Flame 1/1

Kill Brakuus, Lord of Kronk: 1/1

Destroy enemy Elite forces 72/72

~~Capture the city of Kronk: 0/1~~

Destroy the city of Kronk: 1/1

Bonuses will be given for exceeding these numbers.

Reward: Territorial Claim increased, ~~5,000+~~ 9,766 Citizens, ~~Access to City treasuries and capabilities,~~ 6,000,000xp

It was all that I could do to fight down another curse as I saw the little losses marked up again, but that was what it was. Basically, to get the rest, we'd have had to go street by street, fighting most likely. I might have been able to capture the city more or less intact, but the losses incurred to do it weren't worth it.

Also, I'd have ended up with forty thousand ex-slavers and their families and friends as my citizens, so fuck that.

Instead, I felt it as the territory consolidated; the magic crested and crashed down like a wave. I felt the territorial claim snap into place. The boundaries of the Cradle territory suddenly expanded outward to encompass not just the valley but the surrounding deadlands and hundreds of miles in all directions that were already beginning to recover.

Then came the part I'd been looking forward to.

The banishment.

The shock wave that ripped out from me tore through the air and onward, shivering into the ground and away, as I felt the first distant hints that a creature or ten had been a supporter of Illoth.

I shuddered as the notifications went wild again. I almost called out to taunt the spidery bitch, until I realized that as She was banished, She'd never hear it.

More's the pity.

I found the next notification was on my godhood—heh—but it was also "deferred until discussed," which didn't make much sense to me for a few seconds…until suddenly it did.

I needed to talk to the gods about it, as they were clearly holding it back to help me to acclimatize or something. Never mind, I'd sort that tonight.

Regardless, though, I forced myself to go on, and pull up the kill notification. And fuck me sideways with a buttered crumpet and call me a toast rack, that was excessive!

Congratulations!

You have killed the following:

- Brakuus, Demigod of Kronk, Level 56 for a total of 1,576,221xp

- 1,117x Warrior classes of various levels for a total of 1,268,912xp

- 817x Rogue classes of various levels for a total of 1,785,722xp

- 417x Guard classes of various levels for a total of 2,787,133xp

- 143x Cleric classes of various levels for a total of 522,110xp

- 38x Mage classes of various levels for a total of 503,969xp

- 273x drow of various levels for a total of 4,556,117xp

- 3,214,663x Spiders of various levels for a total of 3,587,887xp

- 3x Drow Spiderkin of various levels for a total of 97,114xp

- 16x Drow priests of various levels for a total of 322,301xp
- 89x…

I stared at the notification for long seconds. The list just went on and on and on. I eventually scanned to the bottom and saw the important numbers, shaking my head at just how insane the gain for destroying a *city* genuinely was—especially when you added killing all the drow inside the territory to the list.

The important bit, when I added in the quest rewards, was the final figure, and fuck me, that was worth waiting for.

Forty million and fifteen points of experience.

Forty-motherfucking-goddamn-million points!

Fuck the change, who cared about that?

Congratulations!

You have reached level 52-54.

You have 21 unspent Attribute points and 0 Meridian points available.

Progress to level 55 stands at 417,897/15,000,000

That was nice. Again, I mean, okay, a little disappointing in that was enough to go from what, level zero to level forty or so, at a rough guess, but also, the powers that I was accumulating now made it clear that the higher you got, the less there was about that could fuck with you.

There were a bunch more notifications, but the one that really made me hiss in pain was the next to land.

Congratulations!

**Through hard work and perseverance,
you have increased your stats by the following:**

Agility +20

Charisma +20

Constitution +20

Dexterity +20

Endurance +20

Intelligence +20

Luck +20

Perception +20

Strength +20

Wisdom +20

Continue to train and learn to increase this further.

Congratulations!

You have made progress in a Quest given by the God Sint: Divine Is As Divine Does

The God of Light, Sint, advised that you DO NOT attempt this quest before a minimum of level 50, but as you somehow leapt to 50+ at an unheard of speed, he instead wishes you good luck.

Seek out and acquire fragments of divinity, aiding you in both your ascension of the Crystal Steps to the Imperial Throne and to Godhood.

Seek out and harvest fragments of divinity from those who hold them: 3/10

Reward: True immortality, Ascension to Godhood, 5,000,000xp per fragment

That was another ten million right there, which made my XP just ridiculous, frankly, as yet another five million for each fragment was unleashed into me.

It was the activation of both fragments of divinity.

As soon as I'd unlocked them both, I'd gained the points, but being the way that the system worked, it didn't actually allow me access to it, until I *acknowledged* the change.

Two hundred stat points slammed home in a heartbeat, including enough to push me over the threshold for my century in Strength, and that was just fucking obscene.

The pain that sent me to my knees, teeth gritted hard enough I was at risk of them breaking, was incredible. I barely eked out the words, before I started shaking, bleeding and convulsing.

"Cent...ury...!" I got out, and though I didn't see or feel it, I heard the incoming rush, as Bane reached me, laying a hand on my arm and speaking calmly to me. Reassuringly.

No clue what he said, though; I was too far gone.

By the time I finally unclenched my knotted muscles and stretched again, it was with a whimper. But before me was a single screen that made the pain worth it.

Congratulations!

You have achieved your first century in Strength through point allocation.

As such, you have gained a new Ability!

<u>**Titan's Resolve:**</u>

Your body has become more than mere flesh and bone; instead, it may now transform into a vessel of pure physical dominance. When activated, your muscles compress and their density increases exponentially, granting immunity to forced movement, knockback, and physical displacement. Your strikes carry concussive force that ripples outward, creating shock waves proportional to the force applied. Most significantly, you can channel raw strength through any part of your body, allowing you to perform feats of strength without proper leverage, punching with the force of your entire body from any position, or anchor yourself to any surface through pure muscular tension.

<u>**Passive Effect**</u>: Physical attacks against immovable objects no longer damage you. Instead, the force is perfectly distributed through your enhanced musculature.

<u>**Active Cost**</u>: 100 stamina per minute of use, plus 50 stamina per shock wave generated.

<u>**Note**</u>: Extended use causes temporary muscle calcification, reducing Agility by 25% for one hour after deactivation.

That was fucking *incredible*, and actually suited my fighting style as well, which was a nice change. I'd gained a handful of other abilities of late that although good, they were just…they didn't gel with me, not the way that Hyper Cognition and Mana Overdrive did.

I'd have to learn entirely new fighting styles to take full advantage of them. Frankly, as much as I knew it'd help me, and make me win easier and more solidly, the time it'd take to factor them in just wasn't doable. Not right now.

Mind you, now that I had Flux and the team back? Maybe it was time to start training again.

One thing was for sure, though: the more of this I managed, the further I moved from my mortal beginnings.

As much as it probably sounded dickish, and definitely immodest to say it, I was far from the man Augustus had trained in the arena, and even further from the confused, scared guy who had been forced by the baron to bow and serve.

I was clearly, and truly, becoming a god.

The next notification was probably the only other that I was interested in. I smiled as I read it, even as Bane helped me to stretch out my legs and arms, the knots feeling more like steel cables than anything a human should have.

You have completed a repeatable Quest: Rescue the Legion! (5)

Additional legionnaires have been freed, and not only freed, but rescued from the clutches of such hated enemies! Congratulations, hero, you have given those who had given up hope, a lifeline and a reason to live!

That reason? Punish your enemies and eliminate any threat to the empire!

Reward: 237/200 Legionnaires, 500,000xp

Regardless, the important thing was that the legionnaires were coming home, and the empire was growing—not just in power, but also in safety.

You have received a new Quest: Rescue the Legion! (6)

The imperial legions rise again, buoyed aloft on a tide of rescued warriors. Old friends and old comrades in arms have been reunited in their hundreds by your actions, but there are more still lost. Rescue them, return them to the empire, and feel the pride of a job well done!

Rescue members of the Imperial Legion!

Reward: 37/500 Legionnaires, 1,500,000xp

I accepted it straightaway and moved on, grinning internally at the thought of so many new legionnaires rescued.

I'd also gained twenty-one points. As much as I could slap them in anywhere at this point, there was a genuine need to consider it, as I could hit another century when I did it.

Although, if I were honest, the thought of hitting another had gone from "whoop, that's awesome" into "fuck me, please no, not yet." As much as I needed every advantage I could get, what I couldn't afford now, though, was the period of adjustment, so it was time to get to work. I'd sort the points out later over the next few days.

"Jax!" Ame's voice called out suddenly. "These mer are being difficult. They keep insisting on speaking to you about 'terms.'"

I sighed. Of course they were. Nothing was ever simple.

"Coming!" I called back, then muttered under my breath, "Should have known the oath was the easy part."

As I walked toward the lake where Ame was apparently in a standoff with Vash and half his damn pod, I snorted as I saw the way they were standing.

Most of them were already cowed and uncertain; the runecrafter's force of personality was used more as a battering ram than anything else, but I got it. This was her having basically beaten them into submission, and now she was giving them a chance to retain a little dignity by getting a "win" with me.

Time to go be subtle and lordly.

CHARACTER SHEET

Name: Jax Amon	
Title: Godslayer	
Class: Mage Imperator (Fire Focus)	**Renown**: Imperial Scion, Prince of Dravith, Master of Himnel, Narkolt and Gaij, Godslayer, Mage Imperator
Level: 54	**Progress**: 917,897/15,000,000
Patron: Jenae, Goddess of Fire and Exploration	**Points to Distribute**: 21 **Meridian Points to Invest**: 0

Stat	Current points	Description	Effect	Progress to next level
Agility	120	Governs dodge and movement	+1200% maximum movement speed and reflexes. Gained Temporal Fluidity	N/A
Charisma	81 (76)	Governs likely success to charm, seduce, or threaten	+81% success chance in interactions with other beings.	55/100
Constitution	145 (143)	Governs health and health regeneration	2900 health, regen 190 points per 600 seconds (each point invested now worth 20 health). Gained: Genetic Storage	N/A
Dexterity	120	Governs ability with weapons and crafting success	+120% to weapon proficiency, +120% to the chances of crafting success. Gained: Master Craftsman's Touch	N/A
Endurance	93 (87)	Governs stamina and stamina regeneration	2790 stamina, regen 71 points per 30 seconds (each point invested now worth 30 stamina).	94/100
Intelligence	226	Governs base mana and number of spells able to be learned	2460 mana, spell capacity: N/A (+200 mana from items). Gained: Hyper Cognition & Mana Manipulation	N/A
Luck	99	Governs overall chance of bonuses	+99% chance of a favorable outcome.	N/A
Perception	110 (100)	Governs ranged damage and chance to spot traps or hidden items	+100% ranged damage, +100% chance to spot traps or hidden items. Gained: Essence Sight	N/A
Strength	111 (108)	Governs damage with melee weapons and carrying capacity	+111 damage with melee weapons, +111% maximum carrying capacity. Gained: Titan's Resolve	N/A
Wisdom	125 (115)	Governs mana regeneration and memory	+1600% mana recovery, 18 points per minute. Gained: Mana Manipulation	N/A

CHAPTER FIFTEEN

The familiar thrum of Tenandra's engines filled the air as she returned. The sight of her descending toward us at the makeshift camp, her hull streaming with water as the skies literally tried to wash us away, was a hell of a relief.

Four days had passed since we'd claimed the Cradle. I'd spent most of that time buried in preparations, trying to ignore the constant itch in the back of my mind that counted down every second Oracle was gone.

I stood from the improvised war table we'd set up in one of the temple's upper chambers. Apparently, the old high priests had liked their comforts, judging by the sheer size of their apartments that had been recreated.

The map we'd made was spread out before us, showing what little we knew of the surrounding territories, cobbled together from the memories of those who knew the area, my internal magical map, and old references. But it still had far too many blank spaces for my liking.

"About fucking time," I muttered, staring at the ship through the window as it came in for a landing. That wasn't a complaint, though. Tenandra had made incredible time, all things considered, and I'd not realistically expected her back until tomorrow at the earliest.

Lydia moved over to stand by the window and stared out at the ship as well. "Well, looks like they won't need t'wash t'decks neither…" she muttered, shaking her head. "Ah've never seen rain like it. And she musta bin burnin' t'manastones yer gave 'er all right. Ah thought it'd be another day at least."

"When has Tenandra ever been late?" I asked, already heading for the door. "Come on, let's see what news they bring, and we can get the final plan in place."

The refugees from Kronk had set up a surprisingly organized camp around the temple, with the main group arriving last night. It'd been chaos for a little while, but being that we had Hennen's steady hand to keep everything running smoothly, it was at least organized chaos.

The temple was up against the edge of the lake, but on two sides led into the forest. The trees had been cleared back by a hundred meters or so, and the brush piled up as well.

The legionnaires and ex-soldiers had seen to it that the ground was cleared and where possible, rough shelters had been constructed. But for most people, they were camped out in the temple itself.

The main floor of the temple was fortunately huge, although I seriously doubted when it was originally designed, they ever considered that it'd be filled with thousands of people laid in rows to sleep.

Hennen had split people into three shifts, with the first scouring the area for food, the second clearing the grounds, and the third inside, sleeping. Each "shift" ran for eight hours. I'd expected to be fielding complaints, but instead I saw happy smiles.

The people who were generally the happiest were the ones who wanted to actually live here as well, and that looked like it'd be around two thousand of them, which was *insane*.

The valley could easily support the population. To say it was verdant and overgrown was an understatement. The problem had been the lifespans of the creatures, and that was now dealt with. As such, we were left with a huge valley that was verdant and lush with life, but very little higher order sapient life.

The plan had been made in short order that we'd clear a space around the temple, construct some basic accommodation, and then those who wanted to stay here could. The rest could help until it was time for the march back to Gaij.

I'd thought we might get a couple of hundred who wanted to stay here, but when so many people asked if they could stay as well, the plan had drastically changed.

Now, there was to be a reasonable-sized village around the temple. Considering it would include wisps, the mer, and the ape things that Janae called askanari, there was also going to be a reasonable-sized garrison of the legion deployed here as soon as I could manage it as well.

Thankfully, Hennen, being the outrageously efficient bastard that he was, had—even before they arrived—winnowed through the groups, looking for skills, and had found three carpenters, four builders, and a single tailor, all of which were high leveled, having been kept as slaves specifically for their skills. They were, as of this morning, directing people in the making of the new village.

It might seem that a tailor wasn't as needed as the other skills in making a village, but damn was I wrong on that.

The tailor was the busiest of all the groups, as she was desperately needed to make and teach others to make everything from nets to curtains, blankets, clothing and shoes, to name but a few.

I'd vetoed the first suggested names of Jax's Town and then Emperor's Rest, and several others until it'd been settled on as Godsholme.

Thankfully, there'd also been legion-style planning for everything. Sections were marked out for housing, for paths, a moat, and defenses—and best of all, a large area that was clearly squared off and set aside for the ships to land and be worked on, covered in gravel to help keep it clear of plants and random idiots gaping.

Hennen had been here less than a day, having lead the refuges into the valley last night as the sun began to set, and yet already, by midafternoon, the outline for the new village was laid out, and the ground cleared.

Now, as Tenandra settled onto the marked-out landing area, I could see faces turning toward her with a mixture of hope and worry. These people had learned the hard way that change usually meant trouble, and change was something I typically brought in spades.

From where we were in the temple, I could see the deck. Yeah, as Lydia had said, it was soaked with little streams of water running out of the drainage holes, but the other thing that was clear was that every space that could be used had been filled with crates and barrels. I saw food. Building supplies. Actual fucking tents instead of the makeshift shelters we'd been making do with, and a million more things that I just had to shake my head in relief over.

"Come on, let's get down there," I said to Lydia. The pair of us—along with Bane and Tang—jogged down the stairs and across the main temple floor toward the ship.

It took longer to get past people than anything else, but by the time we were out—the goddamn rain wasn't letting up at all, and I was regretting not wearing my armor, as my clothes were going to get soaked—the ship was fully landed and people were already beginning the unloading.

"Hey, boss!" Jian called out, practically bouncing down the gangplank with Sehran on his arm. Both looked disgustingly pleased with themselves. "You're not gonna believe what we found!"

"A sense of timing?" I shot back, but I was already grinning. Having the squad back together, even in pieces, made everything feel a bit better, and Sehran being Sehran, had lifted one wing over herself and Jian—showing some incredible flexibility—and her other wing over Lydia and me.

Bane was utterly uncaring of the rain as an annoyance, being naturally predisposed to living underwater, and Tang had vanished again, so fuck him…he could get wet.

Sehran laughed, her wings flexing slightly as she stretched. "Better. We intercepted a supply caravan about sixty miles out from Kronk. Turns out the merchants were heading to trade, and had no idea it was…indisposed."

"Indisposed." Grizz snorted from behind me as he hurried in to join the conversation, ducking and trying to get under the wing as well and out of the rain. "That's one way to describe 'reduced to a fucking crater.'"

"The point is," Jian continued, "we convinced them to redirect their supplies to here. That should help with things."

"Convinced?" I raised an eyebrow.

"I was very persuasive," Sehran purred. "Though I think the twenty legionnaires Tenandra picked up from Gaij might have helped make our case."

That got my attention. "Twenty legionnaires?"

Tenandra strode down to stand beside us in her human form, looking pleased with herself. "We gathered an additional twenty full legionnaires, plus another thirty aspirants who've shown promise in their basic training and Daralen felt were ready for additional duties. The primus thought you could use the reinforcements, though we decided en route that having them join the caravan and escort it here was the best use of their time for now. Is that acceptable?"

"Hell, yes. We need everything, after all. Screw this, though—let's get inside out of the rain and we can talk properly."

"Spoilsport," Bane grumbled, and I clapped him on the shoulder.

Twenty minutes later, we'd gathered again in what had been the high priest's private meeting chamber. The room was circular, with windows that looked out over the Cradle in three directions, and enough space for the core planning group without feeling cramped.

Around the table sat a handful of my usual suspects—Lydia, Flux and Ame, Yen, Jian, Sehran, Hennen and Tenandra. We'd also been joined by Varec and Erista, as well as two people I'd been wanting to talk to properly: Borren, one of the Kronk legionnaires who'd survived decades of arena fighting, and more interestingly, a young wood elf named Silviana.

She was pretty in that ethereal way elves always seemed to manage, with bark-brown skin marked by faint whorls that looked almost like wood grain, and eyes the color of waxed spring leaves. She'd been among the slaves we'd freed from Kronk, captured months ago during a raid on her city's territory.

"Okay, first and foremost, Tenandra, updates please. What happened when you reached the refugees and then Gaij?"

"The trip was a pleasant one, though I pushed hard with the additional manastones you gave us and were blessed with favorable winds, so we reached the refugees who have now arrived here well ahead of schedule, as they were making excellent time."

"They had good reason to." Hennen snorted. "Can I just add in that the legion loves the new recruits you've brought us, boss?" He looked over at me.

"I mean, I totally understand that their lives were shit and I'm sorry for that, but they're literally conditioned to work until they drop. They're driven to excel and to prove themselves, and they're over the moon with the rations and facilities available, even when that's literally hard tack and a hole in the ground.

"When you left us with them, I was hoping to make it here in under a week, that was it. I knew that was hopeful, but we dogtrotted for entire days at a time—sleep for three hours and back on the road.

"If we had the supplies for it, I could have run from here to Dravith with these people, they're that solid. We made it here two days early—two entire days! As soon as we arrived, they were ready to work, and damn, I'm proud of what they've accomplished in short order.

"Don't get me wrong, there's some who are doing the bare minimum and have already been caught slacking—of course there are…it's human nature—but still! The vast majority are a delight to work with."

"Glad to hear it." I grinned at his happiness and nodded. "So, you reached the refugees?" I prompted, turning back to Tenandra.

"Yes, we dropped off the additional foods and scouted the area, finding no threats, and then headed to Gaij. We passed several small towns and villages, but sporadically and rarely of more than a few hundred people at a time. On arrival to Gaij, Sehran descended to speak with the mistress of the city…" She turned to look at her partner, who smiled, resting a hand on the wisp's shoulder.

"Seraphina was overjoyed with the news." Sehran took over the narrative. "She'd received a notification that Kronk had been destroyed and she'd already shared that with the city—believe me, the general feeling about you there right now is that if you wanted the day to last longer, you'd just grab the sun and drag it back up—but I'm digressing.

"The mistress understood and got things moving straightaway. It helped that there were caravans fresh to the city that had just come in, so she essentially bought everything they had and loaded it aboard Tenandra. Daralen gave us the extra fifty passengers and we set off again, while Seraphina prepared the main caravan.

"Toren and Annabeth are going to be running it, alongside Daralen, who'll be leading the legion contingent. Apparently Reth wanted in as well, with his outriders, though I'm not sure if they'll all be coming. They were planning to bring all the things you'd need to start a small settlement, mostly things like blacksmithing equipment, a basic forge…you know, all the things needed to make whatever else is needed.

"She was talking about sending everything from alchemy equipment to smelted ingots. She knew there'd probably be a lot of locals here who would want to relocate back to Gaij as well, so expect the caravan to be big and slow. Probably three to four weeks to get here, I'm sorry to say."

"It is what it is." I sighed. "As much as it'd be great to have it all here, there's plenty for people to get along with for now. And then, when the caravan arrives and unloads, it'll be able to turn around and escort the majority back to Gaij anyway, which will make the locals happier."

"The local pod is unenthusiastic about the numbers, that is true," Ame said. "With the facilities still being prepared, the majority have taken to relieving themselves in the lake, and that is…" She paused, then shook her head. "It is disgusting and likely to get worse. Poisoning is a real concern if this continues."

"We've got latrines dug," Hennen interjected. "I know they're small, but we're working on more. The bottleneck is in the equipment needed. For a small group, essentially a hole and being able to squat over it is enough. But for nearly ten thousand, that's just not viable. Proper facilities will be available in around two days, but for now, we're working on it."

"What do you need?" I asked curiously.

"Saws, hammers, and nails more than anything else," he said. "The trees are felled, but cutting the wood into planks and then joining them together is a priority. Then there's the order to build. If we focus on getting the latrines dug, then we're not working on shelter, and vice-versa.

"Although we have some equipment, it's highly limited and in use around the clock. The one saving grace in all of this is that almost everyone was enslaved. Again, I'm not making out that was a trivial thing, but it means that these people are a lot less concerned with certain things that would usually be a prime concern, such as modesty.

"Again, not making light of this, and we have clear separation for the male and female latrines, but it means that where normally there'd be a focus on maintaining dignity for so many people as well…that's just not a driving concern." He looked around before going on.

"Don't get me wrong, that *will* be, and we need to return these people to a position where it's a valid concern, for their self-respect and sanitation if nothing else. But, in this situation, it's actually an advantage."

"We would also like to see a lessening of the destruction of the forest," Erista said carefully. "We understand the need for you to gain shelter, but to see it done in such a destructive way is…distressing."

"I know." I apologized to the wisp. "We shouldn't need to do much more, and once we've cleared the last areas of the ground, then we'll be using the wood that was recovered from the trees to build the houses and more. It's not my intention that we'll clear too much, beyond what's needed to grow the foods for everyone. And, well, only those who are happy to live in harmony with the area will be permitted to stay. I'm definitely not wanting to see a full city grow here."

"Not a human one, but maybe elvish?" Silviana asked in a hesitant voice, and I looked at her in question.

"We live in harmony with the world, or at least my people do, where possible," she pointed out, and I nodded.

"I'd rather that, and frankly, I think the gods would as well. Maybe we need to look at that," I said. "Though there's also a second point that we will need to address and that's going to affect everyone who lives here, and that's that the overabundance of life mana is already dropping thanks to the changes.

"Don't get me wrong—this is always going to be a blessed place, but the prey and predators of the Cradle were driven into a frenzy of accelerated breeding and feeding by the abundance. That's no longer the case. Although those who were benefiting were mainly the predators, we're going to need to actively cull them; otherwise, they're going to wipe out the prey."

"I think it'd be wise to cull both sides," Hennen said after a brief pause as everyone thought about it. "If you cull just the predators, then the prey will still grow in numbers to outdo them, and then you can have a situation where the prey eliminates the predators, and the whole area gets out of balance."

"We'll do both," I decided. "Hunt and cull the predators for the area by half, roughly, and the prey by a quarter or so. That should give us an overabundance that is manageable and that also provides food for our people, as well as hides for tanning and more. Does that make sense?"

"It will, but one quick point, boss?" Hennen winced.

"Yeah?"

"Tanners use a lot of chemicals, or foul-smelling waste when they don't have access to their usual stuff. That means the locals are going to have more of that, rather than less, in the air."

"Dammit, all right, we need to find a way around that. Maybe a market for the furs and so on, instead of making everything?"

"It'd probably be wise, but some tanning will be needed," he agreed.

I shrugged. "We can talk about it, though, and about maybe getting some help, but that's a good start for the next topic." I spread the map across the table. "Let's talk about Lembiq."

Silviana straightened in her chair, clearly nervous but trying not to show it. "What would you like to know, my lord?"

"Everything," I said simply. "Start with the basics. Population, defenses, leadership style, crimes. And please, it's just Jax when we're planning like this."

She nodded, though I could see she was anxious and uncertain. "Lembiq is…*was* my home for forty-three years. The city itself exists within the Heartwood Grove, built into and around the great trees that have stood there since before the cataclysm."

"Arboreal construction," Tenandra interjected. "Defensively sound if done correctly. And if done to high standard, as the wood elves of old had customarily done, then they're actually more effective than most human city walls."

"Very much so," Silviana confirmed. "The outer wall was grown rather than built—thornwood barriers fifty feet high and twenty thick, constantly maintained by our druids. The city proper extends both horizontally through the undergrowth and canopy, and vertically through multiple levels."

Borren leaned forward, looking like he wanted to ask a question, and I gestured him to say it. "Thank you, my prince…uh, Jax. I wanted to ask…I fought a wood elf gladiator once. Bastard could run up walls and leap between platforms like gravity was optional. Is that normal for your people? He was the only one I ever fought."

A small smile crossed Silviana's face. "We begin climbing before we can properly walk. Every child of Lembiq knows the branch-paths by heart. It's common for an elf to cross the entire city without ever touching the ground."

"Population?" Flux asked, ever practical.

"Perhaps thirty thousand within the walls and overhead, with another ten scattered through the surrounding forest in smaller settlements. We—*they* maintain a standing force of around three thousand warriors, with every adult trained in at least basic combat. And we're primarily archers and hunters, rather than straightforward melee classes, which is why you'd have faced us rarely." She nodded to Borren.

"That's a solid force," I muttered. "Archers who have literally the high ground all the time? They'd be a bastard to fight."

Her expression darkened. "We've had to be. The Dark Legion established a fortress in the Bleakwood Marsh a hundred years ago. They constantly raid the area, taking slaves and claiming villages and territory. Sometimes it's worse."

"Worse?" Lydia prompted, though her tone suggested she already knew the answer.

"Conversion," Silviana said quietly. "Those they take either die in their dungeons, return as servants of Nimon, or are sold as slaves. The ones who aren't are used as examples, brought back to us and raised on pikes along the border to die over days. My cousin…" Her jaw tightened.

"I'm sorry," I said, meaning it. "How organized are these raids?"

"Very. They strike at our hunting parties, our perimeter settlements. Repeated attacks meant to bleed us slowly rather than conquer outright. They demand that we swear to the God of Death and that once we've done so, they'll leave us be. But everyone knows it's only the first step. If we did that, then the priests would come and set up their churches, and step by step, who we are will be taken away and all that will be left are dark elves."

"Drow?" I asked, stiffening slightly.

"Dark elves are those who are sworn to Nimon or the dark gods, not just the drow, but those who choose that path…" She hesitated, then went on. "We call them 'Ha'tinaten.' It translates as 'those who have lost their way.' We pity them, even as we kill them."

"And your leadership hasn't done anything about it?" Sehran asked.

"Lord Farendir is…cautious," Silviana said carefully. "He believes that as long as we remain within our walls and don't provoke them, we can endure."

"Sounds like a fucking coward," Jian muttered, earning a sharp look from Lydia.

"He's trying to protect what remains of our people," Silviana said, though I noticed she didn't exactly disagree. "After the cataclysm, we numbered over a hundred thousand. Now? We're dying slowly, and everyone knows it."

I studied her for a moment. "You were taken during one of these raids?"

"A hunting party, yes. I was scouting the southern border of our forests when they ambushed us. Twelve of us went out. I was the only one taken alive, thanks to an unlucky headshot." Her hands clenched on the table. "The slavers bought me from the Dark Legion citadel before…I could be used as an example against my people."

"Lucky," Bane rumbled. "In a way."

"Very," she agreed. "Though I didn't feel lucky. It took them six weeks of me trying to escape to decide to sell me to the arena. My former master had no spare magical collars and couldn't afford to buy one, so when I was caught after the last attempt, I was sold again. That was two days before you freed us all, and I…" She swallowed hard, fighting down tears, before going on. "I had to do things to survive, things I'm not proud of."

"You survived," I pointed out firmly. "That's what matters. We've all done things we regret. Okay, so what can you tell us about Lembiq's politics? Who actually runs things?"

She took a breath, organizing her thoughts. "Lord Farendir holds overall power as First Among the Branches, essentially a prince or a lord, though we don't use that term. Below him is the Council of Groves, seven elders who each oversee different aspects of city life—military, trade, agriculture, magic, crafts, justice, and spirituality."

"Let me guess," Jian said. "They spend most of their time arguing while the city slowly falls apart."

"Not…inaccurate," Silviana admitted. "Elder Morvaine of the military branch constantly pushes for aggressive action against the Dark Legion. Elder Thessarian pushes for greater trade relationships with the other cities and alliances, and Rennmai of spirituality insists we must maintain our isolation to preserve elven purity, and should drive all those who are not of pure blood from the city. The others fall somewhere between."

I shared a look with Flux, who was already taking notes. Politics. Why did it always come down to fucking politics? I mean, my one greatest goddamn weakness!

"Tell me about this elven purity thing," I said. "We've heard the pure elf cities are…selective about who they let in."

Silviana shifted uncomfortably. "Lembiq is…traditional. Non-elves are permitted in Rootside—the ground-level trading district—and even to own homes in that lower level and underground, but ascending into the city proper requires special dispensation. It's not my favorite aspect of home, but after centuries of other races trying to conquer or exploit us…"

"They got paranoid," Flux finished. "Can't say I blame them, but it makes negotiation complicated."

"Exactly what I was thinking," I agreed. "We can't just march up and demand they join the empire. We need a different approach."

"Perhaps not you doing the negotiating at all then?" Ame suggested, and I glared at her.

"What did you have in mind?" Tenandra asked.

I leaned back, thinking. "First, we need to deal with their Dark Legion problem. Nothing says 'we're the good guys' like eliminating the assholes who've been bleeding them dry."

"Just like that?" Yen laughed. "Stroll up to a Dark Legion fortress and knock?"

"More or less." I grinned. "We already eliminated most of their army at Gaij, after all. But first, we need to know more about the fuckers. Silviana, what can you tell us about their fortress?"

She pulled the map closer, pointing to a spot southeast of Lembiq. "The Bleakwood Marsh was corrupted long before they arrived—something about the mana there is…wrong. Dead things don't stay dead. The trees themselves hunger for blood. The Dark Legion built their fortress at the heart of it, where the corruption is strongest, and they use it both as a training ground for their forces and as a place to dispose of the bodies of their failures."

"Of course they fucking do," I muttered. "Numbers?"

"Hard to say. At least a few hundred, I would have thought. They can hold thousands, from what I saw when I was taken through it, but the majority are trainees. The main force, as you say, you already eliminated. Also, the fortress itself is stone, which is unusual for our region. They must have brought in outside builders."

"Or used magic," Lydia suggested. "Wouldn't put it past them."

"The real problem," Silviana continued, "is their commander. They call him the Bleaklord—I know, pretentious—but he's supposedly some kind of death knight. Unkillable, according to the survivors who've seen him."

"Everything's killable," I said flatly. "Just have to find the right person to try it."

"Spoken like someone who killed a god." Jian smirked.

"Two gods," I corrected, grinning. "Well, their avatars. And, to be fair, I do like a challenge. The point is, if we take out this fortress, we remove Lembiq's biggest threat. That gives us leverage for negotiation."

"And if they still refuse?" Flux asked.

I shrugged. "Then we're going to have to come up with a better plan, because from conversations with the gods, there's something there that we need. A library, or a hint to its location at least. That means we can't just give it our best shot and move on. We need the territory, and we can't leave them here if they're going to be hostile. In that situation, we conquer them. But otherwise? I'd rather they agreed to join us, or at the least to be neutral or allied status. Conquering cities that don't want to be conquered is just too much fucking hassle. When they're not dicks, I mean, who deserve it."

"That's…not what I expected," Silviana said carefully.

"What, you thought I'd threaten to do to Lembiq what I did to Kronk?" I shook my head. "Kronk was a shithole that needed burning. From what you've described, Lembiq is just scared and isolationist. Can't say I blame them. They'd be useful allies, and not just because we could do with expert archers who we can call on when we need them."

"So we approach peacefully," Tenandra summarized. "Offer to eliminate their Dark Legion problem in exchange for opening negotiations."

"Pretty much. But we need to be smart about it. Silviana, would you be willing to make initial contact? They're more likely to listen to one of their own."

She hesitated, then nodded firmly. "Yes. I… I want to help. My people are slowly dying. If joining your empire could save them…"

"It could," I said. "We've got human, mer, orc, goblin, gnome, and whatever the fuck else all working together. We have a lot of elves in the empire already as well. Adding an entire city of elves to the mix would barely register as weird at this point."

"The timing works too," Sehran added. "The caravan from Gaij should reach here in a few weeks, sure, but the food that these people currently have, as well as the supplies that are coming from the captured caravan and the available local stuff means they don't need us here now. That means we're free to deal with expanding the empire without worrying about being available for supply runs here."

"Good. One less thing to worry about." I turned back to Silviana and Tenandra. "How long would it take to reach Lembiq from here?"

"Four days, assuming we don't fly to the Bleakwood first to check it out. Six or seven if we decide to loop around and examine the area there as well," Tenandra supplied after confirming the location on the map with the elf.

"Then we leave tomorrow," I decided. "For the rest of the day, we need to make sure everything here is done and up to date. Once we leave, we won't be returning for a while. I've done everything else I can do here for now, so tonight I'll be speaking with the gods, and then dealing with some personal leveling issues."

"What about the refugees?" Borren asked. "I appreciate that there are forces incoming, my prince, but they're a month away, almost. What do they do if there are attacks?"

"You deal with them," I said. "Look, I may not have been clear on this, but I'm planning on most of you and yours staying here, for now at least. You're not all coming with me. I have my squad, and I'll take—what do you think, Lydia, twenty legionnaires?—and that'll either be enough, or it won't."

"Aye, we should take some. Maybe fifty or so?" she tried.

I shook my head. "More people, less experience to go around. Twenty should be more than enough," I pointed out.

"Thirty as a minimum. And if yer don't agree, yer can try leadin' t'buggers and meetin' t'widows after." She glared at me.

Hennen snorted, muttering, "Soul of an optio" under his breath.

"To conquer a city?" Borren asked slowly. "To take down an entire citadel of the Dark Legion? I'm sorry, my prince…I want to be clear. You think a group of what, thirty? Thirty people, even if they're all fully trained legionnaires, can conquer an entire citadel?"

"Uh, Legionnaire?" Hennen smiled. "Not wanting to piss on your parade here, but the boss and Sehran conquered and destroyed Kronk, the two of them. Alone. Sure, they had help once they got going from you all, *once they'd rescued you*, but it was just the two of them who attacked."

"Well, yes, but…"

"But you think I should take you all with me?" I asked bluntly. "Believe me, I'd rather that. If nothing else, it'd make capturing other cities a lot easier. I plan to do that in the future, but right now, what I need more than anything is speed.

"If I didn't worry that there was a risk to our people here if you came with us now, I'd take you and all your people very happily. But, as it is, we need to maintain this location to keep the territory. If we lose this, not only will we lose a hell of a lot of people who are citizens of the empire, but we'd also definitely lose control of the area.

"If we do that, then what? We have to take it back, along with all the losses that would entail. No, Legionnaire, when I have more troops, be assured I'll damn well use you all. But for now, this is all I need."

"But..." He struggled with the words.

"Listen to me," I growled. "What we've found over the last few months is that the entire power of the city, the authority that commands it, is concentrated in small locations, and best of all, nobody on this continent views flying as a serious threat. Why, considering the flying people I've encountered, I don't fucking know, but people tend to think in terms of small numbers and simple spells when it comes to sieges and attacks.

"We're not going to do that. You saw the large boxes on the sides of Tenandra's deck, Legionnaire?" I asked him; he nodded slowly. "Do you know what they are?"

"No, sir."

"They're the ripple-fire cannons," I explained carefully. "They fire spells that can take down city walls in short order. She has four of them, two to a side, on mounts that can turn and aim independently.

"They *alone* could flatten the citadel, and they might very well end up doing that. Their defenses? If they're purely magical, then whoo-boy are they in for a shock, because I'm gonna fuck their shit right up.

"As for enemy cities after the citadel? Sure, it'll be more complicated for Lembiq, but we're hoping that we'll be able to make friends there. For others? Usually, they have a lord or two in charge in a castle, thinking they're safe from everyone, because a few archers are on their walls, or the occasional mage.

"Well, I've got news for them. We can literally fly in and bombard their walls to dust, slaughter their defenders from the ship's decks. We can then drop in and smash through the heart of their defenses, avoiding the vast majority of their forces, capture the leaders, and release all their slaves.

"Once we've captured their leadership, then we can bring their second tier and beyond leaders in and have them swear oaths, or eliminate them and move on to their successors. Is it brutal? Fuck, yes, but this is war. And as far as I'm concerned, I'm at war with the entire continent. These are imperial lands, and by the gods, these people will either remember that, or they'll all die in the process!"

Silence fell as I glared around, and I forced myself back to calmness. "I'm sorry, people. I know I'm on the ragged edge here, but let's be clear on this. By the time the caravan with reinforcements arrives here from Gaij, my intention is to have at least half of the fucking continent sworn and back under imperial law.

"As we go, we'll be continuing to search for imperial ruins, because I damn well don't doubt that there'll be some. Once they're brought under our control as well, we'll be starting the next phase, which is securing the land."

"What do you mean?" Yen asked when silence fell.

"You remember how we kept casting the frostfire circle and burning the rats out of the walls in Narkolt?" I asked her, and she nodded. "Well, I'm planning on the same thing, but for the entire empire, and using runes to do it."

"What?" Ame jerked her head up. "What do you mean, boy?"

"There's a city in the middle of the desert—Romesh, I think it was called—and their walls had hundreds of runes carved into them. They were close by the underground city that Xenefier held. The city had been worked on, and changed, to be a bastion against Xenefier—or at least against something called the 'creeping death' and 'that which walks between' or some such weirdness. I have to think that was the fucker, all things considered."

"Active runes? Intact?" she asked grimly. "You're sure, boy?"

"I am. We passed dozens, and the outer wall was covered in them, though over the course of the city being abandoned after the cataclysm, the runes were failing, occasional ones flaring and collapsing. But that's the point."

I glanced around, seeing the way Ame was fixated on me and the others looked confused.

"Look, Xenefier is real. It's also an oozing tar-like substance, and that means it can get through any conventional defense. I've been setting off flares of the spell over and over the last few days since everyone here swore to me, but it's not enough to make a real difference. But once you've got this worked out?" I looked at Ame. "You're close, right?"

"Boy, you're insane! Do you have any idea how complicated it is to recreate a spell in runic form? Then tying it to a single ideal, which is essentially loyalty to you specifically and the empire generally? Just that part alone could take decades. Then to have it selectively heal some, and injure others?"

She stumbled over her words, clearly trying to explain it in terms I'd understand and yet not just come out and say no, but actually explain why it wasn't ready and wouldn't be for some time.

"Fuck's sake, Ame…seriously, you've had four days and you wait until now to tell me this?" I snapped.

"I've tried to speak to you about it!" she retorted angrily, throwing her arms up. "Twice I came to you and tried to explain this, and twice you told me to simply work on it and you'd cast the spell instead. What, you think that a day or two would make a difference? Boy, this is the first I'm hearing about a city that had this in the walls! Take me there, give me a chance to study the runes, and maybe, perhaps, I'll be able to do this inside a *decade*."

"Fuck," I muttered, rubbing at my temples. "Okay, right, yeah, fair point. I vaguely remember you saying shit like this before, but—"

"We all tried to tell you," Flux interrupted. "You refused to listen and changed the subject."

"Well, there's a lot to get done," I growled. "Fine, though…you can't do this? I'll sort it."

"You think you can do it in a day?" Ame asked me derisively, folding her arms across her chest. Considering, as a mer, she had four of them, that took some complicated layering, which was pretty impressive.

"No, I think I'll speak to the gods," I retorted.

"What?"

"They have a vested interest in this place being free of Xenefier as well, so I'll speak to them." I shrugged. "Leave this with me, and I guess, I'm sorry for not listening," I added lamely.

"Well, fine," Ame grumbled, before sighing and holding out a small panel that she'd had sitting next to her chair. "If you're going to be reasonable, then I suppose I'll do the same. This is a healing rune."

"Okay?" I agreed, not really seeing the point as she angled the panel to catch the light. It was stone, more like a tile than anything else, and about eight inches on a side. The rune itself was complicated, and drawn in swooping, flaring lines of silvery metal, that I instantly recognized as condensed mana.

"What I have done—not that you were listening when I asked for your direction—was create ten of these. They're healing runes, that when connected to a manastone, will heal anyone who stands on the rune.

"While it's not as flashy and attention-grabbing as your own spell, this will—*in theory*—treat the Xenefier creature as an infection and attempt to heal the host if they stand on it, driving it from the body."

"Well, shit, Ame, that's all we needed!" I grinned.

"No," she growled, leveling a finger at me. "No, it isn't and you're not listening! This will *heal* the host. You say that the creature can't bear or interact with mana? Then this would kill it as well, *I think*…but the problem is it's a single point. If the host steps over it, or doesn't see it or the stone is depleted, then it'll do nothing!"

"So, you're saying we need more of these then?" I mused as I squinted at the rune, tilting the tile from side to side and examining the craftsmanship.

"Yes!" she snapped. "And no. We'd need tens of thousands of these on every inch of flooring to have the effect you want, and I made ten over four days. That's it!"

"Fine." I nodded to her. "Leave it with me."

She stared at me in disbelief, then got up and stormed out of the room, clearly too furious to speak.

I let her go, turning with a sigh to Hennen. "So, with the legionnaires you've got here, and the ones who are incoming now with the captured caravan, will you be able to hold this place?"

He hesitated. "It depends, Jax," he said seriously. "I could make this place practically impregnable, but it'd depend on having the time and the right equipment, and the aim for the site. If it's to be a place for the enemy to break their teeth on, but nothing else? Yes. With our people as determined as they are, we could make something truly terrifying. But the bigger it is, the harder that becomes.

"To surround a village, one that has fields and crops, housing and all the things that come with it, not even considering children, that's going to be much more complicated. Frankly, I'd need to destroy half of the valley to do it, strip-mining would be the least of it and…" He looked unsure and nervous as he clearly expected me to explode.

"Fine." I sighed. "Fuck's sake, man, relax. I'm not that bad, am I?"

"No?" he replied uncertainly.

I glared around, before going on.

"I expect, no, I goddamn *demand* that you all be honest with me, all right? If I'm out of control, then you need to tell me, because I trust you all."

"You're on the edge, Jax." Bane spoke up. "Not over it, but constantly dancing along it. We all know why, but…it's starting to be a problem."

"Fine," I snapped, then forced myself to draw a deep, calming breath. "You're all my friends and advisors, so how about some damn advice?"

"Will you listen?" asked Flux grimly.

"I asked for it because I want it." I glared at him.

"Fine. Then I say that you can't do what you plan with just your team and the legionnaires." He shrugged. "I understand the need, but it is an unacceptable risk. Lio and I will come with you. Cheena and Ame will remain here. And I recommend we take a team from the local pod, as well as double the legionnaires as a minimum. We can fly over the caravan that is headed here now—the captured one, I mean—and borrow some from there, if we don't wish to remove any from here. I recommend at least eighty of us as a force.

"With so many here trained and experienced, as well as incentivized, removing sixty from here will make little difference to the safety of Godsholme. Especially considering how many of the ex-slaves here want to fight and are willing to train. So, stop thinking of them as people who need to be protected, and start thinking of them as a large town of *arena fighters*. If the local pod is willing to include scouts to maintain a watch over the area as well, then I believe this place is safer than most cities.

"On the ship, heading to any target city is less risky with enough of a force aboard that you can fight your way free. Also, while yes, Tenandra is intimidating, she is also highly valuable. Anyone who sees her and understands her capacity will also see the potential. With her captured and under the control of a local warlord, they could—much as you plan to—conquer huge areas."

"I'd have something to say about that," Tenandra murmured, and both Sehran and Jian nodded, all three looking fierce.

"I know you would, but they don't," Flux ground out. "Think! For them to understand what you are, it is not for them to decide that they must give up this foolish plan—instead, you become even more valuable to them. They need not learn to pilot you; they simply must break you and then give orders. And that you are also able to teach magic? They will see you as a prize beyond all others."

"So we need to be very careful—" I started. And was cut off by Flux.

"You need to show that there is no chance for the enemy to achieve what they desire. You must cow them *instantly*. As a starter, that includes a significant force of legionnaires on watch at all times. Landing must be done only at controlled times and places, and with little opportunity for any enemy. When—not if, *when*—they attempt it, they must be shown the full power of your displeasure. No half measures, no chance for them to think again, or to use innocents as a bargaining chip. Extreme force from the outset and zero mercy."

We all stared at the usually kindhearted, though professional mer in surprise.

"In addition, I suggest we open negotiations with Lembiq, and ask for an observer to be placed aboard, someone they will trust. You will play nice with them, show them you are more than the rage-addled, distracted fool you can be and you've been showing us all of late.

"Instead, we land there, send someone in to negotiate, open dialogue and then we ask for an opportunity to demonstrate who and what you are. Then, and only then, do we go to the citadel, and we destroy it utterly. Absolute destruction, to a level that there is no doubt how utterly outclassed they are.

"Once this is done, we return to Lembiq, and we let the observer speak to the council and their lord. Let them consider their options, and while they do, we make the most of the visit to the city. Tenandra is incredible, but when we set off, she was yet to be completed, in her new form.

"She has the capacity for over two hundred aboard, and holds less than forty, including your own team and the entire crew. Half her hold was still being reconstructed and her hull sealed while we were in flight here. She is marvelous, and completely untested as anything but a transport. In this situation, you need her to be a warship, and she needs practice with her weapons. Finally, we recruit. There will be others available, mercenaries, and we make them swear the oaths as part of the deal—"

"Mercs!" I cut him off as I clapped my hand over my eyes and groaned. "Fuck's sake, there was a mercenary guild in Gaij. They swore to us, and I sent them to Lembiq to get set up, thinking that it'd be months before I'd be ready to even consider taking the city. They've probably not even arrived yet…"

"What was the reason behind sending them?" Flux asked, and I shrugged.

"I was planning on sending caravans to the city, both to sell stuff and to make contacts, and I figured if there's a band of obviously dodgy mercs available for hire, the people who want to raid the caravans are likely to hire them as extra muscle, and I can put spies in place as well. Then, if there's an attack, the mercs can stab their 'employers' in the back and boom. Nice, easy defensive situation— plus they'll have information for us."

"Seems convoluted," Flux grumbled.

"It was, but considering all we needed was some platinum to get it all set up, it was worth it. I slaughtered a bunch of nobles when I took Gaij, and we've got coin coming out of our ears. Information? Less so."

"Very well. If they have arrived, then perhaps we hire from their ranks, or not. But we hire a full ship's company to defend Tenandra, and to be clearly more than any small attack can see off. You also hire additional staff—a decent cook, for a start—and anything else we need. We were aboard her for months, and although she's incredible, there wasn't much that the team rotating shifts as cook could do with what we had.

"Some fresh meat and restocking from a city that we're not at war with would make a hell of a difference," he finished with a sigh.

"I… Okay." I nodded, sitting back in the chair and scratching the back of my neck as I thought. "I guess you're going to suggest that I don't handle the negotiations as well?"

"Absolutely not." He nodded, as if that was just common sense, and annoyingly, most of the others nodded along as well.

"Fine. Then if not me, who?"

"Yen," Lydia said. Everyone turned to her in surprise, including Yen herself.

"What?"

"Yen?" I looked at the legionnaire.

"Why not?" Lydia grunted. "She's got t'experience, yer know she's got t'empire at heart, an' if they try t'fuck around, she can carve them a new arsehole."

"I also have experience in dealing with nobility and the legal side of things, laws and so on, which would make it easier to spot issues with the way things are phrased." Yen sat up a little straighter.

I stared at her in shock, and then nodded slowly. "Yeah, yes, actually. Damn, I'd not even considered it! I'm sorry, Yen. I'm so used to knowing that you're part of the squad and that you've got my back in a fight that I never even considered that you're perfect for the role."

"Thank you," she said softly.

I nodded, loving the idea more and more by the second. "Do you want Grizz as your bodyguard?" I asked after a few seconds. "I mean, I know you don't need one, but then you've got him there, always at your back with his sword. He's a pretty big threat to anyone who looks at you, both as protection and on the ceremonial side."

"He'd be useful." She smiled. "Especially if you're thinking of leaving me in the city to negotiate while you destroy the Dark Legion's citadel. You're just going to use the ship's weapons, right?" she asked, and I grinned. "You're not going to be attacking on foot?"

"No, I'm thinking that we stand off and bombard the place, reduce most of it and slaughter the troops from the air. And thanks to my new class as a Mage Imperator, I got access to some cool new spells, including one that lets me essentially block everyone else from using magic for a short period. I'm thinking we fly in under cover of darkness, I use the spell, disrupt all their defensive spells and anything else they have, and stop their mages from fighting back, and then we level it."

"But…you can't!" It was Silviana who said it, and she appeared as surprised as the rest of us when we turned to look at her. "I mean, don't you want to try to free their prisoners and slaves first?"

"I…" I stared at her, reordering it all in my mind, and then groaned. Of *course* we needed to free their slaves first. But that was going to make what had been an easy, devastating raid into a nightmare.

Fuck.

CHAPTER SIXTEEN

It was an hour and a half or so later, and most of that time had been spent going in absolute circles.

Yes, I wanted to free the slaves; yes, I definitely wanted to avoid killing any innocents; and yes, most definitely everyone wanted to avoid me losing my temper, diving into the middle of the fight and slaughtering everything I could while screaming that all gods were dicks.

I pointed out that realistically it was one or the other: we save the slaves, or we destroy the citadel. To do anything else was going to cost us a lot of lives, as we didn't have the forces we needed to capture the citadel. And we sure as shit didn't have the same advantage as we would with an enemy city, which was that if we took out the leadership, the others would all panic and fall into line, or so we hoped.

If I tried that with the Dark Legion, the next in the ranks would order the attack, as would his or her successor—on and on until the stableboy was charging me with a butter knife. Because apart from those who were kicked out and mutated through whatever shitty trials they had—like Thomas's old squad—the rest could expect to die by Nimon's hand if they changed sides, and that wasn't an idle threat.

Also, for some strange reason, the fuckers didn't like me very much…not that I could work out why, of course. I'd always been *so* respectful when I'd dealt with Nimon and His chums.

Regardless, I'd dismissed everyone and moved down to the cathedral to kneel in reverent contemplation.

Or so it'd appear from a distance, anyway, as Bane and Lio were keeping people well back from me.

I reached out to speak to the gods.

"Jax, it's about time!" Jenae snapped as soon as I used the spell to reach out to Her. Ten seconds later, I was surrounded by titanic presences, and the others in the cathedral were being lifted and buffeted out of the doors, herded by invisible winds.

"Uh, all right." I sighed, standing and looking around; the room changed subtly as the doors crashed closed and shutters sealed themselves over windows.

Bane was the only other one in the room, and he was crouched by the door, clearly trying to not be noticed, while at least forty people had been lifted by the winds and hurled out—Lio, for some reason, included in that.

"Clearly you're all pissed it took me awhile to reach out," I guessed.

"Pissed…?" Sint rumbled. *"No, Jax, we are not upset. We're highly confused and concerned! You bound both fragments of divinity in a matter of minutes and then did nothing with the resulting power beyond destroy a city. Since then, you've not attempted to exercise your newfound gifts, not even slightly!"*

"Okay, can I have a clue?" I asked. "Because from where I'm sitting, I thought I couldn't access the powers until I fully ascended?"

"You gain a new ability with each fragment that you bind, you understand this, correct?" Jenae asked flatly.

"Yeah, I mean, vaguely. I got that tether thing, uh…Soul Anchor, when I bound the Fragment of Death."

"Exactly!" She snapped. *"You haven't even bothered to examine the abilities you were offered upon binding the other two fragments, and yet—"*

"Well, I tried but it says I need to have a discussion before I can do anything!" I growled, throwing my arms up and pacing. "I mean, what the hell does that mean? I thought it was a discussion with you, but now I'm guessing not, right? So what? Do I need to walk in circles asking the void who I need to talk to until someone marches up and says—"

"You need to speak with me," came a new voice.

I missed a step in my little march, as I spun, looking around to see who'd spoken, as the other gods suddenly paled and seemed worried.

"All right, I'll bite, who or what are you?" I asked the empty air.

"The Arbiter," Sint whispered.

I shot him a glance, before turning back to the empty air.

"Okay, so you're the Arbiter?" I felt slightly ridiculous, but didn't know what else to do.

"The title serves a purpose," the voice said calmly.

"Okay, well, what's the crack, Jack?" I asked after a few seconds of silence. "No offense, but I don't know who or what you are. But if you can stop me getting access to my powers, I clearly need to."

"I am the many-faced judge. I am they. I am the one who watches and the one who renders judgment."

"That's nice," I agreed. "You're not making much sense, though. Are you another god?"

"To your mind, perhaps. I am neutrality," the voice replied solemnly. *"I enforce the balance."*

"Well, you're pretty shit at it," I snapped. "What the hell, dude, were you having a nap when it was the cataclysm or what?"

"The balance must be enforced."

"Yeah?" I tried again, before catching a glimpse of Sint and seeing that he was drawn back as if worried, mouth partly open to say something, and yet he'd stopped, frozen. "Sint?" I asked, a sudden nervousness rising. "You okay there, buddy?"

"He cannot interfere. None may."

"Okay, so what's going on?" A twisty mass of lines and shimmering, morphing symbols slid into being, hovering before me. "Whoa!"

"You appear to require a form to focus on, hence I have taken this one. The others in your mind would be inappropriate."

"Yeah, definitely," I agreed lamely, as Oracle doing the same thing and all the images she'd found suddenly sprang to mind, which then sent my already poor mood plummeting.

"You may call me Arbiter or another name as suits you," the being said.

I nodded. "Okay, I'm—"

"Jax." It bobbed slightly. ***I know what you are and why you are as you are. If not for the intervention of the Xenefier, this discussion would be held until you have acquired your tenth fragment, but I see that this is unable to occur.***

"What? Why?"

"You cannot then speak."

"Uh…"

"Seek not to try to trick knowledge of the future from me. I know all."

"Okay?" I tried, and then because I couldn't help myself, I asked the question. "Is Oracle…?"

"She lives, as does the child in her womb. You have more time than you fear, though less than you hope."

"Is that like a month? Three?" I tried uncertainly.

"I cannot answer."

"Yes you can," I replied quickly. "You just fuckin' did."

"I will not be drawn into the fight on your behalf nor against you, but upon claiming your third fragment, you gained enough power to survive direct contact with me. Understand this, little demigod, what you deemed the cataclysm was but a shiver in the realm, when observed from my position."

"But me getting three fragments of divinity somehow gives me the right to this conversation?" I asked, totally bewildered.

"No, but when you achieve ten, we will be unable to discuss, hence you gain a boon here and now in recompense."

"Why?" I asked.

"You wish the knowledge of why to be your boon?" it countered.

I shook my head. "Fuck no, give me Oracle and our child back here, safe and well," I begged. "Please, seriously I'll do—"

"What you ask is beyond your boon."

"Why?" I asked desperately. "Fuck's sake, why?"

"The Xenefier has both, and it has developed ways to block our interference. For our kind, what you perceive as gods, to be involved at your level will destroy your realm far beyond the minor effect of the cataclysm. We cannot interfere, not until there is no choice left."

"What?"

"If we were to take action, the power to remove Oracle and the child from the clutches of Xenefier would be akin to me removing one of the gods, or a continent and erasing it from existence. We are all bound."

I stared at the floating collection of lines and symbols and tried not to lose my temper, considering this was the one—or so I was guessing—that had punished Baphomet by ripping his power free to reform the temple.

Clearly, I wasn't going to get much sense from it, as it was just fucked in the head. Although there was a good chance I could trick some kind of an answer from it to help us, there was an even greater chance that I'd end up getting squished like a bug.

"The cataclysm was necessary to return balance. The darkness and those you deem evil were out of alignment, and the world of light must be brought into play."

Clearly this thing was batshit, or…

"Ask me of your boon, One Who is Yet to Be, else all must fall to chaos."

"What can I ask for?" I asked, stalling for time.

"Ask for that which you require, and which is you. This boon is your gift to the world."

I suddenly remembered all the slight nudges that Jenae had been giving me—the extra XP and the little unasked-for hints, markers appearing on my map…that kinda shit—and I desperately wanted this thing anywhere else but here, in case it noticed them.

"Do I get to choose my boon?"

It flared; the lines became spikes and symbols flattened out as an eye opened in the center, staring at me with three pupils that roamed and twisted.

"The Question!"

"Dude, what the fuck is going on here!" I snapped as my pent-up anger and confusion ran over the top. "Fuck's sake, you keep saying I have to choose, then you tell me I have to ask you, but you can't tell me shit! What do I want? I want Oracle! I want my love and our child free and safe!"

"You cannot—"

"I know, all right?!" I roared. "But you said you want to know what I want? That's what I want! I want them free. I want all my people free! I want them safe. I want to be able to face anyone who comes after them and tear them a new fucking arsehole! What do I want? I want the power to protect them all!

"I need to free them. I need to be the wall between them and the fucking night, all right? I need to be a father, Like I should have had and I'm terrified I'll never be good enough to be! I want to be there for them when they need me, and I want to be…to be…"

The eye stared at me fixedly.

"You ask for the power to protect," it hissed. ***"To be there when they need you."***

A sudden force seized me, like a fist around my head grabbing onto me and holding me in place as my memories were rifled through, like someone flipping through old LPs in a drawer. *Flick, flick, flick…*

Suddenly, it was as if I was there again, the last dream I'd had before being captured by the baron, the dream that I'd had the night I'd found out about Lou and Martin.

I was there, in the snow, bleeding out, an arrow through my leg, wounded, dragging myself along, frantic to stop the sounds that I could hear nearby, as the raiders…

Then I was back in my own flesh again as the clamp around my brain released, and time juddered into motion again.

"Your boon is granted. A limit removed, a gift that will grow."

I collapsed to the floor, gasping as pain ratcheted through me. My mind shuddered as in a bare brush of our minds against each other, the difference between my existence and the Arbiter's was revealed.

The Arbiter wasn't like our gods—oh fuck no, not even close.

It was a being that spanned entire universes and was the closest thing that I could imagine a "real" god to be. It was horrifically powerful and yet utterly uninterested in us, until we crossed a line. Just like I wasn't overly interested in the ants that roamed in the garden.

I suddenly saw the reaction it had to the cataclysm; it had been a blip.

Literally, that was it: a growing imbalance of life over death in one small segment of its realm was reined in, and relatively smoothly.

Other sides of the veil were thrown into disarray, but they soon smoothed themselves out as well.

Others called for judgment, or for aid, and it watched and waited, maintaining the balance until something was serious enough that it required its attention.

The rules being broken was one such item. And as it looked closer, it saw that one of the Dark-aligned deities had banished its opposites, taking advantage of the confusion. But as this reinforced the swing back to balance, it was judged acceptable, though the power gained was not.

Arbiter smoothed the flow, returning much of the stolen power to the realm again, and sending the one who had enacted the change screaming in frustration, fear, and agony.

I saw it as it opened a way for the other gods to return, eventually, and how it...holy shit, how it manipulated me and Tommy, attaching Amon to us, reinforcing the soul and enabling him to grow to where he could...

"You did it," I whispered, staring into space, seeing nothing, as the god above all, the true god, returned to where it had come from, breaking me free and tossing me aside, content that the balance was maintained, and that the little godlings had learned not to put their fingers on the scales too blatantly again.

It had been named "Arbiter" by the other gods, but there was a different name that suited it better.

Fate.

CHAPTER SEVENTEEN

"So, explain that one more fucking time," I whispered. My head throbbed as I sat on the floor, my face in my hands and this time, even Bane banished from the room as the gods spoke.

"It is the one above all, and one you should be unaware of until you draw its eye," Sint said. *"To draw its eye is both a boon beyond measure and curse everlasting. We did not ask for arbitration lightly, but it was necessary."*

"But why the hell did it speak to me now?" I asked. "Seriously, what the fuck?"

"Who knows?" Jenae sighed. *"Most likely, it was watching us and waiting for you to reach out to us for it to intervene. You're probably too weak for it to focus on—sorry, but it's true—without you directly involving yourself on a level that you really don't want."*

"Tell us again, what did it say?" Tamat whispered, staring at me, and sort of through me in a weird way.

"That it was giving me a boon now because I couldn't speak when it wanted to when I gain my tenth fragment," I said dully. "I mean, that's a good thing, right?" I tried, injecting a grain of false hope into the conversation. "I mean, I get all ten fragments!"

"Perhaps," Lagoush agreed, looking like She didn't believe it at all.

"Well, what the hell else could it mean?" I asked grumpily.

"It could mean that you gain your tenth fragment and instantly die, or that the damage it causes to your mind leaves you unable to communicate ever again," Tamat pointed out. *"What I don't understand is why did it do that?"*

"What?" I snapped. "Fuck's sake, Tamat, you can clearly see something, so what the hell is it? Quit the bullshit and the half hints—just fucking say it!"

"All right, you're broken," She replied coldly.

"Great. You mean emotionally? Yeah, I fucking know, all right, and—"

"No, I mean your power," She corrected.

"I…wait, what?" I looked at her.

"Tamat is correct, though with little tact." Jenae sighed. *"Jax, your powers have been twisted into a knot, one that requires significant work to understand, but it appears that your path has been unlocked, early."*

"Say what now?" I tried again.

"Your path…" She repeated, then sighed again. *"Okay, I can't think that the Arbiter would do this and still prevent us from discussing it. I guess that you gaining the third fragment so soon was enough for it to deem you worthy.*

"First of all, and just in case you can't hear what I say, the Arbiter is all powerful, but also…" She hesitated, looking unsure until Darakin stepped in and spoke quickly.

"The Arbiter is unmoored in time. It sees everything, everywhere, and it guides reality, in a way that none other can, and toward something only it can see. All we know is that things that happen too close together can distract it, and

we certainly wouldn't want that." The last was said in as obvious a 'oh, we really fuckin' do' way as could be.

"Okay, so if there's a lot of things happening in a short period…" I said slowly.

"Then it's possible the Arbiter would pick an event that was close enough and access it." Jenae nodded. *"Hence, you might understand and you might still be blocked."*

"Fuck me, this shit makes my head hurt," I whispered.

"You understand so little and yet you have never been more right." Darakin sighed. *"I, too, wish for the simpler things in life. But regardless…"* He turned to Jenae, who took a deep breath and then plunged on.

"So, the path of a god is their focus, the way that they access and accumulate power, and that they zzzzzzzzzzz." Suddenly, a section of what She was saying was lost entirely to a shimmering chime that drowned out Her words, and I held up a hand to stop her.

"Okay, well, we get to discuss some of it," She grumbled. *"Not like that would have made this much easier, but here we go. Your powers as a god come from specific things, which you might not have realized."* She looked at me as if to say, *This is the first you're hearing about it, so shut the fuck up and don't make it harder.*

"Oh, right, that's helpful," I said slowly.

She glared at my terrible acting before going on.

"So, what it was doing was asking for you to identify the most important part of yourself, the single ideal around which you will make your soul and your power rotate, the heart of who and what you are," She explained carefully.

"Oracle," I said firmly, relieved that I understood that much.

"No," She replied just as firmly. *"What came out when it put pressure on who and what you are wasn't Oracle, though I accept that to you she embodies and focuses everything that you are. No, what came out is the drive to protect.*

"The need to be there, to stand for all that you wish another had stood for, for you. You and your brother Thomas are identical in most ways, but here is where you differ, Jax. Thomas would drown the world in blood to be free, and at his heart, he knows that he would cross lines that you could not. That is why he looks to you for guidance, why he stands proudly in your shadow.

"He seeks to be guided, while for you, your soul searches for the love and protection you lost. As a small child, you saw all that you loved taken away. You watched as she died, and where others saw your mother pass, you saw the loss of the center of your world.

"The one who taught you right from wrong, who was the bulwark against the night. The person who held you when you were afraid and who showed you that nothing in the darkness was greater than her love. Her spirit was laid to rest in a realm that barely knew mana, or else she would have risen to a level few can imagine.

"She was the one you saw as your protector, and your home. You looked to her, and you saw everything that was right in the world. When she was gone, you refused to accept that she was a mortal woman and frail.

"Please understand, Jax, I say this not to be cruel, but you built her up in your mind to be a goddess, someone who would always be there to defend you and others. To instinctively know right from wrong. There is no fault in this— you were a child, and she your mother—but you kept this core tenet of your soul intact forever more.

"You taught and reinforced this in your brother, and you brooked no argument. He loved her equally, but where given time he would have seen her flaws, you convinced him of her sainthood. The result was the iron-clad belief that to honor who she was, you must protect those weaker than you. The heart of your honor and drive is that need to protect, to be the wall in her place, as you unknowingly wished another could have become for you."

"This is honorable, brother," Darakin said in a low voice as I stared at Jenae, tears trickling down my cheeks as my most hidden self was laid bare for all to see. *"Do not be ashamed of who you are, nor of why it came about. In this situation, you gain by it, and now, understanding such a thing, you have the chance to become exactly what you need."*

"I do?" I asked slowly, blinking the tears away.

"When she died, you and Thomas wished for one thing above all else," Jenae said softly. *"You knew that your mother was dead, no power on earth could bring her back, but your father? A figure you knew nothing about, and as such could hold all the desperate desires and wishes of a child?*

"You made him in your mind to be all that you felt you needed—a knight of your old-world histories, a hero, a leader and a protector, a general and a king, and humble enough that he'd care.

"In time, you grew out of the fantasy, forgetting it, as the real world rolled around and you saw more than any child of your world should. But that image remained embedded in your psyche, until you met him at least. Tell me, Jax, do you believe your father is evil?"

"Yeah," I growled. "Through and through."

"Despite knowing that he was entrusted by the emperor in studying the city of Pelath's View?"

I glared at her.

"You know something of what Xenefier is capable of, and yet you still can't bring yourself to look at your father, the man who was once the prince of the empire and Amon's right hand, as anything other than complete evil," she pointed out.

I forced myself to take a deep breath and answer honestly. "I don't know," I admitted. "He and all the others—"

"The other nobles who were once as dedicated to peace and justice across the empire as Amon, you mean?"

I couldn't bring myself to answer.

"Jax, I say this not to bring you pain or to distract you, but you have looked full upon the embodiment of evil, or as close as any creature can become to it, and you know that there were opportunities for Xenefier to interact with others.

"They then fell from grace, becoming twisted, selfish parodies of the leaders they once were, and others, the next generation and beyond, came to be raised by these people. Who else would you believe is responsible for this situation? And where better to deal with the infection, than at its source?"

"I will," I said, grasping for that lifeline. "I'll fucking kill Xenefier!"

"You'll try, and we'll do our best to aid you in this, Jax. But this is the point—if Xenefier can resurrect itself from the smallest sample, as it has claimed to have done in the past, then what do you suspect hides inside these nobles?"

"You think they were infected by it?" I asked hesitantly. "They were driven to do what they did, because of it?"

"I'm saying it's possible, that's all," She answered slowly. *"And Jax, what your focus is, what you asked for and demanded from the Arbiter as it set your path—a path that should have been unlocked as a full god and not before—is something that you need to understand."*

"Right...?" I agreed, getting whiplash from the constant conversational twists.

"Jax, your power is rooted in who and what you are. You are a protector, yes, but what you asked to be, what your soul demanded, is to be a father."

"A father," I repeated flatly. "You mean the thing that—"

"That Xenefier took from you." She nodded quickly, overriding my protestations. *"Yes, Jax—yes, I know. But what you asked for, what you called out with every fiber of your soul for, wasn't to be the emperor. It wasn't to learn, like I did, or to heal the realms like Lagoush. It wasn't to fight forever, as Darakin did, or to bring Order as Sint did. No, what you begged to be, what you demanded to be, was a father. The father of your people, of the empire."*

"But that was Amon," I interrupted, confused. "Amon was—"

"Amon was the Eternal Emperor, and he created the empire. Yes, he led it. He was the iron glove. But a father needs to be more than that, Jax. Specifically, the father you cried out to be was the father you wished, with all the power of a little boy, lost in the world, to have.

"A father who cared, who taught and who protected. Yes, the iron glove is there, but so is the softer touch. A father who isn't ashamed to hold you, and to shout out to all the realm that he is proud of who and what you are. Think on the drive and ability you have to free others from slavery, that absolute foundational need to free those people and protect them. That is your focus. The center of your power is to protect your children—all the citizens of the empire— but it's also to lead them, to guide them and to raise them to surpass you."

"What the fuck?" I gasped. "How the hell do I do that?"

"That's for you to figure out, Jax." She smiled, suddenly, and I glared at Her as She stood slowly. *"We have faith in you."*

"Fuck, no!" I cried, scrambling to my feet. "Dammit, Jenae, don't just drop this mystical bullshit and then fuck off! I need answers!"

"And you have them, Jax. You already know what you need to do," She replied. *"You'd been sliding from the path of your soul since losing her, you'd been growing ever angrier and ever more short-tempered, demanding and abrupt. That's acceptable in a man who has suffered a terrible loss..."*

"Exactly!" I retorted, desperately trying to get a word in edgewise.

"But it's not acceptable in a father dealing with his wayward children," She finished firmly. *"And for your soul to scream that you needed to be what you are, shows that you know it as well."*

"But what the hell does that MEAN!" I roared. "Fucking hell, how do I grow? How do I use my powers?!"

"The way you always have," She said, as the other gods slipped from sight. *"You do it with your heart, and your rage. You act as the one you believe you should be would act, and you fight against your baser urges and needs. Believe me, Jax, you have gained access to power that you should not have managed to yet. It can change the course of this fight, or cause you to fall at the final hurdle.*

"Be true to who you are, and who believe you should be, and there, on the cusp of your rage and love, you'll find your power waiting."

Jenae stepped out of the realm again and left me alone in the cathedral, surrounded by silence and flickering flames, candles that floated in the water here and there giving the room a cheery, warm light.

"FUCK!" I yelled at the top of my voice.

"Everything okay, boss?" Bane stuck his head in the door.

"Fuck! Fuckity fucking fuck's sake!" I screamed. "I'm gonna rip your tits off and beat you with them, Jenae!" I roared at the ceiling, as Bane carefully slid the door shut.

"He's…not very happy. Best we leave him alone for a bit," I heard him explain diplomatically to someone else, and that only served to rile me even more.

It was about another half an hour before I'd calmed down enough to think logically, though internally I was still an absolute mess. That was when I found the last notifications, which annoyed the hell out of me even more.

Congratulations!

You have taken your second step on the path to Godhood, climbing the mountain in truth, but what awaits you at the peak? Who knows, for you have bound a Fragment of Chaos to your soul.

The Fragment of Chaos offers three paths of power, but choose wisely, for Chaos once embraced cannot be contained, and until the choice is made, your soul dances on the edge of madness.

Entropy's Touch

Channel pure chaos through your physical form, causing anything you touch to undergo rapid, unpredictable transformation. Stone may become water, flesh may become crystal, or reality itself may simply…cease.

Note: Each use risks backlash, as Chaos cares not for the wielder's safety. Your own form may suffer unintended changes.

Charge: 1 per 12 hours

Probability Storm

Create a localized field where the laws of probability break down. Enemy spells may heal instead of harm, weapons may pass through targets like mist, or gravity may reverse. Within this storm, only your will guides the chaos.

Note: Maintaining control requires constant concentration. Loss of focus will affect all within the field, including allies.

Charge: 1 per 24 hours

<u>Fractal Mind</u>

Split your consciousness across multiple probability streams, allowing you to perceive and act upon different potential futures simultaneously. See the outcome of choices before making them, and select the timeline that serves you best.

Note: Extended use risks permanent fragmentation of consciousness. The more streams observed, the greater the strain on sanity.

Charge: 2 per 24 hours (duration: 30 seconds per use)

I stared at the notification, still inwardly seething, as I tried to come to terms with what had just happened, and why.

First of all, yeah, all right, nothing much had changed, and yet, oh *so* much had.

First of all, nothing changing, because I was still exactly who I always had been. Fate or Arbiter or whatever could paint himself blue and suck my balls if he didn't like that.

I still had exactly the same mentality and motivations, didn't I? Let's see: free Oracle and the baby; fuck up Xenefier. Have some great sex. Look after my people. Conquer the world. Maybe find a decent bar and relax on the beach for a bit, look at some titties.

Yup, same priorities. No change there.

The change was because when the gods had stepped up with that little goddamn therapy session—that was totally unasked for and nobody goddamn needed either, *thank* you very much—I'd been compelled to look at the single driving force in my life, beyond getting laid.

Protecting those I loved.

That was it, it had always been it, but until I had the layers peeled back in that weird circle jerk of a goddamn intervention, I'd never really seen it so clearly.

I still hated it, though.

Fuck it.

Nothing had changed, except that Jenae had basically called me out on being a bit of a dick with people and being a bit rude. Well, that was fine because I was going to have my diplomat deal with that kinda shit from now on and I was going to deal with what I was good at, which was stepping on throats and making fuckers sorry they crossed the line.

With that in mind, I pulled up the notification and reread the options, carefully ignoring that I'd just spent the last little while screaming threats at a goddess who should have had me smote at the very least.

Smitten? Smited? Fuck it, I was fairly sure it was smote, even if it didn't really sound right to my ear.

Okay, Entropy's Touch was just out. No chance. A section of space that would basically be filled with chaos, including the bit with me in it, and where anything at all could happen? That sounded like playing Russian roulette with three guns and a nuke.

Not happening.

Probability Storm was much the same. It could affect me and my people if my concentration slipped, and being that it was a divine-level ability, I didn't want to think about the fuckups *that* could cause.

I mean, a black hole suddenly popping into existence three inches away was always a possibility; if it was just an infinitesimally small one, but under the influence of chaos? That might happen, and when the spell expired, there was no way of knowing whether the damn thing would vanish or remain.

I could destroy the entire realm the very first time I tried to cast the damn spell. Uh, no. Just…no.

That only left one option, and although it sounded kinda cool, it could also be horrifically bad. Fractal Mind was basically me seeing the future, very narrowly, and seeing all the possibilities of an action, then picking which one I wanted to happen.

It was also possible to totally fuck my mind by doing it. But it was probably worth the risk, if I kept it as a one-off type of ability.

If I kept it to use right before I went for Oracle, then I could check the streams of reality and pick which one led me to her. Then booyah—I got her and my baby back, and I could win the fight.

Simple.

Admittedly, the strain of that might be enough to break my mind instantly, but if it resulted in me freeing them and ending Xenefier? Worth it. I just had to be careful and not use it before then. I chose that, and moved onto the next, whimpering as the fragment burrowed deeper into my soul, settling fully at last.

The second notification was the one for Order.

Congratulations!

You have taken your third step on the path to Godhood, and step by step, you ascend the mighty heights of reality, and a Fragment of Order has been joined to your soul.

You have bound a Fragment of Order to your soul.

The Fragment of Order presents three manifestations of absolute law. But remember: perfect Order tolerates no deviation, and until the choice is made, your soul yearns for its rigid perfection.

Immutable Decree

Speak a single law into existence within a defined area. This law becomes absolute reality that cannot be violated by any means, magical or mundane. "None shall cast magic" or "All must kneel" become inviolable truths.

Note: The decree affects all within range, including the caster. More complex laws require exponentially more power to invoke and to maintain.

Charge: 1 per 24 hours (duration: 10 minutes)

Crystalline Restoration

Impose perfect order upon any object, structure, or being, returning it to its original, intended state. Heal wounds by restoring the body's proper form, repair ancient artifacts, or undo magical corruption.

Note: Cannot restore life to the truly dead, as death is often the "proper" state. Forcing order on chaotic beings causes extreme pain to both sides. Mana required must be supplied or else the divine being using this ability will be drained to power it.

Charge: 1 per 72 hours

Dominion of Law

Create an expanding field of absolute order where your will becomes natural law. Within this dominion, you define the rules: magic functions only as you permit, physics bend to your design, and even thoughts must follow patterns you establish.

Note: Maintaining a dominion drains power proportional to how much you alter reality. Conflicting with other divine domains risks catastrophic backlash.

Charge: 1 per 48 hours (duration: varies by size/complexity)

Okay, reading this one over made me damn glad that I'd already accepted a little chaos into my soul, considering that the "feel" of order was so rigid and unmoving.

Checking out the options, I decided that Immutable Decree was a good one. I could do something like inflict a situation where any liquid not bound behind flesh boiled away in an area with me and Xenefier in it and…

And I'd blind myself and probably die horribly like I was in space, wouldn't I?

Dammit, I wished I knew more of the rules of reality, but physics was such a boring subject and I'd hated school. Fuck it. It was still a contender. I'd just have to be very, very careful about the decree I gave, that was all.

On to the next, but I'd keep that one on the back burner.

Crystalline Restoration was a hell of a drug, I instantly saw. That one…yeah, that was a possibility. The long cooldown on it was a killer, but that I could forcibly recreate, repair, or return anything to its most perfect state was incredibly tempting.

Admittedly, that whole "needs fuckin' mana" side was a bit of a killer, but then they all did—they just hadn't mentioned it thus far—and I damn well knew that.

So, if I found another great tower, as long as I had the mana, I could actually repair it. That was insane, massively overpowered and a true "god" ability. I liked it.

The third option was another "law" option, but an insanely overpowered one. I was tempted, but it was basically a dominion spell, and the end point of the one that I already had.

I could already disrupt all mana use in an area thanks to my Imperator class spells, so this was just a little…well, it was good. All right, it was *great*.

I admit it—it was great and it could be used all sorts of ways. For a start, anything in my dominion that was identified by me as being of Xenefier, as an example, could be destroyed.

I could say that anything linked to that fuckstick was to catch fire and die.

The problem was, how and who defined "linked to"? Maybe I was linked to it as I'd seen and interacted with it. Was that enough? If I said that, would I instantly catch fire and die?

No, there were too many variables and not enough certainties for that one, so fuck it.

I gave myself a few minutes to think about it, then sighed and picked Crystalline Restoration. Then I fucking groaned as the fragment fully settled, then I groaned again as I saw that in being linked to me, I didn't feel a cost in mana the way I normally did. Instead, I felt that they'd linked to the imperial throne, and the highly limited store of mana that it held.

That was good because it wasn't going to rip the mana from me to do the spells, or at least not until that was emptied, but I also knew that the imperial throne's stores were what I typically used to free the slaves. And if there wasn't any mana left there…dammit.

The abilities were basically reduced to utter emergency uses, but I was fine with that. As I grew and gathered more fragments as well as power, I'd be able to refill that store and get the use of these abilities as well.

That made me think about it. For a long moment, I saw the thousands of ways that the gods of history had interacted with people and performed or refused to do miracles.

Suddenly, it all made a little more sense.

Fuck it.

I dismissed the screens, and for the first time in ages, there wasn't a notification blinking away to pester me.

That, of course, just as my temper finally cooled, was when someone thought it was the perfect time to give me some shit.

CHAPTER EIGHTEEN

"What the hell was I supposed to do?!" I snarled at Flux, who shook his head and pointed to the floor again in silent order. "Goddamn sneaky motherfucking…" I forced myself not to continue with what I really wanted to say, instead going on with the push-ups and trying to get the last possible points over the line as we flew.

It had been Ame, of course, who had walked in at just the right—or wrong—point in the damn day for me, coming with her usual brand of subtlety to ask whether I'd found a solution to the problem of protecting the temple. And given that she'd been as calm and polite as she always was, I'd practically boiled the hide off her in my anger.

That meant that when I calmed down and realized that I'd seriously fucked up, I'd then had to go and apologize to her, which had been immeasurably worse than I'd thought it could be. It left me with a feeling that I was both a naughty schoolboy, and the most uncaring and self-centered lout in the world.

How she'd done that was beyond me, but she'd actually managed it.

That was how I'd ended up in the position I was in now, where Flux had given me his recommendation and asked whether I was willing to listen, or whether I already knew more than he possibly could.

I got that he was pissed with me tearing his mate a new asshole, and so I now forced myself to go through the stages to make it up to him, as the others merrily got on with their flight.

Mainly by placing bets and chilling out.

The stress of the flight to reach me had been dealt with, and now everyone had basically fallen back into their old routines, which was why I had Giint sitting squarely on my shoulder blades to "add additional weight" as I continued to work out.

I also wore the extra-weighted armor that I'd gotten so long ago from Augustus, as Lydia had helpfully produced it, making half the rest of the squad panic, until they realized it wasn't meant for them.

Apparently, the armor had seen a lot of extra use on the flight over, as they all wore it—those who could anyway; Bane and Giint, for example, couldn't at all due to extra arms and being a short-arse, respectively—but it'd made a hell of a difference in their training regimens.

Wearing armor essentially made of lead and then being forced to run and do everything you normally did in your regular, much lighter armor certainly burned the calories, I found. And doing push-ups with a mad little cackling gnome on your back while wearing the stuff was even worse.

The final straw, as I hit two hundred and was only mildly out of breath, was when the disgusting little bastard farted on my back.

It was against the naked metal, which meant that it reverberated and echoed, seemingly loud enough to wake the dead, followed by a little "oopsie" into the sudden silence. The ensuing maniacal laughter finally convinced me to give it all up.

Or, more accurately, to leap to my feet, grab Giint as he tried to run, and hurl him as far as I could.

Admittedly, I hadn't planned to throw him over the side, but Lydia was quick enough to catch the smelly little bastard so he didn't die. This time.

When I'd calmed down, and so had the others—Grizz couldn't stand, due to hysterical laughter—I sat with Lydia and Flux and filled them in on exactly what had happened, and why.

They had to stop me several times as things I said were blocked from them hearing it, which was a weird experience, as I heard nothing of the interruption. But they would suddenly stiffen and start shaking their heads, leaving me to work out which bits were forbidden knowledge—how the gods gained their power and used it—and which weren't.

Mainly me screaming abuse about the unfairness and stupidity of it all, and how I wasn't a fucking tree-hugger who wanted to be the world's father and be all sunshine and light, until they both stopped me.

"Why?" Lydia asked me gruffly. "What's pissin' yer off so much about that?"

"It's…well, it's not that… It's…" I tried to explain it, that it was so lovey-dovey, hippie-dippy that it just made my feckin' balls cringe until she went on, with Flux nodding along with her.

"What do yer think yer bin doing since yer came here!" she snapped. "By all that's holy, Jax, yer an idiot sometimes, yer know that?"

"I'm not!" I snapped back.

"You are," Flux agreed with her. "You spend your entire life working to protect people, you train harder than any other, you run everywhere. Any chance to stop and relax? Look at them." He waved a hand generally toward the others, and I frowned, following the gesture.

Yen and Grizz sat on the railing, talking, smiling and looking all right; two of the new starters in the mer warband were training with Lio; Tang stood on the railing farther down, practicing his balancing, while Ronin recited a story for the others, and…

"What?" I asked, not seeing it.

"What are they doing?"

"Nothing?" I shrugged. "They've worked their arses off the last few weeks, so they're relaxing. They've earned it."

"Exactly," he growled, and Lydia nodded vigorously. "They do what you should be doing, and yet you never do! When on a flight like this, usually you ask to train with us for most of each day, and then when you can't take any more, either you mate with Oracle and vanish for a bit, or you're off making potions for everyone."

"And?" I asked, not getting it, but feeling the flare of pain when he mentioned my missing love.

"You. Don't. Stop." He punctuated every word with a jab of a finger into my shoulder. "You never do. You always push yourself. The only time you ever stop working is when you sleep, when Oracle has dragged you off to your room for mating, or if we've forced you to interact."

"Do yer no like relaxin' with t'team?" Lydia asked quietly. "Ah mean, ah can understand it if not. Ah know sometimes they be annoyin' as shit."

"No," I said quickly. "I do like it. I just…" I paused, looking for the words. Lydia said them before I could.

"Yer feel like yer lettin' them down iffin yer not workin' as hard as yer can?"

"Well, yeah, I guess," I admitted. "It's not that I think I *have* to, not all the time. It's just that if I make the potions, if I give everyone the tools they need, then there's a better chance they'll survive. That they'll…"

"That you'll have protected them," Flux said softly.

"Yeah, I guess." I shrugged a bit awkwardly.

"Jax, you work harder than any I know save Restun," he pointed out. "I know you said that the gods think you're going to get stronger if you become the father of the empire, not just its leader—or at least that's what I think you said, so much was blocked or lost that it was hard to get—but if that's the case, you don't have to be the father that you had, or a father in some way that you don't feel and understand.

"You can become the leader you always intended to be. You misunderstand if you think the gods are forcing you to become someone you're not. They told you, whatever else they told you, to help you be truer to yourself!

"You said that your powers would come from what you are? Then don't fear what you do, or hate it—be who and what you are and accept that every minute, every hour of each day that you grow, that you continue to be who you are, is giving you additional power to be who you want to be.

"The protector of the empire doesn't have to be the diplomat; they don't have to be the lawyer or the alchemist. They just have to be the one who steps up and does something about it when the time comes, and they have to care. You are the father of a new empire, even if you didn't set out to be. Accept it and move on."

"'E's right, Jax. Yer just need t'keep bein' who yer are. An' stop being such a miserable bastard!" Lydia growled.

"Oh, well, fuck you very much!" I snapped at her. "Is my missing my love and my fucking child annoying you?"

"Jax!" Flux clapped all four hands together in front of my eyes, making me blink and glare at him. "She is right. You do little beyond snap orders, train, or demand others obey. You must recover the heart of who you are, and this is not a miserable person. Yes, you are sad, and you miss Oracle and you are worried about the child, but you are not only this. We all miss her and worry. We have all lost. You must accept and recover, or you will lose the chance to rescue her."

I forced myself to take a deep breath and then ask him—calmly—what he recommended.

"Asha'tuun, and meditation," he said definitively. "Exhaust your body, and relax your mind. Permit the knots around your heart to relax, and accept that enjoying something, *anything*, is not a betrayal of those you love, if they cannot also experience it."

"My stats aren't improving," I admitted, and he shrugged.

"Not all exercise or activities will increase stats," he said. "It doesn't mean you should not do them."

"All right, but you had me doing hundreds of fucking push-ups this morning to prove that," I pointed out.

"No," he corrected. "I had you do that because you shouted at my mate and annoyed me. Also, it was funny and I was curious to see if it would increase your stats still, regardless. But mainly it was for Ame."

"You rat bastard," I muttered.

He shrugged, a particularly expressive gesture when done with four arms. "It was worth it, though I didn't expect Giint to make such a…memorable…addition."

"You know what the little bastard is like."

"I do, but I also didn't ask him to climb aboard your back. He chose to do that himself."

I thought about that and then seriously considered "helping" him over the side to run alongside the ship for a bit again, until Lydia shook her head and smacked my arm.

"Leave 'im be. Yer know 'e probably thought it'd be funny and might cheer yer up."

"Being farted on?" I cocked my head to the side in question. "You think he thought I'd like that?"

"Well, maybe 'e thought it'd be funny for everyone. 'E is a mad gnome, remember."

"I do," I grumbled. "Fine, whatever. Did he manage to help the other gnomes?"

"Oh, aye. When we left, they were tearin' t'rebuilt version of their airship apart and tryin' new shit again. Looks like they'll be at that stage for a few months now."

"Dammit." I groaned.

"No, they won't," Flux disagreed. "As much as Ame was annoyed with you, she said she had a plan for the gnomes and a wagon design, so expect her to get them whipped into shape."

That started the conversation about the original design of the airship, and why it'd gone so badly wrong, and then we were off on a tangent about gnomes.

After a little bit, I realized that the pair were deliberately asking me questions, and that I'd gone from single answers or cursing, into actually relaxing a little, and I forced myself to dismiss that and keep talking.

Gradually, when the conversation had died down, Flux got me up and training with him and the new mer—he'd brought a group of ten from the lake who had volunteered—and with Lio and Bane joining in. We taught the new recruits a little, and that was the way the hours passed until we landed to deal with the caravan.

It was a medium-sized one, as these things went, with a little under forty wagons, some two hundred guards, and a trio of merchants who had been in charge until Tenandra had shown up, destroying a section of the ground nearby and thoroughly cowing them all, before dropping off the legionnaires to take command.

Now, with me there to take the oaths, the first hour involved some questions and a very simple offer. Namely, "do you want to be given the value of the shipment you were taking to the slave and raiding city and you can fuck off, or do you want a chance to join the empire?"

All three merchants chose the former, and were then highly surprised when their mercenary guards took the option of joining the empire.

Admittedly, that was because I'd pointed out that they'd get superior training, opportunities, and experience, but mainly because the wages that had been settled upon for the legion—back at Gaij, I'd had nothing to do with it, but I was happy with it when it was explained to me—was more than double a merc's normal wage.

So, they were told that they had a choice just as the merchants did: they could be paid for their contract now—by the merchants, who were suddenly a lot less sanguine about the whole deal—and they could join the empire, or they could return with the merchants, and possibly end up on the other side in any fight to come.

That left a grand total of one hundred and fifty-nine of the nearly two hundred guards and mercs joining us, and the rest to march back with the merchants, who had finally realized that they were in the middle of nowhere, and my definition of "everything" included their wagons and supplies.

Was it a bit shitty on my part?

Yeah—yeah, it was, and a bit of a bully tactic as well. But considering one of the first things the merchants had said to me was that they were members of the Caravaneer's Guild in good standing, apparently expecting that would help them, I had zero fucking patience with them.

As they weren't looking to join the empire, I couldn't be sure anything that they told me was the truth, and I also couldn't execute them on guilt by association of being members of the guild. So, instead, I settled on making their lives miserable—as the vast majority of the caravan, and the guards and members of the legion headed on toward the Cradle with their prizes.

Hennen had stayed back at the Cradle—he wasn't happy about it, but I'd decided that I needed someone in charge of the settlement who knew their arse from their elbow—and so the caravan was directed to report to him on arrival. Borren had come with us, to help look after our expanded forces, and so that I had someone in charge of the greater contingent, when I inevitably went off exploring and Lydia and the others followed me.

So now, as we all got sorted out into groups, I was left with the unenviable position of being surrounded by people who had sworn loyalty but who had very little personal experience of me beyond that I was a lunatic who had come out of nowhere and kicked the living shit out of the world in general.

The end result was that they all expected me to do everything perfectly, and seeing me humbled as I tried to help them to train was a new experience.

So, being the bastard that I was, as the mer and the new legionnaires lined up to start training, I shouted for our people to stop fucking around and come and join in as well.

Seeing Ronin perform a spin kick that was a thing of beauty was an absolute surprise. But the biggest shock and the proof that the group had trained incessantly on the journey over was seeing Grizz, the massive wall of muscle and terrible jokes, flow from one stance to the next in asha'tuun like he'd been doing it all his life.

Three hours we trained for, which sounds like a lot to anyone without martial arts experience. In reality, it was an hour of warming up and the basics, an hour of high intensity training, half an hour of sparring, and then half an hour of cooldown.

By the end of that, and then a little meditation, I found myself in a much better mood, my anger over Oracle having changed mainly to a mixture of melancholy and determination, and the evening passed smoothly.

The next day was much the same, though minus the caravan. We trained, we relaxed, and we helped the mer to acclimatize. Their species could live outside of the water, as Bane and the others were a testament to, but it took time, determination, and an absolute fuckload of water.

Fortunately, Tenandra had put sections of the ship aside for the mer team members already, and it was a simple thing to make those a little larger, keeping them sealed from all other entrances and keeping the water in them.

Gradually, over the next two days, they were in and out of the water, training on the deck with the rest of the ship's company and were permitted healing fountains. They got used to it, even if they were never exactly comfortable.

By the evening of the second night, the gentle blur in the distance resolved into the trees and forests, and by the following sunrise, we found ourselves deep into the great forest, hanging over a wide lake, and waiting, as Yen, Grizz, and Silviana approached the city of Lembiq, ready to open negotiations.

<u>YEN</u>

Yen had faced down gods, fought alongside literal legends and the Godslayer, and survived the worst years of the legion's life—apart from the loss of the emperor, of course.

Now, though, as she stood at the edge of the city of Lembiq's walls, watching the morning mist curl through trees that seemed to scrape the very sky, she felt a flutter of nerves she hadn't experienced in years.

Whatever happened, Lembiq was going to swear to join the empire, she silently declared, as there was no way she was failing her first official diplomatic mission.

"Sweet suffering saints," Grizz muttered beside her, craning his neck back to follow the nearest trunk upward until it disappeared into the canopy overhead. "How tall are these bastards?"

"The Great Mothers average three hundred meters," Silviana said softly. Her voice carried a reverence that made both Yen and Grizz turn to look at her. The wood elf's bark-brown skin seemed to glow in the filtered sunlight, and for the first time since they'd freed her from Kronk's arena, she looked…content. "The eldest among them have stood for over two thousand years."

Yen studied their guide carefully. Silviana had been clearly nervous as they got closer to the walls, constantly adjusting her borrowed leather armor and running her fingers through her leaf-green hair. Now, standing before the first checkpoint—a graceful arch woven from living wood and branches that carved a gap in the heavy wall of thorns—she seemed more relaxed in herself, but also was apparently resigned to something happening that she wasn't looking forward to.

"State your name and purpose, travelers," demanded a voice from above.

Yen had to suppress her instinct to reach for her weapon as three figures descended from the canopy on what looked like nothing more than twisted vines. The wood elf guards landed with barely a whisper of sound, their armor and cloaks blending perfectly with the surrounds to make them difficult to spot until they threw the cloaks back, clearly ready to fight.

The lead guard was male, his face bisected with a long, jagged scar that must have been horrific to endure, considering the clear natural healing that had left him this way. His armor was a mix of greens and browns, and a short bow was held ready in his left hand, though the arrows were thankfully still in his quiver.

He looked from one of them to another, clearly noting the legion gear that both Yen and Grizz wore first and then moving to linger on Tenandra hovering over the lake in the distance.

"That…thing," he gestured toward the ship with his elegantly curved bow, "has half the city in an uproar, so you'd better explain before—"

"I am Silviana Moonweaver." Silviana stepped forward with a confidence that hadn't been shown until now. "Sister of Caelum Moonweaver, and scout of the Southern Reaches, taken in a Dark Legion raid four months past."

The guard's suspicious expression flickered. "Silviana? I recognize the name. Though I was told she was killed along with the rest of her unit."

"If only. No, I was sold to slavers. I was forced to fight in the arenas of Kronk at the end, and I was freed when the city fell to the empire." She pulled back her sleeve, revealing the faint scars where slave shackles had rubbed her wrists raw. "I've come home, bringing representatives of the same empire that freed me. They need to speak with the council."

A younger guard, her hair woven with small stars that Yen identified more as functional—if small—weapons than decoration, leaned forward. "Captain, I know her. We trained together under Master Tisan. That's definitely Silviana."

The captain's stance shifted subtly, sweeping a hand out to the side as if adjusting his cloak. Yen recognized the gesture as deliberate. He was signaling to unseen watchers in the trees above.

She carefully kept her hands away from her weapons, noting that Grizz had adopted his "big dumb human" posture that he used when he wanted people to underestimate him, but still stood silent and calm.

"The Moonweaver bloodline was mourned," the captain said finally. "Your mother hasn't left the Grove of Sorrows since you were taken." His voice softened fractionally. "She'll want to see you."

"After I've completed my duty," Silviana replied. "These are honored representatives of the empire. Yen'ma Rultahir, Speculatores Praetoria and diplomat, and Grizz Borrowman, guardian and warrior. They come with an offer of aid against our common enemies."

Yen stepped forward, offering the formal bow she'd been taught so long ago was appropriate for elven culture. She thought she'd done it right, but the truth was that clearly the species divides on Carrmor were totally unlike on Dravith. There, apart from the high elves in their hidden city, the rest of the elven population of the continent was so intermarried and mixed that even her own elven heritage was long lost to her. Only her legion life mattered now.

"Captain, we understand Lembiq's caution toward outsiders. We come not as conquerors but as those who share your enemies. The Dark Legion that has plagued your borders has also struck at our people. We come to offer your elders partnership, and an alliance."

The captain studied her for a long moment. Yen knew what he saw—a "common" elf: her pointed ears marked her as cousin-kin but her features lacked the distinctive wood elf traits. It made her slightly more acceptable where a human might not be, but only just.

When she'd been a child, she'd heard the high elves calling her kind mongrels and "dirty blood" because they were more interbred than those puritan pricks. But fuck it. Either they'd accept her or they wouldn't, and then she'd have to teach the fuckers some respect.

"The council will decide," he said eventually. "You may enter the lower Branch district while I send word above. Touch nothing, harm nothing, and remember—the trees have eyes and very long memories."

The checkpoint's living arch pulsed with a faint green light as they passed beneath it, and Yen had a tingling sensation as a spell washed over her. What it did, she had no clue, but she felt it nevertheless, and Grizz shuddered beside her.

"Did anyone else feel like they just got fondled by a very polite tree?" he muttered under his breath, making Yen snort as she tried to keep the smile off her face. That stupid oaf.

"It's the wardens," Silviana explained quietly. "They remember the scent and soul of everyone who passes. That way, they always know where you are. If you've entered with ill intent…" She didn't finish the sentence, but the hint was pretty damn clear.

The Rootside district was unlike anything Yen had ever seen before. Where most cities built their homes with stone and mortar, here everything was grown from scratch, meaning a level of city planning that had to be centuries in design.

Buildings emerged from massive roots that broke the surface like frozen waves, their walls formed from woven branches that had hardened into something more like granite. Mushrooms the size of shields provided gentle illumination in the dimmer areas, pulsing with bioluminescent blues and greens.

The ground-level marketplace bustled with activity, though Yen noticed the crowd was distinctly more mixed than she'd expected. Humans, common elves, mer, and a few dwarves moved between stalls selling everything from preserved foods to weapons.

For every other member of the races, there were two wood elves, but the heavy mixture didn't match the hard looks she'd gotten from the captain, so Yen kept her mouth shut and kept walking, watching.

"Rootspawn," she heard one mutter as they passed, though whether it was meant as insult or a name or what she didn't know.

Grizz tried very hard to look everywhere at once without appearing like a tourist. His usual swagger—the fucker strutted like a proud goddamn peacock even in armor, for the empire's sake—thankfully lessened as they passed a staircase that spiraled up around one of the great trees, disappearing into the misty heights above.

"How high do those go?" he asked faintly, failing to keep the nervousness from his voice.

"To the Branch district, about sixty meters up," Silviana replied. "The Canopy is another hundred and twenty above that."

Grizz made a sound that might have been a whimper if it had come from anyone else. From him, it was merely a very manly clearing of his throat, and Yen bumped him with her shoulder, reminding the big ox that she was there, and that nobody else knew about his stupid issues with heights.

It was stupid, by any standards, because he had absolutely zero fear aboard Tenandra, sometimes miles in the sky, and yet tall buildings freaked him out.

Even more stupidly, the Great Tower didn't, and the thought of all the billions of tons of stone overhead whenever she walked in the place sometimes gave her nightmares.

The damn fool.

They were led to what Silviana called a "lifting platform," an elegant cage of woven branches powered by some mechanism Yen couldn't see. As it rose, Grizz's knuckles went white on the guide rail.

"You all right there, big man?" Yen asked quietly.

"Oh, you know, heights and I have such a good understanding," Grizz replied through gritted teeth. "I don't like them, and they try to kill me. It's worked out poorly so far."

"You jumped from that tower in Himnel across to a moving airship," she pointed out. "I remember that, and then from the airship to another airship."

"Please don't remind me," he whispered, closing his eyes. "Seriously, I didn't care about heights until then."

"You were dancing along the edge of Tenandra's railing last night," she added.

"I thought I was going to get lucky," he grumbled, making her laugh. "The risk was worth it, and I trust Tenandra."

"You big fool." Yen sighed fondly. "What the hell did I do to deserve you?"

"Just unlucky, I guess." He snorted, but she saw the little smile reflected in his eyes, and she nodded.

"*Lucky*, you meant to say, I think," she whispered, before turning back to stare out across the amazing sight that was being revealed.

The platform rose smoothly through layers of the city Yen could barely tear her eyes from. The Rootside fell away below, the simple wood and well-made, though dimmer and more "down-to-earth" areas, she quickly realized, and they entered the Branch district proper.

Here, the city's true glory was shown off to stunned eyes. Walkways of living wood connected platforms built around and into the massive trunks. Some bridges were wide enough for literal crowds to pass over, with smaller, leafy branches rising on the sides, curving up and around to protectively shield from wind and rain. Others were slimmer, and clearly single-person routes only.

Vines lifted and lowered, people hanging from them, a hand or foot looped into the vine as they called out to friends or shouted the news as they passed.

Buildings hung like insanely oversized fruit from the branches, their windows glowing with warm light. Gardens flowed down from balconies, creating literal waterfalls of flowers and vines.

The air was clean, and the deeper Yen breathed, the more she relaxed, as the air was filled with the smell of growing things and the occasional sound of wind chimes ringing.

And the elves? They moved with the speed and grace of people perfectly used to their homes. She saw children no more than five or six years old racing along branches that would have given her pause, laughing as they leaped gaps that made her legionnaire's stomach clench.

"Show-offs," Grizz grumbled after a single glance, his eyes firmly locked onto the solid platform under him.

The platform stopped at a broad plaza built into a meeting point of three massive trunks.

Here, more guards waited, these wearing armor that seemed to be as much grown as forged, with leaves and thorns of steel and glass blended into a design that looked as much art as anything martial.

"The council has agreed to hear you," one guard announced, stepping forward and nodding to the captain who had escorted them in greeting, but directing his words to Yen. "Elder Thessarian has descended from the Canopy to observe. You should feel honored, outsiders. He hasn't authorized that an outsider be admitted to plead their case in the council chambers themselves in thirty years."

Over the next twenty minutes or so, they were led across bridges that made Grizz's breathing go ragged, through passages that wound through the living wood of the trees themselves, and up on two more lifters, until finally they emerged into the council chamber.

Yen had expected something grand and formal. Instead, she found herself in a space that felt both warm and alive. The chamber was a hollow in one of the Great Mothers—the insanely enormous trees—apparently naturally formed, then presumably carefully shaped over centuries.

Bound in amber, the magelights gleamed with a warm light, giving the entire room a comforting feeling, and the floor was polished wood smoothed by what had to have been hundreds of years of passage.

Seven figures sat in a semicircle, each in a chair that must have been grown from the floor specifically for them. Around the outside were dozens of elves, with more coming as they gathered, clearly curious, but staying quiet in what was apparently their way.

At the center of the room, flanked by the other chairs, and Yen guessed from the description Silviana had given, sat Lord Farendir. She immediately understood why Silviana had described him as "cautious."

Everything about him, from his carefully neutral expression to the way his hands rested perfectly identically on his chair arms and his calm silence, said this was a man who had survived centuries by never committing to anything too quickly.

To his right sat an elder, and from the description Silviana had given, he had to be Thessarian. He was also everything Farendir wasn't.

So old Yen couldn't put a number to him, the whorls of his bark-like skin actually looked like they'd creak when he moved. His eyes, though, were bright and sharp, and they fixed on Yen with an intensity that instantly made her feel like a primus was judging her.

"So," Thessarian's voice was like wind through old leaves, smoothing his little van-dyke beard. "The empire returns, eh? I remember when the true 'Eternal' Emperor walked these very bridges. Amon was full of fire and promises. That was, oh, eleven hundred years ago? Just after we helped him establish the Northeastern Reaches."

"You knew Emperor Amon?" Yen couldn't hide her surprise as she abandoned the speech she'd been working on in her mind in her shock.

A huffing sound was all he managed as laughter, but the smile on his face was genuine enough, she was willing to bet.

"Knew him? Child, I helped train some of his honor guard in our ways of warfare. Fine young men and women, though they never could quite master the branch-dancing. Too much human blood, I always said." His ancient eyes fixed on Grizz. "No offense meant, knight."

"None taken," Grizz said politely.

Yen heard the lack of strain in his voice, meaning that in here at least, surrounded by solid walls and a stout floor, he was clearly okay. That or now that she needed him, he'd gone from worried about little things, to the true knight that hc was.

Lord Farendir cleared his throat delicately. "Perhaps we might address the present rather than dwelling on the past. You come claiming to represent a reborn empire, yet all we have seen are notifications of destruction. Cities fallen. Continents conquered. Gaij and Kronk attacked. Gods themselves struck down. Lembiq has no interest in binding itself to an agent of such chaos."

This was Yen's moment. She stepped forward, drawing on all her training in law and all the oh so many times she'd had to cheerfully speak to fucking nobles all while wanting to gouge their eyes out with rusty spoons.

"Before we begin, perhaps as a starter, we may introduce ourselves." Thessarian sighed, holding a hand out to stop her. "My apologies, child. It has been long years since any we addressed formally were not of the trees. So, I am Thessarian, and this is…" He went around the group, and when their turn came, Yen introduced herself, Grizz, and Silviana, who got wide smiles, and a series of "Welcome back, child" from the elders as well.

Then, the niceties observed, Thessarian gestured back to Yen.

She forced a smile, and she began again.

"My lord, honored elders, we come not as harbingers of chaos but as its opposite. The empire seeks to restore order to lands that have fallen to darkness. Yes, Kronk burned—because it was a cesspit of slavery and murder that could not be redeemed. And to be clear, when I say 'burned,' I mean it was utterly destroyed. There aren't two bricks atop one another there now."

She looked from one to another as she went on, judging the way they took that little tidbit. "Yes, Prince Jax has fought gods—the same gods who brought about the cataclysm and who declared themselves against the return of the empire. However, we also *serve* gods, the Pantheon of the Flame, the nine elder gods who the God of Death tricked and banished, and two more who have joined since then. We're not agents of chaos. Instead, we bring order, and peace."

"Yes. I've heard it's hard to break the peace from a coffin," Elder Morvaine interjected. She was younger than Thessarian but still carried centuries in her bearing. Her hand rested on a sword hilt with the easy familiarity of long practice. "But words won't stop the Dark Legion from bleeding us dry. I've got more to do today than I know what to do with, and little time for this, so let's cut to the chase. What does your prince offer? More empty promises, as so many before him?"

"No, Prince Jax offers action," Yen replied. "Solid, clear evidence of his promises. The Dark Legion fortress in Bleakwood—he offers to destroy it completely. Not raid it, not weaken it. Eliminate it entirely. Free every slave within its walls and end its threat to your people forever."

Yen smiled as several of the councilors blinked in shock; even Farendir's careful neutrality cracked slightly as he gripped the arms of his chair tightly, before forcing himself to relax, as he caught himself.

"I find that hard to believe, child," Farendir murmured, smiling in a gently mocking way.

"The Bleakwood fortress has stood for centuries." Elder Rennmai took up the conversation. She looked to be the youngest on the council, which likely still meant she had half a dozen centuries on Yen. "We do not mean to disparage your prince, young one, but the citadel holds thousands of soldiers, and the death magic of its master is soaked into every stone. Last, and most important of all, the citadel is commanded by something that calls itself the Bleaklord. You speak of destroying it as if discussing tomorrow's weather."

"That's because for Prince Jax, it might as well be," Yen said smugly, looking from one to another as she judged their interest. "He took Kronk with one other of our party, because he was too annoyed to wait for the rest of us to arrive. Note that he took it, freed the prisoners, then destroyed it utterly.

"You're used to lords who try and buy your aid, I'd imagine, who grub in the dirt for gold and silver, platinum and gems and backstab the second they find a better deal. He's not like that. He destroyed the city without bothering to strip the vaults because that form of wealth means nothing to him.

"In his eyes, the people are the greatest wealth he can gather. Each and every single person he saves is a balm to his soul. And believe me when I say it's not bullshit."

Well, there goes the carefully crafted diplomatic talk. Yen mentally cursed herself, then went on.

"He was named scion and prince by the spirit of Eternal Amon, and he's killed divine avatars in single combat. The flying ship you must have seen out over your lake? It carries weapons that can level city walls from the sky, and he drew up the plans to create them. We can and have destroyed entire armies using them, and this is but one ship. Your enemy's fortress was built to withstand conventional assault. What we bring is anything but conventional.

"You talk about the citadel? We had one on Dravith. Centuries it'd stood, the center of the worship of the God of Death. He tore it down personally, with a single spell. Then he took that god's head, when he came filled with fury to punish him for it. That's the man—no, that's the *demigod*, as he has three fragments of divinity—that's the *prince* who offers you aid, and asks for yours in return."

"And in exchange for this service?" Farendir asked carefully.

"He asks that you think of it as an example of goodwill. He wishes for you to remember your old oaths and return to the empire. Yes, he can conquer cities as he goes, and in the main part, he will. The difference here is that Lembiq is a city known to be both against the slave trade and to be a city of honor. Most of those we've encountered don't have either of those reasons for his mercy.

"As such, the prince's offer is this: Lembiq maintains its internal governance, its customs, its ways. But you become imperial citizens, contribute to mutual defense, and you open your gates to trade. Your expertise in woodcraft and archery would be invaluable. And in return, you gain access to magical knowledge, the blessings of the gods and access to them, as well as the protection of the growing empire. A small example of this is the complete destruction of the thorn in your side that is the Dark citadel."

"And I presume this same empire demands we once again swear binding oaths?" Thessarian's eyes narrowed. "I remember those oaths, child. I remember what they meant. We did not forsake them; they failed when no aid came in times of need."

"And the prince acknowledges that, as do we, members of the legion. We come now, and as evidence of the truth of the prince's claims, he will destroy the Dark citadel, just as he destroyed Kronk."

"Those oaths enslaved those who swore them," one of the crowd called out.

Yen shook her head, but addressed her word to the council, not the growing crowd. "The oaths protect all who swear them," Yen said clearly. "They ensure no citizen may harm another, that all have the right to call upon the legion for aid, that justice applies equally to all. They're not the chains you fear, but mutual promises of protection and support. They literally give you the right to call on the Godslayer himself for aid."

Silence fell over the chamber. Yen forced herself to stay still, to not glance around, to keep her posture relaxed and serene—or as much of those as she could manage—and waited. These people had survived by trusting no one outside their trees, and now she asked them to embrace an empire that they had to have thought dead forever. And, more than that, to swear to serve the prince when he called, despite the empire failing them in the past.

She'd thought that they might raise that, considering the long lives of the elves, but they had to remember the advantages of the empire as well, surely?

The seconds dragged out as both sides considered and watched the other. For the first time, Yen felt totally out of her depth. Was she supposed to say something else? Offer something more? Suggest that it was something they could decide in a week?

Fucksticks! She'd not mentioned the observers! Or had she? Oh shit, oh shit, oh shit…

Finally, Silviana stepped forward. "May I speak?"

Farendir nodded slowly, and Yen did her best to maintain an unmoving, uncaring, confident smile.

"Four months ago, I was taken by the Dark Legion. I watched them kill the other survivors of my squad, one by one, for entertainment. They sold me to slavers, as they saw greater value in a woman on the slaver's block. In Kronk's arena, I fought for the amusement of monsters, forced to kill or be killed."

Her voice was steady, but Yen could see the tremor in her hands.

"Prince Jax freed me. Not for coin, not for information, not because I could offer him anything. He freed me because it was right and he could. That was it.

"It wasn't that I was from here; he barely knew the name of this city before I went to one of the legionnaires and offered to act as an intermediary to introduce him to you.

"He freed nearly ten thousand slaves and utterly destroyed the city that profited from our misery. Then he offered us a choice: go our own way with some supplies and coin—that he would provide—or join his empire. No chains, no force. Just an honest choice."

She looked directly at Thessarian. "I know the old stories, Elder. I know the empire wasn't perfect. But I think we've all seen what exists without it. Chaos. Slavery. The strong preying on the weak, with no justice to stop them. The best we've managed to do for hundreds of years is hide in these forests and take down our enemies with constant raids until they gave up, or we fought in pitched battles that did nearly as much damage to us as those enemies could have done themselves. Prince Jax offers something better."

"Pretty words from one who has already sworn his oaths," Elder Morvaine said, though not unkindly.

"Then let me offer proof," Yen interjected, stepping forward again. "The prince offers this, if you're interested. Send observers with him, and I and my companion will remain here so that you can question us. Let your own people witness the destruction of the Dark Legion fortress. See how the empire wages war, how it treats its enemies and those it liberates. Judge us by our actions…not the fear of the past or my poor words."

The council exchanged looks again, conducting one of those silent conversations that only people who had worked together for centuries could manage. But as they did, Thessarian inclined his head slightly in respect to Yen, making her feel a wash of relief that at least he was considering it.

"Who would go on such a fool's errand?" Farendir asked finally, sounding almost annoyed.

"I will."

The voice came from the chamber's entrance. A younger elf entered, bearing enough of a similarity to Silviana that the relationship was obvious even before Silviana gasped, "Caelum?"

"Sister," he replied, and for a moment, his warrior's composure cracked as he broke and ran across the room to hug her tight. "Mother thought you were dead. We mourned you."

"I survived," she whispered into his shoulder, and he nodded, squeezing her tight, and letting lose a shuddering breath as he held her.

"Damn you, little sister…you've always got to be the one who surprises everyone, haven't you?" He snorted fondly. "I thought I had a chance at finally being the best known of the family!"

"In your dreams." She laughed, before letting loose a strangled sob. "I missed you."

Caelum pulled back, studying her with eyes that missed nothing—the scars, the way she stood, the battered and ill-fitting leather she wore. His jaw tightened.

"I'll go as observer," he announced to the council. "And I'll invite others if they're willing. We'll see this empire's truth with our own eyes."

"As will I." This from another elf, elderly but still strong, from amongst those who had gathered to stand on the outer edge, watching. "Silviana was my student. I would see what she has become, and what this empire truly offers."

Others volunteered, seemingly without rhyme or reason, just those who felt like taking part: a handful of warriors, a healer, even a young mage who looked barely past her first century and claimed to be a summoner.

In the end, a dozen wood elves had gathered and offered to witness the assault on their enemy, and Yen felt a sudden irrational worry that Jax might not pull the damn thing off.

"Then it is decided," Farendir said grimly with the air of a man making the best of a situation he apparently couldn't control. "Our people will observe. Based on their reports, the council will speak again regarding alliances and oaths." He fixed Yen with a steady gaze. "I pray to the Heart Trees that you are what you claim to be. Lembiq has survived by giving trust rarely, so understand this: if you play us false and our people do not return, neither will you go free."

"Yen'ma Rultahir will remain as our guest," Elder Thessarian announced.

Yen nodded. She'd expected that they'd want her to, so had offered it already.

It'd taken a little fast talking to persuade Jax of that, but she needed to stay and convince them, if she could, despite it feeling wrong to be parted from the rest of the squad after so long.

She almost snorted. "So long." She'd spent longer with her training cadre and on long marches than she had with Jax and the others. But in terms of battles and events? She could have served him for a century by now, in more normal days.

"You will explain your empire's laws and customs, answer our questions, and we shall answer your own. A fair exchange of knowledge while we wait for proof of the deed." Thessarian smiled at her.

"And her bodyguard remains as well," Farendir added with a glance at Grizz. "We wouldn't want our guest to feel…unprotected."

That was the "joy" of diplomacy: both sides kept hostages while sending their own people into potential danger. Not that she thought of herself as a hostage—she could probably fight her way out if needed, and Grizz certainly could—but the threat was clear.

"I thank you for your hospitality." Yen bowed. "I look forward to sharing knowledge of the empire and learning of Lembiq in return."

And that was that.

Within an hour, she watched from a balcony that made Grizz turn green as Silviana led the observers back to the ship. Her mighty love stood well back from the edge, one hand gripping a support post in the room that they'd been given.

"Politics, and living in a bloody tree," he grunted. "Give me a straight fight any day."

"This is a straight fight," Yen corrected. "Just with words instead of swords. And you damn well know the stakes are higher."

Below them, Lembiq spread out in its glory, a city that defied conventional understanding. Above, the Canopy district was barely visible through leaves and mist, a realm reserved for those who had earned their place through centuries of service or birth. It'd been made clear it was not somewhere that they were permitted, not yet at least.

"Think the boss will actually level that fortress?" Grizz asked, then he snorted. "Shit, better to ask if he'll let anyone else play. The changes in him are terrifying."

Yen nodded slowly, her eyes drawn back to the ship again, hovering in the distance. She thought of Jax, of the rage she'd seen in him since Oracle's loss, of the power he'd unleashed at Kronk. "I think the Dark Legion has no idea what's about to hit them."

"Good." Grizz's voice was grim. "It's about time we wiped that shit stain from the realm. Maybe seeing what happens to slavers will convince these tree-huggers we're worth allying with."

"Maybe." Yen winced absently, hoping that there weren't spies in the walls listening to him.

The pair watched as Tenandra swung around, gracefully landing in the lake, then extended a gangplank that she could just make out in the distance, ready for the observers to board when they arrived.

It took nearly two hours for them to reach the ship, two hours that she and Grizz spent on the balcony, talking softly and watching as their friends got ready to leave.

It was sad, but it was also a bit of a relief when it was done, as well as exciting. For the first time in ages, she was more than just a member of the squad; instead, she had a responsibility of her own, and a chance to rise again.

But as she watched Tenandra lift from the lake, water streaming from her hull as her engines fired harder and she turned southeast toward Bleakwood Marsh, she had a sudden horrible thought: would demonstrating the power that Tenandra could unleash inspire the wood elves to join the alliance or would they run in terror?

Then a worse thought occurred to her, and she bit her lip in genuine fear.

What if Jax unleashed his darker side? The side that Bane had warned her about—the anger, and the bloodlust, the rage and the utter uncaring unconcern about the deaths of those he considered his enemies.

If the wood elves refused the alliance, would he one day decide that this city, this amazing, beautiful, vibrant and above all else *living* city, needed to be conquered? Or worse, outright destroyed? Would she be called upon to march its streets and kill its defenders?

She shook herself and forcibly banished the thought. Only time would tell, and there was no use borrowing worry from another day.

"Come on," she told Grizz, trying to distract herself and the big man. "Let's go find something to eat. Then we can come back and relax a little. We're gonna be here for a few days at least, and we need to make the most of it. I want to learn everything I can about these people before the others return, and make damn sure they want to join us."

"I don't suppose there's any chance of getting some quarters on the ground," Grizz muttered, following her deeper into the large apartment that had been set aside for them. "Or at least get somewhere with actual walls. Solid walls. And no damn windows?"

Yen smiled, then reached out and grabbed his shoulder, turning him to face her as she kissed him roughly.

"You and I are going to get that irrational fear of yours under control, Legionnaire," she promised him, staring into his eyes. "No matter what I have to do to achieve it. We can go get some food after that."

"It's not possible." He groaned, "Even Restun tried and—"

"Oh, I think I can do things I doubt you and Restun ever tried—or at least I hope not," she said in a voice that bypassed Grizz's brain and made him shut the hell up.

Maybe the next few days wouldn't be so bad after all, she decided, as her lover and fiancé started frantically shucking himself out of his armor, as his brain finally caught up with what she was really suggesting.

CHAPTER NINETEEN

"**W**elcome aboard Tenandra," I called to our guests, as the deck tilted smoothly under my feet, and we were all pressed in place by the increasing gravity, as she soared upward.

"Now, you're all here to observe, so if you can pay attention for a few minutes, I'll do my best to keep you all alive for the journey. First of all, I'm Jax. Some call me prince, others call me lord, others just call me Jax. I'm not big on protocol, and I avoid it whenever I can. But make no mistake, if I give you an order, it's for a good reason and I expect to be obeyed. If that's a problem, say so now and we'll turn around and drop you off.

"Any order I give you will be to keep you and my people safe, and that's it. Beyond that, I understand you're here as neutral observers, not my citizens. I respect that, but I expect you to respect my people as well.

"First and foremost, if we get into a fight, you have two options: hide below decks, or observe. If you observe, understand that we'll try to protect you, but it's a battle and sometimes shit happens. Literally, that's life, and… Excuse me, am I boring you?!" I barked to a small knot at the back, where Silviana and two others were in the middle of a heated argument.

"What? No! Just don't interrupt!" a tall and clearly distracted wood elf woman replied, absently waving a hand in my direction, only to be slapped by Silviana, which obviously stunned the little group, Silviana included.

"That is the PRINCE you just told not to interrupt you!" Silviana hissed. "I told you that I'd come and see you after the fight, but that wasn't good enough for you. And then I told you I'd speak to you once the introduction was done, and still you didn't listen! Root and branch, Mother, he's killed GODS, for fuck's sake! Shut up before you get us all thrown over the side!"

The diminutive wood elf spun to face me—the people around the squabbling little group had all quickly backed out of the way, leaving a clear path from me to them—and she dropped to one knee, her fist to chest in the legion style.

"Please, my prince, my mother didn't mean to be so disrespectful. She just…" She faltered, then went on in a rush. "I take full responsibility. Punish me however you see fit."

"The hell he will!" the older woman snapped, before grabbing her daughter roughly by the shoulder and trying to haul her upright. "Stand up, you fool girl. He's just a human. He might be a prince in the empire but he's not in their lands. He's in ours, and—"

"Mother!" It was a male this time, and I guessed by the similar features, it was Silviana's brother who frantically tried to shut her up. "You need to show some respect or he'll punish us all!"

I couldn't help it—I really wanted to laugh. The two kids were frantically worried, Silviana especially, and the mother looked at me like I was a bad influence and needed to be kept away from her kids.

It was practically the same look I'd got when I'd been brought home to meet the family by any of my exes for half my life. Familiar? I could have reeled off the next lines in her speech by rote by now. "Bad influence" and "jumped-up thug"' and more were the traditional ones. But I couldn't afford to let this roll on, even for my own amusement.

"Tenandra!" I barked. "Land, please. Let's drop this good lady off, and she can walk home."

"I will not and—" she started haughtily.

I triggered both Mana Overdrive and Hyper Cognition, blurring through the gap to come to halt a few inches from the much smaller, older woman.

"In your lands, you might not show respect, but aboard my ship you will, or you'll leave," I said softly, as she blinked, stunned. "Release Silviana. She's sworn an oath to me, and either you treat her, and me, with respect, or you can go over the side and swim home." I reached around and picked her up by the back of her dress then carried her—clearly effortlessly—to the side of the ship, then dangled her over the side, where the river grew closer by the second.

"Help!" she screamed, swinging a fist at me. "He's assaulting me!"

"The hell he is!" another of the observers barked, striding forward. "Prince Jax, I apologize for this woman. If I'd remembered how self-centered she was, I'd never have permitted her to come. I'm Tisan. I was Silviana's instructor, and I'm ashamed to admit I was her mother's as well. If there is a cost to landing, I will ask that it be taken from her birthright, but please, I ask that you do not kill her. Death is a poor punishment for rudeness."

"There's no cost," I assured him, before sighing then lifting the woman back across the railing and lowering her to the ground, before cutting my abilities. "She just didn't seem the type to listen if I asked her reasonably to calm down."

"She isn't." He sighed. "Silviana and her brother Caelum are a credit to their father, but their mother…" He shook his head in disgust. "She's always been a witch and a harridan."

"A witch?" I asked, suddenly interested. "Really?"

"I'm no witch!" she shrieked, only to be hauled upright by Tisan, who dragged her to the side, bowed once to me in apology and then spoke to her in rapid, but low bursts I could barely catch.

"Bring shame upon your house…" and "Report to the council…" and so on as Tisan verbally tore her a new asshole in public, literally reducing her to a glaring, red-eyed wretch before us all.

Thirty seconds later, as Tenandra continued to angle downward, heading for a clearing, he raised his voice and spoke again, this time turning to me and bowing.

"I apologize for the distraction and the rudeness, Prince Jax. Might Shanna remain aboard? She does have a genuine desire to heal a rift in her family, and perhaps seeing the empire at work, and seeing the risks that others run to maintain her comfortable life, would be good for her." The older elf paused, looking at me in question, while Shanna, now with her cheeks flaming red, refused to look at me at all.

Mind you, she also noticeably didn't apologize as well.

"She can stay aboard, but if she speaks to me like that again, I will put her on the ground, regardless of where we are at the time," I said firmly, getting a bow of acceptance from the elder elf and a final glare from Silviana's mother.

"Now that the entertainment is over, perhaps I can finish what I was saying," I called loudly, walking back through the now silent group. "As I was saying, the rules we have are for your safety, and are simple. You are not to touch the ripple-fire cannons, those there, there, and similarly placed farther back."

I pointed to the gigantic cannons that squatted, bolted to the deck and covered with tarpaulins.

"Yes, they are magical, and yes, for those who understand such things, they are covered in runes. But they are also highly dangerous and if one detonates, the ship will be lost. Again, do not touch."

None of that was true, but it would hopefully keep people away from them. The runes were clear if anyone actually looked at them, so I'd decided to just say it and get it over with.

"Next, that cabin there…" I pointed to the control room. "This is the control center of the ship, and you are permitted in there by invitation only. No, I'm not trying to hide anything from you, but the captain of this ship, and his partners, will be inside there most of the time. They firmly believe that clothing is optional, so if you walk in there, you might see more than you want to. You have been warned," I finished dryly, and I got a few looks that ranged from curious to disgusted.

"There are rooms belowdecks that you cannot enter as well. Those doors will not open for you, neither will any others, beyond the room that you are assigned, the mess hall, and the common areas. Again, we're not trying to hide things from you, but there are dangerous areas aboard any ship, and other people's private quarters are their personal spaces, so don't go pushing your way into anywhere you don't belong.

"I shouldn't need to say this, but clearly I do, so fuck it. Be polite, be respectful, and my people will treat you the same. Now, you all volunteered to fly into war with us. We'll do our best to keep you safe. I don't expect you to take part in the fight, but please be ready to protect yourself if the need arises.

"That's it. Do you have a leader?" I asked, and the majority looked to Tisan, who sighed and shook his head.

"No, Prince, we are individuals; our society believes in personal freedoms as well as personal responsibility. As volunteers, we are each responsible for ourselves only, and will give our reports and the details that we feel are pertinent on return."

"Great. Well, you'll understand that I won't be permitting you to all wander in and out of meetings and so on, so if I invite any of you to join in on them, then that's fine. Otherwise, I suggest you get used to the sensation of flight, as I think it's about a two-day journey to the citadel from here."

"Depending on the wind, that is correct." Tenandra spoke up, stepping into being by my side, literally forming from the mana of the ship and smiling round at the wood elves.

"Greetings. I am Tenandra, and—"

"An abomination!" Shanna suddenly gasped. "An enslaved wisp, forced to do his bidding and—"

"Excuse me!" Tenandra barked, cutting the wood elf off mid-tirade. "I am a *free* wisp, in fact! Am I sworn to the empire? Yes, I am, but I served the old empire, and then was freed by the prince. I was offered the choice between my freedom and my service, and I was granted this body.

"I am now free to fly the skies, to rescue others of my kind, and to protect them and the rest of the empire. I chose this body, this form, and I chose my life! I am in full control of the ship, and yes, I am sworn to the prince, but I could just as easily level cities with the form he has granted me." She turned to look at the others and clearly forced a smile, as her trio of fox tails continued to flick angrily.

"Should any of you have questions, ask them as you will, and I will form as many bodies as I can to respond, but be aware, that in times of stress, I may be unable to reply promptly.

"Meals are served in the galley at sixth bell, and every three hours after then until midnight. Your rooms are in the foredeck, level three. All other rooms are closed to you. Take this hatch, and proceed to…"

She gave clear directions, assuring everyone that they'd be met on the correct deck—by her—and that they were welcome aboard.

That last comment, though, was finished with a glare for Silviana's mother that suggested she, at least, fucking wasn't.

Fifteen minutes later, most of the wood elves were belowdecks, and Flux started up the training schedule again; the day returned to the usual routine of exercise, training, a little relaxation, and then general maintenance.

It wasn't until the evening meal, which was shared in my rather large private cabin, that the actual planning for the fight at the citadel got underway again.

Some might say that was late, considering we'd be approaching it tomorrow night, or early the day after, but fuck it, that was life.

"That's not a plan," Flux growled at me, and I laughed.

"Feel free to come up with a better one then! I mean, is it a *good* plan? No. Will it work? Yeah, it probably will."

"It has the potential for tremendous loss of life," he grimly pointed out. "Jax, this could be a suicide mission for at least half of our forces, and that's if it goes well!"

"Which is one reason I didn't want to do it," I replied. "I wanted to destroy the fucking place from a distance and show them what 'peace through superior firepower' means, but no. They had to take slaves."

"Jax, you cannot simply bombard the citadel!" Flux growled.

"And I won't," I shot back.

We sat in my quarters, a rough map of the citadel and its surrounding areas on the table nearby. We'd all looked at it, but try as we might, there wasn't a sneaky solution to the problem that I could see.

"My plan isn't great, I accept that, but bombarding the very top of the citadel, attacking in the middle of the night by surprise, and then breaking out, and freeing the slaves is the best option I can come up with, all right?

"If we bombard the place from a distance to wear them down, they'll all know we're there and they'll be ready for the attack when we make it. Hell, if they're smart, they'll threaten to slaughter the slaves to try to get us to land and fight them in a straight-up fight. And who knows what their mages can do?

"I can cut them off from their spells for a short time, maybe five or six minutes, but that's it. If I use that spell in the middle of the night, when they're least expecting it, then we bombard the upper floors…yes, we may kill a few slaves, and I don't like that, but it'll kill most of their leadership, and then we can sweep the main barracks.

"While we do that, I unleash my imperial ability and free and protect the slaves. We do that at the same time as we attack the area, and it should, if we time it right, keep them safe. Then they get to run like fuck, and we land and hold the perimeter. The slaves run to us, we let them aboard and fly them to safety, bombarding the enemy as they try to chase us."

"And if there are hundreds, or possibly thousands of slaves?" Flux asked grimly. "This is a citadel that is devoted to the training of entire legions. It holds upward of five thousand when fully garrisoned, you said so yourself!"

"Then you come up with a better plan!" I snapped. "I'd love to hear it!"

"Will you listen with an open mind?" he asked.

I glared back.

"Will you?"

"Of course I will!" I retorted, and then the rat bastard did exactly what I was worried he would do. He gave us a plan that was much more complicated, but actually stood a better chance of succeeding, with lower casualties.

Not that it was a great plan.

It really wasn't. In fact, I thought it was a terrible plan, considering the risks that it posed. But I had to admit, it was going to be a lot more fun, and would actually, for the first time, mean that we got to make use of the seriously good assassins and stealth fighters of the group.

Just to make sure we had the very best chance that we could have, though, I also finally took the time on the first night to put my points into place, and hit another century. I was a single point off gaining a point in Luck—literally, I was at ninety-nine out of a hundred, on the gradual progress to next level mark. And I was also at ninety-nine out of a hundred overall, but as much as it irritated me, I couldn't afford to wait.

That was when I realized the truth. Being that close to leveling it naturally, was that lucky? Why yes, it was…

Congratulations!

**Through hard work and perseverance,
you have increased your stats by the following:**

Luck +1

Continue to train and learn to increase this further.

Heh. That worked well!

Congratulations!

You have achieved your first century in Luck through natural progression and point allocation.

As such, you have gained a new Ability!

Fortune's Mockery:

Lady Luck doesn't just smile upon you; she actively conspires in your favor. When facing seemingly impossible odds, reality itself develops a sense of ironic humor. Enemy spells randomly select new targets (including the caster), critical failures become contagious among your opponents, and fatal blows inexplicably strike non-vital areas. Most unnervingly, when you're about to die, there's a chance that something completely unrelated will intervene: a structural collapse, a sudden equipment failure, or an enemy tripping over their own feet at the crucial moment.

Passive Effect: Any single attack that would reduce you below 10% health has a 25% chance to instead trigger a "lucky break," dealing half damage and causing a random mishap to befall the attacker.

~~Active Cost~~: Cannot be actively triggered. Fortune's Mockery activates automatically when you're outnumbered 10:1 or face an opponent 20+ levels higher.

Note: The universe's sense of humor is cruel: your allies are not immune to the chaos, and "lucky" doesn't always mean "pleasant." Side effects have included enemies dying by choking on their own victory speeches.

I read it and I reread it, unsure whether this was a good thing, and as much as I was ready for it, there was a total lack of any physical effect, which was frankly nice for a fucking change. I was getting sick of having to surreptitiously Scour myself over and over to get rid of blood in unexpected areas from these fucking things.

That being said, there was one more to go, and I had the points I needed just sitting there, ready to be spent. Fuck it, might as well, after all.

Charisma or Endurance, basically being sexy and speaking better to people, or being able to fight and screw for longer.

I mean, when I put it that way, it was an easy fucking choice.

I wanted to be able to fight and screw for longer any day of the week, but…

But I needed to be at least a little better with speaking to people, and although it was, for example, a hundred percent chance now to gain "a favorable outcome'" as my Luck stat said, it wasn't really that as I understood it.

Or not as I would have thought of it all before this.

It meant I was a hundred percent luckier than I would have been naturally.

That was it. Space and time didn't warp around me so that checking down the back of the couch I'd find a billion dollars that had been accidentally misplaced.

Instead, it meant that if I would have normally had a chance at finding something, now I had a slightly better chance at it.

Money that wasn't there wouldn't suddenly appear.

Instead, if say, I had a hundred percent increase in my chances, and I had a 1:10 chance before, now I had a 1:5 chance. Not an immense improvement, sure, but it was still a hell of a lot better than I'd had before.

If it was simply that I had a hundred percent chance of success, then I'd have opened my door and somehow found that it had magically linked to a room where Oracle was being held, and Xenefier would have a heart attack.

After developing a heart and discovering it needed the damn thing.

I chose Charisma, as much as it galled me and felt like I was being a dick.

Congratulations!

You have achieved your first century in Charisma through point allocation.

As such, you have gained a new Ability!

Imperial Gravitas:

Your presence alone commands the battlefield of hearts and minds. When you speak with true conviction, your words carry physical weight, lies wither, deceptions crumble, and even the most hardened souls feel compelled to listen. Those who hear your voice during pivotal moments (oaths, surrenders, or declarations) experience your emotions as their own, feeling the depth of your rage, determination, or rare mercy. Most powerfully, when you issue a direct command to those who serve you, they temporarily exceed their natural limits, pushing beyond exhaustion, fear, or injury to fulfill your will.

Passive Effect: Intimidation attempts automatically succeed against anyone 20+ levels below you. Your presence causes natural submission responses in hostile creatures below your level.

Active Cost: 200 mana to issue an Imperial Command (affects up to 100 sworn subjects for 5 minutes). Individual commands cost 50 mana per target.

Note: This is not mind control. Subjects retain free will but gain absolute clarity about your expectations and the strength to meet them. Commanding someone to act against their nature causes severe backlash to both of you.

That, I damn well felt.

Why the hell everything from my skin to my throat to my goddamn teeth and hair suddenly hurt was beyond me, but I whimpered and rolled into a ball, shivering and shaking for what had to have been hours, considering that by the time I could finally force myself back upright, to sit on the edge of my bed, the blankets were fit for burning at best, and I had a room full of people.

Again.

"You dumb fuck." Tang snorted, seeing my confusion as I blinked, looking around. "What? You thought we'd not notice the bond being full of pain? We felt it again and again on the way here, so of course we all came running."

"Thank you," I whispered, before summoning a fountain and drinking deeply, uncaring of the water that splashed across the floor, before being absorbed.

"What did yer do this time then?" Lydia asked, torn between worry and hard-bitten annoyance, as she threw me a blanket to cover myself.

"Hit another century."

"That's what, four?" Ronin asked, strumming his lute, and I suddenly remembered the music, at the edge of my memories when I was stuck thrashing and groaning.

"Nine," I admitted.

"NINE?!" He gasped, slipping and hitting a discordant note. "Are you fucking serious?"

"Well, no, sorry." I sighed.

"Oh, thank God..." he whispered.

"It's ten. I've got two of them in Intelligence, but I still have Endurance to hit yet."

"Fuck me!" He whimpered, staring at me. "What the hell have you done since you came here? That's...that's over a thousand points, boss. That's insane! That's like level two hundred plus for most people, and you did it in what? SIX MONTHS?!" That last came out in a squeak.

"Nope, I just reached level fifty-four." I sighed, trying to calm my racing heart, deliberately ignoring it as the rest of the room stared at me in disbelief.

"What one did yer get?" Lydia asked, and I forced a rueful smile.

"Charisma." I shrugged. "Figured it'd help with the speeches and the deals."

"Fuck me," Ronin whispered. "You've gotta tell me everything, boss. Please. Think of the knowledge we can add to the imperial records. Fucking hell, they're never going to believe this shit."

"That's a point." I blinked. "You said there was a bardic college, right? Where is it again?"

"Dai'Amaranth," he said softly, as if half afraid of the name. "At the heart of the old empire, and the heart of the realm."

"I've still not seen a single fucking modern map with that on it," I muttered. "The old ones? Sure, they all show it, but is it still where it was? I mean, a fucking cataclysm turned seaports into mountain ranges, so..."

"It can't have moved that far. And my master said it was still an island, but that a section of the moon hit it dead center, so..." Ronin shrugged. "For anything to have survived, either it was a small section, or the magical defenses must have been insane. But I guess there's only one way to be sure..."

"And that's to go there," I finished for him, before sighing and gesturing vaguely toward the cabin door. "All right, thanks for coming, guys, but I need some sleep, and to recover from this shit. I'll see you in the morning."

"Goodnight…" That started the ball rolling, as everyone else stood and started out of the door—Ronin having to be dragged by the ear by Lydia as he kept trying to question me—until Bane shut it firmly, with him on the inside.

"You need to get some sleep," he told me, and I snorted.

"So do you."

"I sleep enough," he grumbled. "I have the first shift, with Tang taking over soon. So go on, use your clean spell and then sleep. Oh, and use the blanket. It'll be a relief when you stop exposing yourself. I told you, I don't swing that way."

"You wish." I snorted, but my heart wasn't in it. In under a minute—just long enough to use Scour and grab a fresh set of sheets and change the bed—I was back asleep.

The next day was spent in a mixture of training, preparation, and relaxing, which was kinda weird.

Especially because the changes that had taken place on my hitting a hundred in Charisma started to be obvious.

People turned and stared. Commented on my skin or my hair. And I caught people sniffing the air as I passed.

It made me a little paranoid at first, thinking I needed a bath, until I realized that part of the pain I'd felt was apparently my sweat glands and hormones being altered.

Apparently I now smelled fucking delightful, which was weird, as to me, I stank the same as ever.

I shrugged it off and tried to ignore it, including when one of the "neutral observers" made a pass at me. I explained carefully that I was involved with someone and not interested, and got the whole "they don't have to know"' speech. I finally saw that, yeah, it was true: it really is *painful* when a guy gives it—and my memories of trying that line myself in drunken states in nightclubs were forever tainted.

The area we were flying across was heavily wooded, mile after mile of rolling hills and deep valleys with the occasional meandering band of water that glistened below.

The deck was split into three areas—first and foremost, training. That was literally half the deck. Four groups were at work: the mer had been split into two groups and the legionnaires into two, and they were facing off against one another, either belowdecks in room-to-room clearance training, or abovedeck in asha'tuun.

Flux had clearly spent more time training with Restun and was now at least a high journeyman level in the art, if not closing on expert, and he made the most of that, with him, Lio, and Bane leading the lessons.

Tisan and others watched as we trained, and occasionally those with an interest in it would join in as we taught the forms, but mainly they kept to themselves.

Gradually, more and more of the group joined in and the barriers were ground down a little. But the best thing that came out of the trip? Silviana's mother created such an impression that there were now three distinct groups formed by the time the citadel came into view:

the imperial party, the wood elves, and that miserable fucker on her own.

By the time Tenandra was ready to begin the assault, I was seriously considering whether there was a way to harness the general malice that the woman seemed to radiate, as it was incredible for breaking down barriers in the other groups.

The mer and the legionnaires, for example, were solidly integrated by now, and even her own people, exposed to two days of her miserable attitude, were dead set against her being used as an example of their race.

That being said, she still managed to interrupt and try to demand answers about the assault, as she "had a right to know what we were planning if we were going to put her life at risk."

That was when Tisan finally lost his formerly almost endless patience, and tapped her lightly on her shoulder, causing her to collapse bonelessly to the deck.

"Okay, what the hell was that?" I stared down at her, and the older elf showed a small needle concealed in his palm.

"A mixture of nightbane, wheels' blossom, and salven's root," he admitted. "It's a potent sleep draught, and when administered without warning, it tends to result in, well, this." He sighed, then smiled at another elf who grinned and wordlessly picked up the unconscious woman before carting her off to her quarters.

"Well, I'm sorry that you had to do that, but fuck me, how much of that stuff do you have on hand?" I asked.

"Only a little. It's not something that's really useful in large doses. It tends to be lethal if administered in larger quantities, and is quickly cleared if someone is excited or threatened. It merely grants a few minutes of slumber."

"Are you mad?" I snorted. "That sounds fantastic to me. And if it's lethal in larger doses, then I'm fine with that."

"If you're looking for poisons, the forest has a great many other, more powerful substances. But for dealing with an annoyance that you do not wish ill, it is perfect." He smiled.

"No, seriously, how much of that do you have?" I asked firmly. "Or what ingredients was it? Can you teach me? How long does it take to prepare?"

And that was how the assault was put off for another full day, and we ended up spending the next twelve hours flying around the forest, landing in small clearings and running back and forth to harvest ingredients.

By sunset of the third day, we were all in a much better position, and my poisons knowledge had improved drastically, as had our plan.

<u>CHARACTER SHEET</u>

Name: Jax Amon	
Title: Godslayer	
Class: Mage Imperator (Fire Focus)	**Renown**: Imperial Scion, Prince of Dravith, Master of Himnel, Narkolt and Gaij, Godslayer, Mage Imperator
Level: 54	**Progress**: 10,417,897/15,000,000
Patron: Jenae, Goddess of Fire and Exploration	**Points to Distribute**: 0 **Meridian Points to Invest**: 0

Stat	Current points	Description	Effect	Progress to next level
Agility	120	Governs dodge and movement	+1200% maximum movement speed and reflexes. Gained Temporal Fluidity	N/A
Charisma	100 (95)	Governs likely success to charm, seduce, or threaten	+100% success chance in interactions with other beings. Gained: Imperial Gravitas	N/A
Constitution	145 (143)	Governs health and health regeneration	2900 health, regen 190 points per 600 seconds (each point invested now worth 20 health). Gained: Genetic Storage	N/A
Dexterity	120	Governs ability with weapons and crafting success	+120% to weapon proficiency, +120% to the chances of crafting success. Gained: Master Craftsman's Touch	N/A
Endurance	95 (89)	Governs stamina and stamina regeneration	2850 stamina, regen 72 points per 30 seconds (each point invested now worth 30 stamina).	94/100
Intelligence	226	Governs base mana and	2520 mana, spell capacity: N/A	N/A

		number of spells able to be learned	(+200 mana from items). Gained: Hyper Cognition & Mana Manipulation	
Luck	100	Governs overall chance of bonuses	+100% chance of a favorable outcome. Gained: Fortune's Mockery	N/A
Perception	110 (100)	Governs ranged damage and chance to spot traps or hidden items	+110% ranged damage, +110% chance to spot traps or hidden items. Gained: Essence Sight	N/A
Strength	111 (108)	Governs damage with melee weapons and carrying capacity	+111 damage with melee weapons, +111% maximum carrying capacity. Gained: Titan's Resolve	N/A
Wisdom	125 (115)	Governs mana regeneration and memory	+1600% mana recovery, 18 points per minute. Gained: Mana Manipulation	N/A

<u>CHAPTER TWENTY</u>

"**T**his is insane, you know that, right?" It was Ronin, unsurprisingly, who complained. Considering we were rappelling down fixed lines from Tenandra's deck, headed into the blackness of the citadel in the darkest point of the night, I couldn't help but agree with him, even as I barked an order to be quiet, because we were about to drop.

Jenae had apparently forgiven me for the things I'd been shouting about her and the others, because five minutes before we climbed over the side, a quest notification had pinged and the entire ship's company had gotten it.

Interestingly, the observers had gotten it as well, though a lower reward and easier variant, considering they just had to keep their mouths shut and watch.

Congratulations!

You have been given a Quest by the Goddess Jenae: "Gut those motherfuckers and shit on that bastard's altar."

The followers of Nimon, Dark God of Death, have recently crossed a line with Jenae and the rest of the Pantheon of the Flame. As such, please mete out appropriate punishment to them in the heart of their power.

Bonus rewards will be given for additional offense caused.

Reward: 5,000,000xp, possible allies, additional citizens, possible loot, general approval from the pantheon and forgiveness for recent comments.

There wasn't even an option to refuse it, not that there'd been any chance that I would, but reading it—wow. I didn't know what the dark dick had done of late but fuck me, he'd pissed the other gods off.

That raised a point, though: was the Arbiter still hanging around? It was important, because if not, if it'd gone, then maybe things would go back to how it was before, when both sides were cheating, more or less.

What worried me was that a single word in the ear of a particularly high placed priest or that lunatic who ruled the roost here might be all that was needed to really screw up our plan.

"I just got a quest from Tamat," Bane whispered to me, having reached over from his rope nearby and grabbed onto mine, leaning in close. "I get additional XP per kill I make while we're undetected."

I looked at him, working it out, then nodded abruptly, stifling a grin. *Damn*, she was good. In giving him that quest, and leaving it active, she'd basically given him a way to be sure that nobody knew we were coming.

If he suddenly failed the quest? We knew the jig was up.

That caused me to relax—slightly—before my butthole puckered up at the sight of the rapidly approaching citadel ahead.

It was essentially a castle, and a fucking ridiculously large one, especially when seen from the air, dangling from a rope beneath an airship.

We approached at high speed, making me feel like I was about to find out whether it was true that the last thing to go through a fly's mind, when it met the windshield, was its ass.

It was built around the adage of "bigger is better": it had four sets of curtain walls, with six towers in the outer wall, spaced equally around it, all with thankfully silent siege weapons in place.

Inside the walls were row upon row of barracks and training areas, all orderly, perfectly aligned like the spokes of a wheel, marching around the outside. In the next section—inside the second wall—were four more towers, each with a flat roof and more ballistae that squatted atop them like terminally fugly grasshoppers.

Next came the section between the outside and the final, inner walled keep, occupied by a single huge cathedral with a handful of luxurious-looking manor houses.

They took up half the space in the inner walls, and what could only be the slave quarters took up the rest.

When I'd asked Silviana why the hell the slaves were kept there of all places, she'd thought it was obvious.

"For sacrifices, and…fun," she'd said, her face and tone shutting down completely. Clearly, whatever memories she had of the place were exceedingly unpleasant.

Then, when you passed the last wall, you were inside the citadel itself.

"Passed the wall" was perhaps not accurate, as it was actually a single, incredibly heavily built building that occupied the heart of the city.

Its outer walls were connected to the rest, making them more like the outer walls of a building than anything else, and the keep spiraled slowly, with gardens and walkways moving from section to section. And then, standing in splendid isolation, at the top of the building, was the death knight's tower.

It, too, apparently had additional slave quarters. Silviana hadn't seen them; she'd just heard about them from the Dark legionnaires, who'd amused themselves by telling her stories of what was to come, each more terrible than the last.

Personally, I was impressed.

The citadel, from a distance, looked impregnable, but it was built with a single massive assumption in mind.

If their enemies could fly, they'd either not be so stupid as to fly into the citadel, and if they did, they'd set off the wards.

"Okay, here we go…" I whispered, closing my eyes, reaching out, and finishing the spell that I'd been holding in place for the last half an hour.

Tenandra had helped me with it. I could have done it myself—I could—but it wouldn't have been something I could hold, not for long, and the time it was active for would have been about thirty seconds.

With her help, we targeted it to two areas—covering the wards that soared high over the citadel, and more specifically, on the upper keep's private gardens—and then hold it for nearly four minutes from activation.

It was going to totally drain me, as well as seven manastones, which was a lot of what I had left—there'd be a little over a dozen left after this, and still more than a dozen potions—but that wasn't the point. I'd had hundreds recently.

When we'd talked about this, it had made sense for there to be a detection system in place on the keep. But what we'd not expected—and it was fucking wonderful that Tenandra had both thought of it and had been able to see it, being a wisp—was that although the lower levels had detection nets in place to sense anyone who wasn't one of their kind landing in the gardens or passing through the gates, the outdoor areas of the higher floors in the death knight's keep all had a much more insidious spell in place.

The gardens were literally kept knee-deep in a powerful spell of death.

That was it—nothing else. Not "detection" or "trap" or whatever, or at least not as near as she could see—the ship's vision was incredible, but it always had been, in fairness. Instead, it was literally a spell that had to be given by Nimon, because anything that landed in there had its life force ripped free and fed through the veil.

I had one foot braced in a stirrup-type loop in the rope, the rope braced between my elbow and side, and had Flux above and Bane alongside me to hold me in place. My fingers wove intricate patterns and my tongue twisted in the ridiculous loops to pronounce the spell.

Whoever came up with the word "Sathsarathaastra," for a start, needed their ass kicking. But I managed it, unleashing the spell with less than ten seconds to go.

Absolutely nothing happened.

Well, not as far as I could see, anyway—though my mana bottomed out and the stones that were strapped around my left arm in a complicated pattern of knots crumbled to dust.

Then Jian let loose a brief attempt at a whistle—being linked to Tenandra, he was chosen to pass the word for the drop—and then everyone was jumping.

I jumped, too—well, actually I was dragged loose by Bane and Lydia—and as I fell, I saw the ground coming up…but a horrific mana migraine flared bright and vicious, meaning I could barely see it as I fell.

This was the worst part for most of us. Tenandra had approached low and fast, dipping in and then pulling up, her engines flaring dangerously, increasing the chance we would be seen.

The advantage, though, was that we were all hanging from ropes below her and with our bodies well trained and well developed and our magic being what it was, it meant that we should be able to land and run a few steps to break our momentum.

Sure, there were going to be injuries—there were…this was a stupid way to assault anywhere—but we also had magic, and it was judged as the best chance to succeed.

It wasn't like I had time to make parachutes, train everyone to use them and then fucking experiment after all.

I quickly yanked free a mana potion, popping the top—still blind—and chugged it, even as we landed, running into the dissipating clouds of death.

Then, because the hidden and evil god Murphy clearly hated me and I couldn't see, I crashed into the ornate fountain in the middle of the garden, flipped over and nearly drowned, as Lydia, who'd also been helping me, had just lost her grip thanks to a tree root taking her out.

The situation was made worse because I couldn't stop casting the spell, not without it literally stopping and wiping me out through the backlash. So, almost blind with a mana migraine, half drowned, and with the remains atop me of what had apparently once been a small but ornate statue of a boy pissing, I continued to weave the damn thing together.

My mana bounced violently up and down, until I released the outer edge of the spell, focusing only on the garden we were in now, at Tenandra's distant assurance she was clear.

To me, as I regained a little sight and the statue was the first thing I saw…well, it just proved that no matter where you were in the universe, some fuckers were always going to be weird.

I felt it as the others pulled the stone off me, then dragged me out of the water, even as Ronin, the sneaky little shite, cracked the lock on the doors out of the garden and stepped back. The first of the mer blurred from sight and into the darkness beyond.

I was carried, mainly silently, by the others until we were inside. Then I was lowered to my feet, as I continued to cast until the last of us were confirmed as out of the garden, and I could finally stop.

The door was locked again—it wasn't like we couldn't just smash it if needed later—and with a nod from Tang, I released the spell.

"Ah'm so sorry, Jax…" Lydia started immediately, and I waved it aside, too busy chugging the next potion to care, as Flux started separating out his people and sending them hunting.

There were plenty of us. My squad, of course, was me, Bane and Tang, Ronin and Lydia, Jian and Sehran, Arrin and Giint with Bob broken down again and strapped to Bane's back—the bones had been shit and we decided to "acquire" more here.

On top of the usual idiots, we had the ten mer from the Cradle—I needed to learn their names; as busy as things had been, I'd just not gotten them so far, but a few I recognized by sight—and Flux, Lio, Silviana, and Borren, who was leading the legionnaires.

Fifty of them—him included—were casting Heal on one another and the mer. The landing for those who couldn't fly had been rough as hell, and there were a lot of broken bones.

Then the last of the group, the old wood elf Tisan, brought up the rear.

He'd gone from a neutral observer to an absolute bloody necessity when we'd decided to allow him in on the plan. He'd admitted that for the elites of the wood elf scouts—which he'd been a trainer for—a few additional spells were taught that he could use to increase our likely success rate.

Featherfall was an old favorite, and it was something that I'd been damn well holding onto in my bag of holding forever—not for any particular reason, just because since I'd been able to actually learn a spell from a spellbook again, it'd been such a pathetically underpowered thing that it'd not been worth the effort.

Thankfully, Tenandra was able to do—just as Oracle had—the little trick with linking minds, enabling me to pass the spell across to basically everyone in the party, apart from Silviana and Tisan, who both already had it.

It basically did as it sounded; when cast on an individual, it lessened their inertia by thirty percent, changing what could have been a terminal impact into a survivable one.

It cost ten mana a casting and lasted a minute, and so pretty much everyone had been spamming the shit out of it and downing potions like crazy on the way in, just in case, to make sure we were covered.

It was the second spell that had made even more of a difference, though, and it'd been a "just in case" one, and one that only Tisan knew.

Tenandra had offered, and then I and Flux had joined in as well, to persuade the old bugger to allow her to pass his spell across from him to any of the party, but unfortunately, at this time he wasn't willing to share.

All he'd said was that at times, deep in the forest, when the elites needed to drop from the branches above to take out their enemies, there was a need for silence. As such, they'd developed a spell that could provide exactly what they needed, as well as that it was an AOE spell.

He'd not share any of the details beyond that, clearly recognizing that it was an incredibly powerful and valuable spell. I'd twisted my brain in noodles, trying to decide whether this was a perfect example of my Luck stat actually kicking in, and if it was, how the fuck it worked.

To have him, *specifically* him, wanting to join the mission, required so many minor changes in decisions that it was insane.

After all, he was an expert trainer of their elite scouts. For him to just happen to have a spell that would make this shit much more manageable was fantastic, and I did what any other man in my position would have done in my place.

I decided that thinking about it hurt my head and I promptly stopped.

Now that we were on the mission and I had a genuine need to know, I tried again to speak to Tisan, asking how long the spell was active for and the range on it, only to have no sound come out, while he just winked at me.

Rolling my eyes and glad that spells didn't require sound if you could sub-vocalize, I turned and actually took my first proper look around the inside of the citadel.

The room we were in was something like a reception area, or maybe more, considering the entire wall that looked out over the gardens was clear on this side, but had seemed opaque from beyond.

That was where the easily understood style ended, though.

The room that stretched before us was like a mausoleum given life. Black marble floors polished to a mirror shine reflected the pale moonlight filtering through the one-way glass wall, leaving pools of silver that tracked across the blackness with each passing cloud.

The ceiling was vaulted, disappearing into shadows that my Darkvision couldn't quite penetrate and that had to be damn well deliberately shielded. Here and there around the room, as if rising from water, I saw what looked like carved bone formations jutting from the darkness like stalagmites, then flowing into seats or tables.

The walls were worse. What I'd first taken for decorative paintings were actually sections of flesh and sinew, stretched tight across frames of black iron, with brands and tattoos carefully preserved.

They pulsed with a faint, sickly luminescence—some kind of preservation magic at work that kept them eternally fresh, eternally bound. I realized with a start that they weren't just decoration; the way the tissue was arranged formed runic patterns, each wall a massive glyph of necromantic power.

"Don't touch anything," I tried to whisper, the words not leaving my lips before Tisan's spell swallowed them. Right. No sound. I settled for snatching back Ronin's wrist as he reached toward what looked like an ornate candle formation.

The bard jerked back, shocked, and I pointed to the base—the "wax" pooling there was moving, reaching tiny tendrils toward where his hand had been.

Furniture rolled out of the bone sculptures, or *were* bone, carved and joined together in patterns; a dozen spines—humanoid, by the look of them—had been fused together to make a chair; ribs rolled in an eternal circle to make a table… The entire room was filled with islands of seating and sculpture in an ocean of death and it freaked me out because it was so well made I actually really wanted to sit in the chair thing just to see if it was comfortable.

I mean, that would be incredibly stupid of me, but that didn't mean I didn't want to!

Then, off to one side, was a massive desk carved from what had to be a single piece of some enormous creature's femur. It literally dominated one corner of the room; its surface etched with more of those flowing, script-like patterns that hurt to look at directly.

Papers scattered across it seemed to writhe in a breeze I couldn't feel. I caught glimpses of diagrams that made my eyes hurt, construction plans for something that had way too many organic parts.

Spread throughout all this utter weirdness were seats that made everything else almost worse for how normal they were. Plush chairs in velvet sat next to ones that were upholstered in what I desperately hoped was just very realistic leather; they surrounded a low table of polished obsidian.

If not for the skull-motif carved into every wooden surface and the way the shadows seemed to pool too deeply in the cushions, it might have belonged in any noble's receiving room.

Bane touched my shoulder, pointing toward the far wall where a series of doorways led deeper into the keep. Each was framed by an arch of yellowed bone, and I could see through the nearest into what had to be a trophy room.

Weapons hung on the walls—not the death knight's weapons, I was willing to bet, but those taken from his victims. Each had a label with a small description that I couldn't read from here. But the way they were displayed, with such careful attention to detail?

The fuckstick must be the kinda guy who held parties and showed people this shit.

No, this wasn't right.

None of this was right, but…

"Hssst!"

We'd been walking slowly deeper into the building; Ronin had gotten our attention, pointing to one of the side rooms. A mer appeared, slinking out of the shadows, and gestured to Flux.

"Menr senses life," Bane said softly to me, as the sounds of motion around us suddenly stepped up in volume, signaling the end of the spell.

"What?"

"Menr…*her*, you blind fool!" Bane snapped at me, gesturing to the mer who was already leaving the room.

"I meant, 'what did you say, you prick?' I was distracted," I hissed back at him in as low a voice as I could manage.

"Jax, Menr has sensed life. At least three are asleep above us in the tower. I've sent her and her team to inject them." Flux moved over to stand close to me so his voice wouldn't carry.

"Is that enough?" I asked him seriously. "If it's the death knight…"

"Then they'll either take him by surprise or they won't," Flux replied. "Either way, it's already done."

"Fuck's sake," I whispered. "How long until we have a plan of the building?"

"Working on it now," he replied.

I looked around, not hearing anything, but getting a nod from Bane. Apparently, he could feel it as well.

For the mer—or the Tia'Almer-atic, to give them their full name—searching a place like this was child's play, mainly because where we needed to check each room, each nook and cranny and all the shadows, etc., they were blind, so shadows didn't really exist to them.

Mind you, neither did light.

Instead, they saw through a complicated mix of sonar and sound refraction. The tendrils, short stubbly tentacles that ringed their heads, allowed them to build a 3D mental picture of any shape they needed, enabling them to "feel" the world around them from every angle—coincidentally making them fucking incredible at stealth, as they viewed it as they needed to hide from *everything* when they tried.

That made them world champions at hide-and-seek and natural assassins and spies, a skill set that had been sadly neglected by the Dark Legion and the current batch of nobility with their "human first" way of looking at things.

So sad, too bad.

I, on the other hand, was overjoyed about this as it meant I had a much better chance of using the buggers on my enemies, rather than having them used on me.

It also meant that with half a dozen of the group posted in strategic places around any structure, they could send out a low-level pulse that was inaudible and map it, including picking out any traps and hiding guards.

Now, it was possible for just one of them at a time to map out an entire structure, just by unleashing a really powerful blast, and plotting the way it bounced off all the walls.

The problem was that it was loud—or, more accurately, a very *deep* sound—and it came with a serious need to use the bathroom for most species when they felt it.

The "I had a vindaloo a few hours ago and I'm now going to spend the night atop the throne and cursing my poor choices" kind of bathroom break.

So, instead, Flux's multipoint and much quieter version they employed was much more subtle and was unlikely to be noticed by anyone without the appropriate equipment.

I glanced around and then closed my eyes, listening as hard as I could. Despite that, even with my perception as high as it was, I was left unsure whether what I sort of sensed was real, or just my mind playing tricks on me.

"Borren, spread out and start moving down. Lio, go with them. Use the darts and check out how far you can go before you encounter a guard post. If you can take them out while they're asleep, fucking do it and keep going until you find a real risk. Hold there. We need to stay quiet as long as we can."

"As you command, my prince," Borren breathed, and Lio gave me a mocking brief salute and a grin, before vanishing, making me shake my head at how much fun she seemed to be having.

Intaglio was a legionnaire first, but as time had gone on, she'd been entirely split off from the legion to become Flux's right hand and second-in-command, and she fucking loved it.

She and he were also the reason such plans as this had a chance of working. Her specific job, along with two of the mer who slunk off after her, was to use the wood elf soporific poison on anything and everything she could.

Ideally, we'd all stay hidden as long as possible, while she and the others made their way to cookpots and so on and put enough of the stuff in to make the job an easy one. Depending on your perspective.

As they vanished downward, I quickly followed Flux and Bane as they led the way up the stairs to the next floor, passing glossy black stairs followed by bone white, followed by carved red stone that I didn't recognize.

It looked to be lacquered, it was such a deep, vibrant red, and it took an effort of will to look away from the steps, until I noticed the way that the mer, without saying anything, were skipping those steps.

I started to ask why, then shook it off. The less noise here the better.

Less than a minute later, and I was staring in the doorway at the third of the slumbering figures that Menr had sensed.

Each room we'd passed on the next floor had been identical, spaced out and just as big as the others: the same clothing in the wardrobes, the same uniform-like armor on the stand, and the same whips, serrated daggers, and fucking toys dotted around.

The women who slumbered, aided by the poison that Tisan had taught me to make, were identical, presumably a triplet, and the lack of a lock or anything similar on the door made it clear they could come and go as they chose.

Their outfits that stood on their armor stands were blood red, the material a mixture of hardened panels and well-worked leather. The gloves were reinforced, as were the knees, with what felt like knuckle-dusters, or something similar.

There were no helmets, making it clear that they were supposed to be seen and recognized. The long skirts that completed the outfit were made of stiffer leather, with splits to make it easier to walk, and under it were trousers that felt…

I stared at the overall uniform, as the last details clicked.

Jez Cajiao

These weren't prisoners in any sense of the word, unless it was prisoners of their own twisted desires.

They were torturers and enforcers. Checking first that Flux was ready with a knife at the target's neck, I used my spell and examined her.

Cerina Veritsa	
Cerina Veritsa is one of the few surviving graduates of the Dark Legion's Sanguine Mistress Class. When she and her sisters were discovered to have the potential to study and excel with blood magic, their entire family were taken, and the sisters were conditioned over the following decade to torture them to death without mercy or remorse. Graduates of the Scarlet Citadel are renowned as the most sadistic of Nimon's followers, and are adherents of the hidden one, Lorne, known as the mistress of death. Where many classes are taught to deliberately counter magic, only two groups are known to have been fully created from scratch as anti-mages. The Sanguine Mistresses are a highly dangerous and feared class that spread such fear in their passage; that it is said embracing Nimon is a relief.	
Weaknesses: Physical	**Resistances:** Mana
Level: 37	**Class:** Sanguine Mistress
Health: 1000	**Mana:** 0

I stared at her for long seconds as I puzzled my way through the meaning, then looked to Flux and nodded firmly.

I didn't know what these fuckers were, but it sure as shit didn't seem to be a wise choice to let them wake up and fight fair.

He stabbed down, hard.

The blade was a serrated one, and once it'd punched through her windpipe and deep toward her spine, he ripped it sideways in a sawing motion, almost decapitating her, and sending a fountain of blood spraying.

At exactly the same time, as she and her sisters here died, a scream of rage from the two floors below us, somewhere above, and distantly rising from several other points in the citadel rang out, making it clear we'd just massively fucked up.

"Fuuuuck!" I snarled, having damn well hoped we'd be able to get a bit bloody farther than *this* before it all went horribly wrong.

Shouts broke out below us, and I darted from the room, dismissing any attempt at stealth, and tore my way up the stairs, three at a time, as I dragged my naginata free.

Was it the right choice for possibly fighting in a stairwell? Certainly not. But it was my murderstick, and I was damn well using it.

Three revolutions of the stairs I made before I burst out onto the next floor up. A second trophy room had a dozen figures more or less intact and nailed to large stands, blood steadily draining from them, as bags of potions on what looked to be an IV drip slowly healed the poor bastards.

The entire room was a monument to sadism.

As I raced across the floor, headed for the distant stairs, I heard the sounds of another fight breaking out overhead.

"Help!"

"Don't do it!"

"Run!"

"Save yourself!"

The figures on the stands around me were rousing with the sound of my armor clattering and the fights breaking out. Some were desperately begging me to help them, but others were telling me to just leave them and run, to try to escape.

I'd be back for them, I silently vowed, as I leapt up the stairs. The underside of my boots caught just enough traction on the polished stone to stop me going arse over teakettle as I kept going.

From overhead, there were shouts, and then a sudden scream, dying away as if the person had been yanked into the distance. I took two more twists in the stairs—why the fuck this one had to go back and forth while the flights below had been goddamn spiral, I didn't know—but as I broke out onto the next floor, it was to find three mer in a fight with a flesh golem that looked to have shouldered its way out of a storage nook.

The remains of a painting hung ragged, and a panel of black onyx shimmered against the wall, as a second creature slowly resolved from it. Its clawed foot crashed down as it started to escape as well.

"Stop it!" someone screamed, as the first one, standing at least three meters tall and fully made of stitched-together bone and sinew, grinning teeth and staring eyes, dragged a mer toward the same portal.

The mer, bleeding and battered, with two arms broken, feebly stabbed at the creature; it, in turn, ignored the injuries and mechanically lifted an arm, seemingly intent on throwing the mer through, even as its fellow came the other way.

I powered myself forward with a combination of Mana Overdrive, Hyper Cognition, and Soaring Majesty. I flashed across the intervening distance and fed a lick of fire mana into the naginata, whipping it up and around, hacking through the gap where its forearm met the elbow.

The arm came free with a crunch of bone, and the mer fell to the floor with a gasp of relief.

That got the first reaction from the creature: it roared and spun, ignoring the mer—with the detached arm still clutching them—and swung for me instead.

That gave me the chance to see it full-on, and yeah, whatever it was, it was *definitely* a construct, rather than a living creature, as I picked out a dozen places where silver bands were used to lock sections together.

Its left arm had ended with a hand, but in place of a hand on the right— incidentally now shooting toward my face—was a huge maw filled with great, big, pointy goddamn teeth.

I twisted aside as the maw snapped shut where my head had been, teeth grinding against one another with a sound like breaking glass. The construct's momentum carried it forward, and I used that, spinning low and bringing my naginata around in a sweeping arc that caught both its legs at the knees.

The silver bands holding the joints together sparked and shrieked as my fire-enhanced blade hit some kind of an embedded shield.

It flared and popped, but it'd held long enough that it deflected the main force from the bands and they held—barely.

The creature stumbled, giving me just enough time to plant my foot and drive the blade up through its exposed rib cage, searching for a heart or focus point.

"Bane! Get them clear!" I roared as the second construct fully emerged from the portal, this one even larger than the first. Where its companion was a patchwork of organs and muscles, this horror was wrapped in strips of preserved flesh, with dozens of faces twitching and shrieking independently as it moved.

The first construct grabbed my naginata with its remaining hand, trying to wrench it from my grip. I let it take the weapon, instead casting a spell I'd not used in ages and relying on the old advantage of "it's my spell so it doesn't hurt me" as I jumped up, grabbed its skull in both hands, and cast Pyroclastic Blast.

As the spell formed between my palms, the construct's head exploded in a shower of burning bone fragments and whatever foul preservatives animated it; the spell bucked wildly now, but still held tight.

I jumped back, grinning wildly as its body collapsed. My naginata clattered to the floor as I landed then dove forward again, rolling away from the second creature's sweeping claws, before coming to my feet. I hurled the spell at a third monster that was just pulling its way clear of the wall.

Given the hugely damaging result of essentially half liquid lava and TNT combined, the previously cold, enchanted surface shattered in a spiderweb of cracks under the impact, and the creature that was trying to exit it was cut in half.

"These things aren't alive!" Tang shouted from somewhere behind it. "No blood, no life force—they're just meat puppets!"

"Noticed that, thanks!" I snarled, snatching up my weapon as Lydia crashed into the second construct from the side.

Her mace cracked against its knee with the sound of a sledgehammer hitting concrete.

The thing barely noticed, backhanding her with enough force to send her skidding across the polished floor. But it gave me the opening I needed. I blurred forward thanks to Mana Overdrive and closed the distance, naginata spinning in a figure-eight pattern that carved chunks from its flesh-wrapped form.

Ronin's voice rose in song behind me, and the familiar surge of his combat buffs settled over us like armor. The construct moved to grab me, but its movements were even slower now, more than enough for me to duck under its grasp and drive my blade up through what would have been its heart, if it had one.

Nope, tried that before. Dammit, Jax, think! Learn!

A scream of passing missiles blurred overhead, each one impacting a half second behind the last, dead center in its forehead, destroying flesh and exposing bone…bone that was swallowed again as the flesh reformed over it.

"The silver bands!" Ronin called out, protected by Silviana, who loosed arrows that sparked with green energy as they struck home, small but each detonating with impressive ferocity. "They must be the anchors!"

Right. I yanked my naginata free and targeted the joints, the places where silver gleamed between bone and sinew. Each strike sent sparks flying; with each band that shattered, the construct's movements became more erratic, less coordinated as sections collapsed.

A nice, simple, second pyroclastic detonation would have been preferred, but considering my friends were in as close as they were now, that was out. I could have gone all out on it, but I decided that wasn't a good idea either. We needed to understand how these things were built; we needed to know how to take them down, not be stuck when a squad without me encountered them.

Flux and two of his mer had flanked it now. Their poisons were useless against something that wasn't alive, but their blades were sharp enough. They carved away at its legs while I kept its attention, distracting it with heavy blows until finally, with a sound like breaking chains, another of the silver bands burst apart under the strikes. The whole thing suddenly collapsed into a pile of twitching meat and broken bone, whatever animating force had driven it dissipating into foul-smelling smoke.

"Check the rooms!" I barked.

I turned to check on the injured mer—Bane was already working on him with healing magic—when footsteps on the stairs made us all freeze. Not the rushed, chaotic sound of people running to a fight, but measured, deliberate steps. Multiple sets, moving in perfect synchronization.

"Positions," I hissed. My people spread out, finding cover behind the grotesque furniture and displays.

The first figure to emerge from the stairwell was a woman in blood-red armor, identical to the ones we'd seen below but very much alive and alert. Her face was beautiful in that cold, sculpted way that suggested I'd not like her jokes, and her eyes...

Her eyes were pools of congealed blood that shifted and swirled as she looked around the room.

"Three of my sisters are dead," she said in a voice like honey poured over broken glass. "Their blood sings to me of betrayal and blades in the dark. How...disappointing."

Two more emerged behind her, flanking her with practiced precision. Their armor gleamed wetly in the moonlight, as if freshly painted with blood that never dried.

"You know what? Fuck it," I muttered, then raised my voice, marching forward. "Is your boss home? Got some complaints about the décor. Very 'angsty teenager discovers death metal.' Not really my style."

The lead Sanguine Mistress tilted her head, studying me with those horrifying eyes. "Lord Karridan is attending to matters in the south. But do not worry, you will meet him upon his return...those of you unlucky enough to survive. We are more than capable of handling unwelcome guests."

"South? Fuck's sake, trust me to come visiting when he's away. I don't suppose you want to tell me exactly where?" I asked, already calculating angles and distances. "Would've loved to critique his interior design choices in person. I mean, seriously, all the black and bone? The pale skin and the smell? He'd be worshiped as a patron saint of goths everywhere, and that ain't a smell anyone wants to be near."

She smiled then, and I immediately wished she hadn't. Her teeth were filed to points, and blood welled between them as if her gums were constantly bleeding.

"You seek to provoke me with words while your companions move into position. How...quaint." She raised one hand, and the air in the room shifted, becoming thick and coppery. "But blood magic cares nothing for your strategies."

A sudden glow burst to life around her hands as something in her armor flared with power. The trio chanted in fast succession.

I grunted in shock; a sudden, weird tugging sensation started in my veins, as if my blood were trying to answer her call, and my health bar flickered as damage started to climb.

From the sharp grunts and gasps around me, I wasn't the only one feeling it either.

"Fuck this!" I roared, triggering Mana Overdrive and charging forward. Whatever blood magic bullshit she was pulling, the best counter to any mage was usually violence, preferably applied directly to the face.

The room erupted into chaos. Arrows from Tang and Silviana streaked through the air, even as Arrin sent more missiles flying. Lydia's war cry echoed off the walls as she charged from the opposite side. The mer materialized from shadows, blades seeking vulnerable points in that shiny fucking red armor.

But the Sanguine Mistresses were ready.

The lead sister gestured sharply, and Jian—who'd been flanking left— suddenly jerked to a stop, his own blood turning against him. His veins bulged grotesquely as he fought against whatever control she exerted, his face contorting in pain.

The sister gestured and he was jerked into the air, then slammed into the wall face-first. Sehran darted forward, sliding between him and the sister, and let loose with a screech of fury that sent literal shivers through the air, before she clutched at her head and collapsed almost atop Jian.

The second sister moved like flowing water, dodging a strike from Bane and raking fingers lightly across his leather-armored chest. Where her fingers touched, his blood seemed to boil; steam rose from the wounds, as he screamed and collapsed.

The third had drawn a whip that looked like it was made from someone's circulatory system, still wet and pulsing. She snapped it toward Ronin, who barely dove aside in time. Where it struck the floor, the stone cracked and red veins spread through the breaks.

I reached the lead sister just as Sehran's sonic attack had ended.

My naginata came down in a brutal overhead strike that she deflected with a blade that materialized from her own blood, the crimson weapon as solid as steel.

"Predictable," she hissed, twisting to let my momentum carry me past. Then she grinned and opened her mouth wide, vomiting a sonic attack at exactly the same range and power as Sehran's had been, sending me staggering as the world shuddered and my eardrums burst.

I spun, bringing the butt of my weapon around to crack against her temple. She swayed back, but not quite fast enough. The impact sent her stumbling, but she hissed in pain, even as Sehran, laid on the floor, shrieked in agony.

The sister did something; a sudden tether of blood-red light flashed from her left hand to latch onto Bane from behind, and she pulled sharply.

Jian had barely pushed himself to his knees, stunned, when he was hit by Bane, the mer having been jerked across the room by the damn tether. That gave her time to dart backward even as I forced out a Complex Healing into myself.

I'd barely shaken the crackling pain free as my ears popped and healed. On the far side, Sehran, now shaking and writhing, still laid before Jian, shoved Bane off him. "These bitches are anti-mages!" I called out, parrying another strike from that blood-blade. "Physical damage only!"

"No shit!" Tang shouted from across the room, firing arrow after arrow into the second sister even as she snarled, trying to deflect them and Lydia's mace at the same time.

Then she made a mistake, and it was her last.

She focused on the clear and obvious danger—Lydia, as opposed to the bowman; she leapt back, narrowly avoiding a blow from her. That meant that Tang finally got a clear shot. The arrow slammed home in the center of her forehead, and whatever gifts she might have, surviving massive cranial trauma delivered by high-speed, pointy steel clearly wasn't one of them.

She dropped, bonelessly, to the floor and Lydia made sure of the job—by smashing her skull in with a blow of her mace.

The third sister's whip wrapped around Flux's ankle, and where it touched, his scales began to blister and crack. She yanked, trying to pull him off-balance, but three of his mer materialized behind her, blades punching through gaps in her armor.

She laughed—actually laughed—as blood poured from the wounds, then sucked in sharply. The blood flowing from her wounds reversed direction, shooting back into her body and solidified around the blades, trapping them. With her free hand, she grabbed one mer by the throat and squeezed, shaking him like a rag doll as she opened her mouth wide, clearly about to bite down, pointy teeth very much in evidence.

"Oh no you fucking don't," I snarled, and I pushed off *hard*.

The difference in the fight to this point so far had been habit, as much as anything else.

When I was around my people, I knew my capabilities. I knew how strong I was, how fast, and using my crutches, like Mana Overdrive, was instinctive.

The thing was, Darakin had shown me how much of these actions were ingrained, and where my limits were in reality.

I was across the floor before she could get him in close enough, and I sliced through her arm with a single swing, shouldering Flux aside, then snap kicked her in the stomach.

She catapulted backward, slammed into the wall with a sound of breaking bones, then slid down it. She stared at me with a glazed, stunned expression, even as behind her a smear of blood tracked her movement from the damage to her skull.

"Y…ou…" she tried, before making a single wet crunch as her final sound.

I was there before her in a heartbeat, stomping down hard and driving her skull into the ground with a soggy, squelching sound.

"Sister!" the lead of the three hissed in fury, glaring at me as I wiped her off my boot.

Silviana's voice rang out: "The stairs! More coming down the stairs!"

Sure enough, I could hear it now: fighting had broken out again overhead, and distant shouts rang out from the stairwell, suggesting some distance below the legionnaires were adding to it.

"Defensive positions!" I barked. "We hold this floor!"

The lead sister smiled that horrifying smile again, blood still weeping between her teeth. "Hold? You cannot hold against the Sanguine Sisterhood. We are eternal. We are—"

Giint lobbed something that looked like an old school football, all wrapped leather at her, cutting off her monologue as it hit her in the chest. She howled in outrage, then in genuine pain as whatever the mad little bastard had come up with burst across her and burned with a light so bright I had to shield my eyes.

"Boss!" Tang called out. "We got a dozen coming down and half the mer are out of action!"

Thirty seconds. I looked around the room—my people were solid. Already, those who had been wounded were being healed. Jian was upright again and he sprinted forward, his twin blades lopping both her arms off, then her head, even as she capered and shrieked in flames.

As soon as the bitch was dead, Sehran let loose a gasp and started desperately sucking down air, even as she was hit again and again with healing spells.

Four of the mer I could sense on the floor overhead—the party system gave me a small image of them in my mind when I focused in—were badly injured, and Tang had been right to draw my attention to it.

Well, we were off to a shitty start, I reflected, but when had that ever mattered? We still had to clear the rest of this tower, find the slaves, and trash the place.

If anything, although I wasn't happy the death knight was gone, him being somewhere else with a lot of the army was actually a good thing.

"Change of plans!" I shouted, making a command decision. "I'll lead. We take the remaining floors fast, then head back down! Clear the tower from the top!"

"I thought that was always the plan?" Tang called back, bracing a boot against what was left of the sister's head and using the extra leverage to drag his arrow free.

"It was!" I grinned inside my helmet. "But before, I was going to save this for a surprise. Try to keep up, kids!" I shouted, before letting loose with the full force of my boosted body.

I was across the floor and at the foot of the stairs in under a second, leaping up them in bounds of six steps at a time, then ten.

I burst from the stairwell in less time than it took to tell of it, landing and spinning to take in the entire room, in one glance.

Five mer out of the group had come up here; presumably the other sisters we'd just fought had left the three up here to play a little, while they'd moved down to find entertainment for themselves.

They were dressed identically: three women in blood-red armor, leather and gloss standing out as they laughed and played.

Of those five, two were dead or dying…one beyond anything healing magic could do with her head split in two to her chin, the other… needed help fast.

The other three were laid around the room, either unconscious, injured badly, or stunned. One was held, his armor hanging loose, rotted off his chest somehow—a spell, I presumed—and a pair of sisters on either side of him, gripping him by the arms.

The third sister glanced over languidly toward the stairwell, clearly expecting to see another coming to the rescue and to be able to make an impression, as she drew her fingers slowly down his chest.

Blood blisters bubbled up, and she grinned in a deranged way…right up until she blinked as she finally focused on me.

I'd crossed the floor in a blur. The wet *thwack* noise that my backhand slamming into her face made was only eclipsed by the sound of a branch snapping as her neck was broken and she was hurled across the room.

The two sisters gaped.

I didn't even bother to use my naginata this time. I'd felt what they could do, on a small scale, when they'd started playing with blood magic downstairs, and I was in no mood for that shit to be tried on me personally, instead of as a widespread AOE.

I reached out, fast as lightning, and closed my fists over their skulls, yanked them forward and then together, resulting in a sound like eggshells being ground underfoot.

Then I dropped the pair, and turned to the only person in the room who wasn't one of my people, and stared at the black and red clad man, even as I unleashed Complex Healing, one after another, on the mer.

"You get one chance," I ground out, staring at him. "Explain."

"I am Baron—" He drew himself up haughtily, and then let loose a squeal as I blurred across the intervening distance, gripping him by his jaw and lifting him into the air, leaving bloody fingerprints on his face.

"Are you a member of the Dark Legion?" I asked.

He desperately tried to deny it, which I guessed would result in Nimon taking action if he was, so I accepted that.

"Local nobility?"

He got out a muffled *yes*, and I snorted in contempt.

"What are you doing here?" I asked.

"He'd probably be able t'answer better iffin yer put 'im down." Lydia snorted, arriving with a clatter of armor. "Fuckin' 'ell, Jax, yer been hammerin' yer agility?"

"That and more," I assured her distractedly. "Everyone okay?"

"Aye, most o' them. Give 'em a few more minutes an' those that're savable will be anyway."

"Who'd we lose?" I asked.

"Two mer, one legion," she replied grimly. "Fuckin' red bitches are a handful."

"Yeah." I nodded. "Ask Flux to question this piece of shit, then feel free to chuck him out a window if you don't like the answers." I smirked at the terrified expression on the apparent noble's face, then I was off again.

Two more floors were searched in less than a minute, literally. I skidded to a halt at the top of the tower, staring around a single massive chamber: tall windows on one side rose to the roof, a wall covered in bookshelves, as well as ornate and clearly magical weapons. And on the last side, a fucking torture rack. I just shook my head in disgust.

This fucker was going to die painfully, I decided.

The body on the rack was long since dead, left to rot, which I had to assume, given there was unlikely to be any shortage of servants, was deliberate.

I gritted my teeth, then spent another thirty seconds running from side to side in the room, amusing myself by grabbing anything that looked magical or expensive—which was half the room—and tossing it into my bags of holding.

Then I was off, making it down to the next floor just as Lydia arrived on it.

"Nothing?" she asked, and I shook my head.

"Fuck all. Let's get back down. We needed to make sure it was clear, but fucking hell, it was a waste of time. What about the dickhead?" I yelled to her as I ran past.

"Flying lesson!" she shouted after me, and I grinned to myself as I raced onward.

The mer were back in the fight thanks to healing magic—or four of them were, anyway. The fifth had his arms crossed over her chest and one stood over her, the other three having already headed down the stairs.

"I'm sorry," the mer said softly. Her hand reached down to rest once more on the dead one's chest, before she pushed upright. I streaked past her, making her snarl, before she saw it was me; she started after me, already falling behind as I caught up and passed the others.

I had a brief thought about just how goddamn stupid it was of me to run like this in a stairwell, that if I slipped, I'd beat myself bloody bounding down the steps, and then I was out, crossing the next floor and heading down.

I slowed on the next floor, finally catching up to my people, surprising them, feeling the powerful need that radiated out from Bob as he locked eyes on me.

Or, you know, eye sockets.

Giint had been carrying Bob's skull strapped to his back, and apparently the big construct had finally had enough of being luggage. He roared in fury to get everyone's attention, then demanded in that grinding, sepulchral voice:

"Bones!"

I grinned evilly as I got the impression from him that said a lot more than the single damn word had.

"Drop Bob, then make sure the rest of the tower is empty!" I called to Giint, before looking at Flux and Bane, knowing that of everyone, they were the experts in stealth here, with Tang chasing after them. "You two, get moving. If you can't help the others below, or there's any side passages and shit, grab anything that looks fun, kill anyone who deserves it and then catch up!"

"My mother-of-pearl rings against your bracers says that I kill more than you," Flux shot at the younger mer, appearing from stealth, before vanishing again. "Try to keep up!"

Bane snarled something and set off after him, mocking laughter floating down the nearest stairwell.

I spun to the rest of the room, and barked orders. "Get ready to move out. I want archers at the ready. No spells on the red bitches. I'm guessing their counter-mage ability is that they steal your magic. Instead, hold them with skill and fucking steel. Give me a minute and we're moving, but first, we're turning the tables!"

I crackled my knuckles and reached out, triggering my necromantic spells, locking in on Bob. My eyes surged with power and the bones scattered around the room seemed to leap into glowing life for me.

Whatever the Sanguine Sisters did to train their kind, they corrupted them all the way to their core, which as I saw the way their bones glowed, and the marked "Spell Absorption" bonus of at least one point per bone was just a wonderful sight.

"Alrighty then, time to fuck some shit up." I grinned evilly, and guided my spell as it sloughed the flesh from the sister's bones, softening them, and reforming them like putty by my will.

CHAPTER TWENTY-ONE

I *could* say Bob's new form was a thing of beauty, but even with that old adage of beauty being in the eye of the beholder, it would be bullshit.

He was a horrific, terrifying creation, that as soon as he was finished, raced into the stairwell and frankly was off to give nightmares to nightmares.

I'd engineered him into a form similar to his old "knight" version, but then I'd added a layer of flesh from the flesh golems across the outside as a sort of semi-living shield.

Admittedly, it was dying. Whatever had been done to make them before was very quickly wearing off, but much as holding a normal shield between you and the enemy would absorb some damage, the mounded flesh did this now.

When we reached the next fight, it had apparently also given the other side some pause as he sort of looked like their bosses' toys at first, making them hesitate for a split second.

That proved to be a very costly mistake, as apparently the utter disdain by which he punted a sister into the wall as she attempted to use her power on him demonstrated that they'd not, in fact, been trained to deal with three-meter-high, semi-undead monstrosities with their own souls that *didn't* try to use magic on them.

By the time we made it down the next floor, it was to find a half dozen mages and sisters all dead or dying, and the last handful of the nearest defenders of the keep—namely a Dark Legion paladin and a dozen soldiers—all being forcefully introduced to one another.

"Bob, I think they're dead," I called after a minute.

The big construct paused, looked at his makeshift and very bloody club, before hitting the last soldier again with his former boss and then letting loose an earth-shattering roar of triumph.

"So, you like?" I asked him, grinning.

"More bones," he demanded, pointing at the sisters.

I just started up the spell again and stripped them of all flesh. Cursing, I realized that if I wanted to loot them, now we'd need to dig through a literal mound of rotting flesh and…

"Hey Giint, old buddy, old friend of mine…" I said smoothly, turning to face the mad little bastard, who was already rolling his sleeves up and eyeing the piles.

"Giint want…" He paused, apparently thinking about what he could demand for the nasty job, and I spoke up quickly.

"Soooo, I discovered a potion, something that's incredibly lethal and apparently was reserved from destruction by Svetu as it was too powerful a drug. He kept it only for the strongest and maddest of the gnomes… You want some?"

"YES!" he howled, turning on me with a gaze that made me worried I might need a water sprayer to stop him humping my leg.

"AFTER the mission!" I said quickly, pointing at him. "I mean it, you mad little fucker. You do *everything* Lydia tells you, and after, you get a little of it, and only a little!"

"Oh great, why fuckin' me?" Lydia groaned.

"Because I don't want to have to watch the feral bastard." I shrugged, turning back to the sound of shouting that echoed up from the next floor.

"Well, fuck that. Gri… Dammit! Tang!" she said, remembering at the last second that Grizz, Giint's normal "handler," was still in Lembiq.

"No chance, boss!" Tang yelled, running to the other side of the floor. "I can't hear you, lalalalalala!"

"Jian?" she tried desperately.

"Uh, my hands are full!" he replied quickly.

"With me!" Sehran purred, grabbing his hands and planting them firmly on her, before kissing him, showing that she'd clearly fully recovered from whatever the madwomen had done to her.

"Not a fucking chance," Arrin called as he ran past.

"Fine!" Lydia snarled. "Giint, behave yerself or I'll tell Bob t'watch over yer and stop yer getting' any drugs ever again."

"Giint be good," he said mournfully, before pulling a fresh bomb out and sidling up to Jian. "Oi, you want to play?"

At that point, out of existential terror over what he was defining as "playing," I promptly focused as hard as I could on the stairwell and ignored the little bastard as I started to run again.

It didn't take long to find the legion. Clearly the Dark Legion were "ready for anything" in that they all seemed to have died with weapons at hand. But given that they were all dead, it hadn't helped much.

There were clear marks of magic on most of them. Tenandra had done a great job of passing spells around for them, and whatever the Dark Legion expected, it'd not been their archrivals streaming out of the upper floors of their own citadel, wielding magic and steel in the early hours of the morning.

"Borren, how we doing?" I slid to a halt next to him as he levered a hand axe out of the forehead of a dead enemy. "Damn, that's nice."

"Isn't it?" he agreed, grinning widely. "Got it off a paladin over there. Think I might keep it…if that's all right?" He hesitated, looking at me, and I snorted.

"Go for it, mate. But come on, what's happening?"

"The next few floors down are like a maze," Borren replied, straightening and wiping blood that had smeared across his helmet clear. "The floor below was wide open, and Lio went ahead.

"She warned us we had more than double our number coming, and we set up here to make use of the narrow confines to funnel them and reduce their advantage in numbers.

"This was the last of them, and we're ready to move back ahead now. Reports were that the barracks are mostly empty, a skeleton crew at best. We've likely already faced most of them, but the slave quarters…" His jaw tightened.

"How many?" I already dreaded the answer.

"Hundreds. Maybe more. Lio said they were packed in like fleas on a dead dog." He caught himself, shaking his head. "The slaves are in bad shape, my prince. Really bad."

I nodded grimly. We'd known this was coming, but knowing and seeing were two different beasts entirely. "Right. New plan. We clear every hostile between here and them, but we leave the slaves locked up for now."

"What?" Silviana's voice cracked. "Prince Jax, we can't just—"

"We can and we will." I cut her off, bluntly. "Those cells might be hell, but they're also protection. We open them now, while there's still fighting? It'll be a slaughter. We secure the area first, then we free them properly."

She wanted to argue—I could see it in her eyes—but she'd been in those cells. She knew I was right.

"Bob!" I called out, and my beautiful monstrosity of bone and stolen flesh turned to face me, bits of Dark legionnaire still dripping from his makeshift club. "You're on point. Anything that isn't us dies."

"Good," he rumbled.

I swear the bastard was grinning. Hard to tell with a skull, but after all this time together, you learned to read the signs.

I started into the lead, as the legion fell in behind me, and damn, every meter we crossed, it was clear that it'd been paid for in blood.

The Imperial Legion had made the most of better training, better tactics, and the choke points of the building, but it was obvious that it was only thanks to the combination of surprise, decades of brutal experience, and magic that so many of them were alive now.

Not one of them had armor that was fully intact. Most wore dented and even partly rent, badly damaged plate. And those who had fallen…

We passed three of them, each surrounded by literal piles of the dead.

On Dravith, the Dark Legion and the Imperial Legion were roughly equal—in a fight, anyway. The Imperial Legion were better trained and better disciplined, but they lacked the sheer vicious brutality of the Dark legionnaires, and definitely the numbers and backing.

That wasn't the case here. These legionnaires I'd brought had all been enslaved and had been in the arenas, captured by slavers and forced to fight—day in, day out—for the entertainment of the masses.

They were utterly unforgiving and fuck me, they were impressive.

The next two floors blurred together in a symphony of violence that would've made Darakin himself proud.

It was when we found ourselves in yet another long hallway, fighting for every step, that I lost my patience with this bullshit.

We were literally facing dozens of the enemy racing forward, and we were cutting our way through them, fighting to reach the far side and the dubious safety of the narrower doorway.

The Dark Legion had trained for decades to be the ultimate warriors, conditioned from childhood to feel no fear, no mercy, no hesitation.

They were dying—screaming, anyway.

I'd held back at first, some part of me still clinging to the idea that I was just another soldier in this fight, limiting myself to closer to their level. But as we carved our way through the fourth wave of defenders, something crystal clear clicked into place.

I was wasting time.

Worse, and more importantly, I could be wasting fucking *lives*.

Those who had fallen while I was elsewhere, higher up the keep and fighting the sisters, I wasn't to blame for; I accepted that now, as hard as it had been to come to that acceptance.

But those who died here if I was fighting below my capabilities? It was a betrayal, and I wasn't fucking havin' it.

Bane and Flux had taken the side passages, and they'd vanished, working their asses off to make sure that nobody snuck up on us. As I'd passed those passages, I'd seen how Lydia dispatched the other mer to go after them to make sure.

We were in the middle, facing a surge of what had to be the more elite of those forces still here, which made it clear just how fuckin' stupid my plan had been.

We were carving our way through forces that had been awoken from sleep. Although we were winning, clearly, it was as much the fact that they were in much smaller numbers than there should have been here, as it was that we were "just that good."

My determination that we could essentially do anything and just storm the heart of the enemy's power was another symptom of my goddamn instability, and now it was going to cost my people their lives.

Borren had fallen back a few times already, giving up ground he'd taken to get into a position where he could use the narrow areas to funnel the enemy to him in controllable numbers.

If we'd had to face most of their forces without that advantage, even with the rest of the legion elsewhere and their main forces dead at Gaij, this would have been touch and go.

But that was the point, wasn't it.

They'd been nervous, but they'd followed me here for two reasons when I'd asked.

First, I was their prince, and a demigod, and I did this shit kinda regularly.

Second, and very importantly, my squad followed along and had gone with the plan. Clearly, they'd have not done this so happily if they expected it to fail, so that had allayed some fears. As it was, though, I'd been adding to people's stress levels because I'd been fighting as "one of the team," like Augustus, Restun, and all the others had drilled into me.

Everything had changed since I came here, though, to Carrmor. In truth, it'd been changing before that, since the fight with Nimon as well.

I *wasn't* one of the team anymore. And to be fair, I'd always been a bit shit at it. Instead, I decided, it was time to show off a little and make it clear why my people could trust in me.

I'd just decided that, when a dark paladin charged me with a blessed mace that crackled with necrotic energy. I didn't dodge.

Instead, I darted forward and caught it. Bare-handed. The weapon that should've shattered every bone in my hand simply…stopped as I grabbed it below the head in my left hand, grinning at him as he strained.

"My turn," I said softly, and twisted.

The mace was ripped from his grasp as if he were a toddler. The paladin had just enough time to register shock before I smashed it down atop his helmet with sufficient force it not only ended up embedded in his damn *chest plate*, but the mace was also bent.

Crack.

His body slid across the floor; blood sprayed wildly as I released the remains of the mace and snap kicked it backward.

"Holy shit," I heard Tang whisper, but I was already moving.

Three more paladins rushed me, coordinating their attack with the kind of precision that came from years of training together: ice magic from the left, lightning from the right, and a massive two-handed sword coming straight down the middle.

I triggered Mana Overdrive—not because I needed it, but because I wanted this over with—and the world slowed even further to a crawl.

Three months ago, this would have been a death sentence for me, but now? After the lessons with Darakin, they just seemed…weak.

Slow.

Pathetic.

The ice mage's spell was still forming when I reached him. I grabbed his face, reminding him why it was a mistake to not wear a helmet in a fight. My fingers sank into flesh as though it were soft clay, and I crushed his skull.

The lightning user got his spell off. Electricity coursed over my armor and did precisely fuck all as I spun and brought my naginata around in a horizontal arc that separated his top half from his bottom half.

The swordsman actually managed to bring his blade down. But the blade catapulted from his grip as I freed my hand from his friend's face and backhanded the blade aside contemptuously.

"Impossible," he breathed.

"Improbable," I corrected, then grabbed him by the throat and squeezed until things started to pop, lifting him from his feet and starting forward. "But Nimon's not here to argue semantics, so fuck it."

I drew back and then threw him into another of his legionnaires, but my utter contempt was beginning to draw eyes.

"Hold this!" I barked out the order, passing my naginata to the next legionnaire to my right—Borren, as it turned out—and he glared at me as he was forced to juggle his sword and shield, and my weapon…though that annoyance faded as I waded forward.

Kung fu had been a passion of mine, once.

Any martial art was, really. I liked the smooth gestures, the flow that led from what was almost a dance into suddenly ripping someone a new arsehole.

Now, as I marched into the thick of it, Hyper Cognition kicked in and I traced each and every movement. I saw the paths that weapons would take, the speed of the owners, and with a little effort, just how easy it was to change them.

A screaming, bare-chested man wearing a helm, and with impressively hairy shoulders, was the first in line, howling as he brought his greatsword around.

I blurred forward three steps, uncaringly backhanding the two to my left and right aside, then spinning to my left.

As I turned, the three steps had brought me inside his reach. The sword that swung down toward me was no longer about to introduce its pointed end to me but was instead bringing the hilt down in a slow-motion slide.

I snap kicked the blade aside with my right foot, pivoted on the left, grabbed his hilt in my hands, and squeezed, before wrenching it sideways, *hard*.

As his body was catapulted backward, it was without his fingers, which had been reduced to almost jam.

I completed the turn, brought the blade up to head height and added a spin, and I threw it into the incoming Dark legionnaires and their aspirants.

It carved through half a dozen before it hit the wall, glancing off and burying itself in a highly unlucky man who had just ran in.

With almost a third of the enemy down in about three seconds, I went on the rampage. I flowed through their ranks, slapping weapons aside, breaking bones and kicking them into walls.

I even tried a trick I'd done ages ago in a fight where you cupped your hands slightly and slammed them into your opponent's ears, rupturing their eardrums.

Turns out that when you're strong enough to use a car as a barbell, that's kinda overkill.

His skull shattered and blood sprayed everywhere.

One of the enemy nearly got out of the door, screaming in terror, unarmored—clearly having picked a bad day to forget to get dressed first.

Then one of his friend's axes—a nice double-headed design that flew fantastically—hit and passed through him without stopping.

"Fuck yes!" one of the legionnaires bellowed, and I grinned at him, getting a wide smile in return. "Whooo!"

"Right, let's make this quick!" I shouted at the room. "Kill any who are injured. We're not taking prisoners, and none of these fuckers deserve the chance to surrender anyway!"

That got a second round of cheers.

I started down the stairs, well aware that the fucking brutality we showed would be enough to get us all accused of war crimes back home, even though there was no such thing here.

No, here we were following the Canadian model: ask for forgiveness, not permission, and leave the observers glad they were on your side, even as they wrote down the reasons not to fuck with you to make sure future generations got it.

By the time we reached the ground floor proper, the defenders had given up on tactics and fallen back on desperation. They'd barricaded themselves behind overturned tables and chapel pews, turning the main hall into a killing field.

Or it would've been, if they'd been fighting mortals.

"Stay back," I ordered my people, cracking my neck. "This'll be messy."

"Jax—" Lydia started.

"That's an order."

I picked up a dead Dark legionnaire and carried him before me as I stepped out into the open, and immediately two dozen crossbow bolts sprouted from his back.

They made a lot of noise as they crashed into him, and did fuck all to me. I looked down at the bolts, then over the corpse at the suddenly very pale crossbowmen.

"Really?" I tossed the body aside to ring against the stone floor. "This is your plan?"

Someone screamed an order, and a wave of magic hurtled forward, even as I blurred to the right, then replied with a dual cast version of a spell.

Clearly, I wasn't as fucking calm as I was trying to outwardly show, because the gravity seeds that spun up in both hands were kinda excessive.

The spell manifested as a pair of orbs of compressed fire and more, each one roughly the size of my fist. This close, with nowhere to go but forward, and there being a little less than twenty meters between them and me, they erupted from my hands like a missile launch.

The seeds impacted the barrier about five meters apart. Considering the range I'd set on the spell was ten meters for the circles to roll out to, that was just adding insult to injury.

Twenty separate seeds—individual points of gravity that flared up to thirty times the local level then flipped to minus thirty, and then up again, intermittently and unpredictably—spread out across the small area. Everything inside it was reduced to basically what you got when you forgot to put the lid on the blender.

The barricade simply ceased to exist. The defenders behind it fared worse.

When the smoke cleared, the main hall was…well, "renovated" was a polite way to put it. The far wall had a new door—about ten meters wide and still glowing at the edges. Through it, I could see the courtyard beyond, where more Dark Legion forces scrambled to respond…though the look on their face suggested "respond" and "run like fuck" were the same.

"Right then." I turned back to my stunned companions, clapping my hands together and rubbing them cheerfully. "Shall we?"

"You're fucking terrifying at times, boss, you know that?" Ronin asked.

I couldn't tell whether he was impressed or horrified. Probably both.

"Yeah, well, that's what happens when you leave me alone to play…I find new and interesting ways to dispose of my enemies. Bob, you're with me. Everyone else, secure the side passages. Flux, I see you there, you sneaky piece of shit. Report."

"The keep to this point is clear, apart from a handful of prisoners we rescued. I also sent a pair of my people up to free the people on the stands in the upper floors," he confirmed; four of his mer, as well as Bane and Lio, flowing around him as he spoke. "We're ready to take the grounds."

"Fuck, I forgot about them," I muttered.

"I think we all did."

"Well, fuck it, good man, and let's continue." I watched as the forces that had been preparing to run into the building below and back their friends up apparently decided that discretion was the better part of valor, and ran like fuck in the opposite direction.

The next twenty minutes, as we continued to clean out the last few areas on the ground floor, were methodical butchery. We moved room by room, hall by hall, cutting down anyone stupid enough to still be fighting while leaving the slaves locked safely in their cells until we were sure it was all clear.

It killed me to walk past those barred doors, to see how these people backed up and stared in horror. But how some of them pushed forward, yelling in joy and crying out that the legion was ready to return to service was a balm to my soul.

"Last chamber clear," Lio reported, smiling widely. "Found what looks like a command post with maps, deployment records…the usual."

"Grab anything that looks useful," I ordered. "Especially anything about where that death knight fucked off to."

As we finished the last floor, I gave Tang the nod, and he grinned, rushing off to start freeing the slaves. He'd taken a set of keys—triangular-ended things that looked more like they belonged on a weird piano than in a door—from a dead high-level Dark Legion paladin, and he called out orders as he went.

Most of the slaves were ordered to keep well back from the fighting, just to gather up anything they wanted and to get ready, but to stay clear. But the legionnaires?

They were given healing, and were asked to swear the oath, before stripping the dead of weapons and some armor and joining the line.

We regrouped at the massive gate separating the inner keep from the rest of the citadel. It was a monument to paranoia—three feet thick, banded with enough protective runes to make my eyes water, and probably worth more than most kingdoms' entire treasuries.

It was also noticeably abandoned, and could only be locked from our side, which was fucking hilarious. If we didn't know there were other slaves beyond this point, we could have literally locked the gates and called in Tenandra, then fucked off.

Instead, I peered through, as my people formed up, getting ready.

On the other side was a courtyard that had seen better days. Whatever gardens or training grounds had once been here were long gone, replaced by more of the death knight's charming decorative choices. Gallows lined one wall, most still occupied. A fountain in the center bubbled with something that definitely wasn't water.

And arranged in formation, getting ready to repel our assault and attack, stood the remainder of what I guessed was the citadel's garrison.

"Surrender!" A captain in elaborate armor stepped forward, trying to project authority despite the way his voice cracked. "You are surrounded and outnumbered! Lay down your arms and your deaths will be—"

"Quick?" I suggested. "Painless? Boring? Come on, you've got to sell it better than that."

"Mock all you want," he snarled. "When Lord Karridan returns—"

"He'll find a new garden ornament," I finished. "That fountain's looking a bit lonely."

The captain's face flushed. "You dare—"

"Boss?" Tang interrupted. "Not to ruin your fun, but we've got movement on the walls. Lots of movement."

I looked up. He was right. The citadel's defenders were pouring out of barracks, grabbing weapons, racing to defensive positions. In minutes, we'd be facing hundreds instead of dozens.

Well, that was convenient; it'd make it much easier as we wouldn't need to chase them all down.

"Everyone get ready," I ordered. "We're ending this."

"Ah, shit…" someone muttered behind me.

"Fuck's sake…back it up. He's gonna do something stupid," another voice added, making me grin as I recognized Ronin.

They fell back through the gate, and I followed, pulling it mostly shut behind us. Through the gap, I could see the captain's confused expression turning to triumph.

"Coward!" he shouted. "Face us like—"

The grin melted when I undid the lower sections of my armor and took a long and highly relaxing piss in his general direction, before putting myself away and waving at him.

He'd turned a fantastic shade of purple by the end, and I couldn't help it. I took my helmet off and smiled at him, as something in my expression made him take an involuntary step back.

"Jax," Lydia said slowly, recognizing that particular grin. "What are yer doin'?"

"Getting ready to free the slaves." I reached for the power that had been singing in my blood since I'd passed these poor bastards in their cells. "You ready to hold their attention while I do it?"

"Oh, aye. Right, you lot, get ready. This is gonna be fun. All out?" That last part was directed at me, and I nodded as she went on for the others. "Right, 'e's gonna let them charge us, an' the narrow gate means they cannae all get through at once, so this is where we all kick their asses and have some fun. Yer ready?" she barked at the others.

I saw the grins as people moved up to surround our side of the gate in a semicircle, getting ready.

"CHARGE!" the captain bellowed, and the Dark legionnaires ran at the gate.

I took the time to watch, examining a few of the different groups. This lot were mostly made up of either class trainers but elderly, or low-ranked noble types who had clearly bought their way into a position of power.

The last group, outside of the few dozen actual Dark legionnaires, were the aspirants, who, just like the legion aspirants we had, were basically trainees.

I grinned as they closed on the gate, nodding to myself as I decided that this was probably most of the remaining forces in the citadel, and as such, I could get away with this now.

I took a deep breath, gathered the power and focused, and then spoke the most basic and yet important words that these people could possibly hear.

"BE FREE."

CHAPTER TWENTY-TWO

The power erupted out from me, washing over my people and through. It filled the air and thundered past the charging group, just as they reached our people, and the effect was incredible.

Not because they were slaves, though a few dozen of the aspirants were, actually. They were suddenly yanked into the air, their chains and collars shattered, healed, and then dropped back to the ground, stunned.

No, it was incredible because, to the charging enemy, they saw a suddenly massive spell that slammed into them…and through.

They faltered, staring, confused. *Distracted.*

My people, though, weren't.

They'd expected it. And Lydia had made sure that those who didn't know what was about to happen were made aware. So, when the Dark legionnaires stumbled and stared, twisting around and checking themselves, their distraction made even more powerful as some in their midst they expected to use as fodder were suddenly yanked free?

Well, that just meant they weren't paying enough attention to the fight, now were they?

My legionnaires made the most of the distraction, and they literally slaughtered the fuckers. That got the attention of the professionals, who quickly fell in, trying to form a cohesive wall…and that was when Lydia unleashed one of her signature abilities.

She didn't use it much, mainly because it was so horrifically draining, but the Power of Starlight ability was incredible. She launched herself into the air; her wings flared out to the sides as magic held her steady, and rage flowed through her at the fuckers who dared to face her master and threaten him.

The power of the stars above were drawn down. Those tiny, bright lights were focused in and down, over and over. Each time the light that shone from her was halved in size, it grew in intensity, again and again. By the time she unleashed it, it was a little like a laser pointer.

She'd clearly been practicing with it, because she jerked it back and forth across the fourth and fifth rows, then randomly across the mass of figures rushing forward behind them.

The beam was the equivalent of a death ray, carving through the armor of those she targeted and into the flesh, then out the far side.

Where it took a head from someone in the fourth row, it then took out the chest of the guy in the fifth, the guts of the guy in the sixth, angling all the way down until people in the eighth and ninth rows screamed and collapsed to the ground, their feet chopped off.

Then she cut it off, dropping to the ground and gasping for breath as all around her, her fellow legionnaires unleashed their abilities.

Taunt was a classic, of course. Both sides had that, which was almost funny to see how many people ran forward, screaming abuse at one another.

It was made even more so by the number of low-level trainees on their side who staggered and jerked back and forth as the taunts of higher opponents overlapped and confused them.

At higher levels and with experience, Taunt was a weird thing, apparently. You gained a level of resistance to any taunt below your level, but it was also affected by things like your condition. You could taunt a master of Taunt when you were a novice, if you caught them unprepared and in just the right way.

They'd just shrug it off very quickly, that's all.

In this situation, weirdly, Lydia and I were among the lowest leveled with the skill on our side. But she had a degree of protection from her class, and I did from being insanely high leveled in other areas.

That wasn't the case for most of the enemy, though.

Lydia had already cut at least a third to almost half of them into kibble. Our front line went through theirs like a blowtorch through rice paper. And considering it was their actual real, working and fighting legionnaires who were the ones Lydia had focused on eliminating…

Well.

There was a brief pause as our front line counterattacked and hit their few experienced and skilled fighters; then we were through them.

The slaves who had been forced to fight by the collars were suddenly free, and they fell on their former captors with a vengeance. And all the time this was going on?

Several of the highest-ranking noble types, who had been entrusted with the leashes to said collars, had made this known by basically detonating.

It was an absolute *clusterfuck* for them. The fight lasted less than a minute, with only a single serious wound on our side, compared to over four hundred deaths on theirs.

The survivors who weren't slaves ran like their arses were on fire. The few slaves who had been in the fight were now dumping weapons and asking to join us.

It took less than an hour to clear out what was left of the citadel. Those who had run for it had kept going, and Tenandra let them get far enough out from the walls that they didn't have anywhere to go, before she started her strafing runs.

In the end, we were left with what was best described as "an embarrassment of riches" when it came to rescued slaves.

Five hundred and fourteen of them were rescued and offered a place in the empire or to return to Lembiq, as most were from there. Another two hundred were waved off with a general "have fun" as they wanted to return to their homes in the area. And on top of this, three hundred and nineteen imperial legionnaires were rescued.

Three hundred and nineteen of my people.

They went from stunned to overjoyed in seconds as they found out what had been happening. Most of them had been in the "care" of the Dark Legion for a long time, and specifically in the depths of their dungeons, blocked from any notification by an anti-magic field.

Why my divine-based, imperial ability got to them, I didn't know, but I was ecstatic.

They were also pretty pleased about it, and they'd signed up immediately. Then they'd had a whale of a time looting. The Dark Legion citadel had a truly incredible amount of loot available. Most of it wasn't of much use to me personally—I wasn't willing to replace my armor, and didn't need the rings that granted +2 and so on, and not one of them had anything on my naginata in weapons—but it was a massive help to the legionnaires.

In the end, we stayed in the citadel for nearly a day and a half.

In that time, my people were like locusts, stripping the place down to the ground, ripping anything and everything free that they could. I actively encouraged everyone that, instead of the latrines, they were welcome to make full use of the enormous cathedral in the heart of the citadel.

I personally took a highly satisfying shit on Illoth's altar, and then again a few hours later on Nimon's. If I'd had more time, I might have gone for the full set; instead I packed Baphomet's away in a box for later, and made do with just those two, making an offer to the other, lesser altars around the room—which I could feel were being listened to by their owners—to change sides to the winning side whenever they felt like it.

I ticked off a few quests as well.

Congratulations!

You have completed a quest given by the Goddess Jenae: "Gut those motherfuckers and shit on that bastard's altar."

The followers of Nimon, Dark God of Death, have recently crossed a line with Jenae and the rest of the Pantheon of the Flame. As such, you were asked to mete out appropriate punishment to them in the heart of their power.

You certainly did this, and as such, the Pantheon of the Flame gives you their thanks.

Reward: 5,000,000xp, +100 to reputation with Lembiq, 832 new citizens, loot, general approval from the pantheon and forgiveness for recent comments.

Bonus: Locations of Altaic the Red and Hildegaard of Tanis

That was nice. Apparently Altaic the Red was a mage of some renown; the locals had heard of him. Hildegaard on the other hand was a total unknown.

They were both holders of fragments of divinity, and in sharing their locations, it was damn clear that the gods were back on my side and were willing to help me hunt the fuckers down.

You have made progress in a new Quest: Rescue the Legion! (6)

The Imperial Legion rises again, buoyed aloft on a tide of rescued warriors; old friends and old comrades in arms have been reunited in their hundreds by your actions. But there are more still lost. Rescue them, return them to the empire, and feel the pride of a job well done!

Rescue members of the Imperial Legion!

Reward: 356/500 Legionnaires, 1,500,000xp

The real gain for the legion—beyond the destruction of their hated enemies and the rescue of their people, I mean—was that the Dark Legion had been stealing, stockpiling, and smelting down imperial equipment for centuries.

Their own gear was mainly imperial in design and then fucking painted, after all.

They'd had literal imperial equipment produced in our old camp then shipped here to be mangled, painted, and stupid things like faces carved into the armor to make it more intimidating. But it was still mainly imperial gear.

That was simply taken back. Although most of it was a mess, there was enough to provide all my freshly rescued legionnaires with a full set, and well over a thousand more to boot. We took everything that wasn't nailed down. And thanks to the wonders of storage devices taking up most of it, although Tenandra was a little overloaded in the end, she was fine really.

We gathered everyone up in the fields to the north of the citadel, and we cracked open several barrels of ale, some wines, and a lot of good food, and we had a wonderful feast, as Tenandra began to bombard the absolute fuck out of the citadel.

Using her weapons against a building in this world should have been nightmarish, as the mana built into the building could strengthen it. But we'd thought of that, and I spent half a day prepping the spell that took full control of all mana in the area. I then used that wonderful little spell that Amon had taught me.

It'd been created by one of his court mages, Darioush the Great. I used all that insane amount of mana that was available to me, by linking the area of effect mana denial spell to it, and I basically did to the citadel what Lydia had done to the Dark legionnaires.

It lasted three seconds, as the ball I created punched through the outer wall and came to a rest in the heart of the citadel, then it spun up.

The spell had been created when a mage had been trying to fuse different materials together to make better metals for the flying war-cities, also known as the prax.

He discovered—and was bloody lucky to have been able to escape it—that a massive exothermic reaction, when channeled into a perfect circular burst, was essentially like inflicting a hole in reality...or it was, when it was powerful enough.

Everything—such as, in this case, anything around its point of release, about a hundred meters out and one meter tall, at near enough ground level—simply vanished.

When that happened, there was a brief pause, as apparently gravity did a double take, and then the next level up and all that mass that was built atop it, dropped.

Sure, a meter isn't that much when you consider a building that was hundreds of meters high. A minor detail, though, was that when a specific section of the ground floor vanished, the impact of millions of tons crashing down, even with no real buildup of momentum, was kinda significant.

We felt the ground shake where we stood.

The rest of the citadel was suddenly spiderwebbed with cracks. The connections that usually reinforced the structure had been broken, and the mana for the area was denied to anyone who didn't have the right signature, so the structure's normal reinforcement runes and so on just failed entirely.

Now, to most people, they saw me fire something off and do some maybe minor damage to the structure; they missed the tiny shift as the entire building realigned itself to be a meter shorter.

What they didn't miss, though, was when Tenandra screamed in from overhead and unleashed absolute hellfire upon an already weakened building and basically tore it a new arsehole.

As the entire thing started to crumble—walls toppling, ceilings shattering and taking out the lower floors, windows that were already broken simply vanishing under the pounding—I stepped forward. The static electricity and pressure in the air made it clear that the gods were watching.

Jenae and the others had given me that quest to really piss them off, after all, so I decided I might as well go for gold.

"So!" I called out, grinning upward and feeling incredibly ready and really wanting to fight with fucking someone. "Well then, Nimon…I mean, what the hell, dude? Usually you're right here by now, telling me to behave or else!

"You've not given up, have you? Just because I cut your fucking head off, destroyed two of your citadels, and personally took a shit on your altar? You fucking started this, you miserable bastard, you and those you protect. Or is it time that both sides grew up a little?"

There was a roll of growing thunder until I said that last bit. I strolled farther forward, making sure I was far enough away from everyone that if He pulled some shitty trick, then they'd not get caught in the crossfire.

"Is that it?" I called upward into the darkening sky, the rising sun tingeing the clouds pink and coppery as I waited. "You've decided that maybe we need to be adults and move forward with things in a more or less accepting manner? Well, I'm all for it, to be honest!"

Absolute silence filled the air as all the gods involved were listening with manic intensity: my side clearly wondering what the fuck I was playing at, and his side actually interested, I was willing to guess.

"See, the thing is, I never had a problem with you, Nimon!" I shrugged, gesturing as I walked back and forth, staring at the clouds. "Me personally, I mean. Sure, I didn't like the shit you pulled in the past, but that's the *past*. Seven hundred years ago. I'm a big enough man that I'm willing to talk, so if that's what you're hoping for, sure. I'll do it.

"The assault on your sleeping troops back on Dravith? It was a mistake, and it was entirely my own, but it was a genuine mistake, that's it.

"We've killed tens of thousands in the attempt to get at each other since then, so if you want to draw a line under it and let bygones be bygones, I'm willing to listen. I'm willing to help bring an end to the war and start the realm off on a better footing. Are you?"

"Jax, what are you doing?!" It was Jenae, and I went on.

"But, because, you know, let's face it, I'm fucking slaughtering your forces these days, I do have a few little conditions…" I grinned up at the clouds. "Nothing too unrealistic, as you'll understand. Your Dark Legion is to be renamed the 'Dark Disappointments,' which I think describes them really well. All the imperial legionnaires you currently hold are to be released, given their gear back and a personal, fucking groveling apology by each and every member of the Dark Disappointments they encounter, whenever they encounter them—that'll need to be enforced by magic on your side, obviously. And last of all, and this is the one I really want, so listen up, all right?"

The rumbling of thunder and the sudden flashes of lightning in the sky overhead—in a previously barely clouded sky—faded slightly, and I nodded.

"Glad you're listening. All right, I want *Baphomet*. I want him fucking hog-tied, his power restrained to a mortal level, and he's to be served to me on a platter with a fucking apple in his mouth and a splitting wedge inserted in his arse, and I'll bring my own sledgehammer! He gave my love to Xenefier, *motherfucker*!

"He conspired with the creature that wants to end everything, all life. And when that happens? You'll get a great boost in power and then boom, it'll all fade away. Everything will.

"No more life, no more mana; no more mana, no more life—and then no more souls. All of reality will grind to a fucking halt, and all because that hairy-arsed bastard wanted to fuck with me. So here it is, the offer direct from me to you:

"GIVE ME BAPHOMET, AND THAT'S THE PRICE OF PEACE!" I roared into the sky. "Otherwise, you and me? We're at *war*, motherfucker. And let me tell ya—I've been questing and dealing with shit like this as a fucking *side order*.

"This has been a *distraction* to me so far, something I do when and if I get time! Until now, I was willing to leave this low-level, not to rock the boat. But if you want to keep it going? Let's see just how much of your power base I can wipe out, IF I ACTUALLY START HUNTING YOU!

"I know how this shit works now, bitch! I know! When He took her from me, He took the only reason I was willing to be reasonable! The only reason I listened and stopped! You want me to back off? You want me to fucking behave and not take another steaming shit on your altars? Not actively hunt down and destroy each and every fucking one of them I can? FINE!

"GIVE ME BACK MY LOVE OR GIVE ME BAPHOMET! Do that and we're even, you and me. No more shit…no more me hunting you and no more you hunting me. Give me my legionnaires back, and I'll stop hunting your dickheads—all good. But you refuse me? You refuse this single fucking offer of peace? And then it's on. I'll not offer again, and it'll take you kneeling to Jenae and the others to survive what's coming.

"You know what I can do now, and I don't doubt you've been watching me. You know what's coming. What I'll become to rescue her! You want that held off? You want me and you square now? This is the chance, the only chance you'll get!"

"YOU ARE A FOOL." It was Nimon, and the roar flattened the grass all around me, almost making me stagger. ***"What comes is what must be! My former brethren are nothing compared to my might. I am the God of DEATH. Each and every one of my people you kill only feeds me power! They only have to get lucky once, but you must be lucky every. Single. Time.***

"When you enter the house of death, when you cross the veil, I shall pluck your soul free and snuff it out. I shall ensure you never rise again. Your soul fires will be extinguished for all of time!"

"Well, that's it then, dickless. Remember this, and remember that you were given a chance, because now it's on!" Then, because I was just such a reasonable and understanding man, I dropped my pants and started to helicopter my cock.

"COME ON, YOU BIG FUCKER! Get your arse down here and fight me. Send one of your pets to do it, or FUCK OFF!"

The sky went white with power as bolts of lightning in their hundreds slammed into a hastily raised shield, as the gods of the Pantheon of Flame proved they still had my back.

The shimmering dome shield that covered us all shook and twisted, but I didn't care. I'd achieved what I needed to. I'd planted the seed with the bastard: as the days and weeks now passed, every single loss He took, He was going to blame Baphomet.

So, to make sure I kept His attention, I switched from helicoptering to instead give it little thrust and played at "flicking the light switch."

There was no way, realistically, He'd have given up His ally—or, at least, I didn't see how it would be possible. But if He'd gone for it, I'd have fucking taken it.

Handing over Baphomet for me to slaughter six ways from Sunday and take His fragments? Then, for me to continue with my hunt—because fuck you if you think I'd not keep hunting the fragments—would have meant that the God of Death ended up as a footnote in my rise to power.

Sure, He was more powerful than me right now. But if I could collect enough fragments, and then the others that were scattered across the realm?

I'd realized something after my little conversation with Tyosh. He'd been stunned and a little concerned that I could ignore the lure of binding the fragments. For me, it wasn't a big thing. Just like the XP I gained from the quests and the stat points weren't that big a thing.

Not that I didn't want them, or that I didn't need them. Sure, slamming them into place and feeling the increases in power was great.

No, the reason I could do what I did, I was realizing, was because of the power differential between here and Earth.

I'd come here with fuck all—really, I was slightly more powerful than a ten-year-old—and it was because of the usage of that power, and the absolute fucking slaughterfest I'd engaged in since then.

I'd leveled like nothing else. In the span of six or eight months maybe, I'd literally reached a level that had legionnaires with decades of experience staring in wonder.

Some of that was because of my natural gifts—but most was blind luck. I'd gained extra points from being Jenae's champion, and then the gods had basically power-leveled me by giving me extra quests and doubling up the XP.

Was it cheating? Yes and no. But did I care? Fuck to the no.

Then I'd bound three fragments of divinity, and I'd started kicking entire cities to fuck.

Where I was now, I was used to the fact that I'd been leveling and growing constantly day after day. There'd barely been a few weeks where I didn't have levels coming out of my arse, and when that happened, I'd been overjoyed to instead get laid and just relax.

When you slammed a load of points into a stat and increased it suddenly, it was actively painful. That, combined with no fear of plateauing and the absolute certainty that I could beat most giants into submission by now, meant that power was something I just accepted.

I knew—knew in myself, I mean—that if Nimon were to pop up tomorrow and hand Baphomet over, I'd be fine with taking the fragments and binding some, but not passing the threshold into full divinity.

When I did that, when I finally passed that level, I'd be locked into my power. And then, any changes, from what I understood, like absorbing another fragment, would lock me down, hard, for a while.

That wasn't the case when you first fully ascended, though. I had no clue why, but however many fragments you had seemed to form a cohesive whole instantly, or that was what I understood.

If that was true, then most gods, desperate to ascend, would be binding the ten as fast as possible. As Tyosh had said, if I could gather more, a lot more, then I could literally make sure that when I hit the other side, I was far more powerful than the other "lesser" gods.

That would mean that I could genuinely be a threat to Nimon, a direct and real threat, once I rescued Oracle and my child.

I could take that fucker down. And if He had been watching me, He had to know it.

If the cost of ending this war was a reasonable one, I was starting to think He'd take it. Jenae and the others might not be happy about it, but I definitely got the feeling that they'd be willing to consider it, at least.

No, the sticking point was that I couldn't afford to let that happen, not unless I could get a sacrificial lamb like Baphomet handed over. That fucker I'd kill twice over—three times on Sundays—and between the fragments and the satisfaction, yeah, that was my price.

I'd thought of all this, in the time that it took for the light show overhead to die away. And it was only then, as the dome shimmered from view, that I had a sudden horrible, terrible realization.

We were all inside the dome, all protected by the grace of the gods.

But Tenandra wasn't.

CHAPTER TWENTY-THREE

Nimon apparently saw that minor oversight just as I realized it. The skies grew clear and the overwhelming feeling of pressure died away. Suddenly, He shouted out, and it was clear that He'd been pushed a little too far.

"Very well. If this is to be war, then a war you shall have!"

The bolt of lightning that burst from the heavens was at least as thick across as I was tall, and it slammed into the middle of the forward deck like the spear of the gods.

The bar of light hit the ship as it arced around the smoking and collapsing city, and then kept going, entering through the top and erupting through the bottom before slamming into the ground and digging deep.

It lasted maybe half a second, and in that time, it was powerful and bright enough that it left a solid bar of light across my vision.

As soon as the bolt had struck, I felt the outrage from the gods and their fury as the Arbiter was called into play, as well as the sudden feeling as everyone's ears popped as the pressure unexpectedly vanished.

The gods were gone. Where or why, I didn't know, but I was pretty sure that was the Arbiter again. Regardless, though, I didn't care.

I launched myself into the air, even as the screams from Jian and Sehran rose behind me, and I poured everything I had into the flight.

She was over a mile away, and as I rocketed upward, I saw the start of the flames rising.

The closer I got, the more I reached out to her, and the more I panicked when she didn't respond. The impact looked to have been roughly halfway down her deck, which was the first thought that crossed my mind. The angle she'd been at wasn't exactly helping me to see for sure, but I knew she was housed in the control area mainly, wasn't she?

I doubled down, straining harder, screaming through the air and rising higher, pushing to get a clear view.

When I did, I really started to panic.

She was listing, slowly shifting over to the right side. The engines on the left side were firing and dying, over and over, as she angled around, clearly trying to turn back toward us.

I crossed the last few hundred meters in a blur, flipping over and pushing as hard as I could backward, bringing my momentum to a stop, more or less above her. I stared in horror at the hole that had been punched through the deck.

It was at least a meter wide, and I could see the ground below through it. Multiple fires had started on the several decks as various things that had been in the bolt's path smoldered and burned. But the worst part was the sparking conduits.

Flaring pulses of mana jetted out of the hole. The conduits that formed her spinal column were breaking down; the formerly contained crystallized mana was turning into gas, released to rejoin the realm.

I dove into the hole, passing through the thick planking of the upper deck and down.

The damage was horrific, but it was on the third level, as I grabbed the flooring from the level above and flipped myself around to land, that I saw just how badly I'd fucked up.

I'd been *wrong*.

I'd got it in my head that Tenandra was always in the captain's cabin, and that she was always hanging around the control systems there. But that wasn't the heart of the ship.

The crystals that I'd put in place when I'd first boarded her had been put in—according to the gnome who had rearranged them all—back to front and upside down. I hadn't been able to tell the difference, and I genuinely still couldn't, but besides them, we'd also placed Tenandra's core.

It was what she'd been inside and bound to when I'd removed her from the prax and brought her here. And now, the area where she'd been, the area where the fucking majority of the manastones had been, was just…gone.

We were going down, and I didn't see a way to prevent that. Worst of all, I could feel her there still, but also…gone. She wasn't responding to me, and this was where the two halves of the mana conduit were supposed to be feeding into.

The entire space was just…missing. The literal technological heart of the ship, and Nimon had taken it entirely out with a single strike.

I stared, as the ship gradually listed further and further, before coming to a conclusion I didn't like.

I had two choices, that was clear. First of all, get out. Get out and run, and when the ship had landed—crash-landed, to be clear—then I could try to figure out some kind of a fix.

That would not be quick or easy, and the likelihood was that if she crash-landed, Tenandra—as a ship—was definitely gone. She might survive bonded directly to Jian, but in her present form, that she loved?

Not a chance.

The second option was a fast and dirty fix, one that was going to be fucking incredibly half-assed and quite possibly useless, as well as incredibly wasteful. But it had a chance to save her, and if I was honest, the plans we'd made as well.

I'd done this, though. I'd put her in this position, sure that Nimon wouldn't cross the line because of the Arbiter, so I'd been goading him, playing at being Billy Big Balls and confident that the other gods had my back, even as I ran my mouth and risked everything.

Now I was paying for it, and I damn well knew Tenandra already had.

There wasn't a choice, really.

I reached into my bag of holding, pulling out the dozen or so small manastones I had on hand, and I set to work, botching and bodging the job. I rammed the manastones I had into the two sides of the conduits, and started to frantically channel.

The skill I was using now—one that like *so* many others, I needed to spend more goddamn time on—was the one that I'd gained when I hit my second century in Intelligence and my first in Wisdom.

It was created through the juncture of using mana and recovering it, and fuck me was it an impressive skill.

Or it could be.

I'd barely touched it, literally, because like so much else, I just didn't have the damn time, and when I did, I chose to do other things, because there was never enough time in the day.

I focused as I pulled up the description, feeling that it was the only thing that had a chance to help, but reading it to be sure.

Mana Manipulation
The Mana Manipulation ability is exceedingly rare for a mage, despite its common-appearing name. The ability to manipulate mana at its most fundamental level is the ability to interact with the wider magical world. However, rather than simply using mana to cast a spell, as most mages do, it involves the manipulation of the aspect of mana, converting Death mana to Life, Fire to Water, or any one of a thousand variations. An expert mana manipulator can form mana into its physical form, creating manastones, yet forcing them to remain in a set aspect.
Cost: 50 mana per point converted

Yeah, that was what I needed.

Now, there *was* a minor issue: "an expert mana manipulator" I was not. I'd barely fucked around with it a dozen times since I'd gotten it, and that was mainly around the campfire when I'd been relaxing or talking to Oracle.

I'd also had a little mess around with it in practicing guiding it into the potions when I was making them, seeing if that helped. But I'd given up on that pretty fast as it added an extra layer of complexity to something I was already doing by the seat of my damn pants.

So, being the stupid ass I was, I'd left it, and right now was where that was coming back to bite me in the ass. I dredged up the details that Jenae had shared with me about mana conduits, and finally what I'd discovered on my own by acting as a blunt instrument and connection for mana to rejuvenate the stump of the Great Tower of Gaij.

I drew on all of it. I slammed that mana out of myself, into the ship, putting myself in the middle of the two conduits and forming a living bridge.

As soon as I did, I felt the change as the two sides went from leaking mana into fully firing. Mana streamed through me and across, carrying complex orders, details, changes.

I screamed in agony; I burned with the mana that poured through me, but I also felt the sudden nearness of Tenandra.

She was here still! Fuck me, I'd known that she had subsumed herself into the ship, and that the core, the section I'd been panicking over losing, had been reconditioned into a core for the ship to externally accept power. I'd just not been sure that she'd been "out" enough to survive what had just happened.

Giint, that mad, magnificent bastard, had gone up the mast in the middle of a storm and had connected the mast to the core with the magical equivalent of spit and duct tape, and it'd sucked down lightning strikes, recharging the ship as the core filled with mana.

Tenandra had spread out across the ship, but her core had still been left there.

Nimon had seen her, had seen the core, and had taken it out in a single cunning strike.

He'd broken her back, robbed her of most of her power. I could feel it even as the engines started to die, but with me bridging the gap, Tenandra could actually control the ship again.

Reaching out, I tried to speak to her, to apologize, to ask what I could do to help. But I couldn't feel much from her, not beyond a baseline "I'm busy—get over it." She was there, though, and she was leveling out the ship, bringing her around to land.

"Jax, yer mad bastard!" Lydia's voice came from above.

I gasped, looking up. She and Sehran stuck their heads over the edge of the hole and stared at me.

"No time!" I barked desperately. "Manastones! Get them…as many as you can!"

She blinked, then turned, grabbing Sehran by one horn as the succubus tried to push past her, and speaking quickly. Then the pair of them were off.

Thank the gods Lydia still trusted me the way she did; rather than wasting any more time asking stupid questions, the pair just did what I'd asked.

I blew out a breath and kept the gap plugged, no longer trying to do what I had been, in thinking I could somehow use the stones, my own rough understanding, and yeah, blind luck and spells to form a conduit out of nothing.

Instead, I used my own channels as a highway for her commands, bracing myself and just holding the bridge.

It seemed to take hours, but as the ship finally settled, the desperate need to pass a million differently tweaked commands a second vanished a heartbeat later as well.

The last few minutes had also been filled with shouted orders, conflicting advice and swearing, but Sehran and Lydia had come back with the stones to help.

Admittedly, Lydia also blasted me with the rough side of her tongue for the entire time, which wasn't helping how long the flight felt. But for each manastone she pressed into place, a little of the draw on my own reserves lessened and a little more of the conduit was regrown by Tenandra, with me handling the manual bits.

I knew we were "there" when, less than a minute after the ship settled to the ground—I could see the ground a dozen meters below me—Tenandra reformed into her kitsune persona and crouched next to me, glaring as she took more stones from the bag and started work.

"Tenandra, I'm sorry…" I started.

"You're in my way, Prince Jax," she replied tightly.

"I'm sorry," I repeated dumbly, pulling my hands back, and feeling the crack as something like ice crystals but formed of mana, fractured, crumbling away to release my hands. "I…" I was unsure what I could say, and she nodded.

"I know. Now, please, leave me to work," she said as politely as she could.

For the first time since those early hours of our relationship, I could feel the waves of fury at me that were rolling off her.

I hesitated, then dropped to the ground, barely missing kicking Jian in the face as he reached the hole a second after I crashed out of it.

He barely saw me, pushing past with a glare that was distracted, but made it clear he blamed me as well.

As well he should.

Then he was clambering upward, joining Sehran.

Lydia followed me out as I crouch-walked under the lower keel and into the morning beyond.

I'd just snatched a flawless victory away and reduced both our safety and our strength in the damn area, and for what? A chance to piss the gods off even more.

Lydia took one look at my face, then stepped up, murmuring.

"Jax, yer gonna say somethin' yer regret iffin you speak t'anyone, so do us all a favor, and go t'yer cabin. Get a few hours o' kip, an' later in t'day, we'll figure this shit out," she suggested.

I drew down a deep breath, glanced at her, and nodded slowly. I was a hundred percent done with the goddamn day, and the sun was barely up.

What a clusterfuck.

CHAPTER TWENTY-FOUR

When I woke—around midafternoon…and after a particularly shitty sleep—it was to a fast rapping on my door.

I jerked upright, blinking as the blanket fell from me. I stared around the room, trying to work out where the hell I was for a few seconds, before the knock came again.

"Come." I sighed, rubbing at my face, before flinching as instead of the door opening, Tenandra reformed in the middle of the room, standing to attention in a blue jacket and pant set, with a gleaming white shirt beneath it.

"Good morning Jax," she said politely.

I sighed, staring at her. "Are you okay?" I ignored the greeting, shame rising in me.

"I will be," she said. Then, clearly seeing I was serious, relaxed and shifted from the stance of parade rest and instead strode to a chair and sat in it, then reached behind it and tapped one finger down atop Bane's head. "This conversation is for the adults, dear. Run along."

"Jax?" Bane asked, clearly as surprised as I was by the change in attitude. But once I nodded that it was okay, he got up and headed out, glancing back as he closed the door.

"As much as I try to be one of the crew, and of your team when possible, certain events remind me that before you awoke me, and before the long sleep, I was already over a thousand years old, Jax. Situations like this are jarring because of that." She sat forward, resting her hand on her knees, and stared at me, her eyes looking far older than I'd ever understood before.

"What happened was *incredibly* stupid, and something that we should have all seen coming," she said. "And yet…" She held up a hand as I started to apologize, talking over me as I tried.

"And yet, you've done this repeatedly to prove a point and to keep your opponents off-balance. Though whatever you've done this time feels different, so, rather than being angry, I've decided that we'll discuss this like adults.

"First of all, I have to ask: was the risk worth the gain? You need to understand that yes, I am severely damaged, but I can repair it and nothing is permanently damaged, beyond the need to replace internal systems. These will be highly costly, but can be done."

"Oh, thank fuck," I whispered, closing my eyes and taking a deep breath. "Are you sure?"

"The damage was extensive," she said. "My old core is gone, as are many of the lesser systems and the manastone reserves. These will be *very* expensive to replace, but I don't doubt that they can be done. In the meantime, I can fly and maintain power so long as we need, though firing the cannons and anything too mana-intensive is beyond me, should you also wish to continue flight.

"The repair will take at least five days, and that number is predicated on me having access to enough manastones to do it entirely using that as a resource.

Should you provide the raw materials, then it would go faster, but that would depend on your plans from here on out." She fixed me with a glare.

"Don't misunderstand me, Jax. This was *entirely* avoidable and I am furious over the damage to my hull and control systems. That being said..." She paused, then forced herself to sit upright and take a deep breath.

"In war, there are damages that occur, even the loss of lives, and although many are unavoidable, sometimes small losses must be accepted in order to achieve great things.

"This is one of those times, I believe, as you have both a large number of manastones, and a large number of gnomes sworn to you in the area, or at least that can be recruited and made use of.

"Therefore, I suggest we make the most of the situation as well as the resources and use the gnomes you have freed—there were many in the citadel, I believe— and we improve upon my form."

She finally let me get a word in edgewise, and I nodded.

"I agree," I said mumbled. "Shit, Tenandra, I'm sorry. I didn't think about anyone else being a target, not really. I just let my mouth get away from me and, well..."

She nodded. "I know. And for what it's worth, Jax, I understand...truly I do. But this was always going to happen. You've used that same method several times now. Perhaps running along the edge of the razor blade and daring yourself not to slip is a method best put aside? After all, the first time and possibly the second, it was a surprise. Now? I do not doubt that you have less and less effect each time you do it, and neither should you. Originally, you manipulated events by shock and surprise. Do you truly believe that the other side are surprised or shocked by your actions now?"

I stared at her for a few seconds, thinking it through, then sighed and shook my head.

"No. I don't think they are, though I think for now they're still so low on self-control that it's working...a little, at least. I'm sorry, though—genuinely, I am. I should have thought more about you being outside the protective barrier, and that's on me. But keeping them reacting is all that's kept us alive so far," I admitted.

"There are *rules*, Tenandra. I don't understand most of them, but they're not allowed to take a direct hand. And when they have in the past, there's been massive costs involved for them. One of those costs was taken from Baphomet to rebuild that temple, because He crossed a line. It's both injured Him beyond the loss of His fragment to Darakin and further weakened Him doing it.

"Provoking the gods to fight me as I did gives us chances that we just won't get any other way, and there's..." I kept talking, but I felt something change.

Tenandra blinked, staring at me suddenly. "Jax, I can't hear you, and I can't make out your lips." She held her hand up to stop me, and I sighed.

"Yeah, that's what I was afraid of," I admitted. "It's the Arbiter basically deciding that some knowledge isn't for anyone not on the path of godhood. All right, how about this instead? I'll provide you with whatever you need for the upgrade, and I'll do my best not to put you or the others at risk without thinking about it first."

I cocked my head to the side in question as I spoke; she nodded as I went on, forcing a smile.

"I don't like it, but I can't say I won't do it again. Because if I have to, I will. The issue here was that I didn't think, and so you got hurt, and I'm sorry for that. But this is, like you say, a war. Shit happens, and I need to accept that, and so do you."

"I agree," she said with a sudden small smile. "You're growing up, Jax."

"Yeah, well, doesn't mean I have to like it." I snorted.

"And that's an important decision and realization to come to for yourself, Jax," she said softly. "I'm not happy with you—I'm *really* not. That attack was incredibly painful. I nearly lost my body, which could have cost us everything, and it has most definitely cost us our chance at catching the Dark Legion in the field at this time.

"I could have been functionally destroyed, leaving you with the choice of abandoning me in the field as wreckage—which you would have been forced to do, with the largest Dark Legion force in the area no doubt heading here now— or entirely destroying me yourself.

"Had I been captured, they could have forced me to rebuild myself for their use. Or had I not survived, they could have captured another of my kind and begun binding her to my corpse and then stripping me for the knowledge of flight.

"Inside a year, you would have lost the single greatest military advantage you have over your enemies, as well as your primary method of fast transport. And the result would have been catastrophic for the empire.

"That being said, sometimes risks have to be taken, and good things can come out of this. So tell me, my prince, was this risk worth it, and will we come out of this stronger?"

"Yes and no," I admitted. "I don't know what the impact will be until the gods are talking to me again. But for now, it's resulted in them all being driven off, if nothing else. And as much as it pains me to say this, the long-term effect is that you survived, and I'll try to watch my tongue. If nothing else, it's made sure the other side is still being watched for cheating."

"Very well. Then what do we do now?"

I paused, ordering things in my mind.

"We return to Lembiq, and we start repairs," I decided after a few seconds' thought. "Were any of the crew aboard you injured in the attack?"

"Not the crew, but several of the observer team were given minor injuries. Silviana's mother is apparently intending to give you a lecture," Tenandra said with a little smile.

I groaned, putting my head in my hands. "Fine! I'll take care of that. But before we get things moving, is there anything else I need to know?"

"Not from my side. Anyone else, I'm unsure of," she replied.

"Fine again." I sighed. "Right, I'm gonna get some pants on. Not much point with modesty around you considering I've literally 'worn' you already and you see everything around you, so fuck it."

I stood, casting the blanket aside and pulling clean clothing out of the drawers in one wall, loving that there were actual clean clothes here for me as I kept speaking.

"I'd like a meeting for the leadership in here in oh, ten minutes?" I said to her as I dressed. "You, obviously. Lydia, Flux, Sehran, Borren, uh…Tisan as well, and, ah fuck it, that should do."

"Do you wish to invite Silviana as well?" Tenandra suggested. "She is a citizen of the empire now, but as an ex-slave who was once processed through here, she and her brother have proved invaluable in dealing with those who have been freed."

"Yeah." I chewed on my lip. "Do we need anyone else?"

"The citizens, or those who wish to become citizens, are represented by Silviana, the observers by Tisan, the legionnaires by Borren and your squad by Lydia, with Flux for the mer and essentially as both your sounding board and spymaster, and Sehran because you want to have her there. I believe these are enough, though I would warn you that Ronin has been attempting to gain access to these meetings as well."

"Why?" I looked at her, nonplussed. "Fuck's sake, I'd avoid them if I could."

"I know. In his place, however, they are a source of information, and he may currently only prove his worth to you on rare occasions. He is exceedingly knowledgeable of the greater realm due to his class, and he is attempting to compose an epic ballad of your life. Access to such meetings would assist him."

"And it'd result in songs like 'Silly Arnold the Farmer' and worse," I countered with a snort. "Fuck no."

"Lydia has accepted that he is a valued member of the team, and no longer a walking atrocity," she informed me.

"Seriously?" I stared at the wisp, pausing in pulling my top on. "How the hell did he manage that?"

"Continuous effort," she said. "Despite the impression he likes to give, he has been assisting her whenever possible. And, if I am reading the signs right, he is apparently smitten with her."

I stared at her for a few seconds, working that out in my mind. My brain tried to rebel against it, and then I started to smile, in a very evil way.

"Sure, invite the bard along." I grinned. "I mean, what's the worst that could happen, right?"

~~~

"Seriously?" Lydia snarled at me a few minutes later. "Fuck's sake, Jax, yer lost yer senses? Why let that rag-bag excuse for a minstrel in t'meetin'?"

She'd stormed into my room while I was eating, and I'd just directed her to a seat and kept going.

"Because—fuck's sake, that's as dry as Gandhi's flip-flop—" I groaned, shaking my head and pulling out a drink. The travel rations I'd wolfed down were unbelievably shitty, but I'd thought, considering the number of our new people who were going to be forced to eat them over the next few days, I should at least try them.

Fuck that in the future.
~~~

"Because why?" she growled, getting me back on track.

"Because he knows about the wider picture and this, as much as it's shit, is going to be one of those meetings where we put a plan together for the next few months."

"Or an hour an' a half," she groused. "Fuck's sake, Jax—yer know yer plans never survive t'week. Pointless makin' 'em half t' time."

"And yet you still complain when there isn't a plan in place," Flux countered, walking in without knocking, as the big mer could clearly sense around the minor issue of a closed door and hear like a bat.

"Congratulations on your survival, Prince Jax, and your victory," Tisan added, as he and the others followed in on the mer's heels.

"Thanks." I sighed. "Look, everyone, find a seat where you can and eat or drink if you want. This isn't going to be a short meeting, and I'm including you, Tisan, because I don't think there's much point in hiding this from you. I'm hoping a little honesty here will help when we return to Lembiq, so let's get started.

"First of all, for anyone who wasn't aware—yes, I fucked up. My mouthing off at the gods got them riled up enough that Tenandra took a direct hit, and she's going to need some serious repairs. That, in turn, is going to cost us both time and effort, on top of the cost of materials. Now, we don't know where the Dark Legion are, only that they were to the south, and it would take two to three weeks to travel from here to Lembiq on foot.

"Next, we know that the marsh that surrounds us on all sides is a fucking risk. There are a lot of undead and so on out there, is that right?"

"It is, my prince," Borren replied. "The undead have already attacked several times, but due to the constant use of them for 'training' by the Dark Legion, the numbers close by are negligible."

"And if we were to try to march the people we've just freed through the marsh to Lembiq?" I asked.

"We can do it, but it's likely to take at least three weeks, as you said. By my estimate, it could be done in two provided the group was mainly legionnaires and on the understanding of the commander being willing to run risks.

"Instead, I estimate three, on the grounds we would be limited to marching at a speed the refugees are capable of. We aren't familiar with the paths, and we'll need to spread fighters out around the group as we go to keep them safe," he replied without hesitation.

"Okay, but you could do it?"

"We can, but again, it'll cost us in terms of time. The Dark Legion, should they push hard enough, or be close enough, may catch up with us. Without greater intelligence on their numbers, I can't guarantee the group's safety."

It was all very professional and sticking to the facts, and I appreciated it, even as it made me curse myself again for limiting us all.

"Okay, Tisan, will Lembiq have an issue with me bringing these refugees there as a short-term fix?" I asked him directly.

He shook his head. "Not in the numbers you have, and not so long as you don't intend to abandon them to Lembiq's care. Some, of course, would be welcome. Those of our citizens or the people who had come from us originally. Also, those with in-demand skills would have a chance at being accepted. But should you intend on transporting the majority beyond your legionnaires to Lembiq and abandoning them, it would damage the positive impression that you are seeking," he said honestly.

"Thank you." I went on. "No, I won't be abandoning them, and I'm happy to pay for food or whatever they need when they reach the city and until I can get them back to Gaij. My concern was more will they close the gates and think I'm attacking, more than anything else."

"Ah, then no, that's a situation that is easily resolved. When we return, simply make the council aware this is a short-term issue while the group passes through and you intend to cover the costs, and they will instead be impressed by your generosity.

"Much of the lower levels of Lembiq is overcrowded due to failed farms, raiders and lost settlements. The refugees the city has already taken in are a constant drain on the resources it has, hence the reasoning. We are not unreasonable as a people."

"Okay, I get that. Hmmmm, would they be interested in us taking some of those people to Gaij?" I glanced at him in question. "The refugees they want rid of and only if they wanted to, I mean?"

"They'd probably be overjoyed." He stared at me in surprise. "I mean no offense, but why would you do this? The refugee situation is terrible, and all civilized people wish to resolve it. But there are only so many ways, and they can be a terrible drain on any city."

"Only if you think of them that way," I countered. "We have a need for practically everyone, from laborers to legionnaires, mages to chefs. And because the citizens' oath requires that all contribute if they can, we don't have people who don't want to work, or who want to be criminals.

"Don't get me wrong, there's always some crime, but we're working on stomping it out. The oath also requires that our citizens treat each other as family. Stealing from them, injuring them, all that kind of thing isn't something you do to your brothers and sisters, not really, so although a little petty crime still goes on, the vast majority is gone.

"The result is that people know they're safe from one another and the various crimes don't really exist as much in the empire. Then add in that we give the opportunity to learn to all. We have legionnaires who have more spells than most mages, and our mages spend half their time teaching anyone who comes to the classes, for free." I grinned as he stared at me in shock.

"At the minute, it's mainly the legion in those classes, but if there's space, then any citizen can join in. That way, if we come under attack by something big enough, even the regular citizens can help. You heard about the full Dark Legion that the citadel sent to face us, right?"

"Yes, I was told that you defeated it," he agreed, nodding as if it was unimportant.

"No." I shook my head, sitting forward. "We *destroyed* it," I corrected. "The effect of launching several *thousand* Magic Missiles, in volleys, over and over again, as the Dark Legion ran for its life was lethal. Most of the cavalry we deployed never even got close enough to hit them.

"We were at an almost zero risk of losing the fight. We had more than half our forces standing down, hiding out of sight, to keep the enemy from realizing just how easily we were going to defeat them, so we wouldn't have to chase them down later. That's the effect that training *everyone* we can in magic has. Hundreds didn't even have the chance to use their spells, we ran out of targets that fast..."

"But they all got and completed a quest to defend the city, and almost everyone gained dozens of levels as well," Sehran added helpfully.

"That too," I agreed, grinning. "The point is, though, that these people are a drain on *your* society because you haven't processed them and given them anywhere to add to it. I'm not blaming you—I totally get it. Where I once lived, it was the same, though massively worse. The difference is that the empire can make room for them, and even help them establish entirely new cities.

"They can massively improve things for us *and* for themselves. If they're dealt with and offered the chance to gain out of it, then they typically desperately want to. Plus, those rescued from slavery tend to be exceedingly determined to make sure they're never at the risk of that situation again. That means working their asses off at any job they're given. Not all of them, of course—people are people—but the vast majority are thrilled to do it."

"This is a welcome surprise, Prince Jax. Unfortunately, the investment required to provide training and opportunities to those who have failed—most through no fault of their own, I admit—is significant, and the city simply cannot bear it without an expectation of a return. As such, they are left to find their own way."

"So, we're back to making sure the council won't be pissed if we bring them to Lembiq as a staging area, and now we know they shouldn't be, and we can actively make them happier by taking their excess. That's that one concern marked off the list."

I nodded to myself and glanced across at the grizzled legionnaire. "Borren, what I want you to do is take personal charge of the refugees and the rescued legionnaires. You're to take whatever you need from the loot and supplies to make sure you get them to Lembiq as quickly, but *safely* as possible. What do you need from me?"

"Nothing." He smiled. "Beyond the oaths and maybe a little 'welcome' speech? That's literally all we need, and we're ready to leave."

"Fine, get everyone gathered up. We'll do that after this meeting, and then you can get some miles in before you need to set up camp for the night. Leave the gnomes, though, as we're going to need them to help with Tenandra's repairs. And any who are too elderly or infirm for the trip," I ordered. He saluted, and I waved both him and Silviana off as she stood too, letting them both know that I'd catch him up with anything else after the oaths if they needed it.

The pair left the room, and I turned to the group again.

"All right, so here's where we are. We need Lembiq, the gods have told me so, though they're not exactly clear on the reasoning. I'm inclined to agree with them, mainly because I'd rather not destroy or conquer everywhere. This might be as simple as the city is in a great area to launch assaults from and be a central location, but there's also been references to something to do with a long-lost library. Tisan, is there a major library in the city?" I asked bluntly.

"There are three," he admitted, "though nothing unusually large. They are each fairly well stocked, but there is no hidden repository, or not that I would be entrusted with the knowledge of."

"That's fine." I nodded. "No offense, but if you knew of one, I'd have been surprised and frankly suspicious. So, we need to make an alliance if possible, partly to save the knowledge and partly because I'd rather have allies. Will the destruction of the citadel so far accomplish that?"

"Possibly," he hedged, looking out of the back window from my quarters to the massive pile of shattered rock that was all that was left of the citadel.

It still occasionally shifted and fell further, but the combination of my spell and the damage that Tenandra had unleashed meant that the site was now about as far from "functional" as it was possible to get.

"Had you destroyed the Dark Legion as well, then I would have said yes. As it is, it is possible but not certain. I'm sorry," he finished lamely.

"Okay, that's on me." I sighed. "Will they allow us to land and make repairs, though?"

He nodded. "I don't believe there will be an issue. Should you be landing with the entirety of the forces you have here, they may be less sanguine..." He gestured to the gathered legionnaires all around the downed ship currently and partly visible through the floor-to-ceiling windows.

"But the small number of you who will be aboard and to make repairs, yes. I will vouch for the need. And even if you were not asking for an alliance, this would appear reasonable," Tisan assured me. The older wood elf smiled slightly as he said it.

"Great, so we're doing that." I leaned back in my seat and looked at the group gathered around me. "Once we reach the city, we can see how Yen and Grizz have done, and hopefully start searching for something on the hidden library while the repairs take place. Tenandra, how long for that?"

"To restore minimum functionality will take sixteen hours, then three days to return to Lembiq, and probably two more to complete the repairs, though that will leave me exhausted and without the reserves we usually have, including my replenishment system and storage."

She was being very careful not to say anything too detailed, but I waved it away. "Tisan, do your merchants have mana cores?" I asked bluntly. "Are you aware of what they are? Artificial cores, I mean, not monster cores?"

"I believe so. They are similar in nature to the golem cores?" he asked.

I looked at him for a few seconds before nodding slowly. "Yeah. What do you know of golem cores, though?"

"They are self-replenishing and powerful, though limited by size and quality. That is most of my knowledge on the subject." He winced. "That and that the market for them had severely declined until recently."

"And who's buying them all suddenly?"

"The Dark Legion, or so we believe," he admitted grimly.

"You don't know?"

"As a settlement that is frequently fighting and being raided by the Dark Legion, we do no direct business. But those who we have dealt with in the past have then been selling them on; this is known."

"And they know the cores come from you? Ultimately, I mean?"

"Probably."

"And now we get the fucking meat of the matter." I groaned, rubbing at my face. "You stupid fuckers—you've made a target of yourselves for the golem cores for the Dark Legion…because why would they buy them when they can just conquer you?"

"They would have difficulty in locating our source." He smiled.

"Would they?" I asked flatly. "Would they really? Because if that is what the Dark Legion is after, then they'll think nothing of burning your fucking city to the ground, and burning the entire forest down to ash to sort through it easier. Goddammit." I bit my lip, mind racing. "What do you have and where is it?" I knew he wasn't likely to tell me, but it was worth a try.

"I cannot share those details," he replied, resolute.

"Fine. Ronin, were there any imperial facilities near here?" I asked the bard.

He stared at me. "How the hell would I know?" he asked, surprised. "Boss, I know some of the old stories and I could pick out some of the locations on a map if you showed it, but I'd never been farther than the islands three weeks to the south of Dravith before this trip."

"Damn, I was hoping—" I started, only to be cut off by Tenandra.

"The nearest imperial facilities were over a thousand miles from here, or at least those that could have supplied and created the cores."

"Go on," I prompted, recognizing how she hesitated.

"Although the major sites are a significant distance away, there were several trade and transport routes nearby." She reached out and laid a hand on the table, forming a map to draw everyone's attention.

It started as a thing of rolling mist that poured across the table to the farthest edges; it started to mound up, forming peaks and valleys, mountains and rivers, that became more recognizable by the second.

"If the city has been trading in golem *cores*, not full golems, and the cores are intact and easily recoverable, as well as in a quantity that is maintainable long enough for the price to fluctuate, that would suggest a large store of them, but only of the cores.

"If they are not being recovered as damaged nor depleted, and from inactive golems, then logically that suggests they were completed cores en route to a major manufacturing site." She looked around, checking to see whether we were all following as she continued.

"Although some facilities, like the main production facility in Dravith, could create completed units in huge numbers, most facilities here on Carrmor were specialized, with parts being created in multiple areas and then shipped using heavy transports to central assembly points, usually due to material constraints.

"These transports were generally less graceful than my current form, and far smaller than my old. Essentially, imagine a hundred wagons doubled in width and joined nose to tail. They would be flown from the production site to the construction area, and then the transport returned, carrying completed creations.

"In this case, we are between two production sites. Here…" She indicated a glowing dot in the distant mountains. "This was a mining and refining site, and was used to create cores. Then this one…"

She indicated a second site, on the far side of Lembiq in an almost direct line from the mountains in the northeast to the southwest.

"This was a golem production site, specifically servitors, and then they were shipped across the continent and beyond." She drew a line from one glowing dot to the other. "I suspect a transport was en route when the cataclysm struck. If so, much as my own prax did, the sudden warping of all mana would have destroyed or disabled the engines, causing it to fragment and crash."

"How do you know this?" Tisan glared at her.

She smiled. "I was once the primary control wisp for the prax Glorious Retribution," she replied proudly. "My form has changed, but my memories are intact. I remember being supplied from that site," she indicated the southern site, "for my servitor complement, and due to a delay from a storm, we were forced to wait there for three days. My crew enjoyed the additional downtime, visiting the local areas. I remember it well."

"So yer think they're recoverin' broken bits o' an engine?" Lydia asked.

"No. I suspect the main transport crashed more or less intact. Although they were not aerodynamic, they were constructed to survive attacks from lesser dragon kin, who were infrequently drawn by the mana signatures inside.

"As such, it is likely that most of the cores would survive the impact, packed as they would be for transport. They would also have several war golems, advanced models, ready to defend the transport."

"Wouldn't they do something about the crash?" I asked, and she shook her head.

"They would be advanced, so would maintain the site and take action to maintain imperial property. But, provided the cores were protected, they wouldn't take action beyond protecting the cores and awaiting recovery. It would take the next level up, a greater golem, to assess the lack of a recovery response and make a determination depending on that," Tenandra stated unequivocally. "Most likely, if the site was more or less intact, the war golems would simply cordon it off, eliminate any threats in the area and then go into standby to await recovery. Over time, without a repair or maintenance facility, they would run out of mana and simply shut down, leaving the site ripe for looting."

"Okay, so, you want to share anything with me?" I asked Tisan, who continued to glare at the wisp.

"Certainly not."

"Even though those cores are imperial property?" I tried and got a glare, making me snort and abandon that line. "Oh, all right, don't be like that—finders keepers…*whatever*." I sighed. "I'm just glad that you have some. Tenandra, can you use those cores to help you with repairs and upgrades? If we *buy* them from the city, I mean?" I clarified, shooting Tisan a look which he returned with a glower.

"I could, but they aren't capable of replacing my primary core—not unless you wish to devote twenty or more to the project," she clarified.

I winced. "We can, but damn, the old core was that powerful?"

She shook her head. "More like that versatile," she clarified. "A lesser golem core is a much simpler creation, and requires simpler interfaces."

"Okay, so, would it be better to get you one like that, or twenty of the golem cores?"

"Is it too much to ask for both?" she replied after a few seconds, then grinned. "It would enable me to heavily upgrade myself, if both were to be made available."

"Go on." I sighed. "Fuck me, this is like going shopping with my ex. I just know I'm gonna end up poor, as an apology for fucking up."

"If we replace the main core with another of similar or greater capacity, and then include, say…twenty golem cores, I could split them between powering rune script systems and the ripple-fire cannons, both powering them and drawing excess mana away from the firing systems. I could fire for longer without depleting my stores nor damaging the cannon," she pointed out excitedly.

"Then the rune script could be activated only when I need them, using the basic on/off of the golem cores, as opposed to having to switch the mana channels entirely. As an example, I could coat the outer hull in levitation and weight reduction runes, enabling us to lift a far heavier mass, and either move faster or…"

"Or?" I prompted when she paused, looking at me.

"Or, as I say, weight reduction systems could enable me to coat the outer hull in steel and ignore most attacks from anything below that of a lesser dragon.

"Ballistae and the vast majority of spells could be deflected. Even absorption runes could be added, meaning that when we were in a storm or under a magical attack, the hull would act as a connection to suck the mana in and recharge us."

"Could you add that shield rune I got ages ago?" I asked, and she nodded. "I mean, you've still got them, right?"

"The majority melted under sustained use in the war, but we have some. We were fitted to use them if need be, but they're so draining to maintain that we simply don't, most of the time."

"But with this you could?" I asked; she nodded. "A warship indeed." I sighed, rubbing at my chin in thought. I didn't like the time that this was costing me, not at all, but I also knew I had fuck all choice, as this was my fuckup we were working to fix here.

"Fine, plan for that, and we'll get the cores we can where we can. I'll use the information I have from the Constellation of Secrets to hopefully get a new core made for you, though it's going to mean a trip to Gaij."

"Then I suggest we get ready for that." She beamed at me, and I snorted.

"So, am I forgiven?" I asked bluntly.

"You will be." She gave a little toss of her hair. "Just as soon as the upgrades are done."

"Fuck's sake, you sound exactly like my ex." I sighed. "Okay, moving on. That's the plans for the ship and short term sorted. When we get to Lembiq, we try to get this alliance off the ground. But, failing that, we continue with friendly chats and find out what we can. The gods say that what we need to defeat Xenefier is here, or a path to it is. More than that, they don't know, but it's pretty much the most important thing we can do," I said very clearly.

"Once that's done, we have two more targets in the local area, or at least within range." I went on. "Two fragment wielders are heading toward us, or I think so. So as soon as Tenandra is operational for a long flight, we need to intercept them, keeping the fight that is to come as far from Gaij and our people as possible." I left that deliberately vague, and Tisan clearly got the fucking hint, as he clenched a fist.

"That would include far from your allies, I presume? And that would be a concern as to when you intercept them, as opposed to if they're close by any unaffiliated city?" he asked me bluntly.

I nodded. "Of course." I smiled. "We'll be focusing on keeping them as far as possible from *any* imperial subject."

The look on his face said he got exactly what I said and what I didn't: Join us and we'll keep fights like this from you. Don't, and your lands are free game.

I didn't like playing games like that, but that was war.

CHAPTER TWENTY-FIVE

The oath ceremony was both fast and flawless, for a nice change. No shitbags tried anything, nobody tried to avoid it, and frankly, the vast majority of people who were left were so overjoyed at their freedom, and for the slaves who weren't legion to be protected in their march by three hundred plus legionnaires, that their optimism was infectious.

Borren had tried to leave a large guard with us, claiming that I was more important than the refugees, and I put him right by pointing out that if I had to, I could probably bench-press Tenandra now—I'd have to use a fuckton of mana and I wasn't sure my body could handle it, but I was genuinely curious. He accepted it, the whole 'all right, you did attack a few cities for us' hints having the needed effect.

By the time Tenandra had regrown most of the connections she needed and the manastones we needed were all in place—held by a makeshift system she'd clagged together—it was closer to eighteen hours later. But no matter how high I, Sehran, or Lydia went, we couldn't see any armies marching this way, so we accepted the delay.

It gnawed at me, constantly, but it was what it was, and I kept going.

Eventually we were in the air again. The gnomes were mapping out Tenandra's systems, drawing up plans that changed before they finished drawing them. I sat in my cabin—alone, as I'd insisted that I was doing magical experimentation and even Bane preferred to wait outside when I did that—as I focused on splitting my attention.

I'd tried reaching out to Jenae, and She'd sent me the divine equivalent of a busy signal. I forced myself to accept that it was better than a Dear John letter and got back to work.

The first thing I did was concentrate on my meditation. Once I was firmly sure I had it as locked in place as I could, up to the third tier—glowing boxes around me shimmered as the mana was guided in and focused down—I started the second part of this.

This was where it all got a fuckload harder, mainly because the whole point of meditation was to remove the distractions, removing the sense of "me" that got in the way and accepting the mana from all around me, purifying it and guiding it into me.

Now what I was trying to do as well, was improve my Mana Manipulation. I had sort of an idea that this was one way I could train both skills. It was a fragment of an old technique I vaguely remembered, but considering it was a memory from Amon, that didn't mean it was stupid.

Unfortunately, because I was missing some memories, I was also missing some stages of the technique, which wasn't happy making.

I'd really needed the skill when Tenandra was injured. As much as I knew I was incredibly busy over and over again, and just didn't have time to fuck around, that excuse wasn't good enough.

I could have lost a friend and possibly the war because I'd not been practicing, so I forced myself to go back to basics, constructing a hair-thick thread of mana to start with.

Then I floated it out of my right palm, and into the wall of light that hung before me, trying to pass it through and… It shattered and I felt a sting of psychic pain.

Then I reset, got the walls into place again, and started again—because when you had a sudden feeling like someone put a cigarette out on the old grey matter, it kinda shocked you out of a meditative trance.

Still, if I could do this, it would really help me, I knew. So, I kept at it.

That was why for nearly five hours, I tried everything I could think of, before giving up and storming out to watch the stars from the deck.

An hour after I got out there, and ten minutes after I'd tried and given up on "just one more try," Jian joined me, letting out an enormous yawn.

"Hey, boss," he greeted me. "Whatcha up to?"

"Meditating."

"That why the deck looks like you're having a party with the lights?"

I grunted, having forgotten that the light from my meditation could be visible at times. I still didn't damn well know why that was, either. I glanced over, getting a grin from him.

"Going that well, huh?"

"Yeah." I sighed, before turning to him. "Look, Jian, I…"

"Nope." He shook his head.

"I just need to—what?" I frowned.

"This is why Tenandra and Sehran kicked me outta bed and sent me up here, boss." He yawned again, covering his mouth with his hand before settling in to lean on the railing comfortably. "You're still worried about this?"

"I nearly fucking killed Tenandra," I growled.

"Yeah, and me too." He nodded. "Not with that bolt of lightning, but you know…Lydia a few times as well. Hell, Grizz did actually die for you, what, twice? I don't think any of us haven't been nearly killed yet. This was just her turn," he said blandly.

"What?" I stared at him.

"Fuck's sake, boss." He sighed, sounding annoyed. "Look, no offense, but you need to quit this 'blame game' shit. Yeah, she nearly died, and it was your fault. But it's also your fault that she loves her life. That she's not locked in a fucking rotting dungeon, surrounded by necromancers and the undead.

"It's your fault that me and Lydia aren't dead with baby sporelings climbing outta our asses, and it's your fault that Bane and his lot weren't eaten by goblins. As to the legion? Fuck's sake, boss, that's your fault as well—they were supposed to be killed by the nobles and the Dark Legion and who knows what fuckin' ages ago.

"Himnel and Narkolt were pretty much all supposed to be eaten by vampyrs and taken over by the drow as well, so yeah, there's a lot of shit that's your fault. So how about we just draw a line under it and move on, eh?"

"Seriously?" I asked. "You're that chill about this?"

"Well, all I'm saying is that Sehran and Tenandra double-teamed me and then told me I had to forgive you, and stopped at the worst time, until I agreed. Then when I agreed, they went all out. So, yeah. Right now, I'm pretty much all 'peace and fuckin' goodwill,' you know?"

"You're post-sex and happy with the world." I laughed, seeing the tired look on his face for what it was now. Post-nut clarity.

"Damn right, man. Look, a lot of shit could have gone wrong that didn't, and a lot could have gone right that didn't as well. It's life. And right now? What I need is to go to bed, and move on. I think you should do the same."

With that, he clapped me on the shoulder, and whistling a little—as well as clearly lighter on his feet—he strolled off, heading back to his cabin and the women he loved.

I stared after him for a few minutes, then turned back to the stars and silently wished Oracle a good night, sending her all my love and desperate hope, and then went to bed as well.

Strangely, I actually did feel a lot better.

The next day was a weird one, partly because by the time the sun came up, I'd been woken up twice by gnomes—and believe me, the last thing anyone wanted was to be woken by a gnome screaming because he's given himself the mana equivalent of an electric shock.

Mainly because the kinky mad little bastards then argued over what it was, why it happened, and designed some gloves that'd mitigate the effect.

We nearly crashed twice as one particular gnome somehow interacted with Tenandra's central nervous system, while wearing said new gloves, and started having a whale of a time trying to fly her.

That particular little fuckup resulted in Lydia having to catch the gnome, as Giint was told to "deal with this asshole" and promptly threw them over the side to run alongside the ship for a bit.

Someone had introduced him to stories about pirates, and he apparently loved them. Although, where a normal sailor might be savable if they were thrown off the front deck and offered a life raft or preserver as the ship passed by—if they were lucky—the same cannot be said about gnomes thrown over the side of the ship half a mile up.

Lydia only caught the little fucker a few dozen meters from the ground, and she'd been in a foul mood since.

Giint had sidled up to me and pointed out calmly that he'd done what was asked and he deserved a little treat, didn't he?

Considering the other gnome had nearly killed us all and Tenandra was fully on Giint's side in this, I decided that yeah, some actual punishment was well in order, as was some praise, and I got out that little potion that I'd promised Giint.

Mercandor's Delight	Further Description *Yes*/*No*
Details:	Mercandor was an alchemist obsessed with making as much coin as physically possible. The secrets of his "Delight" potion were slow to be revealed, but, when a shipping container was dropped

		at the wrong place and at the wrong time, it was mixed with both nightbloom and arinsinia's bane. The unholy resulting mixture was responsible for the devastation of the city of Narendor. Mercandor was found to have acted irresponsibly and was only saved from the gallows by a personal intervention by Svetu Himself…on behalf of his gnomes, who wanted the recipe.
Rarity:	**Magical:**	**Durability:**	**Potency:**
Rare	Yes	100/100	7/10

I poured a tiny amount onto a cloth and gave it to Giint in front of the other traumatized gnome—he'd barely been on the deck a minute before he'd started telling us all that he thought he'd be able to help pilot Tenandra better now and wanted his gloves back—and to make sure he understood, I let Giint have the cloth, and gave all the other gnomes a tiny amount as well.

But not him.

The sight of all the other gnomes off their tits and having a great time was apparently considerably worse, because he swore off ever trying to mess with Tenandra's systems again and immediately threw the gloves he'd made over the side of the ship.

Then cried and bawled uncontrollably for the next six hours until all the rest of the gnomes came out of their stupor.

That they then went back to work refreshed, invigorated, and apparently with some kind of a buff applied, drove him over the edge.

By the time I went to bed that night, at least three days of work had been done, and Tenandra's systems were essentially as good as they could be, short of us landing and getting the cores.

The next two days were a pain due to the little fuckers coming begging after that, though.

The gnomes were given jobs to keep them out of the way, and then more, which resulted in a third of the ship being reworked, and Tenandra had to land once to collect deadwood and more to use as raw materials.

Finally, I gave in and gave them all a second hit of "the good stuff" and locked them in the hold to keep them from doing something else stupid.

By the time the distant tree top city finally came into view, I was pretty much a hundred percent decided against ever having a multi-day flight with the mad little bastards aboard. I now understood what I'd put Mal through when I set him up with a dozen of the absolutely feral ones from the prax, instead of these—by comparison—upstanding and hard-working members of their community.

That, of course, meant that I'd find it even funnier if I could somehow do it to him again, when I wasn't so close to the situation.

It was also right then when Jenae finally reached out to me, making me jump, then turn and head for my cabin for what I guessed was going to be a very bad conversation.

"I'm here, my goddess," I sent to Her as I closed the door, firmly evicting Bane beforehand.

"Jax, there's not much time," She said bluntly. *"There are a few things to share with you, but one of them is that you personally, and we as a group, are now being observed by the Arbiter. So, I suggest a little more tact in the future. Do we understand each other?"*

I wasn't that surprised that they were, but that it was watching me as well wasn't a good thing. It'd probably mean an end to the extra XP and rewards, and I winced when I realized that.

"Of course, I'm sorry."

"It is what it is, as you frequently say." She sighed. *"It had the desired effect, though. Nimon's direct action against Tenandra was deemed to be excessive, when He failed to strike you directly. To be clear, after the discussion, it's been decided that should He take direct action against YOU in the future, when you goad Him…this is now permitted, provided the level of force is equal to your own.*

"As such, I recommend you cease goading Him, because a pinprick of an injury could eliminate you as a threat, should it be done correctly," She pointed out. *"A single strike by a level-one creature has the potential to eliminate almost any level-one hundred being, provided it is perfectly executed in the right way."*

"A stab to the jugular," I muttered.

"Or through the eye and into the brain," She agreed. *"It is unlikely, but understand, Jax, Nimon's more wildly thrown and unsubtle attacks have been through rage overwhelming his reason. Now He is likely preparing such an attack for you, so please—stop antagonizing Him so much."*

"I'll try," I promised, dubiously. "Wait—can He attack Tenandra and the others…?"

"No," She said firmly. *"That was entirely against the rules, and has resulted in a response, though I cannot discuss it with you. The others, provided they do not personally rile Him, are protected from His direct retribution. I would suggest you do not attempt to take advantage of that, however."*

"Okay." I sighed. "Did we get anything out of it?"

"Again, most of it I cannot share, and would be meaningless to you if I did, but I can share three things. First and foremost, Oracle has been observed— don't ask me how; I don't know—but the Arbiter has given a boon to her directly, slowing her heart rate and her development, as well as strengthening the baby, gaining us at least a few weeks. That is the largest boon, and believe me, I had to fight for it."

She paused as I sank into a chair and stared at the wall opposite, unable to speak.

"Jax?"

I shook my head, unable to speak for long seconds before I managed a single sentence.

"Thank you," I whispered, as tears rolled down my cheeks.

"We are allies…" She tried to pass it off, and I shook my head.

"No, you didn't have to fight for that. And if you did, then you know what you did. Just knowing that you managed this is… I just…" I blundered on, unable to articulate the words, before dragging down a shuddering breath, unable to speak.

"I understand," She said softly. *"I'm sorry that we couldn't do more, and that forcing this issue has weakened our opponents to a point that we—"* A noise like a low whistle echoed as She tried to speak, before She clearly gave up and changed the subject.

"So, let's move on," She growled. *"So far, we don't know a huge amount about where and what is going on with the other side, but what we do know is—"*

This time, it was like a horde of bees had taken up residence in my ears. I shook my head, desperate to make the noise stop.

"Enough!" I shouted after a few seconds as She clearly tried to power through. "Fuck's sake, I…okay, just tell me what you can, please. Jenae, I'll be as good as I can, and what we can do is what we can do," I finished lamely.

"Unfortunately, that's clear," She growled. *"Okay, one point I was permitted to share with you, because it was a point to help you and your people directly, is that the site that you deduced must exist in the area of Lembiq, is only partly looted. I can't tell you what is there, but I can confirm that there are relics and artifacts that could be useful to you. I suggest you negotiate for access to it.*

"Lastly, you'll need the council's help in your quest. It's important that you gain access to their knowledge beyond looting the city. That's it. That's all I can tell you."

"Thank you," I said softly, still processing everything. "I don't know…"

"Just accept the win, stop doing stupid things, and be careful," She replied, a hint of amusement in Her voice. *"Though I also know that part of it was probably because of the quest I gave you, so I'll do my best to maintain a little more dignity in those from now on. Oh, and Svetu suggests you limit the gnomes' access to the Delight potion, as it's apparently addictive. So once in a blue moon, and only when they've really earned it."*

"I will," I agreed instantly.

"Then good luck, Jax. Remember, we have faith in you. Don't forget to plan out your next steps, and using your map is useful when you need to plan things out, but that Tenandra is often going to understand it a lot better than you, and you should just accept that."

She said it, and before I could say anything else, the sense of Her overwhelming presence was gone, like a fart in the wind.

Tenandra would be useful with my map, eh? I nodded and sorted myself out, changing my clothes and checking my armor. It was a bit scuffed and damaged again, and sections of the right elbow joint and left knee were gummed up with what looked like dried blood and hair, but fuck it.

I dressed, then took a deep breath and channeled a load of my mana into the knee joint, feeling it as the armor used that mana to fix and clean itself. Then I facepalmed, and hit my armor with a Scour spell, and cleaned it for a fraction of the cost.

Clearly, excessive mana didn't beat common sense.

By the time I made it to the control room—seeing that Lydia was entering just ahead of me meant it was probably safe—we were less than an hour from landing, and things needed to be addressed.

Tenandra stood at attention, and both Jian and Sehran were in sight as well, all dressed and ready, which made a nice change.

As soon as I entered the room and saw Sehran, I spoke, knowing that with the months here with the three of us alone together, we'd grown much closer than we used to be.

"Oracle's okay." I said it with conviction, and I felt the relief and interest of the room as everyone turned to me. "I'm sorry to interrupt everyone, but I just spoke to Jenae. The punish—" I changed tack. "The gods helped us, and they did it at massive cost. Oracle's development has been slowed down somehow and the baby is stronger. They think it'll gain us a few extra weeks at least, though we still need to not fuck around, obviously."

That was it as the room erupted in questions, most of which I couldn't answer, and it took ten minutes to spread the good news and get ready.

I told the others what our priorities were: make friends, get the alliance, get access to the golem crash site, and use the resources we gained to repair and upgrade Tenandra.

Then, as we finally drifted to the side of the lake—Tenandra chose not to land in the lake as the seals weren't that good yet and it'd make more repairs problematic if she did—it was to find a fair-sized crowd had already appeared, waiting for news.

The observers disembarked, Grizz and Yen boarded, and within fifteen minutes, all was calm again.

Until a gnome did something stupid and a sudden eruption of white smoke burst from the forward hatch, anyway.

CHAPTER TWENTY-SIX

"And that's it for our side," I finished, sitting with the rest of the crew in my cabin, bringing Yen and Grizz up to date. "What happened here?"

"Well, not much," Yen admitted, dispirited. "Essentially, they're willing to listen is about as much as we could get set in stone. Beyond that, they're good at hiding their plans. The more we snooped, the more they got angry, so we held off on a lot of that.

"The details of the golem cores are interesting. I saw a few stores that have things like that, but they're not really considered anything special. Expensive? Yeah. But not valuable or that rare."

"That doesn't make much sense," I pointed out.

"They want a lot for them—a hundred gold each, when I asked—but they don't have anything that can make use of them—no golems around the city. But for four separate stores to have them in, they have to be getting them from somewhere. But they're all covered in dust," she explained.

"So, they've had them for ages, they know they're valuable, but they're not worth much around here." I nodded. "Fair enough. That makes sense. Thanks."

"As to them joining the empire, I'd honestly say it's fifty-fifty, boss." She went on, looking annoyed. "I'm sorry. I've done everything I can, but I constantly get the runaround and they refuse to speak to me about anything properly.

"Instead, they ask about details of your character, your history, and how the empire is doing on Dravith. They want to know everything they can about you and Oracle, and how you treat the other wisps. They also sat up and listened when we spoke about the grove guardians. Apparently, they have a relationship with a grove to the northwest, and that's something that's important to them. But beyond general things, they kept saying that they'd wait and see what happened. When we pushed, we got frozen out of meetings for a full day, so we pulled it back a bit."

She went on, discussing other details…their rough military strength, and their potential benefit to the empire—not just in terms of their fighting strength but their alchemical production as well. The main thing that I got from it all was that she'd worked her arse off, and that she was terrified that she'd fucked up.

"Thank you," I said. "Yen, you've done an amazing job—you too, Grizz—and I've only done half the job I said I would. But we're going to fix that. So, first of all, any idea how long it'll be before we're asked to speak to the council?"

"At least a day," she said definitively. "They might be longer, as they're going to want to interview the observers first."

"And my mother will cause as many problems as she can," Silviana, who I'd also invited along in the end, added morosely.

"Why?" I asked bluntly. "I mean, I get that she doesn't like me, and my methods, but why is she such a bitch?"

"Our ancestors used to be rich, mainly through trade with the high elves and others. We had a trading house, caravans, all of it. We gradually lost it over the years, but I think she hates that others are successful at anything, when she's not," the wood elf admitted.

"You used to be rich and now you're not." I nodded. "Well, that's a simple enough reason, I guess. Any way you see of getting her on our side?"

"Honestly, no." She winced. "Before the trip, I'd have said there were a few, but she hates you now, and most of the others turned against her, meaning the little respect she had is now gone. If anything, she'll blame you more. It's who she is."

"Joy." I sighed. "All right, fuck it. So, moving forward, we need those cores. How many are currently for sale in the city?"

"About a dozen," Yen mused. "I mean, I wasn't looking for them specifically, but we had access to the Branch and Rootside stores and taverns. When I asked around, there were a handful that had them, but mainly in Rootside."

"Rootside?" I asked.

"Shit. Sorry, boss. The lowest level of the city, where the outsiders are mainly kept, so anyone who's not a true wood elf or who's not got a good position in their city are kept on or below the ground level, so 'Rootside.' The Branch level is the middle classes and true wood elves in good standing. And then you have the Canopy, which is reserved for the highest castes and councils, real high flyers, that kinda thing," she clarified.

"Gotcha," I muttered. "All right, so these stores on the lower levels, I want you to hit them with Silviana and... Wait, Silviana, why didn't you mention the cores before?" I asked her.

"I didn't think anything of it," she admitted. "The cores are something that's valuable, like you say, but they're not special. Most of the stores have them because the old 'curiosities' store went bust."

"Explain that."

She nodded, clearly thinking where to start, then shrugged. "It's not that interesting a story," she replied. "There was an old store in the lower levels of Branch. It bought stuff that people found in the forests and that was a bit weird or whatever...things that were curious but that didn't really have a value, like the cores. To the right person, they're valuable. To most people looking for food and to keep a roof over their kids' heads? Not really.

"People from the upper levels liked the weird stuff he had. Every so often, he'd find something really valuable and that'd be enough to keep the shop going well. He set up a shop in Rootside as well, buying from there and selling on Branch, but about ten years ago, he died—just dropped one day—and was gone before the healers could get to him."

"Heart attack," I guessed, then gestured for her to go on.

"I guess." She shrugged. "Either way, he was older than dirt. His kids didn't want anything to do with the store, so they sold it all and that was that. People knew that some of the stuff he had was valuable, so most of the stores bought a couple of things and tried to sell them. But as the months and years passed, people stopped caring."

"Because nobody knew what any of the shit was and if it was valuable or not," I finished for her, nodding. "All right, Tenandra, can you and..." I paused.

"I'll take Jian, Yen, and Grizz," Tenandra said smoothly. "Sehran, will you keep an eye on my body, please, dear?"

"You know I love to." The succubus winked, and I couldn't help but smile.

"Then in that case, I'll need coin." Tenandra looked over at me.

"How much?"

"All of it." She shrugged. "I won't know what they have until I see it."

"I'll keep them under control, boss," Grizz assured me as I reached into my bags, starting to sort through several.

"And who'll keep *you* under control?" I asked realistically, eyeing the big man.

"Me. I will go," Flux said firmly. "If you are to search for valuable materials here, I would ask that anything with runes is included for Ame."

"And I would ask that you don't fucking *bankrupt* me." I snorted, finishing swapping a few things around and then chucked a bag of holding across the room with an under-arm toss. "There's a hundred thousand in gold and platinum in there, and probably the same in looted weapons and shit from the dark dicks. Use whatever you need to, but try not to lose it all gambling."

"I make no promises, boss!" Grizz grinned at me, and I glared at him, before shaking my head and burying it in my hands.

"Who the hell do I send with you to stop you all getting into trouble?" I mused. "I need Lydia with me in case the council summons me…" That had come out in a few conversations with Tisan: apparently, a Valkyrie on my side was a massive thing to the wood elves, and I needed that additional goodwill.

"Giint go with them." The mad little bastard sighed. "For good of the team, Giint will go."

"Now we're fucked." I groaned, before sighing and gesturing vaguely at the door. "Go on then, go. Tenandra, spend what you need to, to sort your body. Silviana, go with them and help them, please."

And that was that; they all left the room, leaving me with Lydia, Sehran, and Bane. As the group left the room, more and more of the team looked from the door to me and back again.

"Oh, just go!" I called, then shouted after Tenandra. "Give our people a hundred in gold from me as well, on top of their own loot. If you need anything else, shout to Sehran and I'll send you more."

There were cheers and the rest of the squad raced off after her.

Ten minutes later, the last of the cheering and running feet had died down, leaving the four of us pretty much alone aboard ship.

The gnomes had already left—apparently, the wood elves liked a little smoke and dust of their own—and by the time we reached the deck, it was deserted.

"I'd have thought yer'd want t'explore?" Lydia asked me.

I hesitated, then shrugged. "Honestly, I don't," I said, subdued. "I just… I don't want to see it without her."

"That makes a lot of sense." Sehran stepped up alongside me as we made our way to the railing, watching as the others walked along the road to the city, some already vanishing beneath hanging lianas. "I didn't care about most of the things I saw in the same way without Tenandra and my Jian."

"Dammit, where's that goddamn bard?" Lydia suddenly hissed, looking around.

"He went into the city." I blinked. "What's up?"

"Nothing," she grumbled, leaning on the railing on my other side and glaring after the group as if they'd pissed her off.

"You can go with them, if you want?" I offered. "I can find you, or…"

"It's not that." She shook her head grimly, before seeing that we were both looking at her. "It's not!" she spat. "Ah'm just used t'little shit being somewhere every time ah turn around an' ah almost have t'kick 'im outta the way. And, if I let 'im outta my sight, 'e gets into trouble, that's all."

"Really?" I asked blandly. "So, he's always around you, is he?"

"Aye. Ah mean it…'e makes me feel like I need t'boot 'im outta the way t'get anywhere," she said. "'E's an annoying little git."

"But?" I prompted.

"But nothin'," she growled.

"All right." I dropped it, letting the silence stretch out.

The three of us—four with Bane, but the fucker was nowhere to be seen— leaned on the railings and stared out.

Tenandra had landed by the side of the lake, close to where a dozen smaller craft, that I'd class as pleasure boats more than actual working vessels, were moored.

That was on the right, if you faced the bow of the ship; we were on that side, with the lake forming a sort of kidney shape, and us by the south edge of it.

It meant that the city was a little farther away, but it also meant that we were clear of any trees and we could see around the ship and easily see the path to the city.

It felt a little weird to me, to not have a group around me dedicated to my safety—not that I felt I needed the fuckers but they were always there—but given that the protector to my left was a demon, the one to my right was a Valkyrie and the Chosen of Vanei, the Goddess of Air, and behind me somewhere was an assassin who was the Chosen of the Goddess of Assassins, yeah…

I didn't feel less safe; it was just strange that it was so quiet.

We watched the few boats on the lake, and two of the ship's crew who doubled as guards for times when we were in port dealt with the lookie-loos who came to the gangplank, but beyond that, it was almost pleasant.

I stared at the glistening water, the sunlight dancing across it and I wondered about those people who went fishing.

Would that have been something that I'd have done? If Oracle was here, I mean, and everything was okay, as we waited to hear something, anything— would we have relaxed and done things like that, or go out on a boat we hired, like normal couples did?

We leaned there for a few minutes, before Lydia finally cracked and reached into her bag of holding and produced three bottles of ale, passing them around, before sighing and throwing one over her shoulder in a devil may care manner.

Bane caught it, appearing from stealth and grunting in laughter as he returned to hiding.

That was the way of the day for almost two hours, before Tisan returned, and this time, he brought company.

"Prince Jax." The normally calm wood elf greeted me, bowing quickly, before stepping aside and gesturing to his companion. "I bring you honor beyond measure. The Elder Thessarian has come to meet you personally, and…"

"Oh, hush, boy." The older wood elf snorted, stepping up onto the deck and pausing, assessing me as I did the same with him.

Easily half a hundred of their guards were spread out across the ground, and more were in the nearby trees, bows half drawn as I looked from them to the elder and back.

"Welcome, Elder." Curious, I asked, "Are you visiting or attacking?"

"Definitely the former, rather than the latter," he grumbled, before turning and gesturing to the guards below. "Go on!" he called. "I already told you lot to bugger off!"

"But, Elder!" one called out, starting up the gangplank and looking flustered. "It is unseemly…you must be protected—"

"Away!" the elder barked, before leveling a walking stick at the younger, yet clearly senior guard. "I remember you when you stole raspberries from my gardens, and I remember when you were on punishment duty for drunken behavior, boy. Don't think I don't remember the report, because I do! Now, either bugger off like I told you, or your men are going to find out why you were called 'Blueberries' for a decade!"

The well-experienced and probably middle-aged wood elf went bright red, then started to bark orders at his people, as the elder turned back to me, grinning proudly.

"I thought that might work. Been holding onto that one for damn near two hundred years," he said. "So, you're the prince then."

"I am." I grinned at the old man. "Want to join us for an ale on the deck and watch the lake?"

"Prince Jax, this is an *elder*, not—" Tisan shook his head, clearly about to go all "honor demands" when Thessarian nodded and smiled.

"You know, I'd like that." He cut the younger man off, before waggling a finger at him. "And you, boy, need to forget that I'm an elder. I fall over when I can't get my pants off like anyone else."

"Lydia?" I gestured to her.

She pulled fresh ales out of her bag, and Sehran called for a few more chairs to be brought by the crew.

"So, what brings you to our little slice of paradise?" I asked Thessarian when he was settled. The five of us sat in a half circle, with me in the center, my people on the left with Lydia first, then Sehran, and Thessarian on my right, then Tisan.

"I thought I'd come meet you personally. Makes it a lot easier to judge a man." He sipped the ale and made a face. "Gah, did you boil it with old stockings? What a taste!"

"It's, uh, what ah had, Elder," Lydia admitted apologetically.

"And if there's no other ale available, it'd be wonderful, my lady Valkyrie." He beamed, looking genuinely pleased to speak to her. "But fortunately for good taste everywhere, I happen to have a few tankards set aside for a special occasion." He reached into his robes, and looking like he was reaching into a pocket, pulled free a full tankard, passed it to her first, then Sehran, then me and Tisan, before finally settling back and taking a sip of his own.

"Oh, that's the stuff." He sighed. "Dwarves make the best beers and ales. I miss the days I used to travel and get it direct from the mountains."

"Long time ago?" I asked politely, before taking a sip. It was actually a damn good clean, crisp lager. Or close enough, anyway.

"Too bloody long." He grunted, before eyeing me sideways, smacking his lips and sighing. "All right, so, what's the truth of the matter then?"

"Which bit?" I asked, unsure.

"Don't play games with me," he snapped, losing the image of a calm and friendly old man. "I remember your ancestor, boy, and you might have the presence, and the viciousness, but it doesn't mean you'll do half the job he did. We've no need to be dragged into your wars."

"No, you don't." I took a sip from the tankard and settled back. "Besides the fact that you're constantly living in fear of being attacked and barely surviving on the trade you can get, I mean."

"We're far from starving." The elder snorted. "You see this forest? It's more abundant than ever."

"It is," I agreed. "And if you noticed the drain to the north that just ended, you're welcome."

"A drain?"

"Life mana."

"Ah." He shrugged. "Couldn't say. Here, it's abundant."

"It'll get a little stronger now," I countered.

"Could be that's a bad thing, boy. You ever see what happens when there's too much of it somewhere?"

"I did." I nodded. "That's one reason I fixed it."

"Fair enough…as long as you're not looking for us to thank you for it."

"No, but I'd be an idiot not to think you could sense it. I can, after all."

"Bah."

A long minute of silence passed between us as everyone drank.

"So." He looked at me.

"So," I replied.

"Don't play coy with me, boy. What do you want?"

"Fuck's sake," I muttered, then looked at Lydia. "You see this, right? This isn't my fault?"

"Ah'll still blame yer," she assured me, and I glared at her.

"What's this?" the elder asked curiously.

"We agreed that I'm shit at negotiation, so I'd stop doing it," I explained, waving generally. "Yen's supposed to sort this out."

"She's good." He nodded. "Polite and conscientious."

"But?" I prompted as he took a long draw on his tankard.

"But I came to speak to you, boy. Better that way, rather than it being between those who have no power."

"Like your lord."

"Bah, he's a good lad really." He snorted.

"But he's a figurehead."

"Perhaps." He shrugged. "Regardless, I asked you what you wanted."

"Allies. Preferably you join the empire, but I'll settle for allies."

"And if we say no?"

"I'll regret it."

"And us too…is that what you're hinting at?" he growled.

"No," I said honestly. "I don't think I need to hint at it. Look, here it is, nice and simple." I gestured to the ship around us. "We're here to make repairs, have a little chat, and then we're going to explore the area. Once we have what we need, we'll move off."

"You think you'll find more cores scattered out in the forest, do you?" He snorted. "They turn up every so often, mainly uncovered by badgers and snoffalumps. Beyond that, there's no great stockpile left, despite what people like to imagine."

"Then you won't mind us searching." I smiled.

"You'll give us half of anything you find, and you'll take a team from my people to make sure you do," he countered.

"I could say no, because there's fuck all you can do about it, and it's lost imperial property, but I won't," I replied. "But on the other hand, I'll happily do that, if we're allies. If I didn't, that'd be rude."

"And if we're not?" he asked amiably.

"Then you get fuck all." I smiled. "Just like you'll be entitled to fuck all protection when your next enemy comes for you. You know, like Kronk did, and we killed them. Or like the Dark Legion did, before we killed them."

"And now there's a force of a few thousand pissed-off Dark legionnaires to the south, heading this way, I hear, boy," he growled.

"Really?" I frowned. "How'd you know that?"

"All-Seeing-Eye." He grunted. "It's a high-level scout ability, leveled over six hundred years of use. I damn well know what they're doing now, and why. That death knight has vowed to catch you and nail you to the prow of your own ship as a figurehead for your heresy."

"Really? And where is he?" My stomach clenched as I worried about our people in the area.

"About two days' march to the south of what's left of his citadel."

"Great, thanks for that." I looked over at Sehran. "When you get the chance, ask Tenandra how long to get the cannons operable."

There was a brief pause, then Sehran replied, smiling, after posing the question to her through their link. "She said two days but it'll be minimum power until we have the new cores."

"Then how about we go take care of that problem in exchange for the right to loot the forest and a good word put in for us?" I suggested.

"The Dark Legion army? You mean, how about you go and finish off the job you said you'd do and then we'll talk when our people are home?" he countered gruffly.

"I mean, I could do that," I mused, as if seriously considering it. "But are you meaning that I take the army out by myself instead of using Tenandra's weaponry? You know, seeing as you're unwilling to let us search the area.

"Now that could mean that I need to use my Fragment of Death to do it, and that would mean that I replace the life mana in an area entirely, suppressing all life for several hundred miles. But that's fine. I mean, it's not like this is my land, so I don't give two shits about it," I pointed out.

"And if you do that, you think we'll still favorably look on the idea of an alliance with you?" he countered.

"Considering I'd have just slaughtered several thousand Dark legionnaires alone, having given you other options first? I think the rest of your council would probably agree to anything to get me to stay the hell away, wouldn't they?"

"No, they'd view you as an enemy of life, and refuse to ever deal with you again," he growled.

"Okay, what if instead I proved myself as an ally of life?"

"How?" he asked curiously, looking over at me, before draining his tankard, then setting it aside and pulling out a fresh one.

"I'd like to explain, but you know, it's thirsty work…" I suggested, showing him the bottom of my tankard mournfully.

"Damn lay-about younger generations…" he grumbled, before sighing and replacing the drinks all round.

"Thank you *very* much." I sighed, settling back after taking another drink. "So, my people are marching here from the remains of the citadel now. But we're gonna need to head south and destroy this army before it can catch up to the people we rescued, so how about this? We stop bullshitting and agree to a little deal here? I mean, that's why you came, right?"

"I came to gain the measure of you," he said noncommittally.

"Exactly, so here it is—a nice, open opportunity to discuss what both sides want and what we're willing to give to get it. And then, if we can't agree, the conversation can be had with the council and me later. But we both know you're here to do that, so why beat around the bush?"

"An interesting saying," he murmured. "Very well, make your offer."

"First of all, you join the empire. Don't worry—I don't want to be involved in your city more than securing the territory," I said. "We respect each other's autonomy in most areas. The only specifics where I won't agree to compromises are that you must swear the oath of imperial citizenship and you accept the Pantheon of the Flame, and banish any worship of Nimon and His pantheon."

"You don't have to worship the Pantheon of the Flame, to be clear. If you don't like the gods, no stress. Just ignore them and don't worship anyone. But we can't have altars to Nimon and worship to Him going on in our lands, or any of his dickhead mates."

"And the citizenship oath?" he asked.

I provided it to him, pushing it out. Unsurprisingly, he didn't take the oath, instead reading over it and musing as he worked line by line.

"I swear upon pain of death, to faithfully execute all that the Emperor decrees. I swear upon my soul that I shall stand for the Empire when it calls. I shall be strong when the weak need me, generous when the poor are at hand, and merciless when my fellow citizens are threatened. I shall worship the Gods of my fathers, respect my elders, and raise up my children to stand tall.

"I am an Imperial Citizen. I claim the right to call upon the Legion in my hour of need, to hold those who wrong me to justice, and to be avenged if I cannot be saved.

"I swear to obey Prince Jax and those he places over me; I will serve to the best of my ability, speak no lie to him when commanded otherwise, and treat all other citizens as family.

"I will work for the greater good, being a shield to those who need it, a sword to those who deserve it, and a warden to the night.

"I will stand with my family, helping one another to reach the light, until the hour of my death or my lord releases me from my Oath.

"Lastly, I will not be a dick!

"The oath would need to be amended, as this, despite you offering an alliance, is essentially a full oath to obey you." He shook his head. "Replace the oath for our people with something like this perhaps…"

"I swear by the ancient trees and the bonds of fellowship, to honor the alliance between our peoples. I swear upon my spirit that I shall stand with the Alliance when unity is needed. I shall be strong when the weak need me, generous when the poor are at hand, and protective when our fellow citizens are threatened. I shall honor the traditions of my people, respect the wisdom of all elders, and raise up any children to walk in harmony with the Empire.

"I am an Allied Citizen under both the council and the empire. I claim the right to call upon our combined forces in my hour of need, to seek justice through our shared councils, and to be aided if I am in peril.

"I swear to respect the Council of Lembiq and its allied leadership; I will contribute to the best of my ability, speak truthfully in all dealings with allied citizens, and treat all fellow citizens as kin of the greater family.

"I will work for our mutual good, being a shield to those who need it, a defender against those who would harm us, and a guardian of both forest and settlement.

"I will stand with the Alliance, helping one another flourish in the light of cooperation, until the hour of my passing or the Council releases me from this Oath.

"Lastly, I will not be a dick!

"I'm happy to retain that last line, as I feel that too many laws are missing it," he mused, with a slight smile.

"I see what you're looking for, but it'd need changing more to be in line with the rest." I shook my head. "But that's an argument for another day, provided we have a clause about mutual aid and something like that. Anything else?"

"The gods I'm personally fine with, though a small minority of our citizens may not be. We have always permitted our citizens to worship as they choose, and for long centuries the choice of god to worship has been… reduced. So, I suggest a modification to this…"

"No," I said firmly. "I'm willing to allow a lot of things, but the worship of Nimon, Illoth, or Baphomet is a hard line. I will destroy those altars."

"We do not wish to offend any of the gods, though I doubt there are many of their worshippers in our lands. Perhaps we could negotiate…"

I shook my head. "No," I said, resolute. "I'm sorry, but having those altars anywhere in lands we control is both a risk and will prevent the territory being claimed by the empire. When we claim it, the drow and any supporter of Illoth will be removed from the territory—and I mean violently removed.

"Like, I usually get a kill notification and XP for them being removed, so that's the level we're talking here. If you have any supporters of Illoth in your territory, when the territory becomes linked to the empire, they'll be yeeted into the next time zone, so you need to accept that."

"Yeeted?"

"Evicted with extreme prejudice," I clarified.

"Very well. Perhaps an amnesty to permit them to leave the—"

"No. As soon as it's agreed, then we'll do it," I said. "First of all, I'm not giving the drow a chance to assassinate everyone. Secondly, I'm not giving up on both weakening Illoth by killing her supporters, and lastly I want the fucking XP."

"That's a harsh way to look at it," he pointed out.

"Have you dealt with Lolly much?"

"Lolly?"

"That's a third hard line." I grinned. "Illoth is to be renamed as 'Lolly the Turd Spider' and can only be referred to by that name."

"Why?"

"Partly just to fuck with Her, and partly because a god's nature is linked to their worship, and it fuckin' amuses me that sooner or later everyone will know Her as Lolly the Turd Spider, and She'll know it was because of fucking with me." I took another pull on the tankard. "Damn good stuff, this."

"You can get me another few tankards when you get your own," he grunted. "I'm running out."

"Ah, but it's worth it for the company," I suggested.

"Well, it's not every day I get to meet a genuine Valkyrie and such a lovely young lady." He beamed at Lydia and Sehran. "Ah, if only I was a thousand years younger." He sighed.

"Dick," I muttered, and he snorted.

"Is that it? You want us to join the empire?" he asked.

"I'd prefer it. Though an alliance is acceptable as well."

"What does an alliance mean to you?"

"It means we help each other. You join us in our war. When I need information you have, you share it. When I need troops, you provide them. You're a friendly trading partner. You'll help when I need it, basically."

"And in return?" He looked grim. "Because that sounds a lot like being conquered."

"In return, I and the empire do the exact same and help you. We put you in touch with the Pantheon of the Flame, and they'll help you with quests and more. I'll help you with protection from your enemies, and give you a trading partner that you know isn't going to fuck you over.

"We'll provide troops when you need them. We'll secure trading caravans. We'll give you access to technology and training, and you gain access to the legion.

"Now, I know you're gonna be thinking 'so what' when it comes to the legion, or at least a lot of other people have been. Truth is that for the last seven centuries, they've been forced by a stupid fucking oath to throw themselves into the fight against impossible odds.

"That's meant that they die in droves, but it also means that the survivors are fucking elite warriors. We have damn near a thousand of them, and around fifteen thousand plus aspirants and trainees. I'm aware that doesn't sound like much, but the plan is that they'll all get further training as the weeks pass.

"They're being taught magic, daily. Within a year, we'll have an army that has the best equipment, the best fighters, and can all use magic. They'll crush any army ten times their size and they'll do it easily.

"In three months, most of this continent will be conquered, if not all of it. In a year? The empire will be close to its old size. Maybe not in numbers of citizens, but definitely in terms of territory. We're strong, we're honest, and we're rich." I shrugged.

"I mean that. If you say that it'll cost me a million gold to secure you all joining as full imperial citizens instead of telling me to fuck off? Just tell me where you want the coin. The truth is, I'd rather have you like that, or failing it, as allies…genuinely, I would. But if I can't get that, then my other alternative is conquering you."

The little group tensed as I continued.

"I can't allow this territory to remain a holdout, so this is how it works: if you agree to even just an alliance, then I can take control of the territory. When I do that, Illoth is pushed out and we move on. If you refuse? And I mean refuse—no alliance, no swearing fealty, just a general 'fuck you'?" I looked over at him, and he nodded at me to continue.

"Then I'll conquer you." The words were simple but honest. "I'll come in with fire and magic and cold, hard steel, and thousands will die. I don't want that, but I won't permit you to be neutral or an enemy. The reason for that is simple: if Illoth and the others can, they'll use your territory as a launching point to attack my people.

"I'll have thousands of my people dying, all because we don't have a firm border, and I won't allow that. I won't allow slavery to continue, nor the shit that I've seen so far. I've had the Dark Legion backstabbing and dealing with shitbag nobles who would as soon burn a city full of innocents to the ground to retain a copper piece more in their pocket.

"I've seen the Caravaneer's Guild literally hiring slavers to attack a caravan that was refusing to use their established routes and pay the taxes. I've seen slavers' guilds and groups that are profiting from the misery of our people, and I've seen the condition of the gnomes…"

One of the mad little bastards chose that time to fall from a tree nearby and faceplant the moss, clearly knocked unconscious on impact. We all looked at her, and then they all looked back at me as I gestured vaguely at them.

"Well, all right, maybe the gnomes aren't the best choice as an example." I groaned, covering my eyes with one hand and rubbing at the bridge of my nose. "Lydia, is she alive?"

"Oh, aye." She snorted. "Comin' round now. No clue how she got up there, though."

I looked over, noting how Sehran and Lydia both hit her with a Heal at pretty much the same time, and I looked back to the elder.

"Look, all gnomes aside, the realm is a shithole. People are stabbing each other in the back, slaving, murdering and worse…all day, every day. The murder rate in my cities is in the single digits, and it's always an outsider involved because, at the end of the day, our people literally can't do that to each other.

"I'm fine with you governing yourselves. Fuck's sake, I don't *want* another headache. If you're willing to ally? Great. If you want to join fully? You rule your people under imperial law, which basically is a common sense, 'don't rape, murder, or enslave your fellows' set of laws. Yen can give you a full breakdown.

"If you do that, I'll do whatever you need…within reason. You want a dozen servitor golems? Fine. A hundred war golems? We can do it. But when I shout for you, you bring your troops and you help.

"Generally, beyond making sure you're not fucking with us, 'I'm not interested' is the honest answer when you ask how you need to rule. Just don't be a dick. The Mistress of Gaij is Seraphina, one of the succubai, and she's basically making the entire city run smoothly. She gets a seat on my council, the imperial council that advises me on the empire, and she gets my full support.

"The fundamental difference between us being allies and you swearing to me as your prince and future emperor is that I will look after my own first. You need to maintain your armies and your borders, you need help? You call to me and I'll bring my people, though it might be a little while if we're already in a fight.

"If you're our people instead of an ally, then I'm responsible to protect you personally, and although you'll have your usual forces here, I'll also send a legion as soon as it's trained, or more if you need them.

"I'll provide training opportunities for your archers—I was told that wood elves are primarily archers and ranger classes, with a few melee frontline fighters, is that right?"

"It is," he admitted cooly.

"Great. So, if you joined us, instead of an alliance, I'd fold your people in with the legion, create and outfit a more defined force, split the archers so that each legion had a larger archer, scout, and ranger team probably, and then provide a hell of a lot more frontline fighters and mages to you in exchange. Truth is, I don't know, though. I came here looking for allies, and I haven't discussed with my heads of the legion how to fold you in."

"Which we're not offering to do," he retorted grimly. "At no point have we volunteered to give up our autonomy and become a part of the empire. Allies? That, we're willing to discuss with an open mind. But subjects? I refuse."

"Keep an open mind." I smiled, as I'd seen something he hadn't. Behind him, Yen and the others were jogging along, and Tenandra was in their midst, lifting a core into the air that sparkled with ruby-red energy as she grinned. "That's all I'd ask. Think about it. You've got a few hours at least, while we get the ship ready. Then you've got a choice to make."

"Oh?"

"Stay here and get a report from your observers, or come with us," I said. "Come with us and see what I do with the Dark Legion when they try to chase down my people."

CHAPTER TWENTY-SEVEN

"I fuckin' love a good ambush," I muttered as I stared into the distance, leaning against the railing on Tenandra's bow and the wind whipping past me. Thessarian stood next to me. His entire honor guard, though almost a third of them were dotted around the deck, was torn between watching him or me, and being noisily sick over the side of the ship.

"Seriously, how are you afraid of heights?" I asked him, seeing the white-knuckled grip he had on the railing, and how he stared fixedly straight ahead. "I mean, I saw the trees you were in before. The Canopy isn't that much lower than where we are now."

"The Great Mothers are firm—they do not bob and weave, nor is there much empty void below them, between my feet and the ground," he explained through gritted teeth, and I snorted.

"No offense, but given the choice of the trees or having Tenandra keeping me safe, I know which I'd pick."

"Hasn't she crashed recently?" he countered.

I glared at him.

"Touché," I muttered. "But that was after I picked a fight with Nimon, and He struck her because He couldn't get to me."

"A point in favor of not allying with you then." He grunted. "How much longer?"

"Until they're in sight?" I asked, and he nodded, once.

"About ten minutes, and fifteen more until we reach firing range."

"And how long until we can land?" he asked plaintively.

"Oh, not long, don't worry. We can even stay a little lower on the way back if you want?" I asked him cheerfully, getting a glare from him as I grinned and contemplated "accidentally" falling over the side just to freak him out more.

The last two days, we'd actually spent most of the flight arguing. Either we were coming to a decent understanding of each other's positions, or we were about to go to war.

It was even odds really, given that although he was aware of what we could do, he'd not yet seen it himself, and seeing was believing.

The trees that made up most of the land we'd passed over were now fewer in number and much smaller, with long groves of something like mangroves, if I was remembering my natural history shows right.

They were trees with thick, strong roots, hundreds of them, that supported them up and out of the marshes.

The water was clearly stagnant, and what had been more regular trees were fallen here and there in pools and streams, rotten through. Thick grasses covered mounds of earth that looked to be barely above the surrounding waters. As we passed overhead, we saw the muck-covered faces of our people as they waved and shouted, whooping at the sight of us so close.

The people who had set off in high spirits from the remains of the citadel were now struggling through waist-deep marsh water—filthy, exhausted, and surrounded by random concentrations of undead.

I saw dozens rising and slogging toward them on all sides, with hundreds more in sight. I could see the state of the legionnaires as well.

They'd been reduced to a foot-by-foot slog. The estimate of three weeks to get back to the city from here?

It looked excessively optimistic now that we saw the marsh as somewhere to trudge through, rather than something to fly over.

It'd been night when we'd passed over it before, and I growled as I saw the state of our poor refugees below.

"Lydia!" I called, then almost shit myself when she stepped up from behind me and let loose with a burst of Explosive Compression aimed at a knot of the undead that had been closing on our people.

"Aye, Jax?" She grinned at me, and I nodded in response.

"As long as we're in sight, feel free to bombard the fuck out of the undead," I said quickly, already turning and looking at the space behind us. "Tenandra, you busy?" I asked, and she formed a body, shifting into reality.

"Never too busy, my prince." She smiled.

"Thank you. Okay, new plan. Once we've slaughtered the Dark Legion, we're coming back this way. We land, load up our people, and shuttle them to the other side of the marsh. This isn't healthy, and I'm not having kids slogging through this mess." I mentally cursed myself for not considering how bad it was going to be.

We'd passed over it twice before but each time, it'd been in the darkness. It'd been a bit marshy, but, in my mind, the threat was mainly the undead. A good strong ring of legionnaires around the group meant that they were perfectly safe. They'd probably get a bit wet on the way, at worst, but it seemed a small price to pay for their freedom.

Now I was seeing this and cursing myself.

"It'll add a day onto the trip," she said. "There are some seven hundred people below, I believe, and we have space for roughly one hundred aboard. The marsh is a six-hour journey for us to clear and return, meaning approximately thirty-six hours to ferry them all to the far side, and a significant cost in mana due to the weight."

"Shit, what about if we have them hole up somewhere reasonably dry and rest, then when we come back we ferry the weakest off and the strongest make their own way with rafts or whatever they need?" I suggested. "And you've got the cores integrated, yeah?"

"To the cannon, yes." She nodded. "They are not, however, connected to anything else, so the mana cost for the trip remains high—as does the risk we run, should the cores be depleted by excessive use of the cannon.

"As to the island, I believe that is the most reasonable method, as a full day or more being lost to transport them out is unfortunately more time than we have to spare."

"I don't like it, but yeah." I grumbled, and turned back. A few of our people fired spells over the side at the undead below. "Want to use a cannon for a test firing?" I asked, and she shook her head.

"No. At this range, if they have any scouts with vision-based abilities, then they may have seen us already, but I don't want to ruin the surprise."

"Well, let's get a move on then, I guess." I sighed. "Those poor buggers."

The people below had stopped waving and shouting, and now they were back to just slogging on; the larger concentrations of undead had been taken out by spells from the ship, and we kept going.

"Should we not land and advise the people that we'll be returning?" one elf asked desperately. "I could stay with them?"

"They'll see us coming back," I assured him. "And it's better that..." I hesitated, then cursed, seeing that there was, maybe an hour's march back along their path, a large knoll that they could rest on, while ahead of them was only more swamp and marshland.

"I'll go," Sehran offered, stepping up to the edge of the railing. "I can't add much to the fight that's coming, but I could help them a lot, and they know me."

That was true. They'd seen Sehran with me before, and nobody with eyes forgot Sehran after meeting her.

"Go, get them back to there..." I gestured to the knoll that was even now sliding beneath our keel. "And tell them that we'll come back and ferry them out of the damn swamp."

"Marsh," the elder corrected absently, before shuddering as Sehran leapt over the side of the ship. "It's mainly grasses and weeds. A swamp is heavily wooded."

"Never knew that," I admitted. "Having seen it, I'm guessing that the undead are the bodies of people who tried to cross it and failed?"

"Mainly they're from a city closer to the center that was taken over by a necromancer." He spat over the side and gestured to the mess we were passing. "The city fell and was cleared out a few times, but considering the undead just come back, it's a mess. And the dam that once served the city failed a century or so ago, turning this from farmland into the marsh."

"So, a failed dam drowned the land, and this is the result?" I asked.

"Essentially."

"Why the hell build a damn citadel here?" I mused, thinking of the Dark Legion, and he sighed.

"Free training, easy access to water, and no need to fight the locals to establish yourself. And it limits the approaches for any enemy force, as all they have to do is close the gates and let the enemy camp in a swamp. Disease and the local undead will whittle away at the enemy until they get reinforced, and then the Dark Legion could destroy them."

He said it as if it were common sense, and I winced, knowing I'd just exposed my ignorance.

"Yeah, I guess," I agreed. "I was thinking more along the lines of why not build a city where someone would actually like to be, though."

"Because no established city that is not already under the sway of the God of Death would allow it, and those that are higher placed in the church and Dark Legion would never care for the suffering of the lower ranks."

"Fuckin' shitehawks," I muttered.

"Well, look on the bright side." He smiled. "Now you get to kill them all."

"I do like that, you know?" I grinned. "Okay, Tenandra?" I looked over my shoulder, and she nodded to me. "I want a fast pass around the outside. Let them all bunch up and watch us. Then I want them blown to fuck."

"Should have kept Sehran aboard then," she countered, before grinning and inclining her head. "I shall blow as many as possible…away," she clarified, adding the last with a twinkle in her eye.

"Oh gods, you've spent too much time with Sehran, haven't you?" I snorted, but the familiar grin was firmly in place as she dissolved back into the ship's systems.

They'd gotten more than enough cores for this. There was a lot more upgrading still to be done, but, as it was, she was excited to show off her full capabilities to the limited observers aboard.

Ten minutes later, we could see them: a dark stain on the landscape, like someone had spilled ink across the horizon. Two thousand Dark legionnaires, marching in formation through the marsh, and alongside them, under and above, marched undead mounts and constructs that plodded through the muck without complaint.

"There." Thessarian pointed with a shaking hand, his other still white-knuckled on the railing. "Their command group, center formation."

I squinted, then nodded that I could see what he meant. In the middle of the army, elevated on some kind of bone palanquin carried by massive undead, sat what had to be their leader. Even from here, the death knight radiated power—black armor that seemed to drink in the light, a helm crowned with spikes of bone, and a sword across his lap that I could feel the wrongness of from half a mile up.

"All right, people!" I called out, getting everyone's attention. "This is going to be loud, violent, and absolutely beautiful. Anyone who doesn't want to see what happens when you fuck with the empire should go belowdecks now!"

Nobody moved. Even Thessarian's honor guard, green as they were from airsickness, stayed where they were, I was glad to see.

"Good choice." I grinned. "Tenandra, take us around for that first pass. Let's give them something to think about."

The ship banked smoothly, and I had to grab Thessarian's arm as he nearly went over the railing in terror. We swept around the army in a wide arc, just out of bow range but close enough that they could still see us clearly.

The effect was instant. The well-organized march suddenly ground to a halt as orders were shouted. Some loosed arrows that fell pathetically short. A few mages sent spells arcing up, but they faded out and fell apart well before reaching us.

"They're bunching up," Lydia pointed out disgustedly. She was right. The Dark Legion's training was kicking in, forming defensive squares, shields up, weapons at the ready as their mages all got ready to throw more spells. I started to put my spell in place as well. "Ah know we wanted 'em, but fuckin' 'ell."

"Perfect." I grinned. "They think we're going to land and charge them. Tenandra?"

"In position, my prince." Her voice echoed from everywhere and nowhere. "All cannons charged and ready. Shall I demonstrate why aerial superiority matters?"

"Light them the fuck up."

The cannons smoothly rotated, lining up, two to a side, and my God were they ready, as Tenandra angled to present her starboard side to them.

They probably appeared weird to anyone looking from below: nine smaller tubes attached in a circle around a single larger one, that was in turn mounted on something like an anti-aircraft swivel from the Second World War.

The cannons fired in a ripple, starting at the nine o'clock position and working all the way around clockwise until it was back to eight. The air itself seemed to scream with each launch.

The smaller cannons were all Magic Missile variants—high-velocity and high-power ones that Ame and her team had spent weeks perfecting. They were built in a circle around the main cannon, each one capable of punching through castle walls.

But the main cannon…

The main cannon was something Ame had named "Dragon's Wrath." I called it a fucking plasma lance, and I *loved* it.

The first salvo hit the Dark Legion's left flank like the fist of an angry god.

Where the Magic Missiles struck, bodies simply ceased to exist. The impacts created perfect circles of devastation, each one maybe ten feet across, where everything—armor, weapons, flesh, bone—was just smashed and burned. Then the plasma lance carved a trench thirty meters long and three meters wide through their ranks, the edges of the devastation glowing white-hot.

The screaming started then, but it was drowned out by the second salvo as it began to fire.

"By the gods!" one of Thessarian's guards gasped, and then promptly threw up over the side again—though whether from the carnage or the fun of flight, I couldn't tell.

"That's what I'm fucking talking about!" I roared as Tenandra brought us around for another pass, angling to let the port side have a go and spread out the cooling for the first two. Then she screamed across their lines, firing again and again.

The Dark Legion was trying to respond, but what the fuck do you do against death from above? Their normal metal shields were useless, their formations worse than that—they just made better targets.

"They're trying to scatter!" Arrin called out. He was right. The disciplined squares were breaking apart as soldiers ran in every direction.

"Good," I said coldly. "Makes this more fun. Tenandra, if you would?"

The third pass was almost surgical in its precision. The ripple-fire cannons picked off clusters of runners, while Dragon's Wrath carved through what remained of their command structure. I saw the bone palanquin explode in a shower of calcium and corrupted flesh, but the death knight himself rolled free, his armor smoking but intact.

"Tough bastard," I admitted. "How many salvos do we have left?"

"Six more at full power," Tenandra reported. "Twelve, if I reduce output to seventy percent."

"Keep going. I want them down to nothing but that death knight and whoever's lucky enough to be hiding under his skirts."

The fourth pass revealed why some of them might actually survive, though, for now at least. In the center of what had been their formation, maybe a hundred soldiers had formed a tight circle, and above them now shimmered a dome of sickly green energy. Our missiles splashed harmlessly against it; even the plasma lance only made it flicker. But as it was hit, on all sides, the running Dark legionnaires collapsed; a sickly green streamer ripped from the bodies and tore back to feed the shield.

"Death magic barrier." Thessarian's voice shook despite his death grip on the railing. "Powered by their own people's life force. They're killing the wounded to maintain it."

"Fucking typical," I snarled. "All right, keep hammering them. Let's see how many lives they're willing to sacrifice. Lydia, Tenandra, take over...I need to concentrate."

That was the kicker for them. They needed to figure some way of dealing with us, after all. Me? If the death knight killed all his forces to keep his own shield going for a little longer? I was fine with that. After all, it meant I only needed to target a single point, rather than chase them all down.

Three more passes, three more salvos that turned the marsh into a charnel house. The water ran black with burned blood, and the screaming had mostly stopped because there weren't enough throats left to scream.

But that fucking dome held. I could see the death knight in the center, arms raised, pouring power into the shield.

"Down to a hundred and fifty, maybe two hundred," Lydia reported, her expression grim but satisfied. "The rest are paste."

I nodded that I'd heard, and kept casting.

I hated how complex the spell was, and that it was so goddamn expensive. But, the one good thing about it was that at least it meant that if I saw someone else using something similar in the future, I knew to run like fuck.

Or, you know, I'd have the time to get up close and personal and stab them in the face before they finished it.

I reached out with my awareness, feeling the flow of magic in the area. The death knight was strong, I'd give him that. His shield was a masterwork of necromantic bullshit, layered and reinforced and fed by the life force of his own troops. But he'd made one crucial mistake.

He was using his own mana to help power it, not an artifact. Admittedly, an artifact wouldn't have helped long-term either, but that wasn't the point. When your mana reached rock bottom, it was painful and disorienting.

Had it been an artifact, he'd have been able to still think and react properly once the shield failed. This way, he wasn't going to be able to.

Still, you know, we all make mistakes, and he was only mortal.

But me? Well, shucks, I was a fucking *demigod*.

"Mine," I whispered as I released the spell, reaching out through the mana of the realm to the huge ambient mass all around us. Then I *pulled*. "Yoink!"

It wasn't subtle. It wasn't elegant. I just reached out with my will and my Fragment of Order boosting me, and used my Imperator spell, Mana Cascade, and fucking *took* every scrap of mana in a mile radius that wasn't already in use.

For those spells that were, you know, like his…well, they had a little teeny tiny problem, in that they tended to fail, break apart, or you know, explode.

Unfortunately, the death knight's shield didn't explode, which would have been my optimal choice—it just stopped existing, like someone had turned off a light switch.

The death knight staggered and his arms dropped. I could practically feel his shock from here, right up until the backlash hit, and he howled in agony, falling to the ground and clutching his head.

"Tenandra, hover us about fifty feet above them," I ordered, releasing the spell and already walking toward the railing. "Time to introduce myself properly."

"Jax, what t'fuck are yer doin'?" Lydia demanded, but I was already vaulting over the side.

"Oh, you know, just going to play!" I grinned, pulling my helmet on. Then I braced myself on the railing, and jumped over.

"TOODLES!" I yelled back up at her, not even bothering to fly. It was time to make my new condition very fucking clear to everyone.

The drop was perfect. Temporal Fluidity slowed my perception just enough to let me aim, and I landed in a three-point superhero stance that cracked the bog-hardened earth, my naginata already in hand. The impact sent the death knight's remaining soldiers stumbling back, and I straightened slowly, grinning at their leader.

"Knock, knock, asshole."

The death knight was everything I'd expected—seven feet of hatred wrapped in armor that probably cost more than most kingdoms. His helmet turned toward me, eye slits glowing with that trademarked bullshit sickly green light.

"Prince Jax." His voice was a grinding, pained mess. "The heretic. The defiler. You will suffer for your abomination! When you fall, I shall resurrect you and—"

"Yeah, about that." I triggered Mana Overdrive, feeling the familiar surge of power. "I've got a strict 'no joining armies led by dickheads' policy. It's worked out pretty well so far."

He moved faster than anything that big had a right to. His sword—a massive two-handed thing covered in runes that hurt to look at—came around in a flat arc that would have cut me in half if I'd been a fraction slower. But I wasn't slow. I was a demigod hopped up on enough mana to light up a small city.

I ducked under the swing and brought my naginata up in a rising cut that struck sparks from his breastplate. The force of it sent him sliding back through the mud, but his armor held.

"Cute sword." I circled him as his remaining soldiers formed a loose ring around us. "Compensating for something?"

"Your jokes will not save you." He raised his blade, and the temperature dropped twenty degrees. Frost spread across the ground between us, and the very air seemed to dim. "I am Karridan Morteus Rakk, Knight-Commander and Fist of Nimon. I have ended heroes and kingdoms alike. You are merely the next name on a very long list."

"Morteus Rack?" I laughed—actually laughed in his face—as my enhanced Intelligence dragged out a sort of version of a Latin translation. Mort I knew was death, and rack? Well, where I came from, a lot of guys would have commented on Oracle's fantastic rack, so yeah. It just slipped out.

"Your name is basically *'Death Tits'?!* Oh, that's fucking *amazing.* Did you pick that yourself, or did Mommy Death Knight name you?"

He roared—an inhuman sound that made my teeth ache—and charged.

This time, I met him head-on.

The clash of our weapons sent out a shock wave that flattened his surviving soldiers and cracked the frozen earth. He was strong, I'd give him that. Death magic reinforced his every move, and his technique was impressive. Years of practice showed in every strike, every parry, every dodge.

But I was done playing fair, I countered twice more, then when he wound up for the big hit, I let him.

I'd held my naginata out to the side, knowing that the wood elves were watching and needing to make this an impressive one. I triggered Titan's Resolve; my strength surged as my mana flooded my body to an incredible degree.

I took the strike on the blade of my naginata, not moving in the slightest. The crash of metal was enough that lesser warriors around the edge of the fight clutched at their heads, deafened.

The death dick staggered, his sword almost jolted from his hands, and I kicked him, with all the force I could muster, right in the crotch.

He collapsed to his knees, bones and armor breaking. If I was honest, I was in pain as well, I'd kicked *that* hard. But that didn't stop me as I strode forward, reaching down and grabbing his helmet. Then I fed mana into the ability even more, doubling and redoubling the effect, until I felt genuine pain as my body started to dance along the edge of what my physical frame could manage.

Then I closed my fist.

The scream as Karridan's helmet began to buckle and crush his skull was a sound that nobody should have to hear: half high-pitched wail, part pleading, and part metal crumpling.

His sword was on the ground, dropped when I'd apparently overwhelmed whatever his armor was made out of and had pulverized his crotch, hips, and lower spine. But he still attempted to get a dagger out, one-handed, as his other arm flopped and twisted.

"Hmm. Looks like the old spine's broken higher up as well, eh?" I muttered to myself as I continued to slowly crush his skull, driving the base of my naginata into the ground to hold it upright. I caught the attempt at a stab, then tugged the dagger out of his hand as if taking a stick from a naughty toddler.

A stick that I then threw to the side uncaringly, and killed one of his supporters.

I glanced over at the scream, seeing the ring of steel that still surrounded me, and the clear, absolute terror in the faces that I could see.

There were priests and paladins, legionnaires and what looked to be several of the Dark Legion elites all standing there silently. My casual un-aimed throw was abso-fuckin-lute evidence—at last—that having a hundred in my Luck stat was paying off.

It'd taken one of the paladins in the thin gap in their helm—literally, the visor had a narrow gap that let you see out, and it was barely narrow enough that the blade could pass through it.

That I'd thrown it, unaimed and unerringly across the gap, had made a second impression on them all; it'd been the priest standing next to the paladin who was screaming.

She was…different, and my attention wandered as I tried to make out why.

That was when the helm in my hands finished compressing to where I could manage, without serious damage to myself, and I glanced back. A mush of blood, brains, snot, and worse dribbled out of the bottom of the helmet.

I shoved it backward and picked up my naginata, then strode to one of the nearby priests—not the strange-looking one—and casually wiped their former commander and death knight's brains off my gauntlet across the front of his robes.

He opened his mouth to speak, and I backhanded him—he was a priest of Nimon, after all—then I turned to the rest of the surviving soldiers. There were maybe a hundred of them, all terrified, all very much aware that their supposedly invincible commander had just been reduced to high-quality fertilizer.

"Right, then!" I called out cheerfully. "Who wants to live?"

The clatter as at least half of the weapons hit the ground rang out so fast, it sounded like applause.

"Excellent choice!" I beamed at them. "Two things. First of all, you all get to renounce Nimon, right now, and call Him a dick. Loud and clear, please, or I'll still kill you… Well?" I asked. "I'm fucking waaaaiting!"

"We…we can't!" one warrior called out.

"Never!" another paladin suddenly barked, grabbing at a secondary weapon, an axe on her hip. She started forward, only to explode as an Explosive Compression spell hit her from above.

Screams sounded out for a few seconds as the ten nearest her—on both sides and close enough to be caught in the spell—were killed as well; their armor rung out as it was crushed. Then silence fell again as the bloody lump of organic materials and broken armor hit the ground.

"Anyone else have a problem with my request?" I asked cheerfully.

"I renounce—" one legionnaire started to say, only to have an elite nearby spin and hack his head from his shoulders.

That started the ball rolling. I grinned to myself, releasing the Titan's Resolve and keeping Hyper Cognition active alone.

It was all I needed to defend myself, as the entire ring fell inward, either attacking one another, trying to get their weapons back, or going for me.

All told, it was less than a minute before the fight was over. Little of that had anything to do with me: my squad had unleashed hell in the form of spells that streaked down on all sides.

From Magic Missiles to Starlight, Explosive Compression to flame lances and even mundane arrows from the archers, the battlefield was reduced to mayhem for that time. And then, as if a switch had been flicked, it was over.

I kicked the last corpse off the end of my naginata, then wiped it on the robe of a nearby priest, frowning. It was the woman I'd noticed earlier, but this time she was a lot less enthralling.

That realization made me chuckle as I put two and two together. She was clearly half-demon; she was probably one of those followers of Asmodeus—a cambion—and presumably the offspring of a succubus or incubus. Then, how she'd been distracting to me…well, I guessed she'd been trying to manipulate me.

That hadn't worked, probably in part due to my high stats, but also because I was used to goddamn Sehran and her antics all day, every day, not to mention Oracle.

As such, the watered-down attempt to draw my eye had barely even registered.

I shook the thought off and then bent down to pick up Death Tits's sword. The thing tried to corrupt me the second I touched it—death magic crawled up my arm like lice. But as soon as it did, I hit it back. The fire that I fed out into the blade almost instinctively wasn't happy making for it, but then the fire, tasting the death magic and interacting with my own Fragment of Death magic, changed it, and set light to the weapon.

I lifted it, staring at the markings. Green fire raced from the hilt to the tip of the blade, licking eagerly at the air around us, drawing heavily on the death magic that surrounded me, and growing brighter and brighter.

I felt the change in the blade, as it went from actively trying to attack me, the death mana leeching out of the blade to try to claim me, into joyful acceptance as for the first time it met a creature that held a true Fragment of Death.

Shifting the blade from side to side, I squinted, reading the carved words that ran down the steel, before snorting. "'Death's Lament.' Pretentious as fuck, but I guess it'll make a nice wall decoration until I find someone who can wield it."

Tenandra dropped closer, and Lydia's face peered over the rail, looking equal parts relieved and annoyed, as I slid the blade into a bag of holding.

"Are yer done showin' off?" she called down.

"Never!" I called back, then I sighed. "All right, Tenandra, can you land, please? And then our people get ten minutes to loot what they want, before we leave. That is, if anyone wants to see what they can grab?"

They couldn't agree fast enough as cheers rang out.

"Ah assume that means t'crew as well?" Lydia called down.

I crouched; then, powering my leap with Soaring Majesty, I arced through the air to land on the ship's deck, before replying.

"Anyone who wants to, can, but they need to be sure who they're looting is dead—that's on them," I said. "Nobody who can't defend themselves can go playing. What do you think, Thessarian? Do your people get to loot as well? As prospective allies, I'll be nice and share."

Elder Thessarian stared at me with an expression I couldn't quite read.

"What?" I asked, accepting a cloth from Arrin to wipe some mud and blood off my armor.

"I've seen many warriors in my many centuries of life," he intoned. "I've seen heroes and villains, legends and pretenders. But I've never seen someone turn the systematic annihilation of two thousand soldiers into…whatever that was."

"Performance art?" I suggested. "Aggressive negotiation? Pest control?"

"Arrogance," he said. "An arrogant demonstration that you apparently believe you can kill anything."

"I kill gods, bitch," I said to him, losing my patience. "Seriously, I fight the Dark gods. These fucksticks? I have to hold my strength back to keep from tearing my way through them all alone. As it is? You're pissed that I can do what I do, I get it, but I'm trying to prove to you why you should join me.

"What was I supposed to do with them all?" I gestured over the side of the ship. "We have very simple rules in the empire. No slavery. No murder. No rape. You think people who joined the Dark Legion and climbed the ranks to the point that dick included them under his personal shield are the nice ones?

"You think that if any survived long enough to actually surrender, we'd have just all laughed and strolled into the sunset, arm in arm? Fuck no. They were mass murderers. And now you're pissed because you're seeing just how powerful and scary they were, and then you've realized that if I wanted to, I could do this to your city as well.

"So yeah, I could raze it to the ground. I could tear your trees apart and kill your people. You know why I don't? It's the same response I once heard to why someone who doesn't believe in the gods, or worships them, didn't go around raping all he wants, whenever he wants.

"He was asked what was to stop him from committing terrible acts, because he didn't worship the gods and obey their commandments, and he said that it was because he wasn't a fucking dick.

"He went around raping and murdering every day just as much as he wanted to, which was not at all. Just like I don't want to hurt people and I don't want to conquer you. Will I do it if I have to? Yeah. Yeah, I will. But do I want to get an alliance based on mutual respect instead? Honestly, I'd rather that.

"Mainly because then we help each other out, but I'm not responsible for protecting you...you are. I don't need more problems—I need solutions. Right now, I keep having to elevate people I can trust to rule cities and territories, just so I can get on with what's important. So, before you mouth off about me being a fucking killer or showing off, understand that, yeah, *I am*.

"I'm both of those things and a lot more, including a demigod who's ascending to true godhood. So, go ask yourself, what do you want out of this? Because I've just done exactly what you wanted, and you're still busting my fucking balls about it."

I took a deep breath, then turned to Tenandra. "Right then, ten minutes for people to loot what they want, then let's go pick up our people. We've got refugees to ferry and a swamp to un-fuck. Bane, Tang, everyone, go have fun...loot yourselves something pretty."

"Already on it, boss." Tang materialized from nowhere, making Thessarian jump.

"Oh, and somebody check Death Tits's armor for anything valuable!" I called out after him. "Waste not, want not!"

"Did yer really have t'call 'im that?" Lydia asked, not bothering to go looting, though she was clearly fighting a smile.

"He named himself Morteus Rakk. He was asking for it," I protested. "Besides, did you see his face when I said it? Fucking priceless."

"The face of a death knight," Arrin noted dryly. "Not exactly known for their expressive features, and he was wearing a helmet."

"Details." I waved him off. I looked around at my team, who were lining up to get off and start looting, and then at Thessarian and his guards. I gestured at the smoking remains of the Dark Legion army below us. "See? Everything's going according to plan."

"You don't have a plan," Sehran observed. "You never have a plan."

"I have part of a plan," I protested. "Very good parts. The best parts."

"Your plan seems to be 'kill everything and hope for the best,'" Thessarian observed, clearly trying to be less assholish.

"And it's working!" I pointed out. "That's the important part, right? Results!"

The elder wood elf shook his head, but I caught the slight smile this time around. "You are absolutely insane."

"Thank you!" I beamed. "I do try. Now, let's go save some refugees and maybe we'll get to traumatize some more Dark legionnaires. Who knows? Maybe we'll get lucky and find another death knight with an even stupider name."

"Please don't jinx us," Arrin pleaded, as he swung over the edge of the ship on a rope. "Hey, boss, any chance we can get Horkesh to give us some soldiers for transport?"

"I'd sooner burn in fucking hell." I gave him the finger, as he laughed and clambered out of sight.

"What's this?" Thessarian pulled out a fresh tankard, passing it over unasked.

"Well...have you ever heard of ancient cave spiders?" I took a sip and then launched into the story.

<u>CHAPTER TWENTY-EIGHT</u>

"What do you mean, we've *lost* Giint?" I asked five days later, sitting in my cabin and staring at Lydia over a bacon sandwich, even as 'Captain Tim' left the room.

Our negotiations for 'hiring the Mercenary's Guild' were still not complete, meaning we had an excuse for him to come and go as we needed him to.

He'd provided a load of little details, but so far bugger all of real use—besides the location of a decent bar and someone who reared pigs, meaning that the glories of bacon were mine again.

Apparently, we'd not given him enough time, was his excuse, so now he was getting to sit back and do 'normal' contract work and get paid twice, as I'd already paid him to be here.

"Ah mean t'little mad bastard found a damn supplier an' bought a bag of that catnip stuff bigger than 'is 'ead, an' 'ammered through it all in less than an hour. Nobody's seen 'im since," Lydia growled.

"Well, that's just fucking perfect." I sighed, setting down my sandwich. "How the hell does a gnome even find catnip in a wood elf city?"

"Apparently they use it fer some kind o' ceremonial tea." Lydia shrugged. "The merchant thought it was funny when Giint started rollin' around in the sample. Less funny when t'mad bastard grabbed up 'is entire stock and ran off, cacklin'."

"Any chance he'll turn up on his own?"

"Oh aye, no doubt. But iffin yer mean before 'e finishes it all, about as much chance as me becoming a delicate flower who enjoys embroidery." She snorted. "We've got 'alf t'crew searchin' fer 'im, but a gnome that doesn't want be found inna city full o' trees? Good fuckin' luck. 'E could be anywhere."

I rubbed my temples, a headache coming on. "Fine. Keep looking, but don't let it interfere with the rebuild or the search for the library. Speaking of which, how'd the talk with the refugees go?"

A bunch had turned up at the ship last night. Now that we were apparently liked by the city council, whatever had been keeping people away had changed, and we were getting people lining up to make requests, including from refugees looking for a chance at life again.

"Better than expected." Lydia's expression softened slightly. "Tenandra agreed t'take ten more on as crew, as well as their families. Poor bastards were so grateful, they were cryin'. Some kids tried t'give us their toys as payment."

"Please tell me you didn't take toys from children."

"'Course not! What kind of monster do yer think ah am?" She looked genuinely offended. "Gave 'em some candy from my stash instead. The looks on their faces…" She cleared her throat roughly. "Anyway, we got the people we brought aboard from t'swamp settled here in Lembiq fer now. The wood elves have been decent about it, set 'em up in some kind of guest quarters, but they're a bit pissed 'cause they were already low on space thanks t'those already 'ere, and the rest of 'em are still marchin' 'ere."

"Good." I stood, stretching until my back popped. "And Thessarian?"

"Been in an' out like a bad curry. Accordin' t'Flux, him and t'other council members have been having lots of locked door conversations. My guess? They're ready t'make their move."

As if on cue, there was a knock at the door. I sighed, eyeing the pile of bacon sandwiches longingly.

"Come in!" I called, and wasn't surprised when Tisan stepped in, looking formal as fuck in what had to be ceremonial robes.

"Prince Jax." He bowed deeply. "The Council of Lembiq formally requests your presence for treaty negotiations."

"About damn time," I muttered; then, louder: "I accept. When?"

"Now, if it pleases you."

"Of course it's now." I eyed the bacon sandwiches again and then snagged one more as well as my good cloak—the one that connected to the shoulders of my armor and didn't have as many bloodstains—and turned to Lydia. "You coming?"

"Wouldn't miss it fer t'world." She grinned, picking a sandwich up as well and under-arm tossing another to Tisan. "Besides, someone needs t'keep yer from calling new people creative names."

"That was ONE TIME!"

"Three times," she corrected. "Death Tits, Baron Cockwomble, and that merchant yer called Princess Pissy-Pants."

"He was trying to sell me 'genuine dragon scales' that were obviously painted fish scales!" I protested as we followed Tisan out.

"Still counts."

The fucker was one of the random people who had turned up to try to do deals with us. Most were fine. Obviously, they were merchants, which meant that they were trying to fuck me at least as hard as a bard would, but they knew the rules: show a little respect and don't lie to my goddamn face.

He'd been the opposite end of the scale, and was apparently on his final warning before being evicted from the city. The scales I'd been called down to see that were "genuine blue dragon scales" and "excellent for armor or potion ingredients" were from a type of fish, and had been painted with such a thick layer of blue enamel that Arrin couldn't identify them, and had escalated it to me.

When the merchant was given the chance to come clean rather than waste my time, he'd doubled down. The scream he'd made less than a minute after I'd met him—as I pitched him over the side of the ship and into the water—had earned him the nickname.

The journey through Lembiq was…different from what Yen had described. Maybe it was because I was actually paying attention this time, or maybe because word had spread about the Dark Legion massacre, but the wood elves we passed looked at me with a mixture of awe and fear that made my teeth itch.

The city itself was incredible, though. Tisan led us along walkways that spiraled around massive tree trunks, past shops and homes that seemed to grow from the wood itself. Everything was organic curves and living buildings, with bridges made of woven branches that were still alive, leaves rustling in the breeze.

"How the fuck do you even build something like this?" I asked, genuinely curious as we crossed a bridge that had to be three hundred feet above the ground. "If you've got builders for hire, I'd love to send a bunch to the Cradle to work on that settlement."

"We don't build," Tisan explained, pride evident in his voice. "We guide. Each tree is sung to from the time it's a sapling, shaped over decades into what we need. This bridge? My great-grandmother started it. I helped complete it in my youth."

"That's actually amazing," I admitted. "In the empire, we just hit things with hammers until they're the right shape."

"Yes, we noticed." His tone was dry enough to start fires. "Imperial architecture has always been… memorable."

As we climbed higher, the social layout Yen had described got much more obvious. The lower levels—Rootside—were cramped and darker, and filled with people of all races, though still beautiful in their own way. The middle levels—Branch—opened up with more space and light. But the Canopy…

"Holy shit," I breathed as we emerged onto a platform near the top. The view stretched for miles in every direction. Other massive trees were visible in the distance, connected by bridges that looked like spider silk from this height. The platform we stood on was easily the size of a small plaza, with the council chambers rising from the center like the tree had decided to grow a crown.

"The heart of Lembiq," Tisan said softly. "The ceremonial heart of the city and our people. Here, it is said, the elders watched the fall of the moon Ishtic."

"It's beautiful." And I meant it. After months of blood and mud and death, seeing something this pure, this alive…it hit different.

"Come." Tisan gestured. "The council waits."

The council chamber was a sphere grown from the living wood, with no straight lines or sharp corners anywhere. Light filtered through leaves that formed the ceiling, casting everything in a green-gold glow. Seven chairs grew from the floor in a semicircle, six occupied.

I recognized Thessarian immediately, sitting to the left of the center. The others were a mix of ages, though with elves that didn't mean much. What struck me was the power in the room—not magical, though there was that too, but the weight of centuries of accumulated wisdom.

Also, for a change, when I was meeting a people's obvious leadership, there were no glares or overt hatred, which was nice.

"Prince Jax Amon." Thessarian stood, and the others followed suit. "We welcome you to the heart of Lembiq."

"Elder Thessarian, Honored Councilors." I even gave a proper bow, not the half-assed ones I usually managed. "Thank you for the welcome."

"Please, sit." He gestured to a chair that definitely hadn't been there a second ago, grown from the floor to match my height perfectly. "We have much to discuss."

I sat, noting how Lydia took position behind me, hand casually on her mace. The council settled back into their seats, and Thessarian began.

"We have debated long on your proposal. The observers we sent with you spoke…passionately…about their experiences, and I have added my own thoughts. Your actions against the Dark Legion were observed by many, and the refugees you saved have shared their stories."

"And?"

"And we are prepared to offer you two choices." A woman to Thessarian's left spoke up. She had that ageless elf thing going on—could have been fifty or five hundred. "Both represent a new chapter for Lembiq, but the terms differ significantly."

"I'm listening."

Thessarian leaned forward. "The first option: a military alliance. Lembiq remains fully autonomous; our forces stay here to defend our lands. In return, you agree to protect us from any who would attack us because of our association with you. We would be allies, not subjects, though you gain the right to search the forest and the city for this hidden library. Once found, the library becomes the property of Lembiq, but you are permitted access rights.

"You would also be permitted to search the forest for the additional cores you believe are out there, and they are to be split equally between yourself and Lembiq."

Yeah, that was a pretty shitty deal, I decided, gritting my teeth and not biting; this was a "if you don't agree to our terms, then this is what you get" kinda deal. Otherwise, they'd never have admitted there were two choices.

"And option two?" I prompted when they stayed silent.

"We join the empire fully." The words seemed to cost him. "We swear fealty to you as our prince and future emperor. Our people become imperial citizens, with all that entails."

"But?" Because there was *always* a but.

"But with conditions." The woman spoke again. "First, Lembiq's council remains in control of Lembiq. We govern our people according to our ways, within the framework of imperial law. We also require a seat on your imperial council."

"Reasonable so far."

"We ask that we receive half of all the golem cores or anything else you recover from the forest, and a dozen of each of the golems you can produce."

"I'll go to five war golems and three servitors when I can. No to any other kinds, because I don't have them. Once there's a link to here from Dravith, we can talk about it, though. And if you have a genuine need, I'm happy to discuss more golems."

"Next." Thessarian's eyes gleamed. "We require full access to the library you seek. When you find it, it comes here, to Lembiq."

I sat back, thinking. "No. The Library of Souls isn't just some building I can pack up and move. It's connected to the gods themselves. I'm not even sure anyone who isn't at least ascending can access it properly."

"Then we have no agreement," one of the other councilors said flatly.

"Hold on." I raised a hand. "I said I can't promise to *move* the Library of Souls. I didn't say we couldn't work something out. How about this: a knowledge exchange program. The library here might not be all of it, but it could hold a way to reach the rest. I'm thinking long-term here—I don't want all our eggs in one basket. Knowledge should be preserved, spread out to prevent total loss if the worst happens."

They exchanged glances, and I pressed on.

"I'll establish a center of learning here in Lembiq. As the main location for now, with satellite locations at the great towers and other sites as we expand. You'll have the right to access and copy any knowledge I *can* share, and have copies that are readable. In return, you share your knowledge with the empire. Fair?"

"Define 'can share,'" the woman said carefully.

"Some knowledge is restricted by the gods, or it's in forms that can't be used by others. Some is too dangerous to spread widely. From what I understand, the Library of Souls is literally a library made by gods for the next generation of gods. I don't know what I'll be permitted to take and what I can share, or even if it will hold books. But what I can share with you, I am happy to do so.

"Some will be taken to the great towers; others would be taken to Gaij or wherever I set up the library to store all this knowledge. But everything else? History, magic theory, spell construction, practical skills? I'm willing to commit to a library on this continent that becomes the home of such things, and that copies of the stuff we've got elsewhere could be taken there. In fact, we could build the greatest library this age has seen, right here in Lembiq."

Thessarian stroked his beard. "And if this hidden library you search for leads to others that *can* be moved?"

"Then we discuss it when we know more. But I'll promise this—Lembiq will become a center of learning for the empire. That's not me fucking around…that's something I'm happy to go along with."

The council turned inward, and a subtle barrier sprang up, hiding their voices. After several minutes, they turned back.

"We have a counterproposal," Thessarian said. "We accept your terms, but we require you to build a dedicated library here. A magical repository that can properly preserve and organize the knowledge."

I kept my face neutral even as I inwardly grinned. Gaij had already started to work on plans for exactly that. "Done. But I'll need you to make two copies of everything I give you—one for Lembiq, one for a second site of my choosing, with the originals returned to me."

"Acceptable." He stood, and the others followed. "We also require your word that the refugees currently in our care will be provided for…training, employment, future prospects. And that the majority will be moved away from Lembiq once they're stable."

"Of course. They're imperial citizens, or will be soon. Their care is my responsibility."

"Then we are agreed." Thessarian's voice carried the weight of centuries. "Lembiq will join the empire, with the conditions stated."

That was when the last figure I'd been expecting entered the room, clearly having been staying out of the way in case the negotiations didn't go well— though why that'd have made a difference, I didn't know.

A handful of others entered with him, taking up a stance by the outer walls and clearly awaiting orders, while Lord Farendir was all smiles and shaking my hand, explaining how honored he was to be leading his people in rejoining the empire. As soon as I met him, I got Yen's comments about him being "cautious."

Everything about him, from his smile that never reached the eyes to the way his hands were manicured, said this was a man who had survived centuries by never committing to anything too quickly, and was a figurehead all the way.

He'd probably hidden outside, listening at the keyhole, ready to run if he needed to.

Well, fuck it, I'd name Thessarian to the imperial council, I decided, and then dealing with the locals would be his problem.

Or maybe I could make them let me name Tisan? He was good people, after all. Or Silviana?

Nah, fuck it. Thessarian had good taste in beers.

The ceremony was surprisingly simple. No grand speeches or complicated rituals. The council stood, placed their hands over their hearts, and spoke the full oath instead of the butchered version we'd gone back and forth on.

The magic of it settled over the room like a warm blanket, before runners were sent to spread the news through the city.

Once they'd done that, I pulled up the notification for the library reward I'd gotten from Jenae through the Constellation of Secrets. I shared it with Thessarian.

Arcanum Library: *The Arcanum Library serves as a repository for magical knowledge, allowing researchers to access a vast collection of spells, theories, and accumulated wisdom more efficiently. Those who study within its walls gain a 10% boost to magical comprehension and spell learning.*

Construction materials required:

- **300 Steel Ingots**

- **150 Orichalcum Ingots**

- **400 Glass Panels**

- **75 Manastones (average or higher in size)**

- **500 Units of Marble**

- **200 Books of Magic (minimum quality: uncommon)**

- **10 Golem Cores**

Note: The Arcanum Library will automatically catalog and organize all magical books and scrolls placed within its walls. When fully operational, it also provides a 5% reduction in mana cost for all spells researched within its confines.

"Now you're gonna have to provide some materials for this…" I said. "Orichalcum is a bastard to get hold of, and we're down to sending out caravans looking for it, so you'll have to help on this. The local golem cores will probably help, though."

"Indeed it will!" Thessarian beamed.

The woman who'd been speaking earlier stepped forward. "There is one more thing. Scholar Eilathen?"

A younger elf—and by younger, I meant she only appeared to be about twenty instead of ageless—moved over from the wall to stand next to one of the chairs. She carried an armload of books and looked nervous as fuck.

"This is Scholar Eilathen," Thessarian explained. "Show him."

The scholar set down her books, picked up one of what looked to be a half dozen blank and clearly ready-to-use identical tomes, and showed me it. Then she closed her eyes. Light built slowly in her hands, and less than a minute later, when she opened her eyes, she swayed on her feet, but smiled.

"I can copy any book," she said weakly. "Perfect reproduction, including magical texts and skill books. Once per day, though it requires specially prepared materials."

She showed me the battered older book she'd been holding, and that the blank one she'd had in her other hand had now been replaced with what looked to be a perfect copy of the first.

"Holy fuck," I breathed as my mind raced. "You can duplicate skill books?"

"With the proper materials and preparation, yes. It's exhausting and expensive, but for building a true library… As I said, Prince, once per day, and it requires a small team to prepare the blanks, but it has been highly useful in the past." She shrugged.

"That's why we agreed," Thessarian admitted. "With her ability and your resources, we can create something unprecedented. A true repository of knowledge, copied and preserved against any catastrophe. Also, should the gods be willing to permit copies of the library to be removed for only a day each—and held here during the process, of course—then, in theory, we could create multiple copies of each book, preserving the knowledge of the ages for millennia to come."

"You beautiful, brilliant bastards." I grinned. "Yes. Absolutely yes. We'll need to establish proper procedures, security, selection…"

"Although we were unaware of the magical building, it fits very nicely with our hopes, so thank you, my prince." Farendir nodded.

"Indeed it does!" Thessarian grinned. "Clearly we chose correctly." He offered his hand, and I clasped it. "Welcome to Lembiq, my prince. May our alliance bring prosperity to both our peoples."

"Count on it." I looked around. "Now, anyone know where I can find a gnome-sized butterfly net? Because we still need to find Giint before he does something spectacularly stupid."

"I'm afraid," Thessarian said with a perfectly straight face, "you are already too late. He was found an hour ago with three live ferrets in his trousers, painted blue, and wearing a particularly expensive cape. He'd somehow attached it to his ankles and wrists and was attempting to fly."

"Of course he was." I sighed. "Lydia?"

"On it." She was already headed for the door. "Ah'll get t'little shite. Yer finish up here."

"So, why the ferrets?" I asked into the sudden bemused silence.

"A better question would be why and how did he steal my favorite cape!" the fucking lord of the city *growled*. "You didn't know? Truly?"

"I had no fucking clue. Why?"

"We thought it was an attempt to force us to decide sooner," one of the other council members admitted. "That we must make a decision or you'd continue to allow him to run amok."

"Well, it wasn't, but I'm glad it worked." I shrugged. "So, shall we discuss the details? We've already searched the libraries that we're aware of and had access to, but…"

CHAPTER TWENTY-NINE

"**W**ell, this is fucking tedious," I muttered sometime later, leaning against Tenandra's railing as we completed our third slow circle around Lembiq. "I thought magical searches were supposed to be all 'Aha!' and dramatic revelations, not flying in circles like a lost tourist."

"Patience, Jax," Tenandra said calmly, her avatar appearing next to me, and a second later getting an arm draped across her shoulders by a grinning Sehran. "Systematic searches require systematic approaches."

"System making Giint sick." Giint groaned from where he was tied to the mast. The little bastard was still coming down from his catnip bender and had tried to jump off the ship twice already, convinced he could fly. The cape incident had apparently just been the beginning. But after seeing the condition of it, well…I'd given the lord of the city some platinum and an apology over the fact that his favorite cape was forever more associated with a traumatic sight for him.

"Yer wouldn't be seasick if yer hadn't eaten three ferrets an' enough friggin' catnip t'kill a horse!" Lydia pointed out unsympathetically.

"Giint not eat ferrets! Ferrets friends! Help Giint fly!" he protested, then went green again. "Oh…Giint think Giint gonna…"

"If you puke on my deck again, I'm dropping you in the lake," Tenandra warned, and another of the crew raced over with a fresh bucket just in time.

I turned away from that particular walking, talking tragedy and focused on the city below. We'd been at this for two hours now, once we'd established that yeah, there wasn't a site deliberately hidden from us in the city, or at least not by the current leadership.

Now we were flying slow spirals out from the center of Lembiq while Tenandra used every sense she had to search for anything that might be a hidden library.

So far, we'd found three illegal stills, two affairs in progress, one surprisingly well-hidden smuggling operation, and what appeared to be an underground fight club that I'd be visiting at some point later with the squad in the hope of at least beers and gambling to distract everyone. No new libraries though, hidden or otherwise.

We had, admittedly, had a good laugh about how traumatized most of the local criminal element was. They'd already seen the drow—there'd been a single group of three involved in the smuggling ring—get literally ripped from their meeting and yeeted across the room.

It was the first time we'd had anyone actually speak about what happened when the territory joined us and the drow were evicted. It turned out that the process was something like grabbing them by the belly button, and then hurling them a speed of 0-5000 mph toward the edge of the territory.

In this case, given that they were in a cave under the city, and there'd been a multitude of walls between the edge of the territory and them, they'd basically hit them and detonated.

The smugglers were easily identifiable by the trait that they tended to scream and cower whenever there was a loud noise nearby, as well as redecorating their trousers if you asked them about the drow.

"Anything?" I asked Tisan, who'd joined us for the search along with a handful of other observers and was leaning on the railing nearby.

"Nothing that matches what you described." He shook his head. "Though I must thank you for locating that smuggling ring. We've been looking for them for months."

"Happy to help," I said dryly. "But unless they're smuggling books, I don't give a shit. I am glad the drow were removed, though. Tenandra, how far out are we now?"

"Three miles from the city center," she reported. "Shall I expand the search pattern?"

"Yeah, but let's change tactics. The council said most of the cores were found to the northeast, right?" I looked at Tisan, who nodded. "Then let's focus in that direction. If the library's not in the city, maybe it's connected to wherever these cores came from."

"The cores were scattered." Silviana spoke up. "Most were found either partly buried, as if they'd been there for centuries, or they were dug up by animals or in gardens and fields."

"Scattered like they fell? Or scattered like someone hid them?"

"I don't know. They have been found roughly in that direction from here, but beyond that they are spread out, though…"

"Though that could be because anyone who finds them doesn't want others going poking around their private looting spot." I grunted and straightened up, looking at Tenandra and remembering the conversation we'd had about the likely source. "Do you think the transport survived the crash?"

"It is likely, as we discussed before, and if it has, we should be able to easily identify it, now that I have the time to search," she assured me.

"Okay then, let's use a little logic…" I sighed. "If it was big and it came down hard, it'd have wiped out the trees, or most of them. Anyone in the city would have seen it, but they'd probably not have gone looking straightaway—all the screaming and the 'end of the world' would see to that. They'd have gone looking soon though, surely?"

"So, look for intentionally hidden, rather than simply crashed…" Tenandra started, then turned to Tisan. "Are there any legends of mysterious deaths in the area?"

"Yes and no," he replied after a few seconds of thought. "There was a tale of deaths in the past to the north of here, but it was found to be a void witch who moved in and had been sacrificing those she could catch."

"In the same area?" I asked.

"Yes, but again, she was caught and executed."

"When was it?"

"Around two hundred years after the cataclysm."

"Could she have been around at the point of the cataclysm?"

"Possibly, though she'd need to have been subtle in her taking of prey."

"So, we have a ship carrying highly valuable cores and shit that crashes, but that would have been identifiable from the top of the canopy. We have it being 'lost' and it's never mentioned, but there's a witch in the area who kills anyone who goes near the site that it went down? Suspicious, ain't it." I snorted.

"You think the witch reached the crash site first and eliminated any who came looking for it?" Tisan scratched at his chin.

"I think it's possible." I nodded. "Hell, she might not have been a witch. Anything is possible. And considering it was five hundred years ago…"

"There are many citizens who endured the cataclysm," he pointed out to me. "Elder Thessarian, for one. And he would have mentioned if he believed the two were connected, or if there was a crashed ship in the forest."

"If he knew about it," I countered. "What I'm thinking, though, is how likely is it that he'd have seen it? I mean, the entire world seems like it's on fire…what's one more sudden shaking of the earth out of the blue? It's not like they're going to say 'Oh hell, that felt like an imperial transport crashing near here!'

"Instead, they're likely just going to hope whatever it was doesn't affect them, and keep hunkered down. If they send out a party to investigate when all this is going on and they go missing, would they send more and more people after the group, or just say fuck it and leave that section of the forest alone for a while?"

"And as the forest regrows, and the centuries pass, a witch is found to have been killing people there." He sighed. "Very well, I accept that many would avoid the area after that until we have stronger forces that could patrol deeper and deeper into the forest again, and around the cataclysm there were multiple great fires that changed the forest horrifically."

"Bad?" I asked Tisan.

"Does 'horrific' mean something else where you come from?" He glared at me. "There was tremendous damage to the lesser giants of the forest and even scarring to the Great Mothers. But yes, I accept that if something crashed hard enough, and there was an ongoing fire, then it may have been lost, buried in the debris and missed, given the timing and that we are already nearly four miles from the city."

"And given the losses that you took around then, the reduction in your people and the shit that was going on, is that unreasonable that people would have left a section of the forest alone for that long?"

"Long enough that the witch could consolidate her hold on the area? If she was subtle, that would explain a lot," he muttered. "The occasional loss here and there, and considering the rise of the monsters that coincided with the cataclysm…" He hesitated, then nodded.

"Those who would have searched the forest on patrols decades later may have missed the crashed ship in the regrowing undergrowth, given that half the forest was burned down at one point or another back then."

"So, let's search for anything that looks likely." I grinned as the ship banked smoothly, and we headed out over the forest. The trees below were gigantic, ancient things that towered over the tallest trees back home, looking like the pictures I'd seen of the massive ones in America. Instead of straight up and down, though, these were more like English oaks: heavily leafy, with wide, twisting branches that I could have ridden a motorbike along.

"Is it just me, or is there a weird gap in the canopy?" Arrin pointed ahead and to the left.

He was right. It was subtle, but there were definitely sections appearing where the trees were younger, smaller. Not a clearing exactly, more like a scar that had mostly healed over centuries of growth.

"That's it." I grinned. "Tenandra?"

"I see it," she confirmed. "I can't currently sense anything below us, not beyond what I'd expect, and no active magic, but there are echoes ahead. Following the line now."

We traced the scar through the forest for another few miles before Tenandra suddenly slowed, moving between trees and as close to the ground as she could. "There. Below us, approximately forty meters down."

All I could see was more forest, but I'd learned to trust her senses. "What are we looking at?"

"Metal. Vast quantities of metal, along with..." She paused. "Hundreds of golem cores. They're inert, but the magical signature is unmistakable."

"Fucking jackpot," I breathed. "All right, everyone gear up. We're going in. Tisan, you and your people can stay up here if—"

"We're coming," he said, determined. "This is our history too."

"Fair enough. Tenandra, can you land?"

"Not without destroying significant swathes of the forest. But I can hover low enough for ropes."

I nodded, accepting that for most people that was the best way. But obviously, those of us who could fly were also going to help.

Ten minutes later, we were all on the ground, staring at what looked like absolutely nothing special. Just more forest floor covered in centuries of leaf litter and moss.

For this little jaunt, given that we were deep in the forest and looking for who the fuck knew what, I'd brought along plenty of our mer friends to make the searching easier.

In addition to Bane, we had Flux and the six surviving mer out of the original ten, as others had apparently died in the fighting already. And between their ability to sense disturbances and voids through sonar, I wasn't worried about anyone sneaking up on us.

"Spread out," I ordered. "Look for anything unusual. Metal, stone, any—"

"Boss!" Tang interrupted from thirty feet away. "Got something!"

"Fuck me, that didn't take long." I snorted.

We gathered around him to find him brushing away moss from what was clearly broken and twisted metal.

"That's old," Tisan muttered. "But not necessarily what we're looking for."

"It is imperial work." Tenandra's avatar materialized beside us, as Sehran somehow shared the mana that she took from Jian to survive here. "Beyond that, I cannot be specific. But the metal is a match for that used in my previous hull."

"'Ow t'fuck do we get in?" Lydia asked, already prodding at the metal with her mace.

"You don't—not here. This is scrap," she admitted, before pointing across the clearing to where a massive mound lay covered by a fallen tree. "I suggest you start there."

"Bane, Flux," I ordered, squinting across the moss-covered and sunlight-dappled clearing.

From above—when Tenandra had hovered in place—the forest looked solid, like it was trees shoulder to shoulder. But a little work with blades on the way down—which hadn't made us better friends with the wood elves—had revealed that the canopy was a lot wider than it looked.

There were huge numbers of trees here, sure, and the canopy was solid, with dozens of trees fighting for space and weaving branches together. But once you were past that, the forest opened up.

We passed multiple layers as we got lower and lower, some with thick branches that I could have walked along comfortably, but most were thinner. Whereas the canopy overhead was thick and lush, below it, there were nowhere near as many leaves.

The lower we went, the less plant life there was, until we reached the forest floor, and that was just…weird.

I knew intellectually why it was like this after a single glance: there was almost no sunlight getting through to the ground level, making the occasional fern or nettle the exception rather than the rule. But the smell, and the constant movement?

What survived down here, so far from the life-giving rays of the sun, was mostly fungus, and everything else was goddamn rotting.

Traveling across the clearing was like trying to cross a bog, with water constantly dripping from the leaves overhead. Because the sun never got down here to evaporate, it meant that for a bug-lover, this was probably heaven.

For us?

There were clouds of stinging insects; glittering things with wings and legs like grasshoppers bounded here and there; stagnant water blipped and bubbled.

Lastly, and most omnipresent, was the humidity. The air felt like you needed to chew it, and I just wanted to lay down the hurt on the entire area with a Flames of Wrath as soon as I tried to cross it.

I'd never been a bug-lover, but the sight of the spiders that sat, enormous and fat in the middle of webs as we passed them, made my butthole pucker.

"Let's move carefully," Yen called out. "This thing's been here for centuries. No telling what might have moved in."

"Only one way to find out." Bane materialized from the shadows, his four arms already holding four daggers. "Give us ten minutes."

"Before anyone gets to play, we'll all need to dig," Flux corrected.

By the time we got there—having slogged through the rotting vegetation—I saw he was right.

The mer started us off, being naturally more agile, even in these environments. They'd reached the mound first, and they started to dig.

It took about fifteen minutes just to uncover a section that was clearly metal, and another hour after that to find something that we could use as a door—a broken section of the wall that had buckled inward, and that creaked as Bob pushed on it. Eventually we bent it far enough that it snapped, breaking free with a resounding *bong* that was about as good at alerting everyone we were there as could be.

It was only made better when Grizz pointed out that nobody had come to answer the door, and Giint took charge.

"This door? Why they no come? Maybe they no hear? Hellllooooooooooooooo!" he yelled into the open gap. His voice echoed around; all of us turned to glare at him and the big legionnaire.

"I expect this idiocy from him," I growled. "But you know better, dude."

Grizz winced and nodded, holding up a hand as if to say "my bad."

The metal groaned as we pried open another section, making it wide enough that we could get in and out easily. A wave of stale air arose that smelled of rust, old magic, and something else.

"Is that…" Flux opened his mouth wider, apparently tasting the air. "Rotting meat?"

"Great, something lives in there," I confirmed. "And it's been eating. All right, combat formation. Me and Grizz up front. Lydia, Yen, and Tisan behind us. Casters in the middle. Flux, Bane, and your people on the flanks. Tang, stay close—I want to know if you spot anything. Bob, bring up the rear. Move slow. Call out anything weird."

"Weirder than exploring a thousand-year-old crashed transport with a giant undead, the prince of the empire, and a mad gnome?" Arrin muttered.

"You know what I mean, smartass."

"I know—this shit practically writes itself." Ronin laughed, and I glared at him as well.

The hatch led to a maintenance tunnel that was barely tall enough for me to stand upright in. Ancient magelights flickered to life as we entered, most dead but a few still clinging to unlife, casting crazy shadows that danced and writhed as we marched past.

The floor was canted downward, making it clear that most of the transport was buried still. But when I looked toward the rear, there was only destruction, meaning that yeah, we were heading down.

"I hate this already," Ronin whispered, his usual cheerfulness now notably absent.

The tunnel opened into what must have been a cargo hold. Massive containers lined the walls, most split open. Their contents—golem cores—scattered across the floor like the world's most expensive marbles, and most of them were dead, which was fucking annoying. But that wasn't what caught my attention.

It was the bones.

Hundreds of them, from dozens of different creatures. Some old enough to be from the crash, others…much fresher.

"Movement!" Bane hissed, his head turning, tendrils extended as he clearly tried to make something out. Several of the other mer let loose with powerful thrums at Flux's order. "Multiple contacts, coming from deeper in."

Then I heard it too: a chittering, clicking sound that made my skin crawl. Like someone tapping bone on metal, but organic somehow.

"Summoning light!" Tisan barked, and magelights bloomed around us just in time to see our welcoming committee.

"Oh fuck me sideways," Lydia breathed. "Fuckin' feenals!"

At first, I thought we were looking at a carpet of moving fur. Then my brain shifted to identify what I was actually seeing—hundreds of the little bastards, pouring out of cracks and crevices in the transport's walls like a hairy, chittering tide racing toward us.

They looked like someone had tried to create the world's most annoying pest and succeeded beyond their wildest dreams. Each feenal was about eight inches long, with a rat-like head grafted onto an insect body, six legs that clicked and clattered on the metal floor, and a pathetic little stinger on the back that looked about as threatening as a toothpick.

What they lacked in individual menace, they made up for in sheer fucking numbers.

"Feenals!" Tisan spat the word like a curse. "The cores must have been keeping them fed for centuries!"

"Questions later, killing now!" I roared as the first wave hit us.

My naginata swept through the air, bisecting three of the creatures in one swing. They died easily—too easily—but for every one I killed, five more seemed to take its place. And worse, they'd started doing some kind of fucking mimicry.

"Questions later, killing now!" A dozen tiny voices shrieked back at me, followed by more: "Oh fuck me sideways!" "Feenals!" "Killing now! Killing now!"

"I hate these things already!" I yelled, which immediately got repeated by a hundred more voices in various pitches and tones as half the squad went straight to magic.

The front of the wave was only a few dozen thick, but the back, where they were boiling up across and over one another, was hundreds deep. If they caught us, we were fucked.

Explosive Compression was the first spell that streaked past over my shoulder, slamming into the pile toward the back. It exploded out, pulping dozens, and then switched to sucking them inward and crushing them.

The success of the first led to a half dozen more like it streaking into the mass before Tisan reminded us why we were there.

"The cores, you idiots—you're destroying the cores!"

And it was true: here and there, in the compressed balls of flesh and bone and fur, there were sections of broken cores, making it clear that the cores weren't holding up to the damage.

"Don't let them bite you!" Flux shouted. "Their mouths are filthy with disease!"

"Would've been nice to know that BEFORE one latched onto my tit!" Sehran called back, frantically stabbing the little bastard, and then finally having to step back into the middle of the group to use a dagger to lever its jaws apart.

"Maybe wear armor then!" he replied shortly.

"Okay, people!" Ronin shouted out from the safety of the middle of the group—and knowing him, probably while trying to get a decent view of Sehran, who was busily pouring a healing potion over her wound. "Listen up! Feenals are hive creatures. Individually, they're as thick as rocks. No survival instinct, no fear at all, and the queen is the only one that can think. If we kill her, the hive will go insane and try to kill anything and everything. Kill her and pull back, and they'll kill one another!"

"That's the play!" I shouted, fingers flicking as I cast. "Drive them back so we've got some space, and then we hunt and kill the queen."

They swarmed Grizz first, probably recognizing him as the biggest threat—or the biggest food source. The big man was swinging his sword in wide arcs; each sweep sent multiple feenal bodies flying, but they just kept coming.

I frantically cast as they started climbed one another, forming writhing towers of fur and teeth to reach any gap in the armor, which fortunately, being legion plate, there weren't many of.

"Grizz, get down!" I ordered, finally finishing the spell.

He dropped without hesitation, then rolled from side to side, crushing dozens under him, even as the Frostfire Circle of Cleansing flared to life, pouring flames across everything.

I swept my naginata in a burning arc over his head. The blade trailed fire and more feenals exploded into flaming, shrieking pieces. Suddenly, the air was full of tiny voices screaming, "Down! Down! Grizz, get down!"

Flames raced everywhere, dancing up across our people—which freaked the elves out completely, despite me telling them earlier that I could do this—and I shook my head as I saw the numbers rising.

"There's too many!" Silviana called out, her arrows finding marks but barely making a dent in the swarm. Each arrow killed one, maybe two if she got lucky, but we were facing hundreds.

"Fall back!" I barked. "I'll make shields—we funnel them in toward the center!"

"All right, everyone!" Lydia barked. "Archers, quit it and 'old yer fire. Anyone with Magic Missile, fire 'til yer at 'alf mana, then 'old. 'Eavy armor on t'front line, scouts on t'sides. Get ready to pick off anythin' that gets past 'eavies!"

I stepped back. As a "heavy," I should be on the front line, but if I was casting shields and holding them in place, there was no way I was fighting at the same time.

Instead, I passed my naginata to Tisan and started to cast, even as Lydia led us back ten meters or so to the entrance to the room.

"We 'old 'ere as long as possible!" she barked. "Yer and yer"—she picked two of the mer—"get back there an' keep t'exit clear! Everyone else, form up, get ready, or catch yer breath. We 'old this point. If it gets 'airy, then we fall back an' Jax makes a shield over t'door! *Move!*"

"Move! Move!" The feenals chorused helpfully, which actually worked in our favor as the swarm seemed to confuse itself momentarily.

"Jax, where's those shields!" she barked.

I glared at her as the last somatic components finally finished and the twin panels slammed into being.

I'd angled them like a funnel, so anything that went around the sides just met the shield wall and the metal walls, while those that came from straight ahead were channeled into a narrow gap.

That gap—or beyond it, more accurately—was being hit repeatedly by a burst of Magic Missiles as the group took turns to fire them over and over, hammering them.

That wouldn't hold them for long, but we didn't need long, because to my left, as I concentrated on holding the shields—the little furry turds were bounding off them and draining them by the second—Yen cast her Flamespear.

It was essentially a massive version of the Magic Missile spell, hugely more powerful, and a bit like using a rocket launcher to deal with a wasp's nest.

When she released it—thankfully firing it all the way to the far end of the cargo bay—I shifted the shields and dragged them together behind it, forming a more or less solid shield before us.

That was lucky, because the goddamn explosion that went off…well, it took care of most of the feenals. And the wall, floor, and everything else.

Fire was *everywhere*, and although it wasn't as effective against me with me being Jenae's Chosen, none of the others were so lucky.

Also, my shields went pop.

I held them to make sure we all survived, but once the flames dropped, I cut the feed for the mana before it could completely drain me.

The cargo hold had erupted into an inferno. Waves of flame rolled across the floor, up the walls, and along the ceiling in an only semi-controlled burn that turned the front ranks of feenals into crispy critters. The stench was incredible— like someone had decided to barbecue a pet store and a hoarder's old sock collection—but it was effective.

The hive mind's reaction was immediate. The swarm pulled back; individual feenals trampled one another in their desperation to escape the flames. Their mimicry turned into a single, wordless shriek.

"Clean up!" I ordered, chugging a mana potion as the flames died down to manageable levels. "And someone please shut them up!"

"CLEAN UP! SHUT THEM UP!" the surviving feenals that were cut off by the flames helpfully repeated as we moved in to finish them off.

"I'm going to have nightmares about tiny voices," Ronin muttered, crushing a wounded feenal under his boot. It immediately started chanting "Nightmares! Tiny voices!" until he stomped harder.

"That a hive survived so close to the city is inexcusable," Tisan growled, looking genuinely disturbed as he wiped feenal gore off his boot. "The scouts will be sent to sweep the area again and again to make sure we get them all."

"You know, it can't be a coincidence that there's one here and all the cores are dead," Yen said musingly, examining the few corpses that hadn't been incinerated. "A small hive must have found the wreck decades ago. With the mana here, and then a constant food source…"

"They made this place their nest," I finished. "Question is, was that all of them?"

"All of them? All of them?" the dying feenals whispered, and I had to resist the urge to set them all on fire again just to shut them up.

"Only one way to find out," Bane said cheerfully, already heading deeper into the transport.

"Find out! Find out!" a tiny voice echoed from somewhere in the darkness ahead.

"I really hate these things," I muttered, but followed anyway.

The transport was divided into sections every twenty meters or so, massive bulkheads that had once sealed independently. Most were open now, their mechanisms long since failed, but they provided decent defensive positions as we cleared each section.

The second hold had fewer feenals but more evidence of their presence—gnawed cores, nest material made from centuries of accumulated detritus, and the bones of various creatures that had wandered too close, as well as holes here and there in the damaged hull that suggested that there was more and possibly worse below us. The mimicry continued, a constant background chorus of our own words thrown back at us in tiny, mocking voices.

The third section was empty except for what looked like crew quarters, long since converted into more nesting space. The smell was indescribable. Apparently, the resident golems had long since shut down, and then had been shit upon.

"Waste not, want not." I grinned as we saw the golems, and I moved over to the closest that was intact. "Hold the line. I need a few minutes," I said to the others.

Lydia stepped up, ordering them all into their places.

It didn't take long—five minutes, maybe less—to channel a thousand of my mana into the golem. Then, as the gem in its chest radiated with power, I held up my bloodstone, making sure it was where the fucker could see it.

"I am Jax Amon, Prince of the Empire, and I hereby assume full control over you. You are not to attack me or my companions. Do you understand?"

There was a long pause, then it nodded. Its eyes glowed brighter and brighter, and I moved back, giving it room.

It was a slightly different design from the usual, in that instead of a humanoid form, this one was four-legged with a barrel body, two arms and a space in the back that was hollow. It was more like a canine version of the war golems, and boy, did the fucker have teeth. But the one thing that it really had going for it as it surged to its feet was that it was low and broad.

I grinned and ordered it to take up station next to me. It trotted along silently, ready for whatever we needed it to do.

Most of the other golems in the room were hidden under mounds of literal shit, and I wasn't touching them until they were cleaned up. But this? This would do fine for what I needed.

The fourth section of the crashed ship when we entered it was nothing like the rest.

"Holy shit," I breathed.

Instead of cargo holds, this was clearly some kind of control center. Panels of dark crystal—some broken but many intact—lined the walls, and in the center sat two chairs that looked disturbingly like pilot seats.

But that wasn't what caught my attention. It was the thing in one of the chairs.

It had been a feenal once, probably. But this was what happened when one of the little bastards got a direct line to centuries' worth of magical energy. It was huge—easily the size of a small bear—with the same rat-like head scaled up to nightmare proportions. Its six limbs had thickened into actual threats. And that pathetic little stinger? Now it was a foot long and dripping with some kind of luminescent liquid.

"MEaT," it warbled. Its voice wasn't a mimicry; it was deep, aware, and somehow worse than if it had just shrieked at us. "MeAt GooD."

It had a good dozen larger things like it standing at the ready to either side, drooling and panting, looking like someone had taken rabies-filled attack dogs and then given them steroids and a history of poor decisions.

Possibly involving alcohol and trailer parks.

"Yeah, fuck this." I turned to the golem. "Kill those things, and minimize damage to the ship, please."

The feenal queen—because what else could it be—moved with surprising grace for something that looked like a rat had hate-fucked a cockroach and the baby had been raised on magical steroids. It flowed out of the chair and up the wall, its six legs finding purchase on surfaces that should have been too smooth to climb.

That really didn't help it though. We just hung back in the doorway, stomping on the few dozen feenals that made it our way, while the golem raced across the floor, then up and along the wall, and the queen's guard tried to intercept the golem.

The queen used small holes that were dotted everywhere in the ship, a few inches deep and on all the surfaces, and as the golem raced up the wall the four-legged but low-slung design was instantly explained.

What the queen was using were presumably designed for the golems to be able to lock into place on the walls and roof to do…whatever.

That meant that while the queen struggled to cling onto the walls, the golem didn't.

It hit her like a heat-seeking fucking missile—or a northerner discovering a free bar.

No deviation, no pause or slowing down—just smashed through everything that tried to get in its way and then bit down, crunching its way through the fucker at horrific speed. The pair of them fell off the wall and crashed to the floor, rolling along the canted deck as the others piled on as well.

The golem finished crushing and chewing its way through the queen, then turned to the guards that were going absolutely feral with rage and hatred.

Needless to say, the golem being constructed out of stone and metal, and the feenals, even the guards and queen, being constructed out of flesh and bone, meant that without them bearing serious weapons or magic, there just wasn't much of a fight.

I ended up summoning a shield again, though it was mainly to stop us all getting covered in goo while we watched.

The feenals had lost all interest in us once the queen was injured. They all streamed straight for her, meaning that anything that had been hiding or injured or whatever was suddenly flopping its way past us, and then being stomped on.

Free XP was free XP, right?

All in all, it took about another thirty seconds to clear the room, and then ten minutes for the golem to report back once I'd sent it out to kill anything else in the ruin that we might have missed.

After that, it was time for us to strip the fucking place to the bone.

CHAPTER THIRTY

"**O**ne hundred and forty-seven golem cores." I shook my head, reading the final inventory; Tenandra stood nearby, beaming and rubbing her hands in glee. "Damn."

"How many golems in the end?" Ronin asked. "You know, if there's a spare, I could do with a bodyguard?"

"If there's any bodies bein' guarded, it's women's an' it's from yer, yer pervert," Lydia snapped, though it was clearly halfhearted as she stared at the debris.

The difficult decision had been made that there was no realistic way of clearing the entire ship and recovering everything without major excavation work.

What we could reach easily, we'd take. What required days of digging through centuries of compressed earth and forest debris? That would have to wait.

"Three engines survived the crash intact and are near the surface," Tenandra cooed, practically vibrating with suppressed excitement. "The majority were crushed or destroyed in the impact, but those three are most likely recoverable without too much effort. With proper integration, they could heavily upgrade my form."

"Right, so we take two, gift one to Lembiq as a gesture of good faith?" I suggested, looking at Tisan and ignoring the crestfallen look on Tenandra's face.

His eyes widened. "That…that would be extraordinarily generous."

"Not really." I shrugged. "We're splitting the cores as we agreed, with you gaining the cores themselves or the value of them to the local treasury." That had been a weird thing in itself. That the city had joined the empire was wonderful—it really was…and yeah, intact and me not having to slaughter half of them was a nice change as well.

What hadn't been so much, was the realization that because I'd not had to do any of those things, well, the city was basically functioning as it normally did. And that meant that the current leadership were staying, and the treasury was theirs, not mine.

Also, I had to play nice with the other kiddies and share my toys.

"Besides, you'll need good engineers to even figure out what to do with it. Consider it an investment in our alliance. The more airships we have, the better." I squinted at the massive golems as they continued to unearth the wreck. "We've got some gnomes at the Cradle who were working on the second airship, and fuck knows what they've built now, but they didn't have engines to work with. They'd built their own from scratch with my descriptions and they were…"

I thought of how to explain it, then just shrugged.

"They were shit. They worked but that was the best that could be said about them. They had about ten to twenty percent of the power of Tenandra's engines, and they cost ten times as much to run. These ones…?" I gestured toward the wreck and left it hanging.

"They should be approximately two hundred percent more powerful than my own," Tenandra said. "Even with the cladding of my hull and the heavier systems being installed, instead of slowing my flight, we should improve upon it."

"And you're still willing to give this up?" Tisan asked curiously.

"Yeah, not happy about it, don't get me wrong," I admitted. "But I'm willing, because if I give this up to you, then it shows that I'm serious about Lembiq beyond just getting access to the library.

"There's a lot of construction and improvements going to be made around Gaij in the coming months, and even your own leadership want the refugees moved on, which I agreed to do. The thing is that most of those people are going to be turning Gaij into an economic and military powerhouse."

I looked at Tisan, thinking about how to say it, then decided blunt was the way to go.

"If Lembiq doesn't do something to even things out, it's going to be left behind. Where it is on the continent, I was thinking, was great to secure the local area. But the forests and the lack of any roads means that unless we're willing to fix that, Lembiq just can't grow significantly. That means either we come up with something that you *can* do here, or we accept that Lembiq is a city in the forest that's about as big as it's getting."

"And you don't believe the library will address that?" he asked.

I shrugged. "Honestly, it might. But the thing that we need to do first is make sure that you're not relying on that. I'd considered moving the gnomes here, if they were willing, and starting an airship industry off. You've got the wood, after all, and Gaij really doesn't. But the truth is, you're not willing to cut the trees down, so that limits it.

"Instead, I think if we leave you an engine, and get some gnomes to move here and start working on the engines, then we can help you become a manufacturing site instead. You make the engines here and you provide some of the wood, the keels and so on, and then you use caravans to move them to Gaij.

"That gives you a seriously important role, but it means you're not providing everything for the ships as well. You've not got the space to have a full-on setup to make them from scratch, but you could make some of the parts and ship them…hmmm."

"Ship them?" he asked. "We have rivers and barges, but no…"

"Fuck, sorry, a term from my past," I muttered. "Okay, we *caravan* them, or we build something like this transport." I gestured to the wreck. "Actually, fuck, Tenandra, what's the chances we could find one of these intact?"

"They are likely to exist, but where they would be are beyond me. Prax manufacturing and assembly was undertaken on Faranthai, the continent on the far side of Dai'Amaranth, and they were then flown to the capitol to be blessed by the emperor. We collected raw materials and golems from this continent, but most of the large-scale production was there."

"Joy." I sighed. "Shame, that. If we could have found a transport and repaired it, then had that ferrying parts back and forth; that'd have been a hell of an advantage."

"It would, but unfortunately, it is unlikely to work out. Also, we must be wary when it comes to golem construction sites." She looked at me and waited, letting me decide whether I was going to talk about it in front of Tisan.

"There are other nobles of the past who have returned," I told him. "If they weren't stripped of their authority, then they can claim imperial sites and take them over—think of the worst of the current nobles, but with imperial golems obeying their orders."

"That sounds horrific."

"It is," I agreed, "but there's ways of dealing with it, so don't panic."

"Boss, I think we're ready to get the first out, but man, they're big," Grizz said, surprising me with the practical point, as he gestured at the engines. Each one was easily the size of a rhino.

"I guess it's time for our new friends to figure this shit out then." I grinned, turning to the golems I'd spent the last three hours reactivating.

It'd been draining, incredibly so. Each golem needed to be uncovered, recharged—meaning I needed to drink more fucking minty mess thanks to the minimum charge being a thousand mana—but we'd gotten eight operational: six servitors and two war golems on top of the one that we'd already activated.

The servitors were a mixture of designs as well. Four were like the ones we had back home: three legs, four arms, and a head that had three faces, each facing in a different direction to give them three-hundred-and-sixty-degree vision and mobility.

The other two were like the dog golem—that was what I was calling it—in that they were shorter, broader, and were clearly designed to work while attached to the walls, ceiling, and floor of the ship.

Those little holes that the golems could insert a limb into and walk up the walls were everywhere, on both the inside and the outside as well. I was willing to bet that the canine war golem and the two servitor versions were to dissuade drakes or repair damage in flight.

The regular war golems were more impressive. Eight feet tall, built like brick shithouses made of enchanted steel and stone, with fists that could punch through castle walls. Two were the standard humanoid type; the other was our new four-legged friend who'd made such quick work of the feenal queen.

"Okay, Tenandra, you happy to guide them for this?" I asked.

She nodded, stepping up to the edge. She'd been formally identified both by me and by the golems—however they did it—as imperial "property."

I *really* didn't like that phrasing one bit, but she wasn't concerned, and it made it easier for the golems to fix her place in the hierarchy to ensure they obeyed her without issue.

What followed was six hours of organized chaos. The servitors were surprisingly efficient, cutting through hull sections with built-in tools and carefully extracting components. The war golems just ripped entire sections free with their bare hands when needed.

"Careful with those!" Tenandra fretted as another piece of irreplaceable tech was hauled out. "They're sensitive instruments!"

"NEGATIVE," the humanoid war golem replied. "CONSTRUCTION SPECIFICATIONS INDICATE SIGNIFICANT STRUCTURAL

REDUNDANCY. ROUGH HANDLING WITHIN ACCEPTABLE PARAMETERS.”

“Did it just…sass you?” I tried not to laugh as I grinned up at the advanced golem, having totally forgotten the fuckers could speak.

“I don’t like it.” Tenandra’s avatar crossed her arms. “Golems should show their betters more respect.”

“THIS UNIT’S COMBAT RATING EXCEEDS AERIAL TRANSPORT VESSEL DEFENSIVE CAPABILITIES BY SIGNIFICANT MARGIN,” the golem noted blandly.

“What?!” Tenandra shrieked. “No you don’t!”

“Okay, I love this guy,” I decided. “What’s your designation?”

“WAR UNIT SEVEN-SEVEN-NINE.”

“Seven it is. Keep up the good work.”

“ACKNOWLEDGED. THIS UNIT ACCEPTS SHORTENED DESIGNATION.”

By late afternoon, we’d stripped everything valuable we could reach: three engines—each requiring multiple trips by the servitors—nearly a hundred and fifty cores, literally miles of mana conduits, and enough rune-inscribed plating to armor a small fort. But the real prize came when we cracked open the cockpit.

“This is entirely intact,” Tenandra actually whispered, peering in. “This is an imperial command interface. Jax, please…if I can integrate this…”

“Do it,” I said immediately. “Take whatever you need.”

“It will take time to integrate, and there may be issues, but Jax, the improvement over my current systems is immense. Using this, I should be capable of significantly greater range, sensing, my flight systems… Oh no.”

“What?” I frowned at her.

“The interface will need to replace my own, meaning possibly days, weeks even that I am incapable of flight. But the advantages…” She tried to justify it as quickly as she could before I could refuse, but she stopped when I held my hand up.

“You do what you can, Tenandra, but only a day of truly being offline,” I said. “You do the rest of the upgrades and updates when you can, but you can’t be out of action for weeks. It’s not happening.”

“The advantages…” she tried to explain.

I shook my head. “It’s not going to happen,” I growled. “When we find Oracle, we’re going to need to move, and move fast. We can’t have you out of action, not for more than a day. I’m sorry.”

“Jax…”

“I’m not risking her,” I rumbled.

“Jax, please, just one point?” she begged.

I glared at her, then gestured to her to get it over with.

“If I had a full imperial interface, we might be able to identify active portals.” She let that hang in the air for a few seconds, before going on.

“I mean it, Jax. If we could identify a portal, then you could capture it, enabling us to link the continents and you could bring the legion through…carry supplies, artifacts. There's no limit to what we could achieve with a fully working imperial interface."

"Why this?" I demanded. "What's the difference between this and any other imperial facility or device?"

"This is a system that was designed to be mobile," she said. "I had a similar, though much larger facility aboard Glorious Retribution, but it was heavily damaged in the crash. I tried to link to it when there and received no response. This one is powerless, but appears intact.

"If I can power it correctly and bypass its security systems, then it's possible that we could gain access to whatever remains of the imperial systems. Each territory had a hub, a primary facility, and although these are likely long damaged and degraded, if they can be powered, then they will provide additional details and capabilities."

"Like the way stations," I muttered.

"Similar," she agreed. "But those stations were intended as local systems for a territory that was not yet fully pacified. Here, the hubs were old, and secured in place. The Great Tower was one. Those obviously heavily damaged and the key systems were destroyed—I could tell that when I visited—but there will be others. Just like this wreck, there will be facilities that were forgotten, buried and lost."

"And you could activate them?" I asked.

"If they have power, then perhaps," she hedged. "If another with higher authority has the system currently claimed, then no…not until you reached it and accessed, then claimed it. But if the system is unpowered, there's a much better chance I can locate it with this. And once we've managed that, you could power it and claim it."

"And if there's a site that's active but unclaimed, you could do that?" I pressed. "And you can sense portals?"

"Yes," she said. "Portals require highly specific materials and construction techniques. Most likely they would survive the cataclysm, and it would be a matter of discovering them."

"Were there many here?" I asked.

"On this continent?"

"Yeah."

"Over a hundred, I believe," she replied. "Some will have been lost to time, and others lost to more nefarious means. Some will have survived, though."

"Nefarious means?" I muttered curiously, still thinking.

"The portals that the nobility used to come here—depending on the level of blood magic used to reach this realm, many will have been damaged beyond repair. Unfortunately, the portals used by the more scrupulous—such as Wilhelm and his kin who you have described to me—will be the most heavily damaged."

"Why?"

"Animal blood and the mana that is released upon death is weak compared to that of sentients. Should they have opened the portals using such a medium, then connection is likely to have caused damage to the portals, resulting in their loss."

"Wilhelm said their portal was destroyed."

"Then it is likely that he was honest about the grade of life used to maintain the connection. Should we identify a portal used by less scrupulous nobility, however, then we could likely take control of it and use it to establish a connection," she pointed out.

"So, basically, we've got no choice. How long?"

"For….?"

"Don't play with me, Tenandra." I glared at her. "How long to integrate the systems you need?"

"The minimum would be three days. If there are significant issues, it could be weeks—and I wouldn't know until I begin," she admitted. "The entire control system for the ship would need to be reconfigured, and I'd have to learn to use it again. Please understand I'm not hiding anything, Jax—this would be akin to a human losing the use of their limbs and you asking how long until they could compete in war again. There are too many variables to be entirely accurate."

"Fuck!" I snarled, before dropping my head into my hands and thinking about it as carefully as possible. "Goddammit."

"I'm sorry," she said whispered. "If there was a faster way…"

"If we do this, do you need to do the rest of the repairs and upgrades at the same time?" I asked suddenly, seeing another issue.

"Yes. Otherwise, I'll need to relearn to function after the next stage of upgrades are completed," she admitted.

"Fuck's sake." I groaned.

"Jax." Lydia interrupted gently, and I looked at her in question. "We need this."

"I know, but…" I started.

She shook her head. "No, yer don't get it. We're 'ere. Thousands o' miles from 'ome, fer yer, an' that's fine, but yer forgetting that everyone else is back there."

"And?" I asked, not getting it.

"And they don't know if yer okay or in a dungeon about t'be beheaded," she said. "All our people are scared, an' this, this would mean yer could 'elp 'em. Yer could bring t'rest o' t'legion through. 'Ell, yer could bring Romanus across an' 'and over command o' t'legion 'im. This Daralen sounds like she'd be overjoyed with that. An' then she and Restun and Augustus could work together and get t'legion back on track.

"Then yer could bring engineers through. They could set up a new shipyard easy, and Oren an' t'others could work on it…get yer a dozen ships in a few months, instead of one." She looked at me, waiting. "Yer know what Oracle would say."

"Oh, thank you very much for that underhanded fucking attack." I threw my hands up in despair that she'd actually gone there.

"She's right," Flux said. "If we can link the continents, we could bring ripple-fire cannons through. We could bring people and equipment, and even golems. Thomas secured the production facility, but it was a close fight. With that under our control, and the capability to march tens of thousands of war golems through, even if your enemies have secured a local facility, you could face them, instead of taking significant damage and possibly losing all you've gained since coming here."

"I hate you all," I growled, before stomping off to my cabin to "consider my next step."

No matter what Bane said later, I wasn't fucking sulking.

The return to Lembiq was…interesting. We were pretty overloaded, considering the sheer weight of the engines, the golems, the cores, and the small number of random materials we'd recovered. But when we landed—carefully—it was to a growing crowd.

Some were there wanting to try to trade—word had gotten around that I had deep pockets and bought what they considered junk, after all—and people kept turning up, wanting to sell complete shit. There were also a lot of people who'd been informed that they'd be moving to Gaij and new opportunities were waiting, etc. They all wanted to know when we were going.

Then there were the people who thought they should be exempted from taking the oaths, and wanted special dispensation. And the list went on and on.

Usually, I didn't get that much of this, mainly because I tended to make very grisly object lessons of the nobility. Most people seemed to take the stance that if I would do that to their "betters," then I'd do worse to them.

It meant I had a growing reputation as a psychopath, but hey, who didn't these days.

"The citizens are going to panic," Thessarian observed, watching the war golems stride down the gangplank and move out to set up a perimeter.

"Nah, they'll love it." I snorted, leaning on the railing as the ship settled fully, the engines powering down to idle. "Nothing says 'we're serious about this alliance' like gifting you a massive magical engine and showing up with a bunch of ancient golems. They'll love it, really."

"That's what worries me."

CHAPTER THIRTY-ONE

As it turned out, he was right to worry. The arrival of ancient golems carrying massive pieces of imperial tech caused quite a stir. By the time we'd set off to the council meeting, planning to fill them in on the discoveries and then reached the city proper, half the population had turned out to gawk.

"CITIZENS OF LEMBIQ," Seven, who was marching next to me, announced unprompted. "THIS UNIT MEANS YOU NO HARM. VIOLENCE WILL ONLY BE APPLIED TO DESIGNATED ENEMIES."

"He's got initiative," I noted as people backed the hell up, clearly frightened. "I like that."

"Please make him stop talking," Tisan pleaded.

"Seven, maybe keep the announcements to a minimum?"

"ACKNOWLEDGED. THIS UNIT WILL MINIMIZE VERBAL TERRORISM OF ALLIED CIVILIANS."

"That's…not quite what I… You know what? Close enough." I grinned. He reminded me of Bob at first. Now, well, I loved Bob; he was partly me and sort of like having a trusted dog around. But after he'd gained his sentience, he didn't seem to want to be too close to me.

Though him spending weeks as a skull with no body probably hadn't helped that. As it was, as soon as we'd landed, he'd set off to continue searching the city for any sign of the hidden library thing.

The meeting with the council went well. They understood my position when I said that no cores were to be sold anymore, regardless of who to, as they were imperial property, and we needed that shit. They took—unsurprisingly—the value of the cores in gold and platinum instead, and let me have the rest.

Then they were overjoyed with the idea I'd suggested about the airships and the engine, and agreed to look into it, with the proviso that the wood they'd provide would be only from younger trees and deadfalls, not living greater trees, which was fine.

There was a little incident with the local arbuton—a sentient giant tree that was basically a bad-tempered Treebeard who wanted nothing to do with humans in any form—as it turned out that a group of the local refugees had trespassed in his territory, and that was, of course, handed over to me, as the new liege lord.

The council took control of the situation themselves, when I said I'd happily deal with it, but that if he wasn't willing to take the oath or enter into an alliance with us, then as his creations—the guardians—had beaten the humans to a pulp and then returned them in that state, that I'd be viewing it as assault on the empire.

They thought about it and after seeing how Tisan and Thessarian had panicked over the thought of me dealing with it *personally*, they handled it "in house" instead.

The next two days were a blur of activity. Tenandra's integration of the salvaged systems was a massive undertaking. The servitor golems worked around the clock, welding, cutting, and reshaping her hull to accommodate the new components.

The command interface from the transport was the most complex part. It required completely rewiring sections of her internal systems, but the payoff would be worth it, or so she kept assuring me.

It also took more than half of the mana conduits we'd recovered. It was only because the golems were incredibly useful that we could do it at all.

"Long-range sensors improving by 300%," she reported during one of our check-ins. "Targeting systems, mana efficiency, defensive capabilities—all significantly enhanced. And that's before we even start on the engines."

The engines were their own challenge. Each one had to be carefully mounted, connected to her power systems, and calibrated. Twenty of the recovered golem cores were installed in a new power hub, their combined output helping to manage the massive mana requirements.

"Weight reduction runes are next." Tenandra was overcome with glee over the upgrades, and I eventually came around to it, though it helped that I was busy searching the city.

Ame would be furious to miss this, and Flux made sure I knew it.

"Jax, these upgrades are…" He struggled for words, as we argued for the fifth time. "Without Ame to observe and document them, we're losing knowledge that could improve our entire fleet!"

"I know," I said. "But we don't have time or a way to fetch her. Oracle needs us, and every day we delay is another day she's in danger. We make do with what we have."

"But—"

"No buts, Flux. Document everything you can. When this is over, Ame can study Tenandra's upgrades directly. For now, we focus on the mission."

He clearly wasn't happy, but he accepted it, throwing himself into documenting every modification with the help of several wood elf crafters and enchanters.

The exterior modifications were the most dramatic. Using the salvaged hull plating from the transport, Tenandra could extend and reshape her form. What had been a respectably-sized airship was becoming something more—a true warship.

"The transport's armor was designed to withstand catastrophic damage," she explained as plates were melded into place. "Integrating it with my adaptive frame means I can slightly extend to give the engines more room, and provide more housing for both passengers and crew, as well as a small contingent of golems."

While Tenandra underwent her transformation, the rest of us weren't idle. The city needed to be searched properly, and there were oaths to administer to new citizens who'd been waiting for the formal ceremony.

Usually, I did them in as large a number as possible, but with Tenandra busy as she was, and Oracle not being there, for obvious reasons, I did them myself in batches of a hundred.

The oath ceremonies had become routine by now, but they were still important. Each new citizen was a step toward rebuilding the empire, and I made it clear I wasn't just a dick who swooped in and made changes. I tried to speak to people, and I did a little light recruiting as well.

Or, you know, Silviana did.

She'd stayed with us, and although she could come on missions with us, she tended to panic a bit anywhere underground or enclosed. Aboard ship, though? She and the small contingent of wood elf archers she recruited were going to add a lot to the security force.

I'd accepted that Tenandra, as she was, was incredible. But upgraded? She couldn't be permitted to fall into the enemy's hands—she *had* to be protected.

I left unsaid that if she couldn't be protected, then she had to be destroyed. As much as I hated it, it was being realistic, and even she had agreed.

The wood elf archers would help with that. Twenty of them had joined, and they were stationed aboard her at all times.

We made time to top off our supplies and hired a new full-time chef and his helper. I spent some time explaining the absolute necessity a full English breakfast was, and that being put over the side of the ship, mid-flight, was well within the range of reasonable responses if someone tried to give me fucking turkey bacon or put herbs in the beans.

I even got some new workout clothes and boots, though the underwear was scratchy. And the tailor had looked at me like I was a sexual deviant when I asked for silk boxers.

"I will not be a dick…" The words echoed through the plaza as another hundred wood elves took the oath. Some were enthusiastic, others clearly just going along with their council's decision, but all were now citizens.

Between ceremonies, we searched. Every old building, every forgotten basement, every suspicious fucking hollow in a tree. We found a lot of interesting things—old artifacts, forgotten caches of supplies, carved wooden plates that were apparently the local medieval version of porn mags, and multiple evidence of affairs that would make Sehran blush—but no library.

"Maybe we're looking in the wrong place?" Arrin suggested after another fruitless day as we sat drinking on the deck, while Ronin sang and played his bloody lute.

"Maybe," I said. "Or maybe we're just not seeing it. It's a fucking library for the gods, after all. I mean, what the hell does something like that even look like?"

It was on the morning of the third day that everything changed. I was recovering from another training session with Flux and Lio when Lydia burst into the room.

"We found Giint," she announced.

"Oh, thank fuck…" I wheezed, using the opportunity to catch my breath. "I mean…where was the little…bastard hiding this time?"

"Aye, that's t'thing…" She looked genuinely disturbed and disgusted. "Yer gonna want t'see this yerself."

"Am I?" I winced, straightening up and wiping a trail of blood from my nose. "Fuck's sake, Lio."

"You should have ducked." She smiled.

"I did!" I snorted, then blew a lump of congealing blood out of my nose. "That's when you kicked me in the face!"

"Well, yeah, that's why I wanted you to duck," she clarified. "I'd have missed otherwise."

"Fuck's sake," I growled.

"And just to make it clear, Jax, this is why you need to continue your training," Flux added. "The difference in your skill and your capacity is staggering. You have grown significantly, but your unarmed combat skill is lagging behind that of your armed."

"I noticed." I groaned. "All right, go on, Lydia," I prompted, following her.

We found him in what could generously be called a den of iniquity in the seedier part of Rootside. The building reeked of stale alcohol, various smoking herbs, and…other things.

"Oh gods." Ronin covered his nose. "It smells like someone died in here."

"More than one, from the smell," Tang corrected, looking green.

We followed the sounds of groaning to a back room, and found…*well*.

"Is that two elves, Giint, and a goblin?" I asked after several long moments, staring at the pile of naked limbs.

"I think so?" Lydia sounded like she was trying not to laugh. "It's 'ard t'tell where one ends an' another begins. That's a high elf at t'back, and I think that's a kitsune elf under t'pile…t'one with ears."

I deliberately looked away from what was definitely a kitsune, and wished that eyeball bleach was really a thing as well, as on the top of the pile, naked and star-fished, was Giint.

"Giint's head is stuck in the goblin's armpit," Bane noted helpfully.

"Why were you looking there?" I held up a hand. "Actually, don't answer that. Fuck me, this is a traumatizing sight. Entire generations of therapists could put their kids through college on this one room."

Thankfully, the sounds weren't from continuing exertion; they were snores, farts, hacking coughs from the one wearing some kind of a mask that apparently made it difficult to breathe—deliberately; the latch wasn't locked and they could reach it if they chose—but overall, there was just an air of absolute sexual depravity, spilled and mostly empty alcohol containers, several bags of drugs, and what looked like a very traumatized seagull in the corner to finish the image off.

A *seagull*.

I'd not even seen one of the beach bastards since I came to this realm, and we were thousands of miles, or at the very least hundreds, from the nearest sea.

All in all, though, I decided the safest thing to do here was to blame Giint and get the fuck out of here.

It took some doing to extract Giint from the pile without waking the others. He was in rough shape—covered in various fluids I didn't want to identify, reeking of catnip and worse, and mumbling incoherently.

"Giint fly… Giint see colors… Pretty lady with ears…" he burbled as we carried him out. "Giint get tail too…catch more ferrets…"

That last bit made me pause as my brain considered what he might have done to get a "tail" of his own and where the twisted little bastard may have stuffed a ferret. Then my brain rebelled and I seriously considered burning anything that had touched Giint.

Maybe I could peel my skin off my hands and heal them again?

"Let's get him cleaned up and—" I started.

Giint suddenly lurched upright.

"GIINT REMEMBER!" he screamed, then immediately threw up on my boots. "Giint sorry," he whined, "but Giint remember the important thing!"

"What important thing?" I ground out between gritted teeth, trying to ignore my footwear situation with a Scour spell as I reminded myself over and over that I couldn't just punt him into the middle of next week.

"The shiny thing! Giint find shiny thing when making the sex!"

We all exchanged glances. Giint's definition of "shiny thing" could mean anything from a bottle cap to a magical artifact, and "making the sex" was just a terrible, terrible thing to hear.

"Show us," I ordered.

Still naked and swaying dangerously, Giint led us through the building back to the room we'd found him in. I had no clue what it'd started out as, but now it was…well, it looked like the aftermath of a particularly ambitious orgy and the others were *still* unconscious despite all the noise.

"There!" Giint pointed proudly at what looked like a coatrack in the corner. "Giint remember! Giint have very good sex with that!"

"I just don't want to even think about that," I muttered, but moved closer to examine it.

It looked like nothing special. Just a wooden post with short outcroppings that I'd taken for hooks. It was also covered in various stains I was trying not to think about. But when I reached out to touch it, carefully picking somewhere that looked to be too high for Giint to have reached and triggering my Essence Sight ability…

"Holy fuck." I jerked my hand back, covering my eyes as they were nearly burned from my head. The thing literally shook with divine energy.

"What is it?" Lydia asked.

"It's…" I deactivated the Essence Sight and reached out again, more carefully this time. The moment my fingers made contact, I felt it, and I didn't know how the hell I'd not felt it before.

It was a divine artifact, that much was clear. Whatever it was, it'd been formed into this shape, constrained to be solid in this realm, and…

"It's aware," I breathed. "This thing is sentient, and it's been stuck here watching… Oh gods, Giint, what did you do to it?"

"Many things!" Giint said proudly. "Giint very creative when high! One time, Giint bent over and—"

"STOP!" I commanded. "Oh, gods no. Just…stop. I don't need details."

"You ask," he pointed out reproachfully, clearly not happy that I would not let him relay the depths of his depravity.

I focused on the artifact, trying to communicate with it. What I got back was the magical equivalent of desperate screaming and demands for bleach.

"You poor bastard," I murmured sympathetically. "Don't worry, we're getting you out of here."

"Boss?" Lydia prompted. "What is it?"

"It's what we've been looking for," I said slowly, pieces clicking into place. "A divine tether point. This is what we've been looking for; it's connected to the library. The Library of Souls has some kind of physical anchor in our realm, and this is one of them. It has to be. I mean, fuck's sake, it's full of divine energy at least."

"You mean Giint found it by accident while high off his ass?" Arrin asked incredulously.

"Giint hero!" the gnome declared, holding his hands up, clearly expecting to be high-fived…then bent over and noisily threw up again.

"We need to get this back to Tenandra," I decided. "Carefully. And someone get Giint some clothes. And a bath. Several baths."

"Giint no need bath! Giint natural musk attractive to—"

"BATHS. PLURAL," I growled, glaring at him.

As we carefully cleared away the base of the artifact—trying to touch as little of the surface as possible—I couldn't help but shake my head. Of course this was how we'd find it. Not through careful searching or brilliant deduction, but because a drug-addled gnome decided to have creative sex with random furniture.

"The poor thing's traumatized," I muttered, feeling waves of distress from the artifact.

"It's traumatized?" Ronin laughed. "What about us? We're the ones who had to see naked Giint!"

"Giint body temple!" the gnome protested. "Very sexy temple!"

"Yer temple smells like shit an' it looks like it's been cursed," Lydia told him.

"Fuck's sake," I muttered as I realized it was literally locked into place in the carved base of the tree. Removing it might actually break it, or who knew what, which meant that we were all going to be spending a lot of time in this room for a bit.

"Wake them up and get rid of them." I gestured vaguely to the still slumbering and drugged-up other participants in Giint's 'experimentation', before making a decision.

"I need cleaning supplies, and this room needs to be scrubbed within a fucking inch of its life," I ordered. "Lydia, go find out whoever owns this building and buy it. Now."

"Aye." She nodded to me, before turning to Yen. "Yen, yer know t'city better than me. Any ideas?"

"I can do it," Grizz said.

"Yer sure?" Lydia glanced over to him.

"I saw the madam of the place running for it earlier. Give me Tang, and we'll get her back."

"She might be long gone," Yen pointed out.

"Nah, she'll be somewhere close enough she can keep an eye on the building." He grinned. "My bet is the tavern at the end of the street."

"There's a coffee shop above the tailors." Tang spoke up, grinning. "I'm betting on there."

"That's because you saw her enter it," Bane pointed out.

"Dammit, I was going to get Grizz to bet push-ups!" Tang groaned. "You wait until he's agreed to it before you drop that in, you idiot."

I ignored the group as the good-natured squabbling carried on, with people moving quickly to deal with the issues.

One of which was that wherever the group had come from, they'd apparently not started in here. There were a lot of random bits and bobs piled around the room: a broken table, damaged chairs, old rugs that looked to have been stained beyond repair…that kinda stuff.

What there wasn't, though, and it was very noticeable, was any form of clothing.

The kitsune seemed epically unbothered, as she woke and stretched languidly, going so far as to ask Giint whether he arranged this, and whether she was going to be 'punished' again.

Lydia growled something and chased her out of the room, while Yen spoke quietly to the high elf, offering her a shirt from her bag, and apparently giving some badly needed advice to the woman.

The goblin was the most confused, and quickly made a break for freedom—bare-arse naked, sprinting down the street—as it wasn't apparently one of the more intelligent variants, like Greg or Cleq.

Instead, it was one of the feral mass-murdering kind. As it ran into the local guard, both sides panicked, as clearly, the guards had no clue there were any goblins in the area.

Fucking Giint.

I was almost impressed.

Either way, though, word spread quickly. By the time we'd cleared the room out and Jian had summoned Tenandra, half the council was hanging around the tiny whorehouse as well, moving aside only reluctantly when two of the golems arrived at my call and started to decontaminate the room.

"Is it true?" Thessarian asked excitedly. "You found the library?"

"Yes and no. I think it's an anchor point for the library, and Giint found it," I corrected. "While high. And had sex with it."

"He had…" The older elf blinked and tried to process this apparent non-sequitur.

"Yeah. It's kinda been a weird morning." I forced a smile.

"I…see." He clearly didn't. "But it will lead us to the library?"

"Once we figure out how to activate it properly, yes. But first, we need to help it recover from its ordeal."

"Recover?" Tisan asked.

"It's at least partially aware, and divine," I explained. "And it's been stuck in this…establishment…for who knows how long. Watching things. Terrible things. Giint things."

"Giint things very good!" the gnome protested, now wearing a makeshift toga we'd fashioned from a tablecloth.

"That's the problem." I sighed.

Tenandra's reaction when she touched the artifact was immediate. "Oh, you poor thing." Her avatar actually looked sympathetic. "The things you must have seen…"

The artifact pulsed weakly; a thread of mana flowed out and around before dying away and conveying what could only be described as desperate agreement.

"Can you communicate with it?" I asked. "Ask it questions, I mean?"

"Given time, yes. But it needs…well, like you said, it needs to recover first. The trauma is extensive."

"Great." I rubbed my temples. "We need to find a therapist for a divine artifact that's been sexually assaulted by a gnome."

"Giint no assault!" the gnome asserted. "Artifact never say no!"

"IT'S A COATRACK!" multiple people shouted at once.

"Sexy coatrack," Giint countered, unrepentant.

I looked at the artifact, feeling its continued distress. We'd found our key to the library, but at what cost? The poor thing would probably need years of therapy to recover from whatever Giint had done to it.

"Right," I decided. "Tenandra, try to help it recover. Everyone else, get back to work and help Tenandra as much as possible to get her body back in order. I bet that while she helps me with the artifact, she's not going to be able to do both jobs. Once it's ready, we'll activate the connection and finally get access to the Library of Souls. I hope."

"And Giint?" Lydia asked.

I looked at the gnome, who was now trying to flirt with one of the servitor golems.

"Gets a bath. And then we never speak of this again."

"Giint legend!" he declared, turning around and beaming at everyone. "Giint find important thing with power of love!"

"That wasn't love—that was drugs and poor decisions."

"Sometimes same thing!"

I couldn't even argue with that. As the group got back to work—and Tang confirmed that the whorehouse had been bought, which clearly annoyed at least two of the council members, who I was willing to bet had been planning to do the same thing—I couldn't help but think that this was definitely going in the history books. The sacred anchor to the divine Library of Souls, found because a gnome got high and got frisky with furniture.

Oracle was going to laugh her ass off when I told her this story.

Even if our divine artifact needed therapy first.

Fucking gnomes.

CHAPTER THIRTY-TWO

I pulled my hand back from the artifact for what felt like the hundredth time. The divine energy was there, I could feel it, but trying to access it was like trying to have a wank wearing boxing gloves.

It was sort of possible, but it really wasn't working for me.

"Perhaps if you tried a different approach?" Tenandra suggested gently. Her avatar sat cross-legged beside the artifact, one translucent hand resting on its surface as she worked to ease its trauma, somehow. "Less force, more finesse?"

"I've tried finesse. I've tried force. I've tried asking nicely." I slumped back against the wall of what was now the cleanest former whorehouse in existence. The golems had scrubbed every surface three times, and I'd personally incinerated anything that couldn't be cleaned. "Hell, I even tried bribing it."

"With what?" Arrin asked from where he was taking notes, probably hoping if he found one, he'd be able to ascend as well.

"Promised I'd never let Giint near it again," I admitted.

"That's not a bribe…that's basic fuckin' decency," Lydia pointed out.

The artifact pulsed weakly, sending out what I was recognizing as its version of agreement. Poor thing was still traumatized as hell, but at least it was communicating in basic concepts now.

"Maybe we need more power?" Ronin suggested. "Like, channel more mana into it?"

"It's not about power." I shook my head. "There's something…blocking me. Like there's a lock on it, but I can't even find the keyhole."

I'd been at this for three hours now. Three frustrating, increasingly annoying hours of trying everything I could think of to activate the damn anchor. Nothing worked. The divine energy was there, teasing me, but I couldn't access it. I could feel it reacting to my own, but each time I reached out, it was like…it was like it didn't know how to do this either, and everything I was trying was completely new to it.

"Fuck it." I sighed as I stood up, my decision made. "I'm calling in help."

"The council?" Tisan asked hopefully. He'd been hovering nearby, clearly eager to see the library accessed, as the others had gradually drifted away. "You'll permit them to access the divine…"

"Fuck no. Higher up than that." I snorted. "No offense, Tisan, but I don't think this is something you can do without divine power, and them attempting to access it without that is like juggling Molotov cocktails in a gunpowder factory. It's just not gonna end well." Instead, I closed my eyes and reached out with my mind. *"Jenae? I could really use some guidance here."*

The response was immediate, as if She'd been waiting for the invitation. The temperature in the room spiked twenty degrees; shadows danced despite there being no change in the light sources, and suddenly She was there. Not just as a presence in my mind, but physically manifested in the room, as She stepped through the wall and smiled at me.

"Well." Jenae looked around, taking in the scrubbed walls, the nervous observers, and the artifact in the corner. *"This is certainly not where I expected to find a divine anchor."*

"My goddess." Everyone dropped to their knees, including Tisan and two of the other wood elves who'd been observing.

"Oh, get up." She waved dismissively. *"I'm not here for worship. I'm here because my Chosen is having difficulties with what should be a simple task."*

"Simple?" I asked incredulously. "I've been trying for hours!"

"Yes, I noticed." She moved closer to the artifact, circling it slowly. *"That's interesting. Very interesting."*

"What is?" I asked grumpily, trying not to show how much that "you're an idiot" reference had annoyed me.

"I can feel it now." She reached out, not quite touching the surface. *"A faint echo, barely there. But only because I'm physically present and you've been hammering at it for hours. Before that?"* She shook Her head. *"Nothing. It was completely hidden from divine senses."*

"Hidden how?"

"That's the interesting part." She turned to face me. *"This wasn't hidden by accident or age. This must have been deliberately concealed from gods. All gods."*

"Why would someone hide a divine anchor from the gods?" Arrin asked, then immediately looked like he regretted speaking.

Jenae smiled at him. *"An excellent question. The answer is less so. I would assume it was to prevent us from interfering. The gods, I mean. This was deliberately hidden from us. Probably because, I suspect, it contains a divine fragment. Whoever created this wanted to ensure that if it was found, it could only be by a mortal, most likely to prevent any other god from taking it."*

I suddenly noticed the way She stood, the way Her fingers twitched and curled, and the way She kept back from it after a single touch.

She was either afraid of it, or She was desperately holding herself back from diving on it. "Fuck," I muttered, as the memory came crashing in, the way the gods could be around fragments, and how desperate they were to consume them. I'd just invited Her to an all-you-can-eat buffet and She was starving, but trying to restrain herself.

"Sorry, Jenae. I understand if you want to leave," I offered, and She shook Her head.

"I will, but not until we've figured this out, partly at least. Your own divine fragments should have been enough; that it's not been so means that this was crafted deliberately to refuse that," She replied. *"In fact, it's probably the only reason you can sense it at all. But you're trying to open it like a god would, with pure divine will. That won't work here."*

"So how do I open it?"

"By understanding what it is." She gestured for me to come closer. *"This isn't just an anchor, Jax. It's a test. A safeguard. Whoever built this must have been trying to make sure that anyone accessing the Library of Souls understood what they were getting into."*

"Great, another fucking test," I muttered. "As if I haven't had enough of those."

"This one's different," She assured me. **"Touch the artifact again, but this time, don't try to dominate it. Reach out with your fragments instead. Let them communicate."**

I moved back to the artifact, placing my hand on its surface. The traumatized consciousness within recoiled slightly, but didn't pull away entirely.

"Now," Jenae instructed, **"instead of pushing your will onto it, let your fragments go silent and instead speak to what's hidden within."**

I closed my eyes and did as She said. Instead of trying to force my way in, I let my fragments—Order, Death, Chaos—show themselves, and then fall silent.

And then I felt it. The other fragment, hidden within the artifact itself, responded slowly. It reached out, felt the fragments, and then seemed to relax when it didn't feel anything else.

"I can feel it," I breathed. "It's…it's what's powering the concealment."

"Very good." Jenae sounded pleased. **"Now, communicate with it. Fragment to fragment."**

I let my fragments reach out more fully, and suddenly I understood. The fragment within wasn't just powering the concealment—it was the consciousness I'd been sensing. The trauma wasn't just from being turned into furniture; it was from being bound into this form and then subjected to Giint's…creativity, after it'd presumably climbed its way to sentience over thousands upon thousands of years.

Trapped here.

"Hello." I sent the thought gently. *"I'm here to help."*

The response was immediate and desperate. A scream of horror, fear, and fuck me, there was a lot of disgust, as well as a desire to die in a fire.

"Yeah, I know," I interrupted quickly. *"I'm really sorry about that. But I can free you now, if you'll let me."*

The voice became more focused, less mindless horror and more "what the fuck, dude," though without words. There was still a desperate need for fire, though.

"It's okay," I pushed out, along with a firm agreement that the entire building and possibly the city attached needed to be fumigated and a full hazmat team called in. *"I'm here to access the library,"* I pushed out toward it. In a heartbeat, the entire world seemed to fade away, leaving only me and the traumatized thing floating in the middle of a dim room.

"And I need to not be furniture anymore." The fragment's tone was decidedly bitter. *"Do you know what it's like being aware but unable to move for centuries? And then when someone finally finds you, they…they…"*

"Giint happened," I finished, wincing. *"I know. I'm sorry. But I can offer you something better now. Join me."*

There was a long pause. *"You'd take me in? Even broken? Even though you have no Fragments of Blood?"*

Blood. I'd never even considered that there was a God of Blood, though the fragments were all from specific ideals or whatever originally, so that meant that somewhere out there, there had to have once been nine more Fragments of Blood. I paused, a little weirded out by adding something of blood that wasn't my own. Then I shook myself and responded honestly.

"I need all the help I can get," I told it candidly. *"And you deserve better than being stuck as furniture."*

The fragment pulsed, considering.

"Or, you know, I could leave you here with Giint…"

A heartbeat later, the concealment shattered. The artifact glowed; divine energy poured out as the fragment freed itself from its prison. As it did so, the wall behind it started to twist and shift, warping to reveal a panel of what looked like polished onyx.

"Extraordinary," Jenae murmured. ***"I didn't expect it to respond so readily."***

The fragment coalesced before me, a sphere of crimson energy that pulsed like a heartbeat. Before Jenae could move, it'd lanced across the space between us and stabbed into me, sinking into my chest like a dagger, aimed for my heart.

I staggered, gasping, hand coming up and feeling…my bare, untouched skin.

My top was ruined—fuck's sake, *again*—but my flesh underneath felt unbroken and smooth, if a little sensitive.

Inside me now, out of reach of Jenae and any other watching gods, I could sense its nature…Blood, with all that entailed: memories, lineages, the ability to manipulate the life force that flowed through all living things.

It was life and power rolled into one, as well as *pain.*

Congratulations!

You have taken your fourth step on the path to Godhood, but where will you end up? As you evolve, each fragment attunes to you, and you to it, your powers, currently dormant, adjust, spread and evolve with you. Who and what will you become. As more fragments are claimed, and your dominion clarifies, you must choose, will you specialize into a single role, growing your path into a narrow but powerful one, or generalize.

Many of the Fragments of Divinity that you accept come with abilities to choose from, and the Fragment of Blood is no exception. Choose carefully, for this choice cannot be undone, and until the choice is made, the fragment, and your soul, are open to the UnderVerse.

Sanguine Mastery: Control the blood within yourself and others, shaping it into weapons, shields, or tools of your will. Blood becomes your servant, responding to your command whether still flowing in veins or spilled upon the ground. Note: Living beings can resist this control with sufficient will or magical protection. The stronger the target, the more mana required to overcome their natural defenses.

Charge: Mana cost varies by complexity and resistance

Crimson Recall: Read the memories carried within blood, accessing the history and experiences of any creature that has bled. Each drop contains echoes of its owner's past, waiting to be unlocked, and souls, if connected to their spilled blood, may be linked to in specific circumstances. Note: Older blood holds fainter memories, and some memories may be protected by divine or magical means. Traumatic memories may backlash upon the reader.

Charge: 3 uses per 24 hours

Vitae Manipulation: Channel life force through blood, either draining vitality from enemies or transferring your own life energy to heal allies. The blood becomes a conduit for the very essence of life itself. Note: Draining life force from unwilling targets requires physical contact with their blood. Healing others depletes your own life force proportionally unless supplemented with mana.

Charge: Continuous use, limited by available life force and mana

I considered carefully. Sanguine Mastery was tempting—the ability to form weapons from my enemy's own fucking blood sounded awesome, but...

"Are you still there?" I directed at the fragment, and I could feel a faint acknowledgment, as the fragment faded into me. Its own rudimentary mind had subsumed into my own, meaning that it was now me who had fucking trauma from Giint, but I dismissed that. *"Are all the fragments blood?"* I asked, struck by a sudden suspicion.

When it agreed that all the anchors were, I cursed, but knew what I had to do.

Memories ingrained in blood, memories that would be right there when I needed them. I had a nasty suspicion that what I was going to find in the Library of Souls wasn't going to be rows upon rows of books that I needed to read. If the anchors were all blood fragments, well, that was a fucking hint right out in the open, wasn't it.

Crimson Recall it was, I decided.

The fragment pulsed approval and shifted, before flowing out and splitting into me deeper. The integration differed from the others—where Order had been structured, Death cold, and Chaos wild, Blood was...alive? I could feel every drop of blood in my body, in the bodies around me.

It felt...wrong. Weaker than it should be. And I knew why instinctively. For the others, I'd bound them in places where their mana was in abundance—death mana for the death fragment and so on—but here? There was virtually no blood and I'd still bound it, resulting in a weak-ass result. Fuck's sake.

I shook it off and got on with it. It wasn't as if I had a fucking choice, after all. I took a deep breath and focused on what I could feel.

I could sense the thundering of my own heartbeat, and I staggered, closing my eyes, even as more notifications surged up.

I cut the kill one off; the details of the fights just weren't important right now, not compared to divine fucking details. I pulled up the next one.

Jez Cajiao

Congratulations!

**Through hard work and perseverance,
you have increased your stats by the following:**

Agility +10

Charisma +10

Constitution +10

Dexterity +10

Endurance +10

Intelligence +10

Luck +10

Perception +10

Strength +10

Wisdom +10

Continue to train and learn to increase this further.

Congratulations!

**You have made progress in a Quest given by the God Sint: Divine Is as
Divine Does**

*The God of Light, Sint, has entirely given up on offering reasonable advice,
but agrees that you have at least reached the minimum levels for this quest
now and instead wishes you good luck.*

**Seek out and acquire fragments of divinity, aiding you in both your
ascension of the Crystal Steps to the Imperial Throne and to Godhood.**

Seek out and harvest fragments of divinity from those who hold them: 4/10

**Reward: True immortality, Ascension to Godhood, 5,000,000xp per
fragment**

Congratulations!

You have reached level 55.

You have 7 unspent Attribute points and 1 Meridian points available.

Progress to level 55 stands at 3,145,773/15,000,000

*

Congratulations!

You have achieved your first century in Endurance through point allocation. As such, you have gained a new Ability!

<u>Adamantine Constitution</u>: Your flesh has evolved beyond mortality, becoming nearly indestructible when channeled properly. Upon activation, your skin, bones, and organs temporarily transmute into a living adamantine-like substance, granting near-immunity to physical damage. Blades shatter against your skin, impacts disperse harmlessly, and even internal organs become armored. You can selectively harden portions of your body or go full defensive mode.

<u>Passive Effect</u>: All physical damage reduced by 25%. Critical hits have only 50% chance to apply additional effects.

Note: While fully hardened, movement speed reduced by 50%. Magic damage bypasses this defense entirely.

Note: Extended use causes temporary muscle calcification, reducing Agility by 25% for one hour after deactivation.

<u>LEGENDARY ACHIEVEMENT</u>

You have achieved perfect centuries across all attributes, a feat accomplished by fewer than a dozen humanoids currently living, and as such you receive a new modifier to recognize this monumental achievement.

<u>Harmonic Convergence</u>: You may select a single attribute to double its attendant pool: Constitution-Health, Endurance-Stamina, Intelligence-Mana

<u>Passive Benefits</u>:

Immune to attribute drain or reduction below 75 (your "perfect floor")

Recovery rates (health/mana/stamina) increased by 100%

I didn't even hesitate as the world around me started to spin. That last one was a simple one to accept. Intelligence all the way. Five thousand plus mana? Fuck to the yes. There was no way I could resist doubling my manapool.

"Fuck." I gasped, steadying myself against the wall as my meridian choices floated before me as well. Despite feeling like I was about to vomit, or explode, I also decided that the best thing I could do would be to get all of this shit show over with as quickly as possible. So I slammed the seven points I'd gained into my Intelligence too, and then desperately shoved the meridian point into my stomach as well, leaving only my nose left to unlock, although the meridian system was probably massively redundant now as I worked to ascend to godhood.

As it faded, I forced my brain to stay active, even as my muscles writhed and an urgent need to redecorate the room swept through me.

I heard Lydia chasing everyone beyond Jenae out and sealing the room, and I felt the soothing pressure as Jenae blessed me with Her "Hearthfire" gift as well.

I forced the breaths in and out, barely able to keep myself upright, but holding on, pushing myself to focus on the meridian system. If I was willing to abandon the activation of all ten points, I could put them into things like my Constitution and increase that by ten points per point or…

PRIMARY

Brain: 1/10 Spell Cost Reduction: -5% (Primary Bonus: 1 spell slot per point.)
Head: Primary Node: Additional points invested will reduce mana cost by 5%.
(Note: Air Elemental Core results in increased mana regeneration by 50%, self-control decrease of 5%.)

SECONDARY

Eyes: 1/10 Vision Improvement (Secondary Bonus: +10% chance to notice important visual details.)
Eyes: Important details will glow to your vision. This will level with the relevant skill.

Ears: 1/10 Hearing Improvement
Ears: Important sounds will become clearer with concentration. High levels will aid in translation.

Mouth: 1/10 Vocal Improvement
Mouth: Your voice will become 10% more likely to have a desired effect on a target—soothing, seducing, persuading as required.

Nose: 0/10 Tracking and Detection Improvement
Nose: Scents will be stronger, aiding in tracking.

Heart: 1/10 Health Increase
Heart: You will gain an additional ten points of health for each point invested in your Constitution.

Lungs: 2/10 Stamina Increase
Lungs: You will gain an additional ten points of stamina for each point invested in your Endurance.

Stomach: 1/10 Sustenance Improvement
Stomach: You will gain the abilities to resist poisons by 5% and to gain sustenance from more sources.

Legs: 1/10 Speed Increase
Legs: You will gain a boost of 10% to your speed, as well as better stability over various terrain.
(Note: SporeMother Core results in a gain of 10% to your speed in darkness. Speed in daylight will be decreased by 20%.)

Arms: 1/10 Strength Increase
Arms: You will receive a boost of 25% to your carrying capacity and your damage output with melee weapons.

Hands: 1/10 Dexterity Increase
Hands: You will develop crafting abilities at a 10% increased rate, along with a greater chance to succeed in crafting complicated items.

I blinked as the pain faded, and realized that we'd killed a shitload of "big" monsters of late. Hell, I'd been sending Giint in to loot things for ages, and not once had I seen an essence core.

Admittedly, as busy as I'd been of late, I'd not been *looking* for them, but that wasn't the point. I'd not been gutting creatures since we killed them, not intentionally; I'd been too busy focusing on survival and Oracle, but dammit!

"Four fragments now."

Jenae broke my train of thought, and I forced myself to straighten, drawing in a ragged breath, and yeah, hitting myself with a Scour as my skin felt doused in filth after the purging of impurities that sometimes came with the century achievement.

"You're almost halfway to true godhood, Jax. Be careful. The more fragments you gather, the more attention you'll draw."

"From Xenefier?" I forced myself to ask.

Her expression darkened. *"Among others. Speaking of which, I still feel your rage over Oracle being taken."*

"Of course I'm fucking raging!" I snapped. "She's pregnant, kidnapped, and probably terrified, and you all act like it's some minor inconvenience!"

"I'm sorry, Jax. That was not what I meant. I simply mean that you must be focused, and calm."

"I'm focused," I growled. "Calm can go suck a bucket of dicks."

"Very well." She sighed. *"Jax, we do believe you will save her. But first, you need to finish what you've started here. The anchor is open—can you sense the way to the library?"*

I could. With the concealment gone and the fragment integrated, I could feel a pull. Not a physical direction, but something deeper. A connection to a space that existed between spaces, and it started at the panel of onyx in the corner.

"I can feel it," I confirmed. "There. Can't you feel it?"

"No, it's still concealed from me, but I suggest you try the same way you freed the fragment." Jenae smiled. *"Reach out with your will, but gently. The library apparently responds to those who have not yet ascended."*

"Okay, let's do this." I took a few deep breaths, then glanced over at Lydia, smiling a reassurance that I was okay. I stepped forward, placed my hand on the shiny rock, and reached out. This time, there was no resistance. Reality bent, twisted, and suddenly I was elsewhere.

The library was…so not what I expected.

I stood in a circular chamber, maybe thirty feet across. The walls were polished black onyx that seemed to absorb light while somehow still allowing me to see. The roof was made of the same stuff and curved around to mesh with the other sections seamlessly.

Mounted at regular intervals and hanging from the ceiling were copper bowls filled with blue flames that cast dancing shadows. The floor was the same black stone, polished to a mirror finish, making it feel like I was walking over a bottomless abyss.

But what really caught my attention were the books. Or rather, the fucking *lack* of them.

"This is it?" I said aloud, my voice echoing strangely. "This is the grand Library of Souls?"

There were maybe two dozen books in total, sitting on simple stone shelves carved directly from the walls. Each one looked ancient, bound in leather that had probably come from creatures I couldn't identify. But two dozen books? I had more than that on board fucking Tenandra!

"There has to be more," I muttered, moving to examine the texts.

I reached out, touching the soft, warm leather of one of the books and I felt…refused.

I sensed that this wasn't meant for me, not at all. It wasn't telling me to fuck off, it just…

It was like I'd picked up a private diary that Oracle had made, or one of my friends like Lydia. It felt personal, and definitely not for my eyes.

I tried to open it. It grew hot in my hand; a warning buzz filled my mind, with the impression of angry fire ants and my private areas, making it clear that, yeah, this book was more or less aware, and it really didn't want anything to do with me.

I decided that okay, maybe there was a reason. As soon as that crossed my mind, the anger faded, and a sort of "over there" sensation, like a nudge in the right direction, was given.

All right, I could work with that, I decided.

A handful of minutes later, and I was done, the entire room searched. Not a single fucking book wanted me to read it.

All of them had been directing me to the others, though.

"Okay, clearly magical, and not for me," I murmured aloud, getting a sense of relief from them all, one that made me consider that I should grab one and try to open it quick; the very air seemed to shiver with warning.

Instead, I explored the chamber, running my hands along the walls, looking for hidden doors or secret compartments. There had to be more. This couldn't be all of it.

As I searched, though, I slowly sensed something else. A presence, or maybe an absence? Like there was something missing from the room that should have been there.

Blood carries memories, the new fragment whispered in my mind. *Blood carries secrets.*

If there was a common theme to the fragments, to the reason that there were all blood fragments in the anchors, then it had to be something about blood. *Where was the blood?* That thought came with a sense of approval and almost a nudge again, though this time it was from all the books.

I stopped in the center of the room, looking down. There was a shallow depression in the floor I hadn't noticed before. Perfectly circular, maybe a foot across and only an inch deep. At first, I'd thought it was just wear from centuries of use, but now…

"A bowl," I said aloud. "For offerings? For light?"

I knelt beside it, scrutinizing it. And there, so faint I almost missed them, were stains. Dark brown, almost black against the dark stone. Old blood. Ancient blood.

Blood carries secrets, the fragment whispered again, more insistent.

"You fuckers want me to bleed into it," I said to myself, and yeah, it wasn't a question.

I drew my dagger, pricking my thumb, and then sighed. The tiny drop of blood that slowly beaded up wasn't going to do anything, was it?

Instead, I held my palm out and sliced across it, deep enough to see the fat and the bones that were exposed along with the flesh. The resulting gout of blood did the trick, even as I hit myself with a Heal, hissing over the pain.

Modern safety standards screamed at me about bleeding into random ancient artifacts, but fuck it. I'd come this far.

The blood hit the depression, and everything changed.

The blood didn't pool. Instead, it bubbled, boiled, then rose into the air. More blood appeared from nowhere—or maybe from the stains in the stone—washing backward and forward, rising into the air in streams that seemed weirdly sapient, joining mine until a finger formed of crimson hung in the air before me.

I reached out to touch it, and the world exploded.

It wasn't the blood.

It wasn't memories in the blood.

It was the soul that had once been linked to the blood. A tether to enable the soul of a god long since dead, and this was their memory. The magic of the soul compressed into a form that was easier to lock into place, then tethered to the blood that had been spilled here.

WITNESS. A voice that was a thousand voices spoke directly into my soul. *WITNESS AND UNDERSTAND*.

I was no longer in the library. I was…elsewhere. Watching events that had happened so long ago that the stars themselves had changed position.

I saw gods. Not the current pantheon, but others. Dozens of them, gathered in a similar, though much larger chamber when it had been new. They were discussing something…*arguing*. And at the center of their discussion was a name that chilled me to my core.

Xenefier.

But they weren't talking about it as an unknown threat.

No, this was an old enemy. An ancient foe that had been faced before. Not once, not twice, but *dozens* of times across the eons.

"It returns," one of the gods said, a huge elf-looking being, with longer arms than seemed normal, sharply slanted eyes that glowed with gold, and veins that stood out against dull skin with ribbons of ruby, his voice heavy with exhaustion. "As it always does. As it always will."

"Then we face it!" another demanded, this time willowy and graceful, though clearly angry. "As we always have. As we always will."

"And if we fall? How many times must I say this!" a third asked, short and dark like midnight, her eyes glowing like fresh banked coals. "What of those who come after? Too many of us fall each time we face it. The knowledge lost takes too long to regain!"

"Then we prepare for that eventuality," the first god decided. "We leave them tools. Knowledge. Power. Everything they need to face the Unending Hunger when it rises again. And should we succeed, then we can recover the fragments, and everyone wins."

"You know our brethren—they'll steal them! How many have refused to aid us, hoping to snatch at crumbs when some of us fall!" the fourth snapped, a creature that stood rail thin, wrapped in a cloak of stars with pinprick, glowing eyes that stared out of a hood of shadows.

"This is why we hide them. We use fragments to hide it all from any of our kin, and reveal themselves only when it rises again. When the first anchor point falls to it, then the others will release, and they will know."

"But they'll ignore it and fight over the fragments!" another screamed. "You weaken us right when we need to be at our strongest! I won't do it!"

"I will," came a new voice, one that tugged at the edge of my memories, but in my confused state I couldn't identify it. "I will guide it. I will lay the breadcrumbs of fate before one with the strength to walk the path, though it shall bring me low, my brothers, and cost me long eons of suffering…"

The vision shifted. I saw them creating this place, and others like it. Six locations, six anchors—each one holding a fragment of divine power. Each of them collapsed, broken, as they sundered their souls, breaking a fragment free and binding the library's entrances with them. But more than that… I saw their *plan*.

"The libraries will be hidden from gods," they decided. "Only mortals or those still ascending can find them. That way, if we fall, others can rise to take our place."

"And the fragments?"

"Six of us will go to face Xenefier directly. If we fall, and before we go, we bind our fragments to that place. Sealed away, waiting for one strong enough to claim them, instead of releasing their power. If we're going to fail, we release all our power and seal the chamber of horrors it calls its home.

"We sacrifice *everything* to seal it, to seal the fragments of our souls and our powers, ready to be recovered by a successor, and we do it so that only a mortal can achieve it before the anchors unlock."

"That's forty-eight fragments," another calculated. "Plus the six in the anchors, and four more hidden in the true library. Fifty-eight fragments of divine power, enough to create five strong new gods to face the threat, on top of the gods who will already be risen."

"And the location?"

"Hidden behind shields that even the other gods cannot breach. Accessible only through the throne portal itself, and only to one who is yet mortal, but has claimed the other fragments first."

The vision faded, but not before I saw two of the gods step forward.

"We will expend half our power to create the prison," they said in unison. "To ensure the fragments remain until they're needed."

"Your sacrifice will be remembered," the others promised.

And then I was back in the library, gasping, on my knees, with blood running from my nose as the power of the place roiled and surged.

It wasn't *mana*.

Mana I could have handled. No, this was worse, so much fucking worse, as I saw the truth of their memories, of the souls of the fucking gods who had been willing to give up *everything* to enable more gods to rise in the future to face Xenefier, if they failed this time around to kill it fully.

"Fuck." I wheezed. "Fuck, fuck, fuck."

The memories had confirmed everything. Xenefier wasn't just some random cosmic horror. It was a recurring nightmare, something that rose again and again across the ages. And each time, more and more of the gods fell trying to stop it.

Each time, it recovered some of their fragments as well. They knew this, knew it couldn't use them; it was burned by them and injured, weakened. But in capturing and locking the fragments away, it ensured that there were less and less gods rising each time to face it.

As a counter to this plan, they literally set themselves up to die if need be. They'd done it in such a way that they were facing the fucker weakened before the fight, making it even more likely that they'd fail…

But they'd *planned* for their failure. They'd left a road map to power, hidden in places only mortals could find. The six anchors, each with a fragment. The four fragments hidden in the true Library of Souls. And, should they fall? Forty-eight fragments more, waiting in Xenefier's prison.

Fifty-eight fragments in total. Enough to create multiple gods, or…one incredibly powerful one.

One god who could rise in the heart of their enemy's power, one god who would come from mortal means, who would ascend in a heartbeat of frozen time as all those fragments were bound into its soul, into its immortal shell.

A single god, a single entity that…

This was what I had to do. If the empire was big enough, if enough of the continents were bound to me, if enough people were funneling their power into the imperial throne, then I could ascend from that alone. I could…

I saw it all: the individual lines of possibility, the lines that had been laid down in my past, the twisting of the rules, the hints and side comments, the need to ensure I didn't ascend before the time was right, and…and…fuck me.

Even the Arbiter, even FATE ITSELF was allowing this… No, it wasn't *allowing* it; it was fucking setting this up! It was making sure it fucking happened because there was a single chance for a god to face Xenefier as it rose.

I needed to be there. I'd needed the incentive, and the fragments ready, but not active, not in hand, not…shit.

My mind boggled as all the tiny hints and details slid into place. The great game of the gods, how they'd been manipulated by the Arbiter, how I'd been led by the fucking nose to this place—all of it made sudden sense, as did the reason it was willing to put me in the position to take it all.

It wasn't because I was "a good man" or the "chosen one" or any such bullshit.

No, it was because I was an absolute bastard. I was mean and violent. I had a heart that, without her, was as hard as a rock. I would do whatever I had to do, to protect and save her—no, *them.*

It was willing to risk it all to let me ascend to be the overgod, because it knew, balls to bones, that if it did, if I had all that power in my grasp, the one thing I could be relied upon to do was absolutely anything I had to do, to protect the woman and child I loved.

I would do anything to destroy Xenefier, and that…that was what they needed.

The gods were too far removed from the drive of mortality, but a mortal who ascended on the day with a family to protect? That…that would do it.

And the key to it all was in Dai'Amaranth, I saw suddenly. The imperial throne *itself* was a portal, but one that would only work for someone still partly mortal. Once I was fully divine, it would be closed to me—to that location, at least, because the gods had other ways to move across the realms.

"Clever bastards," I muttered, struggling to my feet. "Make sure whoever goes after the big prize has to commit before they're fully powered up."

I looked around the library with new understanding. This wasn't the real Library of Souls. This was just an anchor point, a taste of what was available. The real library was elsewhere, probably in a pocket dimension accessible only through the anchors.

But first, I needed to release the other anchors. Five more fragments waiting out there, five more pieces of the puzzle. And then…

Then I'd have to make a choice: go after the forty-eight fragments in Xenefier's prison while I was still vulnerable, or ascend fully first and give up that power forever—and, more importantly, the chance to rescue Oracle.

"No choice at all," I said to the empty room. "Oracle needs me to be strong enough to save her. That means getting everything I can."

I memorized the locations the memories had shown me. Six anchors total—I had one. Five more to find. Then the true library, then Dai'Amaranth, then…

Then I'd be strong enough to face anything. Strong enough to burn the realm to the bedrock and rebuild it after I'd slaughtered Xenefier.

But first, I had to get out of here and explain to everyone what I'd learned.

It was time to get to work.

CHARACTER SHEET

Name: Jax Amon				
Title: Godslayer				
Class: Mage Imperator (Fire Focus)			**Renown**: Imperial Scion, Prince of Dravith, Master of Himnel, Narkolt and Gaij, Godslayer, Mage Imperator	
Level: 55			**Progress**: 3,145,773/16,000,000	
Patron: Jenae, Goddess of Fire and Exploration			**Points to Distribute**: 0 **Meridian Points to Invest**: 0	
Stat	**Current points**	**Description**	**Effect**	**Progress to next level**
Agility	130	Governs dodge and movement	+1300% maximum movement speed and reflexes. Gained: Temporal Fluidity	N/A
Charisma	110 (105)	Governs likely success to charm, seduce, or threaten	+110% success chance in interactions with other beings. Gained: Imperial Gravitas	N/A
Constitution	155 (143)	Governs health and health regeneration	3100 health, regen 400 points per 600 seconds (each point invested now worth 20 health). Gained: Genetic Storage	N/A
Dexterity	130	Governs ability with weapons and crafting success	+130% to weapon proficiency, +130% to the chances of crafting success. Gained: Master Craftsman's Touch	N/A
Endurance	105 (99)	Governs stamina and stamina regeneration	3015 stamina, regen 150 points per 30 seconds (each point invested now worth 30 stamina). Gained: Adamantine Constitution	N/A

Intelligence	233	Governs base mana and number of spells able to be learned	4860 mana, spell capacity: N/A (+200 mana from items x2 modifier). Gained: Hyper Cognition & Mana Manipulation	N/A
Luck	110	Governs overall chance of bonuses	+110% chance of a favorable outcome. Gained: Fortune's Mockery	N/A
Perception	120 (110)	Governs ranged damage and chance to spot traps or hidden items	+120% ranged damage, +120% chance to spot traps or hidden items. Gained: Essence Sight	N/A
Strength	121 (118)	Governs damage with melee weapons and carrying capacity	+121 damage with melee weapons, +121% maximum carrying capacity. Gained: Titan's Resolve	N/A
Wisdom	135 (125)	Governs mana regeneration and memory	+1650% mana recovery, 40 points per minute. Gained: Mana Manipulation	N/A

CHAPTER THIRTY-THREE

Reality twisted again, and suddenly I was back in the cleaned-up whorehouse, surrounded by anxious faces. I must have looked like shit, because Lydia was at my side immediately, the others back in the room as well.

"Jax! Yer all right?" she asked. "What 'ell 'appened in there?"

"I found it." My voice came out rougher than expected. "The library. Or at least, part of it."

"Part of it?" Jenae asked, and I realized She'd stayed to watch. That was…unusual for Her.

"The anchor points aren't the real library," I explained, accepting a healing potion from Arrin and downing it. Despite hitting myself with a Heal earlier, I still felt…off. "They're…fuck, how do I explain this? They're like sample rooms. Teasers. The real Library of Souls is elsewhere, accessible through the anchors once you have enough of them."

"How many?" Thessarian asked eagerly.

"Six of them in total. This is one." I gestured to the now-empty artifact. "Five more are out there somewhere."

"And each one has a fragment?" Jenae's eyes narrowed. *"That's not possible. We would have sensed—"*

"You wouldn't." I interrupted. "They're designed to be hidden from gods. All gods, by ancient gods. Only mortals or those still ascending can find them." I looked at Her meaningfully. "It's a safeguard."

"Against what?"

"Against gods who might fail," I said bluntly. "Look, I need to tell you all something, and it's going to sound insane."

"More insane than finding a divine artifact because Giint fucked it?" Ronin asked.

"Okay, yeah, fair point, I didn't see that coming. And I wish I didn't have the memory of him… Anyway." I took a deep breath. "Xenefier isn't 'new.' It hasn't come a 'few' times before like you thought. The gods who made these anchors…they'd faced it over and over. Dozens, maybe *hundreds* of times. It's ancient, older than any of the current pantheons, and it keeps coming back."

The room went silent. Even Jenae looked shocked at the revelation of how long the cycle must have been going on for.

"That's not possible," She said finally. *"We would know. The records—"*

"The records are gone." I cut her off. "Each time Xenefier rises, loads of the gods die fighting it. I think it's been actively destroying the records each time it rises as well. It's not like it thinks it's in any real danger, after all. It probably let itself be defeated a few times just to destroy the records and let you think you were safe. Each time, new gods rise to take their place. It's a cycle, going back…fuck, I don't even know how long. Tens of thousands of years? Millions? The stars were in different positions in the vision."

"Vision?" Jenae asked.

"Blood can carry memories," I explained. "The fragment I absorbed was Blood. It let me access memories stored in the library. Memories of the gods who created it."

I explained what I'd seen—the gathering of gods, their resignation to their eventual defeat, their plan to leave power for those who came after. By the time I finished, everyone looked stunned.

"Forty-eight fragments," Jenae whispered hungrily. *"They sealed forty-eight fragments in one location?"*

"In Xenefier's prison," I confirmed. "Or what they hoped would be its prison. Spent half the power of two gods just to create shields around it. Shields that even full gods can't penetrate."

"And the only way in?" She asked desperately.

I winced, knowing that She and Her brothers and sisters were going to be searching for it now.

"I need to pass through the imperial throne in Dai'Amaranth," I said. "But only while I'm still partly mortal. Once I fully ascend, that path closes forever, and it leads to a portal somewhere else, far away," I lied. I had no fucking clue, really, but it might keep the gods off my back. Fuck, I should have thought about this!

"That's insane," Arrin said. "You'd be walking into Xenefier's stronghold while still vulnerable?"

"That's the point," I replied absently. "If an ascended god takes the fragments, they'll take anywhere from years to centuries to absorb and integrate the power due to their divine form. I'd need to absorb all the fragments and bind them all instantly. I can carry them until the time comes. But when I have them all and I bind them at once, then I'll form my divine shell, and my power will…what?" I looked at Jenae, who nodded that I was right.

"When your shell forms, when your soul is complete, you won't be able to add more without serious repercussions. But this, Jax…" She shook Her head in disbelief. *"This changes everything,"* Jenae said softly. *"If Xenefier truly is eternal, recurring…we're not fighting to end a threat. We're just fighting to delay it."*

"No. That's the point," I disagreed. "That's what the gods had been doing. Instead, they decided it was better to bring about the Overgod, to give up their fragments and set up the path to follow to enable one to rise who could and would do anything to defeat Xenefier. That's why the Arbiter allowed Baphomet to set up the situation with Oracle. That's why all this came about."

"What?" Lydia stared at me, confused. "Jax, ah can't hear yer?"

I glanced around the room, and saw that nobody could hear me, beyond Jenae, who saw it as well.

"They can't hear it all, but it makes sense," She admitted, clearly conflicted. She wanted the fragments for herself, but She could see the problems if She tried to take them.

"The other anchors," Thessarian said urgently, apparently thinking that was the most important thing. "Where are they?"

I closed my eyes, accessing the memories the blood had shared. Locations flashed through my mind, but they were old. Ancient. The geography had changed; cities had risen and fallen.

"One's in what used to be the Shattered Peaks," I said slowly. "Maybe a week's flight northwest. Another's in the hidden city of the high elves back on Dravith, or I think it is. The third is in the desert where I fucking arrived on the continent, or near enough, far to the northwest. The fourth..." I frowned. "The fourth is on an island to the east, waaay to the east. And the fifth..."

"Where?" Lydia prompted.

"The fifth is to the south, right slap-bang in the middle of the lands that were destroyed by the fucking moon's impact, so there's a good chance that's destroyed..."

"Of course it is." She sighed. "Because nothin' can ever be easy."

"No," Jenae said firmly. ***"They will be intact. Nothing that is this important will be left to chance. The Arbiter will have ensured a path to success, even if it seems as thin as a razor in the dark."***

"Wait." Flux spoke up. "You said six anchors total. You've listed five locations plus this one. But you also said there are four fragments in the true library?"

"Yeah." I nodded. "Once I have all six anchors, I can access the true Library of Souls. That's where the real knowledge is, and four more fragments. Then, with the ten fragments total, I'd be able to enter Xenefier's prison through the throne."

"Where you'd face a cosmic horror while still mortal," Jenae added. ***"This is madness."***

"This is the only way," I countered. "Those gods knew what they were doing. They'd faced Xenefier before, knew how powerful it was. If they thought this was the best way to prepare someone to fight it..."

"Then we trust their judgment," Thessarian finished. "The wood elves will support your quest for the anchors, Prince Jax."

"As will the mer," Flux added.

"An' t'empire," Lydia said. "Though yer not doin' this alone."

"Some parts I'll have to," I warned. "The visions were clear—only one person can enter Xenefier's prison at a time. The throne won't activate for groups."

"Then we get you to t'throne," she said. "After that...we'll figure it out."

I looked around the room at my friends, my allies, even Jenae. They all processed this in their own ways, but I could see the determination setting in. We had a path forward now. Dangerous as fuck, probably suicidal, but a path.

"There's one more thing," I said reluctantly. "The blood showed me something else. The reason only six gods went to face Xenefier directly wasn't because the others were cowards. It was because they were preparing for what came after."

"What do you mean?" Jenae asked.

"They knew they'd lose," I said. "So while six went to fight and die, the others prepared these anchors, created the safeguards, made sure knowledge survived. They accepted their deaths to give the next generation a chance."

"Pragmatic," Flux observed.

"Fucking depressing," Ronin countered. "They just…gave up?"

"They were realistic," I corrected. "They'd seen it happen dozens of times before. Gods rising, fighting Xenefier, dying. New gods rising to take their place. Over and over. They just decided to make the transition easier."

"And now it's our turn," Jenae said quietly. *"We're the gods who have to face it this time."*

"No," I said, resolute. "We're the gods who are going to break the cycle. Because we have something they didn't."

"What's that?"

"Me." I grinned. "A half-mortal smartass with a chip on his shoulder and a pregnant girlfriend to save. I'm not planning to die and leave this mess for the next generation. I'm going to get those fragments, become powerful enough to make Xenefier shit itself, save Oracle, and then retire somewhere nice with a beach and get plenty of head."

"That's your plan?" Arrin asked. "Become a god and get more sex?"

"Best plan I've ever had." I snorted. "But seriously, can you imagine a single fucking driving force more likely to have me dedicated to it? I *will* save them, and if I have to tear the realm and all of reality apart to make sure they're safe, I fucking will.

"So, first step is that I need to get those anchors. Starting with the closest one— the Shattered Peaks."

"My body won't be ready for days," Tenandra said—she was still integrated with her body, undergoing upgrades. "Perhaps three days."

"Then we use that time to prepare," I decided. "Gather supplies, plan routes, maybe see if anyone knows anything about these locations. First step, I want that fucking map, Tenandra."

"Map?" she asked, confused.

"I need a goddamn portal," I clarified. "I need to get back to Dravith to get the anchor in the elven city, and we need reinforcements. You were right. We need everyone."

What I left unsaid was something that surged in my heart—a mixture of terror and relief.

All of this had been set up, incredibly carefully, I was willing to bet, and I was damn well sure that it'd been the Arbiter doing it. That meant that Oracle wouldn't be allowed to give birth, to fall, not yet. She was as safe as she could be, under the circumstances.

That was the relief. But the terror?

If a god who had spent literal millennia setting all of this up, decided that what I really needed as an incentive was to kill Oracle?

I'd not know until it was too late.

Fuck, I still needed to move, and move fast.

"I need those portal markers, Tenandra," I said as we got ready to return to her deck. The revelation about the anchors and the horrible thoughts about Oracle had lit a fire under my ass, and I wasn't about to slow down now. "How quickly will you be able to identify active portals with your new systems?"

"The integration is nearly complete." She looked tired but satisfied. "Perhaps another two days before I can begin scanning. I won't be able to just tell you from here where they are, but as we travel, the detection range should be—"

"Jax, this is for you and your advisors to deal with. The anchor issue is dealt with and I have to leave." Jenae interrupted, and I noticed She was already moving toward the nearest solid wall. *"I must depart. The other gods will have questions about what transpired here, and I need to..."* She paused, studying me. *"You've done well, Jax. Better than expected."*

"Thanks?" I said, not sure where this was going.

"You've discovered something important today. Not just the anchors, but another aspect of soul magic itself. Echoes of Memory." She smiled, and it was the kind of smile that made me nervous. *"The ability to access the memories of the dead through their blood...that's not a small thing."*

"I mean, it came with the fragment..."

"No." She shook her head. *"The fragment bound an echo of memory to the blood. You chose to use it in a way that revealed new truths. That deserves recognition."*

Before I could ask what She meant, She was gone. Just vanished between one blink and the next, leaving only the faint scent of woodsmoke and a noticeable drop in the ambient temperature.

"Well, that was fucking cryptic," I muttered, then froze as I felt something shift. Not physically, but in that weird magical sense that came from too much experience with the damn gods. Something had changed.

"Boss?" Lydia noticed my expression. "What's wrong?"

"Nothing," I lied as I pulled up my magical map, the one that had saved my ass more times than I could count. And there, glowing like a beacon in the middle of that fucking swamp we'd already passed over once, was a new marker.

A portal. Active and waiting. To the south.

"Nothing's wrong at all," I breathed, zooming in on the location. The marker sat in what looked like ruins, the city that I'd been told was responsible for all the undead in the area. But what made my blood run cold were the other markers converging on it.

Fragment bearers. Two of them, both heading for the same location. As I watched, the portal marker faded away as if it had never been. I could take a fucking hint, I decided, especially when I was beaten over the head with it.

"What is it?" Arrin crowded closer, trying to see.

"Ashen Heart." I read the name off the map. "A ruined city to the southwest." I looked up at the gathered group. "And it's about to have a pair of fragment bearers arriving for what I'm betting is a 'kill Jax' party."

"How many?" Flux asked, his tactical mind already working.

"Two." I showed him the map. "They're converging on it. They weren't when I looked at them before—they were to the east and north. Now they're getting closer to the city, so I'm betting that it's not because it's such a fucking wonderful tourist destination neither could pass it up."

I looked at the markers that Tenandra and the elves had added over the last few days by sharing details with me.

Ashen Heart was a city that fell over four hundred years ago. It'd been abandoned for a long time since then, right up until a lich moved in, and that was why the elves had pointed it out.

They'd done it with a certain level of fucking glee that said, *Hey, you're the boss—that makes this nearby city of the undead your problem now!*

"So, we go kill them first," Grizz said. "Problem solved."

"It's not that simple." I zoomed out, looking at the terrain. "Ashen Heart isn't just ruins. Tisan, is this the place you said was crawling with undead, and ruled by necromancers?"

"Sounds like a regular Tuesday." Lydia snorted. "When do we leave?"

I looked around at my people. They'd been running a lot of late, and they were tired. Sure, we'd been in the city for days, but we'd all also been searching the fucker from dawn 'til fucking dusk and beyond. We'd been going nonstop for weeks, and now I was asking them to charge into another massive fight. But I saw determination in their eyes, not exhaustion.

"Three days," I decided. "Tenandra needs to finish her upgrades, we need supplies, and I want to pick up some of our legionnaires on the way. Thessarian, can your people spare fifty guards for this?"

The elder wood elf had stayed to observe, and he nodded slowly. "For such a battle? Yes. But they're not as useful against undead."

"No, sorry, I wasn't clear," I apologized. "I mean, can you spare some guards to help escort the refugees here? We'll fly them south and we'll swap them for fifty of the hardest, most vicious legionnaires we can from the group marching here. Then those legionnaires will help us take out the city of the dead."

"Certainly. Lembiq would be honored." He smiled, leaving unsaid that for the elves I'd essentially asked them to take a few weeks camping and marching through forests with the refugees, instead of battling legions of the undead, and yeah, they'd jump at the chance to avoid that.

I didn't blame him, though: archers and the undead weren't exactly the ideal counters.

"Thank you. All right, people, we've got three days. I want everyone at peak performance. Sharpen your weapons, stock up on potions, get laid if you need to…not you, Giint. I think you need neutering if we can find a veterinarian. But for everyone else, when we hit Ashen Heart, I want us ready for war."

Now with that done, I took the time to pull up my notifications and check for the one that I knew was there from Jenae's comment.

Congratulations!

You have made progress in your Quest: The Deeper Secret

Where once you thought you sensed the truth, now you feel its reality in your heart, and may at last begin to unravel its power.

Echoes is the name you give to the Eighth power, and it sings in your ears as all truth must. Congratulations, young wielder; you have grown, and you make progress in your travels along the road to your destiny.

Forms of Magic Discovered: 8/10

Reward: New forms of magic, 10,000,000xp, Unknown

The next three days were a whirlwind of activity. Tenandra's transformation was incredible to watch. The salvaged components from the transport had been fully integrated, her hull extended and reinforced. The new engines hummed with barely contained power, and the weight reduction runes made her feel almost eager to fly.

Best of all, thanks to the details I'd unlocked, and the servitors, Tenandra and I had worked with them to modify five of the golem cores into a single greater core, one that now made up the heart of her systems.

"The modifications are complete," she announced proudly on the morning of the third day. "Maximum speed has increased by 280%, cargo capacity by 150%, and defensive capabilities…" She actually beamed around at us all. "Let's just say anything short of a dragon is going to have a bad day."

"What about a dragon?" I asked curiously.

"Then we run very fast in the opposite direction," she replied. "But we can now do that faster than before!"

The crew was ready. My core team was there, of course—Lydia, Arrin, Sehran, Jian, Ronin, Bane, Tang, Yen, Grizz, Bob, and Giint. But we'd also gained the mer survivors under Flux and Lio, twenty wood elf archers under Silviana, and fifty guards from Lembiq's forces, as well as the increased crew, and two of the servitors and all three of the war golems, including "Mr. Bitey," the canine version of the golems.

"This is going to be cramped," Yen observed as people filed aboard, and most of the wood elves showed the same issues as others had. They were desperate to get inside and out of the way before the flight began, not wanting to see how high up we were going to go.

"Good thing we're faster now," I replied. "It'll be better once we've swung south. Picking up some of our people from the refugee column will make a hell of a difference."

"T'legionnaires?" Lydia guessed.

"Sure as shit isn't going to be anyone else." I snorted. "Fresh troops dropped off to help them from Lembiq, and then we get to give the legionnaires a little rest, before they can work out some frustration on a bunch of the undead. Plus, I want to check on them, make sure they're okay."

The flight was a revelation. Tenandra's new speed was incredible. What would have taken hours now took a third of the time, thanks to the winds at our back as well. The ground blurred beneath us as she pushed her new engines, laughing with delight at her upgraded capabilities.

We found the refugee column ahead of where we'd expected, they'd apparently given up on waiting on the rise that I'd suggested, and when we'd passed over the local area we'd seen the signs of mass deforestation of the local scrub trees. Then using that wood they'd made what looked like a mixture or rafts and almost laying a road to get everyone out.

"That's Borren's work," Lydia noted proudly as we descended. "Look, 'e's got 'em in proper formations an' everythin'."

She was right. The legionnaire had organized the refugees into a solid column, with legionnaires providing protection to the sides, ahead and behind.

"My prince!" Borren saluted as we landed. "Good to see you, sir. We were wondering if you'd forgotten about us."

"Never," I assured him. "How's everyone holding up?"

"Better now that we're out of that fucking swamp," he admitted. "Nearly lost a few to disease and venomous bites, but we've been keeping morale up, and it's improving a lot more right now."

"I bet it is," I muttered, watching Sehran working her way through the crowd, singing and smiling.

"So, what can we do for you?" Borren asked.

I nodded curtly. Time for business.

"Actually, I need to borrow fifty legionnaires," I said. "We've got a fight coming, and I want fresh troops. But I've brought fifty of Lembiq's scouts and rangers to help even out the loss."

His expression turned serious. "Of course, my prince. The legion stands ready. What kind of fight?"

"The kind where I kill other fragment bearers and claim a portal," I said bluntly. "Probably also involving hundreds or possibly thousands of undead and some necromancers. Maybe a lich or two."

"So, a fun afternoon." He nodded. "If I may, I'd prefer to lead the squads. I have a second here, Hoan, who is of equal rank to me; we've been trading off and he can take over the march."

I glanced over at the legionnaire I guessed was Hoan, and saw his expression. Clearly, he'd been hoping he could come with me, and just hadn't spoken up in time.

"Sounds good." I nodded. "Get your people ready. We leave in an hour."

While we waited for the legionnaires to gear up, I walked among the refugees. They looked tired but hopeful, and many called out greetings or thanks as I passed. It was weird being seen as a hero, but I'd take their hope over their fear any day, and half the time that was all I got in the cities, after all. I remembered Himnel, and the outright hatred I got there, and I forced myself to dismiss that thought.

"Sire?"

A small voice caught my attention. A young girl, maybe six or seven, tugged at my cloak.

"Hey there." I crouched to her level. "What's up?"

"My mama said you're gonna save the empress," she said solemnly. "Is that true?"

My throat tightened at the mention of Oracle and her being identified as that. "Yeah. I'm going to save her."

"Good." She nodded, earnest. "I heard she's nice. She looks after people."

"She does that." I managed a smile. "She likes making people happy."

The girl studied me with that unsettling directness only children could manage. "You look sad."

"I miss her," I admitted.

"Then you should hurry up and save her." She said it like it was the most obvious thing in the world. "That's what heroes do."

Fuck me. That was right out of the mouths of babes.

"You're right." I stood, ruffling her hair. "I should hurry up."

"Prince Jax!" Borren called. "Troops ready!"

Fifty legionnaires stood in perfect formation—armor polished, weapons sharp. They looked eager, hungry for action after days of guard duty.

"Listen up!" I addressed them as I marched over. "We're heading into a shit-storm. Undead, necromancers, and enemy fragment bearers. It's going to be brutal, violent, and probably disturbing as hell. Anyone who wants out, now's the time."

Nobody moved.

"Good." I grinned. "Welcome aboard. Find space where you can, try not to puke on the deck, and remember—we're the good guys. That means we kill the bad guys extra hard, and feel free to use the undead to work out any issues you might have."

"Yes sir!" they chorused, crashing fists to chests in salute.

Loading everyone took time, but eventually we were airborne again. The fifty wood elf guards we'd brought looked relieved to be heading home, while the legionnaires who had replaced them aboard practically vibrated with anticipation.

Grizz already had a dice game going, and Tenandra was organizing legionnaires to trade off relaxing to get spells; although we'd taken most of them who could cast with us, we'd still left ten with the others, just in case.

"So, what's t'plan?" Lydia asked as we turned southwest.

"Hit them before they know we're coming," I said. "The fragment bearers are converging on Ashen Heart, probably planning to group up and dig in. They've changed their direction, so I'm betting a dark dickhead priest or a little birdie told them something. But if we time it right, we can catch them in the city while they're still trying to get dug in."

"Use the environment against them." Flux nodded approvingly. "The undead won't discriminate between targets."

"Unless they've made a deal," I corrected. "If they have, remember that the dark dick is the God of Death, and He's used undead before. Don't be too surprised if that's what we're facing here."

"Plus, if there really do be necromancers runnin' t'place, they might no' appreciate outsiders showing up an' fuckin' t'place up," Lydia grumbled.

"Or they might go all out attacking them and we can hit them from behind," Arrin pointed out.

"Also possible," I said. "That's why we hit hard and fast. No time for alliances or negotiations. We go in, kill everything that moves, claim the fragments and the portal, then see what's what."

"Simple plans are the best plans," Borren agreed. "One point, my prince—if there's a portal, can it be moved?"

"No." I grinned. "That's the fun and second half of the plan. We claim the portal, secure the immediate area through a mixture of excessive force and outright viciousness, and then I'll go through the portal, link up with Dravith, and we'll ask Legion General Romanus to send a force through to secure, claim, and rebuild the city.

"We redraw the map here, people. Claim that territory and the fragments, eliminate the undead curse, and we secure a beachhead. Then we march through a few hundred golems, a few thousand legionnaires, and we teach these fuckers

357

the error of their ways. *Nobody* fucks with the empire." I grinned evilly and saw the same reflected on the faces of my people.

As we flew south, I studied the map more carefully. Ashen Heart had once been a major city, before something terrible had happened. The information we'd had from Lembiq had suggested it'd been a gradual thing—the city had failed, the numbers of undead growing slowly—but the latest reports had suggested hundreds, if not thousands of undead.

"Tenandra, what can you tell me about Ashen Heart?" I asked.

"Only what I remember from historical records and the same reports you were given." She paused. "Ashen Heart was originally known as Batenzour, though since it fell, it was renamed the Ashen Heart. It was destroyed approximately four hundred years ago during what was rumored to have been a succession dispute. Two brothers, both powerful mages, fought for control of the city after their father died. One turned to necromancy, the other to demon summoning."

"Let me guess, everybody died?" I leaned back.

"Essentially. The majority had already left. The ruler's ill health and the people's knowledge of the sons' predilections had warned everyone well in advance. So, by the time the ruler died, most of the city had already fallen into ruin.

"The necromancer won in the end, but at the cost of killing every living thing in the city. The imperial forces of the time cleansed the city, but periodically the undead would gather there again. It's been a dead zone ever since, as there weren't enough people who were willing to move in to stabilize it again. And, frankly, the legion hasn't had the strength to cleanse it over and over."

"And now it has an active portal," I mused. "That can't be coincidence."

"The portal was always there," she clarified. "But it may have been uncovered more recently, or even repaired.

"We have a target." Tenandra suddenly changed the conversation as she apparently spotted something. "Large concentration of undead, two miles to the southeast. They just came out of the trees!"

"Get your game faces on, people!" I called out, scooping up my helmet and standing. "Time to get into the fight!"

CHAPTER THIRTY-FOUR

"Two hundred undead," I muttered, looking down at the shambling mass that Tenandra was showing us. "That's barely worth stopping for. We could just fly over and drop a few fireballs if they get too close to the ship."

The screens in the control room, the wheelhouse, whatever you wanted to call it, had changed dramatically.

Integrating the upgrades from the downed ancient transport had been... Well, you know those Morris Minor cars from the seventies—one of those shitty little cars that when you saw one parked in a supermarket parking spot, and you needed a space, you seriously considered getting a friend and the pair of you could probably pick it up and move it to where they kept the trolleys instead?

The difference in the control room here was as if you'd only ever been in a Morris Minor, and then you went into the house to grab something then came out and instead sat down in your car to find it'd been upgraded to a top-of-the-line modern Mercedes.

Or maybe a Tesla, with all the touch screen crap.

These weren't touch screens, but instead of thin, two-dimensional screens that had ringed the room and that were absolutely incredible—considering most of the ship was made of fucking wood and they were enchanted glass—the replacements were a massive upgrade.

The old screens were a mixture of spells and mist, and meter or so high physical screens that had been attached on all the walls, letting the pilot see around the ship in pretty much all directions, even through the floor for landing, showing the sight on the other side of the hull.

These new ones were three meters tall each, and although there weren't enough to cover all the room, and the older screens were still in place here and there, the picture they relayed was *incredible*.

Again, instead of a TV from the seventies, or dial-up porn from the nineties, this was full fucking 3D HDTV, and the difference was insane.

The zoom function was the same; even though we were still over a mile out from the undead, we could see them as if we were directly overhead, maybe twenty meters or so away.

They were covered in filth, clearly having fallen in the mud and the bogs of the marshes they'd wandered out of. They ranged from what were basically skeletons in rags, complete with broken and missing bones, to what I was guessing were recent additions, including a shambling zombie wearing a once fine red robe.

How did I know they were a zombie? Well, the ripped-out throat and the vacant expression like a social media "influencer" hearing about real work made that clear.

Regardless, I stared at the undead as we closed on them, and I shook my head. "I don't think it's worth the risk," I said. "Bombarding them from here, I mean. If these aren't naturally rising undead and we use the cannons, then we lose the element of surprise with this. Best to keep going for now."

Tenandra banked slightly, bringing us in a wide circle over the concentration of walking corpses. From up here, they looked almost pathetic—rotting bodies in various states of decay, moving with that characteristic undead shuffle that made them easy targets. Some still wore the remnants of clothing, as I said, but most were down to bones and sinew. All of them had turned their faces up to track our movement, empty eye sockets and clouded eyes following us with unnatural focus.

"Prince Jax." Borren stepped up to stand beside my seat in the command room, his expression serious. "With respect, sir, we can't just leave them."

"Why the fuck not?" I asked, genuinely curious. "I'm not saying 'oh fuck them.' I mean, we can hit them on the way back, probably. There's a much larger contingent ahead somewhere. When we take them out as we've planned, then we're going to be massively cutting down on the undead in the area as well."

"Because they're this far north." He pointed down at the undead, then gestured back the way we'd come. "We passed three settlements under the canopy in the last day. Small ones, granted, but still inhabited. Those undead are maybe a handful of days' shamble from the nearest one."

"They're slow as shit," I countered. "The elves can handle them."

"Could they?" Borren's jaw tightened. "Sir, I understand you've got more important targets, but this is what the legion *does*. We protect the innocent. Those settlements might have warriors, but they've also likely got children. Elderly. People who can't defend themselves if a couple hundred undead shamble through their front door in the middle of the night."

I looked at him, then down at the undead, then back at him. The fucker had a point, and he knew it.

"Besides," he continued, warming to his theme, "the legion hasn't had a proper fight in days. The men are getting restless. Let us handle this. Won't take more than twenty minutes."

"You're guilt-tripping me," I accused.

"Is it working?" he asked with a perfectly straight face.

"Fuck." I snorted, trying to hold back the laughter. "Yeah, all right, fine. But make it quick. Tenandra, take us down. Apparently, we're playing exterminator today."

"We can probably set down in that clearing to the east," she confirmed.

"We can draw their attention with arrows," Silviana offered hopefully, and I nodded.

If she and the other archers got involved, even if only slightly like this—arrows were a fantastically ineffective way to fight the undead, after all—then it meant that when the legion slaughtered them, the wood elf archers would get some of the experience as well.

"The undead are already moving to follow us," Tenandra pointed out.

"Of course they are," I grumbled. "All right. Silviana, start peppering them with arrows and draw them to us. Borren, this is your show. Try not to take all day."

There were grins all around now, and I shook my head bemusedly, not sure when I lost the childlike glee of fighting undead.

Mind you, perhaps that said more about the people I surrounded myself with, that everyone was excited to face the undead.

The ship touched down with barely a bump—Tenandra's new control systems were seriously impressive—and immediately the undead began their predictable shuffle out of the trees toward us. They moved like a tide of rotting flesh, arms outstretched and mouths open in silent screams.

"Legion! Form up at the bottom of the ramp, double time!" Borren barked, already moving. The fifty legionnaires raced after him with practiced precision. They flowed down the gangplank in perfect order—it bounced like it was about to give up the ghost under the speed and weight but luckily held—then their shields locked together as they formed a battle line between the ship and the approaching horde.

"Look at 'em," Lydia said admiringly from beside me. "Like a well-oiled machine."

"They better be," I said. "I'm not explaining to Daralen and Romanus why I got these men killed fighting trash mobs."

The legion advanced in lockstep to a point a dozen strides out from the gangplank and then held, shields and swords ready. There were thirty in the first line; behind them and slightly to the right were twenty more, ready if one of their brothers and sisters should fall, to rotate in. It was brutally efficient planning.

The first undead hit their line and simply…ceased to exist. Legion steel carved through rotting flesh like it wasn't even there. Heads rolled, limbs flew, and bodies crumpled. The legionnaires didn't even stop telling each other jokes.

"This is almost sad," Arrin observed, as more of the undead streamed out of the forest, the lines growing thicker. "The undead don't stand a chance."

"Good," I said. "Maybe we can actually get to Ashen Heart before—"

A scream cut through the air. Not from the legion—they were silent killers—but from the tree line to the north. A young wood elf, maybe fifteen or sixteen, crashed through the undergrowth, terror written across his face. Behind him, another dozen undead emerged from the forest.

"Fuck." I started forward, but Borren was already on it.

"Second squad! Flanking maneuver!" he roared. "Advance! Surround and protect the civilian!"

Half the legion peeled off smoothly, racing out as the second line moved up and filled the gap, intercepting the increasing numbers of undead. The young elf stumbled, fell, and one of the undead lunged for him—only to have an arrow slam into it, knocking it back. Then a dozen more flashed out, our archers and those from my squad joining in and thinning the numbers as the kid staggered and screamed, shouting for help.

It took less than a minute for the legionnaires to reach him, and the first undead that tried its luck in following met a legion shield that crushed its skull like an eggshell.

"You're safe now, lad," I heard the legionnaire tell him, as he hauled the elf to his feet. "Get to the ship."

The squad of ten retreated, still spread out and ready, but carving through the undead as they tried to follow.

The boy staggered on, and I met him at the gangplank with Lydia. He was shaking, covered in scratches and dirt, eyes wide with shock.

"Where were you!" he gasped. "My sister…she didn't make it."

"I'm sorry," I said, and meant it. This was why Borren had insisted we stop. This was why the legion existed. Fuck!

I turned to the right, thinking to call for help for the kid, then turned back and started a healing spell, deciding that was the best thing I could do for him.

Before I could do anything, though, he snarled; his face changed as fangs lengthened. He hurled himself at me instead. Fingers grew nails like chisels, even as the muscles on his chest and back surged. In a split second, the little fucker had gone from terrified civilian to hunchbacked feral bodybuilder.

I was in armor, but that fucker was close and I wasn't wearing a helmet. I reacted instinctually, blocking with my left arm and shoving him back before punching out with my right, driving it into the fucker's face.

The head virtually exploded under the panicked reaction, the skull shattering. But as I pulled my fist free, something changed. The skin, which had shifted from the flushed panic of exertion to a mottled grey, suddenly surged again—and this time, something inside was coming out.

As soon as it did, I recognized it, more or less. As the disgusting flesh tried to reform, surging forward across my gauntlet and up my arm, teeth and eyes rolling along it like melted Jello, I snarled and started to cast.

Fire was pretty much my default go-to when I needed something gone. Whatever variant of a vampyr this was, it apparently was okay in the sun—more or less; it was smoking already—although it really wasn't when I summoned my Pyroclastic Blast in its throat.

It juddered to a halt, then burst into flames, frantically trying to disengage and release me before it died.

Spoiler—it wasn't fast enough.

Instead, it flared like a melted candle made of sulfur, fats spitting and popping, clothing and flesh blackening and falling apart. The body collapsed to the ground, burning as something inside frantically tried to drag itself clear.

I leaned down and pressed the spellform into the mass, making damn sure it all burned up. Then I straightened, holding the spell, before aiming at a struggling group of undead in the distance.

With the vampyr's death, whatever cohesion had been holding the undead in such an unusually large group fell apart, as did the limited sense they'd had.

Dozens of them vanished when they stepped off the edge of the land and sank into stagnant pools, instead of swarming around them.

I hurled the spell at a group of about a dozen pressed close in together by the trunk and branches of an old deadfall farthest away from the legionnaires. It impacted a half second later and detonated, destroying half the tree. Wood and bits of undead flew in all directions.

With that done, I kicked the burned and destroyed corpse on the ground once to make sure it was dead, roughly searched it—finding nothing of interest, not even a few coppers—and sighed, before walking back up the gangplank with Lydia by my side.

"Fuckin' 'ell, ah didn't even see it until it were too late," she apologized.

I shrugged, as the pair of us returned to the railing, leaning on it and watching out over what was left of the fight.

"Don't worry about it." I sighed. "At least we know there's a chance of these fuckers here, and it was a weak one. I should have used a spell and checked. Just out of practice, I guess," I muttered.

"Yer cast that fast," she pointed out.

I snorted. "Honestly, I've been casting so much of late that it's second nature," I admitted, going back to watching.

The fight, if you could call it that, was over in fifteen minutes. Two hundred and thirteen undead, reduced to so much rotting meat. The legionnaires hadn't even broken a sweat.

"Casualties?" I asked.

"None, my prince. Few scratches, nothing serious. The men appreciated the exercise." Borren smiled, before straightening and apologizing. "I take full responsibility for the vampyr, sir. We should have contained the unknown figure, rather than permitting him to approach you. I—

"Don't be bloody ridiculous," I said. "It's the middle of a fight. And I was fooled as well. I should have thought about the coincidence of a pack of undead this large and us just happening to find someone ready for a rescue as soon as we landed. They were fucking bait, and we fell for it. If anything, this is a good thing. As I said to Lydia, at least now we know there are some in the area."

"Still, I submit myself for punishment," he tried.

I clapped him on the shoulder, hard, and shook him slightly. "Borren, there's no blame here, and no punishment needed. But if you really feel you need it? I'll make a deal with you. You keep track of any cockups, and when we open the portal to Dravith, and you meet Restun, the Primus Praetoria…you can ask him for punishment. Here's a hint—you'll regret it, and I recommend you don't. But that's a decision a man has to make for himself." I grinned at him. "All right then, now that that's dealt with, burn the bodies. I don't want them getting back up."

"Already on it, sir."

The legionnaires were indeed already building pyres. A few minutes later, I was happy to hit the nearest with a pyro spell, then a second and third. Sure, it spread the flames around as well, but it was both therapeutic and effective. It'd already started to rain, suggesting that any fires we left behind were unlikely to spread.

And if they did? Fuck it. It was a swamp. It wasn't like they'd spread far.

As we loaded back onto the ship, I thought about what Borren had said: *This was what the legion does.* Not just the big battles, not just the wars against dark gods and evil empires. Sometimes it was just stopping to kill a couple hundred undead because innocent people were at risk.

"It were t'right call t'make," Lydia said quietly as we took off.

"It was, and Borren made it," I corrected. "I was ready to fly right over them."

"But yer didn't," she pointed out. "That's what matters."

The next few hours proved Borren had been right about another thing—the undead weren't isolated. As we flew south, we encountered more and more groups. Some were small, just a dozen or so shambling through the forest. Others were larger, organized into something almost resembling formations.

"More there!" one of the wood elf scouts called out. "About fifty undead."

"Slow down for a pass, please, Tenandra, but don't stop," I said to the ship at large, already gathering mana. "No point landing for every group of walking corpses we see."

I leaned over the railing and sent an onslaught of flame lances down. The undead didn't even have time to react before they were reduced to ash. Around me, others with magical abilities did the same. Arrin stuck to precise Magic Missiles, now evolved again into what looked to be a barrage of even smaller versions, but dozens of them. Sehran and the rest of my squad used Explosive Compression. Even some of Borren's legionnaires who'd picked up basic combat magic joined in, as did Lio and Flux.

Most of the legionnaires who could use magic had taken to using it at any opportunity, well aware that additional evolutions would bring greater utility, XP, and improve their chances of learning more.

The driving rain had forced most of the groups off the deck, but the mer were always happy to gather when the heavens opened. So when we passed concentrations like this, the deck was suddenly full of rushing legionnaires, flashes of magic, and then them running back inside, out of the rain again.

"Efficient and good practice," Flux noted approvingly. "Though I notice we're seeing more groups the farther south we go."

"Yeah." I'd noticed it too. "Fuck it, let's hope it's nothing to do with us, but if it is, then we deal with it."

I moved back inside, returning to my cabin with most of the group, once again thanking Tenandra for the thoughtfulness in upgrading it to be large enough for this, and the wide-open rear windows.

My squad was dotted around the room, resuming seats, taking cloaks off and starting up whatever they'd dropped to go play. I sat by the window, staring out, seeing a difference, and then comparing it to the maps I had.

"Is that normal for this area?" I asked Silviana, who'd started joining us so much she was becoming a fixture of the place. "I mean, just look at the forest."

When we'd left Lembiq, the forest below had been vibrant and alive. Massive trees with lush canopies, undergrowth so thick you couldn't see the ground. But the farther south we flew, the more that changed.

The trees were smaller now, sickly-looking. Their leaves were brown and withered, even though it was the wrong season for that. The undergrowth had thinned to almost nothing, leaving bare earth visible between the trunks. And that earth…

"Is it just me, or does the ground look wet?" Ronin asked. "Not from the rain, I mean…like it's bubbling?"

"It's the edge of the marsh," Silviana agreed. "The land itself here is dying, turning to swamp."

"Like where the Dark Legion citadel was," I murmured. "I mean, I knew the marsh was there, and there was some here. It's like a hundred miles long and fifty or so across, but the maps have it a lot smaller and starting to the south, right?"

"It's spreading," Silviana agreed grimly. "All of this area used to be healthy forest, but when Batenzour fell, the fields that surrounded it stopped being tended, the marshes grew, and the Ashen Heart spread. But this…this is just horrible."

"Could it be magical?" Arrin asked. "I mean, Ashen Heart has been dead for centuries. That's a long time for corruption to spread if it's because of the undead?"

"Probably natural," Ronin replied absently, fiddling with a tuning fork.

"What?" I asked.

He blinked, then looked over, and shrugged. "Sorry. I was listening to the strings more than the conversation. What's up?"

"The marsh." I gestured out the massive windows at the dying trees and the stagnant waters that shivered under the deluge. "It's growing quickly, but you said it's not magical?"

"I don't think so." He shrugged again. "When fields get abandoned, the land naturally turns to marshes, that's all." He looked about then sighed, and explained while strumming the strings of the lute. "So, farmers cut the trees down, and they drain fields and so on, growing the crops they want. They take out all the stones they can, and they generally make the land as good for planting as possible, right?"

"Yeah?" Lydia agreed.

"Well, when there's no trees or shrubs or anything to hold the ground together, and it's not being regularly drained or turned over, not being looked after, then it gets waterlogged. When that happens, as more and more time passes, it turns from a bit marshy, to very, and it spreads.

"Over in the marsh near the dark citadel…well, that had trees and plants that were adapted to it, so that held most of the land together. It's not that bad…boggy, but, you know."

"You'd not be saying that if you'd tried slogging through it," Borren corrected. "Speaking of that, thanks for understanding and letting us take the time to do it safely," he said to me.

"No worries." I smiled, then gestured for Ronin to go on.

"Well, there's no trees here to hold the ground together, and there's a massive marsh that way…" Ronin gestured vaguely toward the destroyed citadel and went on. "So, what's happening is that the land is flooding, and the trees that are here are rotting because they're not used to this much water, right?

"Then add in that there's a marsh full of dying things that way, and a massive city that was full of the undead and dead here, and…" He made "what the hell do you expect" gestures with both hands and pushed them together.

"Either way, it's fucking depressing," I said. "Look at it. Nothing should be able to live down there."

But things did live there. Wrong things. We saw them occasionally—twisted creatures that might once have been animals, now clearly undead and as much floating and rotting corpses as moving.

"More undead, one o'clock," Tenandra added suddenly. "Big group this time. Maybe three hundred?"

"Leave them until later," I decided. "We're making good time, and—"

"Sir." Borren interrupted. "We're the legion. We need to—"

"We need to address the heart of the fucking infestation, Legionnaire," I replied sternly. "We can divert over them and bombard with spells, *not* the cannons, but then we're leaving. If things work out the way I'm hoping, first off, they'll see us and they'll start following. That's the immediate hope. But beyond that? When we get things sorted out, I'm planning to have a permanent legion camp here."

"Really?" Tang gestured out the window. "No offense, boss, but can we not be stationed here? The real estate value is shit."

"Up to you." I fixed him with a wry smile. "Personally, I think that when a few hundred golems take up station here, cleaning it up and draining the swamp or marsh or whatever, and once the bodies are removed and burned, I think we're going to find this is a great area for growing crops."

I let that hang in the air for a few seconds, then I shrugged. "I mean, sure, it'll help that there'll be a lot of farmers and so on all moving here to help restart the cycle, and there are literally ruined mansions that could probably be claimed and repaired easily, but don't you worry about it, mate. No land here for you."

"Whoa, maybe we can talk about this, boss." He smiled suddenly. "No need to make decisions in haste, after all. And besides, I think Carmen would love a little holiday home, you know, somewhere she could relax with a handsome legionnaire to work out a little stress."

"Are you trying to bribe me with the promise of you getting laid?" I asked him. "Because, no offense, that's not gonna work out for me."

"I'd owe you?" He grinned.

"Go fuck yourself." I snorted, before turning back to Borren. "We can do one pass, that's it. We're low on fucking time. I'm sorry, Borren, but that's the reality. We need to move it or lose it, and another group of undead is just gonna keep showing up every five minutes. Tenandra, one pass and then full speed for the city," I ordered, as Borren crashed a fist to his chest in salute, standing.

"May I take volunteers to help with the attack?" he asked, clearly not liking it, but accepting the orders.

"Anyone who can use magic is free to do so," I agreed. "Go for it."

"Then I need anyone and everyone with access to an offensive spell to gather on the deck now." He looked around the room, making his position as an optio clear. With most of my squad's position as lower ranks than his, that meant that either I needed to override him again, and damage his authority—which I was betting he knew I wouldn't do—or let him take my people.

I looked at him, holding his gaze for a few seconds, letting him know that I knew what he'd done, then I nodded.

"You heard him, people. Let's make this a quick and dirty one," I decided, already knowing that the gravity seed and dual cast was going to be my choice.

He winced, seeing that I was going to take part, but didn't disagree. Five minutes later, we were back inside, with a smoking ruin being all that was left of the site of the undead.

Three more times that happened, over the next hour, until finally Tenandra appeared in the cabin, standing to attention as she spoke. "We have visual contact with Ashen Heart. You're going to want to see this."

I nodded, moving up to the control room, along with half the squad, while the others moved out onto the deck, the rain having finally trailed off to a sort of cold mist more than anything else.

The city was a nightmare made manifest. It rose from the marsh like a cancer, buildings of grey and black stone that seemed designed to fade into the mist. The outer walls had long since crumbled, but it didn't matter—the real defense was the sea of undead that surrounded it.

Literally thousands of them.

"Okay, that's not good," I admitted.

"You sure?" Grizz asked. "I mean, can we not just stand off and bombard the city into rubble? That seems like the best bet to me."

"Where's the portal?" I asked him quietly.

"Uh…I dunno, boss." He sighed.

"Neither do I." I shrugged. "You know of a way to stop us accidentally destroying it?"

"No," he admitted.

I nodded. "And that's why we need to go in and do it the old-fashioned way."

"Do we have enough people?" Flux asked. "I mean no offense, but do we have the forces to fight this many undead? Even with fifty legionnaires, this is…"

"We attacked a citadel of the Dark Legion with near the same numbers," I pointed out.

"And that was a bloody stupid idea," Flux replied. "That was also a situation where we knew it was unlikely that anyone in the city could go toe-to-toe with you. That's changed."

"Oh?" I asked.

"The fragment bearers, the demigods," he said flatly. "Two of them, both ready to fight you, and frankly possibly more than any of us can face alone. You need to be prepared for the fact that our forces may be insufficient to face them."

"You kicked my ass only hours ago," I pointed out.

"And you were holding back." Lio sighed. "Seriously, boss, as much as I enjoy kicking your ass, you think we couldn't tell? You were going easy on us, using us as training dummies to practice blocks and deflections with your eyes closed. It was obvious."

"You two are the best we have at stealth." I shrugged. "I need practice there."

"You do. But three months ago, you could barely keep up. Since you got the fragments, you had to hold yourself back so as not to hurt us. That's in three months. What's the chances these two have less experience with their fragments than you do?"

"Practically zero."

"So, the chances of us fighting them both at once?" she prodded.

"Not good," I admitted. "But they're likely to be holding a single fragment or, at most, two each. I have four."

"So you might be their equal, but are we?" Flux pressed.

I hesitated, then shook my head. "No," I conceded. "When the fight comes, I need you all to keep out of it."

"You're the prince. Any threat to you goes through us first," Borren said, and before I could speak up, Lydia had joined in.

"Yer t'prince, but we're yer squad," she said. "Nothin' gets a free go at yer."

"Damn right."

"Fuck no."

"We've got your back."

"I'll be sitting off to the side and playing some music," Ronin added helpfully.

I snorted at that, as smiles rolled around the room.

"Thank you all," I said sincerely. "But I mean it. The fragment bearers are going to be a lot stronger, faster, and more experienced than you, so please, leave them to me. You focus on the undead, on whatever else is in there, and leave them to me."

"Until the fight is done," Flux said softly. "Once they are dead, then we will aid you."

"How many undead are there likely to be in the city?" I asked pointedly.

"Ten thousand," Flux replied. "Maybe more. What we can see of the city could hold twice that if they're packed into the buildings."

"The fragment bearers?" Arrin squinted at the screen closest to him. "Do we know what they'll look like?"

"No, and I doubt we'd be able to see them from here." I checked my map and noted that it looked like both dots were so close together I couldn't tell them apart anymore. "But there's definitely activity in that central tower. Lights, movement. Someone's home."

"Or somethin'," Lydia muttered.

The tower dominated the city's heart, rising like a black spear thrust into the sky. It had to be ten stories tall, maybe more, and every window gaped empty, despite the flickering of lights here and there, and frequent movement.

"Think the portal's really in there?" Grizz asked.

"Only one way to find out," I said. "But first we need to—"

"Movement!" Silviana called out. "Eastern quarter, something big!"

I turned and focused on where she pointed as Tenandra increased the magnification there. Something was indeed moving through the packed streets, undead parting before it like water. It was huge, easily thirty feet tall, and...

"Is that made of corpses?" I asked, horrified despite myself.

"Flesh golem," Borren said grimly. "Amalgamation of hundreds of bodies fused together, a bit like the things we saw in the Dark Legion tower. In fact..."

"Yeah?" I prompted.

"I doubt that's a coincidence," he finished. "Fuck's sake, no wonder there's so many here. What's the chances that the death knight just happened to learn to make these on his own?"

"You think he was trading with whatever or whoever lives here," I said. "Seems likely."

"'Ow tough is that gonna be?" Lydia asked.

"Very. And there's more than one. Look, western quarter."

He was right. Another flesh golem was visible there, and as we watched, a third emerged near the tower.

"This is going to be fun," I said with a confidence I didn't feel.

"Define fun," Ronin muttered.

"The kind where we probably die horribly but take a lot of the enemy with us."

"Oh goodie. My favorite kind."

I looked around at my people. They were scared—they'd be idiots not to be—but they were also ready. We'd faced worse odds before. Maybe. Well, I couldn't think of when, obviously, and yeah, all right, probably not "worse," actually. But fuck it, no point dwelling on that.

"So, we've got ten thousand undead, at least three flesh golems, whatever's in that tower, and someone with a piece of a god in their soul," Ronin summarized. "Did I miss anything?"

"The other fragment bearer," I reminded him. "They're around here somewhere."

"Right. Mustn't forget them."

"Plus probably a lich or three, some necromancers, and whatever other surprises they've got waiting," Tang added helpfully.

"Thank you, Tang. Very helpful." Ronin groaned.

"Just trying to paint a complete picture."

"Can I take leave?" Ronin asked hopefully. "You know, just for, oh, a year or two? I'll come back and you can tell me how it all got worked out and we'll laugh about this?"

I stared down at the nightmare below us. This was going to be brutal. We were outnumbered hundreds to one, heading into a city of the dead to fight enemies who could probably raise their own casualties as reinforcements.

But those fragment bearers were down there. The portal was down there.

"Fuck it," I decided. "We've faced worse odds."

"Have we?" Ronin asked. "When?"

"I'll let you know when I think of something." I turned to address everyone. "All right, people, change of plans. We're not charging in like idiots. We're going to be smart about this. Tenandra, take us up and circle wide. I want to know everything about this place before we make our move."

Whatever happened next, it was going to be one hell of a fight, I had to admit.

"Think we'll make it outta this one?" Lydia asked quietly.

"Always do," I said, still faking confidence.

"First time for everything."

"Yeah," I admitted. "But not today. Today, we remind these fuckers why I'm the Godslayer."

Down below, as if in response to my words, a horn sounded from the dark tower. Long and low, it echoed across the dead city like a funeral dirge.

They clearly knew we were here. That was good though. Let them prepare. Let them gather their forces and ready their defenses.

It wouldn't matter. I was getting those fragments, claiming that portal, and then securing a beachhead for my people.

But first, I needed a plan that didn't involve all of us dying horribly.

"Ideas?" I asked the group. "Because charging in seems like a bad idea now."

"When 'as that ever stopped yer?" Lydia asked.

"Fair point. But maybe, just this once, we try thinking first?"

"Miracles do 'appen." She snorted, then she groaned as I grinned at her. "Ah shit, yer've got a plan, 'aven't yer?"

CHAPTER THIRTY-FIVE

"All right, here we go. You know me…I like to keep it simple—less to go wrong." I grinned at the assembled group. "We're going to use Tenandra as a mobile artillery platform. No cannons yet, though. I want that to be a lovely surprise for later, so save those for when we really need them. Instead, everyone with magic is going to rain hell down on these fuckers while we circle."

"That's your plan?" Arrin groaned. "Fly around and shoot spells like we've all been doing already?"

"The first part of it, yeah," I confirmed. "We thin their numbers, take out at least one of those flesh golems—maybe all three if we're lucky. Make them think that's all we can do from here, and that we waste our mana doing it."

"Then what?" Flux asked.

"Then we land and do what we do best: kill everything that moves—until either they come to us and we unleash Tenandra's real powers in a lovely surprise, or we go to them. And if we end up shit creek, we fall back and give her a nice target." I turned to Tenandra. "Can you make it look like we're barely keeping aloft as we're circling? I don't want them understanding how easily you can get in and out when we need you."

"Oh, *please*. I can do anything you need." She sounded offended. "With my new engines, I could do barrel rolls while you cast. Though I won't, because most of you would throw up."

"Or fall off," Arrin added cheerfully.

"Please don't," Ronin said weakly. "I'm already imagining ways to try to hide from this."

"All right, everyone with offensive magic to the rails," I commanded. "Tenandra, take us in. Let's start with that flesh golem on the east side."

The ship banked smoothly, dipping lower as we approached the city's edge. The undead below turned to track our movement. A sea of rotting faces and empty eye sockets all focused on us, and more and more drifted out of the shadows and ruined buildings to stare upward.

"What's likely to be the best range?" I asked.

"Give me thirty seconds," Tenandra said. "I'll slow and present the starboard side."

"Everyone, get ready then," I ordered, already gathering mana. "Focus fire on the big bastard!"

It swayed slightly, clearly unbalanced and surrounded by dozens of smaller undead. It was roughly humanoid again, similar to the last ones we faced, but this time, instead of three to four meters in height, it was around twenty.

Twenty fucking meters of misshapen, fugly monstrosity, with its left arm much longer than its right, the end of it swollen out into a lumpy club that rested on the ground.

The right arm ended in a collection of claws that were all different lengths, and looked to have been made haphazardly by an amateur.

My own work on Bob hardly made me out to be an expert, admittedly, but if you're crafting something with a fucking hand, at least make it so the hand can close, you know?

Some claws looked to be so long they'd stab it if it tried to close its fist. Others were so short they'd be tickling its palm.

Around it in the plaza, surrounded by semi-fallen buildings, ruined walls, destroyed balconies and roofs that had collapsed inward already…were the dead.

Hundreds of them wandered this way and that, unable to function or process the world around them, like millennials searching for a coffee shop.

Then the air lit up with magic. Dozens of spells streaked down from the ship: flame lances, Magic Missiles, Explosive Compressions, gravity seeds. The concentrated barrage slammed into the flesh golem like the fist of an angry god.

The creature staggered, huge chunks of its amalgamated form blasting away. It tried to move, to escape the bombardment, but we had the advantage of mobility. And every step it took resulted in the smaller undead gathered around its feet being crushed, which was a win by our standards. Tenandra easily kept pace, maintaining perfect distance as we poured destruction down on it, as it lumbered for the cover of a nearby building.

"It's regenerating!" Silviana called out.

She was right. Even as we blasted pieces off, I could see corpses from the surrounding area being drawn to it, melding into its form to replace what we'd destroyed.

"Burn it!" I roared. "Don't give it anything to regenerate with!"

I changed what I'd been about to cast, a Pyroclastic Blast, and instead went for a gravity seed, though this time I didn't aim for it. Instead, I aimed for the building it'd been headed for.

It was half ruined, like the rest of the city. The street was ankle-deep—or knee-deep, really—in garbage and fallen building materials. Three walls were intact, and most of a roof was still there, but an entire section of the fourth wall had fallen in.

That was where it was headed, presumably being prodded to get out of sight—which would have been great, except that I fired my spell into the corner of the building closest to it, and opposite the damaged section.

The explosion did some nasty damage, sure, but the warping of gravity was the kicker.

The ten seeds twisted and pulverized the building to the point that the walls and roof tilted almost as soon as the first seed activated. By the time the tenth was going, that entire section of the plaza was a mess of flying bricks, bone, and wood.

That was when the golem lumbered to a halt, as it presumably received new orders, and standing there was exactly the wrong place for it to wait. The next salvo was almost entirely flame-based. The golem went up like a torch. It flailed, trying to beat out the flames, even as more spells hurtled down and slammed into it.

Within minutes, it was nothing but a burning heap in the middle of a charred circle, with hundreds of smaller fuckfaces reduced to bones as well.

Admittedly, as we arced around to the side and lost sight of the plaza, there was the minor issue of a second, and then third building starting to collapse, but that was a problem to be sorted out later.

"One down!" Lydia called triumphantly.

"Western side, second target!" I called out. "Same thing again, people! Pop potions if you need to, but remember this is gonna be a long day."

We swept around the city, raining death from above as we went. The second flesh golem tried to be clever, ducking into buildings for cover. But we had a simple solution for that, and after we brought down the second building, trapping it in the rubble, it learned its lesson.

Admittedly, it was a bit late by then, trapped under tons of rubble and taking concentrated fire, but that wasn't a problem for *us*. The second golem fell even faster than the first.

"This is too easy," Borren said suspiciously.

"That's because you're used to everything you do being a fight," Yen snorted. "Believe me, we were the same!"

"Yeah, well, let's not complain about it," I replied, though I agreed with him. Where was the resistance? Where were the enemy casters?

"Third golem is moving!" Arrin pointed toward the tower. "It's...fuck, it's fast!"

He was right. This one wasn't lumbering like the others. It moved with purpose, almost gracefully for something made of corpses. And it headed straight for the tower.

"It's trying to get under cover!" I realized. "Hit it now!"

But this golem was different. When our spells struck it, they seemed to slide off, deflected by some kind of magical protection.

"Shielded!" Yen observed. "Someone's protecting it!"

"Then we hit it harder!" I countered, pouring more mana into my attacks. But the golem made it to the tower's base, disappearing inside before we could bring it down.

"Two out of three ain't bad," Tang offered.

"It'll have to do," I decided. "All right, phase two. Tenandra, find us a clear spot to land. Eastern side where we destroyed the first golem should work."

"It has more than enough space," she confirmed. "Though I should mention, the undead are massing in that area."

"Good. We can whittle them down...and it's not like there's many other options closer to the tower." I turned to the group. "Everyone, drink up—mana potions, stamina potions, whatever you need. When we hit the ground, it's going to be nonstop, so make sure you have plenty."

The next few minutes were a flurry of preparation. Potions were consumed, weapons checked, armor adjusted. The legion formed up near the ramp, ready to deploy the moment we touched down, and I made a mental note to speak to Marta, as I'd basically ignored her for days, and I'd just found out she'd been merrily working away most of that time in isolation.

Thanks to her work, we now had more potions than we knew what to do with, including buffs for everyone.

"Here we go!" Tenandra called out as she swung around and fired the engines hard, taking us in fast. "Landing in ten seconds!"

The ground rushed up to meet us, then suddenly seemed to stop dead as the engines fired hard again, this time reversing and making us all feel three times as heavy as we were pressed into the deck.

The moment the ship settled, the legion moved. They flowed down the ramps in perfect formation, establishing a perimeter around our landing zone. Not a moment too soon: the undead were already closing in. As soon as we were off—Borren and his fifty, Flux leading his handful of assassins, and Lydia leading our people—Tenandra fired her engines again and lifted off, backing away.

"Form turtle and hold the line!" Borren bellowed. "Let them come to us!"

That was a style we were familiar with, and we fell in as well. The rest of the squad took available slots, pulling their legion shields out to fit into the shield line.

I took my place in the middle next to Borren and Lydia, with Ronin behind us, already playing "Luck's My Mistress."

The legionnaires formed a square, seven on a side at the front and back, and six to the left and right, with those in the middle behind the front line ready to lift their shields overhead and shrug off a conventional arrow or rock attack, or to take the place of those who were injured or exhausted on the front line.

Grizz, being Grizz, had already laid claim to a slot in the front, while most of the rest of the squad were around me, getting ready for the fight.

"We need to see how they react before we know which plan to adopt," Borren advised Lydia and me. "If they're standard brainless undead, then it's a wave that will hit us, trying to wash over. In that situation, we brace, take the impact, and then destroy them. We hold until the front lines are so thick with the bodies that they're running over them. Then we slowly step back, half step at a time, and we bleed their forces.

"Second option is semi-aware undead; they'll hit us with the fodder and then the more powerful will come in and think to hold back until we're weakened. Then they'll take part. This is the most likely scenario, from my experience. When they show themselves, we wait until they commit, and then those who have access to magic eradicate them.

"That should also remove any controlling and guiding sentience with the undead fodder, and we can mop them up.

"The third and least likely is that they'll have a higher-tier commander close by, one that leads them as if they were experienced troops. At that point, we'll know it by the difference in the fight—much more dangerous and much harder. But if you can take the leader out, they'll often be linked to the lesser undead, meaning that they'll all either collapse as soon as the leader is taken down, or they'll revert to mindless.

"In this situation sir, I'd appreciate you taking the lead and taking the enemy down fast and hard," he finished, before turning and barking out orders to two of the legionnaires to tighten up their formation.

"Sounds good." I nodded that I'd understood and did my best to ignore the low-grade arguing that was going on behind me.

"What do you mean, a platinum? Where the hell am I gonna get a platinum to gamble?" one legionnaire was asking.

"I'll take your word," Tang assured him in a friendly tone. "We're all legionnaires, right? So, when you get the platinum will be fine, and the bet should be easy, right? You heard him—the third is the least likely, so I think odds of two to one are reasonable…"

The cheeky fucker was betting that it was going to be the worst-case scenario, and he was confident enough he was collecting from the legionnaires around him already.

"Here they come!" one legionnaire called out.

And come they did. Hundreds of them, pouring from every street and alley. Skeletons with ancient weapons, zombies in various states of decay, and lumpy, rotting things I didn't want to identify. They crashed against the legion's shield wall like a putrid tide.

But the legion held. Their training showed as they worked as a team, each soldier covering their neighbor, rotating fresh fighters to the front as needed after ten minutes. It was brutal, efficient, and absolutely beautiful to watch.

"Archers, thin the rear ranks!" Silviana's voice drifted down from above and behind us aboard Tenandra, and twenty elven bows sang in unison. Arrows found gaps in ancient armor, shattered brittle bones, and dropped targets before they could even reach the rest of us, even if most did clamber back to their feet if they hadn't been lucky enough for a headshot.

"Charged shot!" she shouted. Ten seconds later, a streak of twenty glowing arrows lit the afternoon air before detonating against the undead.

They destroyed them this time, bones reduced to dust and fragments, rotten armor and clothing catching fire or shattering.

I stood in the center of our formation, watching for threats, conserving my mana for when I'd really need it. And that's when I saw him.

He strode through the undead like they were beneath his notice, and they parted before him like a sea of bones. A figure in tattered robes that might once have been purple, now faded to the color of old bruises. His face was just a skull, but his eye sockets burned with green fire. I knew we'd found someone who was going to be a little more fun.

A lich.

Even better, the half dozen figures around it that hung back, under cover of hoods and more—those I recognized after our little meeting with the elf in the marsh. Vampyr.

He stopped a hundred meters or so beyond our formation, raising one skeletal hand. The attacking undead immediately pulled back, forming a rough circle around us but no longer pressing the assault.

"Parley!" The lich's voice was like grinding millstones. "I would speak with your leader!"

"That'd be me." I stepped forward, though I didn't leave our lines. "What do you want, bone boy?"

"Such disrespect. But what else should I expect from the living? I am Nethys the Eternal, lord of this city and master of death itself."

"That's nice," I said. "Still didn't answer my question. What do you want?"

"Straight to business then." The green fires in his sockets flared brighter. "You have something I desire. That ship. Give it to me, and I will allow you to leave this city alive."

I blinked. Then I laughed. I couldn't help it—the sheer audacity of this walking corpse demanding Tenandra was just too much.

"You want my ship?" I managed between laughs. "Seriously? We land and destroy half your army in what, an hour, and you think you're in a position to dictate terms?"

"Do not mock me, mortal!" Nethys raised his voice, and the temperature dropped twenty degrees. "I have need of a vessel capable of flight. Yours will suffice. Surrender it, or face annihilation."

"Counteroffer," I said, still grinning. "You take ten percent of your undead—your choice which ones—and you fuck off to somewhere the living don't go. Bottom of the ocean, maybe. In exchange, I don't turn you into bone meal."

"Insolent whelp!" The lich took a step forward. "Do you have any idea who you're speaking to? I have ruled here for hundreds of years! I have mastered magics you cannot even comprehend! I am death incarnate!"

"And I'm the guy who kills gods for a hobby," I replied calmly. "Want to try again?"

"Surrender, bend the knee and I will—"

"Listen, I'm not interested." I sighed, gesturing people aside and then walking forward, ignoring the conversation that had struck up behind me as Tang tried to convince his fellow legionnaires that it was just bad luck on their part, and that they still had to pay up.

"You have two fragment bearers in this city. It's them I came to see, but you also have vampyrs, and the undead have been spreading out and destroying the area as well.

"So, that's why I'm here. Pull back the undead, destroy all but ten percent and leave. You can go to the depths of the ocean, the heights of the mountains, or fuck it, go burn in the deserts. *I don't care.* But I'm an imperial prince, and you don't get to threaten my lands."

"Then you have chosen death." Nethys spread his arms wide, and power built around him. Death magic, thick and cloying, gathered from every corpse in the city. "Foolish mortal. By agreeing to this parley, you've given me all the time I needed."

"Oh no," I said in the most monotone voice possible. "Whatever shall I do. The scary skeleton is gathering power. Someone save me."

"Mock me while you can!" The lich cackled as a sphere of pure death magic formed around him. "This shield is impervious to any attack! And while you stood there like fools, I've been drawing in every scrap of death mana in the city! Soon I'll have enough power to—"

"Yeah, about that." I interrupted. "See, you said you were lying about the parley. That you never intended to negotiate in good faith."

"Of course!" He seemed confused by my calm. "Only an idiot would trust the word of a lich!"

"Funny thing." I grinned as I fed my magic into and triggered my tattoos, feeling them flare to life under my armor. My own shield sprang up, but this one was different. Where his repelled, mine *absorbed* the mana. "I was lying too."

"What?"

"About the parley," I explained patiently. "I never believed you'd take the opportunity to leave. I just wanted to see what you'd do. And gathering all that death mana in one place?" I grinned. "Thanks for that."

"It matters not!" Nethys poured more power into his spell, death magic so thick it became visible as a black fog. "I shall reduce you and your pathetic force to dust. I shall reanimate you, forcing you to serve me, and..."

"Which is it going to be?" I asked curiously.

"You will scream for eternity and... What?"

"I said, which one?" I asked. "You know, reanimate my bones or reduce me to dust. Pick one. You said you'd kill me, but you're going to leave me screaming for eternity?"

"Your soul will be torn from your body! Your flesh will rot from your bones! You will—"

"Blah, blah, blah." I held up one hand, and my Fragment of Death sang in response to all the gathered power. "Fuck me, your evil monologuing skill is low, isn't it? I've had more believable threats from toddlers."

The lich unleashed his spell: a wave of pure death, enough to kill everything in a hundred-foot radius. It slammed into my shield...and sank into it, as I sucked it in and pushed it back out, grinning evilly.

"What?" Nethys sounded genuinely confused. "That's not possible!"

"Oh, you sweet summer fuckin' child..." I snorted distractedly. My hands shifted as I smoothed the death mana out, feeding it into my shield as I'd done so many times. I smiled, as a new plan occurred to me. There was a lot of mana here, and although I could let it power the shield for a while, there was no point in wasting it all, after all.

"See, that's your problem," I said conversationally as my shield absorbed every bit of death magic he threw at me. "You think death is your ally. But me? I have a Fragment of Death itself. I'm a demigod of death, you fucking idiot, and you sent a wave of uncontrolled and unguided death mana at me?"

I shook my head in amusement as he doubled down, trying again, channeling everything he had into an attack that should have rotted me and my companions where we stood.

The tattoos on my body burned now, working in concert with my death fragment. Every bit of power the lich threw at me was caught, contained, converted. My shield didn't just block his attack; it ate it.

"No!" The lich poured everything he had into the assault. "I am the master of death!"

"Oh, fucking *please*. You're middle management at best," I corrected. "Now, let me show you what real death magic looks like."

I turned to Bob, who'd been standing perfectly still beside me, and laid my hand on his arm. "Hey, buddy. Want some juice?"

Bob's skull turned toward me, eye sockets flaring with interest.

I took all that death magic—every bit of power the lich had gathered, everything my shield had absorbed—and pushed it into Bob. Not as an attack, but as pure energy, shifting it into the Bonemeld spell, and powering it past the limits I'd felt before.

The lich had stopped now, seeing it wasn't working, but I hadn't.

He'd gathered a huge amount of death mana here, and fuck me, I wasn't letting it get away. I drank it down like a hamster with a water bottle.

Bob's bones shook. Then they changed.

"*POWER.*" Bob's voice was like an earthquake in my mind. "*YES.*"

I focused on him, using the massive influx of death magic to fuel it beyond anything I'd attempted before. Bob's form shifted, compressing, refining. What had been a massive skeleton condensed, bones becoming denser, stronger, more perfect with each passing second.

"What are you doing?!" Nethys screamed, actual fear in his voice now.

"Necromancy at its best. Recycle, reuse, reanimate," I replied absently. "You know…waste not, want not."

Bob continued to shrink, but I could feel his power growing exponentially. By the time he stabilized at just over six feet—large for a human but no longer monstrous—he practically vibrated with contained might.

"Bob?" I asked. "How you feeling?"

Bob flexed his fingers experimentally. Then, moving faster than any skeleton had a right to, he blurred forward. His fist connected with the nearest undead, and it didn't just destroy it—it obliterated it. The skeleton exploded into powder so fine it looked like mist.

"*Good,*" Bob decided. "*Very good.*"

"You must serve me!" Nethys barked, casting something that looked like a magic tether, lashing it out and wrapping it around Bob's throat, before backing away. "This is impossible! I am eternal! I am—"

"You're done," I said. "Bob? Clear a path."

Bob moved like death itself given purpose. Every strike didn't just destroy undead—it unmade them. Bob grabbed onto them and drained them of their mana, causing them to collapse into their components. And when you did that to a necromantic army? Well, in seconds, he'd carved a corridor through the packed corpses, straight to the lich.

Nethys turned and ran. His undead army shifted to let him past, and then fell in again to slow my buddy. Two of the vampyr rushed forward, as the rest backed away with him.

"Bob, that's enough," I called. "Fall back and clear the area, please."

He paused, snatched a vampyr out of the air and gripped it with one hand closed over its face, turning back to me, even as the vampyr started to screech and writhe as he drained it of its death mana.

"Fuck me, that's a hell of a skill," one legionnaire muttered, and I didn't disagree. In feeding him so much mana to upgrade his bones, I'd clearly imbued him with some kind of local control over the mana, and that was going to make him a disaster for any undead.

"Oh, before you go," I called after the fleeing lich. "I should mention—I lied twice."

"What?" the lich yelled back, confusion pretty clear as he saw that I wasn't chasing him and we were waiting. He stumbled to a halt, glaring back at us. "What do you mean?"

"Tenandra!" I shouted. "Make it rain!"

She twisted to the side, angling her deck slightly as she brought the ripple-fire cannons to bear, and they both spoke as one. The sound was like the world tearing apart. And then the undead started dying. Really dying. The concentrated fire carved through their ranks like a blowtorch through rice paper, each impact creating a circle of absolute destruction twenty feet across.

"NOOOO!" Nethys screamed as his army was shredded. He tried to run, but there was nowhere to go. The cannons tracked him with mechanical precision. Dragon's Wrath kicked in just as the last flesh golem ran out to help its boss, and the massively overpowered plasma cannons basically rendered that entire section of the nearby streets to glass in seconds.

"Think that got him?" Ronin asked hopefully as the cannon finally fell silent.

"You know, I think it did," I mused. "But he's a lich. So we need to find his phylactery or he'll just reform."

"And we lost the loot," Grizz said mournfully. "There's no way anything is recoverable there."

"Goddammit." I swore. "Fuck, I never even thought about that!"

"And that's when you know you have your priorities backward, boys and girls," Tang called from the back. "Always know where the loot is!"

"Later," Borren said. "We've got more company!"

He was right. The bombardment had cleared vast swaths of the undead, but more poured from buildings, sewers…anywhere they could hide. Not as many as before—we'd probably destroyed half the city's population already—but still enough to be a problem.

"Form up!" I commanded. "We push for the tower! Tenandra, give us covering fire but watch for friendlies!"

"*Acknowledged*!" Her cannons cooled and recovered on the starboard side; she pivoted to port, presenting the other two and then continued their deadly work. Instead of focusing on a single area, she dragged the explosions across the city with more precision, picking off clusters of undead as they formed.

We regrouped and started to march, the legion maintaining their shield wall while the rest of us dealt with anything that got too close. Bob was a one-skeleton army. His new form allowed him to move with incredible speed out ahead of us, grabbing and slaughtering the undead as soon as they came within reach.

"Wights on the left!" Yen called out as three ghostly women, dressed in long, flowing robes appeared inside a building, their mouths more like a snake's than a human, and their skin pale as a very pale thing indeed.

"Mine!" Sehran called, before unleashing a concentrated sonic scream into the building and canceling out the ethereal wails that they'd begun, as Tang fired arrow after arrow into their heads, dropping them before they could close.

"Bone wheels!" That was Arrin, pointing at horrible constructions of skeletons formed into rolling death traps.

"Mine!" Yen darted forward. A single massive spear like a lance of flaming light formed over her right hand. She hurled it at them; the resulting explosion sent bone fragments flying in all directions.

We pushed forward street by street, building by building. Every hundred yards or so, we'd stop to consolidate, check for wounded, redistribute potions. The legion had taken a handful of casualties—not many, but some—and Tenandra had already swept in to evacuate the worst injured after a literal building collapsed on three legionnaires, fucking their armor up beyond fixing.

"How we doing on mana?" I asked during one such pause.

"Running low," Arrin admitted. "Maybe a quarter left."

"About the same." Several of the other casters reported similar levels.

"Then we conserve from here on," I decided. "Melee fighters, take point. Casters, support only. We need to save strength for whatever's in that tower."

"Speaking of which." Flux's voice carried from where he was stealthed nearby. "We're almost there."

He was right. The black tower loomed before us, maybe a hundred yards away. The space around it was surprisingly clear of undead, like even they didn't want to get too close.

"I don't like this," Borren said. "It's too quiet."

"Yeah," I agreed. "Bob, you sense anything?"

"*Death,*" Bob said helpfully.

"Specific as always, buddy." I sighed. "All right, everyone ready? Because whatever's in there, it knows we're coming."

CHAPTER THIRTY-SIX

The tower was big—not "great tower" big, obviously, but it was still impressive. Maybe thirty meters across and eighty to a hundred high, or so it seemed from this angle, which made it look squat but powerful.

Stone steps led up to it from a wide and imposing plaza that it occupied the middle of, and what would once have been hundreds of shops and buildings, homes and more were clear in the buildings that faced onto the plaza as well, with the streets that led off from it laid out like spokes in a wheel.

The buildings here were clearly better made than those out in the main city, and where they'd collapsed—some looking like it was from fighting rather than simple degradation—the debris had been cleared away or piled in the building itself.

It was still a ruin, sure, but the tower was more or less intact. It was clear that anything that came here was supposed to behave itself.

Unfortunately for the previous master of the city, I wasn't very good at that.

On the trip here, we'd been hit continuously by the undead, mainly utterly brainless ones that were incredibly easy to deal with. Thanks to the width of the streets, we'd reformed into a narrow, oblong formation and had simply marched through them.

The more unusual undead—the occasional vampyr…two of them, and they were weak, suggesting the more powerful were the ones that we'd reduced to greasy smoke with the lich…the wights, and a single banshee that had been unpleasant as hell—were exclusively dealt with by Bob.

He was having a whale of a time. His new ability to rip the death magic from anything he touched and then absorb it into himself was helping him to evolve in real time. The fragments of his soul, I could faintly sense, were binding together ever more finely, and he was…well, he was exactly what he needed to be.

He was protecting his people, as he'd always wanted to, and it was becoming clear that we'd accidentally created the perfect counter to the area.

He was going to march around, hoovering up the death mana, and as had happened when I absorbed the Fragment of Death, life was surging in its wake.

Not much, and not yet, but we were in the middle of an undead city, and we could all feel the difference.

I was going to need to have a conversation with Ashante about him when all this was over.

Either way, though, we were now drawn up and staring across the open plaza at the large doors ahead. All around us, the constant push of undead had died away.

It was slowly getting quieter, but the most obvious thing here was that since the loss of the lich, there was a lot less coordination from the undead. They were coming in ever increasing waves, though, meaning that we had to make the difficult decision to leave the legionnaires here to hold the area.

We'd hoped that we'd all be able to continue as a group, and ideally for the undead to have collapsed without the lich in command. But until it was fully dead, we were clearly stuck.

We knew the lich would have a phylactery, and until that was destroyed, the fucker wasn't truly dead. I'd checked my notifications and seen that although I had a load of undead marked in there, they were, well, regular. Tenandra had examined the area with every sense she had, confirming that beyond what was now basically a lot of low-grade charcoal with some unusual impurities, there was nothing else there.

That meant either that fucker had escaped the bombardment—possible but highly unlikely—or it was dead and the phylactery was going to be absorbing mana even now to reform him.

That was fine. As long as we found him in the next few hours, he was going to be, at best, as weak as a kitten. But if this was the previous lord of the city who the legion had thought they'd killed long ago, then there was a chance there was a hiding place somewhere that hadn't been found last time, and we'd have to dedicate a lot of effort to that.

What we needed to do, though, was get in there and slaughter the fuck out of the fragment bearers, or have them join us. I was betting that was unlikely, given the hunger I'd seen for power so far, but also, well, you never knew.

Mind you, that they'd come to an undead city and then apparently had taken up station in the heart of it and kicked the lich out of his home, using him as little more than a door guard, I wasn't overly hopeful about them turning out to be really cool people who just wanted to help.

I paused, trying to remember their names, then shrugged and pulled up the notification I'd gotten awhile back and reread it.

Altaic the Red and Hildegaard of Tanis.

When I'd asked around, Altaic the Red had been some kind of powerful fire mage, like insanely powerful, so I could guess that his fragment was going to be fire or something connected, which was cool. That slightly opened a door, as maybe he'd be more willing to discuss and make a deal, with me being Jenae's champion and Chosen.

Hildegaard of Tanis, though, nobody knew much about—or if they did, they weren't saying. I'd mentioned it to Captain Tim, and he'd looked at me like I was making shit up, before telling me that Tanis was a coastal city far to the south and was apparently a complete shithole.

It was basically Kronk, but with money and style. Although that didn't usually equate to "shithole" for anyone, it did for me when he pointed out that it didn't bother to raid other cities; it made them pay tribute by sending assassins that went *way* over the line.

Like "nailed the target's family to the walls of their city and flayed them" as a greeting.

A first contact.

Their. Entire. Family.

The example he'd told me about had included the family dog, and if there was ever a situation where I totally understood going full-on John Wick, it was when someone flayed a puppy alive and nailed it to a wall.

I'd marked that on my list as "kill it with fire" as the best way to deal with the city.

Anyone who willingly used that place instead of a surname or title? Yeah, I wasn't feeling a friendly conversation was likely.

Regardless, standing out here and staring at the doors wasn't achieving anything.

"Okay, people, remember: the aim is to secure the city. We kill anything that wants a fight, we capture the portal, and I deal with the fragment bearers. You are to stay the fuck out of the fight, all right?" I looked around, waiting until everyone had agreed in one form or another.

Lydia looked pissed and mutinous, and Ronin relieved to the point I was half expecting a puddle to spread beneath his feet. But beyond those two extremes, it was all good.

"An' t'lich?" Lydia growled.

"Have fun." I shrugged. "Seriously, I trust you to do what needs to be done. But in there, if there are two fragment bearers who are in full control of their powers, you're not going to win that fight. Trust me, and please, stand back. Let me deal with it."

"Ah'll not watch yer die," she rumbled. "So yer better win."

"Well, yeah, it's on my to-do list." I grinned.

"Dyin'?"

"No, for fuck's sake, you idiot—living!" Glaring at her, I gestured to the doors ahead. Bob took the lead, clearly deciding that if there was a death magic trap— as seemed most likely in a necromantic lich's city—then he was the best placed to deal with it.

There were two, it turned out. One gave him some nasty charring on his legs as the CorpseFire trap burst to life beneath him as he opened the door. But considering a second later, the death mana was ripped from the flames, it left normal fire to blacken and mark him up, but that was about it.

The second trap was a needle that was attached to the handle, and it injected a poison of some kind. What it was we didn't know, but considering that Bob just snapped it off and tossed it into the dying flames, we never got to find out.

An advantage of being undead was, well, poisons just weren't a big thing for you.

He threw the doors wide and marched inside, revealing the ground floor, and letting the echoing *boom* as the doors hit the walls ring out.

It was a bit anticlimactic, as there was fuck all waiting for us, but it looked cool.

Instead, a passage, to the left and built into the wall, led to a stairwell that ringed the floor. We took that, even as Flux dispatched a pair of the assassin team along with Lio to the stairwell that led into the basement instead, just in case.

We marched upward, passing ancient paintings that were lost under a coating of mold, windows that had long since lost their shutters and glass, and the occasional lit magelight.

The vast majority were long dead, though still valuable, and I pretended not to notice Ronin pocketing as many as he could as we went.

Fucking bards.

The next floor and the ones after were the same: large floors, a circular area in the middle that looked to be a sort of common area or gathering point, and rooms that led off it. Nothing new or interesting…just occasional furniture, and more often, debris and the signs of long neglect.

We passed signs of frequent passage, such as dust in the corners but none on the center of the steps, but beyond that, the damn tower could have been abandoned in truth.

Flux and the other mer—besides Bane—moved onto each floor, scanning it with their Worldsense and then returning, shaking heads as we continued.

Bane stayed close by me, absolutely silent.

Twenty minutes later, we approached the final floor. At last, there were signs of life—though, admittedly, not the kind that I was hoping for.

They were screams, and they came from behind a pair of sealed doors.

Between us and the doors were two creatures I'd never seen before. But one of the party had.

"Fuck me, fire elementals," Ronin whispered. "This one's all on you, boss. Sorry. Left my fireproof undies on the ship."

"Dude, the only time we expect you to take the lead in is in whoring, staying in fucking bed, or lying." Grizz snorted. "Boss, you mind me taking these fuckers?"

"Be my guest," I agreed.

They were already moving forward, hands gathering flames.

They were slim, maybe a similar build to the elves, and humanoid, but beyond sections of their body that appeared to flow like magma, in the center of their chests, and spread out across their bodies like a thin skeleton, the rest was all roaring flames.

The first suddenly surged forward, skating across the floor and leaving a trail of blackened stone behind it, even as it reached for the big legionnaire.

Grizz grinned, his massive sword and shield at the ready. The carved and enameled red dragon inlaid into the blade suddenly glowed brighter.

I focused, unable to remember the details of the two weapons, and pulled them up after using my identify spell.

Knight's Revenge	Further Description *Yes/No*
Damage:	**5-500**
Defense:	**+12-50**
Details:	This Imperial Legion Shield has been reinforced with banded steel and Orichalcum, then overlaid with a thin patina of Francicanin Scales. **Shieldwall:** Able to take part in a standard Legion Shieldwall, but will add +12 defense to the overall defense instead of the standard +5.

	Revenge: Any attacks blocked by this shield will result in a 10% reflection of the damage defended against being redirected upon the attacker.
	Knight: The Imperial Legion Knights were a specialist team; when a confirmed Knight wields this shield, the Defensive properties are doubled.

Rarity:	**Magical:**	**Durability:**	**Charge:**
Legendary	Yes	97/100	100/100

Flame of the Righteous	**Further Description** *Yes/No*
Damage:	**50-500 + 25-250 Fire Damage**
Details:	This Imperial Legion sword has been constructed from Chromium and Electrum, with the hilt wrapped in Francicanin Scales. **Punishment:** The ability Punishment allows a Confirmed Knight of the Empire to use a charge to deliver a single blow that results in 10x the weapon's maximum damage, but the Knight will be drained of all mana and stamina in the use of this Ability and will be stunned until they recover 10% of their loss. **Last Stand:** A Knight stands alone at times, outnumbered, and without hope. In these dark times, they may consume their own health, mana, and stamina at a rate of 3 points per second, to increase the damage they wield by the same, and until one of these pools are depleted, the damage will continue to build. **Bulwark:** The Imperial Legion Knight is a Legionnaire who stands between the innocent and all that would do them harm. For so long as they stand in defense of another, their Constitution gains +10.

Rarity:	**Magical:**	**Durability:**	**Charge:**
Legendary	Yes	96/100	100/100

I hesitated, about to mention to Grizz that his sword did fucking *fire* damage, but it was too late. I darted forward as the flame elemental leapt at him; its claws swiped down and across the shield as if expecting to cut through it like butter.

Instead, there was a second as something apparently cracked—and it wasn't the shield. Grizz took the impact, then shoved back, yelling, "Shield-bash!"

The shield slammed into the elemental as it staggered, and nearly threw it through the closed doors behind it. The other elemental dodged its companion, looked back in confusion at it, and then forward, right into the sword that split its head from crown to chin.

It collapsed to its knees, its head being kinda important, but clearly not vital. It reached up uncertainly, trying to push the two sides of the head back together, as Ronin shouted out from behind us.

"Cut its head off and it's weaker, but you have to take the heart out! It's an elemental core!"

Grizz nodded and flipped the blade around to lop its head—and its hands— off with one strike, then reversed the swing and hacked through its waist, before snap kicking its chest.

The upper half of it was hurled backward, clear of the rest…which suddenly collapsed to the floor, the molten rock splattering even as the flames whooshed out.

Then Grizz was moving. The tip of the blade lanced out to skewer the second through the heart as it stood. It froze, then its own flames whooshed out again. A second load of molten rock splattered down, the temperature in the room higher than it had any reasonable right to be. But the windows that were empty to the sky, on either side of the exit from the stairwell, helped to draw the heat away.

"We really need a water mage…" I muttered, then almost facepalmed, and cast my healing fountain spell.

It came up under both the wriggling torso of the second, and the smoking core that sat in the middle of the magma that had been the first, and the room was engulfed in steam.

I barely had time to see the shadow that moved through the steam before I was shoved aside. Bane deflected a strike that was clearly meant for me.

Then he and Flux were moving, blades flashing.

I cursed, not seeing anything beyond a faint shadow that flashed in and out of the steam. I started to cast immediately, and though it only took seconds, that was enough time for Flux to go down with one of his lower arms severed at the elbow, and two of the other mer to die.

Bane was fast and deadly, but he was on the back foot, defending and trying to keep whatever it was back from me and the others. Clearly only the mer could see it, and even he was having trouble as the steam faded.

I almost canceled the spell and started with a fresh fountain, but held on, gritting my teeth as I subvocalized, then slammed a Frostfire Circle of Cleansing down under us all.

The room we were in was clearly only intended as an entry to whatever was beyond that door, shaped like a capital D from above, with the stairwell ending in the middle of the curve, and the doorway into the room beyond in the middle of the straight section.

On either side of the stairwell were the two windows, but they were behind us. That meant that beyond the doors into the next area was the only place to go, as the floor under us all lit with flames.

They rushed to Flux, Bane, and the shadow, the dead mer getting a cursory flicker as flames passed over them, but evidently found nothing fixable.

One was missing her head, and a second had been stabbed through the eye and lay on the floor in a pool of blood and cerebral fluids, so I wasn't surprised.

Bane let out a sudden blast of Worldsense. The narrow room bounced it off the walls and made us all stagger, but the figure he faced suffered a lot more.

Already burning, they were becoming visible as whatever control they had over their concealment failed, and then the Worldsense, which I knew from experience could rupture eardrums and a hell of a lot worse, slammed into them point-blank.

They staggered, slashing at him desperately with two shortswords; he twisted, allowing one to go wide, and then caught the other with both of his left-hand blades.

The right arms snapped out and his opponent screamed, as they cut through their forearm.

A sudden massive overpressure sent Bane flying back; the assassin reached for their fallen forearm, only to dive aside as an arrow as long as my arm passed through the gap they were about to inhabit.

Tang drew back again, and, cursing, the assassin spun and ran for the door behind them, truncated right arm clutched to their chest as they shouldered it open.

The next arrow slammed into their right shoulder. But instead of going down, the image poofed into black smoke, and the real assassin was revealed a good two meters to the right, inside the room, and sprinting.

I darted forward, as did the others. Yen was already casting, pulling up her flame lance. But a dozen images of the assassin appeared, sprinting in all directions to give them cover. It was Lydia who dispersed them, her wings flaring with bright white light and the light of the stars. Where it passed through a glass roof overhead was suddenly folded down and down, until a tiny section of it was dragged across the floor where the assassin had been, in a zigzag, unpredictable, darting pattern.

Ghostly illusions poofed into shadow over and over, but none fast enough to reveal the assassin before the only other inhabitant in the room made themselves known.

Fire suddenly raced from one side to the other, forming a wall that started halfway into the room, and then sped toward our end, burning anything and everything that lay before it.

I leapt forward, both hands coming up. I triggered my shield again, hands outstretched as I triggered the tattoos as well. I allowed the fire to slam into me, so that I could absorb it and feed that mana into my shield.

The firewall bent around me, but my shield was wide enough and the room here narrow enough that it couldn't pass. A heartbeat later, the flames collapsed, leaving me panting and staring through the heat haze, at the partly ruined room before us.

It was a throne room, clearly, and yeah, we'd found the portal as well.

It was pressed into the wall on the left of the room, about three-quarters of the way along toward the far end, and just as clearly deactivated, considering how it stood, doing absolutely fuck all at the minute.

The rest of the room was taken up by a load of smoldering furniture, several large windows, and what I assumed was a defunct creation table off to one side.

I guessed it was defunct because otherwise nobody in their right mind would have basically been using the top of it as a normal table, but these fuckers had been, and we'd clearly interrupted dinner.

There were three other notable things in the room that demanded attention—not the throne, though that was gaudy enough that a third world dictator would have been clutching himself and panting at the sight of it.

No, it was the recovering lich who had already been relieved of its arms and legs and *nailed to the wall*, then the pair of fuckers who stood facing us.

One was clearly Altaic the Red, judging from the red robes, the flaming red beard and hair—that had to be fucking dyed; there was no way that was natural—and the staff he clutched grimly.

It was clearly painted red as well.

The other was the assassin we'd been facing. They were wrapped from head to toe in leather; even their face was hidden by a hood. Although they only had one hand, they clutched a health potion, even as wisps of smoke rose from their armor.

"We finally meet!" Altaic the Red boomed, slamming the base of his staff down with an echo that filled the air. "I am Altaic, sometimes known as Altaic the Red, and a master of fire. My companion is Hildegaard. And you?"

"Seriously?" I strode forward. "You fucking know who I am."

"Ah, a whelp who's unable to summon common courtesy, eh? Very well, then in that case…"

"Jax!" Tang roared, letting loose with an arrow to the left of the room.

As we spun to track it, the arrow split in midair, the "slayer" arrow streaking across the room.

How did I know it was a slayer? Well, it split in midair, into six smaller arrows, and fuuuuuck me.

The first, which punched straight through the shield that had been thrown up, was appropriately enough and totally unsurprisingly, an anti-shield arrow, specifically designed to destroy them. The second? A stun and silence. It hit the fucker as he was revealed, Altaic the Red…but no longer where he had been; the illusion that we'd seen faded.

He staggered, stunned and confused; his mouth flapped but no sound escaped. He clutched his head and stomach, the impact having driven him back as the arrow vibrated.

The third arrow, chainfire, lived up to its name. Six chains of iron and blue flame appeared, bursting out of the end of that arrow as it hit him an inch higher than the last, and pinned his wrists to his lower chest.

As they tightened around him, he clearly wailed in pain, though still, we heard not a sound.

Fourth was a firestorm, which created a zone two meters around him filled with swirling flames, which then vanished as he sucked them into himself—gaining a little healing and relief with that one, which sucked.

Arrow five though, hit him and shattered. All six little hollow glass "teeth" burrowed into his flesh and extended needles, causing blood to literally gush from their entry points.

The sixth, was yeah, sort of overkill by this point. Banshee's Wail, it was identified as. Although we were behind it and well out of the way, we still all winced and shook our heads, trying to get our ears to pop from the sudden, horrifically high-pitched noise.

For him, though?

His eyes exploded, as did his eardrums; he staggered sideways and blood gushed from basically everywhere.

I grinned. Looks like Tang was getting a fucking fruit basket.

Or he was.

Because, right then, as I took my first step forward, the assassin appeared and cut Altaic's head off with a single strike, killing him—and claimed Altaic's fragment for their own.

<u>CHAPTER THIRTY-SEVEN, THE LAST CHAPTER</u>

I gaped, then cursed, as the assassin stiffened, clearly accepting the fragment. I started to run.

I triggered Mana Overdrive, Hyper Cognition, and Temporal Fluidity, and I fucking let loose with everything I had. I knew what was happening, and that I had no time to catch the fucker. Indeed, as I closed the last few meters to them, having crossed the room in the blink of an eye, they were already coming out of it, and they saw me approach.

The assassin jerked back, then exploded into a black cloud of smoke as I swung my naginata sideways at their head, and triggered Fractal Mind, my chaos fragment's ability.

I saw a sudden surge of a hundred possibilities of where and how I could and would move from here, as well as where they would be.

Only two showed as catching the fucker, and I slammed my mind back together with a force of will that could have made boulders weep.

They were behind me, and already aiming with a dagger.

I yanked backward with my naginata. Its length gave me all I needed to slam the metal-clad end into the assassin's face, breaking bones and sending them to the floor, stunned.

I twisted, allowing myself to fall backward, away from them, to ensure I could lock my gaze onto them. I triggered the one ability that I knew was going to decide this fucking fight: Soul Anchor.

A crackling light erupted from my chest and slammed into the assassin, presumably Hildegaard.

They tried to dodge, throwing themselves sideways and rolling. A shadow burst from the folds of their clothing and roiled across them like oil, but it was too late.

A connection was made, and in a heartbeat, half the room was surrounded by a dome of crackling blue light, with the two of us stuck in the center, a tether tying us both together.

"Fool!" a clearly woman's voice snarled. "Light-bound fucking idiot!"

"Yeah…well, fuck you too, Hildegaard," I ground out, climbing to my feet and glaring at her.

"You can't claim them both!" she snarled at me. "Fighting me now? Even if you win, you can only claim one fragment, and one will be lost forever!"

"What?" I squinted at her, setting myself and glad that the tether was still clearly visible connecting us, meaning no more fucking illusions were going to be messing with the fight.

"The fucking fragment, you idiot!" she snapped. "What, you think you can claim them both? You can't! One per fight. The gods can recover and fight and lose one again later, but we can't! You kill me here, and yeah, you'll gain a single fragment, but the other is lost! So come on—what's it worth, hero?"

"What?" I watched her.

"Peace," she spat. "You want me to take an oath and serve you, is that it?"

"So that you can keep your life and the fragments?" I asked, and she nodded.

"Of course, you fucking fool!" She tucked her injured arm closer to her side, and turned slightly away from me.

I'd noticed the pale flesh that was at the end of the arm now. The glove and wrist guard were still missing, but the way she hunched down made it clear that she didn't want me paying attention to it.

My first instinct therefore was to look at it, but Hyper Cognition was still active. As my mind raced, three things came to light.

First of all, the description of Soul Anchor:

Soul Anchor
Create a spiritual anchor between your soul and that of your target, forcing them to remain in close proximity to you.

Note this bond cannot be dissolved, and it must end with a Fragment of a Divine Soul attached to that of the originating Soul Anchor. Should you lose this fight, your own Fragment will be drawn into your opponent.

Charge: 1 per 24 hours

That meant that there was no way out of this fight without one of us losing our fragment. And for us, as semi-mortal demigods, *without* an immortal body, that meant only one of us was walking away from this, as I was willing to bet she knew.

Second: she was a fucking *assassin,* and there was no way she was that obvious about trying to hide anything. And lastly?

Whatever the fragment was that she'd claimed, it'd have come with a power, sure, but she seemed to think that all the others would be dropped, meaning that this place was about to become ground zero for an insanely powerful concentration of a form of mana.

If a fragment couldn't be claimed, it dissolved into the ether, forming a connection with the world around it, increasing that mana form's strength and basically flooding the world with it.

The Cradle of Feshcan'un was one such spot, where a fragment of life had been released, and now it was a place that was basically overflowing with it. Plants grew faster, stronger and healthier, as did anything alive.

Yeah, when someone had fucked it up and messed with the balance and doubled down on that, it'd resulted in uncontrolled mutations, but hey, shit happened.

All those things flashed through my mind, and a half second later, a dagger nearly joined them.

I twisted to the left as a dagger slammed into the corner of my helmet's slit, the section I saw out of, and it very nearly impaled my brain.

Fortunately, not that she knew that, but there wasn't an empty space there. It held something like enchanted glass, and the strike was a hair off, skittering across the gloss of the side of my helm, as I stabbed out with my naginata.

She'd twisted and darted to her left, letting the blade pass between us. She dropped to the ground, her stump of a reforming hand—the fucker must have had some insanely good potion—was already braced to catch her, as she stabbed up. The tip of a needle-pointed dirk slammed into the black chainmail hauberk that was under and between my armor plates.

It skittered across two links, then found a gap, sinking in, and went for my right knee.

I dropped forward, not bothering to aim. Instead, I came down on her hard with the full weight of my plate and me behind it, driving her to the floor and stopping the dirk getting much deeper. But I also saw the sudden flare of my health bar and a "poisoned" notification pop up in the corner of my vision.

She twisted, abandoning the dirk and trying to get free of me even as my health dropped faster and faster. The green "poisoned" symbol suddenly shifted to a bright red and black that flashed repeatedly.

Not good.

A wave of pain ripped through me, but I ignored it as Hildegaard tried to shove me off her. Her palm and nub of reforming flesh pounded against me in repeated strikes, but the weight and solidity of my armor meant that all she was doing was breaking her own bones.

I grabbed her wrists, then saw the fingers, how she was flashing them in a pattern. A sudden whoosh of flame rolled over me, focusing on my head, and then poured down my body. My armor heated at a horrific rate as she apparently cast some kind of flame spell I wasn't familiar with.

I pulled back and nutted her.

My helm had a blade in place of the crest, and fuck me it was vicious. But the angle was wrong, and I couldn't bring it to bear. The effect of having her nose go from its usual shape and size to millimeters thick and smashed inward gave me a second's respite as she was stunned.

I activated Titan's Resolve, and then Adamantine Constitution, the pair reacting to each other as my body hardened further.

My health was still dropping, but it faded from black and red to green again, as the Adamantine Constitution kicked in, armoring my organs, bones, and skin.

The dirk was still in my leg, but as I moved, I felt it being pushed free. Hildegaard drew back and then spat in my face. It hit the helm again…but it wasn't spit or blood. Whatever it was, it was noxious as hell. I frantically held my breath, refusing to breathe it in. Instead, I twisted her arms and squeezed with all my might.

Her bones snapped like toothpicks, and she screamed. I reared back, releasing her right arm and planting that hand over her heart instead to hold her in place, then punched her in the face.

Her head bounced off the ground, but her eyes suddenly flared with light—light that flashed from all her body a second later. I crashed to the stone floor, blinking, the afterimage left seared into my vision.

I blinked, trying to see, but it was no use. Something hit me from the side; a second blow hit the armoring around my neck as she tried to stab me there. This time, I closed my eyes, my perception enhancing my other senses enough that, combined with the tether, I felt her before she could strike.

I slammed my right hand down as I lashed out blindly with my left to drive her back; my right flicked as I cast the spell. By the time I'd taken two more steps after her again, the spell was done.

Frostfire Circle of Cleansing roared to life under my feet, and I heard her cry out as she tried to get clear.

The spell took up over half of our little dome, meaning that although she got free—leaping over a set of already smoldering leather couches—she'd taken several burns in doing so. I blinked and grinned, the flames already searing free the poison that she'd gotten me with, and repairing my eyes as well.

Still, she didn't need to know that.

I staggered, then fell to my knees, waving my hands frantically as if trying to catch her, blinded. She apparently took it, darting to the side, bending over and grabbing at my naginata…

As I triggered Soaring Majesty, I hurled myself across the few meters between us and slammed into her.

The naginata went flying, and so did we, rolling over and over as she frantically tried to land a blow that would do more than smear her blood on my armor.

She came up on top. Her healing potion or whatever she was doing had repaired her limbs enough that she tried to drag my dagger free, hissing in pain, her broken fingers catching on the hilt. But it was too late.

I still had Titan's Resolve active, as well as Mana Overdrive, and Hyper Cognition. Risking it all, but determined I'd not fail, I triggered Fractal Mind.

The myriad possibilities flared again for me. I felt suddenly sick to my stomach, pain ripping through me, but I'd seen what I needed.

I lashed out, punching her in the stomach with all my strength. My fingers extended into a blade of bone and metal, ripping through her damaged armor, her stomach, and upward past her lungs.

I felt the fluttering of her heart as I locked my fingers around it and crushed it like a grape. For a long moment, we stared at each other. Then she let loose a last gasp, and my vision exploded with notifications.

<u>EPILOGUE</u>

"Are you okay?" Bane asked me, awhile later, as I sat on the throne, staring at my hand, deep in thought.

"What?" I blinked, looking up.

"I asked if you're okay, you stupid bastard!" He reached out and flicked me between the eyes, making me jerk back.

"Fucker, that hurt!" I snarled.

"It was supposed to. And stop being such a baby!" he growled. "So?"

"Yeah, I'm all right," I grumbled, before straightening up and looking around the room.

It'd changed a lot in the last hour or so. The legionnaires had cleared a lot of the general crap out, the lich had been killed—I'd told Lydia to give the kill to someone who'd earned it as a reward and she'd surprised everyone by giving it to Ronin—and now the throne room looked almost livable.

If, you know, you ignored the empty windows and the blood everywhere, and the smell of burned flesh and the…

It wasn't the worst place we'd been in but it wasn't the nicest either, and that was probably the best that could be said about it.

"Then why are you still staring at your hand?" Bane asked.

I shrugged, then hit myself with Scour. "It's not my hand…" I said, unsure of where to go with it, until he spoke up.

"Then whoever's hand it is, is already traumatized."

"Oh, fuck off." I snorted a laugh, then felt guilty, as I always did when I felt anything but anger or sadness, since they'd been taken. "I'm just trying to decide what to do, that's all."

"About?"

"The two fragments."

"What are they?"

"Shadow, which I know I can trade to Tamat and get her both a hell of a boost in personal strength, and help the pantheon overall, and…"

"And?"

"Magic."

"What about it?" He frowned.

"It's *magic*," I repeated, before sighing. "It's not fire, like I thought it was the way that prick was acting. It's a literal fragment of magic, and that makes no goddamn sense."

"Why?"

"Because everything I know says that the gods don't work like that—that they're fire and water and all that shit, not magic. I mean, 'magic mana'? How would that work?"

"Isn't all mana magic?" he countered, and I waved that off. "What's the problem then?"

"I can only claim one," I said.

"So?"

"So whatever I choose, the other one will be released into the world, with this as its heart. It'll make the area around this much more powerfully magical, and with that fragment, that flavor or whatever, as the influencer."

"Again, what's the problem?" He sat down on the steps of the throne and waited.

"If I accept shadow, Tamat is gonna be pissed. She'll want it. I'm fine with that, sort of, because it'll make her more powerful and therefore the pantheon. But she's already absorbing the last fragment I gave her of that, and it might be a while before she can claim another—like a year, a century…I don't know."

"So, can you hold it for her?"

"No," I admitted. "If I have it, then I need to bind it when the time comes, and she's gonna be pissed about that."

"Okay, so bind it now, or the other one, or trade it to a different god."

"I can't." I waved that aside. "If I trade it to another god, then they'll be weakened while they absorb it. Instead of strengthening the pantheon, I'll weaken it as another is taken out. Plus, it'll really piss Tamat off."

"Okay, so those options are both out, and we're back to absorb the other one, the magic one." He nodded.

"Yeah."

"But you don't want to do that?"

"I do, but…"

"Am I going to have to stab you with a hooked dagger to drag every word out of you?" He showed me the dagger of ripping that I'd given him ages ago. The back was serrated, and the tip doubled back on itself, making sure that when it was withdrawn, it'd do double the damage it'd make on entry.

"If I absorb the shadow one, I'll get a shadow-based ability, and my magic will be turned more into a stealth-based direction," I explained in a rush. "I don't want that. But if I do it, then the Fragment of Magic is released here. Then everyone who lives here, who studies or whatever, their magic is going to be that little bit more powerful and easy to use. The difference could be massive, and it'd help hundreds, maybe thousands."

There was a long moment of silence between us again, before he finally spoke.

"And if you absorb the Fragment of Magic?"

"I don't know," I hedged.

"Liar."

"I don't, all right? I just…" I rubbed at my chin, before going on, sitting back in the throne. "I think it'll make my magic more powerful, faster to use and help me to understand it."

"And the Fragment of Shadow?"

"It'd be released here and it'd help people who were going down the stealth route. But it'd make those kinds of abilities more powerful, so if an assassin from outside the empire came here, they'd be able to use their abilities better and easier, and could do horrific damage before they were caught."

"You're an idiot," he said after a few seconds of companionable silence. "You know that, right?"

"It's not that simple," I growled.

"Of course it is." He shook his head. "Pick the one that'll help you the most. You said before that the way you'll ascend as a god is to make choices that resonate with you, that match who you are."

"Did I?"

"Well, something like that." He shrugged. "The simple answer is you'd make a shit rogue. You could barely hide a nut from a blind squirrel, and that's only if it also had no nose and had been dead for a week. Magic? You're good at that. So, the question is, play to your strength and get better, or take a stealth ability and become slightly less shit with it?"

I opened my mouth to respond, and he pointed a finger at me.

"Not become 'good'…become *slightly* less shit. Not even a fragment of the divine can make you stealthy. For a start, you fart constantly when you try to creep around hiding."

"No, I don't!" I snapped.

"Maybe you do, maybe you don't. But you'll always be shit at it."

"Fuck you, Bane."

"I know you've been alone for a while, but you'll need to ask nicer than that," he replied dryly, and I couldn't help but grin at him. "So, you going to make the choice we both know you need to, or you going to agonize over it a bit longer? I can ask Ronin to play something depressing, if you'd like?"

"Fuck you," I repeated. I selected the Fragment of Magic, feeling it forming, sliding free of the dead assassin and slipping into me.

I didn't bind it. I held it inside my soul, ignoring the yearning that I felt, surprised by the strength of it. I let out a long sigh, as the room shuddered at the release of the Fragment of Shadow.

The walls shifted, shivering as it flowed out, painting them in glossy onyx. The glass overhead tinted; the windows filled with blackness.

The entire building shivered as a thousand minor changes were made, and I reached out, moving to the side and laying my hand on the creation table.

The decision made, a weight lifted from me. I knew I was one step closer to freeing my love.

Next came the portal to Dravith, then reinforcements, a real foothold on this continent, and of course, a fuckton of violence. But in the meantime?

Congratulations!

You have reached the control center of the city of Ashen Heart and have the prerequisite authority and abilities to claim it and the surrounding land (891 square miles), adding it to your territory as a claimed location.

BONUS:

This location has been sanctified to the shadow and grants significant bonuses to any who walk the hidden paths.

Location gains a 10% modifier to training stealth, assassin, or rogue based skills, and powers discovered here will cost 25% less to use, and gain 25% to their effectiveness.

Do you wish to annex this territory now?

Yes/No

I stared at the prompt before my eyes, and smiled slowly, even as Lydia called out, asking whether I was activating the portal back to Dravith.

"Why, yes…" I purred. "I *do* want to annex this fucking territory."

Jez Cajiao

THE END OF BOOK 10 OF THE UNDERVERSE

PATREON

Hi everyone! Okay, when this launches in February, all of my Patreon supporters will have already read it, and most will have also already finished book 11, and will be on the final in the series, Book 12: Divinity Denied!

The highest tiers will have finished that long since, and are currently reading a secret project, and will be busily reading literally as I finish the chapters. So, if you want to read them perhaps 4-6 months ahead of release? Come join us on the dark side!

HOWEVER: I do want to point out one thing everyone, the app stores on apple and android platforms have enforced that a 30% mandatory percentage goes to them for any purchasing done through the **app**. So, the app store Patreon subscription has increased by that amount automatically, PLEASE sign up through the website instead, it's still Patreon's website, and the increase doesn't apply there.

There's several of those wonderful supporters out there that I have to thank personally as well; Gary Mischa and Niall, thank you all!

https://www.patreon.com/Jezcajiao

Jez Cajiao

<u>UNDERVERSE 11 : THE SOUL ANCHORS</u>

By Jez Cajiao

The gods left a secret. Jax needs to find it before Oracle's time runs out.

Returning to Dravith should have been a victory. Jax has claimed Ashen Heart, reunited with his forces, and finally understands what he's truly fighting— Xenefier, an enemy older than the gods themselves, holding Oracle and their unborn child captive.

But understanding the threat and stopping it are two very different things.

The gods predecessors knew they might fail in their final battle. So they hid something—knowledge, power, and secrets from those that would come after, in the hope that when the threat rose again, so too would a new hope. All of it locked away in the Library of Souls, anchored to the realm by six ancient sites scattered across multiple continents.

If Jax can find and unlock those anchors, he might gain the power he needs. But the high elf city of Albens guards more than just ancient secrets—it's dying, besieged by slavers who've been murdering children. And when negotiations with fragment bearer Lisandra reveal the price of alliance, Jax discovers that sometimes the hardest battles aren't against gods or monsters.

They're against the clock.

Split forces. Ancient secrets. And a debt paid in blood.

Book 11 of the UnderVerse series—where every choice has a cost, and Jax is running out of time.

<u>*Order now!*</u>

A FOREST OF VANITY AND VALOUR

By Adam Beswick

An aggressive debt collector banished from the kingdom. Now his life depends on his ability to help the less fortunate...

Vireo Reinhold relishes collecting his monarch's proper dues. Working hard to prolong and fund the king's never-ending war, the self-centered official revels in the perks of luxury that come with his unorthodox role. But his world upends when he unearths an ancient spellbook that promises to unlock a shadowy, forgotten magic.

Embroiled in a secret affair with a fellow noble's wife, Vireo is mortified when he's forced to commit an unthinkable act. Driven into exile, no longer able to coerce the vulnerable, and with the powerful tome in his enemy's hands, the fallen agent's only shot at survival hangs on his skills at saving others.

Can Vireo redeem himself as the people's champion before they all fall to a sinister fate?

A Forest of Vanity and Valour is the dark first book in the Tales of Levanthria fantasy-retelling series. If you like fast-paced action, evil-to-good transformations, and classic stories with a twist, then you'll love A.P Beswick's ominous tale.

Buy Now!

Jez Cajiao

BATTLEFORGED: FIRST CLEAR: A LITRPG APOCALYPSE ADVENTURE - BOOK 4

By MH Johnson

How to negotiate in the post-apocalypse:
1. Always try make a strong first impression. — *And few things say strength like an army of undead revenants EAGER to begin slaughtering at your command!*
2. Be clear and concise when making your diplomatic offers. Let everyone know all the wonderful benefits they'll enjoy by doing things your way! — *If they play their cards right, they might even get to keep their heads!*
3. Speak softly, and carry a BIG CANNON! — *Because the best negotiations are when your competitors are looking down the barrel of your gun!*
4. *If all else fails, you can always pull out your **DINOSAUR COLLECTION** to impress all your new friends!*
Eric has a little problem.
Someone he cares about has been kidnapped by sadistic goblins working with corrupt bureaucrats who are eager to make him pay for interfering with their plans of military conquest and economic dominion.
Good thing Eric has a BIG ARMY!
An army that's absolutely PERFECT for crushing ANNOYING little problems that threaten any girl silly enough to fall for a guy like him.
Sadly, his mother has made it clear that negotiation is the best path forward when dealing with corrupt administrators. Especially when SMART negotiations just might give his sister the breathing room she needs to fortify her own growing kingdom.
Eric is forced to agree. If nothing else, this is a great opportunity for him to level-up his Negotiation skills. And he can think of no better negotiating tactic than **GROWING HIS UNDEAD LEGION TO MASSIVE PROPORTIONS!**
Preferably by including everyone's childhood favorite: **DINOSAURS!** - *Lots and lots of hungry dinosaurs!*
Eager for a fast-paced adventure with a survivor determined to get the best of everyone trying to kill him? Then read on!
<u>Order Here</u>

FACEBOOK AND SOCIAL MEDIA

If you want to reach out, chat or shoot the shit, you can always find me on either my author page here:

www.facebook.com/JezCajiaoAuthor

OR

We've recently set up a new Facebook group to spread the word about cool LitRPG books. It's dedicated to two very simple rules;

1: Let's spread the word about new and old brilliant LitRPG books.

2: Don't be a Dick!

They sound like really simple rules, but you'd be amazed…

Come join us!

https://www.facebook.com/groups/LITRPGLegion

I'm also on Discord here: **https://discord.gg/u5JYHscCEH**

Or I'm reaching out on other forms of social media atm, I'm just spread a little thin that's all!

You're most likely to find me on Discord, but please, don't be offended when I don't approve friend requests on my personal Facebook pages. I did originally, and several people abused that, sending messages to my family and being generally unpleasant, hence, the author page:

www.facebook.com/JezCajiaoAuthor

I hope you understand.

Jez Cajiao

<u>LEGION</u>

Okay everybody, if you've not yet seen or heard! My wife Chrissy, and our friend Geneva and I have launched the Legion Publishers!
We're taking on new authors, as well as experienced ones, focusing primarily on the LitRPG side of things, but we're open to anything really, with one very clear rule that guides our company:

Don't be a dick.

That's it. Our contracts aren't hidden behind layers of legalese, you can find them here:

<u>https://www.legionpublishers.com/legioncontract</u>

If you want to reach out and ask any questions, get an idea of the support we offer, and possibly become part of the family? We'd love to hear from you, just tap the link and fill in the form:

<u>https://www.legionpublishers.com/contact-and-submissions</u>

Hope you're having a good one!

-Jez, Chrissy and Geneva

If you want to read any of our amazing authors work then go get them!

<u>Theft of Decks</u> By Lars Machmuller **<u>Buy on Amazon</u>**
<u>Quest Academy</u> By Brian J. Nordon **<u>Buy on Amazon</u>**
<u>Wandering Warrior</u> By Michael Head **<u>Buy on Amazon</u>**
<u>Knights of Eternity</u> By Rachel Ní Chuirc **<u>Buy on Amazon</u>**
<u>Scarlet Citadel</u> By Jack Fields **<u>Buy on Amazon</u>**
<u>Welcome to the Dark Ages</u> by Malory <u>Buy on Amazon</u>

<u>LITRPG!</u>

To learn more about LitRPG, talk to other authors including myself, and to just have an awesome time, please join the LitRPG Group

<u>www.facebook.com/groups/LitRPGGroup</u>

Jez Cajiao

FACEBOOK

There's also a few really active Facebook groups I'd recommend you join, as you'll get to hear about great new books, new releases and interact with all your (new) favorite authors! (I may also be there, skulking at the back and enjoying the memes…)

https://www.facebook.com/groups/LitRPGlegion/

https://www.facebook.com/groups/GamelitSociety

https://www.facebook.com/groups/LitRPG.books

https://www.facebook.com/groups/LitRPGforum/